# *Jonathan's Cross*

A Novel
by
*M. L. Gardner*

*To Patty*

*M L Gardner*

Jonathan's Cross

Copyright © 2009 by M.L. Gardner

All rights reserved. No part of this book may be used or reproduced in any manner whatsoever without written permission from the publisher.

Published by Quillen Publishing
Tacoma, Washington
www.quillenpublishing.com

ISBN-13 978-0615435633
ISBN-10 0615435637
Library of Congress Cataloging-in-Publication Data
Gardner, M.L.
Jonathan's Cross : a novel / M.L. Gardner. 2$^{nd}$ ed.
p. cm.

Manufactured in the United States of America

The characters and events in this work are fictitious. Any resemblance to real persons, living or dead, is purely coincidental and not intended by the author.

www.mlgardnernovels.com

*For Lisa*

A special thanks to musician Steve Smith who wrote the song
"Ava-Maura"
To hear all of Steve's music and music created for
Jonathan's Cross please visit:
**www.spoonsong.com**

## Prologue

*Is ea, is cuimhin liom go maith é*
Yes, I remember it well.

June 1972

"Wake up, lazy-bones." With the chessboard tucked under her arm, Maura walked into the room with a slow, tired gait. She tapped the bedpost as she passed. Jonathan stirred, grunted, opened his eyes a crack and closed them again.

"I didn't think you were coming today," he said, struggling in vain to sit up straight.

"I wasn't planning on it, but Ian kicked me out fer the afternoon." She set the chessboard at the foot of the bed. "Apparently, I'm bein' a bother." Her eyes crinkled with her mischievous grin. She got a good grip around Jonathan's chest and brought him out of his sharp slump to the right.

"You? A bother? I can't imagine," Jonathan said with heavy sarcasm. Maura picked a pillow up off the floor and wedged it under Jonathan's right arm; lame and lifeless.

"Besides, I wanted ta see how yer settling in here," she said as she worked.

"I'm a bother," he said, not entirely joking.

"Ye know yer son doesn't see ye as a bother," she said and sat on the side of the bed, placing the chessboard on Jonathan's thighs. She opened a richly engraved drawer and began pulling pieces out. She raised her eyebrows as she held up a marbled piece and a red piece.

"I don't care." Jonathan's left side shrugged. Maura chose marble for him and set up the pieces.

"He has his own family now."

"Aye. But yer his father. He doesna mind ye livin' with him one bit," she assured. "Can I get ye somethin' to drink before Mr. Caleb gets here to lose another game o' chess to ye?" she asked as she made her way to the door.

"Scotch," he said, eyes closed, resting his head against the wooden headboard. She returned a moment later with a tall glass of lemonade and set it on the bedside table.

"That doesn't look like Scotch." He gave an indignant huff as she opened the bedroom window to let in a cool, refreshing breeze.

"Have ye no faith in me after all these forty-odd years, Mr. Jonathan?" She pulled a flask from her dress pocket, unscrewed the cap, and handed it to him. He took a deep drink and paused with eyes closed to enjoy it. He took another before handing it back. He let out something between a sigh and a growl before opening his eyes.

"Have ye been able to talk to him then?"

"I tried," he said. "He isn't listening." He rolled his head toward the window. The summer sun drenched the ornate chair and hardwood floor below it.

"Give it time, Mr. Jonathan. Keep tellin' him yer life's lessons and one day, he'll see his way to them," she said while fishing a rag from the lower drawer of a bureau.

"What are you doing?" he asked, craning his neck. She straightened, smoothing down her hair, mostly gray with a few remaining threads of red throughout.

"I'm cleanin'. Since I'm here and all." She began to dust knickknacks and picture frames, talking as she went of memories that each piece stirred. She held a deep shadow box, admiring the flag inside which was surrounded by medals and awards. She had made the box herself; a memorial for one of Jonathan's sons, who had died in World War Two. Maura went slowly across the chest of drawers, smiling at each framed picture as she wiped off dust only she could see.

"When was this taken?" she asked, holding one out for him to see.

"That was on a trip we all took to Europe, before–" The door swung open and hit the wall with a thud. Jonathan's son, Robert pushed a small but heavy desk into the room.

"Hello, Maura," he said. "Here's the desk, Dad. And I found that old typewriter in the attic. It's really dusty—" Maura held up her dusting rag in an offer to clean it.

"I don't know why you won't just let me buy you a new one," he grumbled as he pushed the desk against the wall. Jonathan said something under his breath as Robert left the room. He returned shortly with the promised typewriter. A thick layer of dust completely obscured the letters on the keys. Maura gravitated toward it and set to work.

"I picked up that other stuff you wanted, too, Dad." He ducked out and back in with a large bag, pulling out boxes of paper, ribbons, and pens.

"Thank you, Robert."

He patted his father's dead right arm and gave a wave to Maura as he left.

"He's a good boy and the spittin' image of ye, Mr. Jonathan," she said. He nodded in agreement but still held a look of worry.

"An' he's smart," she added. "Keep talkin' to him. He'll listen." Jonathan gazed out the window looking past the yard and fence, to a place only he could see.

"I don't know if I have enough time," he said. She slowly turned to him, her face first concerned, then fierce.

"Fer the love of God, Mr. Jonathan! Ye've had a stroke, but yer far from yer deathbed! I won't hear ye talkin' like that." He rolled his eyes, full of love for her and the scolding, and smiled. He knew there was no point in arguing. She spun back around with a huff.

"Would you do something for me, Maura?"

"An' what would that be?" she asked, cleaning the typewriter keys viciously.

"There's a box under my bed. Will you pull it out for me?"

She tossed the rag down on the desk a little too hard and turned to the bed.

"What is all this anyway?" she asked, pulling one thick book after another out of the box and stacking them by his legs.

"My journals."

"Taking a stroll down memory lane, are we?"

"No. You are," he said. She looked at him curiously.

"I don't need yer memory books, I've a memory sharp as a tack."

"Exactly," he said with a smile.

"Exactly *what?*"

"That's exactly why I need you to do this."

Maura's eyes flashed and she set her jaw, growing irritated. "Do what, Mr. Jonathan, would ye just spit it out already? I've no time fer games."

"I want you to take these journals, add to it what you remember, talk to the others, and write them out."

"Write them out . . . like a book?" she asked, appalled.

"Yes. A book. For my children." He looked down at his useless right arm. "I can't anymore. I was going to, but I never got around to it."

"Well." She looked down at the stack of old journals and took a step back. "I wouldn't even know where to begin!"

"Begin anywhere you want. There are so many stories to tell," he said, smiling fondly. "And you were there. I know you remember."

She ran her hand over the dusty journal.

"*Is ea, is cuimhin liom go maith é*," she whispered. She looked down at the books and paper set around his legs. "How can I possibly put everything we've done and seen and been through in one book?!"

"Then write as many as it takes," he said and laid his head back. She studied his face, deciding.

"Please, Maura?"

"Don't try to be charmin'," she snapped. "Ye still think ye can get yer way with those eyes o' yers, don't ye?"

He grinned. For a moment he looked very much like the young man she remembered from a lifetime ago.

"All right. I'll do it for ye, Mr. Jonathan," she said softly. "But first, I need to clean that old thing." She went back to the typewriter and began distractedly cleaning it.

"Thank you, Maura."

"What on earth do you want me to call it?" she asked. He didn't answer. She turned to look at him and followed his eyes, fixed on the straw cross above his bedroom door.

## Black Tuesday 1929
### 5pm

Jonathan still hadn't found the courage to go home. He finished another Scotch and held his head in his hand, his broad shoulders slouched. He pushed the empty shot glass away and ran his fingers through his dark hair, sighing deeply.

"Looks like you've had one helluva day," the barmaid said with a sympathetic look as she refilled three glasses. "Least you can drink easy for now. All the cops are busy with the riots and the jumpers. Not likely to get raided today."

Jonathan's eyes flickered up and he nodded, barely hearing her. He pulled a bill out of his wallet and tossed it on the table.

"Leave the bottle." He was by no means done. He didn't have the words worked out just right in his head, but he would stay here with his Scotch until he did. He stared blankly, trying to comprehend the incomprehensible. So many people that day were wiped out; riches to rags in a matter of hours, and he was one of them. *How could I have lost everything?* He grimaced, unable to wrap his mind around it. The full emotional impact had not yet hit. A wave of desperate panic washed over him when he thought of Ava. He dreaded her reaction and wondered briefly if she would leave as some wives tended to do when their comfortable lifestyles disappeared. He glanced to his left and right at his best friends and business partners who were sitting with similar shell-shocked expressions.

The brokerage firm he owned had suffered devastating losses since the slide began in September. Even as each trading day worsened, the collective thought was that it could not get much worse. The firm had continued to operate as a functioning brokerage, until today. Those who refused to recognize that the ten year binge of prosperity was coming to a climactic and explosive end, rode the purge to the very bottom. What remained of his firm had been decimated in a matter of hours.

Everything he had ever worked for was gone.

Aryl Sullivan and Caleb Jenkins had joined the firm to learn the nuances of the financial world. They were impressed with the wealth Jonathan had amassed, and each had a good reason to take him up on his offer to bring them on. He took them in, taught them well, and the three quickly gained the reputation of being some of the most powerful players on Wall Street. They worked hard and achieved a ridiculously comfortable life in an alarmingly short amount of time.

The three men had grown up together in a little town on the coast of Massachusetts and had been friends for as long as any of them could remember. Jonathan had been the first to leave, drawn to the fast-paced business world of New York City. The next time his friends heard from him, he was making money hand over fist as a broker and owner of his own firm.

Aryl came from a lineage of lobstermen. He worked during his late teens and early twenties for his uncle who owned a small fleet of lobster boats. He liked it well enough and never really gathered much of a plan for his life, quite happy to go along with whatever adventure life presented. He would work long enough to make what money he needed to travel and explore for a few months then return to Rockport to work with his uncle. His fate had been determined by a combination of impeccable timing; Jonathan's invitation to New York and his falling in love with Claire. If not for that timing, he would most likely be involved with neither one today.

Caleb grew up an only child on his parents' farm. When he was twenty, his grandfather suffered a stroke and Caleb ran the adjoining farm entirely on his own. In gratitude, his grandfather willed him the estate when he passed. Caleb sold the farm and took his time traveling south to discover what each state had to offer. He was still intent on farming but needed a change of scenery. He hadn't made up his mind which state he liked best until he met Arianna. From that moment on, the only place he wanted to be was with her. It wasn't long before fate led them north as well.

Jonathan rested his head on his forearm, his other hand still gripping the glass. No matter how many times he turned it over in his mind, he knew he was responsible for their losses as he involuntarily relived the events of the day.

That morning all three had arrived at the office early. Not one of them slept much the night before. Truth be told, they hadn't slept well for weeks. The markets had gone from wild fluctuations the past month to spiraling out of control in the last week.

Glancing up at the clock, Jonathan paced his office in the moments before the opening bell. Today would make or break him and he knew it.

He prophesied one of two things would happen. Either investors would start a frenzy of buying dirt-cheap stocks that would hopefully cause an amazing rally similar to the previous Thursday, or the massive sell off would continue and God only knew what would happen then. One of his best analysts sat at the ticker, anxious and alert, waiting for the numbers. At opening bell, the tape started streaming out as Jonathan, Aryl, and Caleb gathered around the desk. The analyst began yelling almost immediately. From the second it opened, the markets plummeted. Jonathan paced and anxiously waited for the rally. He could feel it coming, but Caleb and Aryl were nervous.

"Let's get out, Jon. It's not gonna stop," Caleb pleaded.

"It will. Trust me, it will," Jonathan insisted as he paced. Eventually, he began to lose faith that a rally was coming as his firm was quickly filling with panicked clients who demanded what was left of their money. He finally gave the order to sell everything and move into cash and gold. His interns worked furiously on the telephones and telegraph.

A fellow broker, tie loose and jacket hanging off one of his shoulders, staggered into the office. Sweat covered his blood-red face as he screamed the news like a town crier, "It's lagging! It's lagging!"

The sell orders were coming in so fast that the ticker couldn't keep up. The global purging had caused an undetermined delay. When Jonathan had finally given the order to sell, it was at numbers that were completely inaccurate in real time. He grabbed his coat and ran. Aryl and Caleb followed close behind.

Full-blown panic had ensued in the streets. Hundreds of people crowded the entrance of the Exchange. Panic caused bank runs that resulted in the sudden failure of some of the largest banks in existence. Police struggled to control the crowds and keep the peace. As Jonathan ran, something in the corner of his eye caught his attention. A figure was free falling from an adjacent building. The friends pushed through the crowds, inching toward the Exchange.

As he yelled out instructions when they reached the trading floor, Aryl and Caleb struggled to hear him over the roar of the frenzied crowd. Fear and panic reigned inside the Exchange. There was complete chaos as hundreds of men ran from pit to pit to scream orders. Sweat-drenched and red-faced men grabbed handfuls of their hair, clutched their chests and a few collapsed to the floor. Frantic brokers too preoccupied with certain doom to care about their colleagues simply jumped over them. The lower the numbers sank, the louder they screamed. As if they could push the numbers back up by will and volume. The whole world was selling; no one was buying. When the bell rang, a sea of heads collectively turned to see what the closing numbers were. Silence fell as the ticker tapes were still catching up; the numbers kept sinking. It was over. The floor erupted in desperate cries, screams of agony and men running in every direction.

Jonathan stood motionless amidst the chaos, staring blankly, and then slowly sank to his knees.

They took the keys to his cars and office building immediately, informing him that everything he owned was now under bank lien. He didn't remember leaving the Exchange, didn't remember how long they had walked, and didn't recognize the pair of sad suits they followed into the speakeasy. He wasn't even sure how long they had been there.

He lifted his head and looked around. Aryl stared at his empty glass with no expression, and Caleb rested his head on his folded arms. There were many men in suits. No respectable businessman needed to be in a place like this unless he was hiding. A lot of them held their heads in their hands with the same looks of disbelief and horror. A grown man sat unashamedly crying in the corner. They were all there for the same reason. They represented the casualties of this day; their possessions to be auctioned, their homes to be sold, their bank accounts to be seized, their jobs literally vanished. They were now among the poorest in New York City, and they had to go home and tell their families. They were all desperately trying to figure out exactly how to do that.

He had the beginnings of a plan forming in his mind. He just had to sound confident and not shaken. He started to pull something together and mentally rehearsed what he would say until he could recite it without a hint of emotion. He glanced at his watch, finished his last shot, and signaled to the others.

"Let's go home and tell them," he sighed. "Then we'll meet at my house to figure out what we're going to do."

∞∞∞∞

Outside, the air was bitterly cold as they hurried through the crowds of downtown New York. They tried not to look at the newspaper headlines or into the panicked faces all around them. The long walk to the wealthier residential district gave them more time to think. They broke away at the last cross street without more than a nod to each other. Jonathan kept straight, Caleb left and Aryl right.

The Garrett house was one of several mansions surrounded by short, wrought iron fences. It was quieter here. He slowed his pace a little and did a final rehearsal of what he would say. He paused at the door, closed his eyes, and took a deep breath. A trembling hand turned the knob, and he saw Ava in the parlor listening to the radio with a deeply concerned look on her face. She knew. She just didn't know quite how bad it was. Three servants huddled across the grand parlor, anxiously awaiting news. Her head snapped up when she heard the door.

"Jonathan!" She reached to embrace him, and he pressed her body into his in a vice-like hold.

"I was so worried! Where have you been?" she asked. She pulled back to search his eyes for answers. "What they're saying on the radio. Is it true?"

He hesitated, painfully aware of three sets of eyes upon him from across the room. He removed Ava's arms from his neck and made his way over to them. He spoke quietly for a moment, explaining and apologizing. Maura, the Irish housemaid, gasped and her hand flew to her mouth. Sven, the Russian chef, nodded with a solemn expression of understanding. Charles, the house butler, said nothing and showed no expression. Jonathan removed his wallet and gave them what pay he owed them for the week. They turned in silence to gather their things as they joined the suddenly unemployed.

Jonathan turned toward Ava again when he was sure they were alone. He sighed and pulled her close. He opened his mouth to begin his speech but found himself mute. He frowned and looked away before attempting again. His face was pained, eyes narrowed, and brow furrowed. She realized it was worse than she had thought.

"How bad is it, Jonathan?" she asked, visibly bracing for bad news. He had come home before from bad days after losing thousands of dollars, and things would be tense for a while until everything shook out. However, it always shook out. They had gotten through those times and come out on top in the end. *How much worse could this be?* she wondered.

"Everything is gone," he said quietly. "We didn't move in time. We–I, didn't sell in time, there wasn't any time. It all happened so quickly. I'm sorry," he whispered.

*So much for my confident speech,* he thought with self-loathing. It took her a few minutes to process his words, and she sat down numbly in a chair by the fireplace. He followed and knelt in front of her, taking her hands in his. She was staring over his shoulder trying to comprehend. *Everything is gone* echoed in her mind. He didn't say it was a setback or even a huge loss. *Everything is gone.* Silent moments passed save the rhythmic ticking of the antique grandfather clock.

"Ava." He frantically searched for something to say. He had nothing in every sense of the word. The feeling of failure was a crushing weight. He put his head down on their entwined hands and took a deep, ragged breath. "Ava," he exhaled. She seemed to come back to the moment as her eyes focused on him. She pulled her hands from his and placed them lightly on his head. Sighing, she looked around the grand parlor: the expensive art, the velvet drapes, the gilded mirrors, the imported rugs, and the plush furniture.

"I always felt like this was too good to be true," she whispered. He wanted to tell her that everything would be all right, that it would all work out, that he would fix the whole mess, and not to worry. It would have all been lies.

"What are we going to do?" she asked with a shaky voice.

"We're, ah, going to get a plan together, I think. Aryl and Caleb will be over later. We'll figure something out."

Ava suddenly realized that their friends were devastated as well.

"I was so stupid," he whispered. "I was stupid and now everyone is busted." She leaned to rest her cheek on his neck and stretched her arms out upon his back as if to physically shield him from the fallout. They had no words of comfort for each other as they tried to comprehend the magnitude of their life's destruction.

After a long, tense silence, Jonathan startled at the hard pounding on the door.

"Jonathan!" Caleb yelled outside the door. "Open up. I need your help!" Jonathan struggled to his feet and limped to the door, his legs tingling from the prayer-like posture he had held for so long. He opened it to a half-frozen Caleb, whose face held pain and panic. "It's Arianna. She's gone. I've looked everywhere. You gotta help me," he panted.

Jonathan grabbed his arm and pulled him inside. "What do you mean she's gone?" Caleb took a shivering breath before speaking.

"When I got home earlier, she was already in a panic. She was crying, mumbling, and running all over the house, trying to hide her jewelry. I got her calmed down after a while. I thought she was in her right mind. I left her by the fireplace to get Aryl, and then we were going to come over here. I was only gone ten minutes. When we got back, she was gone. Some of her clothes are missing and all of her jewelry. We've been looking for a half-hour now, and Aryl told me to come get you."

"Where's Aryl now?" Jonathan asked as he pulled on his coat.

"He and Claire are still out looking."

"I'm going to go help Caleb," Jonathan said, turning to Ava. "You stay here where it's warm."

"No," she said, reaching for her coat. "She's my friend. I'm going with you." He resigned with a sigh.

"If you get too cold, you *are* coming home," he said firmly as he helped her into her fur. He handed Caleb another of his coats, and Caleb slipped it on gratefully, although his shorter compact frame swam in the bulky wool.

∞∞∞

*It* was fully dark now, and the wind blew light snow flurries in all directions. They had no idea where Arianna might have gone but started the search with a social club, restaurant, and a ladies' salon they knew she frequented. Aryl and Claire caught up with them near Arianna's favorite café.

Caleb paced while Jonathan flagged down a policeman on horseback and explained the situation. He grimaced at Caleb and shook his head.

"I sympathize, buddy, I really do. I'll take a description and name, but only to add her to a list of all the other women who ran off today. We only found two, and they were at the train station."

Caleb's head turned slowly toward Jonathan. "She wouldn't." He knew she was fragile, vain, and needed security like she needed to breathe. However, he hadn't thought for a minute that she would leave, that she didn't love him enough to stay if the money was gone.

∞∞∞

Jonathan watched these thoughts play out on Caleb's face as they made their way toward Grand Central Terminal. The rest of them were under no illusions regarding Arianna's character, and it didn't surprise them in the least when they spotted her on a bench. She had on a black fur coat, held a second fur over her arm and two bags stuffed to the gills set on each side of her. Closer now, Caleb jogged toward her, nearly tripping on the hem of Jonathan's coat. Ava turned her face into Jonathan's chest as he pulled her close. He kissed the top of her head, his eyes cast down. He thought briefly that Caleb should just let Arianna go. She required expensive upkeep and was very unpredictable–surely, this wouldn't work for long with a future as uncertain as theirs. Aryl sat hard on a bench and reached for Claire, completely drained from one of the most emotional days of his life.

"Arianna!" Caleb yelled from across the loading platform. Her head whipped to the side, and she stood and looked around for somewhere, anywhere, to run. When he reached her, he grabbed her by the shoulders. "Arianna, what are you doing?" She opened her mouth, but nothing intelligible came out. In disbelief, he asked the obvious.

"Are you leaving me?" Her eyes dropped as she bit her lip, her chin quivering. He stared at her, wounded and humiliated. "So, it's true," he said flatly. "The money's gone, so you are, too." He stared at her for a moment, let go of her in disgust and walked around her to sit on the bench. When she turned to face him, tears were running down her face, and she tried unsuccessfully to wrench out an apology. "So," he said, holding his hands in the air. "Did you ever really love me? Or was it always just the money?" She stared at him pitifully, stuttering to explain herself. "Can't you even give me an answer?" he yelled. "I deserve at least that!" She winced, shivering despite her fur. Caleb looked over at his friends, who stood with their wives a respectable distance away. Suddenly angry and incredibly embarrassed at her behavior, he stood and walked toward her slowly.

"You're not doing this tonight," he said firmly and took her arm. It was the first time, ever, that Caleb had given her a direct order. He called for Jonathan and Aryl to grab her bags and turned, walking her by the arm toward the direction of home. "We're going to Jon's house, and we're going to figure out a plan," he explained. "We'll talk about this later."

*9 P.M.*

"Might as well enjoy this now," he said quietly as he sat down. Jonathan poured Scotch all around and tossed cigars from his collection of the finest money could buy. They sat around the mahogany table in Jonathan's card room, staring in odd directions. They sighed heavily in turn, not knowing where to start.

∞∞∞

Arianna was resting in one of the guest bedrooms as Ava and Claire listened out for her in the attached reading room. Claire curled up in a plush chair set in front of ceiling-high mahogany bookshelves.

"What are we going to do?" She dropped her head to her knees with a hopeless sigh.

"I don't know. But I guess that's what they're trying to figure out down there," Ava said. Claire looked up with swollen eyes.

"How can they possibly figure out what we're going to do when there's nothing to work with? Aryl said there's nothing left except the money we keep at home." Ava shrugged.

"They're smart. It might take a bit, but they'll get a plan together."

"How can you be so calm about this?" Claire asked in irritated awe. "We're penniless, soon to be homeless, our entire life has been destroyed, and you sit there shrugging your shoulders, waiting patiently for them to figure something out."

"What else can we do?" Ava snapped at her. "We wait and hope and see where we end up," she said as she walked to the window. Pulling back the drapes, she watched snowflakes swirl around the streetlamp below. "This is nothing new to me, Claire. Here one day, gone the next." She paused and then decided to divulge a piece of her past, albeit, an edited piece.

"My parents died when I was twelve, and I was sent to live with my aunt. It was all she could do to keep a roof over our heads. One year she arranged to leave me with my cousins here in the city. She was growing too old and weak to take care of me. I hated it and cried for days. I begged to go home to my aunt the same way I cried for my parents. The cousins weren't always nice to me." She sat in a chair next to Claire and pulled her legs up, hugging them. "They really resented my being there, and I wasn't fond of the city at all, but I got used to it. And in the end, I met Jonathan." She skipped over the tumultuous courtship and dramatic ending of her relationship with Victor Drayton immediately prior. "Things have a way of working out. We'll be okay, Claire, you'll see."

Claire looked at her friend with sympathetic eyes and reached for her hand. "I had no idea you'd been through all that, Ava."

In fact, none of them knew much about Ava's past. One day she was just there in Jonathan's life and heart as if she'd been there always. At first, there were questions about Jonathan's apparent obsession with this woman who had no family or social connections, and who very much seemed to appear out of thin air. Nevertheless, a life busy with whirlwind parties, extravagant galas, and overseas vacations easily avoided or redirected the questions.

"It was never worth mentioning until now." Ava shrugged again.

∞∞∞∞

In the card room, Jonathan, Caleb, and Aryl were still cold. Jonathan got up and stoked the fire. Leaning one hand on the wall, he stared at the flames for a long while.

Aryl glanced from Jonathan to Caleb and back. Jonathan's expression was a mix of disbelief and defeat. Aryl was positive his friend had aged five years in the span of a few hours. Jonathan had been defined by his success and was now completely lost. Mentally, he was still on his knees in the middle of the Exchange. Caleb was staring at the grain pattern of the table with his eyes slightly narrowed. Aryl knew his wheels were already turning, looking for answers. Aryl wasn't so much the type to look for solutions but was able to see what others would pass by. When opportunity presented itself, Aryl was the one who knew what to do with it. He focused on Jonathan again.

"We better get started, Jon," he said quietly. Jonathan's head wobbled and he rubbed the stubble shadow on his face. He returned to the card table and sighed deeply.

"Where in hell do we start?" he asked as he poured another drink. The conversation began with recanting the events of the day and the last week with disbelief, anger, and even fear. A long series of *I can't believe* and *If only we had* statements quickly grew old for Aryl.

"We all know what happened," Aryl interjected. "We better figure out what we're going to do." Aryl was never one to look back. He realized that the chips had fallen, and he had to cut the losses and move on.

"You're right. Got any ideas?" Caleb tipped up his shot glass as Aryl sat back and crossed his arms.

"I guess it comes down to two things. First, we secure a roof over our heads. The auction house will send someone out soon to begin the liquidation; the vultures won't wait long. Second, we secure jobs of some kind, any kind. The cash we have won't hold us for long. We have maybe a day or two to go through our things and get together our personal belongings. We can take clothes, some basic household items and sentimental things, as long as they aren't of much value. Everything else will be auctioned to pay our debts."

Jonathan leaned back, rubbed his tired eyes and then rested his hands on the top of his head. "Why the hell did we go all in? We were so stupid. We might have a pot to piss in if we'd–"

"Where do we work?" Caleb interrupted.

"I know a couple guys down at the shipping dock," Aryl offered. "I helped them out a few years back when they got into some trouble. They owe me a favor. Maybe I could get us on there," he suggested with a tentative shrug.

"What guys? What kind of trouble?" Caleb asked cautiously.

"Roman Grey and Harvey Duggins. You don't know them. They got into gambling bad a couple of years ago. They did okay at first but tempted fate and ended up losing a lot. They dipped into the petty cash fund at the dock office because they didn't want their families to find out. They figured they'd win back what they had lost and replace the money. Didn't work out that way, though.

"Long story short, it got so bad they ended up messing with the numbers in payroll, and some accounts came up short. The big boss started getting suspicious, and they came to me in a panic. I pulled an all-nighter and fixed the books to hide the missing money. They gave me some cash the next day. I didn't ask where it came from, but I took it and worked some magic on the Street," he said, smiled and raised his eyebrows twice. "A week later, I gave them back their money ten-fold. They replaced the money to payroll, petty cash and banked the rest. All important parties none the wiser." He leaned forward and poured another drink, obviously proud of himself.

Jonathan looked at him incredulously. "You *do* know that was illegal, don't you?"

Aryl shrugged. "No harm, no foul. Besides, saving their asses back then just might save ours now."

"It's worth a shot. How soon can you talk to these guys?" Caleb asked.

"I'll go in the morning. Dock runs six days a week, and so do we now. No more bankers' hours for us," Aryl said with a gruff laugh.

"Well, I can start scouting for apartments," Caleb added. "I know of some property owners that deal in *affordable* housing."

"I can go with you," Jonathan volunteered flatly.

"I really need you to stay here with Arianna. I can't take care of business if I'm worried about her running off again." Jonathan shifted in his chair uncomfortably.

"It would really help me out, Jonathan," Caleb pleaded.

"Fine," he said, clearly irritated. "Maybe I can pack the drapes and sort through the china. I'm sure Maura's got an extra apron and headscarf around here somewhere."

Aryl stifled a laugh from the mental picture.

They continued to talk for the next hour: possible places to live, what to bring, how much cash each couple had and what bare necessities they would need.

During a quiet moment, Ava came in the room with Claire close behind her.

"Caleb, Arianna is asking for you."

He took a deep breath and finished his drink. "I'll be right back," he said as he lumbered toward the stairs.

∞∞∞∞

Caleb stood outside the bedroom door. Arianna lay curled on her side in the large bed. The bedside lamp dimly illuminated the room. Her crystal blue eyes were puffy from crying and her short, glossy black hair disheveled. Of course, Caleb thought she was still the most beautiful creature who had ever lived. Sometimes he had so much pride in her that he pitied his friends whose wives were more ordinary. There was nothing ordinary about Arianna. Her voice was raspy when she spoke.

"I'm sorry," she whispered, sounding genuinely ashamed. She moved lethargically to the center of the bed, motioning for him sit by her. "I didn't think you'd come. I thought you probably hated me for what I did."

"I don't hate you, Arianna, I couldn't. I know you were just scared." He reached to touch her face, but she turned away.

"It's not just that." She pulled herself up and sat cross-legged, leaning her elbows on her knees. "I don't think I can do this." She hung her head in a combination of shame and exhaustion.

"Do what?" he asked cautiously. *She really is leaving,* he thought, and his heart twisted with pain, beat faster with fearful dread. She mustered the courage to look him in the eyes. Her voice was broken and uneven when she began.

"It's not that I don't love you. I do, Caleb. With all my heart. It's not that." The hysterical sobs started again and he quickly pulled her to him, cradling her, and stroking her hair.

"I don't understand," he said when she quieted. "If you love me, why did you try to leave?" She took a deep breath before trying to explain.

"You love me now–spoiled and pampered without a care in the world. I don't want you to see me desperate. It won't be pretty. I'm positive you won't love me that way. I don't want you to see me depressed, poor, and wretchedly miserable." She grabbed his shirt, desperately trying to convey her point. "You deserve better than that, Caleb. I don't want to make you miserable. But I know I will. I won't be able to help it. I'm a horrible, shallow person. You know it and I admit it. But I do love you too much to put you through that. That's why I tried to leave. I wanted to spare you."

He thought for a moment and kissed her hair. "Let me decide what I deserve and what I don't. Where were you going to go anyway?" he asked.

"My parents," she said with a shrug, avoiding his eyes.

"Ahna." He shook his head, appalled. "We've practically been supporting them for the last few years. Why would you go there?" She shrugged.

He pulled the covers back, gesturing for her to slide back down into bed. He lay beside her and pulled her to rest on his chest. "I love you. You're not going anywhere and neither am I. We'll get through this together. And whether you believe me or not, you will be just as beautiful to me, and I will love you just as much, no matter how bad things get." He looked down at her with conviction. "I'll help you, Ahna, every step of the way. I promise." She attempted a smile and touched her fingers to his lips.

"I don't deserve you," she whispered.

"Nonsense," he whispered back. "I wake up every morning amazed at what I have beside me . . . that you ever gave a second look to a plain old farm boy like me."

"You're short, too," she said with a slight grin and tousled his messy, red-brown hair.

"No. You're tall," he countered and slipped an arm over her waist. "But I love you something awful regardless."

"Show me," she implored, pulling the buttons of his shirt. "Show me how much you love me despite how awful I am."

A while later, he held her and whispered a long list of reasons why he loved her, every beautiful feature and stunning quality she had, until she fell asleep. He quietly slipped back downstairs.

∞∞∞

"Arianna is asleep again. Would it be okay if we stay here tonight? I want her to rest and it's getting late." He joined the others at the table and poured another drink.

"Of course. Actually, we all better think about getting some sleep," Jonathan suggested. Everyone nodded in agreement but no one moved. Claire was by Aryl's side, staring at the floor. He glanced at her frequently with concern. They only talked a short time before Caleb showed up on their doorstep for help in finding Arianna. Ava sat with her hand in Jonathan's, and Caleb felt very alone at that moment.

"Don't think badly of Arianna," he blurted out. "She isn't as durable as some, but she's a good person. This all hits too close to home for her. She was damned near destitute once before. When she was almost eighteen, her father began drinking, gambling, and having affairs. He lost a tremendous amount of money. Her fiancée at the time broke the engagement because his family didn't want their reputation associated with the incorrigible things her father was doing." He paused and took a deep breath.

"When he sobered up, he panicked and took out some loans, so his family wouldn't know the extent of the damage. When I met Arianna, her family was struggling pretty badly. The family hid it from everyone for the longest time. And when I finally did find out how bad her situation was, well, to say she was angry is a major understatement. Her pride was three stories high. I tried to convince her that it didn't matter. I offered to take her away from the shame. I couldn't guarantee a grand lifestyle, but I promised her I'd take care of her.

"We decided to start a new life up north, stopping by the preacher's house before we left Georgia to be married and the rest, as they say, is history."

Jonathan sighed heavily. "I wish I had told you to stay. You might be doing better on your own land in Georgia right now."

"No, you can't blame yourself. How in hell could you have foreseen this? I just don't want you all to think badly of Arianna. She's doing the best she can."

"We understand," Jonathan said.

Caleb stood up and stretched. "I need to get some sleep. We've got busy days ahead of us."

"Night, Caleb," they all mumbled in unison as he left the room.

Claire and Aryl stood up as well and Claire hugged Ava tightly. "I'll come by tomorrow." Aryl helped Claire with her coat, and Jonathan saw them out.

*October 30th 1929*

The next day started too early on too little sleep. Caleb slipped out just at the break of dawn. He stopped by home to change clothes and grab his own coat. He donned his favorite hat, catching a glimpse of himself in the foyer mirror. He hardly looked like a man about to go out and search for a cheap place to live. Lastly, he grabbed a thin wad of cash from a hidden safe behind an oil painting of Arianna. He let out a stress-laden sigh as he realized it was the only money he had left to his name now.

He headed downtown, buying a pastry and coffee on his way. He ate slowly while running through his memory of rental brokers before the businesses opened. He had learned about a few slumlords from other brokers who did investing for them, even though he frowned upon the way those men earned their fortunes. They provided substandard housing to desperate people for a tremendous profit. The buildings were homes only in the sense that they had four walls and a roof. Most of the time. Large, brick tenements contained several apartments, crammed onto each floor. They had unreliable heat sources, shoddy electrical wiring, and leaky plumbing built in long after the original construction. They were drafty, depressing places, and he was not looking forward to having to call one home. Slumlords had made a decent amount of money before the market crashed, and no doubt they would be raking it in now. There were several offices dotted along the downtown area, not counting the one he really did not want to enter.

∞∞∞

"Can I help you?" the receptionist asked. He removed his stylish fedora and smiled at her.

"I'm looking for an apartment. Three apartments, actually, preferably close together."

"I'm sorry. I just rented the last vacancy yesterday. There's been quite the demand in the last month."

Caleb sighed and wrung his hands as he walked a few miles, stopping to inquire at every rental agency. The vacancies available were either too expensive or lacked heat and electricity all together.

Now out of options, he slumped on a bench, elbows on knees, head in hands and reluctant to go back to Jonathan empty-handed. He would have to go to Victor Drayton. He shuddered at the thought of renting from one of the most notorious slumlords in New York, and Jonathan's old rival to boot. From where he sat, however, he saw no way around it. He rallied his resolve and set out for Victor's office. Jonathan's history with Victor was on his mind as he walked.

They had first arrived in New York around the same time. Assigned to the same boarding house, they apprenticed at one of the larger brokerages together. Jonathan had natural talent whereas Victor struggled. He spent extra time in the evenings after work coaching Victor, who should have been grateful, but loathed Jonathan's instinct even as he used him for knowledge. A year into the apprenticeship, Jonathan came across some incriminating information and exposed Victor to the firm for insider trading and playing mole for a half-dozen rival brokerages. The apprenticeship dismissed Victor and later Jonathan became a junior partner. Victor bought his first abandoned building with money he had skimmed, made it barely livable and began his business of taking advantage of desperate immigrants fresh off the boat. He soon built a fortune, and met Ava through some equally cunning friends with selfish motives. Victor might have bullied her to the altar had Jonathan not foiled those plans as well. Victor was controlling and manipulative. When he set his sights on something, it rarely escaped him. Jonathan's downfall would bring outright joy to Victor now. To see Jonathan come to nothing, unable to provide for himself and Ava would be, for him, Christmas come early.

∞∞∞∞∞

Aryl left Claire nestled deep in silken, down comforters and headed to the dock office to talk to his old acquaintances.

He opened the door to an office labeled *Lead Foreman*. Roman sat with his back to the door, talking animatedly on the phone. Aryl cleared his throat, and Roman held up a finger. Aryl smiled devilishly.

"Sir! I'm with the Bureau of Internal Revenue," he shouted with an authoritative tone. Roman leapt to his feet, dropping the phone, his face gone white. Roman recognized Aryl at once, and his head dropped in relief.

"Jesus, Mary and Joseph, you scared the piss outta me, Aryl." He couldn't help but laugh, though, as he wiped beads of sweat from his forehead and hung up the phone.

"It's been a long time, Aryl. How are you?" he asked, reaching to shake his hand. "I heard about all the shit that's happened these last few weeks and especially yesterday. Whew! What a mess. You guys get through that okay?"

"Well, not really. I wish this were a social visit, but I need to call in a favor." Aryl frowned.

"Nonsense. With you, it's always a social visit. Pull up a chair." He walked to the door, glanced both ways in the hall, then closed and locked the door. He returned, pulling a bottle of rum and two small glasses from a bottom drawer. "Can't be too careful, you know?"

"So, lead foreman, eh?" Aryl nodded toward the black stencil on the frosted glass of the door.

"Yeah, I guess hanging around this shithole for so long finally paid off," he said with a laugh. "Now, I know you're not here to celebrate my promotion. What is it, Aryl?"

"Well, remember a few years back when I did some creative accounting work for you guys?"

"Hell yeah, saved our asses. Not just from jail, but from our wives . . . not sure which would have been worse!" he bellowed.

"Well, me and two of my friends, we need jobs. It doesn't matter doing what. We just need them quick."

Roman's face fell somber. "You guys didn't fare so well yesterday, did you?"

"We lost everything," Aryl said without emotion.

"I'm real sorry, Aryl."

"Easy come, easy go."

"Well, as luck would have it, I just got word that two of my men aren't coming back. I was going to replace them with day workers, but I'd be happy to give those jobs to you and your friend."

"That's great, Roman. I really appreciate it. But there are three of us."

"Right. Right," he said, rubbing his chin. "I'll have to get that past the big boss. This company has taken some blows right along with everyone else, you know, but luckily, shipments have to continue. Just shipments of beans and rice in place of radios and clothes, I'm predicting." Aryl could care less what was imported, but he tried not to show his impatience.

"Look, I'll get it past the boss tomorrow. Don't you worry about that. You guys be here day after tomorrow, and come in here to my office, don't go where the day workers line up."

Aryl exhaled with relief. "Thanks, Roman."

"Don't thank me just yet," he laughed. "The job is hard and the pay is shit."

"Doesn't matter, not right now, anyway. Thanks again." He shook Roman's hand and quickly turned on his heel to leave.

∞∞∞

Caleb paused at the front door of Victor's office, shook off thoughts of Jonathan, put on his best poker face and walked in.

"Can I help you?" the receptionist asked, without looking up. Caleb glanced at Victor's closed office door. No light escaped from under the door. Caleb cleared his throat.

"I'm looking for three apartments."

She looked up at him curiously. "Three?"

"Yes, three. Myself and two friends of mine. Do you have any available?"

She looked him up and down in confusion. "Well." She started thumbing through a small stack of paperwork. "I believe we do. We just evicted a few yesterday. Would you like the keys to go take a look?"

"No, thanks. I'll take them."

"You don't even want to look? Who rents sight unseen?" She looked at him, bewildered.

"Someone who sees there's a run on cheap places to live. I'll take three."

"Well, okay," she muttered as she started to gather the paperwork. "Now, you can fill out your paperwork, but your friends will have to come in to fill out theirs."

"What time will Mr. Drayton be in?" he asked casually as he sat down to fill out the paper.

"Oh, there's no telling. Depends on how good of a time he had last night," she said with a wink. He hurried through the paperwork, gave the receptionist a deposit to hold the places, and rushed back to Jonathan's house.

∞∞∞

"Good news!" Aryl called out, entering Jonathan's house without knocking. Jonathan and Ava were talking in the parlor, and he interrupted their quiet conversation. "I found us jobs."

"You did?" Jonathan asked.

"That's great, Aryl, well done." Ava smiled.

"Yep. They're about the crappiest jobs in town, very physical. Farm boy is going to be all right, but it's gonna whip us pretty bad at first," he said, holding up his hands in warning. "The pay really stinks. But it's a job. We start day after tomorrow." Just then, Caleb came bounding through the door.

"Jonathan! Aryl! Come with me now. We have to hurry."

"Where to?" Jonathan asked.

"To sign paperwork. I found apartments. But we have to hurry." Jonathan pulled on his coat and gave Ava a hasty kiss as he followed the others out the door.

∞∞∞

"So, Caleb, you wanna give us some details?" Aryl asked. Caleb stopped short and spun around.

"Here it is." He took a deep breath for words he was sure would have to come out quickly. "I've been to every place that rents anything close to cheap. Everything is filling up fast. There are three apartments available, all in the same building. They're pretty bad, I'm sure. I didn't take the time to look at them, but it's a roof with winter coming. Just a place to land until we figure out something better. I filled out some paperwork and put the money down, but you two have to come in to sign your parts."

"Okay but that doesn't explain the rush," Aryl said. "They're secured, right?"

"No. Well, yes. We just need to get there fast," Caleb replied and turned tentatively to Jonathan. "Look, I tried every other place first. I didn't want to go to him, but he had the only openings I could find, I swear. I'm sorry, but there's been a run on cheap places since the whole damn world fell apart. Anyway, he wasn't in when I was there earlier. With any luck, he won't be in when we get there. We can just run in, sign, get the keys, and leave." Jonathan knew exactly who Caleb was referring to. He stared at him with apprehension.

"You're kidding, *right?*" he asked, barely above a whisper.

"No, I wish I was," Caleb said apologetically.

Jonathan put his hands on his head and turned to walk a few paces in the opposite direction as fury welled up in him. "You went to Victor Drayton for a place to live! Of all people, Caleb?"

"There was nothing else avail–"

"There has to be something else," Jonathan growled through his teeth. "No." He shook his head. "I won't do it. I'll find something on my own. If you two want to rent from that low life, good for nothing bastard, then be my guest." He waved his hand at them and started down the street. His angry pace was so brisk that Caleb's shorter legs had to sprint to catch up to him.

"Jon. You know that I wouldn't have done this if there were any other way. I know your past with him. I tried to do everything by myself, but the receptionist insisted you both come in. That's all you have to do, run in and sign. Trust me, Jon, there's nothing else available in this town right now. I've been all over."

Jonathan continued walking. Caleb stopped and called out, "If you want a roof over your head after Monday, this is it! Hard as it is, you need to take it, Jonathan. Think of Ava." Jonathan stopped suddenly and turned his head slowly toward Caleb. His eyes were blazing with fury.

"*Shit*," Caleb muttered and took a step back.

"And just what do you think I've *been* doing, Caleb? Thinking of Ava and protecting her from that bastard from the first moment I laid eyes on her. And now you expect me to put her in one of his places? Where he can find her whenever he wants? Only I don't have the means to hire security any longer, now, do I?"

Caleb dropped his head in frustration, and Jonathan started walking again. Caleb looked at Aryl and shrugged his shoulders. "Any ideas?"

"Nope," Aryl replied. He knew Jonathan well enough to expect a lot more creative language from him. It always entertained Aryl when Jonathan let loose with a long stream of infuriated profanity. Caleb watched Jonathan walk on for another block and felt helpless.

Then suddenly, Jonathan stopped. Something in the alley to his right caught his eye. He turned and disappeared into it.

They found Jonathan slowly walking toward an older man, sitting on the ground, rocking a limp form and crying. An inch of snow had accumulated on large boxes and wooden pallets that had been strapped together to form a shelter, and a small fire burned in an iron pot. When he stepped closer, he was horrified to see that the woman the man mournfully embraced was dead. Her eyes were still open and they stared through Jonathan. He took a step back, shaken, and put his hands on his head. The man started speaking in a foreign language and reached out to Jonathan with a dirty, ragged hand, tears running down his wrinkled face. Jonathan had no idea what else to do as he reached into his pocket and pulled out a few dollars. He handed them to the man and simply turned and walked away. Caleb and Aryl solemnly followed. Around the corner, Jonathan leaned against the wall, needing deep breaths. When the wave of nausea passed, he turned and began walking toward Victor's office.

"Let's get this over with."

∞∞∞∞

*F*aint noises coming from the guest room pulled Ava from her trance-like state. She walked out to the hall to see the guest bedroom door open. Arianna was sitting in a chair, facing the window, staring at nothing.

"Arianna?" Ava whispered. She walked to the side of her chair and placed a hand on her friend's head, stroking her hair. "I was getting worried," she said. "I've never seen you sleep so long. The guys are out signing papers right now. I guess we're going to live real close to each other still." Arianna just gave her a scarce nod.

Ava came around the chair, knelt in front of her friend, and took Arianna's hands in hers. "Arianna, you need to be strong. Caleb needs you to be brave."

"Caleb." She gave a short, ugly laugh. "I'm the last thing he needs."

"That's not true. He loves you so much, how can you not see that?"

"I know he loves me," she whispered. "He's proven that time and again. I said he didn't *need* me. Did I ever tell you about the last trip we took to Paris?"

"No."

"That look Caleb gave me at the train station. He gave the same look to me several times during that trip. I was really a mess most of the time. Absinthe," she offered. "It was all Caleb could do to just put up with my antics and keep me out of trouble." She shook her head slowly, and Ava thought she read regret on her face. "We were at a party, and things got a little out of hand. I wasn't in my right mind. Caleb stepped out to call for the car to take me back to the hotel, and while he was gone, someone dared me to kiss his wife." She laughed aloud at the memory. Ava waited with a curious expression. "So, I did." Arianna shrugged, her eyes cast down. "I gave them quite the show, actually. Caleb walked in, and I don't know who he wanted to pummel more . . . me or the man who dared me to do it. But he had that same look. Like I'd just stabbed him in the heart." She looked down and picked at the fibers of her cashmere sweater. "I hate that look," she whispered. "He forgave me for that, and for what I did the next night. And the night after that . . . ." She trailed off and leaned her head back on the chair. "I just don't think I'm strong enough to do this."

"Yes, you are. You just don't realize it right now. Claire and I will help you."

Arianna sighed with resignation. "I'm going to drive him away. It's only a matter of time," she said and smiled halfheartedly. "I wish I could be more like you. I'm just self-absorbed and weak."

"You are not weak, Arianna. And you're not quite as selfish as you'd like to think. You talk like it's impossible to change but it's not." She pushed the hair out of Arianna's face. "Now, come on. Brush yourself off and pick yourself up. Claire will be over soon to make lists of what we need to pack. We'll all just take it one day at a time, all right?" Arianna nodded slightly and stood in bare feet, following Ava downstairs to wait for Claire.

∞∞∞

Caleb entered Victor's office building first, and a quick look around the room showed no sign of Victor. He asked for the paperwork, and they set to writing as fast as they could. They handed the papers to the receptionist.

"And none of you have children?"

"No," Caleb replied impatiently. "You already asked me that."

"Just making sure," she said. "Children are extra, you know." She handed keys to Caleb and Aryl and just as she reached for Jonathan's, the bell on the door chimed. All three men visibly tensed when they heard the voice from behind.

"Well, who do we have here?"

Jonathan slowly turned to face Victor, and his friends watched warily.

"Well, I just can't believe my eyes," Victor said and smiled wide. "Are you renting from me, Jonathan?" He eyed the keys the receptionist held out midair and sat down in one of the waiting room chairs. He crossed his arms and tilted his head, anticipating entertainment by Jonathan's answer.

"Only for the lack of anything else in town," Jonathan said through his teeth. Victor put his hand over his heart and made a pouting face.

"Why, Jonathan, I'm hurt. And after all we've been through." He grinned wider. "Lost it all, eh? The whole . . . damn . . . mess?" There was outright glee in his voice as he connected the dots. "How's Ava?" he asked, dropping his voice and his smile. His black eyes were narrow and locked on Jonathan. Jonathan audibly ground his teeth. Caleb grabbed his arm, but Jonathan shook him off.

"I'm fine," he snapped at Caleb. He held his voice steady to Victor, "If you don't mind, we have a lot to do today."

"Oh, far be it for me to hold you up. Maybe I'll stop by sometime. See how you're settling in. Bring you a housewarming gift." His mocking smile returned. "A plant, perhaps?"

"I really don't think that's a good idea," Jonathan insisted.

"Well, it *is* my property," Victor said slyly. "I have a legal right to show up, check on my investment." He smiled with one last stab. "So, is Ava taking to poverty well? And just think, she thought she was marrying the prince, but she ended up with the pauper!" He laughed loudly. "Of course, I'm married now, you remember Ruth." He glared at Jonathan. "But I could make an arrangement of sorts. I'd be willing to take her off your hands. It's not like you can take care of her properly anymore. I could always use a maid."

Caleb and Aryl had hold of Jonathan the second his muscles twitched to lunge at Victor, who didn't even flinch.

"You stay away from her," Jonathan growled.

Victor smiled, walking toward him slowly. "You can't exactly hire armed guards to stand outside her house anymore the way you did after you stole her from me, now, can you, Jonathan?" he whispered.

"No. But I can beat you to a pulp like they did every time you came near her. Remember *that*, Victor?"

Victor unconsciously touched a scar at his hairline above the temple and then smoothed down his white blonde hair above it. Jonathan was visibly shaking with rage.

Victor's receptionist had been watching the whole scene with baited breath and spoke timidly. "Mr. Drayton, will you still be renting to these gentlemen? Or should I tear up the paperwork?"

Victor thought for a moment and flashed another evil smile. "Oh, yes, I'll rent to them. What an interesting twist of fate. Very entertaining." Victor took the keys from his receptionist, held them out to Jonathan, but just as he reached for them, Victor dropped them to the floor. "Oops," he sneered. Jonathan looked at the keys on the floor and back up at Victor with burning hatred. Aryl was quick to snatch them up off the floor and hand them to Jonathan.

"Thanks, Aryl," Jonathan breathed, never breaking eye contact with Victor.

They were careful not to let go of Jonathan until they were several paces from the office.

A few blocks down the street is where Jonathan exploded. He was walking at a furious pace and turned abruptly into an alleyway. He started cursing at the top of his lungs and hurled a metal garbage can through the air. He grabbed a two-by-four from the ground, chased the rolling can and proceeded to destroy it. Caleb and Aryl waited patiently by the opening of the alley for him to dispel his rage. Aryl listened intently to the long stream of obscenities flowing from Jonathan's mouth and made occasional comments.

"Oh, boy, that's colorful . . . What did he just call your mother? . . . Now *that* would make a sailor blush . . . I don't believe I've ever heard that particular combination used before," he said, thoroughly entertained. Caleb glanced at him.

"You're enjoying this too much." Aryl shrugged and then turned his attention to Caleb.

"I got us on down at the docks. We start Monday."

"That's good, Aryl. What does it pay?"

"Crap."

"I figured. What's the job?"

"Manually unloading pallets as they come off the ship, to start anyway," Aryl replied. Caleb ducked as a splinter of wood flew past them and then looked toward Jonathan. He had flattened the metal can and had turned his attention to the dumpster.

"I don't think you're gonna flatten that one, Jon!" Caleb yelled, with a faint smirk. Two more whacks and what was left of the two-by-four broke in half; Jonathan catapulted the remaining half as far down the alley as he could. He paced the width of the alley out of breath with his hands on his head. After a moment, Aryl thought it was safe enough to move in closer. Caleb stayed a few feet behind him.

"That was one hell of a show, Jon," he said cautiously moving toward him. Jonathan stopped and looked up at the sky. Caleb sidled up to Aryl and hesitantly spoke up.

"Look, everything is gonna work out. It's gonna be okay," Caleb offered.

"You're such a damn girl scout, Caleb," Jonathan scowled.

"Excuse me?" Caleb asked as Aryl let out a snicker. Jonathan leveled his head and glared at Caleb.

"It's not all going to be okay, Caleb. It's not all going to work out! This isn't some damn bookkeeping mistake that will be fixed in a day or two. This is real. It's all gone. Everything is gone, and frankly, I don't see how we're ever gonna get it back again."

Caleb sighed. "Jon, I'm just trying to help. I know this is real, and I know it's bad, believe me, I'm not trying to make light, I just— Say, would it make you feel better to hit me?"

"What?" Caleb moved to stand in front of him and patted his cheek.

"C'mon. Right here. Sock me a good one. It'll make you feel better."

"I'm not going to hit you, Caleb."

"No, trust me, I won't feel a thing. I can't imagine you've got much left anyway," Caleb said and grinned.

Jonathan looked at him as if he had lost his mind and walked around him to lean against the brick wall. "I'm not going to hit you." He took a deep breath. "I might hit Aryl, though." Aryl's head jerked up.

"What? What'd I do?"

"You haven't even *looked* anxious throughout all this. How is that even *possible*?" Jonathan asked.

Aryl shrugged. "Well, I'm upset, but I guess I just look at things differently."

"How can you look at this in any way other than a complete disaster?" Caleb asked. Aryl thought about it for a moment before he began.

"You know, if it weren't for Claire, I wouldn't even be here right now. This fast-paced, cutthroat, business world was never my dream. I only came here and joined you so that her family would approve of the marriage. You remember as kids, I was always the one running off for days at a time. I hated staying still. I was always looking for adventure. When I met Claire, she was vacationing at her family's summer home on the outskirts of town. That's the only summer I stayed close to home. I worked for my uncle part-time. We found this cove on the beach, and we'd spend hours there, exploring the caves and tide pools.

"One time, we took off on bicycles and came across a small farm where a bunch of field hands were working. So, we stopped and joined them. They had interesting stories. When the owners found us there, they couldn't believe that we had stopped just for fun, so they invited us to stay for dinner. We had a great time getting to know that old couple and kept in touch with them until they died a few years later.

"And we went to our favorite lake at least once a week. She'd make a picnic basket, and we'd lay on the floating dock for hours as I read to her. That's where I proposed, you know. I found this poem and changed the words at the end to ask her to marry me. We used to go for walks up and down the coast, too. Once we lost track of time and a fierce storm came up out of nowhere. There wasn't time to get home, so we spent the night in an abandoned lighthouse. We found candles and wool blankets tucked in the closet and watched the storm from the lantern room. That's the first time we, well, you know," he said, pausing and smiling as sensual memories flashed through his mind. "The very best memories of my life happened when I was broke, had nothing, was nobody. We came to the city and all that changed. We don't talk much at all anymore, or run off for the day together exploring, or spend time together doing nothing all day. The only candles we light are for formal dinner parties, and the only thing I've read to her in a few years is my weekly schedule. I guess I'm hoping we can get back to those things. The stuff that's important. I'm looking forward to that."

"What about Claire? She's pretty upset over all this. Is she going to see things the same way?" Caleb asked doubtfully.

"I'm going to do my best to help her adjust. I think she'll come around. Eventually."

There was a long silence with Caleb and Jonathan at a loss for words.

"That's a really great way to look at things, Aryl," Caleb finally said.

Jonathan took a deep breath and pushed himself off the brick wall. "I may need some pointers from you, Aryl. I've never done anything for Ava that didn't involve money, staff, and planning. But what you described sounds really nice."

"Why don't we go look at these dumps, so we know what we're dealing with," Caleb said, leading the group out of the alley.

Jonathan was lost in his own thoughts as they made their way through town. He desperately wanted to have Caleb's good attitude and Aryl's romantic ideology, but he shut down his plans for starting a family. He felt a new wave of sadness when he remembered that Christmas was coming. He ticked off the list of what he no longer had: no money, no Christmas, no family, no hope, and no dignity. If it weren't for Ava, he just might have been one of the many that week who had wandered to the top of a building, unable to face their cruel, new reality.

It was a long walk to the tenement, and it got progressively more depressing as they neared the place they would soon call home. They passed scores of destitute folks, who had been down on their luck long before this nightmarish week. People and garbage lay strewn about the sidewalks and alleys. At least once on each block, broken furniture and bags of trash lay piled up on the sidewalk. A skinny, black cat darted out from an alley in front of them with a large, dead rat in its mouth. Hobos and drunks were the least of their worries. Steering clear of the gangsters who controlled this neighborhood, however, was a real concern. A few streetwalkers approached them enthusiastically. They were still dressed like the successful men they had been, and it was assumed they were here for something cheap and easy. A worn-out looking brunette tried to get Caleb's attention.

"Wow. Nothing like Paris, eh, Jon?" Caleb scoffed.

"No, it's not," he replied in disgust as he shook off a skinny blonde, who had grabbed his arm and cooed at him. A half-block away, another set of women saw them and approached eagerly.

"Lookin' for a date?" a chubby redhead offered with her skirt already hiked up. Aryl looked straight ahead and kept walking. Down each alley, they saw lines of dingy laundry drying on cables strung between buildings. Neglected dumpsters overflowed with garbage. Through an open window they heard a couple screaming at each other while a baby wailed in the background. Jonathan felt as if he had just walked into the bowels of hell.

"Here it is," Caleb said, stopping in front of a brick building. They looked hesitant and scared as they walked up three flights of stairs to Jonathan's apartment. He took a deep breath and opened the unlocked door.

The three of them stood speechless. A main room measured about fifteen by twenty feet. A tattered couch set against the wall. Beside it, an end table that looked like it was about to fall over. An upside-down dining table set in a corner. There was a fireplace on the left wall and a door beside it. Jonathan walked in slowly and saw that the door led to the bedroom. His clothes closet was bigger than this room. There was a double bed with a lumpy mattress and rusted wrought iron headboard. Directly across from the front door was an archway that led to a small kitchen which held a gas stove, a sink, and counter with two cabinets. To the right of the stove was a garbage chute with a broken door which allowed the stench from the overfilled dumpster below to waft into the apartment. The dirty plaster walls were riddled with holes, and the stained wood floors needed repair. There was one window in the main room and a small one in the kitchen. Both were cracked. Jonathan turned, speechless, to his equally horrified friends.

"Dear God, how can I bring Claire here?" Aryl asked aloud.

*So much for the romanticism of poverty*, Jonathan thought sarcastically. They walked down the dank hallway and opened the door to Caleb's rental. It was in much the same shape. He walked through quickly. Aryl took more time walking around his. As creative and talented as Claire was, he just couldn't see her being able to turn this pit into a home.

Caleb turned abruptly and stomped down the stairs. He sat down on the stoop with his head in his hands. Jonathan and Aryl walked around him, stood on the sidewalk with nothing to say and simply waited.

"We need some plaster to fix those holes," Caleb started, "and at least some tape for the windows with winter coming. I'll bring some tools and nails for other repairs, furniture, doors and such. Rugs will cover the damaged floors. And if you think we can get away with it, we can smuggle in some things from the house tonight after dark."

"Sounds good to me," Aryl said.

"Okay. Well, I don't know about you guys, but I'm tired, hungry and I really need to see my Ahna. Whatdya say we head home. Well, home for today," Caleb said, as he glanced over his shoulder. "I guess, starting tomorrow, this is our home." The others nodded and they began the long walk home.

∞∞∞

"Welcome home, sir," Grayson greeted with a nasal English accent. He helped Victor out of his coat and waited for his hat and scarf. "Mrs. Drayton is waiting in the dining room for you, sir."

"Thank you." Victor walked through the marble-floored foyer and the arched entryway into the parlor. The lighting was low and a roaring fire warmed the room. He entered the lavishly decorated dining room that bestowed expensive art and dark blue, velvet drapes that perfectly matched the Victorian style wallpaper. A darkly stained, oak chair rail separated the design from ornately engraved wood paneling that encircled the room. The long, formal dining table seated twelve and was always set to perfection with the finest china, crystal, and linens. A vast floral arrangement was set in the center.

Victor loosened his tie as he walked toward his wife, who sat at one end of the long table. He quickly kissed the top of her head and asked an obligatory, "How was your day?"

"Fine." She didn't look up as she poured another glass of wine. Victor usually sat at the other end of the table, which served to limit conversation and eye contact to a tolerable level for them both. Tonight he sat directly to her left. She glanced up at him as he pulled the chair out.

"You don't mind?" he asked, smiling.

"By all means," she replied, waving her hand at the chair. He held up his wine glass and Grayson filled it promptly. Victor looked at Ruth over the glass. He loved her, he supposed, as much as he was capable of loving someone anyway.

"So, what did you do today?" he asked.

"Well, Mildred and I went out shopping earlier today, and then I spent the afternoon arranging flowers." She gestured toward the arrangement sprawling out of a gilded vase.

"Very nice," he said, casually looking over toward them.

"I had to fire the maid today," she continued. "She left the guest bedrooms in horrible states, and we're having our party tomorrow night. Surely, people will stay over. I guess tomorrow I'll spend my day looking for another one," she said with irritation.

"You're too hard on the staff, Ruth." She answered him with a hard glare, and he held a hand up and made a face as if to say, *Fine, do whatever you want with the staff.*

Grayson set their dinner before them, refilled their water and wine glasses, bowed and turned to leave, closing the mahogany doors behind him.

"Have you found a dress for tomorrow night?"

"Yes, but it's dreadful. It's a dreary brown and tan, and the shoulders are set all wrong. I'll look hideous," she seethed.

"Well, it *is* a Halloween party," he said. She glared at him with blue eyes, narrow and hateful, and she continued her complaining.

"All the good dresses were taken, and there isn't time to have one made. It'll do, I suppose."

"After enough to drink, it'll look good to you. And everyone else for that matter," he added under his breath. He could no more help being a cold-hearted bastard than she could help being bitter and jaded.

"What about your day?" she asked, with a sigh of returned obligation.

"Oh, pretty fair. The units are nearly full. By the end of the week, the few remaining will be occupied."

"That's good. I'm glad you had the sense to stay out of stocks. I read today about the outlandish situation that's going on with all that. Mildred's husband was hit hard but not wiped out, thankfully."

"Indeed," he said, wiping his mouth with his napkin. "Of course, the value of the real estate is horrendous on paper, but I've more than made up for that in gold investments and rental income." She held a glassy-eyed smile at mention of gold and was well on her way to drunk. He decided it was time.

"Speaking of a bad situation—" He paused to take a bite of steak. "You'll never guess who wandered into my office today, completely wiped out, stripped of his dignity and hours from homelessness." He chuckled.

"Hmm?" she asked, barely interested.

He watched her closely as he spoke the name. "Jonathan Garrett."

Her fork stopped mid-air, eyes fixed straight ahead.

"You remember him, of course."

She dabbed the corners of her mouth with her napkin daintily before taking three gulps of wine. "What do you mean wiped out?" she asked quietly.

"I mean broke. His little empire is gone. Lost everything and took his friends down with him, too." He gave her a minute to absorb that while he chewed another bite. Slowly, he reached out to pat her hand. "I know he was special to you at one time, but aren't you glad now you didn't end up with him, my love?" She forced a smile and nodded but didn't meet his eyes. Special was an understatement. Ruth had been completely in love with him. Jonathan had cared for her, but he had never loved her, and he never led her to believe he did. Regardless, she believed fully that they would end up married. Mutual hatred of Jonathan had brought she and Victor together. Their relationship was based on little else.

Victor asked cheerily, "What's for dessert?"

"I'm really not hungry anymore," she whispered. She took the wine from the chiller and left the room, swaying slightly. Victor finished his dinner alone, dismissed Grayson and retired to the parlor. He settled in his chair and opened the newspaper with a smug grin. He would give Ruth a while to drink herself to sleep before he went up to bed. He had no interest in witnessing her grief over Jonathan Garrett.

∞∞∞∞

"Ahna!" Caleb yelled as he burst into their home. "Arianna!"

"Up here!"

He breathed a sigh of relief and took the stairs two at a time. He found her on the bedroom floor, legs tucked under her, sorting small piles of jewelry.

"What on earth are you doing?" he asked as he sat down beside her.

"I'm checking the jewelry against the insurance paperwork. We can take or sell anything there's no record of," she explained, eyes focused on the neatly arranged piles.

"Good thinking, Ahna."

"How did it go today?" she asked distantly.

"About that. I need to talk to you. There are some things you need to know concerning where we're going–"

"I found some drapes and linens in the attic and packed them," she interrupted. "But I need help getting them downstairs."

"Okay, I'll get to that. But I really need to talk to you about where we're going. It's going to be somewhat of a shock." He touched her arm to get her attention. She stopped sorting and looked at him numbly with swollen eyes.

"I'm sure it's bad," she said quietly. He nodded with eyes full of dread. She took a deep breath and squared her shoulders. "Okay. Tell me."

∞∞∞∞

Jonathan bent down to help Ava pack a few sentimental pieces. He was thankful for something mundane to do for a moment, having no idea of how to begin to tell her where they were going and whom they were forced to rent from. Jonathan looked up suddenly. "What's that smell?"

She smiled. "It's Sven. He's cooking dinner for us. Charles and Maura are here, too. They came a couple hours ago to see if they could help with anything."

Jonathan stiffened. "I can't pay them," he told her in a low voice laced with shame.

"They know. They want to help anyway. Let them, Jonathan. They feel awful about what's happened to all of us." His brow creased in frustration. Just as he was about to protest again, Charles appeared in the entryway of the parlor.

"Hello, sir."

Jonathan turned and tried to smile. "Hello, Charles."

"I hope you don't mind us coming unannounced today, sir, but we thought it only fair that we assist you right up until you have to leave."

"Only fair?" He swallowed hard. "I can't pay you, Charles."

"We're not here for pay, sir. We're here as friends." His old eyes were kind. "You have been very good to us. You helped each of us in different ways over the years."

Jonathan stared at him, expressionless.

"Last Christmas, for instance, do you remember what you did for us, sir?" Jonathan searched his memories of the last Christmas but nothing involving his staff stood out in his mind.

"No, I'm afraid you'll have to remind me, Charles," he said, a little embarrassed.

"You gave each of us a Christmas bonus that was more than generous. That bonus made all the difference in our families having a Merry Christmas."

Maura was beside him and spoke her piece. "An' you'll remember the time me wee Scottie was terribly sick. Ye paid for his doctoring and didn't dock my pay none whilst I stayed home to care for him."

Jonathan smiled. He remembered now, but these things seemed nothing more than the decent thing to do at the time, and he had never given the decisions any second thoughts. Ava squeezed his hand and smiled at him. Jonathan looked over to see Sven looming in the doorway.

"You've not eaten a decent meal since yesterday," he accused with his hard Russian accent. Jonathan smiled, realizing he hadn't eaten since breakfast the day before.

"Actually, Sven, I haven't. I'm starving."

"Roast and potatoes. I will call you when ready." He turned to the kitchen with a nod. Maura and Charles continued sorting and packing necessities, and Jonathan realized that this was his first taste of charity. He didn't mind it as much as he thought he would, as it was coming from sincere souls.

"Well," he said, turning to Ava and pulling her into a hug. "I guess this gives us some time to talk. There are some things I need to tell you about today. And about tomorrow." He walked her to the couch, turning slightly so he could look her in the eyes. Taking a deep breath, he began to recount the day, omitting details about his assaults on the garbage can and dumpster. He gave her a full description of the apartment and location in a somber tone. He had decided to give her every detail, so there would be no surprises tomorrow, but he spontaneously decided to keep the fact that Victor was the owner from her for as long as possible. She listened and maintained a neutral expression, nodding periodically. When he was finished, there was a long silence as she tried to picture what he described.

"Are you all right, Ava?" he asked, breaking her concentration.

"I am." The crackling snaps of logs in the fireplace filled the room while they both sat deep in thought. She asked some carefully worded questions, pausing for several moments after his awkward, uncertain answers. Finally, she let out a heavy sigh, closed her eyes and rubbed her forehead.

"What's wrong, Ava?" he asked, thinking it an absurd question.

"I was actually thinking about Arianna," she said suddenly. "I'm worried about her. She hasn't been right."

"There's a lot about Arianna that isn't right."

"No, Jon, really. After she woke, we talked today, and she told me about some things that happened in Paris. I knew she was on the wild side, life of the party and all, from the times when we were with her but . . . ."

He put his arm around her and leaned them both back to rest on the back of the couch. He was grateful to talk about anything other than the hovel they were about to call home, and that Ava hadn't fallen apart when he told her of the conditions.

"Arianna acts on emotion and doesn't give a care what society deems appropriate. That's not to say that Arianna doesn't enjoy shocking people because, truly, she does, and she often acts on that. She is also the vainest creature that ever lived. She needs to know that every living thing on earth loves her because, truth be told, I don't think she loves herself at all. She has to stand apart from the crowd. She has been known to go out of her way to make someone's heart race or blood boil just to prove that she can."

"Well, how does Caleb feel about her acting like this?" she asked, still confused.

"Everything about Arianna fascinates him." He shook his head in pity. "He is so completely smitten. She is most comfortable in Paris with friends who consider themselves free from what we consider proper behavior. Caleb told me of some of the wild evenings they've had. Arianna would play cards, drink and smoke cigars right alongside the men. She was right at home. I can guarantee you that the hardest part of all this for her is that she has no idea when they will be able to get back to Paris."

"Will she be all right?" Ava asked.

"Honestly, I don't care. It's you I'm worried about," he said, touching her face, his blue eyes full of concern.

"I'll be all right, Jon." She gave a brave smile. "I'm worried about you."

"I'll be fine," he said with eyes that betrayed his lie.

Sven's booming voice pulled them both away from their distractions. "Dinner is served."

Jonathan turned to Sven, Charles, and Maura. "You will be joining us, of course." He wasn't asking. The three sat down hesitantly for the first time at the same table. Charles began to pour the wine.

Maura put her hand over her glass and scoffed, "I'll have none of that grape juice. Charles, fetch your flask, so I can pour meself a proper drink."

Charles squirmed in his seat.

"Maura," he said nervously. "I've no flask in my possession."

"Yer a bloody lyin' Brit. I've seen ye swig it every day I've been in service here!" Jonathan smiled and went to fetch the cut glass decanter of brandy from the parlor. He set it before Maura.

"Have your fill, my dear," he said and smiled as her eyes lit up.

"Now that's more like it," she said, filling her glass to the brim.

There was a knock at the door, quickly followed by Caleb's voice.

"Sorry we're late!" he called from the foyer.

Charles looked at Jonathan. "I forgot to mention, sir, that Maura went over earlier and invited the others to join us tonight."

"No, that's quite all right," Jonathan said.

Caleb, Arianna, Aryl and Claire entered the dining room quietly and took their seats. They passed the food clockwise around the table. The atmosphere was somewhat lighter; the circle of close friends complete. It was tempting to forget for the moment their worries and fears as they ate, drank, and talked. Arianna, who was sitting next to Maura, helped herself to the brandy which Maura kept protectively close to her plate. She downed a glassful and then poured another.

"We would like to return tomorrow if we could be of some help," Charles offered. Jonathan sighed uncomfortably and ran his fingers through his hair.

"We'll be leaving tomorrow. Caleb, Aryl, and I were going to make a few trips over this evening, actually, to get things started." This was news to Ava, who glanced at Jonathan with a surprised look.

"I'm sorry," he whispered close to her ear, his dark, blue eyes apologetic as he pulled back. "I'll get home as soon as I can, I promise."

"How are you intending on transporting your belongings, sir?"

"We'll walk them, I suppose."

"I hope you don't mind, but I arranged the use of my brother's automobile. It is parked out back if you'd like to make use of it until the morning," Charles said. Jonathan was at a loss for words; grateful yet embarrassed.

Caleb smiled and said, "That's wonderful, Charles. It'll help us out a great deal."

∞∞∞∞

Jonathan carefully set a blanket-covered box into the backseat of the borrowed car. It was the last of his secret stash of alcohol. He leaned on the car and waited for the others. He didn't want to leave the car unattended for fear of theft. That new feeling of vulnerability is what caused him to push off the back of the car and turn quickly toward the approaching footsteps on the sidewalk. He recognized the man immediately; Milton stopped short when he saw Jonathan.

"Milt, how are you?" Jonathan asked, somewhat reserved, wondering how Milt had fared the last week.

"Jonathan. I'm okay. You?" he replied tentatively, knowing exactly how Jonathan had fared.

"I've been better." He cast his eyes down and scuffed the concrete with his shoe. "It's been a rough week. How'd you fare through it all?" Jonathan looked up with genuine concern as Milton looked down uncomfortably again.

"Listen, I heard what happened, and I wanted to tell you that I'm really sorry. What you're going through has to be hard. Those of us who are left feel awful for you." Jonathan looked away, embarrassed and eager to change the subject.

"Listen, Milt, I've been meaning to ask you–"

"Look, Jon, I feel real bad about what's happened, but we've all been hit to some degree. I'm sorry, I really wish I could help you out, but we took a decent loss, too, and with the new baby and all . . . I just can't. Good luck, though, buddy." He gave Jonathan two hard pats on the arm and rushed past him. Jonathan watched him walk away, stunned. He had intended to ask about Milton and Sarah's baby, born just a few weeks ago. He was curious if it had been a girl or boy. Then it hit him. *He thought I was asking for money. Thought I was begging for a handout.*

His face flooded crimson with angry embarrassment. He was tempted to chase Milton down and set things straight. Before he could decide whether to do just that, Charles spoke behind him.

"Excuse me, sir, I found these in the humidor. It's the very last of them, but I thought they might be a small luxury for you under the circumstances." Charles held out a box containing Jonathan's Cuban cigars.

"Yes, Charles, thank you," he said, smiling slightly. If memory served, he had ten, maybe twelve, cigars left. He would make those last as long as he could. When Jonathan opened it, he found the box packed full. Those of a cheaper, locally made brand surrounded the expensive, imported ones. He recalled that the brand was the same as he had given to Charles last Christmas. He looked up at Charles and smiled.

"Thank you," he said quietly.

"You weren't supposed to open it just yet, sir," he said, smiling with a twinkle in his old eyes and turned quickly toward the house. Jonathan smiled, glanced down the road at Milton's distant, foggy silhouette and his smile faded.

∞∞∞

"Stop here," Caleb ordered. The car was crowded with Charles and Sven in the front, Jonathan, Aryl, and Caleb in the back. They tucked the first load of belongings from Jonathan's house into every open space of the interior. "We've got to pick up a few things from the hardware store. Come on," he reminded him, unfolding himself out of the car. They slipped into the store just as the clerk was about to lock up.

"I'll just be a few minutes, sir," Caleb assured the clerk who looked annoyed at a last minute customer. A small, old man appeared from the back of the store.

"Nonsense! Take your time, gentlemen. Take your time! You let me know if I can help you with anything, all right?" he said cheerily with a Jewish accent. The older man placed his hand on the young clerk's shoulder and scolded him for his bad attitude. Jonathan and Aryl followed as Caleb quickly searched the three narrow aisles. He picked up a round, wooden bucket and began to fill it with various items. Caleb held up three mousetraps.

"We'll have to reuse these," he said and dropped them in the bucket as Jonathan gave a look of revulsion. He picked up two bags of plaster powder and handed them to Jonathan, who immediately handed one off to Aryl. He tossed in two trowels and a roll of tape. He also added bleach, steel wool pads, three hasps, a box of screws and three key locks to the bucket before walking to the register.

"And how are you gentlemen this fine evening?" the clerk asked respectfully, his attitude now adjusted.

Caleb paid for the supplies and nodded to the clerk. "It's gonna be a long night," he said. Jonathan rolled his eyes and trudged back to the car.

∞∞∞

Walking through the door of his apartment, Caleb dropped the supplies on the floor.

"I'm going to start patching the holes in the walls. Why don't you guys work on unloading and getting another trip done?"

Jonathan nodded with his hands shoved in his pockets and turned to leave.

"I stay here. I help with walls," Sven said matter-of-factly. No one was going to argue with the Russian giant.

"Great. It'll be good to have some company, and the work will get done twice as fast." Caleb tossed him a trowel and started to mix a batch of plaster in the bucket.

∞∞∞

The others soon returned to Jonathan's house to get another load, this time smuggling the oak floor radio out the back door. Ava had gathered a few small rugs, linens, and some towels. Maura added a box of basic cooking necessities, having rearranged the cupboards behind her. It was impossible to tell that anything was missing. Ava gathered one last crate of their personal items: Jonathan's straight razor, a bottle of cologne, a bottle of her perfume, a book that contained a few irreplaceable pictures of her parents and her aunt, along with addresses of their friends. She took her silver-framed wedding picture, and a wooden jewelry box that had belonged to her grandmother; other than some clothes, these were the only things they would take with them. She gazed over the few belongings.

*How do you take your entire life with you if you have to walk out the door with only what you can carry? How?*

∞∞∞

Caleb had screwed hasps into place on the outside of each of their doors. This would make them all feel better about leaving their only worldly possessions alone overnight. Caleb and Sven worked at an amazing pace and had nearly completed the patching in his apartment by the time Jonathan's second load arrived. It wasn't the prettiest job in the world, but the white spots did look better than gaping holes. Caleb and Sven began repairing the holes in Aryl's apartment as the others went to gather Aryl and Claire's belongings.

"So, Sven. Where do you live?" Caleb asked.

"In an apartment," was his monotone answer.

"You got a family at home?"

"Wife."

"How long have you been cooking?"

"Since little boy." Sven stared straight ahead with a hard face and worked diligently.

"How long have you been working for Jonathan?"

"Five years." There was a long pause, the sound of trowels scraping the walls echoed in the empty apartment.

"You know, Sven, I don't know if I can concentrate with your constant yapping over there," Caleb joked. Sven said nothing, but glanced over at him with an infinitesimal grin.

∞∞∞∞

Arianna dropped very unladylike into the armchair, holding a drink in one hand as she dug in her handbag for something with the other. Ava and Claire were sitting on the sofa across from her, legs crossed with hands neatly folded in their laps and watching her with raised eyebrows. Arianna lit a cigarette, leaned back into the chair, and crossed her legs in a masculine manner. Claire looked at her in horror.

"Arianna! Proper women don't sit like that!" she scolded, looking her up and down in reproach. Ava just smiled, wondering if Claire knew the extent of Arianna's antics on other continents.

"Well, the thing about that, Claire," she paused to exhale, "is we're not exactly proper women anymore, now, are we? On the societal scale, we're no more proper than back-shanty, hired help. No offense, Maura," she said genuinely.

Maura raised her glass. "None taken," she assured and sipped her drink as Arianna continued.

"My mother used to preach about the silver lining. 'Always find the silver lining in a situation, for no matter how desperate it may seem, one can be found'," she said, mimicking her mother's southern accent. "I always thought she was an optimistic simpleton."

"A smart woman, she was," Maura piped up.

"But then I got to thinking that without the dreaded pressures of proper society bearing down on me, I am free to have my drinks when I like, smoke when I like and damn well curse when I like," she said and smiled. "There's no worry of shocking one of Caleb's clients or hurting the firm's reputation by his wife's bad behavior." She paused to flick her cigarette and accidentally spilled her drink on the deep-green Persian carpet. Ava gasped and jumped up.

"Ava, it's not your carpet to worry after anymore," Arianna reminded her. Ava thought about that and slowly sat back down.

"You're right," she said, somewhat saddened.

"Well, that's a relief!" Maura chimed in loudly, who had placed herself in front of the fireplace with the decanter of brandy securely by her side. "Because I spilled me Bloody Mary behind Mr. Jonathan's favorite chair, and I'm afraid it's gonna stink somethin' awful tomorra'."

Ava laughed at her former maid and shrugged her shoulders. "Like Arianna said, it's not my carpet anymore, Maura."

"So, *anyway*," Arianna said, "I decided this morning that, by the end of today, I would find one silver lining in this whole mess. And I did," she said, holding up her glass and taking another drag from her cigarette. Claire and Ava weren't quite sure what to say. Ava had expected her to further fall apart, not actually find a glint of good out of the whole situation.

"Maura, why don't you make Ava and Claire a drink to celebrate my new found freedom? And no grape juice," she said and smiled at her devilishly.

"I'd be happy to, love." Maura returned the sinister grin, wobbled her way to the liquor cabinet to pour two shots of whiskey and delivered them to Ava and Claire.

Arianna held up her glass.

"To good friends and silver linings," she toasted. Ava and Claire were hesitant and glanced warily at each other. They were accustomed to a single glass of wine with dinner and nothing more. After a moment, they gave each other a 'why not' shrug and quickly tilted up their shot glasses.

Claire squeezed her eyes shut and shook her head, hard. Ava's eyes watered, lips puckered, and then she gagged. Arianna and Maura laughed hysterically at them.

"Aye, tis the first shot that burns. The next'll be easier," Maura assured them, patting Ava's head and laughing.

"I think I'm quite all right, thank you," Ava said with a gasp, wiping her eyes.

"Nonsense!" Arianna yelled. "We've only just started! We're celebrating, remember? Maura, let's have another all around."

∞∞∞

The mood was somber as Aryl directed Jonathan and Charles toward the few boxes and crates Claire had organized. Much of the same basic items were included with the only extravagances being Claire's box of paints, her wooden easel, and a few canvases.

It was getting late and Jonathan was eager to get this depressing task over with and get home to Ava. Aryl took Caleb's place repairing holes, and Jonathan helped Caleb transport his and Arianna's belongings, which took three trips because of extra things Arianna couldn't *bear* to part with.

When they returned from the last trip, they began cleaning the bathrooms and kitchens. Sven tackled the cast-iron, claw foot tubs, scrubbing off years of black grime from the chipped, white porcelain finish. Caleb fixed the screw plates on the metal garbage chute doors and lined the wall with layers of masking tape to create a seal. Jonathan worked on the sink and gas stove by scrubbing off years of neglect and checking connections. They put Charles in charge of sweeping the floors. He was, after all, in his sixties and had put in more than a full day already. The others admired his tenacity and devotion. The work went on late into the night.

∞∞∞

"*Just* one more." Ava giggled and held out her glass, her swaying arm making it hard for Arianna to pour. They were all sitting on the floor cross-legged in a circle.

"I don't know for the life of me why I never tried this before!" she slurred and tilted her glass back.

Claire leaned close to her and whispered loudly, "We were proper women before, that's why!" Claire burst out laughing and fell over on her side. Arianna could barely hold herself up, not from intoxication, but from hysterical laughter at witnessing her friends in a very drunken state for the first time.

"I think this be the last drink o' the night for ye, my dear," Maura said, pouring a wobbly Ava another peach brandy.

"But why?" Ava asked with half-opened glazed eyes. "I'm having so much. . . ," She had to stop to remember the word. "Fun," she said triumphantly.

"Yes, my dear, but ye'll be fallin' over on yer face fore long. Yer not used to this strong a drink," Maura said.

"I wonder what's taking the men so long," Claire wondered aloud.

"Caleb told me they would be making some repairs and doing some cleaning so it's not quite so bad when we get there tomorrow," Arianna volunteered.

"That's so wonderful of them," Claire squeaked and looked as if she would start crying, but a long, loud belch erupted which caused everyone to roll with laughter again. Arianna didn't like talking about tomorrow. Or yesterday, for that matter. She knew the men would have a late night which is why she secretly planned this little party. Arianna watched her friends, and she was glad that they were a little less miserable.

Claire was giggling at an off-color joke Maura was privately telling her. Ava was slumped over, patting her face with a confused look.

"Ava," Arianna called to her, smiling. It took Ava a few seconds to find the voice calling her and focus on it. "Are you okay?"

"It's the strangest thing. I can't feel my face. I know I have a face, but I can't feel it," she half-whispered.

"Definitely time for you to stop, my dear," Arianna replied. Ava nodded dizzily in agreement. "C'mon, off to bed with you," Arianna ordered. "It's very late." Ava nodded again and tried unsuccessfully to stand up. Arianna and Maura helped her upstairs and into bed, leaving her fully dressed. She passed out before they even left the room. Claire was lying on her back, singing and waving her arms as if she was conducting a symphony. Arianna smiled. Despite her less admirable qualities, she did care for her friends. She felt happy that they would sleep soundly, the sadness of their misfortune far from their minds, even if only for tonight.

∞∞∞∞

"Arianna, what have you *done?*" Caleb asked, with a look and tone that was all too familiar as he surveyed the room; toppled over glasses, empty decanters, cigarette butts strewn about, and a very intoxicated Claire lay on the couch. Arianna turned to see Jonathan, Aryl, and Caleb looking rather shocked in the doorway of the parlor. Maura excused herself quickly and hurried toward the door as if she were dodging invisible bullets.

"We had a going away party. It was fun. I wish you could have been here," she said and smiled ever-so-innocently.

"Where's Ava?" Jonathan asked with a frown, as he peeled of his coat, now smeared with dirt and bits of plaster.

"She's upstairs," Arianna answered.

"C'mon, Claire, let's get you home," Aryl said, pulling her to her feet and steadying her.

Caleb pulled Arianna aside. "This is not funny, Arianna. Jon and Aryl have been itching to get home for hours and not to watch their wives *sleep*," he said, raising his eyebrows.

"Caleb, don't you dare scold me. You men have been busy thinking, running, and doing, and we've all been stuck here with nothing to do but wring our hands and be scared. We may have gotten a little carried away tonight, but we had fun. This night, by all rights, should have had us crying ourselves to sleep, knowing we have to leave our beautiful houses tomorrow." His face softened, like it always did, and she snuggled up to him, wrapping her arms around his neck. "Besides," she whispered and smiled seductively. "*I'm* still wide-awake." Caleb looked over at Jonathan. He would make apologies for his wife another time.

"See you tomorrow, Jon," he called.

∞∞∞∞

"Sounds like you girls had a hoot tonight, eh, Claire?" Aryl made his way down the street with Claire pulled to his side.

"Maura is so funny!" She giggled. "She told dirty jokes all night. And Ava told us all about her life growing up and losing her parents to the big flu and how her mean ole cousins arranged for her to meet that awful man," she paused to take a deep breath. "Arianna told us about Paris, the dancing shows, and the operas and all the fun you guys had there and the beautiful women that run around scantily dressed."

Aryl stiffened. "Oh, yeah? What, uh, else did she tell you about that?"

Claire shrugged sloppily and stumbled over a root distorting the sidewalk. She couldn't remember many details, even with the cold wind's sobering effect. The women had taken turns bearing their souls to each other during that uninhibited time between tipsy and thoroughly drunk.

"Where's Maura?" Claire asked, looking around.

"Charles took her and Sven home. They'll be back tomorrow to drive us over to the new place."

"Arianna told us that you guys were cleaning and fixing tonight." Claire smiled up at him.

"We were," he said, helping her navigate her way up the steps to their front door.

"That was really sweet of you, Aryl. But we could have done that tomorrow. You have to leave something for us women to do."

"It wasn't much. And there's still plenty to do. You remember what I told you before dinner about the apartment?" he asked as they stepped into the foyer.

"Uh huh," she said, trying to hang up her coat but missing the knobby end of the hook. He took the coat from her, shaking his head with a smile.

"Let's get you to bed. I'll talk to you in the morning before we head over there," he said.

"Why don't you talk to me now?" she asked, carefully making her way up the staircase with Aryl's hands on her waist, keeping her steady.

"I doubt you'd remember a word I said. This is the first time you've ever been truly intoxicated, isn't it?"

"I'm not intop-sir-cated," she said with a frown.

In their room, he helped her quickly out of her dress and slowly into her silk sleeping gown, taking a few minutes to admire her nakedness as she lacked any kind of modesty in her current state. He helped her into bed, stripped off his own clothes and slipped under the covers. He dreaded the coming day and realized how much he would miss this house and this room. They had made many, many good memories in this room. He rolled over to face Claire.

"You know, Claire, we're going to have to start all over."

"Start what over?"

"Making memories. At the new place," he said, tugging the covers away from her. She grabbed them and pulled them up tight to her chin.

"We're not at the new place yet," she said sleepily. He propped himself up on one elbow and pushed the blond hair out of her face.

"Do you remember the lighthouse, Claire?"

"Of course," she said, yawning.

"What do you remember?" She opened her eyes and tried to concentrate.

"I remember watching that terrible storm from the lantern room. The drafts kept blowing out the candles, and there was lightning and loud thunder . . . the smell of the sea and the musty, wool blankets. And I remember you and me," she said and smiled, slightly embarrassed and closed her eyes again.

"Do you remember being happy?"

"Of course. I was with you," she said simply.

"Do you remember being cold and hungry?"

"Yes, now I do." She snuggled deeper into the covers.

"But you were happy."

"Yes. Why are you asking me about our lighthouse?"

"Because it's important, I want you to remember it. I want you to keep those memories in the front of your mind tomorrow. Will you remember that, Claire?" he asked and kissed her forehead.

"I don't understand." She yawned wide.

"You will," he whispered, slipping one arm under her and pulling her close. They were both asleep within minutes.

∞∞∞

*J*onathan assumed Ava had only barely drifted off and did not attempt to be quiet while changing and stoking the fire. He flopped into bed, making it wiggle considerably. Her back was to him and she still hadn't moved. He put one hand on her shoulder and shook it gently.

"Ava," he whispered. "I'm home, love." Her response was two loud snorts as she rolled onto her back. She inhaled deeply, as her head rolled, and she exhaled directly into Jonathan's face.

"Whoa!" His nose wrinkled and he squeezed his eyes shut as he turned away from the peach-tainted stench. He looked back at her in disbelief. *She's as drunk as a skunk*! He couldn't picture his quiet and reserved wife throwing back drinks with Arianna and the others. He looked at her for a moment, astounded and finally kissed her cheek, carefully timing the peck to avoid her exhalation. "Sweet dreams," he whispered and lay back on his pillow with his hands behind his head. Only two days had passed, yet he hadn't eaten much, slept even less, and the events had been so emotionally exhausting that he felt as if deprived of sleep for weeks. He couldn't get comfortable, and his mind wouldn't stop reliving events he would prefer to forget forever: the scene at the Exchange, Ava's face when he told her, the confrontation with Victor, seeing the horrendous apartment for the first time, his longtime friend turning his back on him. Moreover, despite Caleb's optimism, Jonathan knew deep down that there was no possible way to recover from this. Their lives would never be the same. Not even close. It takes money to make money, and they were fresh out of that commodity. It would be a hard life now. Struggling, sadness, and frustration would be daily staples. The room was still and quiet with nothing to distract him from crushing hopelessness. He berated himself for not seeing the warning signs, not saving more cash at home, and for over-extending his credit. All of this ignorance had combined to create the perfect storm that destroyed his life. *Hindsight is twenty-twenty*. He glanced at the clock. It was after four o'clock in the morning. Ava shifted beside him with a whimper as he got up and tied his robe around his waist. Arianna's impromptu party hadn't left him much to console himself with downstairs, but three drinks on an empty stomach, along with little sleep, had him heavy-eyed enough to return to bed, closing his eyes to his old life.

October 31<sup>st</sup> 1929

Jonathan finished pulling the carpetbags from the trunk. He turned to Charles, extending his hand.

"Thank you for your help. Thank your brother for the use of his automobile as well," he said, glancing back at it. He had owned one very similar to this, and he would miss it.

As Charles drove away, they noticed that people had started to gather in small groups, staring and whispering. They weren't dressed in their best, but they were still dressed in finery that no one in this neighborhood would be wearing. Picking up the carpetbags, they began up the three flights of dirty stairs to their new homes.

∞∞∞∞

"That will fade," Caleb told her. Overwhelming bleach odor burned Arianna's nose. "Now that we're here, we can open a window for a while."

She noticed two cracks in the windowpane covered by masking tape. A cold burst of air filled the apartment and began to dissipate the smell. Arianna lowered her hand from her mouth and nose, her eyes inspecting the room. There were boxes, crates and a few bags piled in the corner of the room.

"We patched all these holes last night, Sven and me. I'm going to repaint the whole room so that the white patches don't stand out as much. These walls are impossible to clean. It's in much better shape than the first time I walked in here. Definitely cleaner. There's the kitchen," he rambled, taking her hand and leading her in. "Small. It has everything we need for the most part. No electric icebox. We'll have to get used to that. Here's the garbage chute." He hoped she would notice his repair job on the rusty door.

Her face was still set in stone as they walked out of the kitchen, and he led her into the bathroom. "Sven gave himself blisters scrubbing this tub. It looks a lot better . . . ." His voice trailed off as he looked up at the round, metal ring by the tub. The wall mounts needed reinforcing before it would hold the weight of a towel. He added that to his mental list of things to do. He walked out of the bathroom and around the corner to the bedroom, towing Arianna behind.

It was a small room with no window, and a lone light bulb hung from a wire in the center of the ceiling. A lopsided, stained mattress on a broken frame set close to one wall. Caleb had squeezed Arianna's vanity in the small space left. All of her make-up, perfumes, brushes, hats, and hair accessories were arranged on it almost the same as they had been in their old home. Her eyes softened when she saw it. It was a dark oak, richly engraved vanity table with an adjustable oval mirror held up on either side by elaborately carved wood that wound down and around the table. Between the glass and the wooden frame, Caleb had wedged pictures; some taken of her while on vacation, some of the two of them taken professionally and a few postcards she had collected from Paris. The ornate vanity looked terribly out of place in this dreary room.

"How did you get this here?" she asked in amazement. She hadn't even noticed it missing this morning. Last night, she had been rather preoccupied with other things, but this morning she thought surely she would have noticed it missing. She remembered waking up, putting on a dress and simply walking out of her bedroom for the last time without looking back.

"It wasn't easy," Caleb said and smiled, happy she had noticed at least some of his efforts. "Jonathan practically had to sit on my lap in the front seat with this thing wedged in the back."

"Thank you for bringing it," she whispered.

He walked over and turned her to face him. "Arianna, you know this is temporary, don't you? Don't get too cozy because we won't be here for long. I'm already working on three different ideas that are going to take off like a shot and catapult us right out of this dump." She nodded, avoiding his eyes. "You do believe me, don't you, Ahna?"

"I do, Caleb. I believe you."

He relaxed a little. "Good. I'm completely serious. Me, Jon, and Aryl are meeting together this week, and we're going to get to work on a plan. With my ideas, Aryl's creativity and Jon's leadership, I'll be surprised if we're here past the first of the year," he said confidently.

"I guess we should get to work putting things away," she said quietly, turning toward the living room.

"Hey, I'll go down, buy some wood, and we'll have a fire tonight. How's that sound?" he asked, tapping the mantel of the ragged fireplace. Two bricks came loose from just below the mantel and crashed down onto the hearth. Caleb sighed heavily, adding that to his growing fix-it list.

"That sounds fine," Arianna said, picking up the bricks and handing them to Caleb. He wedged them back in and hoped they would stay until he could fix them permanently. "Can we close that window now? I'm freezing," she said, crossing her arms.

∞∞∞

"I tried to warn you," Jonathan said. Ava slowly walked from room to room. He leaned against the wall by the front door with his hands in his pockets, staring at the floor. She walked slowly back toward the door and stood in front of him. He hesitated to look up at her. If she were silently crying or had a horrified expression on her face, he didn't know if he would be able to stand it.

"I tried to warn you, Ava," he repeated quietly.

"I know. And you gave an accurate description." Her voice was even and calm. "I can see you worked hard last night," she said, looking at the white spots on the walls and recognizing the smell of cleanser.

"It was a group effort," he said, silently wishing that he had thought of and organized the work party instead of Caleb. There was a long silence as each of them stared in opposite directions.

"Will you help me get these boxes unpacked?" she asked, breaking the silence.

"Sure," he said, still staring at the cracked window.

∞∞∞

"So, I was thinking you could paint a mural all around the fireplace," Aryl said. "You could have the beach on this side, and the ocean on the other. Maybe you could paint our lighthouse right over the mantel." Her eyes darted to him, full of tears.

"This is why you wanted me to remember the lighthouse?" she asked, unable to conceal her horror.

"Yes."

"What in the world does this horrible place have to do with our lighthouse?"

He paused a moment, taking a deep breath. "Well, it's sort of the same, Claire. We were so cold and hungry that night and into the next day as well. We spent almost twenty-four hours in that dirty lighthouse and rode out the storm together, and we'll ride out this storm, too. It'll just take a little longer, that's all. I know it's bad, Claire, but we can spruce this place up. We can make it a home for the time being. This isn't forever, I promise. We won't be here a day longer than we have to be."

She nodded and wiped her tears, thinking about that night in the lighthouse. They were so miserable yet so happy together. However, it had only lasted a day, and they knew they could go back to their comfortable homes as soon as the storm passed. She wondered when this would pass. If this would pass. She tried to appreciate Aryl's attitude and hoped that she hadn't let him down by being so upset. With a deep breath, she decided she would show a braver face.

"I can paint the whole wall?" she asked with a sniffle.

"Every wall in this apartment if you want," he said and smiled. "C'mon, let's set up your easel. Where do you want it? Maybe over in the corner? Or closer to the window for the natural light?"

∞∞∞

It didn't take long for Ava to put away the dishes, make the lumpy bed, and cover the tattered couch with a sheet. Neither of them said anything for the next several hours.

"Now what do we do?" she asked. Jonathan had returned from buying firewood and sat on the couch, which they had moved closer to the fireplace.

"I have no idea," he said flatly.

"I'm glad you brought the radio," she said, walking over to turn it on. She adjusted the tuning dial until she found good reception.

"Maybe dinner?" he asked. "I could go out and get something. I think the deli downstairs is still open."

"I'm not hungry. Just get something for yourself."

"Nah. I'm not hungry either," he said and went back to staring at the fire.

∞∞∞

"Who could that be?" Claire asked from the kitchen. Aryl shrugged. He opened the door and looked down to see a small boy, maybe six years old with shaggy, brown hair and big, brown eyes. He was dressed in a man's plaid shirt, baggy and rolled up on his tiny arms. He held a stick with a red bandana tied to it over one shoulder and a grubby pillowcase with the other. Shoe polish was smeared on his face to mimic a beard.

"Trick or Treat!" he yelled up at Aryl.

"Well, isn't that cute. You're a hobo, aren't you?"

"Yep!" the little boy yelled, thoroughly proud of his costume. Claire was behind Aryl, looking at the boy and instantly felt sorry for him.

"Poor thing. I completely forgot that tonight is Halloween!" she said, amazed.

"Me, too," he said, pausing to think a minute. They hadn't bought groceries, much less candy or treats to give out. "Okay, I've got it," he said.

He took a penny out of his pocket, put it in the palm of one hand, and closed his fists, holding them behind his back. The little boy giggled with excitement as Aryl held out both fists. "Pick the hand with the penny, and you can have it," he said. The boy squirmed, grinning from ear to ear, trying to decide which hand to pick. Finally, he chose the right fist. Aryl opened it to show him an empty palm, and the little boy's face dropped.

"Tell you what," Aryl said. "I'll give you one more chance." The boy's face lit up again, and he reached out to tap Aryl's left fist. Again, he opened it to show an empty palm.

"You dropped it behind you!" the boy yelled with a grin. Aryl shook his head no, reached behind the boy's ear and pulled out the shiny penny. He was thoroughly amazed as Aryl dropped the penny in his grimy pillowcase.

"Oh wow!" he yelled with excitement. "Happy Halloween!" He took off like a bullet down the hall.

"Cute kid." He gave a light chuckle as he closed the door. Claire stared at him, smiling.

"That was very sweet of you, Aryl. You made him very happy."

Aryl shrugged. "It's bad enough for us to have to live here. Imagine what it's like to grow up here."

Claire walked over and hugged him, unable to put into words a compliment worthy of how she really felt about him. "I seem to vaguely remember something you said last night," she started.

"I'm surprised you remember anything at all from last night," he said with a laugh. "But what do you vaguely remember?"

"I remember you telling me that we would have to start all over making memories in the new place. Well, we're in the new place. I say let's start making those memories."

"I think that's the best idea I've heard in days," he growled playfully, backing toward the bedroom slowly without letting her go.

A moment later, there was a loud pounding on the door. He pulled his lips away from hers. "You've got to be kidding me," he groaned.

"Ignore it. They'll go away," Claire whispered and quickly reclaimed his mouth. The knocking continued.

"Lemme get rid of them, okay? Don't go anywhere," he said and kissed her again.

"Where am I going to go?" she said, surveying the tiny apartment.

Aryl opened the door to a gaggle of at least fourteen children, all dressed up as either hobos or bed sheet ghosts, which were the easiest and cheapest costumes in the world to make. He laughed aloud and clapped his hands on his head.

"Hey, Claire, you've got to see this," he called. She popped her head around him and laughed as well. Aryl looked at the original trick-or-treater. "You went and told all your friends, didn't you?" The little boy smiled shyly and hid behind the group. "All right, Claire," he sighed. "I'm gonna need more pennies."

She dug through her handbag, passing off pennies and Aryl repeated the penny trick for each trick-or-treater. After receiving their treat, each one stayed to watch the trick repeatedly with eyes wide and excited. Then they collectively turned and ran away.

"Tell the rest of your friends I'm out of pennies!" Aryl yelled after them. He turned around and Claire was right behind him.

"If anyone else knocks on this door, Aryl Sullivan, you are going to ignore it, understand?" she asked, kissing him before he could answer.

∞∞∞

The rag-tag group of trick-or-treaters worked their way down the hall, knocking on every door. Outside Jonathan's apartment, the group knocked loudly, pulling him from his distant stare into the fire. Opening the door, he beheld the large group of hobos and ghosts and couldn't help but smile ruefully.

"Trick or treat!" they shouted in unison. Jonathan rubbed his forehead and grimaced.

"Sorry, guys, I don't have any candy," he said, suddenly feeling worse than he did before. Something he thought wasn't possible.

They chattered as Jonathan closed the door.

"Awww!"

"Dang it."

"Told you so."

"Let's try the next floor."

Last Halloween, he had ordered four cases of chocolate bars from the Hershey factory and handed them out to children in clean and adorable costumes. He decorated the walkway elaborately and had dressed up as a pirate to pass out the bars. After dark, he and Ava had gone to a Halloween party at Milton and Sarah's. His friends spared no expense and threw a fantastic party. Jonathan looked around the shabby room before sitting back down.

"This is definitely the scariest Halloween I've ever had," he said, setting his eyes listlessly back on the fire.

"What was that?" Ava called from the bathroom.

"Nothing. Where did you put the books I packed?" he asked.

"They're stacked by the door," she replied and went back to rearranging the personal items Jonathan had unpacked. He flipped through the small stack of books. Deciding which ones to bring with him had been difficult; he had wanted to bring them all. He settled on bringing his favorite dozen and now tried to decide which one to reread. He sat back down with a war novel and tried to ignore the pounding coming from upstairs and the loud voices of the neighbors through the thin walls. He didn't think that anyone lived to the left of them, not having heard a peep from that side. But the neighbors who lived across the hall constantly talked at a raised volume, laughed, and slammed things around. He tuned the radio to jazz music, turned it up to drown them out and sat back down with his book. Ava emerged from the bathroom, smoothing her hair. "Well, that's done. It's not perfect, but it will work well enough for now." He nodded without looking up. Another knock at the door caused him to slam down his book, cursing.

"I don't have any damned candy," he grumbled, swinging open the door.

An older, slightly pudgy woman with beady eyes and short, gray hair started talking before Jonathan had a chance to acknowledge her.

"Would you mind turning your radio down? If you haven't noticed, these walls are terribly thin." She spit the words at him and he simply stared at her. "It's all nice and fine that you're well off enough to own a radio but just because you own one doesn't mean we all want to listen to it, and I hope you don't plan on blaring that thing late into the night. My husband has enough trouble sleeping with the arthritis, and I don't sleep well for long stretches anyway. I suffer from the anemia. I'm prone to taking naps throughout the day from weakness and that causes spotty sleep at night. It's the draft that runs through these apartments. We're always taking sick with that draft carrying sickness from one apartment to the next. I hope you're clean people. I don't want any sickness floating across the hall. You got a wife?" she asked, trying to peek past him. Ava was hiding behind the door, trying to suppress her laughter. "If you do, I hope she's good at keeping a clean home. I could come over and help her, I suppose. I know how to clean proper and could give her some pointers, make sure it's done right. And I hope she don't cook with a lot of spices. Strong smells and spices tend to make my stomach turn–"

Jonathan slowly closed the door as she continued to ramble. "Dear God." He couldn't help but laugh. "Avoid that one at all costs."

"Did she even take a breath?" Ava asked.

"I have no idea. But if there're folks on our other side, too, I'm almost afraid to meet them now."

∞∞∞∞

"Wow, that was . . . ." Aryl fell back on the bed, wiping sweat from his forehead.

"Yeah, I know," Claire replied breathlessly.

"A hell of a way to start off the memories," Aryl said, grinning. They stared at the cracks in the plaster ceiling, listening to the unfamiliar noises of the new building. When the idea came to Aryl, he sat straight up in bed. "That's perfect! Claire, I need your help," he said as he got out of bed and began digging through her bag.

"What on earth are you doing?" she asked, slipping her dress over her head.

"You'll see," he said, grinning.

∞∞∞∞

"Didn't you tell those brats we didn't have any candy?"

"Yeah, I'll tell them again," Caleb said, opening the door and immediately doubling over with laughter.

"Trick or Treat!" Aryl yelled. He stood before Caleb dressed entirely as a woman. He wore one of Claire's dresses with the top stuffed to create a hefty bosom, a strand of pearls, pink curlers snapped into his short hair and a full face of makeup. Claire stood behind him, giggling. Caleb laughed for several minutes and every time he got control of himself, he would look up at Aryl and begin laughing again. Even Arianna was smiling and soon began laughing at Caleb, who couldn't stop laughing at Aryl. After a while, they all regained composure.

"Sorry, Aryl, I don't have any candy," he said and started laughing again.

"Rum?" Aryl asked.

"That I might have," Caleb said, and got an idea of his own. He pulled Aryl inside.

"Wait here. I'll be right back," he said and dashed out the door and downstairs to the deli and bought a roll of sausage, a half-pound of cheese, a loaf of sourdough bread, three candied apples, and a small pumpkin. He dashed back to the apartment, out of breath.

"Okay, Ahna, you gotta do the same thing to me. Then we'll go over to Jon's," he said, holding up the bag of groceries he bought.

Arianna shook her head. "I'll do my best, but I don't know if I can make you look as good as Aryl." She laughed as she set to work dressing Caleb up. "He's pretty cute," she admitted.

∞∞∞∞

"*What* are you reading?" Ava asked, sitting closer to Jonathan. She looked at the title before he could answer. "I haven't read that yet." Jonathan's mind flashed back to the conversation in the alley the day before.

"Better yet, why don't I read it to you?"

She nodded and curled up next to him, her head on his shoulder, and watched the fire as he read.

Just as he started the second chapter, hard rapping on the door interrupted him.

"This is getting ridiculous," he groaned.

"Don't answer it. It might be that woman again," Ava whispered.

"And if it is, I'm going to tell her exactly where to take her problems," he said, pushing himself off the worn-out couch.

"Trick or Treat!" Aryl and Caleb yelled together, as Jonathan opened the door. He took a step back and shook his head, then laughed.

"You've lost your damn minds," Jonathan said when he stopped laughing.

"It's Halloween! Don't tell me you're turning into Scrooge," Caleb said through beautifully painted, red lips.

"Don't you have your holidays confused?" Jonathan asked.

Caleb shrugged. "Same difference. Here, I brought party food," he said, holding up the bag of groceries.

"And I brought Caleb's rum!" Aryl said, holding up the bottle.

"For what party?" Jonathan asked, confused.

"Our party," Caleb said, pushing past him and handing the bag to Ava. "However," Caleb started with one eyebrow cocked, "all of us are not properly dressed for the occasion," he said and smiled at Jonathan.

"What exactly do you mean?" he asked cautiously.

Arianna handed him a balled up wad of fabric. He held it up to see that it was one of Arianna's dresses.

"Oh, no. I think not," Jonathan said, tossing it back.

"Party isn't starting until everyone is in costume," Caleb said matter-of-factly.

"Forget it," Jon countered.

Aryl held up the bottle. "No party, no rum," he said, shrugging.

"C'mon, Jon! It'll be fun," Ava said, hugging his arm. He covered his eyes with his hand and shook his head.

"I can't believe this."

Arianna clapped her hands. "I'll help you with the makeup," she offered as they dragged him off to the bathroom, still protesting.

Claire cut up the sausage, cheese, and bread. She set the pumpkin in the middle of the table, turned off the glaring, overhead bulb in the living room, lit some candles, and stoked the fire. Aryl went to fetch more chairs from their apartment.

Finally, they shoved him out of the bathroom, and the whole room roared with laughter.

"Damn, you're beautiful!" Aryl yelled. He stood there patiently while everyone laughed and complimented him on his make-up and curlers, which barely clung to his short black hair.

"Where's my drink?" he said when the laughter died down. Caleb handed him a glass then held up his own.

"To six of the most beautiful gals in the world!" he toasted.

Jonathan looked over at Aryl. "I don't even need to ask whose idea this was." He relaxed a little and smiled. "This has you written all over it, Aryl."

For the next few hours, they talked, ate, and spontaneously erupted with laughter. The soft candle and firelight combined with copious amounts of rum masked the dreary apartment somewhat, and Jonathan's mood lightened considerably. Caleb glanced at his watch, walked over to the radio, hiked his dress up and squatted in front of it to adjust the tuner until he found a Halloween special. They moved to the living room and sat on the couch and floor near the fire, listening to the show, which turned out to be more funny than scary. When it was over, Caleb stretched, straining the seams of Arianna's dress.

"We better get going. We've got a big day tomorrow, fellas."

Jonathan's heart sank as this brought him back to reality. He didn't want to think about tomorrow. He was perfectly content to stay in the present moment, where the mood was light, the drinks were plentiful, and his friends surrounded him, no matter how strangely they were dressed.

*November 1st 1929*

Jonathan stared at the ceiling as the shrill ring of the alarm clock sounded at six-thirty. Glancing at the annoying noise, he wished he had brought a different clock, any other clock. He preferred the soft chimes of the ornate grandfather clock that used to sit just outside his bedroom door. But that was his old life. In this new life, he silenced the clock and tried to stretch out his sore back and neck muscles. Ava stirred and stretched, wincing as she woke to protesting muscles as well.

"How'd you sleep?" he asked her, rolling over to give her a quick kiss.

"Horrible. It feels like I slept on a pile of rocks."

"I might have slept better on a pile of rocks."

"Maybe we should move to the floor. At least that would be a flat surface." She poked at the lumps and divots in the mattress. "Or maybe this weekend we can try to stuff the holes, even it out a bit," she said.

"Or we can buy a new mattress."

"I don't know if we should spend the money." She walked to the bathroom, rubbing her lower back. He dug through a pile of clothes to find the pants he wore the day before and pulled on a wool sweater.

"Hey, I'll be right back. I'm going to grab us something to eat," he called to her. While he was gone, she needed to take a quick shower but hadn't had the forethought to bring soap, so she simply rinsed off and made a mental note to buy some when she went out. Dressing for the day was also somewhat challenging. She was accustomed to dressing her best when she left the house, but now she had to dress simple, so as not to stand out. But even her plainest dress was nicer than what other women in this neighborhood were wearing. She settled on a pink dress, which had a low ribbon waist and a three-tiered skirt. She covered it with a long, cream-colored sweater. She heard Jonathan return as she was buckling the straps on her shoes.

"Did Maura pack the percolator?" he called out. "I picked up a pound of coffee."

"I think so," she said. "I'll make some while you take a shower," she said, taking the small bag from him and giving him a passing peck. He grabbed her before she could pass him and hugged her tight. He let go of her after a moment and turned without a word to get ready for the day.

She found two sweet rolls and four large breakfast sausages wrapped in butcher paper. She set to frying them, after struggling with the pilot light of the gas stove. Jonathan emerged from the bathroom in a dress shirt, tie, and black pants. She poured their coffee and set the sizzling sausages and sweet rolls on the small table. They ate in silence, not quite sure what to talk about. He dreaded the day before him, and she had no idea what she would do with herself once she bought soap and a few groceries. A knock on the door interrupted the uncomfortable silence.

"I figured as much," Caleb said, glancing over him as Jonathan opened the door.

"Figured what?" Jonathan asked.

"Here." He handed him a blue work shirt. "You don't need a shirt and tie for what we're going to be doing today. The pants will do, I suppose, but they'll get ruined," Caleb warned.

"I don't really have anything suitable for manual labor," Jonathan said, irritated. Caleb pointed to the shirt in Jonathan's hands.

"That's why I brought you that."

"Thanks," Jonathan muttered and went to the bathroom to change.

"Would you like some coffee, Caleb?" Ava asked.

"No, thanks. We're going to have to get a move on, or we're going to be late." Ava nodded and started clearing the table. A few moments later, Jonathan appeared in the blue shirt, which didn't look right with the dress slacks or black shoes.

"Did you pack a lunch?" Caleb asked.

"No." Jonathan hadn't packed a lunch since high school. He wasn't sure why, but he found the idea utterly demeaning.

"We'll buy something today, but from now on, we're going to want to bring lunch. It'll save money. Aryl's waiting outside so we better get going," he said, smiled politely to Ava and turned, leaving them to their goodbyes.

"Don't go out alone today," Jonathan said, walking over to Ava. "Make sure you girls stick together when you go shopping. And don't wander too far. If you need to go more than a block or two away, I'll take you after I get home," he said, pulling money out of his wallet. "This should cover whatever you need to pick up today," he said and laid a ten-dollar bill on the table.

"That will more than cover it," she said. She straightened his collar and smoothed down the shoulders of the thick shirt. "Try to have a good day," she added sympathetically. She could see the toll the week had taken on him. The normal brilliance of his blue eyes was dulled, his face sullen, his brow furrowed, dark circles shadowed his eyes and his rounded shoulders sagged; the picture of an entirely defeated soul. He nodded, unable to promise an effort aloud and simply pulled her close.

"If it wasn't for you, Ava," he whispered in her ear. She didn't want him to finish the sentence, already having a vague idea of what he meant. She pulled her head back and smiled.

"I'll make a nice dinner tonight, all right? What would you like?"

"Hmm." He looked up at the ceiling while he thought, his hands still laced together on the small of her back. "Steak and lobster." She laughed, shaking her head at his ridiculous request.

"I'll see what I can do," she said, rising up on her toes. A kiss goodbye quickly turned fervent. It was the first decent kiss they had shared in a week, and he savored every second of it. Lifting her at the waist, he took two steps forward, pinning her against the wall and continued to kiss her with growing intensity.

Caleb knocked on the open door twice, clearing his throat while respectfully looking down at the floor. Jonathan pulled away reluctantly and sighed.

"I'll see you tonight," he said quietly and squeezed her one last time. She smiled, her eyes following him until the door closed. Still leaning against the wall, she took a deep breath and folded her arms, looking around the drab apartment. It seemed larger and colder now that she was alone. The hollow day loomed before her, and the last thing she needed was more time to think. There was busy work she could occupy herself with, but even if she took painstaking detail with each task, she would never fill the day. She tuned the radio and began her mundane chores.

∞∞∞

The walk to the shipping dock was brisk. They passed the gate where the day workers gathered and heard the supervisor announce how many men were needed for the day. The workers clamored and yelled over each other in hopes of being chosen. Caleb swatted Jonathan in the chest with the back of his hand as they walked past.

"We're lucky," he said, gesturing to the frenzy of desperate day workers. Jonathan was hardly in a frame of mind to consider himself lucky. They walked around the corner, dodging delivery trucks, vendors haggling deals and men selling apples from crates. They passed a man standing beside his new automobile with a defeated look on his face. There was a cardboard sign set on the windshield; shaky handwriting offered the Packard for $100 cash. A newspaper boy shouted the day's headlines that the worst was over and recovery had begun both here and abroad. The friends paid no attention to this, especially Jonathan. He shut his eyes tightly as he walked by. He knew in his soul nothing would ever be normal again.

Aryl led them through the side entrance of a brick building and made his way back to Roman's office.

"Aryl, good to see you. These the friends you were talkin' about?"

Aryl nodded. "Roman, this is Jonathan Garrett and Caleb Jenkins." Roman nodded at each of them before he turned to his desk.

"Got some paperwork for you boys to fill out. Just basic employment stuff. Should only take a few minutes. I didn't have near as much trouble getting the big boss to approve the third guy. You know the positions I was trying to fill when you came to see me, Aryl? Well, I found out later that two of our guys took a flying leap off a tall building. Put every hard earned cent into those stocks and lost everything they ever worked for." He paused, shaking his head. "Nice guys, too. Anyway, a third guy busted up his arm pretty bad yesterday, so it all worked out I guess," he said, handing out the small packets of papers. "Get that filled out and I'll show you around. Then I'll get you boys to work."

Ten minutes later, Roman was leading the trio out the back of the office building into the bustling shipping yard. "The large cranes lift crates and pallets off the ship deck and lower them to the platform here. These forklifts carry each load to different areas. These little inventions sure have made life easier. Anyway, once inventoried, it's hand-loaded onto the trucks for delivery. That's what you boys will be doing." Jonathan was visibly irritated at Roman's repeated use of the term *boys* and resented being spoken to as if he had no idea how a shipping yard operated.

A tall, thin man with a very weathered face appeared next to Roman.

"These the new hires?"

"Yeah. Harvey, this is Caleb and Jon," Roman said, pointing to each. "And you remember Aryl. This is your supervisor, boys. You'll report to him and he'll show you what to do. I've got a meeting, so I'll let you take over, Harvey. See you around, boys."

Harvey turned to face Aryl. "Good to see you again."

"You, too, Harvey. How's the family?"

"Good. Guess we better get you boys started on the day. Don't know if Roman told you, hours are eight to six, Monday through Saturday. You get an hour for lunch. You bring gloves?" Only Caleb pulled a pair out of his back pocket.

"Well, you'll live one day without them," he said to Aryl and Jonathan. "But I'd get some soon. This job'll tear up a pair of hands quick, and," he laughed lightly as he gestured to Jonathan, "those fancy slacks won't make it through the day." Jonathan's face burned red with embarrassment and frustration. "Loading area's down here. Follow me."

He ordered Jonathan and Aryl to start unloading a pallet of hundred-pound sacks of flour onto a delivery truck and took Caleb down to a different area to work on a pallet of sacks of potatoes. There was no shortage of work. As soon as one pallet was cleared, the forklift would position another near a waiting truck. Jonathan's back was aching before the first hour was up, and Aryl's hands had started to blister.

∞∞∞

Ava paced the living room, having finished the breakfast dishes, made the bed, wiped down the bathroom, and cleaned out the fireplace from last night's fire. She had swept the floors twice and cleaned the windows around the masking tape. She buttoned her sweater and put on her hat, having decided to go up and see Claire. She paused at the door, listening for the beady-eyed woman, whom she knew wouldn't stop talking once given the opportunity to start. She slipped out the door and up the stairs to the next floor.

Claire opened the door and hugged Ava before moving aside to let her in.

"I was just about to come down and see you," she said, as Ava walked into the living room.

"I couldn't bear to just sit there any longer," Ava said, rolling her eyes. "I thought we could go out and get some shopping done together. There's a few things I need. We'll get Arianna, too." Ava walked over to the fireplace to look closer at the wall where Claire had started outlining. There were pencil sketch beginnings of a beach and waves on one side, an outline of billowing clouds on the other side but nothing in the middle.

"I'm working on our beach," Claire said proudly. "Just over the fireplace I'm going to paint the lighthouse. And on the other side of the lighthouse, I've outlined storm clouds. I can't work on those until I get some black paint," she said, tracing the pencil drawn outline of the waves with her finger. "I can work with pencils for now."

"It's going to be beautiful, Claire. I can't wait to see it finished," Ava said, admiringly.

"Personally, I think you should paint on canvas, so you can take it with you when we leave here." They both turned to see Arianna in the doorway. She had dressed to the nines in a blood red, silk, straight dress, black shoulder fur and matching cloche hat with jeweled beadwork adorning one side. She did not even attempt to dress plainly for the sake of blending in. Claire shrugged and looked back at the wall.

"I'll enjoy it while we're here, and hopefully it'll be enjoyed by the next tenants. Right now, I need it to be larger than life," she said with a sigh and turned to her friends. "So, do you want the grand tour?" she asked sarcastically and took them through the three tiny rooms. It was similar to the others' apartments, only the floor plan was inverted.

"I was pretty horrified when I first walked in here. Aryl offered for me to paint every wall in the apartment, and I just might. It might help cheer the place up a bit." There was a similar, ragged couch covered by a sheet, a wooden chair in the corner by a small, slightly lopsided bookshelf, and a small, wooden table with two chairs near the entrance to the kitchen.

"Well, I'm not spending a dime on this dump. We're not going to be here that long," Arianna said with a snort. "Caleb is already working on some ideas. I'm sure they'll have us out of here by New Year's," she said confidently.

"That would be nice," Ava said quietly. Something told her that Arianna was floating on false hopes, but she wasn't about to ruin what bit of optimism she was managing to cling to.

"Why don't we get out of here for a couple hours? I have a list of things I need to pick up, and maybe we can grab a late lunch out," Arianna suggested.

"Yes. That's sounds wonderful," Ava said and smiled.

On the way out, they passed the beady-eyed woman talking incessantly to a young woman who was juggling a bag of groceries in one arm and a baby on the other hip while a toddler clung to her dress. She was trying to unlock her door without spilling the bag or the baby. The beady-eyed one offered the struggling woman no help but continued to rattle on about curing a baby's colic and her own intestinal ailments. The red-haired woman smiled politely as the three passed, and Ava was debating whether to stop and help her when the beady-eyed woman noticed them and turned. Ava put her head down and walked faster, practically running down the next set of stairs. Once on the street, Arianna started laughing.

"Please say that wasn't one of your neighbors?"

"She is," she said grimly. "I haven't met the other one yet, the one with the baby."

Arianna changed the subject abruptly. "Let's catch the trolley. We'll head uptown to have lunch and do our shopping there."

∞∞∞∞

*The* lunch whistle blew much to Jonathan's relief, who not only was starving but also positive his back was going to snap in half if he lifted one more sack of flour. Aryl rested on the bumper of the truck and looked at his hands. There were already several blisters on the palms of his hands, and his fingers ached. He flexed them, trying to relieve some of the stiffness and regain some feeling. Caleb joined them, and they all headed out of the yard to find lunch. They chose a deli close by and ordered sandwiches. They ate by the window and watched the chaotic scene of the passersby rushing in every direction.

"When's quitting time again?" Jonathan asked, while stretching his neck from side to side.

"Six," Aryl said flatly. Even his normally good mood was muted today.

They finished lunch in silence and headed back to the yard. Jonathan had a hard time keeping up a decent pace. He was already exhausted from the morning's work and adding a full stomach to that caused him to feel sluggish and mentally foggy as well.

∞∞∞∞

Arianna perked up noticeably once back on familiar streets surrounded by fashionable storefronts and restaurants. The appetizing aromas of gourmet creations floated in the air, and the relaxed pace of immaculately dressed people going about their daily errands delighted her. She led the trio into "La Petite Bouchée". She animatedly greeted the waiter in French, whom she obviously knew well. They chatted like old friends, inquired about each others' spouses, and flattered each other with compliments. Finally, she ordered crepes and coffee for them all. The waiter went to prepare their order, and Arianna sat down, smiling as she glanced around. In this place, it was easy to pretend all was right with the world; those not destroyed by the crash had continued with their lives. "I think we should have lunch here once a week," she suggested. Ava and Claire looked hesitant. "Oh, come on, we don't have to spend a lot of money. We'll just get coffee, but it's so nice to be here rather than there. We can almost pretend that nothing ever happened," she said quietly. Claire patted her hand.

"Once a week it is then, even just for coffee. Every Friday."

"I thought of something for us to do to occupy ourselves at least for tomorrow afternoon. We can write to friends and family and let them know, delicately, our change of address. I'm going to stop by the stationer today to pick up some letter paper. Why don't you both come over, and we'll write letters together?" Arianna finished just as the waiter delivered their coffee.

"That's a good idea. We haven't heard from Jonathan's parents in several weeks, so perhaps a letter from them would cheer him up a little," Ava said.

"How is he?" Claire asked, concerned.

Before Ava could reply, Arianna changed the subject. She had no interest in glum conversation. She was only interested in pretending that nothing had ever happened, and she played the part well.

"Oh, look! There's Sarah!" She half-stood, waving to get her friend's attention. "I wish she had her baby with her. Oh, I've wanted to see it so badly. Her baby shower was the end all, wasn't it? Her organizer did a fantastic job . . . ." Her voice trailed off as Sarah caught sight of her and turned away as if she hadn't seen Arianna.

Ava knew exactly what was happening. She had seen through Sarah's shallow personality from the first time they met. She tried to distract Arianna.

"What style of stationery did you have in mind, Arianna?" she asked, suddenly appearing to be terribly interested in writing paper. Arianna ignored her and continued to try to get Sarah's attention. When it became obvious to Arianna that Sarah was ignoring her purposefully, she shouted Sarah's name so loud that it was impossible to ignore her. Everyone in the café turned to look, and Sarah, embarrassed, hurried over to Arianna.

"Sarah, did you not see me wave at you?" Arianna demanded, putting a hand on her hip.

"Yes, I did. I just thought it best if I . . . well," Sarah stammered and nervously looked around her, ashamed even to be speaking to Arianna.

"If you what? Ignored me? That's hardly polite, Sarah."

"Well, Arianna, things have changed, you know. I've heard, well, we've all heard about what happened. And we feel terrible for you, me and the other wives, but things just aren't the same now and we thought it best to leave some things in the past, you know? Thought it might make it easier for you. I'm sure you understand." Sarah tried to wrap her cruel words with a smile.

"No, Sarah, I'm afraid I don't understand. We have been friends for going on five years. Are you pretending like you don't know me because I no longer have money?" she asked incredulously.

"It's not only that," Sarah snapped impatiently. "I've heard where you've had to move to . . . surrounded by illegitimate and vile society, streetwalkers and the like. Milton heard through a friend that your husband is doing manual labor now." She dropped her voice to a whisper, "I mean, honestly, Arianna, what would we possibly have to talk about any longer?"

Arianna's face was a mixed expression of hurt and disbelief as she slowly sat down. Ava and Claire, while taken aback at how quickly details of their situation had spread, glared at Sarah with hateful looks that made her uncomfortable, and she rushed away. Arianna stared down in disbelief for a moment and then looked up from the table slowly, her eyes pinned on Sarah. She stood with as much grace as she could muster as fury welled up inside her.

"Oh, no," Claire said quietly, covering her face with one hand. Ava looked at Claire desperately, but they both knew that it was too late to stop whatever blitz Sarah had brought on and rightfully had coming to her. Arianna smiled a large smile until Sarah was almost, but not quite, to the door.

"Oh, Sarah, dear!" Arianna called loudly. Sarah stopped abruptly but didn't turn around. "You're quite wrong about something. We would have much to talk about over lunch, you and I. Take Milton, for instance. I could tell you all about our affair toward the end of your pregnancy when you were, well," she shrugged with an evil smile, "not up for the deed."

Ava choked on her coffee, spewing it over the lace linen and her dress. Claire's head snapped up so fast, it was painful.

"But you'll be relieved to know that it was indeed a very brief affair. After all, he is quite the clumsy lover and very poorly equipped." She narrowed her eyes. "And we could also talk about the streetwalkers I now live in close proximity to. Didn't a streetwalker give Milt that terrible rash while you were recuperating from childbirth recently? That's the word around the gentlemen's club, anyway. I really would see to it that it heals before you think about lying with him again."

Sarah spun around in mute horror, huffed and turned on her heels to stomp out. Snickers and whispers rose up from all parts of the café. Arianna sat down and took a dainty sip of her coffee. Claire's face quivered, not knowing whether to laugh, cry, or run away.

"Dear Lord, Arianna!" Ava cried out and leaned over the table toward her. "Now this whole café thinks you've had an affair with Milton!" she whispered loudly.

"I don't care what these people think of me. Besides, I couldn't exactly insinuate that her husband was an inept lover with a minuscule appendage simply by rumor. It has much more credibility coming from the horse's mouth," she said and grinned maliciously.

Claire sat, shaking her head. "Life with you is never boring, Arianna. Let's get going before we're thrown out." Claire put her share of the bill on the table and stood up.

"It wouldn't be the first place I've been thrown out of," Arianna said quietly. They didn't ask any questions, but Ava and Claire had no doubt that it was completely true.

Next, they went to the stationer where Arianna picked out beautiful, heavy-weight, handmade paper, which had the slightest pink tinge to it and rose petals of a darker pink pressed along the bottom edge. Of course, she had to buy specially made envelopes as well and enjoyed acting as if it were just another shopping day. As they were leaving, something near the display window caught her eye. She walked over to see a hardbound notebook with a gold cover and a silver fleur de lis engraved on the front, and she left with it tucked under her arm.

∞∞∞

Ava was in the kitchen putting the final touches on dinner when Jonathan walked in carrying a package with him. He had stopped on the way home and bought proper work pants, boots, a second work shirt, and a pair of gloves. He limped to the couch and sat down hard, letting the package drop to the floor. Ava turned to see him and her smile faded. She had been remembering the events of the afternoon, particularly the scene in the café, which had been horribly embarrassing at the time, yet now seemed absolutely entertaining. Jonathan rested his head on the back of the couch and closed his eyes.

"That was the worst day of my life," he moaned. Ava sat down beside him and noticed his dress slacks riddled with small tears and dirt, his shoes now scuffed beyond any hope of repair and his shirt dingy with sweat stains around the neck and underarms.

"Oh, Jonathan." She took his hand; he winced and pulled it back slightly. She turned his hand over and gasped when she saw open, bleeding blisters covering the palms and fingertips.

"Jonathan, what happened?" she asked with frightened concern.

"Work. Hard work," he said with eyes still closed. He was so tired that he wondered if he could summon the energy to get to the lumpy bed that he would be grateful to fall into.

"But, Jonathan–"

"I bought gloves on the way home. I'll wear them tomorrow," he said.

"But tomorrow's Saturday," she said quietly.

"I know," he said, hardly moving his mouth. Ava went to the kitchen and wrung out several cloths in hot water. He winced when she wrapped them around his hands. Eventually the sharp stinging on the open sores eased as the warmth soothed his aching joints. He rolled his head toward her and watched her as she worked.

"Thank you," he said quietly. She turned away quickly, so he wouldn't see her tears and busied herself in the kitchen. He lacked the energy to show it, but he was truly happy to be near her again. He'd never consider the shabby walls that surrounded him home. The only place he considered home was near Ava.

∞∞∞

"Arianna," Caleb called as he walked in the door. It was dark and quiet, and he was just about to turn to look for her at Ava's or Claire's when he heard a noise in the bedroom. He pushed open the door and saw Arianna sitting in the dark on the floor against the wall, head on her knees, arms covering her head.

"Arianna. What happened?" he asked with alarm, and quickly sat down on the scuffed, hardwood floor in front of her. She lifted her head to look at him. She was sniffling, and he could see she was at the end of a hard cry.

"I don't want to talk about it," she said with a whimper.

"No, Arianna, what happened?" She took an uneven breath and told him about Sarah and the scene in the café, how embarrassed she was, how horrible she was made to feel for suddenly being poor. She detailed her outburst at the end that left Sarah speechless. Caleb had trouble suppressing a smile.

"You actually said that?" referring to her comments about Milt, the rash and the streetwalker. The fact that she had publicly announced stepping out on Caleb flew right past him as many of her words and actions did. She nodded and blew her nose with a handkerchief, which Caleb handed to her. He let out a little laugh. "Well, sounds to me like she had it coming." Then he said more seriously, "That was awful of her to act that way toward you. I knew she was on the petty side, but still–"

"It's not just that."

"There's more?" he asked, his eyes widening.

"Everyone's talking, Caleb. They're all talking about me, about us, where we have to live and about where you have to work. I can't believe how fast bad news gets around." He sighed with a hint of frustration.

"Why do you care, Ahna? They aren't real friends. Let them talk."

"Me, Claire and Ava were planning to go back to the café once a week, and now we can't do that. I'm sure I'll run into people we know, and they'll be nasty and make me feel horrible." She dropped her head on her knees again. Caleb tried to be understanding, but he was tired and hungry. He was at a loss for what more to say. Shallow people would be nasty. They'd talk and say hurtful things, but this was the least of his worries. He simply decided to change the subject.

"Why don't I run down and get us something to eat? You clean up, and I'll be right back." He kissed the top of her head as his stiff legs lifted him off the floor.

∞∞∞∞

Aryl had been quieter than usual on the walk home. The others had noticed, but assumed he was simply as exhausted as they were, too exhausted to complain. But he was already rolling around a few different ideas. Always perceptive when it came to opportunities no one else noticed, he was even more desperate to find something to cultivate now as every muscle and bone in his body ached.

Misery motivated him more than money ever had. He'd off-loaded bulk flour and rice all day. Most of it directed to repackaging and redistribution plants, but some bulk orders went to large bakeries and restaurants. There had to be a way to get in the middle of that and turn a profit. Find the supplier overseas and undercut the competition on this side.

He was still lost in these thoughts while he and Claire ate dinner. She took his silence as not wanting to talk about his day, which by the looks of him, had to have been a hard one. She decided to tell him about hers. When she started to explain the scene at the café, he fully pulled away from his thoughts and was laughing heartily by the end of the story. Aryl shook his head, smiling.

"How Caleb puts up with that girl, I'll never know." He turned to the wall over the fireplace. "I see you've started the mural," he said, looking over the rough pencil outlines above the mantel.

"I picked up more black paint, so I could start working on the storm clouds."

His smile faded slightly. "Do you have yellow?"

"I think so, why?"

"For the light. It needs to have a very bright light," he said quietly. "One that can shine through to other side of the storm."

∞∞∞∞

*Ava* sat down next to Jonathan on the couch, balancing two plates. He lifted his head to see a tiny piece of steak, a lobster tail, a baked potato with butter, and smiled.

"I wasn't really serious," he said as he removed the cloths from his hands and reached for the plate. "But it smells wonderful." Just then, they heard a few thuds coming from the far wall of the apartment. Jonathan raised an eyebrow.

"There are people living over there?"

"I saw her today. Poor thing was cornered by that woman," she said, squinting her eyes to imitate the beady eyes of the overbearing neighbor. "She was trying to manage her babies and groceries and trying to get in her door."

"They have children?" He shuddered at the thought of having to raise a child here.

"Two that I saw. A little girl of maybe two or three years old and a small baby. It was in a blanket, so I don't know if it's a girl or boy. Cute thing, though; fat, little cheeks and big, brown eyes." He didn't answer, his mood suddenly dropping again. It had been unspoken between them but understood that the plans they had to start a family were to be postponed indefinitely. They ate the rest of their dinner in silence. Ava took the plates to the kitchen and cut a piece of the small cake she had bought that afternoon. She brought it over to see Jonathan, his head resting on the back of the couch again, sound asleep.

∞∞∞∞

"*I* bought you something today," Arianna said as they ate the sandwiches Caleb bought from the deli. They sat on the floor in front of the fireplace with the harsh overhead light turned off.

"Oh, yeah? What is it?" he asked, inhaling his sandwich. She hopped up to get the notebook from the bedroom and held it out to him as she sat back down.

"What's this?" he asked, turning it over then opening the hard cover. "It's for your ideas," she said enthusiastically. "I thought it might get hard to hold so many ideas and plans in your head, keep them all straight, so I bought you this." He stared at it for a long time, feeling the slightest bit of panic come over him.

"What's wrong? Don't you like it?"

"Of course, I do. Thank you, Ahna. It's perfect," he said and smiled at her, hoping that she couldn't see through him at that moment. In truth, he had absolutely nothing to write down.

*November 2ⁿᵈ 1929*

The morning brought pain and stiffness the likes of which none of the men had ever experienced. Overworked back, arm and leg muscles stung and cramped in protest as each man agonizingly pulled his body from bed to begin another day of grueling labor.

Ava found herself doing the same monotonous housework as the morning before. She was tempted to do more but decided it wouldn't make any improvement on the appearance of the apartment, so she sat down to read by the fire. She couldn't concentrate and gave up after reading the same paragraph several times. She stared into the fire for a long while. Even though only three days had passed, her lovely home, her idyllic existence, and even her normally amorous husband all seemed like distant memories now. With nothing to distract her, she was unable to prevent the torrent of emotion that had been building for the last week from surfacing. Memories crept to the forefront of her mind. Details of the life she used to have, and the harsh contrast of her present reality hit her with full force. She covered her face with her hands, folded over onto her knees and sobbed.

∞∞∞

Word travels fast in poor and rich circles alike, and the buzz around the shipping dock revolved around the three new hires. A scruffy-looking man with a full beard poked Jonathan in the shoulder during the brief morning break as he leaned against a partially unloaded pallet of flour sacks.

"Is it true what they been sayin' bout you and your friends?" Jonathan looked up at him.

"What who's been saying?" he asked, confused and sounding uninterested.

"That you're a bunch of rich boys turned poor. Lost it all when the market took a dive last week. Now you're tryin' ta be one o' us." Jonathan grimaced at the insensitive and boorish man standing before him.

"Yeah, something like that," he said looking away, wishing Caleb was here. He had a way with people and would handle this confrontation with more tact than Jonathan could manage right now.

"Well, don't think that you're gonna get treated special, or you can get away with slacking off. I don't care how much money you had, you gotta pull your own weight round here," he said with fictitious authority. He walked away without waiting for a response. Not that Jonathan was about to give him one. He added coping with the resentment of the poor toward the rich, the previously rich in his case, to his ever-long list of adverse working conditions. He looked up at the dark clouds threatening rain. He stared at the churning sky, astounded at how a life could change so drastically and so quickly.

∞∞∞

Claire glanced at Ava, noticing her slightly puffy eyes but didn't say anything. They sat at Arianna's table, which she had arranged with the letter paper, pens, envelopes, little desert cakes and flowers.

"I have no idea how we're going to discreetly inform our families of our situation without too much embarrassment. Anybody have any idea how to start?" Arianna asked.

"With honesty," Claire said.

"No need to put perfume on a pig." Ava laughed lightly.

"But people might think we're looking for sympathy or charity. I can't have family thinking I'm looking for a handout," she said firmly. Ava didn't feel like debating with Arianna about what was and what was not charity. She was still fatigued from her crying jag that had lasted most of the morning. Claire looked at Arianna with irritation.

"If it's family, it's not a handout, and we're not asking for any help. Why don't you focus on asking them how they are? You can drop subtleties about your own situation throughout, without outright saying anything."

"Claire is right. You should be honest," Ava spoke up. "Hiding behind niceties and false perceptions isn't going to do any good for them or you. I plan to inform Jonathan's parents exactly how desperate our situation is. I won't ask for it outright but, if they offer help, I'll take it. I'm not too proud," she said and started her letter. They spent the majority of the afternoon working on their letters until they were satisfied enough with the wording.

The evening went much the same as the previous with Jonathan falling asleep shortly after dinner, Aryl lost in his thoughts trying to piece together a plan, and Caleb going out to buy dinner from the deli. Again.

*November 3rd 1929*

"You're alive," Ava joked, getting up to hug Jonathan. It hurt to lift his arms to hug her back, so he settled for a kiss on the neck. They had slept late on Sunday. When Jonathan emerged from the bedroom, it was after one o'clock in the afternoon.

"Yeah, but I slept half-way through my only day off," he scoffed. "I'm starving. What do we have around here?" he asked, looking toward the small kitchen.

"Go sit. I'll make you something."

She made him a large bowl of oatmeal with fried bread on the side. "My aunt and I used to have this often. I had forgotten all about it until yesterday," she said, sitting down close beside him. "The oatmeal gets old after a while, but I'll pick up some jam to flavor it. And you'll love the butter-fried bread. It's wonderful." He dug in without answering, not remembering ever being this hungry. If he'd taken the time to taste it, he would have remembered that he really didn't like oatmeal. However, he did like the fried bread and asked for seconds.

"What do you want to do today?" she asked as she put thick slices of butter-laden bread in the frying pan.

"I don't know. I honestly didn't expect to wake up, so I didn't make any plans."

"Jonathan, that's not funny."

"I'd really just like to relax. Maybe we could start a fire and read."

*Well, that's a start anyway*, she thought. Jonathan painfully trudged downstairs to buy another armload of firewood. It was cold, and the gas furnace could barely keep the chill off. He started the fire and ate a third helping of fried bread. Then he settled on the couch with his arm around Ava, who curled up beside him. He took the book and began reading where he left off on Halloween. The wind howled outside, rattled the broken windowpane, and rain pecked at the glass. With her head on his chest, Jonathan absentmindedly rubbed Ava's arm but stopped quickly when the blisters on his hand snagged on the material of her sweater. Ava causally placed her hand on Jonathan's knee, left it still for a moment, then drew small circles with her finger very slowly up his leg. He noticed her feather light touch when it reached mid-thigh, stopped reading, and glanced down at her. She looked up at him with a shy but devious smile.

"Ava," he hesitated. Her eyes dropped from his, and she recoiled, feeling slightly rejected. "It's not you, Ava." She nodded without making eye contact. "No, I swear, it's not you. I just don't know if I can. You have no idea how badly my entire body hurts. My arms feel like lead. I'm not sure I have the strength." He nudged her to look up at him. "I couldn't bear to start something I was unable to finish," he assured her.

"Is that all?" she asked with one eyebrow raised. "You're sure that's the only reason?"

"Yes. I swear to you." She thought for a moment, steeling herself against possible rebuff and raised her head again more boldly than she had ever dared, craned her neck to kiss him and began pulling his white t-shirt up over his chest. He moved quickly to hold her wrist.

"Ava," he whispered, clearly tormented and trying to pull her hand away. She clutched a fistful of his t-shirt and refused to let go.

"You may be hurting too badly to hold yourself up, but I'm not." His eyes widened slightly as she continued to push his shirt up and moved herself over him. Stunned by her overt demands, he grinned his approval.

After a brief but intense encounter, Ava lay on his chest, her face hidden in his neck and drifted off to sleep while he ran the back of his fingers up and down the length of her bare back. A hard knock at the door shook them both from their serene respite.

"Well, I guess the timing could have been worse," Jonathan said with a sly grin. "It's probably Aryl. He mentioned yesterday that he needed to talk to me about something." Ava groggily lifted herself from Jonathan's chest and reached for her dress, which hung off the corner of the fireplace mantel. "Do you know where my pants are?" Jonathan looked around, amused. He found them by the door and slipped them on with difficulty in bending his sore legs.

He was still smiling when he opened the door but dropped it quickly as his serene afternoon shattered in an instant.

"What are you doing here, Victor?" he growled.

Victor stood in the doorway with a malicious smile, looking Jonathan up and down. He was shirtless with wrinkled pants, messy hair and still unshaven for the day. Jonathan was immediately self-conscious of his appearance and angry that he should even care for a moment what Victor thought of him. "I said, what you are doing here?" Jonathan repeated. Victor held up a few sheets of paper.

"Your paperwork is missing some information." He glared at Jonathan. "Under 'current employer', you didn't write anything down. You do have a job, don't you, Jonathan?" he asked, enjoying this completely.

"Yes, I do," Jonathan said through his teeth, holding his hand out for the paperwork. Victor looked slightly disappointed.

"I brought a pen," Victor offered with false politeness. "Didn't know if you still owned one," he said, glancing toward the barren apartment. Jonathan's blood boiled as he filled out the details of the job he detested. He shoved the paperwork back at Victor and started to close the door.

"Do your friends work at the shipping dock with you?" Victor asked, looking over the paper.

"Yes. And I'm sure you know where they live, so you can verify that," Jonathan scowled.

"Oh, no, I wouldn't want to bother them on a Sunday afternoon." He looked up at Jonathan with a smirk. "I'll just fill in their paperwork back at the office. Give Ava my regards, will you?" He oozed with phony politeness.

Jonathan slammed the door, furious and humiliated. He turned to see Ava standing in the bedroom doorway with her hand over her mouth, eyes wide. He dropped his head and sighed. This wasn't how he wanted her to find out.

"Tell me that wasn't who I think it was."

He walked over and reached for her hand, but she jerked it away.

"I was going to tell you, Ava. I was just waiting for the right time."

"The right time?" she mocked. "You should have told me from the start!"

"I know. But there was so much happening . . . I didn't want to give you that to worry about, too, on top of everything else," he pleaded.

"Why would you do this, Jonathan? How could you rent from him? Of all the places! You know almost better than I do what a horrible person he is! Why would you purposefully?" her voice trailed off in disbelief, and she stared at him. He sighed and winced as he attempted to raise his hands to rest them on top of his head.

"I didn't do it on purpose, Ava. I didn't seek this out. Caleb was in charge of looking for a place to live, remember? He went to several places, and no one had anything available. Not anything we could afford, anyway." She shook her head angrily and tears filled her eyes.

"No. No, this city is *enormous*. There are thousands of apartments. You could have told Caleb no. You could have kept looking the next day, the next week if you needed to!"

"And risk having the auctioneers show up and take the very chair out from under you! I had to get you out of there fast, so you wouldn't have to see that. Watch people take everything we owned. I couldn't stand to watch that. Could you, Ava?" Ava's fists balled up at her sides, and her face reddened.

"I would rather have watched them take and sell everything we owned than to have to live here under his thumb! How can you stand *that*, Jonathan?" she screamed at him.

"Damn it, Ava! I didn't have a choice!" he screamed back. She took a step back and slammed the bedroom door in his face. He stood for a moment, in disbelief of what just happened. They hardly ever fought and had never screamed or slammed doors. He knocked on the door after a moment.

"Ava, let me in, honey," he said in a kinder tone, his forehead on the door.

"Go away!" she screamed, and he jerked back slightly when something hit the other side of the door. He sighed in frustration and sat on the couch, dropping his head in his hands. He had never shouted like that, nor had she ever yelled at him. He began to wonder if this small part of their miserable situation could have been avoided. Maybe they could have taken one more day to look. Maybe the bank would have waited a day or two. Madness was happening and no one knew which way was up. They might have had more time. Maybe even a week. Maybe he should have kept walking that day and told Caleb to go to hell. After all, Victor wasn't going to bother *him*. Suddenly, he was furious as he mulled over the possibilities.

"Dammit!" He stormed out of his apartment before he could think rationally and stomped down the hall to bang on Caleb's door. Caleb opened it, much the way Jonathan had answered his door, moments ago.

"Do you know who just showed up at my door, Caleb?" Jonathan seethed.

"No, who?"

"Victor. Victor Drayton just showed up at my door." Caleb rubbed his forehead, his eyes squinting as if in pain for his friend.

"What did he want?"

"Does it really matter, Caleb? Honestly, does it matter? He found a reason to come to my door and taunt me. And he'll find another and another, until I lose my mind." He turned, took two steps, then turned back to face Caleb. "Exactly how many places did you go to, Caleb, to look for apartments?"

"Several before Victor," he said cautiously.

"And you honestly couldn't find anything else? You couldn't think of any other agencies to go to. You got a few 'no' answers and just gave up and went to Victor." Caleb started to realize that Jonathan hadn't come here to vent to a friend. He was actually mad *at him*. Caleb folded his arms and narrowed his eyes.

"What are you getting at, Jon?"

"I'm getting at the fact that you were the one to go to him and set all this up. But you don't have to deal with that bastard. So, it didn't really matter who you went to, did it? Did you ever stop to think how this would affect me? Or Ava?"

"Of course, I did, Jon. I didn't take going to him lightly. I knew it would be hard on you, but our backs were against the wall. We had to move fast. We talked about all this at your house the night before."

"We never talked about going to Victor." Jonathan clenched his teeth.

"We had no choice, Jon."

"That's not true and you know it. We could have stayed a couple more days. You could have thought this through better, found a better place to live."

"I guess we could have stayed a couple more days and risked being thrown out on our asses without warning. Not to mention watching the auction house pick through our things. How hard would that have been on Ava?" Jonathan didn't have anything to say immediately but pointed a finger at Caleb.

"It didn't have to be like this," he said through clenched teeth. "You could have tried harder. You didn't do everything you could have. If you'd kept your eyes open, not given up so soon, and seen what was going on around you, just taken more time to think things through, think ahead, plan ahead, not gambled everything, not risked everything." He stared at Caleb, trembling and then walked back to his apartment. Caleb looked down at the floor, realizing Jonathan wasn't so much yelling at him as he was reprimanding himself. Arianna stood behind Caleb with her hand on his back.

"Is he going to be okay?" she asked quietly. Caleb shook his head while he closed the door.

"I don't know."

"Well, he owes you an apology for yelling at you like that, Caleb."

"He knows. He will when he can." He leaned against the door for a moment.

"Ava is probably pretty upset, too," Arianna assumed.

"I think we can bet on that. Maybe you should go see her in a little while. But do me a favor and don't say anything to Jon."

"I won't," she promised. Caleb sat down, started writing in his notebook, and Arianna snuggled close to him.

"Can I see?" she asked eagerly. He lowered the book and tilted it to block her view.

"Um, well, it's just outlines right now, lots of scrambled notes, it's all in process, and it wouldn't really make sense." She grumbled a little as she got up to stir the beef stew Caleb had started for dinner.

∞∞∞

Jonathan paused at his door, leaning one arm on the doorjamb. He could hear Ava walking, heard her sniffle, get a cup from the cabinet, and turn on the water. He couldn't believe how thin the door was, and how every sound echoed from inside. He could hear a pin drop inside the apartment from the dank hallway. He suddenly felt sick when he thought of the possibility that Victor could have been outside the door while he and Ava were together, just on the other side. He quickly scrubbed that thought from his mind. *No, he couldn't have been. The sick bastard would have purposefully timed his knock for the most intimate of moments and enjoyed ruining that for me, too.* He walked in the apartment to see Ava finishing a glass of water. She sent him an angry look, walked back into the bedroom, and slammed the door.

He fell onto the couch without a care of how his back and thigh muscles screamed when he did so. He stared at the dying fire, disheartened, and wished he hadn't woken up that morning. Or at least not bothered to get out of bed.

An hour went by and Jonathan just sat, staring and brooding. He ignored the knock on the door at first, but it became more persistent; Caleb called from the other side.

"Jon, it's me. Open up."

Jonathan hesitated before he got up mechanically, swung the door open and turned away without acknowledging him. He sat back down on the couch while Caleb closed the door.

"Where's Ava?" he asked. Jonathan pointed to the bedroom door without looking up. Caleb stoked the fire and added the last log. He sat down and the two were quiet. Another knock at the door caused Jon to sigh heavily. It hurt his aching thigh muscles to keep getting up from the sagging sofa, and he grumbled as he raised himself. Aryl stood with Claire beside him.

"We brought a pie," Aryl said as Claire held it up. Jonathan nodded and stepped aside so they could come in.

Aryl looked at him then at Caleb. "What'd I miss?" he asked.

"I'll fill you in later," Caleb said.

"Where's Ava?" Claire asked, looking around. Jonathan again pointed to the bedroom door.

"I'd be careful, she's liable to throw something at you. Let her know it's you first," he warned Claire. "She isn't quite herself today."

She knocked and called to Ava through the door. The knob turned and Claire slipped in. Aryl took a seat in between Jonathan and Caleb, looking at each of them in turn.

Jonathan began speaking rapidly and with irritation. "Victor found a reason to show up this afternoon just to remind me how miserable my life really is, and I wanted to kill him, but I can't kill him because I'll go to jail. Unless I hide the body really well, and frankly I hurt too badly to dig a ditch right now, so I have to wait to kill him. In the meantime, I have to sit and wonder when he's going to show up again. And this is how Ava found out that we had to rent from him, and now she's furious with me because I didn't tell her, and she's holed up in the bedroom and won't talk to me, and then I went down and yelled at Caleb for this whole mess." He paused to take a breath. "Sorry," he grumbled, glancing slightly toward Caleb.

"Apology accepted," Caleb said quietly and looked to Aryl, "I guess I won't need to fill you in later," he said and grinned.

"No," Jonathan said firmly, hearing yet another knock on the door. "I'm not getting that."

Caleb stood. "It's probably Ahna," he said as he opened the door. She peeked in cautiously.

"Everything okay?" she whispered. Caleb nodded her inside.

Arianna hated yelling and confrontations unless, of course, it was her doing the yelling and confronting.

"Ava and Claire are in the bedroom," Caleb told her.

Aryl turned to Jonathan. "I've got an idea," he started.

"Does it involve you and a woman's dress? Because if it does, count me out this time," Jonathan said flatly.

"Hey, you have to admit, that was fun," Aryl said and grinned. "But no. No dresses and lipstick involved."

"What is it then?" Caleb asked.

"We've been wrestling bags of flour and rice the last few days–"

"Don't remind me," Jonathan interrupted and dropped his head back.

"Well, I was thinking that flour and rice has to come from somewhere, a bulk supplier, probably from down south, or overseas."

"Go on." Caleb's ears perked up.

"I say we try to find out where it's coming from, find out the names of as many suppliers as we can, what they're selling at, and then find out who the major purchasers are over here. If we can start buying and steal some of the larger accounts by selling it cheaper, we could come out ahead."

"That's a possibility," Caleb said distractedly, his mind turning over the idea.

"You want to start dealing in flour?" Jonathan mocked.

"Well, yeah. I want to look into it anyway. See if it's viable at least," Aryl defended.

"Do you have any idea how much we'd have to buy to turn a decent profit? Where would we store it? And what about delivery? Are we supposed to carry the flour bag by bag to the bakeries and restaurants?"

"I just want to look into it, Jon. I don't have all the answers. And when Caleb and I get all the information together, that's when we're gonna count on you to work out the numbers. You can tell us how much would be needed to turn a profit or if it's even worth trying." Jonathan thought about it for a moment.

"I just don't see how something like that would work," he said, discouraged.

"Well, you don't need to right now. I'll get with you again after me and Caleb have had some time to poke around."

"Fine," Jonathan shrugged, uninterested. Aryl turned to Caleb and gave him a list of things to look into by asking around the yard. He had his own mental list he would work on as well. Caleb was eager to do something, anything that might lead them out of this place.

There was a light rapping at the door.

"It's Grand Central Terminal around here!" Jonathan yelled as he pushed himself up off the sofa again. "Who the hell can that be? Everybody's here!" he said, throwing his arms out, flabbergasted. He opened it to see Maura standing on the threshold, holding up a clean and freshly plucked chicken by the neck, a beady little eye staring right at Jonathan.

"Good Lord," he said, flinching when he saw it.

"Weel, hello to you, too, Mr. Jonathan," she said and smiled. "I see you've missed me. I brought ye a housewarmin' gift," she said, holding out the chicken. He started to reach for it but pulled away when the chicken's head flopped over to the other side of Maura's hand.

"Maybe, ah, you could just put it in the kitchen, Maura?" She laughed at his squeamishness and walked into the tiny apartment.

"Better yet, why don't I put this on to cook? So it doesna go bad. Nothin' stinks worse than a rotten chicken carcass."

"I really wouldn't know, Maura," Jonathan said, slightly disgusted at the dead animal in raw form. She said hello to Caleb and Aryl and set to work in the kitchen. If she had been shocked to see the dilapidated place they now called home, she did a very good job at hiding it. *Surely, Charles must have warned her,* Jonathan thought gratefully.

"Where's Miss Ava? I don't suspect she's out and aboot by herself?" she asked Jonathan, who was standing near the kitchen entrance.

"She's in the bedroom," Jonathan said, staring the chicken in the eye and thinking on what a truly strange day this had been.

"Is she ill?" Maura asked with panic.

"Oh, no," he said. "Maybe a little sick of me," he added under his breath.

"Aye, I'll go in to see her straight away," Maura said, putting the large pot of water on to boil.

"Mr. Caleb, be a love and whack that chicken's head off fer me?" she asked. "I'll be back out to put it in the pot directly. We'll eat in an hour."

"Sure, Maura." Caleb didn't think twice about it, having slaughtered chickens his entire childhood. Jonathan's eyes were wide, and he went to sit down, not wanting any part of chicken-head-whacking.

Caleb raised the butcher's knife, then paused, getting an idea that made him smile ear-to-ear. He put one hand into the cavity of the chicken, grasping the back of the chicken's head with the other, turning it side-to-side. He suppressed his own laughter as he quietly snuck into the living room. He walked behind the couch where Jonathan sat and held the chicken very close to the side of his head. Aryl watched this unfold and could barely keep a straight face.

Caleb thrust the chicken in front of Jonathan and moved the head to peck wildly at his face, making loud, clucking noises. Jonathan screamed a girlish scream that set Aryl into hysterics. Jonathan smacked at the chicken, and the carcass flew across the room, skidded on the floor, and hit the wall with a thud.

"Maura's gonna kill you!" Aryl howled at Caleb. Caleb picked up the chicken and dusted it off.

"It's fine," he said, laughing, although the rough, wood floor had torn bits of skin off. Caleb rinsed it and chopped the head off, still laughing. He propped it on the counter in a way that Maura wouldn't notice the torn skin and dust he couldn't rub off. Just then, she poked her head out of the bedroom door. "Fer the love of God, what's goin' on out here?" she cried out.

"Oh, nothing, Maura, Caleb just told us a joke is all," Aryl said, wiping his eyes. Caleb stood to block her view of the chicken.

"Everything's fine," he said, his face quivering. Maura eyed them suspiciously and withdrew into the bedroom.

"What were they doing out there?" Claire asked.

"Lord only knows," Maura said, shaking her head and sat on the bed with the other women. "Now, you're all in here, and they're all out there. Who in here is mad at who out there?" she asked. Claire and Arianna pointed at Ava.

"What'd he do, love?" Maura laughed lightly.

"It's a long story, Maura," Ava said with a tired sigh.

"Now, I've got time fer it, and it's probably not a man-mistake I've not already heard of, either," she assured.

After a moment's deliberation, she spoke with a frustrated tone, "I'm mad at Jonathan for not telling me who he had to rent from." She went on to explain what a horrible person Victor was, and briefly about how they had a relationship right before Jonathan.

"A'right, I see why yer mad at him for that. But my first question is, love, how in the world did you ever find yourself with someone that awful in the first place?"

"Another really long story," Ava said, sighing. Maura raised her eyebrows, waiting. Ava relented.

"My cousins introduced us. At first, I thought they were being kind by arranging for me to meet so many people, but I soon realized they didn't really care what kind of man they arranged for me to meet. They just hoped one would marry me so I would leave. Well, they arranged for me to meet Victor."

Maura poked her leg. "Go on, my dear." Ava took a deep breath.

"He was fun, at first, and he was nice enough. But things started changing very fast, and, after only a couple of months, he asked me to marry him. I wouldn't give him an answer. He kept asking and I kept dodging. I knew I couldn't marry him. I didn't love him. Something was missing and no matter how nasty my cousins got, I was going to wait and marry someone I loved. Anyway, my constant refusal to give him an answer upset him. He started telling everyone we were officially engaged. One night at a dinner party, I asked him to stop telling people that we were engaged when I had not said yes. And I said this in front of all of the guests. So, he demanded an answer right then and there, and I said no. That *really* upset him." She raised her eyebrows and looked down, twisting her skirt around her finger. "Jonathan was sitting right across from me. Every time I looked up, he was looking at me. Victor noticed that and stormed off, dragging me into the parlor, yelling and cursing. I told him that it was over. And just when he pulled back his arm, someone grabbed it, spun him around, and laid him out right there." Ava smiled despite her anger. "It was Jonathan. He had followed us out of the dining room." Claire gasped in romantic awe.

"I punched someone for Caleb one time," Arianna bragged.

Maura smirked at her. "That doesna surprise me, dear." She turned back to Ava, prodding her to continue.

"We left together, and he took me for coffee while I calmed down before going home. The whole time he kept looking at me with this off-kilter smile, and we talked very late into the night. Later, he walked me to my door and explained to my cousins where I'd been. They weren't happy that I had ended it with Victor, but I think they hoped for something to come about with Jonathan because they didn't give me too much trouble about it. The next evening, my cousin called me downstairs and Jonathan was standing at the door with that same silly smile. There were two, large men standing on either side of the front steps. He never explained to my cousins who those men were, but asked me to dinner that night. Later, he told me not to worry about Victor ever bothering me again because those men he hired would protect me. And they stood there every night until we were married a year later." She let out a deep breath and smiled. "See, I told you it was a long story."

"So, after yer telling me all that an' how Mr. Jonathan went to such great lengths to protect ye from that odious bastard, did ye honestly expect him to just casually mention whilst movin' yer things in that the previously mentioned bastard was now yer landlord? I'm sorry, Miss Ava, but I do understand why he would save ye from that as long as possible. Especially seein' how he can't be providin' the big men to stand at yer door no longer. Imagine how helpless that makes him feel now."

Ava looked down, suddenly feeling guilty for her actions that afternoon; the second half of the afternoon anyway. Claire and Arianna remained very quiet, having only occasionally patted Ava's hand through the story that was difficult for her to tell.

"I tell ye what, Miss Ava. I'm going to go put the chicken I brought in the pot to boil, and I'm going to send Mr. Jonathan in here to talk to ye. When ye come out, I expect things to be right between ye both. Understand?" Ava nodded obediently. Even if she didn't want to make up with Jonathan, she wouldn't refuse Maura's orders. Although she was only a few years older than Ava, Maura had an authoritative and wise, motherly tone. Claire and Arianna followed Maura out. A moment later, Jonathan appeared sheepishly in the doorway. Just as he was closing the door behind him, Maura screeched, "What's happened to me chicken?!"

∞∞∞

The boredom of the first days in the tenement ended abruptly, replaced with monotonous and time-consuming tasks. Doing laundry was a daunting undertaking; scalded hands wrung out clothes in the sink and then hung them close to the fireplace on a rope strung across the room to dry. Constant mopping was required under the clothes as they dripped during the first hours. Firewood needed to be fetched to keep a decent fire going, yet the clothes would still take all day to dry. They were taken down at night and replaced the next morning with more soggy shirts and dresses. Baking bread was another daily task that Ava and Claire found frustrating. Having no experience, they either burned or undercooked most loaves. Claire had gotten so discouraged that she resorted to making biscuits for every meal. Ava kept trying, and Jonathan was very kind about it, blaming the oven or commenting that her gravy fixed everything, reminding her she could cook gravy well. Constant sweeping was necessary as the draft brought in dust, and the leaky bathroom needed cleaning daily to prevent mold. Daily trips to the grocer for food that created dinners consisting more and more of a bread-base and vegetables with a small meat addition for flavoring. They habitually checked the mailbox on the way back in from shopping to find only an occasional letter from family. Most of the time, the three would venture out together, although Arianna had made more excuses lately not to go out with them. When she did go out, she tended to buy superfluous things, such as food from the deli and bakery or decorations for the house. She had yet to attempt to make bread.

*November 6th 1929*

Ava was sewing buttons onto one of Jonathan's work shirts and planned to repair several tears in his work pants. One of the sleeves on a dress needed repair as she had caught it on the metal corner of the garbage chute door. It was silent while she worked, and she pricked herself with the needle when someone knocked on the door.

She looked through the peephole that Jonathan had drilled for her as part of his long and sincere apology the weekend before. Now, neither of them would be surprised at who was on the other side. She saw the young neighbor, who had been juggling babies while the beady-eyed one talked on, standing on the other side with something in her hands.

"Hello, I'm yer next door neighbor, Shannon," she said pleasantly as Ava opened the door.

"I remember seeing you talking with our other neighbor."

"Well, I dint do much of the talkin' that day, but I did see you pass and wanted to wait a proper amount of time to let you get settled in before introducing myself." The door handle on the apartment across the hall jiggled. Ava stepped aside, quickly waved Shannon in and closed the door as softly as possible. Both women giggled quietly as they listened to the beady-eyed one investigating with heavy footsteps up and down the hall. They heard her slam her door and they let out a breath of relief.

"I brought you this as a welcome gift," Shannon said, holding out a round loaf of soda bread.

"Thank you. How kind. I'm Ava." She shifted the bread to extend her hand. "Would you like to sit down?" Ava asked, suddenly flustered and very embarrassed of her home. Shannon was unaffected by the drab surroundings and commented on Ava's green velvet drapes covering the living room window as she sat on the edge of the couch.

"How lovely," she said, pointing to them.

"Thank you. Would you like some tea?" Ava offered, having not completely forgotten how to be a polite hostess.

"That'd be wonderful," Shannon said and smiled. She had light-green eyes and strawberry-blonde curls that bounced when she made the slightest movement. Her frame was small but sturdy, and her accent reminded Ava of Maura.

"So, are ye settlin' in good?" Shannon asked. Ava almost laughed, but quickly remembered that this woman knew nothing of her former life. She set the water on to boil and walked back in the living room.

"I think so. It's been an adjustment, to say the least."

"We've been here a little over a year," Shannon volunteered. "We didn't want to move, it being farther away from Patrick's work and all and the rents' much more, but our last building flooded, so we had no choice. It isn't very bad. There's the talkative one with all the ailments across the way from you, and another new couple down the hall, and then there's a really nice Italian family on the next floor. The wife taught me how to make pasta. She mostly showed me because I could hardly understan' a word she said. There's another family upstairs, but they keep to themselves and then that new couple."

"Oh, those are our friends, Claire and Aryl and down the hall are Arianna and Caleb. We all came here together."

"Really now? Did you live close by before, too?"

"Yes, we all lived within a block of each other."

"In what building? Maybe I know of it?" Shannon asked.

"Well, we didn't live in buildings. We lived over near, well, uptown." Shannon's eyes widened slightly as Ava handed her a steaming cup of tea and glanced back at the velvet drapes and stylish floor radio. She started to put the pieces together.

"I had a much different life a couple of weeks ago," Ava offered.

"Was it the crash I read about in the paper?" Shannon asked intuitively. Ava nodded, her eyes automatically focusing on the fire. "I'm so sorry. I hear there are a lot of folks like that." Ava nodded but couldn't talk more about it, knowing she would break down. She felt her eyes sting and needed to change the subject.

"How old are your babies?" Ava asked quickly.

"Aislin is just three years last month, and Roan is three months. Aislin is the spittin' image of her Da and just as energetic. She runs all day and then just drops for a nappie, out solid for two hours. And smart, too. And Roan is truly the most well-mannered baby that ever lived. He's had a touch of colic but still doesn't fuss much, and he already sleeps through the night," Shannon said proudly. "And you?" she asked, although she hadn't noticed any obvious signs of children.

"No, we don't have any," Ava said, again touching on a subject that made her eyes sting momentarily.

"Aye, newlyweds. That's all the more tragic for what's happened to ye," Shannon said sympathetically.

"Oh, no, we've been married over three years." Shannon suddenly looked uncomfortable and fidgeted with her teacup handle.

"Oh, I'm so sorry," she said solemnly.

"Sorry for what?"

"Well, I dint mean to be insensitive, talking of my own, when ye can't." It took Ava a few seconds to realize Shannon was under the impression she was unable to have children.

"Oh, no, it's all right," she said, smiling. "I'm fairly certain everything is in working order."

"But then how have you managed to not have a babe for three *years*?" she asked, baffled. Then it came to her before Ava could find a dignified answer, and she blurted it out, "Ah. I know. Surely you were able to afford those fancy man covers. We couldn't afford those even if the Church allowed it," she said, casually taking a sip of tea. Ava turned three shades of red, played with the hem of her apron, and Shannon laughed.

"I'm so sorry, I dint mean to embarrass you. Sometimes I just spit out exactly what's on me mind without thinkin'." Ava smiled.

"Why don't I cut us some of that bread?" She stepped quickly to the kitchen, eyes misting for the third time. Shannon's accent and mannerisms made her miss Maura terribly. She looked up at the bread recipe that Maura had written in pen directly on the cracked, whitewashed cabinet door. She remembered what she had said that night after they all ate the chicken dinner. *Since I won't be round to find all the things ye tend to lose, Miss Ava, I'll write it on here. Doubt ye'll be misplacing an entire kitchen cubby.*

She looked down, horrified to see a bug scurrying close to the soda bread. She swiped it off the counter with a dishrag and tried to step on it discreetly, hoping Shannon wouldn't notice. She cut the bread, buttered it, and then put the remaining loaf in the oven to be safe from insects until dinner. She carried it back to the couch where Shannon was eying the drapes and radio.

"That's the loveliest radio I think I've ever seen," she said, stepping behind the couch to admire it closer. "Can we listen?" she asked eagerly.

"Of course," Ava said and smiled as Shannon turned it on and tuned the dial before Ava could do it for her. She found an Irish music program.

"My little radio doesn't get good reception in this building, so I don't get to listen as much since we moved here." Shannon made her way back to the couch, not wanting to take her eyes off the oak box.

"If you don't mind me asking," Ava began, trying to find proper words for her question. "If your church doesn't allow the, the–"

"Man covers," Shannon helped.

"Yes, the man covers, how on earth do you avoid it?" Shannon laughed.

"Well, now, we really haven't avoided it, have we? Married five years with the two babes sleeping next door. And no, even if we could afford such things, tis against the church." Ava waited for an answer to her original question for a reason. The small supply of protection they had brought with them two weeks ago was almost gone, and they were no longer able to afford to run to the druggist to buy more. Even if things continued in the infrequent pattern that they had, they would be gone by the end of the month.

"Well, we try, anyway, to pay attention to the calendar. We have to wait for the safe week."

"The safe week?"

"Aye. There's one week that tis safe with little worry of bringin' a wee one. Hardest part is waitin' for that week."

"How do you know? When the safe week is, I mean?"

"Well, you count starting with yer— Do ye have a calendar? Tis easier to show you." Ava jumped up to get a calendar she had drawn on one of Arianna's sheets of pink stationery.

"Okay," Shannon said, scooting closer to Ava, holding the calendar and pointing. "Start with the first day of the curse. Say if that's here."

"Wait," Ava interrupted, "Can I go get my friends? They need to know this."

"Of course, I'll wait here, you go run and get them."

Arianna looked like she had just crawled out of bed, dark smudges under her eyes and matted black hair. She threw on a sweater and hat reluctantly and trudged behind Ava. Claire was in her paint-splattered smock, and her eyes were still red from a morning cry, but she put on a cheerful face. Ava briefly and tactfully explained what the impromptu ladies' meeting was about.

"Sure, I'd love to," she told Ava. "I've been worried about that myself. Three more strikes and we're out." She laughed as she pulled off her smock. Arianna stood numbly in the doorway, and Ava waited in the living room while she changed dresses and found a sweater. Ava looked over the mural above the fireplace. The lighthouse was beginning to take on a life of its own. Red and white stripes wrapped around the tall chimney with a large, lantern room above it, not yet colored. The light coming from the center was a most vivid yellow, which stretched out several inches from the pencil-sketched lamp source and illuminated a path in the face of the squall. Claire had been working on the rocks at the base of the lighthouse; jagged, menacing-looking black and gray rocks, swallowed in places by crashing, white-tipped waves. The billows to the right of the lighthouse had fully taken shape and the clouds furthest out, jet black and ominous, swirled like those of a hurricane over the ocean, taking direct aim at the lighthouse.

"The cottage on the beach, I can't get it right. I keep having to start over, so I decided to work on the storm for now. I'll fill that in later."

"It's amazing, Claire," Ava whispered in awe.

"Thank you. C'mon, let's go meet your friend."

Ava made introductions all round, quickly made more tea, and hurried to join the others in the living room. Arianna had pulled a chair from the table and sat close to the fire. The others sat on the couch with Shannon in the middle holding the homemade calendar. "Now, here's how you do it." She then detailed to the women how to keep track of female cycles to find the safe week and pointed out the least safe days of all. "It's pretty easy to map out. Hard part is rollin' over and goin' to sleep when you should," she said with a grin.

"Well, there's always–" Arianna stopped abruptly. Her naive friends had had enough sexual education for one day, and she wasn't in a flamboyant teaching mood anyway. This information was nothing new to her, and she found herself rather bored. She would save for another time revelations that her friends would consider shocking alternatives. Claire leaned forward with an elbow on her knee, her hand cradling her forehead.

"*Seven days*," she said in frustration. "That's all? Really?"

"Yes, outside the curse, that's all, so make 'em count," she said out of the side of her mouth. "My question is how you girls got to this age without knowing of this?"

"My aunt," Ava started, "would never speak of such things. And, of course, my cousins were of no help."

"And my family, well, they bought anything they needed to prevent babies. They never talked about all this," Claire added.

"I knew," Arianna said flatly. "I have a book. I made Caleb buy it for me in Paris. It's technically a banned book, but he managed to find me a copy. It was written by one of the most famous and successful madams in France. It has everything you'd ever need or want to know in it. With illustrations," Arianna boasted. Ava and Claire looked at each other and back to Arianna with wide eyes. She laughed and got up to leave. "I'll see you all later. I'm tired. I think I'll take a nap. It was nice to meet you, Shannon," she called out as she closed the door behind her. Claire left a short time later, remembering bread she had left to rise in the oven, and Ava talked with Shannon until they heard her baby wailing.

"Well, nap-time's over," she announced, standing up. "Ava, please come over for lunch tomorrow. It would be so nice to have a visitor."

"I'd love to," Ava said with a smile.

∞∞∞∞

Ava paced the floor while waiting for Jonathan to get home. She was anxious to share with him details of Shannon's visit and news of a letter from Jonathan's parents as well. She kept glancing at the little, knobby clock by the bed and began to worry when he was nearly an hour late. Just as she was putting on her coat to look for him, the door flew open, and he backed in slowly, balancing the bottom and side of a mattress between his hands. Caleb was at the other end dipping it below the top of the door frame.

"Hey," Jonathan said, giving Ava a quick peck as he passed by her on his way to the bedroom. They set the mattress down against the bedroom wall and he ripped the blankets and sheets from the old mattress. He and Caleb carried it out and leaned it against the side of the building.

"Good riddance," Jonathan muttered as he walked away. He thanked Caleb for his help; Caleb nodded, and then hurried down the hall to his own door.

"What is this?" Ava asked when he came back in.

"It's a mattress, Ava," he said, peeling off his coat, gloves and hat.

"Well, I can see that," she said. "What I meant was, where did you get it?" She walked over to the bed and bent over to put her nose to the fabric. "It smells new."

"That's because it is new. Tonight, we are going to sleep like babies," he said blissfully.

"I thought we agreed not to spend money on a mattress. I was still working on stuffing the holes on the other one."

"I don't remember agreeing not to buy one." He picked up a sheet, stood on the opposite side of the bed from Ava and shook it out. Once they had the new bed made, he fell back on it and sighed. "I don't know that I'll be able to get up in the morning." He rolled his head toward her. She stood at the doorway with her arms crossed, glaring at him.

"Come here," he said, patting the bed. "You gotta feel this." She sat down reluctantly, still upset that he hadn't talked to her first. She had to admit it felt wonderful, and it wasn't long before she gave in and lay beside him, their legs dangling over the side.

"Still angry?" he asked, rolling over toward her with that silly smile she loved. His short, black hair was somewhat tousled, and his evening stubble gave him a rugged look. She glanced at him and then at the ceiling. He looked utterly delicious.

"I just don't know that we should have spent the money is all."

"We have to get decent sleep, Ava. You have no idea how hard I work. I need to feel rested for a change. I'll have two things now—two *whole* things, in this world to look forward to coming home to. You and this bed." She sighed, unable to stay mad at him as he reached over her, pulling her by the waist onto her side to face him. "And if I'm really lucky, I'll get to enjoy both of these things at the same time," he said and grinned devilishly.

"If you're lucky," she replied casually.

"What?"

"I just don't want you making promises you won't keep."

"It's not that I don't mean to, or want to honey, I'm just tired. And I get really angry at this life. This isn't what I had planned for us." He reached out and touched her face. "I'm doing the best that I can, Ava."

She smiled weakly at him. "I know you are. We got a letter from your parents today," she said, changing the subject.

"Really? How are they?"

"They're good. They want to know if we could come for Christmas. They offered to buy train tickets for us." Jonathan stiffened.

"If we did go, we'd buy our own tickets," he said stubbornly, sitting up.

"Well, they would consider it a Christmas present, I'm sure, Jonathan." She sat up beside him and put her hand on his leg. "It would be good to see them again."

"Well, it wouldn't be good for them to see us. Not like this. Besides, I can't take any time off work." He stood with a small grunt and reached for a sweater. "It's cold in here. I'll go stoke the fire. What's for dinner? I'm starving." A disappointed Ava walked past him out of the bedroom and into the kitchen to serve dinner.

"Stew. And the neighbor I met today brought over soda bread," she said.

∞∞∞

Claire explained over dinner the delicate details of the calendar planning to Aryl.

"Seven days?" he repeated, looking up from his dinner plate. "Serious?" She nodded soberly.

"I'm getting a second job."

"You can't get a second job. Then you'd never be here, so what would be the point?"

"That's intolerable," he scoffed.

"I'm not thrilled about it either." Not seeing a solution, she decided to change the subject.

"Ava's neighbor is really nice. We had a good visit today."

"That's nice. I wonder if her husband works down at the dock. Maybe I know him."

"We didn't talk too much about him. Mainly she just explained about the calendar and talked about her two babies."

"Wait." Aryl stopped eating. "The woman who taught you how to avoid babies *has* two babies? Are you sure her little plan is credible?"

"Well, she admitted that for it to work, you have to go to sleep when you're supposed to go to sleep. If you don't, *Waa, Waa.*"

"We just can't have that right now, Claire." His mind touched on the consequences of such an event, and he shuddered.

"I know." She stood up to clear their plates. She wasn't in a rush to start having children anyhow. She enjoyed this time with just the two of them. Wanting that to last a while longer, she was fine with postponing a baby.

Whenever the subject of a baby came up, however, Aryl found himself pulled into the same daydream. He pictured the possibilities; a tiny boy with brown eyes like his own or maybe a baby girl as beautiful as her mother, whose bright-blonde hair would triumph over his own dark curls. He imagined himself holding the baby in a grand nursery where no expense was spared to provide every luxury imaginable for mother and child; a set of oak shelves across the room holding stacks of folded linen, sleeping outfits and quilted blankets and hand woven baskets brimming with toys and rattles. A carousel music box spinning slowly, playing soothing music and an oak rocking chair sits next to a window facing a blooming, cherry blossom tree. A fresh, spring breeze causes colorful shapes hung on the window's frame to sway, and cheerful animations painted on the walls of the room occasionally steal the baby's attention. Then Aryl speaks softly, and the little eyes focus on his face again. The infant gives a toothless grin.

"What's that smile for?" she asked. Aryl straightened in his chair, his smile fading along with the vision. He shook his head to imply it was for nothing and stood, digging some folded papers out of his back pocket.

"I need to run these down to Jon. I'll be right back."

∞∞∞

"Aryl saw Jonathan's blue eye on the other side of the peephole and smiled. He put his own eye to the door to stare back at Jonathan, who pulled his head away, laughing.

"Here, I brought you these," Aryl said, smiling when Jonathan opened the door.

"What's this?" he asked.

"I told you that when Caleb and I got some information together, I'd bring it to you to look at. You can let us know if this is feasible."

"Right, right. The flour idea." Jonathan shook his head, looking at his friend with pessimistic eyes, but relented. "I'll look at it," he said, tucking the papers in his pocket.

"Listen, did Claire mention anything to you about a calendar tonight?" he asked in a hushed tone with one eyebrow raised. Aryl nodded slowly with a grim expression. He looked back in the apartment as he stepped out into the hall, closing the door behind him. "Ava just told me about that over dinner." He looked at Aryl, appalled, waiting for him to provide a solution. Both men stood staring at each other for a moment. "What are we supposed to do?" Jonathan finally asked.

"Apparently nothing," Aryl said and laughed, even though he didn't think it was funny at all.

"Well, this just gets better and better, doesn't it?" Jonathan grumbled.

"We'll figure something out. Maybe we can trade a bottle of rum or something," Aryl suggested. Jonathan pointed at him.

"That's a good idea!" he exclaimed. "We should start asking around."

"I'll see what I can do," he said and grinned, turning toward the stairs. "See you tomorrow, Jon."

∞∞∞

On the way up to his apartment, he passed the open door of the family across the hall from him. He unintentionally looked in as he passed and saw a baby positioned by the fireplace that was starting to fuss in a makeshift crib made of a large fruit crate. Several well-worn and stained cloth diapers hung on a line across the room to dry. The faint smell of urine met Aryl's nose. A tired mother crossed the room speaking soothingly to her baby in Italian. Aryl quickly turned his head away. He preferred his idyllic vision to the depressing reality of having a baby in the tenement. The sight reinforced his resignation that a baby could never happen here.

Inside the apartment, Claire was taking down the five or six pieces of clothes that hung on a rope in front of the fireplace. She found that if she did the previous day's laundry each morning, it wouldn't grow to an unmanageable pile that caused her to spend the entire day scrubbing and wringing. She lit candles on the mantel and table, turned off the overhead light, and tuned the radio to a mystery program. She had extra firewood on the hearth and a blanket on the couch, now moved closer to the fireplace, which filled the room with flickering, radiant light. They snuggled under the blanket as they listened to the program and watched the fire dance.

Afterward, they ran across the cold floor on tiptoes to the bedroom, jumped under the covers and, after much struggling, chose to conserve certain precious resources.

Well after midnight, Aryl woke up shivering fiercely, fully covered with Claire curled close to him. She jumped when her leg moved to a freezing cold section of the sheet. Aryl turned on the light, and he could see his breath.

"Heat must have gone out in the whole building," he assumed and immediately thought of the baby across the hall. He pulled on an extra set of day clothes over his nightclothes. Claire followed suit, shivering as she piled on two sweaters and a pair of Aryl's wool socks.

He went out to the living room and saw that there were still some embers left from the fire. He stoked them a bit, so they could breathe and come back to life. He added more wood and crouched by the hearth, blowing warm breath into his hands until it caught.

"We're not g-going to g-get any h-h-heat in the b-bedroom, Aryl." Claire shook in the doorway with her arms wrapped around herself.

"We're not going to sleep in the bedroom," he said as he walked by her, pulled the blankets off the bed and drug the ragged mattress into the living room. Claire pushed the couch against the wall of the living room, and he laid the old mattress in front of the hearth. She picked up the blankets from the bedroom floor and spread them out while Aryl brought the pillows. They hopped under the covers, and Aryl placed the poker on the floor next to him, so he could stoke the fire when needed. They burrowed as close to each other as they could, shivering and waiting for the fire to fully roll and start putting out some appreciable heat.

After fifteen minutes or so, Aryl crawled out from underneath the covers. "This isn't working," he complained. He pushed the couch up to the foot of the mattress and dragged the two dining chairs to the sides of the mattress. "Do we have an extra blanket?" he asked. She nodded, too cold to speak, and went to the small closet to pull out a bedspread.

He tucked the bedspread under the cushions of the couch and then draped it over the backs of the chairs. He arranged the edge on the mantel, piling books on top to hold it there. He lifted a corner, crawled under his tent creation and Claire followed. Within minutes, they began to warm as the tent directed the heat into their cove.

"This was a good idea, Aryl." Claire snuggled close to him and resented the layers of clothing between them.

"It's like camping," he said and smiled, kissing her forehead.

*November 7th 1929*

Victor stood outside the gate of the shipping dock early in the morning, watching the stream of men that filed in. He surveyed each one, and when he found one that he thought would do, he stopped him and introduced himself. The scruffy worker looked Victor up and down warily. After a quick moment of casual conversation, Victor got to the point. He stepped closer to the man, whose small eyes were as black as his own.

"Do you know a worker here named Jonathan Garrett?" Victor asked. The worker nodded. "He's one of them rich boys. His friend, the one with the red hair, he's an okay guy. But Garrett's got a chip on his shoulder. Not real liked 'round here." He bobbed his head in synch with his accent, a combination of old-Italian and new-New Yorker. Victor smiled and held out a twenty-dollar bill. The man's eyes bulged.

"What's your name?" Victor asked.

"Tony."

"You want to make some money, Tony?" Victor said and smiled cunningly. The man nodded, eyes still wary.

"Mess with him," Victor said and handed him the money. The man looked from the bill to Victor and returned the devious smile, nodding his agreement. Victor simply turned and walked away, leaving the details to Tony's imagination. Tony watched him walk away then tucked the twenty in his pocket, looking all around him to make sure no one was watching. He was happy to start earning every cent. He raced to clock in and find out where Jonathan would be working for the day.

Close to lunchtime, one of the yard leads called Jonathan over. While he was distracted, Tony walked by, pulled out his pocketknife, and knifed the bottom layer of a couple of flour sacks. Jonathan had laid his gloves on the bumper of the truck, and Tony stole them. He had more in mind, but made off in haste when he saw Jonathan turning back toward the pallet. He strolled past with a grin. Jonathan reached behind him for his gloves, but felt only metal. He turned and cursed under his breath when he saw that they were gone. He lifted a sack of flour by opposite corners and swung it around. Just as it cleared the pallet, the bag burst and flour spilled onto the ground, piling on his shoes and covering his shirt and face in a white dusting. Before he could even begin cursing, one of the yard supervisors appeared near him, yelling and cursing at the top of his lungs.

"What in the hell did you do, Garrett?" The heavyset, lead supervisor waddled over, a lit cigar hanging out of his mouth.

"I don't know. It just busted," Jonathan said with indifference, brushing flour off his coat and face.

"Don't let it happen again," he barked at Jonathan. Jonathan grabbed a second bag while glowering at the supervisor, and it happened again, creating a massive pile of flour on the ground at his feet. The supervisor turned when he heard the bag rip and began yelling and cursing again. He ended his tirade with, "Those two bags are coming out of your pay, Garrett!" Jonathan threw the torn bag on the ground and took off his coat to shake it out while glaring at the supervisor's back. He laid it on the pallet and started smacking flour from his pants and bent to clean his shoes with a piece of torn bag. When he stood, his coat was gone. He looked in all directions, but there was no one around. It seemed to have disappeared into thin air. He couldn't see Tony, who was hiding on the other side of the truck, slinking his way to the front bumper and then running off.

At the lunch whistle, Jonathan ran to the room where many workers kept their lunches in wooden compartments. The honor system was used as there were no doors or locks to the cubby-type, square openings. It was warmer in this room, and he was starving. He reached into his compartment to find his lunch missing. He looked around the room and found it smashed in a corner by the garbage can.

"You have got to be kidding me," he fumed. Others filed in for lunch, not saying a word to Jonathan but talking heartily to Caleb. He noticed Jonathan's expression as being one of a man on the edge and pulled him aside.

"What's wrong?" he demanded. Jonathan recounted the events of the morning. Caleb shook his head, irritated, and grabbed his lunch, splitting it with Jonathan. "Some of these guys can be real assholes," he commented, ripping his sandwich in half and handing it to Jonathan. He would still be hungry eating only half but knew what to expect at home, so he planned to buy dinner from the deli anyway. Caleb had on several layers and peeled off one of his wool shirts for him. It was small, but it helped a little.

After lunch, Aryl asked around to try to find out who was messing with Jonathan, but no one seemed to know anything. He put the word out anyway that when he found out who it was, he would settle it with them personally. The rest of the afternoon went without incident.

∞∞∞

*Ava* tiptoed out, careful not to alert the beady-eyed one and knocked softly on Shannon's door. She heard a child squeal on the other side of the door. Shannon opened it, half-holding the baby as it nursed, covered by a cloth sling.

"I'm so glad you came," she said. "Please sit down. I'll be done with the baby in a moment."

Ava looked about the room as she sat. It was the same sized apartment, but much more crowded with the additional necessities for two children. The sofa set close to the fireplace with a square table on one side. A full-size bed was crammed in one corner behind the door. There was an older bureau on the right of the bed, a small radio on top, and the square dining table tucked into another corner. Under the table was a large travel trunk, presumably for storage. Glancing in the only bedroom, she could see the foot of a small bed and a cradle in the corner. The kitchen was the same size as hers, but she noticed hanging shelves in the middle of the kitchen ceiling.

"Those are interesting," Ava commented, walking over to take a closer look. Shannon was working at the sink, the nursing baby still nestled in the sling that was tied in a large knot in the center of her back.

"Patrick made those for me. We got tired of the rats gettin' to the food and either stealin' it or makin' us sick to our stomachs."

"Rats?" Ava asked uneasily.

"Aye. Haven't you seen them at your place? We catch a few a week in the traps, but they're all throughout the building, can't get rid of 'em. Patrick made these hanging shelves, so I can put my bread or fresh food on them, and the rats have a heck of a time reaching it. It works well. Ye just have to mind not to bump yer head." Ava studied the simple contraptions consisting of a square piece of wood with thick twine nailed to the bottom of each corner. The twine was knotted about two feet above and nailed directly into the middle of the ceiling. There were three of them hung exactly at Shannon's eye level.

"You were getting sick?" Ava asked curiously. During the brief time she and Jonathan had lived there, they had had intermittent nausea and diarrhea.

"Aye. Get the runs something awful."

Ava thought for a moment that she would be sick making the link between their intestinal ailments to dirty rats, which had most likely crawled on and nibbled at their food. She would have Jonathan make her some of these shelves as soon as possible.

Shannon went to lay the baby in the cradle and returned to the cramped living room, closing the bedroom door softly behind her.

"Aislin is already down for her nap. We might get a few moments peace," she said, smiling and pulling a plate of shortbread cookies from one of the hanging shelves. She poured tea and balanced two cups and the plate back to the couch. "It's so nice to have neighbors I can actually talk to. The ones that were there before you dint speak English. Seemed nice enough but couldn't do more than wave or nod. Patrick's a firm believer in knowing yer neighbors. Looking out fer them and they fer you. Back in Ireland, we knew everyone for miles and could call on them for anything at any time. And they us. It's not like that here." She paused in obvious homesickness. "When I told Patrick about you and your husband, he was so excited. You look nice and clean and, well, normal. He wanted me to invite ye over for dinner, would ye come?"

"Oh, that would be nice. I'm sure Jonathan would like that," she said and smiled, as she looked around, wondering just how they would all fit to have dinner together. "Just let me know when."

"How about Saturday?"

"Sure. We'll be here, but only if you make that delicious bread again." Shannon looked pleased.

"Better yet, how about I teach ye how to make it?"

"That would be wonderful. Maybe I could bring my friends, so they could learn, too?"

"Aye, the more, the merrier." Shannon poured more tea. "Where does your husband work?" she asked.

"At the shipping yard. He, Caleb and Aryl all work there together."

"It's good that you and yer friends could stick together," Shannon said.

"I'm glad," Ava said sincerely. "Only now there seems to be so little to do beyond the same monotonous chores, and the whole day just stares me down. There's nothing to really look forward to, and every morning it seems like I'm only going through the motions to get to bedtime, so I can go to sleep and not worry for a bit. It's all very depressing. Claire, Ahna and I have spent a lot of time together the last two weeks. I guess we've been feeling a bit smothered by each other."

"Aye. T'was that way with some neighbors we had in our old building. I made a couple of friends right off, and we had a wonderful time together. The first week or so it was wonderful, but if ye spend day after day together, ye run out of things to talk about eventually. Boredom makes you begin to notice the uglier side of folks. You begin to pick them apart and get very annoyed with them." Ava nodded in complete agreement.

"Exactly!" she exclaimed. "I love my friends, but Ahna's whining is starting to bother me, along with the fact that she doesn't do anything all day."

"How can someone just not do anything all day?" Shannon asked, amazed.

"I don't know. But Jon told me that Caleb told him that he buys dinner every night and has taken to doing the laundry, too." Shannon stared at her.

"How'd she get her husband to do *that*?" she asked in awe.

"It's not a matter of getting him to do it. He has to do it if he wants clean clothes. If he doesn't have time, he pays a neighbor to do it. Arianna claims she doesn't know how to wash on a washboard. Well, I didn't either, but I figured it out. It's really not that hard." Ava suddenly realized that she was gossiping, something she detested.

"And your other gal, Claire, was it? How is she?"

"Oh, Claire is struggling so much. Her husband doesn't know it, but she cries almost every day. She hides it when he comes home, and he does a great job of helping her see things the way he does. It's enough to keep her from falling apart, I think."

"He sounds like a good man," Shannon said admiringly. Ava nodded, secretly envious that Aryl was strong enough to keep him and Claire going when Jon seemed barely able to get up in the morning and not just because of the new, comfortable mattress. He was getting worse, angrier and more distant. She'd had enough of gossip and touching on subjects that made her eyes sting.

"Where does Patrick work?" Ava asked, helping herself to another shortbread cookie.

"At the dry docks. He rivets on new ships and repairs the old ones. Aye, he does a variety of things. When we came to America, he took so many jobs. He learned to rivet, some carpentry, metalworking, plumbing and painting. He never stayed at any one job longer than to learn the skill, and then he moved on."

"Oh, I'm sorry," Ava said sympathetically. She had heard of job jumpers and the hardships their families had to endure.

"Oh, no, dear, that was the point. He learned as many trades as fast as he could ta increase his chances of gettin' a long-term job. And he did. And if this job falls through, he can try to get one as a painter or carpenter or plumber. Puts the odds more in his favor of stayin' employed, ye see." Ava nodded.

"That's a really good idea," she said, impressed.

"I was gonna get on at the cannery or at Mr. Finklestein's sewin' factory, but then I found out I was to have Roan, so it had to wait. I guess we better pay more attention to the calendar, so I can get to work." They both laughed and Ava glanced over at the calendar by the bedside. Most all the days were marked with a line in black, save seven or eight days.

∞∞∞∞

*J*onathan came through the door, a few minutes earlier than usual, shaking violently with cold. The sun had set, the temperature had dropped markedly, and the two wool shirts did not provide enough protection from the bitter-cold wind.

"Jonathan! What happened?" Ava asked as she grabbed a blanket from the bed and wrapped it around him. She pulled a chair over close to the fire, added a few pieces of wood, and sat him down, rubbing each hand between hers alternately to warm them.

Several minutes passed before he could talk, teeth chattering too violently to form words. He rocked back and forth with his eyes closed, willing the cold away. Finally, he began to feel his hands and could speak without his teeth slamming together.

"Someone stole my coat and gloves," he said, frowning.

"What? No!" she cried.

"Do I look like I'm joking?" he asked, still rippling with small tremors.

"Why on earth would someone do that?" she grumbled and rose to put on water for tea. "This will be ready in a minute, and dinner's almost ready, too," she called.

"I'll eat when I get back."

"Where on earth are you going?" she asked. "You're still half-frozen!"

"I have to go buy a work coat and gloves before the store closes." He went in the bedroom, shook off the blanket, and put on his dress coat. He rummaged under the bed for the jar where they kept their savings. He looked at it, sighed, dumped it out on the bed and counted through it. "Damn," he cursed aloud, rubbing his face with one hand. Ava stood in the doorway, watching him.

"What's wrong, Jonathan?" she asked with a weary voice.

"I didn't realize it would be so expensive to be poor."

∞∞∞∞

Caleb counted through the change in his pocket and decided to buy fresh ingredients for dinner rather than more expensive ready-made deli food. He would have to have a talk with Arianna tonight about her spending and lack of effort at domestication. He dreaded it. It didn't take much to set her off, and most days he came home to her crying anyway, but it had to be done. They were dangerously low on money, there was nearly none left of what little they brought with them, and they couldn't afford to waste another cent. He bought a small roast of the least expensive cut, two potatoes, two carrots, and a loaf of French bread. He also bought a tablet of yeast and ten pounds of flour. It would save them money if Arianna would make bread.

He pushed the door open to their apartment and was glad to see that at least a fire was going. Arianna sat on the sofa, staring at it.

"Honey, I'm home." He set the groceries on the table and went to sit by her. "God, it feels good to sit down," he moaned. "How was your day, love?" he asked, pulling her over to him and kissing her cheek. She shrugged and grabbed onto his hand. "Are you still having a hard time?" he asked quietly.

"We're still here, aren't we?" she whispered.

"Yes." He pulled her chin up to look at him. "But you know I'm working on some ideas right now. You can't get lost in this, Ahna. I need you strong to help me pack when it's time to leave." He kissed her on the end of her nose.

"I'll try again tomorrow, all right? To be strong."

"Okay." He got up off the couch, trying to shake her gently off his arm. Lately, when he was home, she attached herself to him and didn't want to let go. It made it hard for him to work on his fix-it list with her needing to be right next to him. He usually just let her hang onto him in the small apartment as he worked and talked to her. He did that tonight, pulling her off the couch and walking her to the kitchen. He handed her a small knife and a large potato.

"I hate potatoes," she grumbled.

He took the potato out of her hand and replaced it with a carrot. He took the loaf of bread and cut several slices, biting through the stack. "Sorry, but I'm starving. Someone stole Jon's lunch today, so I shared mine with him," he said with a full mouth.

"Stole his lunch?"

"Well, stole it long enough to throw it across the room and stomp on it. He's having a real hard time at work. Some guys are messing with him." He cut the meat in cubes quickly and dumped them in the frying pan. Arianna finished peeling the carrots, he chopped those, then cubed the potatoes and added those to the mix. He sprinkled in spices. Arianna watched him intently.

"Where did you learn how to do that?" she asked, impressed.

"I remember my mom making this when I was a kid. Only instead of getting the vegetables from a corner store, she would send me out to the garden, and I'd dig 'em up fresh. Do we have any grease?" he asked. Arianna handed him a small plate with a lump of white lard on it. "That'll do. I also bought some yeast. I thought it'd be better if we made bread every day instead of buying it."

"And by *we*, you mean *me*, right?" she asked suspiciously.

"Well, I can't exactly make it from work, now, can I, silly?" he said, kissing her forehead. She sighed heavily.

"You know I don't know how, Caleb."

"Can't you learn? What about Ava and Claire, maybe they can teach you? It's not that hard. My mom did it every day." She shrugged her shoulders, clearly uninterested. He stirred the meat and vegetables and took another large bite of bread. She stayed very close to him but didn't say anything more until dinner was ready.

Caleb set a heaping plate of beef and vegetables in front of her and sat down across the table. He wolfed down half his plate of food before he began the dreaded task of talking to her about finances.

"You know, honey, I have some ideas that are starting to take shape, and I've been doing the math, and we really need to save every penny that we can if I'm going to get anything off the ground. That means that we're going to have to do some things a little differently around here."

"Like what?" she asked, unable to imagine where they could further cut any corners.

"Well, we need to cook at home more. A lot more . . . like every night. You would not believe how much it costs to get dinner at the deli every night. And we need to make bread, like I mentioned, and we really have to do our own laundry. It costs too much to have someone do it for us. That's something we can do for ourselves for free."

"And again, you mean *me*, right?" she asked cynically. Caleb shifted uncomfortably in his chair.

"Yes. I do. I can't do everything. You're here all day and," he took a deep breath and steeled himself, "it's kind of your job, Ahna." He fought the instinct to duck under the table after he spoke, expecting a plate of meat and vegetables to come flying at him from across the table.

"I don't know how to do all this stuff, Caleb." She waved her hand at the apartment, glaring at him.

"I know. But you need to learn, honey. Just start trying, please. We'll get Claire and Ava to help you, too. The most important thing is that we start to save money."

"I guess this means no more shopping, too."

He nodded. "There's a lot already here that we could have done without," he mentioned carefully and glanced over at the matching end tables, lamps with linen shades, two gold framed pictures and velvet couch cover in the living room. All bought second hand, but needless expenses just the same. "I thought you said you weren't going to spend any money on this place?"

"I wasn't. But it's so depressing. I needed to cheer it up a little," she said helplessly.

"Okay, but I think it's about as cheered up as it's gonna get. Let's put decorating on hold, all right?"

She nodded, clearly unhappy and pushed the food that she wasn't hungry for around on her plate. He cleared the plate from in front of her and returned to pull her to her feet.

"I also have another idea for saving money," he said, pulling her close and kissing her slowly from her ear to her collarbone and back up again, sending a shiver through her and making her a little weak in the knees.

"How does this save money?" she asked, smiling for the first time that day.

"Well, showers, for example. We both take one every day, and I think we should save hot water." He raised his eyebrows insinuatingly and started backing her up toward the bathroom.

"Well, maybe we should shower every *other* day?" she teased.

"Not exactly what I had in mind."

The bathroom quickly filled with balmy steam, and it was soon warm enough for Arianna to undress. She stepped around the liner to a waiting Caleb, who stopped lathering suddenly to look her up and down, grinning. "Saving hot water is definitely my top priority." She looked down quickly and his mouth fell open.

"Did you just blush?" he asked in amazement. She didn't say anything, just turned away, pretending to look for the washcloth. He turned her face up and examined the reddened patches on her cheeks. "I'll be damned. You did. I've never seen you blush in all the years I've known you. Usually *you* are the cause of red faces." He laughed lightly.

"It's hot in here," she said, pulling her face away and hoping he'd leave it alone. There had been many changes in her in the last few weeks, and this one was the one she liked the least. Lately, she was unable to hide her emotions or play the perfect poker face. He left it alone and put his head back to wash his hair. Arianna leaned against the wall and traced the outline of his chest and stomach with her eyes, aware of the physical changes in him that had taken place in the last couple of weeks. He had never fully lost the solid build of a hardworking farmer that had been bred into his small frame, but several years of comfortable living and relative inactivity faded the cut of each muscle and filled out a few inches at the belt. Those inches were gone now, and a tight waist wrapped around to individual muscles lining the plane of his abdomen, which had become more prominent now. The lowest of the abdominal muscles, starting just below the hip, were the hardest cut, raised and pointing like an arrow to what made Arianna flush with heat again. Her eyes followed the flow of water and errant tufts of lather washing over him, and a tight knot started to form in her lower stomach. She had always been torn between loving and hating someone who had this much effect on her. Unexpectedly, she reached out and pinched his nipple.

"Ow!" he yelled. He lowered his head at her, pushing back soggy hair and shook a finger at her. "You're gonna get it now," he snickered.

"No, no. Caleb, don't!" He grabbed her anyway, tickling and pinching while she half-halfheartedly screamed and yelped, trying to squirm away. He didn't stop until she was breathless and then pulled her up from her sinking position and pinned her against the wall.

"Now, do that again," he said, slowing his breathing. She reached up toward his chest and he grabbed her arm.

"Not that!" He laughed. "The blushing thing." She leveled her eyes at him.

"No."

"Please?"

"No, Caleb. It's not like I can turn it on and off at will," she said, looking down, trying to keep the spray of water bouncing off his shoulder out of her eyes. He slid his arms around her slick waist and pressed himself into her leg. Her eyes widened slightly, and she looked up at him with another flash of involuntary heat throughout her face. He grinned victoriously, holding her around the waist firmly with one arm and yanking her knee up alongside his hip with the other. It was all business now. She leaned her head back, closed her eyes and let Caleb take her far away from the dismal tenement.

*November 8th 1929*

Aryl stood outside the lunchroom, waiting for Jonathan. He was anxious to find out if he had run the numbers to see if his idea was viable. Glancing to his right, Jonathan stood out in a small crowd of men, who were walking toward the brick building.

"What in hell have you been doing?" Aryl asked.

Covered in coal dust, he looked more disgruntled than ever.

"Shoveling coal all morning," he said with disgust while trying in vain to brush the dust that clung to his shirt and pants. It smeared in long, black trails where his hands wiped, and he quickly gave up. He washed his hands the best he could in the lunchroom but still got sooty fingerprints on the sandwich Caleb handed him. He had taken Jonathan's lunch that morning on the way to work and hid it inside his cubby, so it would be safe. There was normally an unspoken respect for personal belongings among these men; a camaraderie of sorts that usually prevented theft and vandalism. But the fact that, instead of eating it, someone had smashed Jonathan's lunch told Caleb someone had a personal problem with Jonathan. Caleb had continued to ask around about who it was, but had yet to find out.

"So?" Aryl asked impatiently. "What did the numbers say?" Jonathan looked around and led the trio to a corner of the small lunchroom that was starting to fill quickly.

"I'm really sorry, Aryl. I can't see how it'll work," he said between bites.

"I didn't ask if you could see it, I asked what the numbers said." Aryl knew Jonathan could barely see the step he was about to take, much less how a small business would rescue them from the ghetto.

"The numbers said that it would take at least forty tons of flour, bi-weekly, bought at the lowest price possible, and if we undercut competition to steal clients, we'd only profit around thirty dollars a month."

"What if we didn't severely undercut competition? What if we sold at just under the going price?" Caleb asked. He, too, had pinned some hope on this.

"There wouldn't be enough incentive for businesses and restaurants to buy from us. Besides, the bigger dealers could undercut us a hell of a lot easier. We aren't in a position to be competitive enough, and we'd be stuck with forty tons of flour. Which, by the way, I have no idea how we'd buy in the first place."

"I was just going to have us all save every cent until we had enough for the first shipment," Aryl said, disheartened.

"Then there's storage and delivery, I'm sorry, it's just not going to work."

"I'll find something else then." He looked at Jonathan's soot-covered clothes. "So, why were you shoveling coal all morning?" Aryl asked, starting on his second sandwich.

"The crane accidentally dumped a ton, literally," he scowled, "of coal all over the ground instead of inside the coal car, and apparently someone told one of the yard leads I called them a," tilting his head up to remember the words, he quoted bitterly, " . . . *'lazy, loudmouthed, fat bastard'*. So, I got shit duty."

"Who said that?" Caleb demanded. Jonathan shrugged.

"Who knows," he grumbled.

"Jon, who did you piss off around here? Me 'n Aryl get razzed, but you're getting downright abused." Jonathan just shrugged his shoulders again, glancing around the room.

Tony was in the opposite corner of the room talking to a few other men and occasionally glancing at the trio. He eyed Caleb and Aryl, sizing them up and decided maybe he better back off a little.

Harvey Duggins was in the doorway suddenly, rapping on the frame loudly to get everyone's attention. The chatter died down and everyone looked at Harvey.

"Looks like you boys get a day off tomorrow. Shipments are down, so we're suspending Saturday work," Harvey announced.

"For how long?" a worried German asked from the back of the room.

"The next two weeks. We're hoping it picks up after Thanksgiving. I'll keep you posted. I also wanted to let you know we are holding a raffle for Thanksgiving turkeys. We got ten of 'em. You can buy raffle tickets for ten cents at the payroll window." He turned to leave without waiting for questions.

The whistle blew, and the three went back to their work areas, worrying about what a missing day on their paychecks would mean.

∞∞∞

They met up as usual by the gate to walk home together. It was fully dark at quitting time now. Caleb handed Aryl and Jonathan a red ticket. "A raffle ticket for a turkey. I bought us each one. Whoever wins it has to host Thanksgiving," he said. Jonathan handed it back.

"My luck hasn't been that great lately. You better hang on to it." Aryl put his ticket in his pocket, preoccupied with the news of losing a day's work each week. With the holidays coming, the first gas and electric bill arriving soon, and their savings dwindling, he was starting to get extremely worried. Caleb stopped by the mouth of an alley and pointed to a pile of broken pallets around a dumpster.

"Hey, look at that," he said.

"Look at what? It's a busted pile of pallets," Jonathan said and started walking again. The streetlight he stood next to was the only one on this particular block that wasn't broken, and it illuminated the corner of the alley where the pallets were stacked like a spotlight.

"Free fire tonight," Caleb said, walking toward the heap of ragged wood. He lifted one, leaned it against the wall of the alley and kicked it hard, causing several of the wood planks to fall.

"Good idea, Caleb," Aryl said and joined him in kicking pallets apart. Jonathan huffed and positioned a pallet against the wall, even though his back was aching from shoveling all day. Later, the three men walked home with a load of pallet boards on their shoulders.

"This should be enough for two days," Caleb said proudly.

Aryl shook his head. "I can't believe I didn't see that."

"I feel like a tramp," Jonathan grumbled as he shifted the load, hating the idea of scavenging in an alley for anything.

"Get over it," Caleb ordered. "It's two days of free firewood."

"And with the heat bill coming soon, every day we can keep the gas turned down, the better off we'll be," Aryl added. Jonathan relented and picked up his pace, wanting to get home to Ava.

∞∞∞

Jonathan walked in to find Charles and Sven sitting on the couch, talking with Ava.

"Hello, sir," Charles said cheerfully and stood to greet him. Jonathan started to correct him, but Charles had said and done this for over five years whenever Jonathan had walked in the door each evening. Sven stood as well, towering over everyone in the room.

"My wife sends black bread," he said and smiled ever so slightly.

"Thank you," Jonathan said, setting the wood by the hearth. "It's good to see you both. How have you been?" Jonathan asked, shaking his hand and then removing his coat. Ava took it, and he grabbed her long enough to kiss her cheek before she went to put it away.

"Good. I have new job. Large family. Lots of work, less pay. Good enough for times like these." He glanced down at his palm, now covered in black smears from Jonathan's soot-covered hand.

"Oh, sorry about that." He had forgotten that he was filthy. "I tried scrubbing it off at work, but it doesn't come off easily."

"Lard. Rub lard on hands, then soap," Sven informed.

"Huh. I'll try that," he said, walking to the kitchen to look around for the bowl of lard.

"I'll be damned, it worked." he said, rejoining the others in the living room a few minutes later. Ava brought him a large piece of the bread that Sven's wife sent, a hot cup of tea, then sat beside him in a chair pulled from the table.

"Well, the reason for my visit, sir, is this. I have a proposition for you. My new employer is holding a holiday party, the Saturday after Thanksgiving, and I could use a little extra help. I have permission to hire one more man as it will be a large party. I wondered if you might be interested. It would be extra money before the holidays. I'm sure I can arrange a spare black suit, should you need it," Charles said and smiled hopefully.

"I'm not sure what you mean, Charles? What would I be helping you with?" Jonathan shifted uncomfortably and sipped his tea.

"Well, you would be performing the duties of a butler for the evening. Serving guests, taking coats, providing drinks."

Jonathan cringed inside. "I'm not sure I would know what to do, Charles. I've never . . . ."

"Well, it really isn't hard, sir. It would be, how do they say? 'Easy money'." Jonathan felt all eyes on him as he tried to find a dignified way out of the offer. He struggled between the humiliation of becoming hired help and earning extra money. He thought about adding it to the savings jar for when Aryl found an idea that would actually work and finally nodded, conceding to the voice in his head that yelled at him to make and save as much as he could.

"Sure, Charles. And I still have a black suit." Charles handed him a piece of paper with an address written on it.

"If you'll be here at six o'clock, sir, I'll meet you at the back of the house." Jonathan glanced at the address, noting it was only a few blocks from where he used to live. He sighed heavily, already regretting his agreement. "Well, we don't want to keep you from your dinner, so we'll be on our way."

"So soon?" Jonathan asked, disappointed. "Maybe you could stay for dinner?"

"My wife is waiting," Sven stated. He reached out for Jonathan's now clean hand.

"I will see you in two weeks, sir," Charles said to Jonathan. "And we'd like to plan an evening to get together. Maura wanted me to ask you if the Saturday after next would be a good night."

"Oh, that would be wonderful. Tell her yes," Ava said.

Ava went over to her homemade calendar and wrote down Maura's visit eight days from then. With that and their dinner plans with Shannon, she had two things to look forward to.

∞∞∞∞

Caleb walked in to the smell of burnt bread, a room full of billowing smoke and Arianna trying to clear the air at the window.

"What happened?" he asked, helping her wave the smoke out.

"I tried, Caleb, that's what happened. I tried, and like I told you, I don't know how to do this. All I did was waste flour," she growled at him.

"You tried. That's what matters. It'll get better. And easier." He walked in the kitchen and saw the oven dial turned to the highest setting. "Here's the problem, Ahna," he said, pointing to the dial. She grabbed the sheet of paper that had Maura's bread recipe, wrinkled and stained.

"No, see right here." She pointed to the temperature on the recipe. "Five hundred-seventy-five degrees. The dial didn't go that high, so I just put it as high as I could." Caleb started laughing.

"No, Ahna. That's a three. It got smudged." She looked closer and threw the paper on the counter in frustration and crossed her arms to pout. "Don't worry about it. I'll go get some dinner," he said, and holding the back of her head, kissed her forehead. "Thank you for trying."

"Good evening." He walked into the shop where Mr. Goldberg greeted him happily. Caleb was his most regular customer since moving in, and the old man was always gracious.

"What will you have today, Caleb?"

"Oh, how about a loaf of that rye bread and a half-pound of salami. Maybe a quarter-pound of provolone, too." They would have sandwiches again tonight. He was too hungry to wait for dinner to cook.

"Coming right up," he called as he set to work slicing and wrapping. "Not that I mind your business, but you know, if there was a Mrs. Caleb, you wouldn't have to come here every night for your dinner. You should be thinking on finding a nice girl and getting married," he said with a Jewish accent and waggled a crooked finger at him. Caleb simply looked down and laughed.

*November 9th 1929*

Jonathan knocked on Shannon's door while Ava held a small cake.

Shannon smiled when she opened it. "Welcome!"

They stepped inside as Shannon's husband came around the corner.

"Babes are asleep," he told Shannon.

The table now set away from the wall. The two regular chairs were set on one side for Ava and Jonathan, and the luggage trunk was on the other for the hosts to sit on. Wonderful aromas filled the apartment.

"Dinner's almost ready," Shannon said cheerfully. "Can I get ye anythin' to drink?"

"Thank you," was all Ava said, unsure of what to ask for. Shannon had already prepared mugs of fresh coffee, to which she now added a generous helping of cream, sugar and Irish whiskey. She passed the mugs out, and the kick caught Ava off-guard.

"Whew!" She laughed with watering eyes, took another sip, and gave Shannon a nod. "Delicious."

Patrick stuck out his work-weathered hand to Jonathan. "I'm Patrick. Me wife has no manners to introduce me proper." He smirked at Shannon. He was a lanky man with sandy-blond hair grown out just over his ears. His brown eyes were deep set and kind.

"Oh, I'm sorry, Patrick, I'm just so excited to have company," she said apologetically.

"Don't fret, woman," he said and smiled, giving her a hard pat on the bottom.

"Jonathan. My friends call me Jon. Nice to meet you, Patrick."

"Come sit. Shannon said you work at the docks. That'd be the shipping docks or the dry docks?" he asked, folding his long legs over the chest across from Jonathan.

"Shipping–" Jonathan began.

"Patrick, would you do me a favor an grab me some more butter?" Shannon interrupted. He twisted his legs from under the table, went to the living room window and opened it. Frigid air blew past him, and he worked quickly. He reached out to the fire escape, used a key to open a lock on a box chained to the bars and pulled out a round of butter wrapped in paper. He handed it to Shannon, who paid him for the favor with a quick kiss.

"You like it there?" Patrick asked when he returned to the table.

"Honestly, no," Jonathan snorted.

"What don't you like about it?"

"Too many things to mention. What about you? Where do you work?"

"Dry-docks. I rivet mainly, but they often call me to do other things. Lately, I've been working on a section of wood deckin' an' week 'fore that I was putting in pipes for the privies." Patrick was proud of his versatility.

"You like it down there," Jonathan assumed.

"Yes." Patrick nodded. "I've had much worse. Good people I work with for the most part. Don't catch too much trouble for bein' a mick."

"Patrick Michael Mulligan!" Shannon cried, her accent rolling as deep as her anger. Patrick jumped and mockingly cringed as if being scolded by an angry mother with a switch.

"Don't ye dare use that profanity in me house!" She was by his side and glaring at him.

"T'isnt profanity, woman. Just slang," he rebutted with a boyish grin.

"Offensive slang at that. An insult to our Irish heritage. I know all too well what's implied when it's said and it's only said out a' meanness. I'll not hear it in me own house. Not when I have to hear it on the streets in insult."

Patrick nodded. "Fine, fine. You'll not hear it from me in our home." He pulled her over and stretched up to kiss her cheek. "Now don't go showin' yer temper to our guests."

"Don't give me cause to," she chided back, glancing at him from the corner of her eye. Her face was hard, but her eyes teasing.

"The way I see it, people are too damned sensitive." He looked at Shannon but was speaking to Jonathan. "I once seen a fight break out between two fellas at work, Jewish and Italian, I think, or maybe Jew and German. Anyhow, they started with talkin' and callin' each other names like feckin' schoolgirls then started boxin'. Both their daft arses lost their jobs. Now what's the sense in that? Losin' a job over words," he said, shaking his head.

"It's the meanin' behind tha' words, Patrick," Shannon called from the kitchen.

"Aye, but there still just words. An' if people stopped takin' offense, the words would have no power a'tall."

"Where you work, are they hiring?" Jonathan asked casually. Ava eyed him from the kitchen.

"Nah. There's rumors of layoffs because of what happened last month. Got everyone on edge."

Patrick and Jonathan continued talk of work while Ava offered to help Shannon, who stirred a pot of ham and pea soup and pulled a sizzling, cast-iron skillet out of the oven filled with small cakes.

"What are those?" Ava asked. "It smells wonderful."

"Boxty. Potato cakes of a sort. I'll teach you how to make 'em, if you and Jonathan like 'em," she said and smiled while slicing a heavy loaf of soda bread, and they set the dinner out on the table. Both Shannon and Patrick crossed themselves and mumbled a prayer, and then Shannon lifted the ladle to serve soup to her guests.

"How long have you been in America?" Jonathan asked.

"Near five years. Me n' Shannon here came over together. Married the day 'fore the boat pushed off," Patrick said, smiling.

"Honeymoon trip," Jonathan commented.

"Well, I wouldn't say it was a honeymoon," Patrick said, laughing. "The first days were exciting with the prospects of coming to America and all. But tis hard to find a bit o' privacy when yer crammed in with a couple hundred other emigrants in steerage day after day." Jonathan shook his head, unable to imagine.

"Is it all you thought it would be? America, I mean?" It wasn't Jonathan's words, but his tone that caused Ava to give him a hard look and poke him in the thigh. Patrick laughed.

"Yes and no. Everything always looks better from far away. Take Shannon, for example." He recoiled before she could even raise her hand to slap his shoulder. Her green eyes flashed, and she hit him twice in the arm, hard. "Now, now, woman," he howled. "Shannon here was the most beautiful lass in all of Enniskerry." He pulled her close to his side and kissed her on the top of her head. She pinched him for good measure. "There was talk back home o' opportunities that any man willin' to work hard would have his own land in no time. Dint turn out to be that easy. But I'll get it. One day," he said contentedly.

"That's what you want? To own land?" Jonathan asked.

"Aye. Tis what every Irishman wants," he said quietly.

"Where?" Jonathan asked, having stopped eating, watching Patrick intently. He shrugged.

"Maybe upstate, maybe out west. Not sure just yet."

"How will you go about that? Obtaining land, I mean?" Jonathan asked, curious at what strategy he had in mind.

"Work hard, save, and it'll come. Maybe before lil' Roan is old enough for schooling."

"How can you be so sure you'll get it?"

Patrick raised his head and looked Jonathan straight in the eyes. "Because I want it bad enough."

Toward the end of the dinner visit, Patrick arranged a night to get together with the other men to show them how to build the hanging shelves, and Shannon promised to come over to teach Ava how to make boxty.

*November 13th 1929*

The days passed without much else to break the monotony until midweek when Caleb came home to a quiet apartment that distinctly lacked the smell of food, burnt or otherwise. Arianna sat on the couch in the dark, staring at a dying fire. She remained motionless as he walked through the door and greeted her. Sitting carefully on the couch beside her, she held something against her chest with folded arms.

"Ahna, what's wrong?" he asked gently, reaching for her hand. She jerked it away. "Did you have a hard day, my love?" He tried again for her hand. She pulled away again, her gaze remained on the fire.

"Ahna, you're scaring me. Tell me what's wrong."

After a long moment, she turned her head slowly toward him and silently stared at him with vacant eyes. The dying light intensified the dark hollows under her eyes, sunken cheeks and the drawn lines of her mouth. The focus of her lifeless eyes locked onto his, and her stock-still posture caused the hairs on the back of his neck to rise. He remained trapped in her startling gaze until she glanced down at what she held to her chest. Uncrossing her arms, and turning Caleb's hardbound notebook over, she opened it slowly.

"You lied," she whispered. She flipped the sheets, exposing page after page of meaningless doodling, drawings of his childhood home, ocean beaches and an entire page crowded with her name, written in every size and script, surrounding a poem. He looked with dread from the notebook to Arianna's face and back to the book. "First of all," she spoke slowly in a too-calm voice, "You said you had ideas, plans. You said you were writing those ideas down, working on them until one of them would work. And you said we would be out of here by the first of the year." She stared at him again with frighteningly empty eyes, waiting for an answer. Caleb took a moment, rubbed his eyes and ran his fingers through his hair. He stared at the floor while he spoke.

"Ahna, I," he paused to take a deep breath, "I had to tell you all that. I needed you to hold on, to make the best of things until I was able to figure something out. To be completely honest, Aryl has been the only one with an idea and, well, that one didn't turn out to be practical. For us anyway," he said dejectedly. "I do know something will work out. I just need more time."

"You thought I'd run again," she assumed.

He nodded. "Are you telling me you wouldn't have? If I had brought you here and told you, right then and there, that I had no idea how we were going to get out of this place? If I had told you just how hard life would be for us? You wouldn't have run the first chance you got?" He turned toward her on the couch. "Ahna, I told you that I would find a way out for us, and I will. But I can't work miracles. I just need more time. It's not even been a month," he said, pleading. She turned her head toward him in disbelief.

"It feels so much longer than that, Caleb."

"I know. It does to me, too. This life is exhausting." He searched for something to say and remained quiet for a long time.

"Don't ever lie to me again, Caleb," she finally said firmly. "Every day for two years, my father came home and reassured us all that everything was fine. Right up to the day when the bank showed up to take our things and give us notice to leave. Do you remember what you said when you came home that day, almost a month ago?" He shook his head, too tired to remember. "You said everything would be fine. It would all work out. But I already knew the truth. The neighbor's wife had come over, crying. Her husband invested everything with Jonathan. He got home before you did and broke the news to her. And when you got home, all I heard was my father's voice. *It's fine, it'll all be okay, there's nothing to worry about.* It's the other reason I ran. Not because we were suddenly penniless, not because I don't love you. I just couldn't be blindsided like that again."

He nodded, his eyes acknowledging. "All right. From now on, no sugarcoating. I promise." He took her hand, and she didn't pull away this time. She leaned over slowly and laid her head in his lap, watching the last of the burning embers in the fireplace. He stroked her hair, trying to smooth her wild, raven tufts. "You look like hell," he said with a smile. She whipped her head around, mouth open in shock. "Hey, I thought we were going for honesty."

*November 23rd 1929*

"Now it's a party!" Maura cried as Arianna and Caleb walked through Ava's door the following Saturday night. "How've you been, love?" Maura asked as she hugged her.

"All right," Arianna said, smiling.

"Yer losin' weight, ye sure yer feelin' a'right?" Maura asked, concerned, feeling her forehead and touching her gaunt cheeks. Arianna nodded.

"My stomach is upset, but I'm fine." Arianna handed Ava a plate of biscuits and a small jar of honey. She had managed to master biscuits well enough to be edible as long as she sat in front of the oven the entire twenty minutes. Ava added the plate to the table of food. Everyone had brought a dish, so there would be plenty to go around. The room was fairly bursting and it quickly grew stuffy with so many bodies in the small space. Aryl shared his last bottle of brandy, and after a while, Maura grew frustrated with the occasional loud outbursts from the men gathered on one side of the small room.

"A'right!" she yelled, getting everyone's attention. "Seein' that all the men are gathered over thar, and all the women are over here, why don't we split this lil' party up an' you men grab a plate o' food an' go find somewhere else to be. Let us women alone to talk about ye, and don't be stealin' the brandy on yer way out," she ordered with hands on her hips. All the men looked at each other and nodded in agreement. Jonathan took the box of cigars from under his bed before they filed out the door as Aryl offered his apartment and Caleb offered his last bottle of whiskey.

"Now that's better," Maura said, plopping down on the couch after the door closed. "Ye girls gather round, and let's get on with the gossip. And bring the brandy." Ava skipped over with the bottle and sat close to Maura. "Now as I was askin', what's gone on since I saw ye last?" she asked, pouring herself a glassful.

"I got to know our neighbors," Ava started.

"The annoyin' one?"

"No, no, next door here. Shannon and Patrick. They're very nice. They're from Enniskerry."

Maura's eyes lit up. "I know Enniskerry!" she exclaimed. "Me family lives not too far north a' there! Good people, is she?" Ava nodded.

"She's very nice. She's teaching me all kinds of helpful things."

"Well, why isn't she here with us? Go get her to join the party!"

Ava jumped up, grinning and went next door, rapping impatiently. Shannon opened it and smiled.

"I'm having a get together at my house, and I was wondering if you would come?" Ava blurted out.

"I'd love to, when'll it be?" Shannon asked.

"Right now."

"Oh. Well." She turned to look at Patrick. "I do have to get the babes down for the night." Patrick scoffed.

"Go, Shannon, I'll put the wee ones to bed." She looked from Ava to Patrick and smiled.

"A'right, let me get my sweater." She put it on and started giving instructions to Patrick. "Now if Roan won't sleep, give him some warm milk and sing 'im that lullaby, an' if he fusses, walk the floor pattin' his back and—" Patrick hushed her.

"I think I know how to care for me own babes, Shannon." He gave her a quick hard kiss and squeezed her bottom.

"Don't be too late," he whispered, glancing at the calendar.

"I'll see to you later, don't ye worry." Her eyes flashed wickedly, as she and Ava scurried away.

Ava made introductions, and Shannon settled in right away with a drink and talk of Ireland with Maura. With nothing overly pleasant to talk about in their own lives, Arianna, Ava, and Claire listened to stories told by Maura and Shannon that had all of them doubled over with laughter. Arianna handed her drink to Maura after taking two sips. Her stomach was still disagreeable, and she didn't want to have to leave early from sickness.

An hour passed and Ava's side and cheeks hurt from laughing so hard. A harsh rap at the door suddenly interrupted their carousing.

"If that's the men tryin' ta get ta the last o' the brandy, shut the door quick!" Maura called as Ava opened the door to the see the beady-eyed one looking very irritated.

"The noise coming from over here is keeping the whole building up! Have mercy with the yelling and the laughing, how's a body supposed to get some sleep with all this carrying on, there's noise ordinances, you know. It's nearing nine o'clock an' most impolite to hold a party when there's been so much sickness and folks are tired with recovery, sickness probably floated across from over here anyhow–"

"Jaysus sufferin' Christ!" Maura grabbed Ava's arm, pulled her out of the doorway, and met the beady-eyed one nose to nose.

"Yer a yapper, aren't ye?" she yelled, clearly taking the woman by surprise. "What's the meanin' of coming over here distruptin' our good time with yer whinin' and carryin' on? If yer so damn sick, maybe ye should be in bed! And if yer not and our carryin' on is botherin' ye so much, why can't ye come speak to Ava civil-like? Stead of bellowin' on. I've heard a heifer giving birth to twin calves make less racket than you!" The beady-eyed one's eyes were wide, her mouth hanging open. "Now," Maura said with her arms crossed. "You'll do one of two things. Either ye'll shut yer trap and carry yer disagreeable arse back to yer apartment, or ye'll shut yer trap an' join us for a drink, leavin' yer problems at the door." Maura tapped her foot and looked her up and down quickly. "What'll it be?" It took the woman a moment to speak and when she did, her tone was in check.

"Well, now . . . I'm not the drinking type," she said and turned to her apartment. Maura closed the door, and Ava pulled on her arm.

"Why would you invite her in to join us?" she asked, appalled.

"If you can help it, never make an enemy of a neighbor, Ava," she said. "Now that doesna' mean that ye shouldn't put 'em in their place when they cross the line, mind," she said and smiled. Ava couldn't help but laugh, thinking that Maura could put a hardened criminal in his place and send him crying to confession.

*November 24th 1929*

Sunday morning, Jonathan and Ava roused at noon. Jonathan stumbled to the shower, and Ava went to the kitchen to make coffee; both had a mild headache from the previous evening. Rubbing sleep out of her eyes, she reached for the coffee from the hanging shelf Patrick helped Jonathan build the week before.

"We're almost out of coffee," she called. Jonathan didn't hear her, having his head fully under the stream of water. He had had a good time last night, and just like at the end of the Halloween party, he hadn't wanted it to end, forcing him to return to the doldrums of reality. The brandy provided a soothing blur to the truth of his circumstances, and the presence of his friends was reassuring and amusing.

In what was a blend of male bonding and therapy, the five managed to get thoroughly lit with what little alcohol was available, rationing having lowered their thresholds. Mostly it was a night of hilarity, and when conversation became too deep or gloomy, someone would crack an irreverent joke. Caleb was particularly good at timing loud and meaningful bodily emissions to break any quiet tension.

They sat around the small table, playing cards, and smoking cigars and even created an imaginary barmaid that they would periodically call out to for refills. And Sven, Jonathan remembered with a smile, was the most comedic of them all. Jonathan had only ever seen the hard, serious side of Sven. He laughed heartily, teased the others, and taught them all to swear in Russian. He was the highlight of the evening.

Of course, they all presumed that the women were talking about them, and Aryl's only reverent moment was when he secretly hoped that Arianna wouldn't divulge more details about the trips to Paris. One trip in particular had left him with a pressing burden of guilt that he carried every day. Jonathan remained in his reminiscence under the steaming spray until the last of the hot water ran out.

When he walked out of the bathroom in muslin boxers and a white, sleeveless t-shirt, Ava was in the doorway of the small kitchen with coffee in one hand and a plate of biscuits in the other. Her head fell forward slightly and her mouth gaped. She raised one eyebrow as he walked by, looking him over from top to bottom as the biscuits nearly slid off the plate.

"*Wow*," she whispered. Strenuous labor had given his arms and chest masculine definition, and his shorts hung loosely on his hips. He rubbed his wet hair with a towel, glancing over at her with strikingly sapphire eyes.

"What's for breakfast?" he asked, leisurely crossing the room toward her.

"You," she said, eying him this time from shoulder-to-shoulder.

"What?"

"Get back in there," she said quickly, nodding her head toward the bedroom. She set the plate on the table and pulled off her apron with a yank. He looked at her, confused for a second, until she ran her hands up his arms, over his shoulders and down his chest, grabbing two fistfuls of t-shirt material that was already stretched tight, and he smirked as he got her meaning.

"Well, you know, honey, they say you shouldn't perform strenuous exercise on an empty stomach," he said, grinning slyly.

"Fine. Eat then." She loaded the plate with biscuits, shoved it in front of him and sat across from him to wait impatiently.

He smiled, shaking his head. He enjoyed the newly assertive side of her and ate very slowly, just to tease. She huffed her breath at him to hurry him along.

"I wouldn't want to eat too quickly and get indigestion, Ava," he said seriously but with a mocking look. He still had lingering buoyancy from the night before and smiled at her with more life in his expression than she had seen in a long while, and it made him all the more appetizing. She watched him as he ate; his wet hair tousled and glistening, lingering on every movement and muscle twitch of his hands and arms. She stared at his mouth as it opened for each bite, his tongue occasionally licking his lips and his eyes, deep as the abyss, flashed under dark lashes. She swallowed hard. Unconsciously, her breathing was shallow and fast through her nose as she admired, gripping her own hands like a vise in her lap. He flashed an amused smile.

"You gettin' started without me over there?" he teased, relishing in her torment. She flushed scarlet, but didn't look away.

"Well, if you'd just hurry up," she insisted.

He was being downright cruel when he began casual conversation about the night before and the day ahead, their friends and his to-do list, dragging breakfast out as long as he could. As he ate the last bite, he wished that it could be like this all the time; lighthearted and teasing. By the time he looked up from his wish, she was by his side, reaching for his face with both hands and leaned down to kiss him. He stood without breaking their kiss and wrapped his arms around her waist, pulling her so tight to him that she could hardly breathe. When she pulled away to catch her breath, he teased her further.

"You know, they say you shouldn't exercise on a full stomach."

"That's swimming," she said, pulling the t-shirt over his head so ferociously a few of the stitches on a seam popped.

"But I might get cramps," he whined.

"You'll live," she said sternly and attacked his mouth again, ravenous. He put up no more false excuses, returned her greedy kiss and lifted her up by the waist, shuffled toward the bedroom and kicked the door closed behind him.

*November 25th 1929*

Monday morning came with the shrill ring of the alarm, and Jonathan pulled himself from his bed to begin another disciplined week of strenuous work, ravenous eating, and restless sleep. He was particularly discouraged that Thanksgiving interrupted the week. No dinner plans existed yet, and he felt torn between hoping they would furlough the day and working so he wouldn't lose pay. They had been hemorrhaging cash, setting up a new home that required purchasing several primitive tools for day-to-day life, supplementing heat with bought firewood, and shopping daily for food as they lacked the convenience of an electric icebox. He made a mental note to find a box to put on the fire escape, some chain link and a lock to secure it to the bars like Patrick had devised. It was cold enough outside to keep milk and butter, and when the temperature dropped further, they could freeze some meat. But the box would cause a further dip into their dwindling savings for yet another expense of poverty. He kissed Ava goodbye and she felt saddened by the dejected expression that had returned to his face. She sighed heavily as she closed the door behind him and began her routine.

∞∞∞

Tony walked slowly, waiting until Jonathan passed him on his way into the yard before doubling back and jogging across the street to Victor, who was waiting by a lamppost. "I messed wit' dat guy like you said to," he told Victor proudly. Victor nodded.

"Good. What did you do?"

"Well, I cut some flour bags, made 'em spill, and he got docked pay for it, an' I stole his coat an' gloves, bastard froze the rest of the day an' got blisters, too, wit-out his gloves." He could see Victor was not impressed. "An' I told a supervisor he was talkin' disrespectful-like 'bout him, so he got coal duty for a coupla days, boy, that pissed him right off." Victor gave a tight smile.

"Anything else?"

"Well, not really, sides tellin' some of the bigger fellas at work 'bout his talkin', too. They get in his face and threaten him regular now, he gets real embarrassed." Victor nodded.

"That's a start, I suppose."

"Say, not that it's any of my business, but what's ya' beef wit' this guy anyways?" Tony asked curiously.

"You're right. It's none of your business. You weren't able to do more than that?"

Tony shifted uncomfortably. "Well, no. See, he's always got these two uttha guys wit' him before an' afta' work. It's not that they're big guys er nothin', but wit' three of 'em, I'm just not wanting to get my ass kicked, if I'm found out, ya' know?" he explained, hoping Victor wasn't too disappointed.

"Do you have any friends, Tony?"

"Well, yeah, course." He bobbed his head.

"Big friends?" Victor quizzed.

"Yeah, some of 'em are."

"Lastly, Tony, do you and your friends want to make some more money?"

He eyed Victor cautiously. "For doin' wat?" Tony didn't frighten easily, but something about Victor did frighten him. He started to feel dread well up in his stomach as he expected Victor to ask him to kill Jonathan. Victor could sense the apprehension and took a step closer to him, smiling as he pulled three fifty-dollar bills out of his pocket. Tony began bobbing his head, suddenly not so concerned with morals.

"Yeah, yeah, I'll off 'im for ya'," he volunteered before Victor could ask.

"No!" Victor said, loud and stern. "I don't want him dead, you understand?"

"Yeah, I understan', but if ya' don't wanna off 'im, wat then?"

"I have a very simple but specific request, Tony." He waited for Victor's instructions, glancing from his face to the money in his fist and back again. Victor could see he was itching for the cash and would do anything for it. "You gather a couple of your bigger friends. Catch Jonathan alone. Here's where it gets specific, so listen closely, Tony. I want you to beat him, but strike where it counts. The ribs, kidneys, stomach, but not the face. I don't want his pain to be obvious. I want it to be his alone to suffer through. And not so badly that he can't work. I wouldn't want him to not be able to pay his rent, after all." Victor said and smiled cruelly. "But for a couple of weeks, I want him to feel lingering pain with *every move he makes*."

"I can do that easy," Tony reassured and reached toward the money. Victor snapped his wrist away.

"No. You get this when the job's finished. I'm going to be out of town for a week, and you have that long to catch him alone. Next Monday, I'll be waiting here. If it isn't done by then, don't bother to approach me."

"It'll be done. Don't you worry 'bout that," he said with his eyes on the money as Victor stuffed it back into his pocket.

"Good. I'll see you in a week then."

Tony hurried through the gate just as the whistle blew, thinking about which of his friends he would recruit.

∞∞∞

Patrick knocked softly on Aryl's door.

"Patrick, how are ya'?"

"Good and yourself?"

"Good. We really appreciate you showing us how to make those hanging shelves last week. It's a great idea. Hopefully now there'll be no more cases of the runs." He laughed, patting his stomach.

"No bother a'tall. I was wonderin' if I could speak to yer wife real quick. Shannon's puttin' the wee ones to sleep, and I snuck out on the sly." Aryl stepped aside.

"Come in. Claire, Patrick needs to speak to you."

"Hello, Patrick," she said, smiling and wiping her hands on her apron.

"Ma'am." He nodded. "I had a question to ask ye, if ye have a moment."

"Of course, what is it?"

"Well, I know tis a bit early, but I've been thinkin' on Christmas for Shannon. The babes are young and don't know better, but I wanted to do something special for Shannon, and well, when I found out you painted and then seeing this," He pointed to the mural in progress above the fireplace. "I've got to say, that's some talent. Absolutely amazin'."

"Thank you," Claire said modestly.

"Anyway, I was wonderin', an' I kin pay ye, if ye'd paint a picture for Shannon." Claire beamed.

"I'd love to, Patrick. What a sweet thing to think of. What do you think she'd like?"

"Well, I have this picture." He pulled a folded piece of newspaper out of his back pocket. "It's a picture of a statue, an angel that sits in the gardens of Powerscourt Manor in County Wicklow near where we grew up. She found this picture in the newspaper and tore it out to keep as a reminder of home 'fore we left. The paper's gettin' mighty tattered. I'd love to have it painted for her." He handed Claire the faded scrap of fragile newspaper carefully. She laid it flat in the palm of her hand and took it over to the light.

"Yes, I can do a painting of that. It's beautiful. I'd be happy to."

"That would be wonderful, just let me know what would be the cost."

"Oh, I don't know? How about I trade you for black paint?" she offered.

"Black paint?" He looked confused.

"Well, I'm almost out from painting the storm, so how about I do it for paint?"

"That would be fine. Could it be ready by Christmas?" he asked.

"Of course."

"Oh, that's wonderful, Claire, thank you so much, you have no idea how much this will mean to her. I better go now before she notices me gone." He waved goodbye, joyful at the thought of having something so special to give Shannon on Christmas. Claire carefully laid the faded paper between two pages of a book, then sorted through the remaining canvases Aryl had brought with them until she found the right size.

"I'll start working on it tomorrow morning," she decided aloud.

Aryl had moved to the window, tuning out much of the conversation, looking out as a light snow began to fall. He loved the quiet hush that came over the city when snow blanketed the streets but was unable to enjoy it thoroughly, knowing he would soon have to turn up the heat. He looked back at the dwindling supply of wood on the hearth and sighed. He decided he would have to go out and look for more broken pallets or any form of firewood after work tomorrow.

*November 26th 1929*

Aryl broke off from the group a few blocks from home in search of firewood while Jonathan and Caleb continued home. Caleb mumbled about feeling guilty for not helping Aryl, but Jonathan had a hard time hearing him over the crunch of their work boots on the iced-over snow coating the sidewalk. He pulled his wool hat down lower on his ears and shivered.

"It's really getting cold," he commented.

"What?" Caleb asked.

"Nothing."

They walked on in silence until they were about a block from their building. Caleb stopped and pointed.

"Hey, look at that. I used to have one just like that!" he said, pointing to a black Packard parked on their side of the street. "Wonder what it's doing in this neighborhood?"

"Maybe they're moving in," Jonathan said sarcastically. Caleb didn't take his eyes off the car even as they passed it.

"Damn, I miss that car," he said longingly. They were a few steps beyond it when the rear car door opened and a woman exited, taking several strides to catch up to the men.

"Jonathan!" she called when she was a few paces behind him. He looked back and did a double take. He took a deep breath before he turned to face her fully.

"Hello, Ruth," he said flatly.

Caleb's eyebrows almost hit his hairline.

"Hello, Jonathan," she said sweetly and took slow steps toward him. "It's been a long time."

"It has."

"How have you been?" she asked casually.

He looked around the neighborhood and then back to her with a phony expression of glee.

"Wonderful. Just fabulous, Ruth. Just thought I'd spend some time seeing how the other half lives," he said mockingly.

"I heard. I'm so sorry about what happened to you. I know how hard you worked. I watched you pour your heart and soul into your brokerage," she said soothingly.

"I'm sorry, why are you here?" he asked her, slightly annoyed.

"I just wanted to make sure you were all right. Like I said, I heard what happened and I just feel awful."

"Does Victor know you're here?" Jonathan asked coldly.

"Oh. I didn't know you knew we were married. No, he doesn't. He's out of town. It's best that way, given our history. You're not his favorite person."

"Believe me, the feeling is mutual."

"I only married him because I was pining over you," she blurted out. Jonathan didn't know what to say to that, so he focused on the ground in front of his feet. "I was brokenhearted." She touched her heart and attempted a pout.

"I sent you a letter." He looked up at her impatiently. "I explained everything."

She waved her hands. "You know what? None of that matters. It's all in the past. I came here today to let you know that I still care for you, Jonathan, and if you need anything, anything at all, you can come to me. I have money, resources, and people. I could have you out of this neighborhood tonight if you wished." He glared at her. "Here's how you can get a hold of me without having to deal with him." She held out a piece of paper. He reached out and took it even as the voice in his head screamed at him to turn and walk away.

She was inches away from him now, looking up at him through her lashes.

"I do mean anything you might need, Jonathan," she cooed and reached one arm around his neck, the other around his waist to hug him.

He didn't return the hug and pulled away after a brief second. Before he could say anything, Caleb stepped in.

"Ava's waiting at home, Jon."

"Maybe I'll see you again sometime?" she asked hopefully.

At the top of the landing, Caleb reached into Jonathan's left pocket and pulled out a folded piece of paper, holding it up for Jonathan to see.

"She slipped this in when she hugged you," he informed. Jonathan opened it up and read it aloud.

"*Thanks for the memories. I will always love you, Ruth.* She put a lipstick kiss on it." He looked at Caleb in frustration. "I really don't need this shit right now."

"I know. Here," he said. "I'll get rid of them for you." He held his hand out for the second note.

"Thanks. See you tomorrow." Jonathan turned toward his door just as a woman's scream echoed in the hall. Caleb snapped his fingers.

"Arianna – Rat." Caleb knew that yell in particular, and he broke into a jog to rescue Arianna from the vermin.

∞∞∞∞

Ayl spent an hour looking in alleys and behind stores. It only slightly paid off. He got enough splintered wood planks and broken crates to last for a few hours. He was freezing when he walked in, set the wood on the hearth and warmed his numb hands by the fire that Claire already had glowing.

"Dinner's almost ready," she told him as she handed him a mug of steaming tea. He nodded, too cold to converse. A few minutes later, she brought a big bowl of soup over to him, so he could eat while warming.

"What kind of soup is this?" he asked.

"Chicken noodle," she said, handing him a fat chunk of bread.

"Where's the chicken?"

She leaned over and poked around with her spoon.

"Oh, there's a piece," she said and grinned. "Shannon showed me how to make three dinners out of half a chicken," she said proudly.

"I really appreciate you being so good about this," he said affectionately. "Even though this latest idea didn't work out, eventually something will and we have to be ready."

"I know." They sat on the brick hearth, eating their soup and talking about every possible way to increase their savings.

*November 27th 1929*

Jonathan got home amazed that he had made it through the day *without* a confrontation, *with* his lunch, *without* a prank, and *with* his coat. They had even walked after work to Victor's office to pay December's rent before the Thanksgiving holiday, and Victor had been out of the office as Ruth had mentioned. It bordered on a good day.

"They furloughed tomorrow," he told Ava over dinner.

"Don't they always?" she asked referring to the Thanksgiving holiday.

"I have no idea. I've heard they do and they don't, depending on who you ask. For now, they are consolidating shipments to save on labor. We get tomorrow off, without pay, of course," he said, his brow furrowed with worry. He pushed the mix of cubed potatoes and ham around with his fork. "Caleb won a turkey in the raffle, so I guess he's hosting Thanksgiving. He asked each of us to bring something. I'm not sure what you want to bring."

"I'll figure something out," she said, not exactly looking forward to the first major holiday in the tenement either. They ate while listening to the radio.

Later that evening, Jonathan sat reading on the couch, and Ava joined him after she finished another letter to his parents. Picking up a blanket on the way, she nestled next to him, covered them both and closed her eyes trying to ignore the sounds of the city outside. She concentrated on the slow, rhythmic sound of Jonathan's breathing and the soft crackles of the fire. She was just drifting off on his shoulder when they heard angry shouting coming from down the hall. They looked at each other then quickly toward the door, identifying one of the voices immediately as Arianna's.

"Think we should go over there?" Ava whispered.

"No. And why are we whispering?"

"I don't know," she whispered back and giggled. Jonathan intended to let Caleb and Arianna work out whatever had her shrieking today, but he changed his mind when he heard the crashing of what sounded like shattering glass.

∞∞∞∞

*L*ooking down the hallway, he saw Caleb backed up against the wall of the hall with his hands up, trying to calm Arianna. She stood in her own doorway with a frying pan.

"Hey, now!" Jonathan inched his way in front of Caleb and faced Arianna. "What's going on here?" he asked her and glanced back at Caleb.

"This son of a bitch is stepping out on me!" she screamed, pointing at Caleb with the pan.

"Arianna." Jonathan held up his hands. "If he's not with you, he's with me, and I can tell you that all he leaves this apartment to do is work. I swear to you."

"Oh, yeah? Then what in the hell is this?" She threw Ruth's notes in Jonathan's face and then tried to get around him with the frying pan aimed at Caleb. Jonathan grabbed her from behind and held her back. "Arianna! Calm down!" he yelled.

"Let me go!" she screamed, kicking behind her, aiming at his shins.

"Arianna, those aren't mine!"

"Liar!" She wriggled and grunted, trying to get out of Jonathan's grasp.

"I swear to you, they aren't!" Caleb pleaded.

"Not yours, huh? Then who the hell do they belong to? They were in your pants pocket, Caleb! Well, whose are they then?" she demanded. Caleb looked helplessly at Arianna.

"I can't tell you," he said.

"You're lying! They're yours! I know they're yours! I'm leaving! Soon as Jon lets me go, I'm packing and going home!" she sobbed. Jonathan closed his eyes and took a deep, frustrated breath.

"They're mine, Arianna," he said through gritted teeth. She stopped fighting him immediately.

"What!?" She twisted her head around to try to look at him.

"Jon–" Caleb started but didn't know how to finish. Either way, one of them was in trouble tonight.

"They're mine, Arianna. Caleb was just getting rid of them for me, so Ava wouldn't see them." He slowly let Arianna go, sliding his hand down her arm to take the frying pan from her. Just in case.

"Yours?" she whispered in disbelief. He nodded.

"You son of a bitch! Stepping out on Ava!"

Now Caleb grabbed her to keep her from pummeling Jonathan, who raised his arms to protect his head and spun around. Ava was standing behind him with a strained expression. Arianna stopped fighting, and they all watched Ava cautiously. She walked past him and picked the notes up off the floor.

"Ava. Don't," Jonathan begged. "Let me explain first."

"You should have explained in the first place," she snapped at him and unfolded each note, her spine stiffening as she read them. She walked by Jonathan with a hard face, dropped the notes at his feet as she passed and then slammed their apartment door. Jonathan leaned against the wall.

"This is great, just great," he growled, and banged the back of his head on the wall twice.

"Jon, I'm sorry. I should have thrown them out the window first thing," Caleb's voice trailed off.

"You were helping him hide an affair!" Arianna's voice was scratchy from screaming.

"It's not an affair, Ahna. It was a set-up. Don't you remember Ruth?" Caleb asked her. Jonathan took over the explanation.

"Blonde, blue eyes, talked a lot, I was with her just before Ava. She was always going around with us, and then suddenly she was gone?" Arianna's eyes lit up.

"I remember now," she whispered.

"Well, she found Jonathan," Caleb interrupted. "Not that hard to do being married to Victor. Well, she showed up outside last night. I guess she's still smitten. She slipped a note in Jon's pocket, and I saw it. I pulled it out and offered to get rid of it for him, so it didn't cause any problems. Like this," Caleb sighed. Arianna looked toward Ava's door.

"Oh, boy," she said, understanding fully now. "Maybe I should go talk to her first and explain things."

"I think that's a good idea," Caleb agreed.

He pulled Jonathan inside, where he sat down hard at the dining table. Caleb poured hot coffee and sat down across from him silently.

"I had just let myself relax, too," he said with a mocking laugh. "I was sitting on the couch reading and had the passing thought that I'd gotten through *one day* without some sort of dramatics." He shook his head helplessly.

"I'm sorry. If I hadn't been preoccupied with trying to catch that rat yesterday, I wouldn't have forgotten to toss them out the window," Caleb apologized.

"How'd she find them anyway?" Jon asked.

"I was changing, and they fell out of my pocket. She picked them up, and, well, you saw the rest," he said, cringing.

Jonathan nodded, and they sat in silence until Arianna returned a half-hour later.

"All right, I explained everything to her. Everything you guys told me anyway. I think she'll at least talk to you. You'll have to fill in the details, Jon. There's a lot more she wants to know."

"Thanks." He patted her back as he walked past her.

She sat next to Caleb at the table, quiet for a moment and then took his hand.

"I'm sorry," she said quietly.

"It's okay. I know how it must have looked," he admitted.

"It didn't look good, that's for sure."

"You were really gonna club me with that pan, weren't you?" he asked, half-smiling.

"Yes. Yes I was."

"I would never do that to you, Ahna. Step out on you, I mean."

"I know that deep down, Caleb. I don't know what came over me."

"A woman scorned is a very scary thing," he breathed.

∞∞∞

Jonathan sat down on the far end of the couch, eying Ava tensely. On her end, she sat with crossed legs and her arms crossed over her chest, staring at the fire.

"If I had a nickel for every hour we've spent staring at this fire," he said quietly.

"Who is she?" Ava demanded. He took a deep breath and sat back, attempting to get comfortable. He had a feeling he would be there a while. "She is someone I was with before you."

"Why have you never mentioned her before?"

"There was no need to. The minute I met you, she was ancient history."

"You were with her when you met me?" she asked with a look of surprise.

"Yes. At the dinner party. I deserted her when I left the party with you. She was the drunken annoying one, remember?"

"I was upset that night. But you took me for coffee later, and you didn't mention that you were seriously involved with someone."

"I'd already forgotten about her, Ava. I'd already decided that I was going to end it with her, and I wasn't going to say anything to you that would make you think twice about seeing me again. If I had told you that I was involved with someone else, would you have gone to dinner with me the very next night?"

"Probably not," she answered honestly.

"See? I wasn't going to risk that."

"I would have told you to end it with her and then come see me." She glanced at him sideways. "That's the proper way to do things. Technically, I was the other woman from the time you met me until you ended it with her."

"Which was all of twenty four hours, Ava. I wrote her a letter the very next day. I didn't even see her again. I had Charles turn her away when she came to the door and my doorman turn her away at the office. Eventually, she accepted it and I hadn't heard from her again. Until now."

Fury welled up in her at the thought of this woman approaching Jonathan on the street to slip him a note smelling of perfume and imprinted with a lipstick kiss.

"How did she find you then?" she asked through tight lips. Jonathan hesitated, not wanting to say the name.

"She's married to Victor," he finally said bluntly. Her head whipped to face him.

"Are you serious?"

"Yes. She mentioned he was out of town and felt bad about what happened to us–"

"To us? Or to you?" she asked with an accusing tone.

"Well, she said to me." He fidgeted uncomfortably at the questioning.

"All right, Jon, just start at the beginning," she sighed and listened as he gave her every detail of the meeting, starting with Caleb noticing the car and ending with them on the landing and hearing Arianna scream at the rat. Her eyes flashed livid when he told her that Ruth had hugged him when she slipped him the note. She took a minute before she said anything in return. "So, you were just going to let Caleb get rid of the notes and never say anything to me about it?" she asked, appalled. He nodded grudgingly.

"Do we honestly need more problems?" he asked.

"No, but that's not the point."

"I'm sorry. I should have told you. But just like when I first met you, I wasn't about to let her come between us. If I had walked in here and told you, what would you have done?" She thought about it for a moment.

"I don't know," she admitted. "But I do know that if she ever approaches you again," she spoke with penetrating eyes, "you will tell me about it right away."

"I promise." He nodded, relieved that the confrontation was over. She was distant, though, when she changed into nightclothes and got into bed with her back to Jonathan for a night of restless sleep.

*November 28 1929*

Tension still hung in the air as they ate breakfast quietly. Afterward, Ava searched for something to make for Thanksgiving dinner. She pulled out a bucket of potatoes from under the cloth skirt that hid the sink pipes, which had been snuggled up against the wall to keep them chilled.

"I'll make boxty," she decided aloud. "It's not traditional, but I think they'll like it."

"I think that would be fine," Jonathan called from living room. He was trying to stuff small scraps of newspaper into the spaces between the window and the frame. He unsuccessfully attempted several times to start a conversation with Ava the rest of the morning. Neither of them were looking forward to the dinner that would be embarrassing compared to previous feasts. He walked with her to Caleb's apartment with a heavy heart.

Thanksgiving was a subdued evening that was more a gathering of physically tired and emotionally weary souls for dinner. Caleb and Arianna worked to make a well-prepared turkey despite the old gas oven's tendency to fluctuate wildly in temperature. Claire and Aryl brought bread rolls, a vegetable mix of carrots and peas, and Ava added her plate of potato cakes. They all squeezed around the dining table that Arianna decorated with a lace tablecloth and dried flowers. Everyone now assembled, Caleb pulled out a bottle of wine from under his chair.

"Hey, you've been holding out on us!" Aryl cried in delight.

"No, not holding out. Planning ahead. I have one set aside for Christmas, too," he said and smiled, pouring everyone a glass; the bottle was gone with one round.

Aryl held up his glass. "Never drank wine from a water glass before," he chuckled. Caleb carved the turkey, and no one mentioned that Caleb skipped over the traditional Thanksgiving blessing.

Every year, for as long as the couples had been together, they had taken turns hosting the holidays and saying a blessing of simple, respectful words of no particular religious denomination that expressed gratitude for the food and the company. Easter was Aryl's for hosting, Caleb had Thanksgiving, and Jonathan performed the duties on Christmas. In their old life.

Everyone ate quietly, occasionally complimented a contribution and only stayed together for an hour after dinner, listening to the radio by the fire. The other couples sat as close as possible to each other with intertwined hands and arms, but Ava sat several inches away from Jonathan, and the tension was obvious. Arianna felt like she was partly to blame for going to extremes the night before, Caleb felt it was his fault for not getting rid of the notes in time and Jonathan assumed it was his fault simply because he was breathing. Regardless of whom the fault belonged to, they were all depressed even further by such a somber holiday compared to previous years.

They said goodnight at seven; everybody going to bed early with work the next day as the excuse.

∞∞∞

Friday blurred into Saturday, and Ava finally started talking to Jonathan again with some normality as he was getting ready to meet Charles for the extra night's work.

"Maura wants us to go to midnight mass with her," she told him as he was shaving at the bathroom mirror. He stopped to throw a confused look her way.

"We're not Catholic, Ava," he said flatly.

"I know that and we don't have to be. She wants to take us as guests." She looked down and dropped her tone. "Besides, what else do we have to do?" Her words stabbed at him whether she meant them to or not.

"I figured we'd get together with Aryl and Caleb like we always do."

"Well, we saw how festive Thanksgiving was, didn't we," she said sarcastically. "Besides, she already asked them and they said yes," she continued.

"When was she here to ask them?" he asked, calling her bluff.

"It was during our girl's night. She asked and Claire and Arianna said they would."

"Ah, I see. So, Caleb and Aryl haven't necessarily agreed?"

"Well, no, but I'm sure they will. Aryl will be up for it because it's something new, and after Maura was able to convince Arianna that she wouldn't spontaneously combust near holy water, she agreed. And we both know Caleb will do anything Arianna wants," she said triumphantly.

"Why did you even ask me if I had no choice in the matter?" He quickly went from despondence to irritation.

"You do have a choice. All I said was that she had invited us. I didn't get to the part where I tell you that I'm going and would like you to come, too. If you don't want to, however, you don't have to," she said indifferently.

"What time is it at?"

"It's *midnight* mass, Jonathan."

"Oh, right, right. I guess if everyone else is going, I wouldn't want you to have to go alone." He made a mental note to start looking for a way out of it as soon as possible.

"We're supposed to go to her house for drinks in the afternoon, then to the church for the children's mass, back to her house for dinner, and then back to the church for midnight mass," she informed. "Look on the bright side. It will make the day go faster," she said, sensing his anxiety over the holiday.

He finished getting ready for the dreaded night before him.

"You look nice," she said genuinely. He looked handsome and dignified like he used to when they would go out to the theater or to a dinner party.

"Thank you. I'm taking some change out of the money jar, so I can take the trolley. I'll replace it with the money I make tonight."

She straightened his coat collar and brushed some lint off the arms. She kissed him a quick peck and then stepped away. He grabbed her arm before she could turn.

"When are you going to forgive me?" he asked with begging eyes.

"I have."

"No, you haven't."

"I have. It's just that I keep wondering what else?" She crossed her arms and looked at the floor. "What else haven't you told me?" she asked, exasperated.

"There's nothing else," he chose his words carefully as he took a step forward to close the gap between them and lifted her chin to look at him. "There is nothing else that has happened since the day we met that I have not shared with you. I swear." She wanted to believe him, but something nagged. She pushed it aside and gave him another slightly more meaningful kiss goodbye.

"Be careful tonight."

"I will. You keep the door locked and a chair under the handle till I get home. I don't like being gone at night."

"I'll be fine," she reassured as he walked out the door. He waited on the other side until he heard her turn the lock and then headed down the stairs.

∞∞∞

It was cold, and he walked briskly from the trolley. He had arrived uptown early and decided, against his better judgment, to walk down his old street three blocks away. Except for hair slightly grown out over the ears, he looked like he belonged here. There were many houses up for sale and some with auction notices listing dates and times that the houses and belongings would be up for bid. Only about half the houses on the street gave the soft glow of life within. The others stood sad and dark. He looked around, amazed at the transformation the neighborhood had taken in just one month. He stopped in front of his old house and had mixed feelings when he saw that it, too, was sad and dark. Part of him was glad, for it would hurt to see someone else through the windows living a life that used to be his, but he also hated to see the beautiful house showing signs of neglect. He went back and forth and finally decided that he was happier that it was empty.

He walked up the front steps and stood in front of the bay window. That was where he and Ava had put their Christmas tree for the last three years. He could make out the stately mantel that once held glowing candles and pine boughs of scented garland. They had hung quilted stockings from the mantel, which they stuffed for each other in secret. And even though they were grown adults, each insisted Santa Claus had visited. He pictured the sofa, angled toward the fireplace, where they had sat many times and discussed moving their stockings over, one day, to make room for smaller stockings of pink and blue. His memories played out in front of him like a picture show, and when he couldn't watch anymore, he turned away as sad and dark as the house he loved.

∞∞∞

"Hello, sir." Charles waited outside the rear entrance and greeted Jonathan cheerfully, knowing that it would be an especially difficult night for him. He took him in the back door, showed him around the kitchen, and introduced him to the chefs. One needed no introduction as Sven turned away from the stove and smiled. Jonathan now felt a little better with two familiar faces to help him get through the evening. He hoped there would be no more, however, in the ballroom where almost two hundred guests chatted, laughed, and drank merrily. Charles handed Jonathan a large, silver tray piled with small sandwiches, crackers, and pate'. As he lifted it onto his shoulder, Jonathan inhaled deeply and his mouth watered. He missed exotic food with spice, having survived recently on a diet consisting mainly of bland carbohydrates.

"Follow me with this, sir. There are large banquet tables at the far end of the room. We will swap these for trays that are empty or low, and on our way back, we'll pick up used glasses and plates. That's mainly it unless there is a request from one of the guests," Charles explained.

Jonathan nodded and followed him down a hall and through the servant's door into the ballroom. There was a lavishly decorated Christmas tree in the middle of the room that glistened majestically and a quartet in the corner playing elegant music. He glanced around and recognized some of the faces. He put his head down and hoped none of them would recognize him. He managed to get to the table, swap out the tray, and get back to the kitchen unnoticed. He relaxed a bit while he waited for one of the chefs to fill a new tray. If he could manage to get back and forth quickly without being noticed, this would indeed be easy money.

The first half of the evening went just as he hoped. He even got to enjoy some of the foods he missed so much as the chefs' assistants set aside items from returned trays for the kitchen staff to enjoy. Jonathan saw this and brought back a tray with plenty of crackers and pate' on his next trip.

When Jonathan was returning near the end of the party, someone called his name. He glanced with his eyes but kept his face forward with the hope that the man was calling someone else.

"Jonathan!" A small, round man took several penguin-like steps to catch up with him. He was short and bald with kind eyes and a wide smile. "Hi, there, Jon. How are you? I haven't seen you in quite a while. How's Ava?" he asked glancing from his face to the tray he held and back.

"I'm fine. She's fine. Thank you. I'd love to talk, but I have to get back to—" He looked toward the servant's door. "work," he finished.

"Well, it was good to see you again. You look great. Look all big and strong. Say hello to Ava for me, will you? You take care, Jon."

Jonathan gave a faint smile back as he quickly walked toward the kitchen. He was relieved his former acquaintance hadn't made a scene or been rude or insensitive. Actually, Jonathan realized he had been quite kind. He mentioned nothing but good things, compliments and well wishes. He hadn't mentioned his humiliating position, and Jonathan was grateful.

On the next trip, however, several men recognized him. One nodded with a piteous expression. Another simply whispered to others the news that one of their own had fallen and was now reduced to hired help, which caused stares and a few snickers that made Jonathan burn under the collar. The last one was the worst. He confronted Jonathan in the middle of the ballroom.

"Hey, Garrett!" he yelled from several feet away. "Thanks for losing a boatload of money for me." He staggered over to where Jonathan was working and leaned in close to him, whispering loudly with putrid breath.

"Thanks to you, I don't get to retire next year. And I had to sell a couple of my homes on the coast." Jonathan looked at the belligerent drunk and recognized him well enough as one of his former clients. Before the crash, his firm had made a massive amount of money for the man. "Lucky for me," the man continued, straightening his posture and returning his insults to full volume, "I didn't hand everything over to you to destroy. I spread it all over and kept plenty of cash. I got hit. Oh, I got hit hard, but I'm not out. Not like you. You got what you deserved."

Jonathan snapped up, took a step toward the man and just as he opened his mouth to speak, Charles was at his side.

"Sven needs your help in the kitchen," he said calmly and politely as if nothing were going on. Jonathan hesitated and then turned away seething.

"Yeah, get me a drink while you're in there, Garrett!" the drunk called out after him. It took every ounce of self-control Jonathan had to keep walking. Charles kept him in the kitchen for the last hour while he continued to work.

When the guests had all left and Jonathan, Charles, and Sven had finished the last of the cleanup in the kitchen, Charles held a few dollars out to Jonathan.

"I'd say you more than earned this, sir." Jonathan took out his own wallet and tucked the bills inside.

"Jon, catch!" Sven called and tossed a bottle of vodka across the room to him. He dropped his wallet on the counter beside him and caught the bottle just in time.

"We have drink before you go," Sven ordered. "Sit." He, Charles and Jonathan sat at the table the chef used for food preparation, and Sven poured. "I had good time with your friends. They are funny," Sven said smiling.

"They are. We all had a good time, too. But Sven, you were the funniest one of us all," Jonathan insisted.

"I'm no funny. I'm Russian. Is impossible," he teased in a stern voice.

"Say what you want, but I was there and you were hilarious. We'll have to do it again sometime," Jonathan offered.

"Yes, we do again." Sven nodded and Jonathan turned his attention to Charles.

"Charles, you're always so quiet. Why is that?" Jonathan remembered that even in the middle of the men's night hoopla that he had been the quietest one.

"Mainly habit, sir," he replied. "But I also enjoy watching people."

"Watching people?" Jonathan asked curiously.

"Yes. I like watching people; how they interact, their body language and facial expressions, and in some cases, their strangeness. It's most amusing," Charles said and smiled.

"Amusing, huh? Maybe I'll try it sometime. I'm getting real tired of fire-watching. It'd be a nice change of scenery."

"Well, I also learn a great deal about people that way, sir," Charles added.

"Really? How's that?" Jonathan asked before finishing off his drink with a large gulp.

"Just by paying attention. That impolite man in the ballroom, for example. I could tell what he was preparing to do before he had fully crossed the room."

"Thanks, by the way. I'd probably have laid that guy out and gotten thrown in jail," he said.

"I can tell other things, too, though, not just the bad." Jonathan stared at Charles, waiting. "Well, how much you care for Mrs. Garrett, for example. In both your old and new life, anyone with eyes could see that you love her more than your own soul. I remember the ones before her and not one of them consumed you the way she does."

"Maybe you could drop by and tell her that sometime? She's not very happy with me right now," he said, staring at his empty glass.

"And the other night, for instance," Charles continued. "I have been aware that Mr. Jenkins and Mr. Sullivan are your friends through my long service to you. But I was able to see the way you interacted with each other on a different level that night. You finished each other's sentences, so in tune with each other, you can communicate without words. I got the distinct feeling that I wasn't with a group of friends, but brothers. The three of you could not be more different, in personality and attitude, but the three of you complement each other's strengths and give where the next man might be weak. It was wonderful to watch."

Jonathan sat quietly, having never consciously considered the way the three were around each other. But it was true, if he were being honest. Since they were young, they had been like brothers. Although he still carried the guilt of their losses, he was selfishly grateful that they were in the trenches with him. He stood up and reached for his coat.

"I'd better get home. Thank you, Charles, for everything."

"You're most welcome, sir." Charles nodded.

"Night, Sven. Don't be a stranger," he called as he closed the back door behind him.

∞∞∞

The frigid northern wind made Jonathan turn up the collar of his coat and keep his head down as he walked. Turning the corner onto his street, he didn't notice the man leaning against the lamppost, waiting patiently. Just as he was about to pass him, the large, dark-haired man who towered over his own six feet stepped directly into Jonathan's path.

He stopped abruptly. "Excuse me," Jonathan said and took a step to the side. The man sidestepped with him, once again blocking his attempt to pass. Jonathan realized then that this was a mugging and reached back for his wallet to surrender but felt an empty pocket. Adrenaline rushed as he tried to think of what he could barter to get away from the mugger with his life.

"Look, I don't want any trouble," he told the big man. A voice carried from the alley to Jonathan's right.

"This the guy?" A smaller man emerged from the shadows of the alley, pulling on leather, fingerless gloves.

"Yeah. That's him," another voice laughed from behind Jonathan, grinning at his payday. Dread and fear balled up in Jonathan's stomach as he realized this was much more than a simple mugging. He might have had a chance with only one, even the big one, with his recently added bulk. But not three. He glanced frantically for an open spot as they closed in around him. His only chance of escape was between two parked cars to his left; he knew he was close to home. The big one in front of him looked over at the one emerging from the alley, and Jonathan took his chance. He turned and sprinted three steps into the street only to come inches from death by a speeding delivery truck.

The two seconds that Jonathan was blocked were all the men needed to catch up with him. One pulled on his left arm, and Jonathan spun around with a clenched fist, realizing instantly the only option left was to fight and caught Tony on the eyebrow. He growled and swore, holding the bony ridge over his eye as blood trickled down his face. The big one grabbed Jonathan from behind, and the third man from the alley centered himself as Jonathan struggled to get free. With a sadistic grin, he pulled back his fist and punched Jonathan in the stomach. His mouth opened wide in a silent scream as the wind rushed out of him, his knees went weak, and his head pulled down toward the pain. Hard alternating blows to his ribs took his breath again. He pushed Jonathan up by the shoulders, holding them against the big one and kneed him hard in the groin. Everything went white as he doubled over, and his legs gave out. The big one let go his grip on Jonathan, allowing him to fall forward, his face scraping the icy concrete of the sidewalk where it landed. His eyes floated around in their sockets, and he was unable to focus on anything but pain. He instinctively curled into a fetal position, which left his back entirely vulnerable. Tony kicked him in the kidney with vengeance for his own bleeding face. Jonathan's back arched toward the pain, and the one in front took advantage by giving another hard kick to the stomach causing Jonathan to writhe forward again. One jumped around completely caught up in the adrenaline. He landed a kick to Jonathan's face that sent him over onto his back, and he screamed through clenched teeth.

"Not the face!" Tony yelled a split-second too late as the man leaned down and delivered a punch directly to Jonathan's nose. Blood flowed down both sides of his face, his vision went from blinding white to pitch black and finally he saw the dim light from the lamppost above him fading in and out intermittently with his heartbeat.

He heard what was going on around him now as if it were very distant; a gagging sound when someone grabbed the man from the alley by the throat with one hand and delivered a blow to the head with the other, which rendered him instantly unconscious.

Tony took several steps back with his hands up, terrified and then made a break for the alley, scurrying like a rat. The big one hit the ground after three lightning-fast strikes that carried the force of a half-dozen men; one to the face, a second to the ribs making a horrible crunching sound, and a third to the stomach. Stepping over the big one as he lay whimpering on the ground and heaving with a loud grunt, Sven pulled Jonathan onto his shoulder and carried him home.

∞∞∞∞

"Oh, God!" Ava's hands muted her cry as she opened the door. Sven walked inside with Jonathan hanging over his shoulder. He leaned down to deposit him on the couch as carefully as he could.

"What happened?" Ava cried, sitting beside Jonathan and looking from him to Sven and back with horror.

"He was mugged. He didn't have wallet. So, they did this," he explained.

"Go get Caleb, please," she told him and ran to the kitchen to wet a handful of cloths.

She knelt on the couch beside him and began wiping away the blood. He winced and her hands shook as she first attended to the ragged cheek and then the kicked, swollen other. Caleb came bounding through the door ahead of Sven and stopped abruptly in front of the couch where Jonathan sat, half-slumped over. He was barely conscious. Caleb stepped back to pace the floor a few lengths.

"Who did this, Jon?" he finally growled. Sven explained again that it was a mugging gone badly, and Caleb noticed out of the corner of his eye Jonathan gingerly shaking his head no.

"It wasn't a mugging?" Caleb asked. Jonathan moved his head side-to-side again.

"Go get Aryl," he told Sven. "Save your strength, Jon," Caleb told him. Jonathan nodded slightly with eyes closed.

Aryl was through the door a moment later, and his eyes flew open when he saw Jonathan's condition. "What'n hell happened?"

"Sven says it was a mugging, but Jon is trying to tell us something," Caleb replied.

"All right, Jon. Go ahead. What happened?" Aryl asked anxiously, waiting to find out who he needed to start looking for. Jonathan opened his eyes, and his vision was still blurry. "There were . . . three. One asked if . . . I was the right guy, one . . . I tried to get away but . . . ," he said with great difficulty.

"They were waiting for you? Did you get a good look at their faces?" Aryl asked.

"Saw two . . . got one in the eye," he explained.

"One of them is hurt. Good. That'll make him easier to find." Caleb turned to Sven. "You found him?" he asked. Sven nodded.

"I was minutes behind. He forgot wallet on counter. I return to him. If I was sooner, he would not be so hurt," he said regretfully.

"No, Sven." Ava looked up at him. "If it weren't for you, he might be dead," she said with gratitude and went back to cleaning Jonathan's face.

"I hurt them good. One ran but others," Sven said, shrugging. "Not so lucky."

"You got a hold of them?" Aryl asked.

"Yes. One block north."

Aryl and Caleb glanced at each other for a split-second, and then the two of them ran out the door.

Down the block, they found a man just returning to consciousness, disoriented and woozy. Caleb pulled him up and slammed him against the wall. He and Aryl took turns convincing the man to tell them who recruited him for the beating. They got the names of the other men involved, dropped the man on the ground like garbage, and walked away.

When they returned to Jonathan's apartment, Ava asked them to help her remove Jonathon's coat. They helped to lift him up and then steadied him. As she took his coat off carefully, she gasped when she saw the dirty imprint of a boot on the side of his shirt.

"Get his shirt off, too," Aryl told her. Sven approached Jonathan, inspected the dark and swollen areas, and then felt his ribs, pressing his chest; pressing the front, back and sides. Jonathan winced and groaned, but didn't scream.

"I don't think broken. But much bruised," he announced.

"That's a miracle," Aryl said with relief.

"He needs rest," Sven said insistently, and they helped Ava get him to the bedroom and through the painful process of putting him into bed. She kissed him so lightly he didn't feel her lips brush his forehead.

Caleb and Aryl stood at the foot of his bed.

"We're gonna find who did this to you," Caleb said.

"And God help them when we do," Aryl finished.

Ava hugged Sven, her head barely to the middle of his chest.

"Thank you so much, Sven," she said with tears in her eyes.

A few moments after seeing them out, she heard a soft knock at the door. Ava opened it to the beady-eyed one.

"I can't be bothered with you right now," she said wearily and closed the door in her face.

"Please," the older woman called from the hall. "I have medicine for your husband." Ava opened the door a bit and looked at her.

"What medicine?" Ava asked suspiciously.

"Pain medicine." She held out a bottle of clear liquid. "Give him two teaspoons every few hours to help him get through the first few days. Make sure he eats something because it can make him powerful sick if you give it on an empty stomach. And if–" Ava held up a finger to quiet the woman. She took the bottle and read the label.

"Thank you very much. I'll give him some now." She turned back into her apartment. For the first time ever, the beady-eyed one went home quietly. She held Jonathan's head while she spooned the foul liquid into his mouth.

Within minutes, it had taken the edge off his pain, and he was asleep soon after. She lay next to him as close as possible without bumping his sore body and cried. She now had a new reason to hate this horrible life.

Through the night, he woke twice, moaning, and she fed him the medicine both times; it sent him back into the merciful deep sleep.

Caleb and Aryl checked in with Ava several times throughout Sunday. Jonathan had remained asleep the whole day.

*December 2ᵈ 1929*

Victor waited on the corner for Tony and watched from a distance as Caleb and Aryl arrived at work early and alone. Tony casually walked up to Victor, and the two began to walk away from the gate. "Everything work out?" Victor asked as they walked.

"Yeah, worked out fine," Tony answered.

"Why is he not at work today? I left you with specific instructions, Tony," he said, irritated.

"Well, we didn't catch him 'til Saturday night. He's messed up, but should be back to work tomorrow, maybe the next day," Tony explained, thinking back on the attack and hoping he was right. Victor nodded, turned to him and held out three fifty-dollar bills.

"I'll leave it up to you how to split this up for the job."

"You got anything else you want me to do?" Tony asked hopefully. Victor shook his head.

"Not now. But I'll be in touch." Victor smiled in a way that told Tony he would be making more money in the future. "I have some ideas," Victor said as he walked away.

∞∞∞∞

𝓑efore work began, Aryl spoke with Harvey and informed him that Jonathan would be out sick for the rest of the week. When he began to sound like the absence would be a problem, Aryl glanced at the accounting office and back to Harvey, and he relented. He felt bad for a moment as he had never wanted to hold that favor over Harvey's head.

Caleb and Aryl ate lunch outside, inspecting every face as it passed. Tony put his head down to pass them, but Aryl caught sight of the cut over his eye. They dropped their sandwiches and caught up with him, one on each side.

"You Tony?" Caleb asked.

"Who's askin'?" Tony replied with attitude.

"We are," Aryl said and stopped in front of him.

"Yeah. My name's Tony," he said, nervously looking back and forth at each one.

"Let's go for a walk, Tony," Caleb said. They both took an arm and led him away. They stopped several feet away in an area that held empty storage containers and slipped in between the rows.

Caleb let go of his arm, and Aryl shoved Tony against the side of a shipping container.

"We got word that a guy named Tony helped organize an attack on our friend," Caleb started.

"Hey, now, this is N-New York. There's a m-million guys named Tony," he stuttered nervously.

"Yeah, but there's only so many who have a fresh cut on their forehead *and* works with Jon," Aryl pointed out. "Not bad, actually. Looks like he got you good."

"Look, I don't know nuthin' 'bout attackin' nobody. I got this over tha weekend when I pissed my brudder off," he said, pointing to his forehead. They stared at him with straight faces and crossed arms. Tony got increasingly nervous.

"You got the wrong guy. I don't know what you're talkin' about," he pleaded. They stepped closer to him, crowding him against the side of the container.

"You better give us some answers, Tony," Caleb warned.

"I ain't sayin' nuthin'."

"Wrong answer," Aryl said and pulled his arm back.

"Okay! Okay! Some guy paid me to do it."

"Why?" Caleb asked.

"How da hell should I know? I asked 'im what his beef was wit' this guy an' he said it was nunna my business. Just gave me instructions and said he'd pay me when it was done," he explained.

"What instructions?" Caleb demanded.

"He told me to get a couple uttha guys, catch 'im alone. An' he made it real clear to keep it to his stomach an' back. Didn't want us to mess with his face. One of my guys went too far, but dat wadn't me," he said, holding up his right hand as if under oath.

"Who was it that paid you?" Aryl insisted.

"Dressed fancy. Blond hair and eyes damn-near black. Only gave his first name."

"And what is that name, Tony?" Aryl pressed, growing more impatient.

"Victor."

Caleb and Aryl locked eyes.

"I should have guessed," Caleb growled.

"So, let me get this straight, Tony," Aryl started. "You took money from this man, Victor, to beat a man you didn't even know?"

"Well, yah, it was fiddy bucks." He bobbed his head and shrugged his shoulders as if needing the money justified the act.

"Well, that's unfortunate," Aryl said, pulling his fist back, "because I'll do it for free."

*December 3rd 1929*

Aryl and Caleb stopped to see Jonathan after work Tuesday evening. "How is he?" Caleb asked.

"A little better. The bruising is worse, but he doesn't need the pain medicine as much now." She paused, looking toward the closed bedroom door. "He isn't talking much. He only answers my questions and goes back to staring."

"We'll talk to him," Caleb reassured with hand on her shoulder as he passed.

Jonathan was sitting up in bed, picking at a bowl of stew.

"Hey, looks like you're feeling better," Aryl said. Jonathan shrugged without looking up.

"Well, we found the guy that set this up. It wasn't hard with that gash you left on his forehead," Caleb said.

"Who was it?" Jonathan asked.

"Guy named Tony. Works at the ya–"

"Well, he *did*," Aryl interrupted. "I have a feeling he won't be back to work for a while." Jonathan finally looked up at them.

"Why?" he asked flatly.

"Well, because Aryl, here, beat the living sh–"

"No," Jonathan interrupted. "Why'd he attack *me*? I don't even know anybody named Tony."

"We're not exactly sure," Caleb lied. "You know how ignorant people can be. Give them any reason to get riled up and it can spiral out of control." He let Jonathan assume that it had been simple harassment carried over from work. They had decided to keep any knowledge of Victor's involvement to themselves.

Jonathan glanced at Aryl's hand; it was swollen with red cuts on the knuckles. Aryl noticed and folded his arms.

"Like we said, Jon, we took care of it," Aryl said.

"*You* took care of it," Caleb said resentfully and looked at Jonathan. "I tried to get in on it, but Aryl here didn't leave me much to work with." Jonathan sighed with annoyance.

"You shouldn't have done that. Either one of you. You could have landed yourselves in jail," he said, glaring at them.

"Never been in jail," Aryl commented as if it were something he wouldn't mind trying sometime.

"Yes, you have," Caleb reminded and grinned. Aryl ignored him and looked at Jonathan seriously.

"You would have done it for us."

"You *have* done it for us," Caleb corrected. "How many sets of ears did you box in school because I was always getting picked on for being the smallest?"

"That was different," Jonathan said.

"Regardless, Jon, I don't think you'll be having any more trouble at work next week," he said confidently.

"I'm going back tomorrow," Jonathan said flatly.

"What? But I cleared the whole week for you." Aryl glanced at Caleb and back at Jonathan.

"I'm going back tomorrow. I can't sit here in this bed, staring at the wall anymore . . . I can't *afford* to sit here and stare at the wall anymore. Just got the first heat bill." They couldn't argue with him about that. They had gotten a heat bill, too. They staggered at the amount and panicked at how they would pay it without depleting their small savings.

"Caleb and I were talking about that. We're going to start looking for firewood each night after work. That should help a little. It'll start warming up in a few months."

Jonathan went back to picking at his stew, unable to think about living in the tenement that long.

"I'd better get home," Caleb said, standing. "You sure about going back to work tomorrow?"

"Yeah, I'm sure."

"Okay," Aryl said hesitantly. "I guess we'll see you in the morning." Jonathan called to them as they were leaving, "Hey."

They both turned to look at him.

"Thanks."

Ava came in after they left and moved his bowl of uneaten stew. He didn't look any better after the visit. She sat very close beside him with her hands in her lap and leaned her head over onto his shoulder. He was staring again and didn't acknowledge her. Several moments of silence passed.

"Jon, let's leave." Her words snapped him out of his daze, and he looked toward her.

"What?"

"Let's leave," she repeated. "Let's get out of here and leave this whole mess behind."

"How can we possibly do that?"

"I don't know. We'll find a way. We could go stay with your parents 'til we figure something out," she suggested.

"I can't go live with my parents," he insisted.

"Why not?"

"There is no way I am crawling home, a complete failure, to live under my parents' roof, bringing the wife I can no longer support," he said, angry with her for even suggesting it.

"They know that's not true, Jon. They know what happened, and they know it happened to half the world. You act like you were the only one that day," she said, slightly irritated. She expected him to jump at the idea of leaving the tenement no matter what amount of pride he had to swallow.

"I can't," he said firmly.

"Jon, it doesn't have to be like this!" she yelled suddenly, getting off the bed and standing next to it.

"No, it didn't," he said, mentally scolding himself again for his mistakes. She knew well enough what he was doing, and it infuriated her.

"There is no way you could have stopped what happened, Jon. No one could. Deep down you must know that, yet you continue to be a martyr." She was fully angered now. "We have a way out. But you won't take it because of your *pride.*"

"Living with my parents is not a way out, Ava. What about jobs? They weren't plentiful when I left that small town ten years ago, and there are even less now. We'd be fully living on their charity without a job, and I won't do that." She stood with her arms crossed. She had already written his parents a letter explaining the situation and suggesting the idea and she wouldn't give up trying to convince him to leave. "Besides . . . would you honestly leave Claire and Arianna?" That sent a jolt through her heart. She hadn't thought about leaving them, living without them. Just the thought of it was painful. She sighed and left the room, frustrated.

While washing the dinner dishes, she decided on an alternate plan. She would get Claire and Arianna to join her in insisting to their husbands that they all leave the city. She was certain that they had had their fill of life in the tenement.

∞∞∞

After his visit with Jonathan, Caleb came home to a quiet, dark apartment and found Arianna in bed. He sat on the side of the bed and felt her head. Her fever had gotten worse, and she coughed loud and wet when she stirred. He stayed with her until she was asleep again.

He wandered to the kitchen and was surprised to find a bowl of vegetable stew in the oven. He ate it cold and then quickly got ready for bed.

Lying on his side, he wiped the sweat from her forehead with a cloth and wondered if they had enough savings left to take her to the doctor if she continued to get worse.

He got up quietly and dug in the back of the dark closet till he found the hidden money jar. He hated to do it, but Arianna would continue to spend money if he hadn't; especially when she felt sad, which was most of the time. He took the jar out to the living room and sat on the hearth to count it by the light of the remaining embers. He was relieved to find that there would be enough to take her but prayed he wouldn't have to. If he didn't have to, then there would be enough for the heat and electric bill and groceries. After that was gone, they would have to live on his weekly paychecks. He couldn't see how that would be possible; every week they had needed to dip into the jar just to make ends meet. He lay in bed several hours worrying before he finally fell asleep.

∞∞∞∞

"You found who beat up Jon, I take it," Claire said, pointing to Aryl's swollen hand.

"We did." She took his hand in both of hers and examined it.

"Well, you know I don't like the idea of you fighting," she said like an exasperated mother. "But I'm glad you found him. C'mon, dinner's ready."

"What's this?" he asked excitedly when she set the bowl in front of him. It was brim full with chunky vegetables. He didn't wait for an explanation before digging in.

"Well, technically, I could call it vegetable beef because there is a little bit of beef in it, but it's vegetable soup. Shannon took me down to a cannery today. She's friends with the owner. He lets her buy the dented cans for half-price. I bought a dozen. I used some for this soup and put the others away."

"That's a great idea. Can you go again?"

"Shannon goes every other Monday. She said I could go with her anytime."

"You should take Ava and Arianna, too," he suggested.

"I will. That reminds me, Arianna is sick."

"Sick with what?" he asked, worried it was something that might make rounds and cause them to miss work. She shrugged.

"She has a fever, and her cough sounds horrible. Ava and I took turns today checking on her." He nodded his approval while finishing off the soup. "That was great. Is there more?"

"Sure." She carried his bowl back to the kitchen and refilled it.

"You don't think there will be any trouble, do you?" she called. "With you and Caleb taking care of that guy who attacked Jon? I'm worried he has a big brother that'll come looking for you guys," she half-joked.

"Well, if he does have a big brother, then that might be more of a challenge," he said, grinning.

"I'm serious, Aryl," she said, setting the bowl in front of him. He debated a moment before he spoke.

"Can you keep a secret?" he asked.

"Of course."

"No, I mean, really keep this to yourself. Never breathe a word of it to anyone, especially to Ava and Arianna."

"I promise. What is it?" His expression was starting to worry her.

"Well, you already know the history between Jon and Victor," he started. "We got it out of this guy that Victor paid him to do it." Her eyes widened in question as he continued. "We're not sure why exactly. I'm wondering if he found out that Ruth showed up, throwing herself at Jonathan. That might be enough to drive him to do something like this."

"Well, what would stop him from doing something like this again?" she asked, truly afraid for all three of the men now.

"The message we sent through Tony," he said gravely and left it at that. He was quiet while he finished his second bowl of stew. He pushed his bowl away and leaned back.

"That was great," he complimented. Although it was rather bland, it was hot and filling; therefore, in Aryl's mind, it was great. She took his bowl, still worried and walked to the sink.

"You don't need to worry, Claire," he said, reading her. She nodded, unconvinced. He held his hand out and she walked back over to him. He held her by the waist and looked up at her.

"I promise you. There is no need to worry. If it makes you feel better, Caleb and I agreed that we wouldn't go out alone."

"Then you're worried, too," she said accusingly. He shook his head.

"No. We thought it would make Jon and you girls feel better, that's all. What's for dessert?" he asked, changing the subject.

"There isn't any," she said, looking down at him apologetically. He grinned and looked her over.

"Nonsense. There's something sweet and tasty right here." He hugged her waist and tugged at the material of her blouse with his teeth. She pulled away, sighing in frustration.

"Aryl." He pulled back to look up at her, a button between his teeth.

"Hmm?" She nodded toward the homemade calendar pinned on the wall. The day had a black line through it. "You're kidding!" he groaned, letting the button pop out of his mouth. "I thought that started tomorrow!" She shook her head with remorse. He dropped his head in disappointment and she put her hands on his head.

"I'm sorry," she said, frustrated at the situation herself. He brought his head up and pulled her close, buried his face in her breasts and let out a long, agonizing scream. She threw her head back laughing and, after a moment of muffled screaming, growling, and swearing, he pulled away composed.

"Are you going to be okay?" He nodded with a strained face and let go of her.

"Fine. I'll be fine."

∞∞∞

*J*onathan was quiet on their walk to work, despite Caleb and Aryl's attempt to pull him into conversation. He had a knit hat pulled low in an attempt to hide the bruising that spread from his nose to both eyes. Even though he ached incredibly, he decided he would rather endure the protesting of the damaged muscles in his body than stay home. If he had been there today, he would have continued to stare at the wall, the minutes ticking by, as he relived events of the last six weeks. Ava would have fluctuated between doting on his injuries and flying into fury for his unwillingness to consider moving back home. Even the stares and commentary from ignorant men at work would be better than dealing with that.

He didn't notice that no one looked at him as he entered the yard. And the ones that did, by accident, looked away as quickly as possible. People stepped aside to let him pass, and whispers uttered well out of ear shot confirmed that this was the man to stay away from. Word had traveled about Tony, rumored still to be in the hospital. Jonathan didn't know it yet, but he would never receive another insult, be the butt of any practical joke, or receive words without respect for the rest of his days at the yard.

∞∞∞

*A*va gathered Claire and went to Arianna's where Ava sat on the end of the bed. Arianna was still slightly feverish.

"We need to talk," Ava told them. "I have an idea. I presented it to Jon, but he turned me down flat. I'll keep pressuring him, but I have a feeling that he will have to relent, if you both put pressure on your husbands as well and if they agree."

"What's the idea?" asked Claire, who was simply excited there was something new to talk about.

"I think we need to leave. Leave this place and leave the city. We should go to Rockport." They stared at her for a moment, not sure what to say. "Oh, come on, aren't you sick of this? We don't have to stay here! We can leave on the next train. Wouldn't you give anything to get out of here?"

"Of course," Arianna said with a hoarse voice. "I'd love to leave, but where would we live? Where would the men find work?"

"I've already thought about that," Ava said excitedly. "You and Caleb can stay with his parents on their farm, and you and Aryl can use that summer home your parents have, and Jonathan and I can stay with his parents. Jonathan is fighting me about that part. His pride is stopping him from asking them if we can come. But he'll have to agree to it if we're all on board together. There's no way he would stay here without Caleb and Aryl. As for jobs, something will work out," she finished insistently.

"Ava, Caleb and his father haven't spoken in several years. Ethel writes, but Hubert is still incredibly angry with him for selling his grandfather's farm. There's no way we could stay with them," Arianna told Ava regretfully before going into another coughing fit. Claire turned to Ava.

"My parents sold the vacation home shortly after the crash to pay some debts. They aren't as bad off as we are, but they only have a fraction of what they used to, and it seems to be getting worse. I guess we could go to Boston and stay with them there, but then we all wouldn't be together, and I don't know how long that would last. She talks in her letters as if they are weeks from living in a place like this themselves."

"What about Aryl's parents? They love you. They would love to have you both," Ava pressed. "They sold the house when Aryl's younger brother left home, and his father built a small cottage. They wanted to save everything for retirement, and they put lots of money into investments like everyone else. Now all they have is that little cottage and his fishing boat. They're hand to mouth, too."

"There has to be a way," she insisted. "There has to be. I'm going to keep trying to find it," she informed them willfully.

"We'll try to think of something, too," Claire reassured her but knew deep down the reality of it. She and Aryl had talked of going home in the beginning but decided it wasn't feasible. Claire turned her attention to Arianna.

"Have you eaten anything today?" she asked while feeling her head. Her fever had come down slightly.

"No, I'm not hungry."

"Nonsense. You need to eat. I'll go make you something." She went into Arianna's kitchen to find something to make and called Ava to help her.

∞∞∞

Caleb and Aryl went to look for firewood together after dinner. They came home with only a few pieces each.

The next evening, Caleb stopped in his tracks a block from the building and hit Jonathan on the arm with the back of his hand.

"There's the Packard again," he said with a nod.

Jonathan looked up and grumbled under his breath.

"Let's just keep walking. No matter what, just ignore her," Aryl suggested. Jonathan nodded, put his head back down and walked fast. She exited the car before he passed this time and blocked his path.

"Jonathan! What happened to you!" she yelled, trying to reach out to touch his face. He pulled his head away and tried to side step her. She kept up pace beside him.

"Jonathan, why won't you let me help you? Why won't you let me take you away from all this? You deserve so much better," she whined. He stopped and glared at her.

"Go away, Ruth," he snapped before he turned onto the stoop of his building.

Inside, Caleb stopped him at the door with a grab of his coat.

"Now if I were you, I'd go right in and tell her Ruth showed up," Caleb suggested. Jonathan looked irritated.

"Caleb's right. In fact, why don't we go in with you?" Aryl insisted.

∞∞∞

"I have to tell you something," Jonathan started. Ava was surprised and slightly confused to see all three men walk through the door. "Ruth showed up again outside this evening." Ava's smile dropped, her ears burned red and she crossed her arms tightly. "The only two words I said to her were *go away*. And then I walked away."

"He's telling the truth, Ava. We saw it," Aryl said.

"What did she say this time?" Ava asked. He shifted uncomfortably. He hated repeating Ruth's words.

"She just went on like she did before, just a few sentences . . . ." He trailed off, praying she would drop it.

"What were her exact *words*, Jonathan?" Ava insisted. He looked at Caleb and Aryl helplessly, but they could provide no relief.

"She asked what happened to me. She asked why I wouldn't let her help me get out of here and said that I deserved better than this," he said, finishing with a sigh. Ava said nothing. She stared at him with clenched teeth and took a moment to remind herself that Jonathan had been honest, so she shouldn't be angry with him. Her anger was with this woman, who wouldn't stop approaching her husband.

When she could speak with kindness in her voice, which took several minutes, she looked at Jonathan.

"Thank you for telling me," was all she could manage.

Jonathan and Ava spent another tense, silent evening eating dinner, watching the fire and then trailing off to bed separately.

∞∞∞∞

After Jonathan left for work the next morning, Ava sat down with pen and paper. She closed her eyes to better visualize Ruth's notes. Having only looked at them briefly and in anger, she had difficulty recalling the details of the information. She wrote down what she could remember: a park, fountain of lovers, something about a dog, three o'clock in the afternoon. What days? She huffed her breath in frustration and threw the pen down. She suddenly remembered that Arianna had seen the notes, too. She threw her sweater on, grabbed the paper, and prayed that Arianna would remember enough to make a difference.

∞∞∞∞

"Ava." Arianna opened the door, still a little sick but on the mend.

"I need your help," Ava said before Arianna could greet her. She walked in and spun around to face her. "Those notes," she started, "from Ruth. I'm trying to remember the information, but there are pieces missing. I was hoping since you looked at them that you might remember the things I can't."

"Why would you want to do that, Ava?"

"I plan on going there. I'm going to tell her to her face to leave Jonathan alone," she said, and handed her the paper. "Here's what I remember. Can you add anything to it?" she asked hopefully.

"I can do better than that," Arianna said, smiled and went to the bedroom. Ava followed and leaned on the doorjamb while Arianna dug in a drawer of her beautiful vanity. She pulled the original note from under her delicates. She held it up between two fingers, and Ava's mouth fell open.

"You have it! Why did you keep it?" she asked, amazed and grateful.

"I thought you might want it eventually. If it were me, I would *definitely* want to make an appearance," she said. Ava opened it and saw she would be there on Monday, Wednesday, and Friday at three o'clock to walk her dog around the fountain in the center of the park. Arianna was reading it from over her shoulder.

"You know, today is Friday," she said and grinned deviously.

"It is," Ava said. "I think I'll take the trolley there today and make my appearance."

"Be careful. Unless you don't want to go alone."

"No, I wouldn't mind, but you're still sick, and this won't take long. I'll just show up, introduce myself and tell her she needs to stop approaching Jonathan. I'm sure that will put a stop to it. Any decent woman wouldn't continue to pursue a man after being confronted by his wife."

"I wouldn't count on her being a decent woman," Arianna said with a snort.

"Oh! I have no idea what she looks like. How will I know her?" Ava asked, suddenly worried.

"She has blond hair and blue eyes, full lips and a round face that's more cute than beautiful. She's very tall, almost as tall as me. And she has really big . . ." She put her hands up to her chest and grabbed her breasts.

"Lovely," Ava commented under her breath and rolled her eyes.

"You sure you want to do this alone? Claire and I would be happy to come." Arianna raised her eyebrows, hopeful. Ava shook her head.

"This is mine to do. Thank you, but I'm not going to burden you or Claire." She hurried home to get ready to catch the trolley that would put her at the park just before three o'clock.

∞∞∞∞

Ava found the fountain in the center of the park easily enough. A beautiful, marble bowl's edge held four cherubs with harps that faced inward. The water to the center spray and the cherubs long since had been shut off for the winter. A gravel path dusted with snow encircled it. A few pair of snuggling lovers strolled along it despite the cold. Park benches built intermittently around the path faced the fountain and shrubbery hugged the backs of the benches all around, which provided a protective barrier from the wind. The manicured shrubbery broke at the north and south of the circle for entrance and exit.

Ava sat on a bench with her back facing west in order to view both entrances. She sat, nervously fidgeting with her gloves, bouncing her crossed leg, and still unsure of how much she intended to say to this woman. Her heart racing, she wasn't sure whether she was more nervous because this woman was from Jonathan's past or because of whom Ruth was married to. She toyed with the idea of abandoning her plan but resolved to do what she must to keep Jonathan; what was left of him anyway.

At three o'clock, a tall blonde in an earth-colored fur coat entered the circle with a white poodle on a leash trotting ahead of her. Just as Arianna remembered, she had striking blue eyes, a cute face with pouting lips and the longest legs Ava had ever seen. Her own self-image took a vicious beating as she looked her over bottom to top and then suffered a final blow as she saw her undeniably substantial and perfect breasts. She hadn't bundled up like the other park walkers. She let her fur coat and dress top hang open; as a result, both her cleavage and legs could be seen from a mile away. Ava watched her glance around the park in anticipation, her eyes only briefly rolling over Ava and then continuing around the circle. She closed her coat with a flash of disappointment on her face, shivered and continued on with her dog. Ava's heart was beating in her ears when she stood and walked up close behind Ruth. She took a deep breath.

"Excuse me," she said with a shaky voice.

"Yes?" Ruth turned around, smiling.

"Are you Ruth?" Ava asked, shoving her hands in her pockets nervously.

"Yes. Who are you, dear?" Ruth asked sweetly. "Should I know you?" Ava straightened her posture and met Ruth's eyes.

"You should. My name is Ava," she said with the slightest hint of anger in her voice. "Ava Garrett," she clarified and Ruth's eyes widened slightly. Her angelic smile faded.

"So, *you're* the one," she said under her breath.

"I'm here to talk to you about approaching Jonathan. It needs to stop. He's my husband, you have no place tracking him down or talking to him," she tried to sound authoritative, but her slightly faltering voice undermined the attempt.

"I think you underestimate me. And the lengths that I will go to. Not that I expect I'll have to."

"He is *my* husband. And you will leave him alone. He doesn't want anything to do with you." Ava pulled off the commanding tone now that she was fully angry at Ruth's arrogance.

"But he does want what I have, and he will realize that sooner or later. I can offer him money, security, and a return to dignified living. He'll only be able to resist that for so long."

"He won't leave me. He loves me."

Ruth looked at her with pity. "He felt sorry for you, Ava. Isn't that what you wanted? You played quite the victim that night from what I hear. Taunting and teasing Victor, and then playing coy. And after tempting him to madness, you ran away with Jonathan. He always did have a soft heart for pitiful creatures. He was always bringing home stray dogs when we were together. And much in the same way, he picked you up, brushed you off, found himself in too deep before even he knew what happened and then couldn't find a way to end it with you."

"He found a way to end it with you easily enough."

"Enjoy him while you can," Ruth warned. "Luring him away from that filthy, rundown dump will be easier than luring a drunk to wine," she said. "I'll bide my time, Ava. I'm very patient. He will eventually get sick of the life he thinks he has to live, and I will be right here waiting when he realizes that it doesn't have to be this way."

Ava glared at her, mulling over her possible responses. She was surprised as she watched Ruth's face transform from a smug smile with mean eyes to a look of slight shock as she caught sight of something over Ava's shoulder. The slightest hint of fear flickered in her eyes.

Ava turned to see Arianna sauntering up in typical fashion with her head down and her eyes fixed on her prey. Claire fell out from behind her, as they walked the last few steps and stopped on each side of Ava. Then Ava turned and smiled at Ruth with pity.

"Ruth," Arianna greeted. "How completely unpleasant to see you again." A nervous Ruth didn't respond. Arianna looked over at Claire and smiled. "It's funny, I could have sworn Jon took the trash out that night." She looked back at Ruth. "I guess the garbage men couldn't lift the can."

"This isn't any of your business, Arianna," Ruth said politely.

"Oh, but it is Ruth. I can assure you that you are under the delusion that you have what Jon wants, but you couldn't be more wrong. Jon knows that you don't really have anything of your own, that any valiant rescuing or love-laced charity would, in fact, ultimately boil down to being on Victor's dime. And we both know he would rather die than hold one of Victor's dimes." Ruth's face showed the truth in Arianna's statement, and she nervously searched for a rebuttal. "Now Ava's request is simple." She spoke slowly, with insistence. "Stay away from her husband."

"And what if I don't?" she challenged, defiantly tossing her blonde hair out of her face and puffing her chest out. Arianna opened her mouth to speak, but Claire interrupted, taking a step forward.

"Ruth," she began sweetly, "we are three women who have had our entire lives ripped away from us overnight. We've struggled with depression and suffered from going without." Arianna threw Claire a furious look for spoiling an opportunity to wound Ruth verbally in what sounded like an attempt to gain sympathy. "My point, Ruth, is this. We stick together. We are three women on the edge with nothing to lose. And if pushed too far, well, do you *really* want to see what that looks like?" She dropped her voice with the last sentence. Arianna smiled and the friends turned to walk away. Arianna couldn't resist one last stab after a few paces and turned back.

"You remember that trip to Paris you took with us, don't you, Ruth? Of course, you do. And you remember the board meetings that Jonathan went to, which left you in the hotel alone in the evenings?" She chuckled, shaking her head. "Silly Ruth, powerful businessmen don't hold board meetings at nine o'clock at night! He was in a meeting, all right. Just not one with any *board members*."

∞∞∞∞∞

"Thank you," Ava said to them both as they boarded the trolley.

"You honestly didn't think that we would let you do this alone, did you?" Arianna asked, smiling.

"Well, it was mine to deal with, and you're just getting over being sick and all."

Arianna waved her hand as if none of that mattered and stared out the window. Ava turned back to Arianna. "Ruth went to Paris with Jon?" she asked. Arianna nodded. "You were there?" she continued. Arianna nodded again.

She turned to Claire. "What about you?"

"No, that trip was right before Aryl and I got married. I was still in Boston," she explained. "I only knew Ruth very briefly. Remember, Aryl and I got married shortly before you came along."

"It was Caleb and I, Jon and Ruth, and Aryl," Arianna offered. "That's the only time she ever went with us. Jon found an excuse not to bring her the other times," she explained. Ava was slightly relieved to hear that. She had been to Paris twice with Jon. However, the last time was a quick trip with no time for sightseeing and fun, and he had gone without anyone.

"Was he with another woman? When he told Ruth he was in meetings?" Ava asked directly. It was impossible for anyone who heard Arianna's insinuation to think anything differently.

"How the hell should I know? I was drunk most of that trip." Arianna laughed through her half-truth. Ava left it alone, confident that Ruth wouldn't be popping her head up anytime soon.

*December 14th 1929*

On Sunday, Aryl spent the afternoon looking for firewood. Broken pallets and crates were getting harder to find, but he went regardless as he needed the quiet time to think. He had some ideas that he had been considering, but there seemed to be a roadblock for each one that he couldn't find a way around. He collaborated with Caleb often, and they talked about endless possibilities that were just out of their grasp. He peered down alleys where he normally found at least a few broken boards and planks. He was looking, but he wasn't really seeing. Caught up in his ideas, worries and fears, he felt as if his life was going to disintegrate even further at any moment, and he was running out of time.

Ava had told him how Claire cried every day but put on a smile in the evening. He could only keep her hanging on for so long. Her hope was pinned on his plan to rebuild their life, and he had yet to come up with anything solid.

And then there was Jonathan. He was literally sinking into oblivion right before Aryl's eyes, and he was clueless how to help him. He and Ava were cracking under the stress of this life, and he could do nothing but watch. Caleb was so consumed with Arianna's mood swings and near daily sobbing that he could hardly think about anything else. He was starting to show signs of fatigue from constantly pulling her up.

Aryl stumbled backward off-balance, holding his aching forehead and stared, dumbfounded, at the lamppost he had walked directly into. He rubbed the rising lump and looked around to find he had wandered a good distance from home. A sudden gust of icy wind pushed Aryl back a few inches, and he turned his face away from the arctic blast. The gust continued and he turned up his collar, shivering. He glanced up at movement in the window next to him and saw an old man placing a sign in the window of one of the front apartments of the small building. The sign read 'For Sale by Owner Contract.' Without making an allowance for how ridiculous it was to inquire about buying an apartment building while out scavenging free firewood, he climbed the steps.

"Can I help you?"

"Hello. I saw your sign and I wonder what your terms were?" Aryl asked.

"Well, I'd like to ask a hundred dollars down and ten-percent of the monthly rents after mortgage," he said.

"Why don't you just sell outright?" Aryl asked, wondering his motives.

"Even if I could find a buyer, I owe more than the building is worth. And I would be out of an income."

"Why do you want to sell at all, if it's your income?" Aryl asked.

"I'm barely making mortgage. The building is not fully occupied, and I can't make the repairs needed to get steady renters. But someone like you–" The old man looked at Aryl and smiled. "Someone young and strong, who could put effort into making this place real nice could attract good renters," he said with hope that Aryl was interested.

"So, you're looking for someone to assume the building with a down payment, take over management, repairs, and maintenance?" The old man nodded. "And after collecting rent, paying the mortgage and giving you your ten percent, the rest is my profit?" he asked. The old man nodded again. Aryl smiled widely. "I think we can talk. My name is Aryl Sullivan," he said, holding out his hand.

"Arnold Fuller. Come in, please," the old man offered and soon had him seated at a dining table with a cup of coffee. Aryl pulled a pen and paper out of his back pocket, which he kept on him at all times for jotting down ideas.

"How many units are there?"

"Twelve. Plus the two storefronts on the first floor." Aryl wrote the details down as he asked Mr. Fuller a barrage of questions: the total mortgage due, average rent, number of bedrooms in each apartment, current vacancies, heat source, and recent work done. Last, he asked if he could look around the property. The old man was happy to give him a tour.

They started with the two empty storefronts at the bottom of the building. They were half-sunken; the store window at street level, with six steps down to the store entrance.

"These could command higher rent if they were fixed up," he commented, unlocking the door to the first one. The window had been broken, and it was filthy and neglected inside. It looked to Aryl that this had been a bakery with rounded, glass cabinets and a wood fire oven at the rear of the store. It needed wall repair, paint, fumigating and deep cleaning.

The second storefront wasn't as badly run-down and looked like it might have been a general store with shelves along both walls and a display counter in the middle. Mr. Fuller took Aryl through each vacant apartment, introducing him to a few tenants, who poked their heads out to investigate. Two of the apartments had two bedrooms, and Aryl knew, if the price was right, there would be a tremendous demand for those. He hadn't seen anything in the building that scared him away from the idea. Walls with holes, doors hanging from the hinges, bugs, and rats were all things he had been used to dealing with for the last couple of months. They ended the tour and settled back down at Mr. Fuller's table.

"Well, sir, I can tell you that I am extremely interested." Mr. Fuller's eyes lit up. "I do need to talk to a couple of friends of mine. This would be a joint effort."

"That's okay. You know where to find me."

Aryl had one last small but crucial detail to inquire about.

"This would be a *legal* contract?" Aryl asked, as he stood to leave.

"And binding," Mr. Fuller added. "I would draw up the papers indicating the terms. You are protected from me changing my mind or demanding more than ten percent, and I am protected from you changing your mind or not giving me ten percent," he explained.

"But technically, it would be a private transaction?"

"Yes. Until the building is paid off and then the deed would carry your name," he explained. Aryl liked that plan. They all still owed the bank money as their homes and furnishings had not fully paid off their debts. If it were on record that they had any kind of asset, the profit would most likely be seized.

"When are you looking for someone to take over?" Aryl asked.

"Honestly, as soon as possible," Mr. Fuller said. Aryl sighed and pulled out his notepaper, estimated the three couples' dwindled savings and calculated how long it would take to save for repairs. He shook Mr. Fuller's hand again and promised to be in touch. It was snowing, and he hurried home.

He would keep the prospective arrangement to himself, not wanting to raise false hopes if somehow it didn't turn out to be a feasible plan. He went over every detail in his head and on paper to look for a roadblock of some kind.

He couldn't find one, so he decided to bring Caleb up to speed a few days later. He explained the opportunity as they walked one evening. After every detail was hashed out, Aryl showed him the figures, and Caleb offered to rerun the numbers and to secure renters. He knew Shannon and Patrick would jump at the chance to have a two-bedroom apartment in a slightly better part of town for no more than they were being charged now. Caleb was anxious to get home and tell Arianna.

"No," Aryl said. "Let's wait a little while. Let's tell them on Christmas. We'll get Jon on board then. It's less than two weeks away. That will give us time to work out every detail," he suggested. Caleb agreed, although it would be hard to keep the excitement to himself.

∞∞∞

That evening Aryl did, however, call the couples together for a meeting at his house. Arianna and Caleb arrived first. Caleb knew what the meeting was about, and his excitement was obvious.

Jonathan and Ava arrived later, and Jonathan's reluctance to leave his apartment was obvious. His bruising was significantly better, but his mind-set hadn't recovered.

"Okay," Aryl started when everyone was settled. "I wanted to talk to all of you about something. I have come across a possible opportunity, and I really think this one will work, although I'm still working out the details." Claire's eyes lit up and Arianna looked at Caleb. He smiled, patted her leg, and wished he could tell. It would help her so much to have something solid to hold on to. He found restraint since this would be the only thing he could give her for Christmas. All eyes were back on Aryl.

"So, what is it?" Claire asked excitedly.

"Well, that's the thing. I'm not ready to give any details right now. I can tell you that it looks very promising, and it's very attainable if we work hard," Aryl explained.

"What is it this time, Aryl? Rice?" Jonathan asked sarcastically as he looked up for the first time.

"No, it's not rice, Jon. I can't explain it just yet, but I will soon. I promise. For right now, I need us to save every single penny," he said, looking at everyone individually. "Christmas is coming, and we may be tempted to buy something for each other, but we just can't. And I'm not just talking about presents either. We have to save, conserve, and improvise with everything. When it's time to do this, we will need to put together every cent we have. Please trust me on this."

Everyone agreed, but continued to pressure Aryl into explaining his plan. He changed the subject to something that he and Caleb deemed necessary and unavoidable, despite his speech on saving money just a few minutes earlier.

"Now, my second bit of news, Caleb and I have decided that we are all going to go see a show uptown tomorrow night."

"I thought you just said we needed to save every penny!" Ava exclaimed.

"Well, yes, we do. However, we also haven't done anything fun in a long time. We thought it would be nice to have a night out before we dive into unprecedented frugality. It'll boost morale," he said, looking at Jonathan. "So, ladies, be powdered and beautiful tomorrow night by the time we get home. We need to catch the trolley at seven."

Arianna was smiling and Claire was worried about spending money, but excited to go to a show. Ava patted Jonathan's hand.

"Doesn't that sound like fun, Jon?" she asked.

"Sure. Sounds great." His voice was monotone as he looked over and faked a smile.

∞∞∞

The next afternoon, Ava, Claire, and Arianna went back and forth between their apartments for approval while trying to decide on outfits and hairstyles. Finally, they gathered at Arianna's, so they could take turns in front of the vanity's mirror.

"What do you think it is?" Ava asked. "Aryl's idea, I mean."

"I don't know. I tried getting it out of Caleb for a few hours last night, but he wouldn't budge. I think he knows more than he wants me to believe he does," Arianna said.

"Aryl won't tell me either," Claire added. "But I haven't seen him this excited about something since we got here. I hope whatever it is really does work out."

"Do you think it has anything to do with leaving the city?" Ava asked hopefully.

"I don't know," Arianna said. "All I know is I am going to thoroughly enjoy tonight because Caleb made it clear that money will be spent only on necessary things after this. I sure hope Aryl reveals his plan soon because life is going to be downright miserable after tonight," Arianna said with dread.

They waited anxiously for the men to get home and hurried them along in getting ready. They dressed in clothing that they had had no reason to wear since moving, and they looked utterly elegant as they left the tenement and walked to the trolley.

∞∞∞

They ordered coffee and crepes in a small café uptown. Ava glanced at Jonathan repeatedly as he started to show signs of life in the cozy café.

He talked more than he had in the two weeks since the attack and even laughed at some of Aryl's jokes.

When they left the café, Jonathan slipped an arm around Ava and pulled her close to his side as they walked a few blocks down Broadway. They had been to many stage shows and motion picture premieres; they knew the area well.

Once tickets were bought, they walked into the elegant, mahogany paneled lobby of the Capitol Theater and stood before the marble staircase that led up to the mezzanine. Just as Arianna started to take the first step, Caleb stopped and gestured toward a man in a tuxedo at the other end of the lobby.

"Is that the guy you needed to talk to?" he asked Aryl.

"It is. Listen, you all go up and get settled. I'll catch up. I need to talk to someone," Aryl said and walked over to the manager of the theater. The others watched for a moment as he spoke with the man, shook his hand, and began talking animatedly.

"Maybe he's investing in the theater," Arianna whispered to Claire excitedly. Claire gave her a hopeful smile as they headed up the staircase to their seats.

Claire began to look around nervously when the theater had filled nearly to capacity and Aryl still hadn't joined them. "Maybe you should go look for him," Claire suggested to Caleb.

"Nah. You know how Aryl gets. He'll be along," he said.

The lights dimmed and just as the newsreel began, Aryl appeared, tapped Caleb on the shoulder, and leaned down to talk to him. "We need to go talk to this guy. This could be a good opportunity," Aryl whispered a little too loudly. Caleb leaned over to whisper to Arianna that he would be back in a few minutes. She pouted and whined. However, when he told her it was business, she relented. Aryl apologized to Claire and kissed her cheek.

"I'll be back as soon as I can. This is really important," he pleaded.

"Fine. Hurry back or you'll miss the whole thing!" she said. Neither of them said anything to Jonathan who was absorbed in the newsreel.

"Well, that worked out well," Caleb commented as they headed back down the marble staircase to the main lobby.

"It did," Aryl agreed. He introduced Caleb to the manager. They talked of meaningless things before Aryl commented that they were probably missed by their wives and had to get back. Someone called the manager's name from across the room and he turned and waved, signaling he would be there momentarily. When he turned around, Caleb and Aryl were gone.

∞∞∞∞

Victor pulled on his gloves and adjusted his hat. His car sat parked alongside the road, and he tapped it twice as he continued down the street. The driver remained in the parked car near the entrance of the gentlemen's club, so that anyone wondering Victor's whereabouts, mainly Ruth, would be cleverly fooled. He paid his driver well for his silence and boredom.

Victor began walking the four blocks to his waiting mistress. He never saw the man who grabbed him from behind. With his hand over Victor's mouth, he pulled him back into a dark alley. Victor's arms flailed wildly as he tried to get away. A second man came from behind the dumpster. Victor couldn't make out the face that stood before him who wasted no time in delivering two hard punches to his gut, ending Victor's struggling.

"No," the man behind Victor said. "Just the face."

∞∞∞

"Where have you been?" Claire complained. "It's half-over!"

"Sorry," Aryl said, settling in his seat. "We just got to talking, you know." He turned his attention to the show.

As they were leaving, they stopped to introduce Jonathan and the wives to the manager, and Aryl promised he would be in touch. The girls didn't notice the manager's confused expression as they left the theater. They hurried home, shivering as the temperature had dropped below freezing. They talked about what a great evening it had been, and Caleb promised they would do it again as soon as they had saved enough for Aryl's idea. Jonathan's mood was lighter in the theater, but as they passed the streetlamp where he was attacked, he returned to his previous depressed state.

∞∞∞

Aryl woke early to a loud pounding. He stumbled to the door and opened it to two policemen.

"Are you Aryl Sullivan?"

"Yes," Aryl said, rubbing sleep out of his eyes.

"Sir, there was an attack last night, and it was implied by the victim that you might have been involved," the first officer said.

"I don't see how I could have been since I was at the Capitol Theater last night with my wife and friends," he said calmly.

"Do you have proof of that, sir?" the second one asked suspiciously. "See, that isn't far from where the attack happened."

"Sure," Aryl said and turned to dig the ticket stub out of his coat which hung on a nail by the door. He handed it to an officer. "If this isn't good enough, you can talk to the manager of the theater. My friends and I spoke with him about investing in the theater before and after the show," Aryl said with a yawn.

"This Mr. Smith will vouch that you were there the whole time?"

"Of course. Go talk to him."

"Investing, huh?" the first officer said, glancing around the tenement with a mocking smile. "All right. We're going to go talk to the others implicated and see if their stories match yours. If this Mr. Smith confirms you were there last night, you won't hear from us again."

"Fair enough. Say, who was it? Who thought I had something to do with this?"

"Victor Drayton."

"From what I hear, he has plenty of enemies. Good luck finding the guy," Aryl laughed and the policeman nodded knowingly.

"Yeah, but we gotta follow up first on whoever the victim implicates as a suspect. Particularly with an attack this vicious," the officer explained. Aryl waved, closed the door, and turned to see Claire standing by the sofa with crossed arms and an angry face.

"Investing, huh?" she repeated the officer's comment.

"Yeah. Investing in a peaceful future," he commented and walked past her to put on a pot of coffee and get ready for work. She spun around, out of patience.

"You really are playing with fire, Aryl. Going after some petty thug for this is one thing, but Victor Drayton is not someone you want to mess with. Especially since we are currently renting from him," she said, infuriated.

"It'll be fine. Victor is not going to show his face around here for quite a while." He wouldn't be showing his face anywhere for quite a while. "And he certainly will think twice before messing with us again."

"He didn't mess with us. He messed with Jon," Claire clarified. Aryl hurled her the angriest look that Claire had ever seen.

"When somebody messes with one of us, he messes with all of us. I thought you of all people would know that, Claire. Wasn't it you in the park last week standing with Ava, even though it had nothing to do with you?"

∞∞∞∞

Caleb's story matched beautifully and the timing couldn't have been more perfect with Jonathan's bruises having faded to the point where he simply looked violently hung over when he answered the door to the policemen. He also produced a ticket stub, and Ava insisted he was by her side in the theater the entire time. Jonathan figured out what really happened quickly enough and promised that his friends were in their seats near him for the whole show. The policemen left and found no reason to return.

Caleb insisted that everyone come over for dinner that night after work, and they each brought something to add to the table. Everyone except Jonathan was more talkative than at their last gathering for Thanksgiving. Their morale was slightly lifted from their evening out. Each one took turns suggesting ways to save money further, weekly meals together being one of the ideas. Jonathan sat across from Aryl and Caleb. He looked each of them in the eye for a few seconds. Caleb's eyes narrowed slightly, and one side of Aryl's mouth twitched. Their silent conversation went unnoticed by the rest of the table. Jonathan nodded once.

∞∞∞

Ava was unable to get to sleep. Every noise from the apartments, the sirens and screeching tires from the street jarred her every time she started to drift off. It was nearing the early hours of the morning as she stared at the ceiling, longing for sleep. Jonathan had been very restless all night. Grunts, flailing legs and talking in his sleep added to the list of things that kept her awake. Much to her relief, he finally settled into slow and deep breathing. She closed her eyes, grateful for the silence and began to drift off.

"*Elyse*," Jonathan whispered and Ava's eyes popped open. She propped herself up on one elbow, and he repeated the name quieter this time.

"*Elyse*." he said again with a sigh. Ava kicked him under the covers. He snorted, mumbled, and rolled to his side. She stared at him for a long time waiting to hear him repeat the name during the hours left of darkness.

The next morning, Ava was up before Jonathan and sat, waiting at the table with her coffee. When he sat down across from her, her glare was set in stone.

"Morning," he said, spooning some jam into his oatmeal.

"Who is Elyse?"

"What?" he asked, choking on a sip of coffee.

"Who . . . is . . . Elyse?"

"Where did you hear that name?"

"You said it in your sleep last night. Twice." Honesty had worked with Ruth's second visit, so he decided to take that approach again.

"She was someone I knew before you," he said causally.

"Another one. When can I expect her to show up?"

"She's not going to show up, Ava."

"How can you be so sure? She must have left quite the impression on you for you to dream about her all these years later. I'm sure the feeling was mutual."

"She just won't."

"Bet you thought Ruth wouldn't show up either."

"She won't show up because she's in Paris, Ava."

"Oh," she said, sitting up straighter in her chair, beginning to put the pieces together. "Was that who you were with when you told Ruth you were in board meetings?" she asked.

"How do you know about that?" he asked quietly.

"I confronted Ruth."

"When?" he exclaimed, finally looking at her.

"Over a week ago. I went to the park and confronted her. Arianna and Claire showed up to support me, and that was the last thing Arianna said to Ruth. That you were with someone else when you told Ruth you were in board meetings." Jonathan looked clearly shaken, and he cursed Arianna under his breath.

"Yes. I was with Elyse," he said, digging deeper into his proverbial grave. Just him saying her name made Ava's blood boil, and she resisted a violent urge to hurl her plate across the room.

"Well, part of me is relieved to know that Ruth never meant that much to you."

"Of course, she didn't."

"But someone else obviously did. You're still dreaming about her." She seethed with jealous rage. He opened his mouth to argue but couldn't.

"I didn't mean to," was his pitiful reply. "It was long before you, Ava. I haven't even thought about her in ages." He desperately wanted this whole conversation to end and be forgotten. She didn't say anything else but sat stewing with crossed arms as he left for work silently.

∞∞∞∞

Ava walked down the hall and pounded on Arianna's door. Ava pushed her way past and spun around on her heels.

"You were in Paris with Jon. You saw what went on. Tell me about Elyse." she demanded. Arianna looked suddenly as if she wanted to crawl under the table and hide.

"Well? I'm waiting," Ava said impatiently.

"Why do you want to know, Ava?" Arianna asked cautiously.

"Jon dreamt about her last night. He said her name. I asked him about it this morning, and he told me about her. I just want to hear it from you," Ava said convincingly, so that Arianna wouldn't see through the lie.

"Sit down," Arianna said hesitantly. She poured both some coffee and sat across the table from her. "Where do I begin?"

"Try at the beginning, Arianna."

"Okay." She took a deep breath. "You know that Jonathan's more wealthy clients overseas threw enormous parties for him when he visited three or four times a year. They were always regal events with the most famous and important people attending," Arianna started. "Well, every luxury was provided. Elegant suites, exotic food, expensive wine . . . beautiful women." Ava felt her face flush with anger. "I can't say anything about the trips before I came along, but I went every time that he and Caleb went, plus the few times when Aryl joined us."

"But you can tell me about the trips you *did* go on with them," Ava insisted.

"Elyse was one of the women provided for the parties. She was one of at least a dozen women from the most elite and respected brothels. Real high priced entertainment." She waited for Ava's reaction, but she showed none. "Well, Jon spent some . . . time with Elyse. Since she was a regular at the parties, I guess you could say he got to know her." Arianna was getting more uncomfortable telling the story, and Ava could hardly hear her through the pounding of her heart in her ears. Her hands were shaking in her lap. She told Arianna to go on.

"Well, Jon worked it out with the brothel owner that she was not to be available for any other clients. She was to be reserved just for him when he came to visit."

"He *what?*"

"M-Maybe Jon should tell you the rest," she said nervously.

"No. *You* will tell me the rest. Right now," Ava demanded. Arianna was not used to being put on the spot or being ordered what to do, but she obeyed.

"He paid the brothel a large sum of money in exchange for Elyse being reserved for him. And he saw her every time he visited."

"Every time?" Ava asked, thinking specifically of the last time he went to Paris, alone.

"As far as I know. Of course, after you came along, we never heard another word about her," Arianna tried to reassure her.

"But you never heard that he ended his agreement with the brothel either, did you?"

"Well, no, but that almost goes without saying. You have to understand, Ava. Once you came along, there were no other women on earth as far as Jon was concerned. And you may not like to hear this, but he did have needs and a life before you."

"I know that," she growled, even though she didn't like the idea. "But he should have told me about this. After all, he's still dreaming about her. He must have really loved her."

"He didn't love her, Ava. She was supporting her family and trying to save to go to a women's college one day. He was trying to help her out is all." Ava thought back to Ruth's statement about his pity for her being the reason why he took care of her, and she thought her head would explode with rage. It explained why he was so distant, showed no interest in her, and spent his evenings staring at the fire. He was thinking of this woman now that he had grown tired of her, and she refused to believe that he hadn't loved Elyse.

"What about Caleb and Aryl? Did they have whores on retainer, too?" she said, clearly disgusted.

"Caleb and I were married before he ever came to work for Jon. I was with him during all of his trips. And Aryl's stories are not mine to share. However, I will say he didn't do as Jon did and actually tried to talk him out of it." Ava's eyes flashed up to Arianna, turning her anger on her.

"Why didn't you ever tell me?"

"Ava, that was another world, another time long before you."

"Apparently a lot happened before me. How dare you call yourself my friend!" Ava stomped out the door, slamming it behind her.

∞∞∞

Later that evening, the tired and cold men trudged up the stairs. Jonathan opened his door to a torrent of screaming and crying that caused Aryl to stop on the stairs and look back towards Jonathan's door. Aryl's head fell, worried for his friend, but was too tired to intervene.

"Don't talk to me! Don't you dare touch me! Don't even look at me!" Ava's shrieking was followed by a loud crash.

∞∞∞

Caleb came home to a sobbing Arianna, who was so upset about Ava that she forgot to make dinner. She told him everything that happened, and he reassured her everything would work out. On the way to the deli, he stopped at Aryl's to give a word of warning.

"Ava found out about Elyse," he said gravely. "She backed Ahna into a corner and got the whole story out of her."

"What all did she tell her?" he asked.

"I'm not sure. Arianna was hysterical. But I thought you would want to know in case you wanted to do some damage control of your own."

"Okay. Thanks," Aryl said.

All through dinner, Aryl wrestled with himself and finally decided that telling Claire the truth now would ultimately be the best thing to do. She would, he hoped, forgive him eventually.

"Claire," he called from the couch, and motioned for her to sit. "I need to talk to you."

"What's wrong?" she asked.

"I need to tell you something. And I know it's not going to go well, but I'd rather you hear it from me than hear it from anyone else. Some things have come to light," Aryl started. "Things that happened a long time ago. For the most part, it involves Jon and Ava. I'm sure you're going to hear about it, so I'll just give you a quick rundown." She sat down beside him. "Before I even came to join him in New York, Jon had a relationship with someone in Paris. She was one of the women that Jon's wealthier clients provided for entertainment at their parties." By his raised eyebrows and tone, Claire assumed easily enough what kind of entertainment he was referring to. "Well, it turned into a long-term relationship, and the circumstances of that relationship are what he and Ava are downstairs, no doubt, hashing out right now."

"What does all this have to do with you?" she asked. He hesitated, fidgeted with his cup, adjusted in his seat, and then continued.

"This trip in particular was the time when Jon brought Ruth with us. Elyse saw the two of them together and was very upset. She hadn't known about Ruth, and had become very attached to Jon after a couple of years, so it was hard for her. Of course, Jon had to act as if he didn't know her in public, but he made excuses to Ruth of meetings, and he would go see her in the evening. I guess the reunion with Elyse didn't go well that trip. They argued a lot. Jon told me later that Elyse suddenly started pressuring him to marry her and bring her back to America. There is no way that Jon could have done that, and they both knew it. But she was insistent. He ended up walking out during an intense argument with her one night.

"Later, she showed up at the door of my hotel room. She was crying and looked a wreck. I had had too much to drink with Caleb and Arianna and was on the verge of passing out, but I let her in and tried explaining to her that Jon couldn't marry her even if he wanted to. It was socially unacceptable and would have ruined his career. She had enough money to go to a women's college by then, so I told her she should leave the business she was in behind. I think she really loved Jon and was completely devastated. I talked to her for a long time." He paused to take a deep breath before passing the point of no return. "There's no easy way to say this, so I'll just spit it out. I made a mistake," he said simply.

"What do you mean, you made a mistake?"

"I needed for you to hear this firsthand. Not in a roundabout way, like with Ava. Jon was afraid he would lose her if he told her the truth back then. And I'm afraid I'll lose you if I don't now." He finally looked over at her and she was staring at him, not fully comprehending.

"What are you saying, Aryl? Exactly?"

"You're really going to make me say it," he said agonizingly. He didn't dare look up to see her face frozen, staring at him in shock. "I was drunk and I missed you so much," he said with a heavy sigh. "I spent the night with her, Claire . . . I know what you're thinking. But it was the only time, I swear. I only went on a few trips that year we were apart. And although it was difficult with Caleb and Arianna, Jon and Elyse, and then me, the odd man out, I behaved like an already married man. Every night I went to my hotel room alone and stayed there, thinking about you. I swear. All those letters I wrote you, I wrote those late at night in my room. Alone.

That night, though, I just wasn't thinking. I let my guard down, and I didn't realize what happened until after . . ." She hadn't moved her statuesque expression. "Claire, I know you–"

She interrupted him, holding up her hand. "I need a minute, Aryl."

He sat quietly, unconsciously wringing his hands while his stomach twisted. The burden that he was partially relieved to be rid of was a thousand times heavier now, as he waited for the fallout.

Almost an hour passed, and the ticking of the clock echoing in the living room seemed to grow louder and louder. The fire had died out, and the room was only dimly lit from the kitchen light. He wondered where the screaming, the crying, the harsh words and even a cup or plate thrown his way were? He would have deserved it. But she was so deep in thought that he grew more afraid that this was the calm before the storm. And he had no idea what that storm would look like. *Even her yelling*, he thought desperately, *would be better than this*. When he couldn't stand the silence any longer, he turned to her on the couch.

"Can you ever forgive me?" he asked quietly, assuming that was what she was debating. She looked at him for a long time and then held out her hand. He took it readily and wondered if it would actually be this easy. Could she love him enough to forgive this indiscretion that, after all, happened before they were married?

"Only if you can forgive me. I have something to tell you, too," she said, preparing to unload a burden of her own.

∞∞∞

"Ava, what in hell?" Jonathan stood by the door, taken aback by Ava's ranting. She glared at him with detestation, went into the bedroom and slammed the door.

Awhile later, she came out when she was sure she could do something other than scream. She was instantly irritated to see him on the couch. Jonathan bent to unlace his boots and asked, without looking at her, "Do you mind telling me what's going on with you?"

"I found out about Elyse. That's what," she snapped at him. He rolled his eyes impatiently.

"You're still mad about that? It was long before you, so I don't see why you're making this such an issue, Ava. Was I not allowed to have a life or a girlfriend before you? I guess I should have acted like a monk until the magical day when you showed up," he mocked.

"No. I found out more about her today. From Arianna."

Jonathan stopped unlacing his boots and sat up straight.

"Well, if you know everything, then you know that I ended it with her when I met you," he said, wondering how much she really did know and not willing to divulge any more than he already had. *Arianna would never do that to me. Tell her everything*, he thought.

"You ended it with her over there and with Ruth here. Any other women on any other continents I should be aware of? Exactly how many of them did you have going at a time, Jonathan?" He sighed and rubbed his forehead.

"Again, Ava, it was before you. You can't hold anything against me that happened before I ever knew you existed," he said, exasperated.

"You should have told me about all of it," she insisted.

"Now, there's some great first date conversation. Listing off all the women of my past," he said sarcastically. It became obvious to her that he didn't realize that she did, indeed, know the whole story.

"You must have really cared about her to pay so much money to keep her just for yourself," she said with a dark tone. He stared at her.

"How did you find out about that?" he asked, already knowing what her answer would be.

"Arianna."

"She had no right—"

"She had every right. And more over, she didn't have a choice. If I had to beat it out of her, I was going to find out who Elyse was," she said.

"I was trying to help her out," he started to explain. "That's all. She shouldn't have been forced into that life. I set it up so that she could continue to make the same amount of money without having to—"

"*Act* like a whore?" Ava finished for him. She could see a flash of anger in his eyes when she referred to Elyse as what she truly was, and that infuriated her to no end. "Did you feel sorry for her?" she asked through her teeth.

"Yes."

"Like you felt sorry for me," she assumed.

"No, that was completely different. I was trying to help her get out of that work for good."

"But you didn't just set it up as a kind gesture. You got your money's worth, didn't you?" He didn't answer, but stared at the fire. "How long did this go on?" She felt compelled to ask, even though she really didn't want to know.

"Three years," he said flatly.

"When did you end your arrangement with her?"

"The very next time I went to Paris after I met you. But it started falling apart before that." His tone was softer now, as he attempted to be reassuring.

"And what about the very last time you went? After we were married. You were alone. I'm supposed to believe that after a long relationship with what must have been a very exciting companion, you actually managed the whole trip without seeing her?" If he lied now, he knew that it would come back to haunt him like everything else had. As much as he hated the backlash it would bring, he was honest.

"I did my best to steer clear of her. But the concierge didn't know that our arrangement had ended, and he let her into my room. She was waiting for me the last night of my stay. She didn't want the arrangement to end. I told her that I was married. I made her leave. Nothing happened."

"I don't believe you."

"What can I say to make you believe me?" he said hopelessly.

"There's nothing you *can* say, Jon . . . I've written Maura to ask her if I can live with her for a while after Christmas until I can figure something else out." She turned and slammed the bedroom door again. He stared at the fire for a moment before he got up and stormed out angrily.

∞∞∞

Jonathan pounded on Caleb's door steadily until he opened it. "Your wife has a real big mouth, you know that? She promised me she would *never* speak of Elyse to Ava," Jonathan yelled.

"She didn't speak of her first, Jon, you did," Caleb reminded him. Jon stepped around Caleb and pointed a finger at Arianna.

"You had no right!" he shouted. "Thanks to you, she's leaving me!" Caleb stepped in front of Jon and backed him up a few inches.

"Don't yell at my wife, Jon. This is ultimately your doing. You chose to have an unconventional relationship with Elyse, and then chose not to tell Ava about it. It would have come out eventually, somehow. Now you go home and do what you can to fix things with Ava. And don't you ever show up at my door to yell at my wife again," Caleb ordered and closed the door in his face. Jon turned and headed upstairs to talk to Aryl, who might see a way to get this straightened out.

∞∞∞

Aryl answered the door on the third knock, and Jonathan saw it was dark inside his apartment.

"It's really not a good time, Jon," Aryl said somberly.

"What's going on?" Jonathan pried. Aryl stepped out into the hall and spoke in a low voice so neighbors wouldn't hear.

"I came clean about Elyse."

"You what?" Jonathan cried.

"I heard that Arianna spilled it all, so instead of Claire finding out later, I told her myself."

"Ava's leaving," Jonathan said pitifully, unable to focus on Aryl's crisis.

"I can't do anything about that right now, Jon. I'm in the middle of this with Claire. Look, I'm sure she's just mad. I'll talk to you tomorrow," he said, leaving Jonathan standing in the hallway.

∞∞∞

He sat down beside Claire and took her hand again. "Now go on and tell me what it is you need to tell me," he said. Secretly he was relieved. Claire had had many admirers in both Boston and Rockport, so he waited patiently for her to tell him of some incident of hand-holding or a stolen kiss. He would act very troubled and then forgive her. She would forgive him and it would all be over.

"I was miserable, Aryl, the whole time we were apart. My mother did her best to keep me busy with charity work and parties and introduced me to everyone she could think of. She insisted I go out with my friends and didn't even mind when we went to the dance halls. My mother introduced me to her friend's daughter. We spent a lot of time together before she left to do some charity work overseas. My group of friends accepted her fiancée, Steven, and tried to help him along the same way they tried to help me. It didn't take long for him to fit right in with us, and we were all having a grand time. Most importantly, time was flying by and before I knew it, it was almost time for you to come back. My mother thought Steven was the perfect escort for me since both of us were spoken for. She considered it a safe alternative to going unattended." She hesitated and Aryl mentally steeled himself, waiting for the confession of a rogue kiss between them. It wasn't going to be quite as easy to hear as he previously thought. He remained focused on having this whole thing behind him by morning.

"We went to a winter party at the Governor's Mansion," she continued. "It was an enormous gathering, and I lost track of Steven toward the end of the night. I wanted to go home and went to the coatroom only to find the attendant wasn't there. I went in to gather my things, and Steven was there looking for his coat as well. Aryl, I should have stopped with one glass of champagne. I wasn't thinking. One thing led to another and . . . ."

"What do you mean, one thing led to another?"

"I mean that I'm guilty of the same transgression as you. For the same reason." He stared at her baffled while her words sunk in, and dropped her hand, rising to his feet, jealous and angry.

"Tell me you're not saying what I think you're saying," he demanded, and now she was the one not willing to look at him and remained silent.

"You mean to say that you . . . and Steven . . . in a coatroom? While I was working night and day to make a life for us here!"

"Well, if your definition of working includes spending the night with Jon's high-priced whore, then yes!"

"How could you do this, Claire?" His eyes and voice were heavy with betrayal.

"I could ask you the same thing!"

"That's different," he said, shaking his head.

"And just *how* is it different?" she yelled, pushing off the couch in shock at his double standard. "We both had the same reasons, not that they were right, but we both missed each other terribly and both had too much to drink. We both weren't thinking and—"

"And you never told me all this time."

"You never told me either!"

Fuming, he turned and left, slamming the door behind him. He paced the length of the hall several times, trying to decide where to go.

∞∞∞

Aryl banged on Caleb's door with his fist.

"Doesn't anyone knock anymore?" Caleb griped as he opened the door.

"I need to talk to you."

"Look, I know a lot of stuff is going on right now, but if you're here to yell at Arianna, you can just go the hell home now," Caleb said protectively.

"I'm not here to yell at Arianna. I confessed on my own," Aryl admitted. Caleb did a double take.

"You what? Are you talking about—?"

"Yes," Aryl said with residual dread. "I told her. And then she told me a little something of her own. I guess she figures we're even now."

"Uh-oh. Come on in," he sighed. Caleb went to the bedroom, brought out a bottle of brandy, and poured Aryl a glass at the table. "All right, what happened?" Caleb asked.

"Well, I decided to come clean altogether. I was almost relieved to be rid of this guilt. So, I confessed, and then she told me about something that happened at a party with some guy named Steven. And when I find that bastard . . . ." He gulped his drink and slammed his glass down.

"You're not going to want to hear this."

"I know what you're going to say, Caleb, so don't bother. You're going to say that we're even, and we need to just forgive each other because it was before we were married."

"You said it, not me."

"Well, I can't, Caleb. This is unforgivable." He sat back in his chair, shaking his head.

"And spending the night with Elyse is?"

"It's different. You know it's different, Caleb."

"No. It's not," he insisted. "Listen. You both really messed up. But it was a long time ago before you were married, and a lot has happened since then that means a hell of a lot more than two serious lapses in judgment. Now, you can either keep that in mind, forgive each other and forget about it, or you can let it eat you alive, stay angry and end up like Jon and Ava. She's leaving Jon over this, by the way."

"She's just angry. She'll come to her senses when she realizes that Jon actually remained faithful."

"Go home, Aryl. Forgive each other and let it go. It's not worth it to let it destroy your marriage."

"That's so much easier said than done," Aryl said, reaching for the brandy, but Caleb snatched it out of the way.

"I'll pour you one for the road, and you can drink it on your way *up* the stairs."

"Well, maybe we should think of a way to help Jon out of this mess?"

"Aryl. It's my week. Go home."

"It's your week and you're the only one who's not in trouble. How do you rate?" he said, seeing himself to the door.

∞∞∞∞

The next morning, the men were exhausted on the walk to work. Jon and Aryl slept poorly from silent tension that hung heavy in their homes, and Caleb had hardly slept, trying to make the most of the safe week.

"You know she'll come around, Jon," Caleb said out of the blue. Jon didn't answer, still angry at him for slamming the door in his face.

As they walked into the shipping yard, there was a restless look on many faces and a nervous bustling as everyone hurried about their work. Caleb noticed it right away and suggested Aryl go talk to Roman to see what was going on. Aryl went to his office only to find him in a meeting. Roman looked very upset and was extremely animated in whatever he was trying to convey to the suits.

Aryl walked back out to the work area and stopped a couple of guys.

"What's going on?" he asked, looking around at all the uneasy faces and the noticeable lack of day workers being let in the side gate.

"There's talk of layoffs. It's got everyone on edge. Saturday work isn't going to resume any time soon either." They continued on their way and left Aryl with a fresh worry to add to his pile.

∞∞∞∞

Jon and Aryl quietly worked together. Close to lunchtime, Jon turned to Aryl.

"You know, I was thinking about the night I got jumped. I was pretty lucky, I guess, with Sven being there and all."

"Yeah, I guess you were," Aryl agreed.

"But what if there's a next time? And what if I'm not so lucky?" Jonathan asked calmly. Aryl looked at him, bothered by his comment.

"There isn't going to be a next time, Jon. Don't worry about it." He went back to pulling bags of flour off the top of the pallet.

"But what if there is? I got to thinking; I wondered what would happen to Ava if something happened to me? I never really thought about that before."

"Nothing is going to happen to you, Jon. Except maybe get fired for talking when you should be working," he snapped.

"Okay, but what if?" He went back to slinging bags of flour while he talked. "If something did happen to me; I get jumped, hit by a bus, an accident at work. It would be nice to know that Ava would be taken care of. I mean, you would, right? Take care of her like a sister until she remarried?" Jon asked outright. Aryl was visibly uncomfortable with the topic.

"Of course, Jon," he said, wanting him to talk about anything else.

"I mean, I'd do that for you. Take care of Claire like a sister, if anything ever–"

"I know you would, Jon. And I would take care of Ava."

"You promise?" he asked almost childishly.

"Yes, I promise, Jon. Now please get back to work before you get us both fired," Aryl pleaded.

"Okay." Jonathan doubled his pace. "Hey, don't say anything to Caleb or anyone about this, okay? I guess I'm just a little paranoid with what happened recently."

"I won't say anything," Aryl promised. "Lemme ask you something. Say, for example, after Ava found out about Elyse, she then told you about something similar that she had been hiding. How would you feel?"

"I'd probably feel a little strange if she'd kept a woman in Paris."

"I'm serious, Jon. Say you stepped out and begged her forgiveness, but then she told you about her stepping out as well. You're both guilty. What would you do?"

"Jump up and down, thank my lucky stars."

"Dammit, Jonathan, I'm serious!" Aryl yelled.

"So am I. If it were even, it would be over. We would have to forgive each other to be forgiven. All the chips wouldn't be on her side of the table. I wouldn't be stuck trying to figure out a way to convince her of something I have no way to prove. I'd take even ground any day. She says she's going to Maura's after Christmas," he said. Aryl searched for what to say.

"She'll come around, Jon. She's just angry. Caleb and I can talk to her."

"Nah. It won't do any good."

∞∞∞∞

*C*laire spent the morning working on the mural. She had finished Shannon's angel, wrapped it in brown paper, and set it against the wall by the door. She had run out of black paint while completing the angel. Patrick hadn't paid her with any yet, but she found that the cooled embers from the previous night's fire worked well as a substitute for the paint. She spent the entire morning extending the storm front until it completely surrounded the lighthouse and loomed over the beach cottage menacingly. She amplified the torrent of the white-tipped waves to show them churning and swirling out in the open ocean, thrashing the sandy shore and painted the crashing water higher around the rocks at the base of the lighthouse. The once vibrant light from the beacon was made dimmer and extended now only a few inches before being swallowed by the storm.

After admiring it for a few moments, she felt satisfied and then decided to visit Ava. She debated all morning whether or not to go, knowing that Ava needed a shoulder right now, but also knowing she would learn details about Elyse that she wasn't sure she wanted to know. She washed the black soot off her hands and changed out of her painting smock.

∞∞∞∞

Claire sat with Ava on the couch while she cried and told Claire everything.

"You honestly don't believe him? That nothing happened?" Claire asked.

"No. And even if I did, he felt sorry for me the same way he felt sorry for her, and I can't live with that. Ruth said he was always taking in pitiful things he felt sorry for. It's no wonder he acts like he does around me and then dreams about her," Ava said with a sniffle.

"I don't think it's you, Ava. I think it's this life that makes him act this way." Ava shook her head, unconvinced.

"I wrote Maura and asked her if I can go to her after the holidays. I want to go now, but I won't interrupt her family's Christmas."

"Ava, are you sure you want to do that?"

"Yes," she said, resolved.

"All because he didn't tell you about an arrangement he had long before you?" Claire asked.

"Yes. And for the reason that I will never know what really happened on that last trip."

"I know Jonathan. He wouldn't lie to you, Ava." Claire said with confidence, but Ava didn't answer. "This affects Aryl and I as well, you know," she said quietly.

"How?"

"On the trip with Ruth. When things didn't go well with Elyse. Aryl was there, and at some point, I guess Elyse found him. She was all broken up about Jon. Aryl told me they spent the night together," Claire said through her teeth. Ava's mouth fell open.

"What?"

"And then I told him about Steven."

"You didn't!"

"I did. And he was furious. I'm not sure anything will be the same after this. He didn't say anything to me all evening or this morning."

"I guess all the cats are flying out of the bag this week," Ava said sarcastically and sat back, crossing her arms. "What are you going to do?"

"I don't know. All I can think of is this woman, who from thousands of miles away, managed to completely disrupt two homes."

"Destroy is more like it," Ava said gravely.

"Don't you wonder what she looks like? All morning I wondered. And the more I tried to imagine her, the more furiously I painted. I had to try to think of something else when I realized my whole wall was almost black with storm clouds."

"I need to come see your mural. I haven't seen it in a while," Ava said. "And yes. I wonder what she looks like."

"I guess we'll never know," Claire said. "I doubt the men would give us an accurate description."

"But you know who would? Someone who saw her several times." They locked eyes.

"Arianna."

∞∞∞∞

"You're the only one who will tell us the truth," Ava pointed out while sitting at the table waiting for answers. Arianna was hesitant to provide any more information. She procrastinated by making tea as slowly as she could before sitting down at the table with her friends.

"Yes, but last time–"

"Last time I got mad at you. I know. What happened isn't your fault. I just felt betrayed that you never told me."

"Would you have told me?" Arianna asked.

"Yes. Absolutely."

"You would have looked me in the eyes when I was the happiest I had ever been, when I was completely in love with someone so perfectly compatible, you would have told me?" Ava looked down, seeing her point. "I couldn't, Ava. Even if Jon *hadn't* begged, pleaded with me, and made me swear that I wouldn't ever breathe a word of it to you, I couldn't have done that. He was so happy, and you two were so perfect for each other. I decided the first time I ever saw you together that I could never ruin that." Ava nodded, understood now, and silently forgave her.

"Did you know about Aryl as well?" Claire asked.

"No, what about him?" Arianna asked. Claire filled her in on Aryl's confession, and Arianna's eyes grew wider and wider.

"Claire," she straightened, intent on saving at least one marriage today and looked Claire directly in the eyes. "He was always so good on all the trips with us. I felt sorry for him with couples all round, and he missed you so much. There was even one time," she began with a laugh, "when a woman did approach him. She sat down next to him at our table, clearly enamored with him. Well, he went on so much about you that she got bored and left on her own. He talked about you all the time, Claire. I don't know what happened on that last trip, but I can reassure you, I saw nothing out of character from him all the other times," Arianna promised. Claire was grateful for her reassurance and remembered times when her friends in Boston would groan and complain because of the amount of time she spent talking about Aryl.

"We came here for a description," Ava reminded Arianna.

"C'mon, no good can come of this. Just please go home and try to make things right. Leave the details alone."

Claire was willing to do that as her heart was already softening. She just wanted all of this to be over, but Ava was insistent.

"I need to know," Ava pushed.

"You're not going to like it, Ava. I wish you wouldn't make me do this," Arianna begged.

"I know she's more beautiful than me. That won't be a shock," she said, casting her eyes down in humiliation.

"No. It's not that. That's the thing. She looks just like you, Ava," Arianna said with an apologetic tone.

"What do you mean she looks just like me?"

"She has dirty-blond hair, light-brown eyes, she's the same height as you, and even her build is the same. Of course, she wore wigs and a pound of makeup, but her natural look is very similar to yours."

Ava didn't know what to think or feel. She sat dumbstruck at Arianna's table; her tea growing cold in her hands. Part of her was relieved that there was nothing to be jealous of in a physical aspect, but this revelation planted the seed of doubt that Jonathan didn't really love her so much as he loved how she reminded him of Elyse.

∞∞∞∞

This new insecurity preoccupied her thoughts the rest of the evening, and she didn't acknowledge Jonathan when he came home, as they ate, or as she went to bed early, leaving him on the couch with his far off gaze. He silently watched her walk into the bedroom and then fixed his eyes on the fire again.

He went over the small list he had compiled in his mind. He had gotten Aryl's promise to care for Ava today, and he would easily get Caleb's tomorrow. He knew how, but he still needed to figure out when and where. He could take a walk one evening, slip into an alley and hide behind a dumpster, but the small, tattered shred of dignity he still held turned him from the idea of being discovered by strangers, gawking with pity. No, he wouldn't hide in an alley, he would do it here. He needed

Ava to be gone. She couldn't be allowed to find him. The only time she would be gone for any amount of time would be Christmas Eve. She would be at Maura's for dinner and mass. It would be easy to make an excuse to catch up, and then leave a clue for Aryl to find later, so he would prevent her from coming home.

It all fell together in his mind as he went over the final details of his plan. He felt a wave of relief wash over him with his final decision. He only briefly worried about what would come after, knowing the widespread belief of what happens to the souls of those who take their own lives. He remembered the truth Charles spoke on the night he was attacked. He loved Ava more than his own soul. So, he supposed it didn't really matter what happened after the fact.

He peeked in the bedroom to watch her sleep. She would, in time, remarry into better circumstances and be happy again. He was sure of it. He quietly readied for bed and lay down at peace with his decision. It would all be over soon.

∞∞∞

Caleb trudged home, completely worn-out. He had worked at a rapid pace all day, working through lunch and breaks. Aryl had started feeling poorly earlier that morning, and Caleb had tried to do some of his share of the work, so the supervisors wouldn't notice the lag. It wasn't wise to stand out in a negative way or you risked being let go. With the plan Aryl had cultivated and organized this last week, Caleb knew neither one of them could afford to miss a single day of work. Aryl had everything worked out down to the penny, and it looked more promising than anything they had talked about previously.

As he fumbled for his key, he could hear Arianna's sniffles and whimpering from the other side. He threw his head back and sighed heavily. *What now?* He simply didn't have it in him to contend with her hysterics because someone was foul to her or something lovely was seen that they couldn't afford. Every day he found patience to handle some sort of crisis or emotional outburst. But not today. He opened the door, and although it was dark, he could see she was on the couch, hugging her knees.

"Oh, Caleb!" She burst into sobs and reached her arms out for him. He stared at her for a moment with a tired, indifferent expression and turned, closing the door behind him.

He went to the deli around the corner. He hated to spend any money, but he was starving, and he knew there was no dinner at home.

∞∞∞

Arianna put on her sweater and headed down the hall to Ava's apartment. Her knock on the door was weak, but Ava managed to hear it over Aryl's heated debate with Jonathan. She had been sitting by the fire with Claire trying to get warm and tune out the men, both of whom they were still not speaking to. Aryl had followed Jonathan in straight from work to finish the debate that had started on the walk home. He was trying to get Jonathan interested in real estate without giving away the plan he would reveal on Christmas. Jonathan wanted no part of it.

"Arianna!" Ava gasped with one look at her. "What's wrong?" She was leaning on the doorframe, her forehead beaded with sweat, the color drained from her face.

"I'm sick," she started. Ava helped her inside and sat her on the couch.

"Are you in pain?" Ava asked, looking for an explanation for the tears.

"My stomach, but it's better than it was. It started this morning. I didn't want to come here and risk making you sick, too, but I didn't know what else to do. I don't have the strength to chase after him."

"Who?" Claire asked, taking her hand.

"Caleb. When he came home, I was crying, and I know he must be tired of that, but this time it's serious. I went to the doctor today . . . but he didn't know that, he just turned and walked away when he saw me. I don't know where he went." She started crying again and reached to hug Ava.

"Did he say anything? Do you have any idea where he went?" Aryl asked, very concerned. This was completely out of character for Caleb. She shook her head.

"He didn't say a word to me. I didn't even have a chance to tell him what the doctor said."

"What did the doctor say?" Aryl asked, presuming her diagnosis was the same stomach flu that was spreading fast around work and the tenement.

"He said I have a stomach flu." Aryl moved to the door and put on his coat. He was opening the door as Arianna finished her sentence. "And that I'm pregnant," she blurted out. Aryl stopped short in the doorway, stunned for a moment, then looked back toward Arianna.

"I'll go find him, all right? And don't worry, I won't say a word about this," he promised.

"Caleb should have been the first to know," she said, disappointed.

"Well, he didn't exactly give you the chance now, did he?" Claire said, smoothing her hair. Both she and Ava were at a loss for words. This was something they all worried about; bringing a baby into this dreadful place. But with little means beyond a calendar to prevent it, they supposed they shouldn't be too shocked. Sooner or later, it was bound to happen to one of them.

"How are you doing, Arianna?" Ava asked.

"I don't know. I'm still in shock, I suppose," she said quietly. "I feel horrible. The doctor said it's baby sickness on top of stomach sickness. A double whammy. He gave me a tonic to settle my stomach and iron pills. Dr. Westley said he was worried about my diet, under the circumstances.

And he gave me the address of a midwife near here. He said she's well experienced and doesn't charge as much as a doctor. She can give me check-ups and see to the baby after it's born. I hate the idea of bringing a baby home to this place. And I'm so worried that Caleb will be upset," she said quietly.

"Well, it's just as much his doing as yours, you know," Claire said in defiance. "He would have no right to be angry."

"I know, but it's one more worry. And one more expense."

"Listen," Ava said and smiled. "Why don't we help you get up to your apartment, so you can get some rest? Aryl will be back with Caleb soon." Arianna agreed, feeling utterly exhausted. Jonathan hadn't moved from his seat at the table, staring at the floor. He couldn't imagine how devastated Caleb would be, and he was grateful it wasn't happening to him.

∞∞∞∞

Aryl checked in the deli, and Mr. Goldberg told him Caleb had been there but left. He walked a few blocks in each direction, trying to think of where he might have gone. Finally, he stopped a streetwalker across from the deli.

"Where can a guy get a strong drink around here?" The tattered blonde looked him up and down and smiled.

"You're the second guy to ask me that tonight."

"Well?" he asked impatiently. She smiled but kept silent. He huffed his breath impatiently.

"Nothin's free, honey," she said finally.

"How much then?"

"For the information? Or for something else?" Aryl was getting very frustrated. It was cold, and his stomach was cramping worse than earlier.

"Just the information."

"A quarter."

"Fine," he said, digging a quarter out of his pocket and dropping it into her hand, not wanting to touch her.

"Keep walking down a block, turn into the alley and walk to the third metal door on the right. Knock three times, stop and then knock twice more. They'll let you in."

He walked off without saying another word, found the door, and knocked as she had told him to. A large man opened the door, gave him a quick look up and down, then stepped aside to let him in. He spotted Caleb toward the back of the makeshift bar.

"Caleb."

He looked up, slightly surprised to see Aryl. "What are you doing here?"

"I'm here to bring you home."

Caleb shook his head. "Not just yet. In a while," he said and turned back to his drink.

"No, Caleb, you need to come home and deal with this."

"Deal with what? Her whining and crying all the time? If it's not one thing, it's another, and none of what she cries about is important in real life. Almost every single day, she is falling apart about something. And I have to make it better, but I just don't have it in me right now. Maybe not at all. Almost every single day, I come home to a cold apartment that distinctly lacks the smell of dinner cooking."

"Are you done?"

"You know how I spent my days off this weekend, Aryl? Doing laundry. She said she didn't know how and won't attempt to learn, even though Shannon offered to teach her. I've spent too much money buying dinner every night, and I have to hide the money jar, which she threw a fit over. She has wasted more of our pitiful savings than I care to think about." Caleb tossed back his drink.

"Are you done?"

"And for the last few days, she had gone on and on about this thing with Elyse. Falling apart because she feels like it's her fault. Then last night she broke down because it doesn't feel like Christmas without a tree, presents, and parties. Even after your speech on saving money. I can only deal with so much. And I've had my fill."

"Are you done?"

"I suppose," Caleb huffed.

"Okay, good. Now you need to come home and deal with your wife. This time, I can tell you that her tears were well warranted."

"How do you know?" Caleb asked.

"She came to Jon's while I was trying to talk some sense into him." Aryl hesitated. "She's sick, Caleb. She went to the doctor today, and she was crying because of what he told her." Caleb's face fell into sudden concern.

"What did he tell her?"

"It's not my place to say," Aryl insisted.

"Is it serious?" he asked as he put his coat on.

"I think it is."

"You gotta tell me what's going on," Caleb ordered. Aryl shook his head.

"I can't. I promised her I wouldn't."

Caleb hurried faster now, worried about Arianna and angry at himself for walking out in frustration the one time he shouldn't have.

"I had no idea she was sick, Aryl," Caleb said as they walked toward home.

"I know."

∞∞∞∞

*A*yl was shivering hard by the time they got back to the tenement, his face flushed from his spiking fever. Caleb ran past him to his own door, as Aryl knocked on Jonathan's to tell him they would have to finish their discussion another time.

"Aryl, you don't look well." He hadn't heard Claire walk up behind him. It was the first time she had spoken to him since their argument.

"I don't feel so well," he said. She put her arm around his waist and helped him upstairs.

"Come on, let's get you home."

"I have to tell Jon–"

"He'll figure it out," Claire insisted. She walked him straight to the bedroom and helped him into bed. "I think you're getting what Arianna has," she called while wringing out a cloth in the bathroom. She turned as he pushed past her and was extremely sick. When he was finished, she helped him back to bed and sat beside him, wiping his face.

"It's one week to Christmas," he said suddenly.

"Where'd that come from? That should be the last thing on your mind. You need to get some rest," she said.

"I have something to give you on Christmas, but you can't touch it. Not yet anyway," he said apologetically.

"Some of the best gifts are the ones you can't touch . . . like forgiveness." She pushed a few fallen curls away from his forehead.

"I was going to talk to you about that. Before I started feeling so sick."

"Then it can wait." She wiped his face again, noticing that he was very hot to the touch.

"No, it can't." He took her hand away from his face and held it. "I don't want this to ruin us like it's ruining Jon and Ava. I won't let it. I shouldn't have gotten so angry with you for something I was guilty of myself. It's hard to explain why it seems so different to me."

"I think I know," she said quietly.

"Do you? Do you have any idea how crazy it made me to think that just for those few minutes you weren't mine?" he asked.

"Yes and I felt the same way. You weren't entirely mine that night with Elyse, either."

"Do you have any idea how important you are to me?" he asked.

"No more important than you are to me. I never told you because I couldn't lose you, Aryl. It simply wasn't an option. And if that meant living every day with guilt and regret eating me alive, then it was worth it as long as I could have you forever," she explained.

"Exactly," he said with a relieved sigh. She saw his weak smile in the dim light, leaned to put her head on his chest, and listened to his heartbeat for a long time. "Forgive me?" he asked.

"Yes. Do you forgive me?"

"Yes," he said, placing one hand on her head and the other around her shoulders.

"I blame my parents, actually," she said after a long silence.

"Why?"

"Because they were so hard on you. They insisted that you make some vast fortune before you would be good enough to marry me. If they hadn't, we wouldn't have spent that time apart."

"What would we have done? If I hadn't left to make a life for us here," he asked curiously.

"Oh, I don't know. Maybe we would have borrowed one of your uncle's boats and sailed around the world. Just gone from port to port, working long enough to be able to get to the next exotic place."

"That would have been *wonderful*." He closed his eyes to envision the alternate reality and soon drifted off to sleep.

∞∞∞

"Are you sure?" he asked. Caleb sat on the side of the bed trying to process Arianna's words. She nodded, still hiding under the covers.

"What are we going to do, Caleb?" Her muffled voice was desperate. He didn't answer for a moment, still taken aback by the words 'I'm going to have a baby.'

"Dr. Westley is positive?" he asked. "This couldn't be a mistake?"

"No. He's sure." She sniffled, sat up, and pushed the covers off her head, her hair clinging to her face with static and her eyes sunken from dehydration. "What are we going to do?" she asked again.

"Well." He stopped to wonder if Aryl would be mad if he told her about the apartment building now. "It's going to be all right, Ahna. It'll be fine, I promise, we ha–" He saw panic take over her face and realized what he was saying and how he was saying it. "No, Ahna. Listen to me." He held her face in his hands and looked her in the eyes. "I'm not saying that everything is going to be fine like I did that day in October. Or like your father did. Do you understand me? I'm telling you it's going to be all right because I know that it is. I wasn't supposed to say anything until Christmas. But I think Aryl would understand under these circumstances." She waited for him to finish, not fully relaxing the panicked expression. "Aryl has a plan that is real, Ahna. It's viable. It's going to happen," he said excitedly.

"What's going to happen?" she asked cautiously.

"We're all three going in on a small apartment building," he began.

"How on earth can you possibly do that?" she almost yelled and felt panic welling up inside again. This didn't seem practical or possible to her. He let go of her face, grabbed both of her hands from her lap, and held them together tightly.

"It's all Aryl's doing. He met the owner of a building that is looking to sell on private contract. We take over the building, pay the mortgage, pay him a percentage of the rents and the rest is our profit. Aryl has it all worked out to save the profits, buy more small buildings and build it up from there."

"When is this supposed to happen?" she asked.

"The first of March. That's the tentative date set for us to move in."

"Move in! We get to leave this place?" she asked surprised.

"Yes. It's not a whole lot better," he warned. "But we can fix it up as nice as we want. It'll be ours. After paint, trim, and new windows, we can start saving for nice furniture and appliances. And the best part," he said and smiled wide. "There are some two bedroom apartments. We can take one of those and this little guy," he said as he pointed to her stomach, "can have a room of his own." She was at a complete loss for words and sat with wide, tear-filled eyes. "I told you," he said, squeezing her hands, his eyes convincing. "I told you it will be all right." He moved to lie beside her and pulled her close under his arm. She was quiet, relieved, and almost hopeful as she listened to Caleb talk for a long time of his plans for the new place. "We could have Claire paint the baby's room," he said suddenly, interrupting his own thoughts on building improvements. "She could paint a mural on every wall. Maybe she could paint a countryside scene, so he won't even know we live in the city!" Arianna giggled at that idea.

"Thank you, Caleb," she said with a sigh. He kissed her hair and squeezed her shoulder. "It might be, though, that *she* won't even know that we live in the city," she countered.

"We have plenty of time to work out the details," he assured. "By September, we'll have everything in order . . . for *him*," he teased.

"About that." She sat up on one elbow to look at him. "It won't be next fall," she said. He counted on his fingers and looked up confused.

"Well, it can't be too much later than that," he laughed. "Unless things have changed."

"Not later. Earlier. More like mid-June."

"What!" he exclaimed.

"According to Dr. Westley, it will be mid-June," she repeated.

"Oh, wow," he said soberly.

"There's still enough time, right? To get everything ready?" she asked, suddenly concerned.

"Yes, there is, I just thought I had a little more time. Wow. Six months."

*December 23rd 1929*

*Monday* didn't bring a letter from Maura but a visit from her instead. "You mind tellin' me what this is all about, Miss Ava?" she barked, holding up the letter as Ava opened the door. Ava threw her arms around Maura and started sobbing. "All right now, whatever it is this time, it'll be fine," she said, patting Ava's back. "C'mon, let's get inside before yer interferin' neighbor pokes her nose out her door an' I gotta handle her, too. I dint bring me flask with me, so I might not be so nice to her this time." She sat Ava on the couch, pulled a handkerchief out of her pocket, and handed it to her. "Now explain this letter to me."

"I want to come and live with you after Christmas," Ava cried. "I want to come now, but I won't ruin your family's holiday." She sniffled and snorted, with little gasps of breath.

"What on earth did he do this time?" Maura asked, exasperated. Ava went through the whole story of Jonathan's sleep talk leading to the revelation about his relationship with Elyse that was kept hidden from her and the question of infidelity during the solo trip. She finished her long-winded story with a whiny and frustrated, "And she looks *just like me*!" She fell on Maura's shoulder crying. Maura patted her back patiently.

"So, yer mad because he never told ye about her, even though he ended the arrangement when he met you?" Maura asked. Ava nodded against her shoulder. "An' yer worried something happened on the trip he took alone with . . ." She paused trying to remember her name.

"The *whore*!" Ava sobbed from her place on Maura's shoulder. Maura couldn't help but smirk.

"My, what language, Miss Ava. Now what did Mr. Jonathan say about the trip in question?"

"He admitted that she was waiting in his room the last night of the trip but says nothing happened."

"And why don't ye believe him?" Maura asked while pushing Ava off her shoulder to look her in the eyes. "I can't imagine Mr. Jonathan lyin' to ye, Miss Ava. I just don't think he has it in 'im."

"I don't believe him because he kept the relationship a secret. He hid it from me all this time."

"Hidin' and lyin' are two different things, love," Maura said. "Just when would've been a good time ta tell ye about his kept woman across the ocean? The first night he met you? Or the next night when he came to ask you to dinner? Maybe right before yer first kiss? Or right before he proposed? Or right after? The day before yer wedding? The day after? Then there's always yer one year anniversary. I can see that going over quite well with dessert."

"You always take his side!" Ava yelled and dropped her head down in Maura's lap, sobbing again.

"I'm not takin' sides, Miss Ava. I'm just tryin' to get ye to be honest with yerself. I don't think this has so much to do with ye not believing him as ye being mad at him," Maura assumed.

"I'm furious with him."

"But it's not all about this woman, is it?" Maura asked, patting her head. Ava thought about it for a moment and then shook her head in Maura's lap. "What else are ye mad at him for then?" Maura asked. Ava knew, but she couldn't quite put it into words and was quiet for a long time. "You think about that while I go make us some tea," Maura said and pushed Ava back up to a sitting position and busied herself in Ava's kitchen. Ava stared at the dark fireplace, and that was the first thing on her list.

"He sits and stares at this blasted fireplace for hours on end," she said. "And he doesn't even act like I exist. He hardly says two words to me anymore." She stood and started pacing the living room. "And believe me," she started with a huffing sarcastic tone, "I have no worries of ending up in Arianna's position." Maura had no idea what she was talking about but didn't interrupt her now that she was getting to the real core of her anger. "And he isn't looking for a way out. He doesn't talk about ways to rebuild our life. He doesn't have any hope. He just sits. And stares. And sleeps. He's an empty shell, and he's never once, the whole time since we've been here, taken how I feel about this nightmare into consideration! He isn't like Caleb who always sees the tiniest bit of good. Or Aryl who is always looking, always thinking." She was fully ranting now with flailing arms and a livid tone. Maura stood in the doorway of the kitchen, listening.

"He built a business from the ground up ten years ago from nothing. *Nothing*, Maura. He came here with a hundred dollars," she yelled through gritted teeth. "He fought his way to the top, and although I hadn't met him until after he made a name for himself, I've been told about the tenacity and determination that got him where he was. Where is all that now? When he needs it the most?" she asked, holding her arms out. "I've been to his town. I've met his parents. They aren't rich, and they don't put on airs. Jonathan acts like he was born with a silver spoon in his mouth, and now he has no idea how to live without money and assets. Happiness isn't possible without a large house, a Packard, parties and trips overseas," she finished exasperated. Maura came back to the couch with two cups of tea.

"He's not adjusting well to this new life then."

"Not at all. It doesn't even seem like he's trying."

"An' now that ye know what yer really angry about, what are you going to do?" she asked, handing Ava her tea and patting the seat cushion for Ava to sit by her.

"I have no idea," she said, sitting with slumped shoulders.

"Yes, ye do, love. Yer going to tell him the real reasons yer angry. So he knows it's not all about this woman."

"Whore," Ava corrected. Maura smiled.

"Whatever you want to call her, dear."

"Oh, I've got some other things to call her as well," Ava assured.

"But do ye believe him now, after getting to the root of why yer so angry, about that trip?" Maura asked.

"Yes," she sighed. "I do. But I still need to know that he doesn't see her every time he looks at me . . . and that he didn't feel sorry for me like he did for her."

"Then ask him those two questions and get that out o' the way. Take his answer ta heart and don't ye question it again. Ye'll only drive yerself mad. Then get on with the real problems. He may not even realize the extent to which he's fallen in spirit." Ava conceded to Maura's suggestion and resolved to talk to Jonathan as soon as she could do so without anger.

"What would I do without you, Maura?" she sighed, taking her hand. Maura dismissed the credit quickly.

"I will see ye on Christmas Eve at me house. I expect things ta be better between you and Mr. Jonathan, do ye understand me?" Maura reached out to hug Ava before standing to leave. "He'll come around, Miss Ava. Just give him time and be here for him 'til then. Right now's when he needs ye the most."

"That's so hard to do when it feels like he's pushing me away," Ava said with tears stinging her eyes again. Maura squeezed her tighter.

"I know, love."

∞∞∞∞

That evening after dinner, Ava sat away from Jonathan on the couch.

"I need to talk to you."

He grunted an impersonal acknowledgment and she was instantly irritated with his indifference. "It would be nice if I could steal your attention from the fire for a few minutes." He looked over at her with vacant, despondent eyes. "I need to talk to you first about . . . Elyse," she said. Just having to say her name set her into an even fouler mood. He exhaled heavily, dreading the conversation to come.

"Arianna said she looks like me. Is that true?" she asked pointedly.

"Yes, somewhat." His answer was barely audible.

"What does somewhat mean? Arianna said she looks just like me."

"I really don't want to have this discussion," he said, shifting his eyes back to the soft glow of the fireplace.

"Well, I do. I need to know."

"There are similarities and there are differences," he said after a long silence. "What does it matter, Ava?"

"It matters because I need to know that you don't see her every time you look at me." She couldn't help but snap at his listless tone.

"That's ridiculous," he scoffed. It wasn't the answer she needed to hear and, despite her efforts to stay calm through this, she grew angrier by the minute.

"Did you feel sorry for her the same way you felt sorry for me? Is that why you married me? Pity? Poor, orphaned, country girl lost and alone in the big city? Did it make you feel valiant to swoop in and save me from Victor the way you saved her from having to bed a thousand strangers?" He turned to her with harsh eyes.

"Who's putting this garbage in your head?" he snapped. Her anger boiled up and spilled over at his inability to reassure her.

"What's happened to you anyway?" she started, her anger getting the best of her and the conversation contorting into something she hadn't intended. "You just stare at that damned fire every evening, and you have completely given up, Jonathan! Not that you ever tried that hard in the first place! You're just this empty shell anymore. A shell that doesn't talk or feel or care."

"You have no idea how hard I've tried," he said, growing furious at her complete lack of understanding.

"Really? Well, I haven't seen it. From the minute we got here, I haven't seen it. You can't even answer my questions about your whore!"

"Stop calling her a whore," he growled, glaring at her. Ava stared at him, taken aback.

"I see. I wasn't sure until now, but–" Tears blurred her vision as she stared at him and her chin quivered. "You still love her," she realized aloud.

"No, Ava, I don't. That's not true," he said, unable to explain further. She waited, hoping he would clarify and set things right somehow. When it became clear that he wasn't going to do that, she stood. The conversation that should have put things going in the right direction had been a complete failure. She walked slowly to the bedroom, more scared and insecure than before, and closed the door softly.

As she cried herself to sleep, Jonathan found himself unable to leave the couch to go to her, which reaffirmed his decision as the only option. He looked forward to not feeling the heartbreak of being a disappointment and not feeling the guilt of being unable to reach out to her. His only relief was that she would be happy again one day.

∞∞∞∞

*J*onathan finally spoke to Ava during breakfast on Christmas Eve morning.

"They furloughed today."

"I assumed," she answered curtly.

"Did we give Christmas cards this year?" he asked unexpectedly, looking up as if they had forgotten something terribly important. Ava shook her head. "I'll go pick some up after breakfast."

"But Aryl said—"

"Yeah, I know, but a few cards aren't going to make a difference," he insisted. She waited for him to continue the conversation, hoping that he was using the Christmas cards as an opening to try to set things right before their evening with Maura. However, he wasn't. He merely set out to buy the last minute Christmas cards without another word.

He returned a while later and laid them on the table before shaking snow off his coat and hat. She picked them up to look them over, and he took them from her hands abruptly.

"I'll take care of it this year," he insisted and searched for a pen. He began to write cards to the handful of special people in their lives. He penned generic openings, greetings and closing signatures on all of them except one each for Aryl and Ava. Aryl's was simply a request and an apology with no explanations. He felt Aryl knew him well enough to know the reasons. While Ava made shortbread cookies and mashed potatoes to take to Maura's dinner, Jonathan sat at the table for a long time deciding on just the right words for Ava's card. He decided to keep it simple and tell her the one thing he knew she needed to know; the one thing that, for reasons he couldn't understand, he found impossible to say.

*Ava,*

*I have always loved you more than anything or anyone in the world.*

*Jon*

A few hours later as Ava readied to meet everyone at Aryl's for drinks before Maura's, Jonathan made a last minute excuse to stay behind, claiming he needed to shower, shave and look around for a missing bottle of brandy to take to Maura's. He handed her the Christmas cards with instructions to be sure Aryl received his.

"I'll see you at Maura's then?" she asked, looking him in the eyes for the first time in days.

"I'll see you later," he said, remaining expressionless. He kissed her cheek and turned, not wanting to watch her leave. When the door closed, he waited a few moments before he dragged a chair over to wedge it under the doorknob. He put Ava's card on her pillow and walked to the bathroom, rolling up his sleeves slowly. He pulled the straight razor out of his leather bag on the edge of the sink and stepped into the bathtub. Sitting down, he unfolded the straight razor and stared at it for a few moments. Then he closed his eyes and ran through his memories of Ava. He wanted his last thoughts to be of her.

∞∞∞∞

"Where's Jon?" Aryl asked, letting Ava in.

"He'll be along. He had to take care of a few things, said for us to head over to Maura's and he would meet us there," she said, her mood muted despite the pleasant atmosphere of Aryl and Claire's apartment. "He also said to give you this." She held out the Christmas card labeled 'Don't open until after midnight.' Aryl took it, slightly puzzled. Jonathan's attitude had improved this last week, but Aryl hadn't expected him to be in the frame of mind to give Christmas cards. Ava handed one to Caleb as well and held a few in reserve intended for Charles, Maura, and Sven.

Claire sat by Arianna, putting finishing touches on a long, last strand of garland. She had spent hours wiring together scrap tree branches that Aryl had brought home, tying in red bows that she had made from the ribbons of one of her dresses. She had draped a length of it over the fireplace mantel, the cracked living room window, and the doorway to the kitchen. She had set candles around, and Ava was amazed at how such small touches could improve the look of the place. The radio played Christmas carols in the background and the mood, despite their subdued celebration, was contented. A light snow fell outside, and Aryl had saved extra firewood for a roaring fire.

Arianna remained quiet; she had been for much of the last week. Caleb had been watching her closely, waiting for a complete breakdown, but it hadn't come. She remained calm and lost in her thoughts.

"Hot buttered rum, anyone?" Aryl asked, making good use of his last bottle of rum for the holidays. Caleb was the first to jump up.

"Right here." He held a colored, chipped mug out to Aryl, who led him a few steps away from the others, so they could talk privately. He talked as he poured.

"What do you make of Jon's sudden turnaround?" Aryl asked, holding up the card before tucking it into his back pocket.

"Maybe he's finally coming around." Caleb shrugged. "Dealing with what happened last fall, or it could be the Christmas season, or maybe he knows what we've been planning, so he's excited? He did come up on us a few times while we were talking things through."

"Maybe . . ." Aryl shrugged. "There's something else, though. I know getting jumped by those guys kind of messed him up, but you know what he asked me the other day?"

"What?" Caleb asked, sipping his drink.

"He asked me, if anything ever happened to him, would I take care of Ava. Like a sister, you know. Kinda caught me off guard. I mean, those guys did a number on him, but he was nowhere near dying."

Caleb looked at him with one eyebrow raised. "He asked me the same thing a couple days ago," he volunteered warily. "Made me promise that

I would and promise again that I wouldn't say anything about his asking."

Aryl leaned back on the counter with crossed arms, thinking.

"What time should we leave here in order to be on time? It's a bit of a walk, and Maura will skin us alive if we miss her son's choir performance," Claire called from across the room. Aryl barely heard her as he pulled out the Christmas card, turned it over slowly, and opened it. It wasn't a Christmas card, but a folded piece of paper; on it only two sentences.

'Don't let Ava come home after midnight mass. I'm sorry.'

"Keep everyone here," Aryl ordered, ran out the door and down the staircase to Jonathan's door.

∞∞∞

"Jon!" He yanked on the doorknob, which turned freely, but the door wouldn't budge. Aryl burst through the door; the chair blocking it broke into two pieces at the joint of the back and the seat. Jumping over it, Aryl checked the living room, then ducked his head into the bedroom, but saw no sign of Jonathan. He threw open the bathroom door, and his face went white with the scene laid out before him. He leaned on the door handle to steady himself.

Jonathan didn't look up, didn't even flinch when the bathroom door had slammed into the wall behind it.

"Put it down, Jon." It was all he could think of to say, his voice shaking slightly. Jonathan didn't acknowledge him, his eyes fixed on the straight razor pressed into his left wrist. "Jon, don't do this . . . give me the razor," Aryl said softly, taking a cautious step away from the threshold. Jonathan's set expression was that of an already dead man. His only response was to press the blade slightly harder into his wrist, causing the skin to puff up on each side of the blade and a small drop of blood appeared. Aryl's eyes darted frantically as he tried to think of anything he could say that would prevent Jonathan from pulling the blade sharply to the right.

"Go away, Aryl," Jonathan whispered, his eyes still fixed. Aryl took another small step forward.

"I'm not leaving, Jon. Now give me the razor." Aryl saw the muscles in Jonathan's right arm tense and his fingers gripped the handle of the blade until his knuckles turned white. Aryl's mind raced. "Jon!" he boomed, grabbing Jonathan's attention, although he didn't look up. "If you do this—" He paused briefly and tried to keep control of his voice. "If you do this, I swear to God Himself, I will take Ava and personally deliver her to Victor." Jon's dead eyes flickered.

"You promised you'd take care of her."

"If it were an *accident*, Jon. But if you do it yourself? Forget it. I can't deal with Ava grieving a husband who took his own life. Especially after watching you do it." He hesitated as Jon looked down at the blade and began to breathe deeper and harder.

"You already promised," he growled, eyes fixed on the task he had decided upon.

"I lied," Aryl said flatly. Jonathan shook his head tightly in denial.

"Caleb will do it," he whispered.

"Caleb's got his baby to worry about now. And it's just a matter of time before Claire comes to me with the same news. We have to take care of our own first, Jon." Jonathan was quiet for a moment before he looked up at Aryl. He unconsciously let some of the pressure off his wrist.

"You wouldn't do that to me, Aryl," he said pitifully.

"I could say the same thing to you."

Jonathan lowered his head, his face slowly fracturing into a thousand, painful pieces and started to shake. His grip was loose on the straight razor, and Aryl took two quick steps and grabbed it out from under his fingers. He let out a heavy sigh of relief, folded the razor, and put it in his pocket with a shaking hand. Jonathan covered his head with his arms as whimpers and grunts turned to loud, uneven sobs. His guttural cries were heartbreaking to Aryl as he collapsed on the bathroom floor. He bent his knees and held his own head.

He wasn't sure how much time had passed when he caught a glimpse of Caleb standing at the bathroom door, looking worried and confused. Aryl made a few motions and expressions that Caleb understood. He was to take the others and go on ahead without them. He turned to leave but looked back at Jonathan anxiously. Again, without words, Aryl told him it would be all right.

A long time passed before Jonathan's sobs started to quiet, and he wiped at his face, keeping his head down, not wanting Aryl to witness any more of his breakdown than he already had.

"Jesus Christ, Jon, it's Christmas Eve," Aryl finally said quietly. "You were really going to do this . . . on Christmas Eve?" he said in disbelief, staring at the side of Jonathan's head with betrayal on his face. Jonathan sniffled, cleared his throat, and wiped his face on his sleeve.

"I just can't do it anymore, Aryl."

"Yes, you can, Jon. You have to. Every day we all wake up and struggle to put one foot in front of the other with no promise that at the end of the day, life will be any better. But you get up anyway. You keep breathing and hold on to faith that somehow, someday things are going to change for the better. Probably when we least expect it."

"That's a problem, then," Jonathan said, with a ragged sigh, "because I don't have any faith that anything is going to change. I can't see how." He shrugged and slowly moved his head helplessly. "Every time I find the strength to stand up," he said through clenched teeth, "I get knocked back down again." He looked at Aryl, confounded. "I don't understand. But I can't get up again, Aryl, not when I know exactly what's going to happen. It's just a matter of time," he finished, leaning his head against the wall beside the tub. Aryl thought for a moment, poignantly, about his friend. He had always been the one in charge; the organized, fearless leader of the group. He had been powerful, successful, and confident. Now he sat hopeless in a bathtub ready to end it all.

"What about Ava? How the hell do you think this would affect her?" Aryl asked. Jonathan shrugged.

"She'd get over it. I'm not the man I used to be. She said so herself, I'm just a shell. You and Caleb would care for her until she met someone. She'd forget all about me."

"I don't think you've ever been more wrong about anything in your life," Aryl scoffed. "This would destroy her, Jon. She'd always blame herself, maybe even follow you." Jonathan's head turned toward Aryl, absorbing the possibility he'd never considered. Aryl fed into it. "I don't know if you've noticed, Jon, but she's been pretty low herself lately. She has no real family, barely clings to shreds of hope, all of which revolve around you. So, how long do you think it would be before she climbed into this bathtub herself?"

Jonathan's mouth was gaping slightly and his eyes fearful.

"She wouldn't," he whispered.

"What would stop her? What would she have to live for without you?" Jonathan couldn't think of anything to counter Aryl's prediction. His head fell back, and he stared at the ceiling in defeat.

"She's never going to believe me about Elyse. Or forgive me. She's still going to leave," he said, tearing up again.

"You have to make her believe you, Jon. And with enough devotion, she will forgive you, and she won't leave."

"You think she won't?" Jon asked meekly.

"Jon. It looks like you're going to have to get out of that bathtub and put one foot in front of the other just like the rest of us," Aryl announced with modest victory. Jonathan didn't move. "We'll help you, Jon."

Jonathan shook his head. "I've leaned on you two enough," he said, aware of how little he had contributed from the start.

"Nonsense. We're friends, Jon. Practically family." He paused looking for the right words. "I wouldn't have Claire if it weren't for you. You know her parents would have never allowed the marriage if it weren't for joining your firm."

"Sure," Jon said sarcastically. "And look what joining my firm got you."

"That's the point. It got me Claire. I don't care how it ended as long as it ended with her. And look at Caleb. You know as well as I do that if life had continued unaltered, Arianna would have gotten more and more out of control. She would have put off starting a family, probably indefinitely, so the parties could continue. Caleb would have only been able to put up with that for so long. I know it's only been a week since she's known, but there's a change in her, Jon. *A visible change.* And I have never seen Caleb this happy. Not happy like with money and power and security, not happy like when we would win over a key client. But deep down to his very soul happy." Jonathan shook his head in amazement.

"How the hell do you do that, Aryl?"

"Do what?" he asked as he stretched his legs to stand.

"I see destroyed lives, and you see a baby that otherwise wouldn't have been born. I curse this building when the heat goes out, and you pitch a tent in the living room with Claire and pretend you're camping . . . I just don't see things the way you do."

"You never started looking, Jon," Aryl said perceptively. "But for now, you don't have to. Right now, just keep breathing. That's all I'm asking." He reached a hand out to help pull him up from the bathtub and then stepped aside to let Jonathan move to the sink. He leaned on it for a moment, took a deep breath, and bent to wash his face. His left wrist was red and swollen along the line where the blade had pressed and he was sure it would scar. He washed a few drops of dried blood away. He felt guilt wash over him, like he had committed some horrendous felony.

"Please don't tell, Ava," he asked quietly, looking over but not meeting Aryl's eyes.

"I won't," Aryl promised. "Keep your sleeves down and no one will notice." Jon nodded numbly. "I'll be right back. There's something I want to show you." He slowly raised his head to face his reflection after Aryl left.

He didn't recognize the man who stared back at him.

Aryl returned a short time later with his coat and gloves. "Get your coat. We're going for a walk," Aryl announced.

A light snow fell as they briskly walked in silence.

∞∞∞∞

"Here it is," he announced. Aryl stopped suddenly and turned toward a dilapidated, brick building.

"Here what is?" Jon asked, confused. Aryl pointed to the building.

"A way out," he said, starting to brim with excitement. "Caleb and I have been working on this for a few weeks. We were going to wait to tell you until tomorrow, sort of a Christmas present. You don't have to do anything but say yes. We've already got everything worked out." Aryl was beaming now.

"Say yes to what?" Jon asked warily.

"The owner of this building needs to sell. He's too old to take care of it anymore."

"Doesn't look like he took care of it in the first place," Jonathan said, looking over the ragged building.

"Anyway," Aryl continued, "he offered to sell it to us on time. We assume the loan, and give him a kickback of ten percent of the total monthly rents, so that he maintains a small income. If he outright sells, with the value of real estate being so little, he'll owe money." Aryl was excited now and talking fast. "If we each take an apartment, that will leave nine to rent, plus the two ground floor shops once we get them fixed up. We live rent free, and after the mortgage is paid plus the kickback to the owner, we save the profit, plus what we make at the shipping yard. We save everything and do it again. There's got to be more deals out there like this, until we have enough rentals that we don't have to work at the yard anymore. It'll take time, but it can be done," he finished proudly.

"Renters," Jonathan said flatly. "We can't pay a mortgage without renters."

"There are already four long-term renters that have agreed to stay if we fix things up. And as for the rest, we steal them right out from under Victor. Caleb has already talked to several people in our building, and even if we didn't undercut Victor's prices, they agreed to move. But if we do cut rent even a few dollars, we'd have people lined up to save some money, and we'd always be full." Jonathan took a minute to roll all of this around in his mind.

"How sure of a deal is it?"

"Very sure. We have a tentative agreement to take over March first. We need the money down, plus money for repairs, and I won't lie, it's pretty bad. It'll be a lot of work. Other than that, we need you on board." Aryl waited for his reaction with baited breath. Jonathan started to feel a spark of life creep back into his chest. He didn't recognize it yet as hope.

"Have you told the girls yet?" Jonathan asked, looking over the broken down building.

"No. We didn't want to get their hopes up. We wanted to wait until we had you on board."

Jonathan suddenly felt a wave of relief that almost brought him to tears, as he realized this meant being out of Victor's building and having something of his own again.

"We'll tell them tomorrow," he told Aryl with a hint of strength in his voice. Aryl smiled wide.

"Okay, then. We'll do it."

∞∞∞∞

"Oh, Mr. Jonathan, Mr. Aryl, ye missed me Scottie, singin' like an angel in the choir!" They heard Maura's loud brogue from down the street. Having missed the children's mass and choir performance, Aryl and Jonathan walked to Maura's to wait on the stoop for everyone to return.

"I'm sorry we couldn't make it," Jonathan apologized quietly.

"Well, you must be freezin'. Come in and I'll make us all hot drinks before dinner," she said, making her way to the door. Ava was relieved to see Jonathan for reasons she didn't understand. She stood in front of him. He wouldn't make eye contact and she could see the red, swollen rims of his eyes and blotchy face.

"What's wrong?" she asked, standing closer to him. He avoided her eyes and tried to appear convincing with his lie.

"Well, I was shaving." Aryl eyed him cautiously. "And this jackass here scares the hell out of me. I got lather all over my face and in my eyes." He attempted a rough laugh and shoved his hands in his pockets.

"Sorry," Aryl said sheepishly. "And to make matters worse, when I was running from him, I tripped over your chair and it broke. I'll fix it, though," Aryl offered.

"You boys. I swear," Ava said, shaking her head. "But you didn't finish shaving," she mentioned.

"Jonathan has decided to grow a beard," Aryl interjected matter-of-factly, holding the razor in his pocket that would not be soon returned to its owner.

"Shall I be servin' drinks out in the street, or are ye goin' to join us inside?" Maura yelled from her door. Maura's home was one of only four apartments in a brick building that might have once been a single home, but it was warm and friendly. She introduced everyone, going around the room, pointing as she said the person's name. Between friends, cousins, uncles, aunts, nieces, and nephews, there were almost two dozen gathered in the small living room. The girls offered their help in the kitchen and filed in behind her. Maura pulled a turkey from the oven and smiled.

"Oh, it's beautiful!" Arianna exclaimed.

"Tis," Maura agreed and pulled her flask out of her sweater pocket. "To another perfect turkey!" She toasted with a swig and passed it around. Ava and Claire took a dainty sip but Arianna waved it away. Maura looked at her and her hand flew to Arianna's head. "Are ye feelin' poorly, Miss Arianna?"

"No, I feel fine."

"Well, what then? Tis not like ye to turn down a drink. If I'm rememberin' correctly, yer the one that *starts* the pourin'!"

"Well, it appears that I won't be doing any pouring for a while. At least six more months." Maura's eyes opened wide when she made the connection, and she grabbed Arianna in a tight hug.

"Oh, Miss Arianna! How wonderful! A wee babe! Does Mr. Caleb know yet?" she cried.

"Well, if he hadn't, he would now." Arianna smiled at her loud enthusiasm. "But yes, he knows." Maura reached under the sink and pulled out a large bottle.

"Been savin' this for a special occasion, and thar's nothing more special than celebratin' news of a new babe." She cradled the bottle and walked into the living room. "We have more cause to celebrate!" she called out, getting everyone's attention. "Miss Arianna and Mr. Caleb are expectin' their first wee bairn!" The whole room erupted in cheers and applause and even Jonathan couldn't help but smile. Arianna moved from the kitchen to Caleb's side, somewhat embarrassed. He put an arm around her while everyone around the room, even those who didn't know them, took turns toasting and soon the large bottle was empty.

Arianna looked truly happy, although slightly self-conscious, and Ava couldn't help but be happy for her, feeling that this is the way the news should have been announced. Not with tears and anxious concern for the future. Caleb grinned proudly as if he had accomplished some fantastic feat.

Jonathan stood next to Ava against the wall of the small room by the window, which had been opened to relieve the stifling buildup of body heat. Claire and Aryl found a spot in the corner near the fireplace to watch the loud and jovial crowd as cousins teased cousins, aunts scolded nephews and nieces, and later the oldest family members told embarrassing stories of the younger generation.

Maura produced a modest but beautiful dinner that filled the entire table. She announced it was time to eat, said a quick blessing and proclaimed that the oldest and the youngest be allowed to the table first. They gathered to form a line and then found whatever spot they could to settle and eat. The room filled with chatter, the clinking of dishes and glasses, eruptions of laughter and a few more toasts in Caleb and Arianna's honor. Maura made it a point to walk by Arianna several times with a bowl or platter to heap more food on her plate, ignoring her protests that she couldn't eat another bite.

"Maura, that was wonderful," Aryl told her as she took his empty plate. He sat down on the floor, and Claire sat beside him, taking his hand in her lap.

"Are you okay?" she asked. He rolled his head over to look at her.

"I'm just so tired, Claire," he said, not sure he could make it to midnight. She slipped her arm around his shoulders and pulled him over to rest his head in her lap. She put her hands on his head, playing with the unruly curls and massaging his head lightly until he was quite tempted to fall asleep.

Jonathan remained quiet against the far wall, standing beside Ava, grateful to be removed from the center of conversation and commotion. He was exhausted as well and on the verge of passing out himself, if not for the lingering excitement of Aryl's news and wanting to talk to Ava to explain himself, beg her forgiveness, answer all her questions and convince her of how he really felt. The bustling room provided no privacy; he would have to wait until they got home.

Maura announced that her husband, Ian, would read The Christmas Story while she prepared dessert and everyone gradually settled down. Ian sat on a thatched stool by the fireplace, balancing Scottie on one knee and the Bible on the other. He had a wonderful voice for storytelling, and, even though everyone in the room had heard it many times, the way he spoke held everyone entranced. Maura passed out plates of pie, stepping over legs and bodies in the crowded living room.

Toward the end of the story, Maura gathered empty plates from guests and began clearing the table of empty, serving dishes. By the time Ian finished the story, Scottie was asleep on Ian's chest. Maura lifted him carefully and took him to bed. Three other relatives with sleeping toddlers of their own followed her to settle them for the night.

When she returned, Maura stood in front of the fireplace to make an announcement. "As most of ye know, me young niece, Tarin, arrived from Ireland last month. She will be stayin' here to watch the babes while we go to mass, but 'fore we leave, she is goin' to honor us with singin' one o' our favorite songs," she said and smiled with pride, stepped aside and Tarin took her place in front of the fireplace. Ian picked up his guitar, and began playing the soft and gentle opening to Ave Maria.

When the first words of the song were heard, everyone was impressed by the powerful and majestic voice that erupted from the tiny girl. It completely filled the room, drowning out the city's noises of barking dogs and wailing sirens. When Jonathan closed his eyes, he felt that he could easily have been sitting in the balcony of a fine opera house. It was the consensus of the room that an opera house was exactly where this voice belonged. Maura watched both Tarin and Ian with pride. She glanced around the room at her guests, who were completely spellbound at the performance. She watched Jonathan reach blindly, his head leaned back with eyes closed, for Ava's hand and held it tightly, once found. Caleb stood behind Arianna with arms locked around her waist and his head next to hers, and he had the same look of awe at Tarin's angelic voice. Arianna was intently watching the youngest guest, a baby of only a few weeks, sleeping in the arms of Maura's cousin. Glancing to her right, Maura saw Claire looking down adoringly at Aryl, who was lying on his side with his head still resting in her lap. His eyes slowly closed as he drifted off to Claire's touch and Tarin's hypnotic voice. Maura watched the couple; Claire serene and contented to watch over Aryl as he slept with an expression so peaceful that it almost moved Maura to tears.

Tarin sung the crescendo that caused the few dry eyes to blink with welling tears and others to swallow hard against the rising lump in their throats. She finished the song with a long note and her audience was completely silent. Maura cleared her throat and wiped a tear, stepping toward Tarin.

"That was absolutely amazin', Tarin," she said. The other guests fell in with compliments and admiration and shortly after, Maura announced it was time to leave. The room burst into a flurry of activity as everyone began to gather coats and hats in preparation for the chilly walk. Aryl stirred, yawning and stretching, and Caleb held Arianna's coat for her. Only Jonathan remained motionless against the wall, still holding Ava's hand with closed eyes. Ava stared at their entangled hands, ignoring everything else around them.

Maura gathered Jonathan and Ava's coats and made her way over, saying his name gently to get his attention. He opened his eyes and as he reached for his coat, his sleeve rose just enough for Maura to catch a glimpse of the angry, red score on his wrist, and her eyes flickered from it to Jonathan's red-rimmed eyes and quickly away again. She was the last to leave, after seeing all of her guests out, and she stretched up on tiptoe to take the straw cross off the nail where it hung above the door.

∞∞∞

On the street, they were a large, loud bunch with Jonathan, Ava, and a very sleepy Aryl lagging behind. Jonathan took Ava's arm and laced it through his without explanation. Claire walked ahead with Arianna toward the front of the group, holding her arm and talking about the wall murals Caleb had already asked her to paint. Maura came up between Jonathan and Ava, removed Ava's arm from Jonathan's and replaced it with her own.

"Ye go chat with yer girlfriends about babies and knittin' and such. I'm goin' to steal yer husband for a bit," she ordered. Ava took Aryl's arm and did as Maura told; hurrying ahead with relief that everything would be all right once Maura set Jonathan straight.

"I've been meanin' to talk to ye, Mr. Jonathan," Maura started, clinging to his arm with both of hers.

"Maura, just Jonathan. No mister is needed any-"

"I'll call ye whatever I damned well please, and I'll thank ye to leave me alone about it," she barked lovingly. Now that authority was established in the conversation, she continued. "I never told ye the story of the night of the big wind, did I, Mr. Jonathan?"

"I don't believe so, Maura," he said, patting her arm.

"A long time ago, when me grandmother was a small girl, there was a great storm that swept over Ireland. It came down so swiftly and with such force that there was no time to prepare, not that any amount of preparations could have done much given the ferocity o' the storm. Hundreds of lives were lost, homes destroyed, fields flooded and stores of food for livestock were ruined. Folks said that the storm was so enormous that it almost covered all o' Ireland. Me grandmother woke in the middle of the night ta howling winds that shook her family's small cottage. Her mother gathered all the children in the kitchen by the warmth of the stove while her Da' went out to secure the animals. He barely made it back to the cottage with the wind and drivin' rain such as they were. As the wind became more violent, it ripped off large pieces of the thatched roof and rain flooded the fields and the floor. Me grandmother and her family believed that the end of the world was at hand. They ran from the cottage when the storm took the rest of the roof. They tied the smaller children together with a rope to help get them safely ta the barn where they remained the rest o' the night. The storm made such a deafening roar that it sounded as if the whole world was bein' torn apart. They huddled together in the barn, cryin' with fear, sayin' prayers and waitin' for the end to come." She paused with a far off gaze and Jonathan jostled her arm.

"What happened after that?" he asked.

"Well, obviously, it was not the end of the world. The storm passed, and the next day, the sun shone bright. They lost everything, although most of the barn survived, and they had a few animals left that hadn't run from the thunderous noise. Their cottage was scattered in bits as far as the eye could see. Only two things survived the night. Everything else was gone."

Jonathan was quiet, all too able to relate to the feeling of devastating loss.

"Is that when your family came here? After losing everything?" he asked.

"Nay. They remained. They buried their dead, rebuilt their homes, bartered skills and services to help one another along. They cared for their fields and reset the boundary stones. Families crammed together under one roof as life was slowly restored. It was a great deal o' tiresome work. And it wasn't without tears and sorrow, mind ye. But in time, babes were born under newly thatched roofs, couples were wed in green meadows of summer and crops were harvested in fields of gold the following fall.

"My people survived the greatest storm in over three hundred years and came out stronger and more resilient for it. And when hard times come now to my family, here and back home, when compared to the devastation and heartache of that day, it truly puts it into perspective for us." She stopped walking and turned to face Jonathan, still holding his arm. *"Tis not the end of the world*, Mr. Jonathan. Babes will be born, you're to be an uncle. Homes and marriages can be rebuilt if you work hard enough. And love, hope, and faith are things you can harvest all year long. If yer in the right mind to." Her words were gentle and sincere, and Jonathan fought the sting in his eyes and the tightness in his throat, realizing the intention of Maura's story. He cleared his throat, looked away from her, unable to speak for a moment, and then asked her a detail she omitted from her story.

"You said two things survived that storm. What were they?" he asked, still looking away.

"The stone foundation of the cottage, and wedged between, near where the door once hung, a small cross made by her mother." She pulled the straw cross out of her pocket and showed it to Jonathan. "That cross remained in our family, passed down and protected as a great treasure for generations. One year my mother carefully unwove the fragile and delicate fibers, which were by then over seventy years old and beginning to show wear. She wove new crosses for each of her children and within each, one of the original fibers was woven in from the cross that survived that storm. And this," she said, holding it out to Jonathan, "is one of the crosses she made. She gave it to me the year before I left Ireland with Ian, and I want you to have it, Mr. Jonathan."

Jonathan looked at her, stunned. "Maura, I can't take this. This is far too special–"

"I insist and I won't hear another word about it. I have the story in my heart, Mr. Jonathan. And, I know the lesson within the story. It needs to be with someone who needs it. And that someone is you." He opened his mouth to protest again, but she quickly interceded. "If ye don't take it, Mr. Jonathan, I shall have me mother on the next boat from Ireland to argue with ye herself, and I promise ye I am a mild-mannered angel compared to *that* woman."

Jonathan smiled, finding it hard to believe someone could be more brazen and stubborn than Maura.

"You are an angel, Maura," he said, holding the cross in the palm of his hand for a moment before tucking it in his pocket. "I'll take good care of it, I promise."

"I know ye will," she said, patting his cheek.

Ava and Ian waited for them on the front steps of St. Brigid's Church. Maura gave Ava a pat on the arm and a wink as she passed her. Jonathan and Ava followed, unsure of what to do once inside. The church was packed with only a few seats open in the pews toward the back. Maura found a small open space a few rows behind Claire and Aryl and asked people to make room for the four of them. Jonathan looked around nervously, having no idea what to expect. He watched Aryl and Claire. He had a clear view of Aryl's face and could see the fatigue in it for the first time. Dark circles around his eyes and lines on his forehead that weren't there a few months ago. His eyes weary as Claire put an arm around him and pulled his head down on her shoulder. He marveled all the way down to his core at how Aryl had been holding the hope for the entire group for all this time. He had been looking for a way out since the first day and had been doing it alone. Always looking for an opportunity and, more importantly, believing he would fine one. He had just as much determination to escape this life as Jonathan had guilt for putting them in it. He admired Aryl now more than any one other man he knew. And Jonathan knew that if it weren't for him, he would not be sitting here now.

Jonathan was broken from his fixation on Aryl as there was a collective shuffling and everyone rose. Jonathan rose with them, although he didn't know why he was doing so, and noticed the sharp smell of the incense as the priest made his way down the center aisle. He caught sight of Caleb, a few rows up and to the right, and his eyes stayed on him as everyone sat.

Caleb sat with his arm around Arianna and she leaned in close, whispering to him. She turned suddenly toward Jonathan, as if feeling his eyes on them, and smiled. *Aryl's right,* he thought. Caleb turned, gave him a hearty grin and waved, and Jonathan, like Aryl, couldn't remember a time when he had seen Caleb so happy. He didn't even look tired. Instead, he looked like a boy in line for a ride at a carnival. *But that's Caleb,* he thought with affection.

When everyone stood again, Jonathan's eyes were pulled from Caleb and Arianna. He looked down at Ava and felt overwhelming guilt swallow him whole; guilt for almost leaving her, almost abandoning her to fend for herself in this world, for asking Aryl and Caleb to look after her in his place. Only six, short hours had passed since he sat in the bathtub, certain of his choice. But now, as he sat in this beautiful cathedral, he was astounded that he could have ever considered it. He had almost left her. He let her believe he cared for another more than her. He let her cry, feel scared and alone when his own pain paralyzed him. He looked around unsure as everyone moved to kneel in front of each pew. He did as the others did and bent his head in prayer. He didn't know who or what he was apologizing to for almost taking his own life, but he did so sincerely. And while he possessed only a shred of faith that was engulfed by doubt, he asked for strength and promised in return to wake up every morning and try.

Simply try.

∞∞∞∞

When they returned home, it was after two-thirty in the morning. Jonathan was reminded of what he had almost done when he walked into his apartment and saw the broken chair in pieces scattered about the living room. He looked at the splintered wood for a moment and then turned back toward the door.

"I'll be right back. I have to, ah…do something," he told Ava awkwardly.

∞∞∞∞

"Aryl, wait!" he called. Aryl poked his head out.

"What?"

"I, uh, just wanted to say thanks. For earlier, you know." He shifted uncomfortably and shoved his hands in his pockets. "I also want you to know that I'm going to start pulling my weight. You and Caleb have carried it for too long. I never meant to be a burden, I just-" He shrugged, lacking the words to explain himself.

"You weren't a burden, Jon. You would have done it for me."

"I would," he said, staring at Aryl's shoes.

"How's it with Ava?" Aryl asked with concern.

"Well." He rubbed the back of his neck and grimaced. "Not great. But I'm gonna work on that," he said, not exactly sure how he would begin the process of mending their relationship.

"That's good to hear. You do that," Aryl said and smiled.

"Listen, one more thing, can I get my razor back? I'm gonna look like a lumberjack by tomorrow," he smirked with bloodshot eyes, rubbing his stubble. Aryl looked wary and his smile partly dropped.

"Not just yet. Besides, the rugged look suits you. I was thinkin' about trying it myself," he said, grinned and stepped back into his door. "Night, Jon."

"Night." Jonathan turned to leave, too tired to convince Aryl to return his razor and understanding Aryl's hesitation.

∞∞∞

When he returned, Ava was walking out of the bedroom with the Christmas card he had left on her pillow. She looked at him, her expression mingled confusion and hopefulness.

"Thank you for the card," she said a little too quickly as he closed the door.

"You're welcome," he said and taking a deep breath, still standing by the door, grateful that his goodbye note had become the proverbial icebreaker. "I mean it. I really do." His eyes were sincere and Ava felt overwhelming gratitude to Maura for whatever it was she said or did to make Jonathan soften toward her.

"I love you, too," she said quietly, looking down at the card in her hands. "More than anything."

"I know tomorrow we're supposed to go to Aryl's, but after that, I really want to talk to you. I feel like I'm going to drop I'm so tired, or I would talk to you tonight," he said apologetically.

"No, it's okay. I'm tired, too. We'll talk tomorrow." She turned to the room, read over the card once more, and put it in her small, wooden box of precious things before changing for bed.

∞∞∞

"I think everyone knows why we're here," Aryl started. "And actually, I'll be amazed if everyone doesn't already know," he said, unsure that his friends were able to keep the secret. "I've told Jon and Caleb, they've been helping me work out the details."

"I told Arianna last week," Caleb confessed. "I didn't want her to worry about the baby coming home to this place."

"That's understandable," Aryl said, knowing that probably had kept her from a complete breakdown. "I have to admit, I told Claire last week as well," Aryl added and turned to Jonathan for his confession. Ava looked around in disbelief.

"Am I always the last one to know anything around here!" she cried, frustrated.

"Jon, why don't you tell her?" Aryl suggested with a grin.

"Well, I have to give Aryl the credit." He turned to face Ava while he spoke. "He found this and worked out the initial details. I just found out last night, actually. We're moving," he said bluntly. "We're all going in on a small building, a little better than this one, but, with a lot of hard work, it'll be a lot better than this one."

Ava's eyes lit up as she gasped. "Really? How? When?"

Jonathan smiled at her excitement. "Yes. We're signing a private agreement with the owner, and we move in on March first. We plan on taking the profit, adding it to everything we can manage to save, and do that repeatedly until we don't have to work at the yard anymore and can manage buildings full-time. It'll take a long time, but we might be able to one day have our own house again."

Ava stared at him speechless, not so much at his words but at the genuine smile that touched his eyes, and the spark of life that had returned to those eyes. She laughed a hard laugh and threw her arms around him. She pressed her face into his neck, fighting tears that had nothing to do with the building. Grateful to be close to him again, smell his familiar scent, see life in his eyes, and feel his arms tight around her, the building didn't matter. *This was her home.*

Jonathan kept his head low to her shoulder, his eyes closed. Aryl watched them for a moment, turned to Caleb and they both exchanged a look of relief. Jonathan didn't let go of her as Aryl started talking again.

"I thought we could eat first. Claire is warming up the leftovers that Maura sent last night, and then we could take a walk and go see the place," he offered.

"Sounds good," Jonathan said and pulled away but kept one arm around Ava's shoulders, needing her close. Her head was low as she wiped a tear; her head on his shoulder and her arm around him.

Arianna followed Claire to the kitchen while Caleb and Aryl talked of improvements, repairs, and ideas for the new place. Jonathan distantly overheard their discussion – 'white paint' - 'flower boxes' - 'brickwork to the stoop' - words that slipped in between his thoughts that all revolved around Ava.

Claire called everyone to dinner, and they gathered around the table. The mood by far the most jovial it had ever been at one of their gatherings. Ava sat as close as possible to Jonathan, who sat on her right side so he could keep an arm around her and eat with his right hand.

"There's good news, good news and bad news," Caleb announced as they started passing food around the table. "What'll it be?"

"Good!" everyone said in unison.

"All right. The first good news is that I have that last bottle of wine I promised for Christmas dinner," he said as he put it on the table.

"What's the second good news?" Jonathan asked.

"Arianna isn't drinking, so there's more for us," Caleb said, grinning and Aryl cheered as he poured everyone a glass.

"Very funny, now what's the bad news?" Arianna asked.

"Well, since we haven't done an actual cash count, we need to do that tonight. But I know that we have spent a lot of what little cash we brought here. Regardless, we have to save. And I mean save like mad. We need to take our expenses down to only what's necessary to stay alive," Caleb said as he glanced toward a very uncomfortable looking Arianna. "We need to save well over the down payment. We need money for repairs and renovations and furniture. We have two months to make this happen. And I really think we can do it if we try."

"I do, too," Aryl added. "It'll be hard, but it's only two months. And however miserable it is, it'll feel great to leave this place and move into our own."

"Truer words were never spoken," Jonathan said, raising his glass and tapping it to Aryl's.

"Oh, I almost forgot!" Claire jumped up to tune the radio to carols. "It is Christmas, after all."

∞∞∞

"Here it is," Aryl announced. The others stood looking slightly surprised at the old, brick building. It was considerably better than anyone expected. At least they could see the potential in it. Aryl pulled a ring of keys from of his pocket.

"The owner lent me these, so I could show everyone today," he said, holding open the door as they filed in. The first vacant apartment they looked at was a two bedroom and was in the best shape of all the units. "We discussed it, and we think Caleb and Arianna should take this one."

There was a living room only marginally larger than their current place, a kitchen with a small nook for a dining table and a bathroom in between the two bedrooms. The fireplace was in better condition. Although the walls were filthy, there were very few holes to repair. Caleb took Arianna's hand and led her into the smaller bedroom.

"We can put a cradle here and a rocking chair there," he said. She glanced around the room trying to see what Caleb was seeing. "We'll make it really nice, Ahna. Claire can paint all of the walls and even the ceiling. And I've already written my mother. I've asked her to send the cradle she used for me when I was born," Caleb said. That pulled her from her quiet apprehension.

"That'll be really nice, Caleb. It'll brighten the room up so much," she said, looking around. They looked at every vacant apartment after that, and Caleb took more notes on repairs needed.

"Which one do you think we should take?" Jonathan asked Ava during a brief moment alone.

"I'm not sure. Maybe the one next door to Arianna?" she suggested.

"Why that one? It's in bad shape."

"I know. We can fix it up, and that way I'll be close to help her when she has the baby."

"That's really thoughtful. I guess we can always take one of the larger units later," he said and smiled.

"Well, we don't need two bedrooms," she said flatly.

"Not yet," he said, taking her hand and leading her downstairs to look at the apartment next to Arianna's again.

Claire had chosen the apartment across from Arianna and each couple spent some time in their future home, taking notes and making plans for improvements.

∞∞∞∞

It was nearly dark when they began walking home; they were happy, chattering and joking as they walked through the frozen snow. Along the way, Aryl and Caleb started pitching snowballs at each other, and Claire and Arianna quickly crossed the street for safe territory. Aryl jogged ahead to hide behind a garbage can and made more snowballs. He jumped out and threw one as hard as he could toward Caleb, who ducked, and the snowball hit Jonathan square in the face. Caleb laughed hard and Aryl waited for Jonathan's reaction. Jonathan wiped snow from his eyes, shook his head, looked up at Aryl menacingly and warned Ava.

"You might want to join the girls across the street." It was each man for himself as they hurled snowballs through the air at each other and burst into laughter when they hit their targets. Caleb and Jonathan teamed up and launched a barrage of snowballs at Aryl, who went scrambling down the street, looking for cover. Claire, Ava and Arianna stood across the street, watching them take turns ganging up on each other and shook their heads.

"They never did fully grow up, did they?" Arianna asked.

"Nope," Claire answered.

∞∞∞∞

"You should get in a hot shower," Ava told Jonathan as she helped him out of his coat, which was dripping from the snowball fight.

"No. I want to talk to you. But I will change clothes," he said, shivering. She went to put tea water on while he changed clothes and leaned on the sink, wondering what he wanted to talk to her about specifically. She had been so happy to see him with life and hope in his eyes and to be close to him that she forgot about the details of their fight; forgot about Elyse, forgot about how defensive he was of her, forgot how he never really denied still loving her. She forgot that he never did explain what was said between them on that trip he took alone, when he was supposed to have ended the relationship much earlier. She started growing anxious and angry as she recalled all the things that remained unresolved. He saw the uneasy look on her face as he came into the kitchen.

"What's wrong?" he asked cautiously. She looked away, turning toward the stove.

"I was just thinking," she said.

"About what?"

"The last few weeks."

"That explains the troubled look," he said, stepping behind her and putting a tentative hand on her waist. "I hope looking at the building today and knowing that it's just a matter of time before we're out of here helped a little. I know it's just a small step, but it's a step toward getting our life back. A small piece of it, anyway." She turned around, slightly irritated.

"It has nothing to do with this building or that building. I was thinking about the last few weeks with you," she said, looking up at him.

"Oh," he said, suddenly scared that he misinterpreted her body language, that maybe she was putting on an act for the sake of the others and was still planning on going to Maura's. "Well, that's part of what I wanted to talk about," he said. She poured two steaming cups of tea and handed him his, then walked around him to the living room and sat on the couch. He sat beside her and took a deep breath. "I know I've been . . . out of sorts. I've had a really hard time with everything that happened. Losing everything and all–"

"But you didn't lose *everything*, Jon," she said quietly, not looking up at him.

"I know that now. And I'm sorry it took me so long to realize it," he said, taking one of her hands. "Aryl and Maura have really helped me . . . ." He wasn't sure how to finish the sentence. "Before I go into all that, I know you have a lot of questions you want answered. Things I couldn't explain before but I'm ready to explain now." She sat back and thought about what she wanted to know most of all.

"Do you still love her?" she asked, not looking up at him.

"No. I don't," he said with conviction. "I didn't really ever. It's complicated," he said with a sigh.

"Then why were you so upset when I called her a . . . ." She couldn't bear for him to be defensive of Elyse again, so she left it at that.

"I probably better just start at the beginning and tell you the whole story. It'll make more sense that way, all right?" She nodded, slightly apprehensive about hearing every detail about this woman. "It started at one of my client's parties three years before I met you. She was new to the business of entertaining and stayed in the background a lot, not mingling and flirting like the others. When I was returning from the restroom that evening, I overheard someone scolding her for not being friendlier with the guests. I saw her standing at the bar, looking very uncomfortable, so I went over and started talking to her about pointless things just so it looked like she was being sociable.

"Later that evening, I did take her back to my room, but we just continued to talk. She told me about her family and that her lifestyle was a last resort. Her parents were old and broken and barely keeping a roof over their heads. She had managed to get through her first four parties without having to, you know, personally entertain anyone. For the remainder of the trip, she stayed near me at all the gatherings, and the other men left her alone. She was really grateful for that."

"Forgive me if I don't pat you on the back for your kindness," Ava said snidely. Jonathan let the comment slide and continued with his story.

"Nothing happened on that trip. But before I left, I did visit the brothel and spoke with the owner. I made it appear as if I wanted to reserve Elyse for my visits only and offered compensation. They accepted the arrangement, and she was really appreciative."

"And you made this arrangement before anything happened with her?" she asked cynically.

"Yes. I never really planned on anything happening. I just wanted to help her," he said uncomfortably.

"But it did. Eventually."

"I spent a lot of my free time with her on subsequent trips. Nothing happened until the third trip, almost a year after I had first met her. I did care about her, Ava. But I didn't love her. I may have thought I did at the time, but I didn't. I liked having someone to spend time with on my trips. She didn't have to live a sordid life, and I wasn't alone when I went overseas." He paused to let her absorb what he had revealed so far. "A year or so later, I met Ruth and we started seeing each other regularly. I took Ruth with us the next trip, and Elyse was not happy to see me with someone else. I guess I looked at our arrangement as more of a humanitarian deal than she did. I went to see her that night and tried to talk to her, but she was furious that I had brought Ruth and demanded that I send her home. I told her that was ridiculous, and I would still try to spend some time with her before I left.

"The next night, I told Ruth I had a meeting and went to another hotel where Elyse was waiting. She was acting strange, demanding that I marry her and take her back to America. I told her I couldn't do that, and she said that if I didn't, then she wanted our arrangement to end. I told her I would end it, if that's what she really wanted, and that's when she went hysterical again, crying, demanding and I walked out."

"That's when she went to Aryl looking for sympathy," Ava assumed.

"You know about that, too," he said with an uncomfortable laugh and ran his fingers through his hair.

"We girls tend to talk."

"Apparently. I did see her one last time that trip. I spent most of the night talking to her after she explained her erratic behavior. She told me that on my previous trip, two months earlier, she had found out she was pregnant."

Ava froze, staring at him with wide eyes and his words echoed in her mind. He could see her shock and gave her a minute before going on. She stood up clumsily, spilling her teacup on the floor where it shattered, opening her mouth to say something but couldn't find the words.

"Ava, listen to me. Let me finish, please. Just let me finish," he pleaded. "Please sit back down." She continued to stare at him. "Hear me out. Please." He sighed heavily and forged on. "She told me that's why I had to marry her, why I had to take her with me. I told her I couldn't do that, but I promised her that I would see to it that she and the baby had everything they needed. She told me if I didn't marry her then she would get rid of the baby. I begged her not to do that. But she laid down her ultimatum." He stood and walked over to Ava. She was still visibly shaken. "I didn't love her. I couldn't marry her. So, she went to the doctor and took care of it," he said solemnly. "I ended the agreement with the brothel and she refused to see me after that. She was still angry at me for what she felt like she had to do. The next time I saw her was after I married you when I went alone. She came to my room and tried talking to me, but I stopped her cold. I told her I was married and everything we had was in the past. She screamed and yelled, threw a few things at me and then left. I never spoke to her again after that."

"So, why is it that you were so defensive of her? If you didn't love her and didn't want to marry her?" Ava asked.

"Because that's not who she was. I spent a lot of time getting to know her, and she was a good person. But I still feel very guilty over what she had to do."

"But that was her choice, Jonathan."

"I know. But I still feel responsible. So, that's the whole story," he said, letting her mull it over and waiting for her questions. She didn't want to talk of Elyse anymore and went on to the next concern on her list.

"Ruth told me something that day in the park when I confronted her," she started. "She told me that you felt sorry for me, and that's why you married me. Is that true?" she asked.

"No. Absolutely not," he said. He took her hand, led her to the couch, and pulled her down onto his lap. "I never felt sorry for you. I fell completely in love with you. By the time I took you home late that night, not only were Ruth and Elyse the farthest people from my mind, but I knew you were the one. I knew I would marry you," he said sincerely with tranquility in his voice.

She leaned over and rested her head on his shoulder, relaxing somewhat. He sighed with relief and locked his arms around her.

"But you still dream about her," she said with lingering insecurity.

"These last few weeks I spent a lot of time thinking about the past. Most of it was too painful to revisit, so I thought a lot about Paris and the fun I had there. Not so much about Elyse," he added quickly. "But me and Caleb and Aryl. It was sort of my escape, thinking about those times," he explained. "I spent so much time in those memories, some of which were combined with guilt. That's actually what that dream was about that night. I wasn't dreaming about what you think. I was begging her not to get rid of the baby again."

"But if she kept it, you'd always be linked to her. And if you didn't love her–"

"I know. I just felt that it wasn't the baby's fault. And as shallow as this may be, if it had come to light after I met you, I most likely wouldn't have felt so strongly about her keeping it. That probably makes me a horrible person." He put his head down on hers and waited for the next question.

"No, it doesn't," she assured, although she loathed herself for a moment, being glad he would have chosen her over Elyse and their unborn baby.

"I'll tell you anything else you want to know, Ava," he said after a long stillness. She shook her head against his chest.

"No, that's enough for tonight," she said, feeling there had indeed been sufficient explanation for her to feel confident of her place in his heart again, and she would sleep soundly.

Ava slept through Jonathan's alarm the next morning and he quietly dressed for work, kissing her on the forehead before leaving.

∞∞∞∞

*I*nsistent pounding on the door woke her, and she stumbled to the door, wrapping herself in her robe. She smiled when she looked through the drilled hole and saw Maura's dark, auburn hair piled high on her head, still in her uniform and looking rather impatient. Ava opened the door and hugged her before she could fully step inside.

"Thank you, Maura. Whatever you said, whatever you did, thank you so much," Ava said, squeezing her tight.

"I dint do a thing, Miss Ava. 'Cept lose half a day's wages to come help ye bring yer things to me house. Yer still movin' in with me, are ye not?" she asked, breaking Ava's hold on her neck. Her face was stern but her eyes smiled, already knowing. Ava closed the door and turned to Maura, smiling.

"No, Maura. I won't be leaving, after all."

"Well, imagine that. You seemed pretty intent on leavin' last week. Twas it some Christmas miracle that changed your mind perhaps?" she teased.

"Something like that. It was whatever you said to him on the way to the church, Maura. It completely changed his attitude and outlook, and last night he was so sweet, he was more himself and he explained–"

"Hold on, Miss Ava," she said, waving her hand to hush her. "First of all, I don't believe I had much to do with it a'tall. Tis my belief that it was what happened before and after my talking that brought about the change."

"No, Maura–"

"I'm not finished," she interrupted. "Lord Almighty, yer manners, morals and schedule have gone to hell without me around to look after ye! Now I want ye to tell me all about it, but first, go get yourself dressed proper and wash yer face. You look like you just crawled out of bed what with the linen lines all over your face, and it's almost noon!" she scolded.

Ava touched her face self-consciously and admitted she had, in fact, just woken up.

"Go. I'll put on some coffee."

Ava huffed her breath impatiently, wanting to tell her all about the talk with Jonathan, the whole story about Elyse and thank her a thousand times more. She went to dress quickly, washed her face and ran a brush through her hair and fairly ran back out to find Maura sitting at the table with two mugs.

"How did you make that so fast?" Ava asked, stunned at the fresh, steaming coffee waiting for her.

"Irish magic," she said flatly. "Now sit down and tell me everythin'. I know yer dying to," she said with joyful eyes and Ava began her long and animated narrative, including details about the new building at the end. "Well, Miss Ava, I am truly glad for ye. I was beginnin' to worry about the two of ye," she said, shaking her head. "But I won't be takin' any credit, so stop thankin' me. Now I need ta go see yer friend, Miss Arianna." She lifted a bag from the floor that Ava hadn't noticed her bring in. "Point me in the right direction, would ye, darlin'?" Ava saw Maura out, telling her Arianna's apartment number and hugged her twice more, making her promise to come back again soon.

A moment later, Arianna opened her door and Maura held out the tapestry bag. "I dropped by to bring ye some things, Miss Arianna." Arianna welcomed her inside and invited her to sit, curious as to what was in the bag.

∞∞∞

"Hey, Aryl, are we getting together for New Year's Eve?" Caleb asked, tearing into his sandwich. The three ate lunch outside, standing in between a stack of boxes and the building to block the icy wind.

"I'm not sure. I'm pretty sure there's work the next day, at least, I hope they don't furlough it," he said, slightly worried. He looked around at the men who broke for lunch, and their numbers seemed to be dwindling.

"Well, we always spend New Year's Eve together," Caleb reminded him. "It's no big deal to lose a little sleep, is it?"

"Let's do it at my place," Jonathan offered.

"Yeah?" Aryl asked, pleasantly surprised.

"Sure. Why not?" He shrugged. "It won't be a big ordeal, but we can have a few drinks, listen to the radio."

"Are there any more drinks to be had?" Aryl asked. He doubted any of them had anything left of the supply they brought.

"I have a full bottle of brandy at home," Jonathan said and smiled. "I guess I hadn't felt like celebrating much these last few months."

"You know what we could do?" Caleb asked excitedly. "We could have a Charleston dance-off, and we could come up with a prize for the winning couple."

"Well, what prize do you want because you and Arianna always win," Aryl said sarcastically. "I stopped competing with you guys a long time ago."

"Who would judge?" Jonathan asked, liking the idea even knowing he would lose.

"Oh, I don't know. Maybe Shannon and Patrick would want to come over, too," Caleb suggested. "Or Ian and Maura."

"I don't know, I only have the one bottle of brandy and if Maura comes?" Jonathan teased.

"It's about time to get back, fellas. We can talk more about this on the way home," Aryl said, tucking the cloth that had wrapped his sandwich in his back pocket. "And don't forget," he reminded, "we still need to get together to do an official cash count. And we need to agree on a place to hide it. I'm not so sure opening a bank account is the best idea at this point."

"Neither do I," Jonathan added. "But we could get a safe deposit box. And we could put it in one of the girl's names."

"Good idea," Aryl said, pointing at him. "Would you mind looking into that? Hopefully it won't cost too much."

"Well, it may cost a little, but what's it worth to protect what we've saved and what we want to do?" Jonathan debated.

"He's got a point." Caleb turned to Aryl. "We need to start protecting this now."

"Okay. It's agreed then. And you'll take care of that, Jon?" Aryl asked.

"Sure," Jon said, content to have something to do toward the venture.

They headed back to their separate work areas just as a burst of freezing rain fell, lasting only long enough to pelt their faces and necks painfully and soak their work coats.

∞∞∞

"I brought you some baby items, Miss Arianna. A few things from when Scottie was a babe, and after I told me friends and family the happy news at the party, they all sent something as well." Maura situated herself on Arianna's couch and put the bag between them.

"That was very thoughtful of you, Maura," Arianna said as she watched Maura empty the bag. She laid out two quilted blankets and several cotton swaddling cloths, a half-dozen sleeping gowns, a pair of blue, handmade, knit booties with a matching cap, and a dozen cloth diapers that, despite their thickness, had obviously served their purpose for several babies in their time. Maura added to the top of the pile two diaper pins.

"It's not much, but it's a start," she said confidently. "I've put the word out and I expect to be bringin' more things over the next few months. And I know it's borderin' tackless to do, I should be asked, after all, but I was wonderin' if it'd be all right if I gave yer baby shower?"

"I would love that, Maura," she said, moved by her thoughtfulness. Arianna smiled at her appreciatively. It hadn't crossed her mind that she would even have a shower under the circumstances nor had she begun to think about collecting needed things for an infant. Arianna sat, staring at the pile on the couch apprehensively. Maura stood and buttoned her coat.

"I best be leavin', but I'll be in touch. Ye take care of yerself, Miss Arianna," she said, smiled and reached to hug her.

"Thank you, Maura. This is just so sweet of you."

"'Tis nothin'. I don't mind a'tall," she said.

Arianna closed the door behind her, walked back to the couch, and stared for a long time at the pile. Despite all her gratitude for Maura's generosity, she couldn't help but feel sad looking at the pile of used baby clothes. She had never spent any appreciable amount of time thinking about having a baby, but she was sure that if she had, she wouldn't have imagined welcoming it into the world with so pitiful little to offer it. Her eyes misted in spite of her efforts not to think about it, and she felt irritated having promised herself that Caleb wouldn't come home to tears yet again. She left the pile of clothes where Maura set them and went to the kitchen to start dinner.

∞∞∞

"*Damn*, it's cold today," Caleb said, shivering as he turned up the collar of his coat and pulled his hat down lower. It didn't provide much relief; he was soaked through to his shirt from the brief but heavy rain shower after lunch.

A few blocks from home, something caught his attention out of the corner of his eye, and he stopped the others. He stepped a few feet into an alley where transients stood around a metal can, warming their hands by the fire inside.

"Hey, how's it goin'?" Caleb nodded to one of the transients, who grudgingly moved over to let Caleb hold his hands over the glowing drum. Jonathan and Aryl eyed the scruffy men warily.

"C'mon, Caleb. Let's get going," Jonathan said, cold and hungry himself, wanting to see Ava and very uncertain about intruding into the group uninvited.

"Just give me a minute, Jon, my fingers are numb," Caleb said, shivering.

"All right," Jonathan replied, his eyes flickering over to the destitute souls who lived in this alley. They met his gaze straight on, and he looked away uncomfortably. He wished Caleb would hurry. After all, they were close to home, a place Jonathan was suddenly grateful to have to go to after spending a few minutes standing near the alternative. He stepped up to the fire next to Caleb, hoping to hurry him along and saw his hands, swollen and red with cold.

"My gloves got wet earlier," Caleb briefly explained. Jon pulled his off.

"Here. Use mine."

"No, you need those." Caleb pushed them away.

"My pockets are dry. I'll be fine. We're close to home," he insisted.

Caleb pulled them on, and the three started for home again.

∞∞∞∞

"*What's* all this?" Caleb asked, looking at the pile of baby things. He hunched down next to the fire, still trying to get warm. The hot shower had stopped the shaking, but hadn't relieved the cold he felt clear to his bones.

"Those are things Maura brought by today. Baby things," Arianna said with uneasiness.

"Really? Well, that was nice of her." He moved the blankets aside and held up one of the gowns. "It's so tiny. Have you looked at these?" he asked, amused at the miniature outfits.

"Just when she was taking them out of the bag," she called from the kitchen. "Do me a favor and put it all in the box in the closet, would you?"

He put them away and sat down to dinner.

"What are you smiling at?" she asked, sounding slightly annoyed from across the table.

"You know, not touching the clothes won't make you any less pregnant," he chuckled, seeing right through her apprehension.

"Well, I know that," she snapped. "I just didn't have time to put it away is all."

He was still grinning as he tried to cut the meat on his plate. The table shook while he sawed at the tough chunk. Finally he stabbed at it with his fork and tried gnawing off a bite.

"Sorry," she said with a huff. Arianna sat back and crossed her arms.

"No, it's okay. The potatoes look good."

"I'm still learning," she reminded him, insulted by the strained faces he was making as he struggled to chew.

"I know. It'll get better," he reassured and swallowed the lump of charred meat. "It's tricky to get cheap beef tender."

She glared at him. "It's pork."

*December 30<sup>th</sup> 1929*

The following Monday, Arianna went downstairs and knocked on Shannon's door. She opened it with a smile and invited Arianna in.

"What's the occasion, Arianna?"

"Well, Shannon, several weeks ago you offered to help teach us things that we never had to do until we came here. Ava and Claire have caught on pretty well, but I was wondering if you would help me. I promise to pay attention this time."

"Why, I'd love to. What is it that yer havin' a hard time with?"

"Well, laundry, cleaning in general, cooking, making bread . . . ."

Shannon suppressed a laugh as Arianna tried to think of anything else she was incompetent at.

"Why don't we just start at the beginning?" Shannon suggested. "I'm gettin' ready to start some bread and then some laundry. You can help me a bit, then we'll go up to yer place, and I'll help you a bit. You'll get the hang of it, don't worry."

Arianna smiled gratefully and turned to the bedroom when she heard a baby's cry. "That's Roan, up from his nap. I'll just go get him and then make us some tea."

She emerged a moment later with a tiny bundle and laid him on the couch to change his diaper.

"How old is it?" Arianna asked over Roan's wailing.

"He's three months now," she replied as she quickly changed him out of the wet diaper and rolled it up. "Would you do me a favor and put this out on the fire escape? There's a bucket, just drop it in."

Arianna hesitated, took it between her finger and thumb, and ran it over to the window. "That's a lot of stink for something so small," she commented as she tossed it out into the bucket.

Roan settled down, and Arianna watched Shannon as she slipped off the cotton sleeper and slipped another clean, dry one on with hardly any effort.

"Can I see it?" Arianna asked, sitting down on the couch by the baby's head.

"See what?"

"The . . . your . . . it," Arianna stammered, pointing to the baby.

"His name is Roan, and yes, you can see him."

She swaddled him quickly and scooped him up. Holding him out to Arianna, she could tell she had no idea how to hold a baby. She positioned her arms and then put Roan in them.

"I guess I better practice this, too," Arianna said aloud to herself.

"Are you expectin'?" Shannon asked in a neutral tone, knowing if she was, it would be a bittersweet event. It always was in neighborhoods like this.

"June."

"Well, feel free to come down here and practice to your heart's content. I might take advantage, though, and sneak a nap while you're here learnin'," she teased. She went to put on tea and left Arianna on the couch holding Roan. He started fussing and flailing, and Arianna looked over at Shannon with panic.

"Just rock him a bit," Shannon called out from the kitchen.

Arianna started a rocking, bouncing combination, and he quieted quickly. "Hey, that worked!" she called out to Shannon and looked back down at Roan. His mouth was drawn in a tight line; his face was turning blood red.

After a moment, it became obvious that he wasn't breathing, and Arianna screamed for Shannon. She flew over just in time for the foul odor to reach Arianna's nose.

"What *is* that?" she yelled.

"He was just finishin' his poo."

Arianna coughed and gagged, shoving the baby back toward Shannon.

"He wet on me!" she cried.

"They tend to do that. Don't worry, I'll get you a cloth for your dress. It don't seem to stink so bad when it's yer own."

"I think I've had enough baby practice for one day. Can we move on to bread now, please?"

∞∞∞

"*I* invited everyone over for New Year's Eve," Jonathan told Ava over dinner.

"You did?"

"We're always together for New Year's, so why should this year be any different?"

"Well, okay. I just didn't think you would feel like having a party is all."

"It won't be a huge deal, but we'll all be together. Caleb wants to have a Charleston contest," he said and grinned.

"Oh, no," Ava moaned. "They always win! What's the point?"

"I know. But it'll be a good time."

"I guess I can make something," she offered.

"How about those fried potato things Shannon made for dinner?"

"Sure," she said, surprised he even remembered.

"This weekend we should walk down and look at different shades of paint for the new place. We can't take any of this stuff with us, not that I would want to, except the mattress. That's coming with us. But we'll need to look at buying some more furniture," he said with a hint of excitement.

"That sounds like fun," she said and smiled.

"We'll window shop away the months of January and February. It'll make it go faster and give us something to look forward to," he suggested.

Over the last several days, things had slowly gotten back to what Ava considered normal. Jonathan smiled more and when they sat on the couch after dinner, they talked about many things; he had spent very little time staring silently at the fire.

"Where are we?" he asked unexpectedly, nodding at the calendar.

"Next week," she answered casually. Inside, she was ecstatic that he was wondering. It was cruel in her opinion that their reconciliation happened so far from the safe week.

"Think we can make it?" he taunted.

She looked up to see the teasing eyes and devious smile that she hadn't seen in months, and her heart fluttered lightly in her chest.

"I'm beginning to wonder," she said, breaking away from his sultry stare.

"It wouldn't be the worst thing in the world to happen, would it?"

"Would what?" she asked, concentrating on her food.

"A baby."

"Whoa! Hold on." She looked up at him, taken aback. "What on earth are you talking about, Jon?"

"I'm just saying that, if it were to happen, it wouldn't be the worst thing, that's all."

"Jon," she said seriously. "We can't. You know that."

"I'm just worried that Caleb's going to get a decent head start on us, and then his kid will grow up thinking he's the ringleader of the next generation." He smirked.

"Oh. And that's coming from the ringleader of the current one," Ava chided.

"I'm not the ringleader," he denied with a smile. "I'm just the oldest. They looked up to me when we were kids."

"You're the oldest by six months. And they still look up to you."

"I don't know about that, but nice try on changing the subject."

"I didn't change anything. You know we can't take any risks right now, Jon."

"Caleb and Arianna are managing. It would work out for us, too. Especially with the new building."

She answered him by shaking her head with a stern look.

"Well, I didn't want to have to resort to this." He leaned back in his chair and crossed his arms.

"Resort to what?" she asked suspiciously.

"Seduction," he replied nonchalantly and she laughed aloud.

"Tempting as that would be, sir, the reward is not worth the risk."

"I'll take that as a wager," he said, grinned and ran his eyes over what he could see of her above the table.

"Don't even think about it, Jon. This is so unfair." She was visibly flustered now. "I don't want to talk about it anymore."

"Why not?" he said and grinned sinfully.

"We're going to talk about something else," she said firmly.

"Okay. What shall we talk about? Your choice."

"I think I'd like yellow paint in the kitchen," she said, after thinking about it for a moment. "And maybe we can use part-wallpaper and part-paint in the living room."

"Okay. We can do that. What color do you want to paint the bedroom?" he asked with raised eyebrows.

"Jon, I said we weren't going to talk about it anymore."

"I'm not talking about it! I am talking about paint. You, however, are obviously thinking of something else."

"No. I am not!" she insisted.

"Okay, love. Whatever you say. Listen, I have to run up to Aryl's. We need to do an official cash count and fine tune a budget. I shouldn't be too long. Do you want to come along?"

"No. I think I'll stay here." She was entirely frustrated and needed to put a little distance between them.

"Suit yourself," he said as he walked around the table. "Can I have a kiss goodbye?" he asked.

"That depends," she said indignantly.

"On what," he asked with a laugh.

"On whether you're going to play fair," she said, crossing her legs and arms before looking up at him.

"Ava, I promise . . ." He leaned over, lingering a fraction of an inch from her lips. "I have no intentions of playing fair," he whispered and gave a light peck on her lips.

∞∞∞

Aryl answered the door on the third knock, and when he did, Jonathan looked him up and down, amused. His shirt was unbuttoned, his belt hanging open and his hair a mess.

"I need to cancel that meeting, Jon, can we do it tomorrow night?" he asked slightly out of breath.

"Sure. Why would you even plan a meeting if it's your week?"

"That's the thing. It's not my week," Aryl whispered.

"Oh, great. Not you, too. Now my kid's gonna be the youngest," he said, exasperated. "He's gonna get picked on like Caleb."

"No, no kid, not yet anyway."

Jonathan looked at him, confused. Aryl looked back when Claire called for him. "I'll be there in a minute," he called and stepped into the hall, pulling the door behind him.

"Arianna loaned Claire her book," Aryl said with a huge smile.

"You mean the *book*?"

"Yes, *the* book from Paris. So, I gotta go," he said, ducking back into his apartment.

"Hold on." Jonathan grabbed his shirt. "You have to help me out," he said insistently. "Have Claire give the book to Ava the next time we get together for cards."

"All right. But I'm going to let you in on a little secret. They knew about this stuff all along," Aryl said, grinning.

"Then why didn't they ever say anything? Why have we all been suffering?"

"Oh, all that prim, proper society-hooey. According to Claire, who would kill me if she knew I was telling you this, decent women pretend to not know of such things and would never suggest them." He rolled his eyes.

"I'm beginning to see why Arianna loved Paris so much," Jon said.

"And why Caleb is rarely in a bad mood," Aryl added with a smirk.

"Okay. The girls can get together over here while we have our card game. I'll let Ava pretend like this is all new and keep up her proper appearances," Jonathan said, already scheming.

"Okay. I really gotta go." Aryl slammed the door before Jonathan could say anything else.

∞∞∞

"Well, that was fast," Ava said as Jonathan walked through the door.

"Aryl couldn't meet tonight. Something came up," he said and grinned. "We're going to meet tomorrow night instead."

"Tomorrow night is New Year's Eve," she reminded him.

"That's right. Well, I guess we'll have the meeting here."

"Would you like some tea?" she called from the kitchen.

"Yes, please." He picked out a book and even though he had read it a half-dozen times, started it again.

She sat down on the other end of the couch with a magazine that the women had bought together a few weeks ago and shared.

"How many times have you read that magazine?" he asked, eyeing her over the top of his book.

"Five. How many times have you read that book?"

"Six."

"Aren't you tired of it?" she asked.

"Sort of. Are you?"

"Yes," she huffed.

"Well, we should definitely try to get you something else to read besides that old magazine," he said and grinned behind his book.

### *January 1st 1930*

"Good afternoon, Mr. Drayton, and Happy New Year. Please come in." Victor took his coat off and folded it over his arm before sitting. "How can I help you today, sir?"

"I'd like to review the insurance policies for my properties. And possibly adjust the coverage."

"Certainly, sir."

He opened a cabinet and found Victor's file. "Here we are. Now which properties were you interested in reviewing?"

Victor answered him by holding out his hand for the file. The agent handed it over hesitantly.

"Is there something I can help you find, Mr. Drayton?"

"No, I'm perfectly capable," he said, flipping through the pages until he found the one he was looking for. "Here it is." Victor held out the paper. "I'm concerned about this property. I'd like to increase the coverage."

"Well, we can certainly do that for you. Do you have any particular concerns?"

"Yes. Fire. A few tenants there are careless with their fireplaces," he explained with a smile.

"I see. We can increase the policy to cover loss of the building due to fire."

"What if there was only partial damage?" Victor proposed.

"Well." The agent eyed him suspiciously now. "We would compensate according to the extent of the damage and the estimate to repair."

"Very well. I'd like to increase that protection as much as possible."

"Certainly, sir. I do have to inform you that there is a sixty-day grace period for policy changes of this nature. Just a preventative measure to protect against arson, you understand. Especially in times like these."

"Of course. I understand completely," he said and smiled, hiding his disappointment well.

"Then I will be happy to make these changes for you and have the updated policy sent to your house by courier."

Victor held his frustration until safely inside his car.

"Everything work out, sir?" his driver asked as he pulled into traffic.

"No. Not yet," he snapped.

∞∞∞∞

One week into January, just after dinner, the building lost heat again and with subzero temperatures outside, it didn't take long for Jonathan to notice. He checked the thermostat as he pulled on a second sweater, and they watched it fall for over an hour. When it registered forty degrees, they were full on shivering, and he got an idea.

"Tack a blanket at the kitchen and close the bedroom door," he told Ava. "I'll be right back."

"Where are you going?"

"To get the others."

Once everyone was inside, they put towels at the windows and base of the door and added a heap of wood to the fire until it was burning intensely.

"Good idea, Jon," Aryl said, smiling. "I would have just pitched another tent and suffered smoke inhalation again. But we wouldn't have had enough wood to last the night by ourselves, that's for sure."

They made pallets across the length of the living room floor, and snuggled under piles of blankets, fully clothed in layers and still shivering. The only light came from the bright, glowing fireplace. Jonathan kept the fire roaring, and the room slowly warmed to a livable temperature.

"We haven't had a camp out in a long time," Caleb said from under the blankets.

Jonathan couldn't help but laugh. "Yeah, about twenty years. I think we were ten the last time we went camping."

"Hey, remember when we rowed across the way and camped on Thacher Island?" Aryl asked.

"No," Jonathan said.

"I remember, but you weren't there for that one, Jon." Caleb said. "And that's probably good because we got in so much trouble when we came home on Sunday."

"I remember the trouble," Jonathan said, poking his head out from under the blankets. "That was one trip when I was grateful to have to work for my old man."

"How'd you get in trouble?" Arianna asked.

"Well, we told our parents we were going to go camping on the beach. We were what–twelve, thirteen? There was one spot we always camped at as kids but this time, we decided to borrow a boat and row over to Thacher Island to camp there. Only we didn't tell anyone."

Caleb continued, "Aryl's mom hiked down the beach to our usual spot just before dark to bring us some food and couldn't find us. His dad found his boat was missing, and they had the whole town looking for us. We sort of forgot to ask him if we could borrow it."

"Since he would have said *hell no*," Aryl said. "All weekend, they figured we took the boat and got into trouble out on the water. They had search parties out for us and everything. Thought something really bad happened."

"I remember that part. I was helping in the search for you two. Had me scared to death," Jonathan added, remembering the panic as he helped search for his missing friends that weekend, fearing the worst.

"Well, Sunday afternoon, we row home unaware of what had been going on and found the whole damn town down at the dock, all over the beach, and out in boats," Caleb finished.

"I think your dad started beating you before you were even out of the boat," Aryl said.

"Yeah. Some welcome home that was."

"Well, if it makes you feel better, I got whooped, too," Aryl said. "Just not as bad."

"That was the last camping trip we ever took as kids," Caleb explained.

"Why weren't you with them?" Ava asked Jonathan.

"I had to work."

"Work? You were twelve."

"Yeah, but as far as my dad was concerned, I couldn't start learning early enough."

"How old were you when you started working for him?"

"Eight. By fifteen, I was doing the work of an accountant and learning business taxation on the side," Jonathan said quietly and leaning on one elbow, pulled the covers up higher around Ava, tucking them in around her back and shoulder as she moved onto her side to face him.

"But you were still a child. Why did he push you so hard? I never got that impression from him when we went to visit."

"Because when we went to visit, I was a successful man. I had surpassed even his wildest expectations for wealth and accomplishment."

He was whispering now, the community story having moved to private conversations. He lay back down but turned his head to look at her. "He was proud of me and of himself. He figured pushing me so hard from an early age had paid off."

"Did it?" Ava asked, wondering if Jonathan was grateful for the early motivation or resentful of it.

"I don't know. It's hard to say. Part of me thinks I would have ended up the same, and the other part thinks I would have gone to college and then stayed in Rockport. Started my own business like my father. But then I wouldn't have met you. So, that alternate reality is unacceptable," he whispered, looking back at her.

The resolution in his voice and the sincerity of his eyes made Ava warm and content, despite the apartment's chill.

*January 9th 1930*

Thursday evening, Arianna stood at the sink, peeling potatoes and hating every one she put into the pot of boiling water. *When this is over, when things are better, I never want to see another potato again.* She then remembered the fish in the oven and pulled it out, only slightly burned, and set it next to the sad, little, crooked loaf of brown bread and went back to the potatoes.

Caleb came through the door with his usual chipper tone.

"I'm home, Ahna," he called. She turned and her smile was mostly from relief that she had help now. He glanced over at the saggy rope in front of the fireplace, with clothes thrown over it in careless clumps and the small puddles of water under each on the floor. "You've done a lot around here today," he complimented.

Secretly, he used the same tactic with Arianna that he'd used with a stubborn dog he'd had as a teenager. He would praise and reward the scruffy mongrel for the tiniest bit of obedience or effort, and just like with the old dog, he was beginning to see progress with Arianna.

"Dinner's going to be late," she huffed. "I think I did it out of order again." She glanced at the over cooked fish and the still-hard potatoes.

"That's fine," he said, grinning as he walked toward her.

"What?" Her eyes narrowed at his wily smile.

"I just realized something on the way home from work today. Can't believe I didn't think of it before."

"What's that?" She turned back to the sink.

He closed in behind her, wrapped his arms around her, and placed his hands over the now obvious bulge of her stomach.

"We don't have to worry about getting pregnant anymore," he whispered in her ear. Before she could answer, he gasped.

"What was that?" he asked soberly.

"You felt that, too?" she whispered.

"Uh-huh. Was that . . . him?"

"I think so."

Another flutter and Arianna's eyes grew wide. They both stood statuesque, waiting for another kick. It happened and Arianna laughed a hard, quick laugh and turned to Caleb, who was ghost white with a startled expression.

"I guess that's a good sign, right?" she asked.

He didn't answer, his eyes just flickering from her face down to her stomach and back.

"What's wrong, Caleb?"

"Nothing. I guess that is a good sign. You better go see that midwife soon." His voice was quiet and monotone. He shoved a hand through his hair. "You said dinner would be a while?"

"Yes," she answered, still staring down at her stomach waiting for another bump.

"Okay, then, I'll be right back." He walked calmly to the door, closing it softly behind him and then tore down the hallway, nearly tripping over his own feet and banged on Jonathan's door.

He answered it with a smile that faded slightly when he saw Caleb, visibly shaken; leaning on the doorway with one arm and holding his stomach with the other.

"It's moving," he said in a deep voice.

Jonathan looked him over. He was pale and sweating with a slight tremor.

"Did you eat something bad?" he asked.

"No." Caleb shook his head. "The baby," he whispered.

"She felt it move? Well, that's great . . . What's wrong, Caleb? That's a good thing," Jonathan reminded him. Caleb had a very serious and dazed look on his face.

"Nothing's wrong with it, it's just–"

"It's just that it's real now," Jonathan assumed. Jonathan knew Caleb better than he knew himself. On more than one occasion, he had witnessed Caleb's somewhat innocent perception of things throw him for a loop once the reality of a situation truly hit him. Like with the tenements.

"Caleb. It's going to be fine, okay? We have the building to look forward to, and there's still plenty of time to get everything you guys are going to need. We're all going to pitch in."

Ava stood at the stove, eavesdropping with a smile. She loved hearing Jonathan in a better mood; to hear him reassuring Caleb was even more wonderful to hear.

"I don't know, Jon, maybe this wasn't such a good idea?"

"Well, there's nothing you can do about it now. Besides work your tail off to get ready for that kid. Go home. Eat dinner. Spend some time with Arianna. You'll feel better about this in the morning, I promise. Cards tomorrow night, right?"

Caleb mechanically walked back down the hall, his mind buzzing with worries.

Jonathan closed the door, smiling again. "Well, I can't say I didn't see that coming. He'll be fine, though," he said aloud. "You might want to go see Arianna tomorrow," he told Ava.

"Why? What's going on?" she asked, pretending she hadn't heard every word.

"She felt the baby move, and Caleb's a little overwhelmed with the reality of it, I think," he said and grinned.

She put a plate in front of him with a heap of diced potatoes with pepper gravy and a side of beets.

"Well, this is interesting," he said.

"More importantly, it's cheap."

Their meals had gotten progressively smaller, meatless and starch laden over the last few weeks.

"Whose turn is it to start tonight?" she asked.

"Yours."

They had, for lack of entertainment or fresh reading material, sat together each night after dinner and took turns asking each other questions for an hour or so. One question led to another, and the conversation always took interesting turns.

"What's on your mind?" he asked.

"Your childhood. I was thinking back to the story Caleb told when we all slept here the other night. I was thinking that there's a lot about your childhood that I don't know about."

"There's not a lot to talk about really. Just a normal childhood," he said, shrugging it off.

He preferred the questions and conversations that bordered racy topics and caused repetitive blushing on her part.

"What was your favorite thing to do as a child?" she asked, beginning the questioning early.

He thought about it for a moment before he answered. "Probably exploring with Aryl. He always discovered neat places and met interesting people. I learned a lot of my people skills from him. It just came naturally. Everybody in and around town knew him."

"What about Caleb? What did you learn from him?"

"How to birth a calf. Messy and unpleasant stuff. Made me glad to go into business. One Saturday, I walked over to his place to continue work on the tree house we were building, but he had to tend to a calf that was being born. The mommy cow—"

"The mommy cow?" Ava interrupted, laughing.

"Well, yeah, I don't know what you call it, but she was having a hard time, and it was taking forever. So, I stayed with Caleb that day, and it was finally born by dusk. I remember that Caleb, even though he was a kid, was so serious and concerned about that cow."

"Like how he's concerned about the baby moving?"

Jonathan almost choked on his dinner, laughing. "I hadn't thought of that, but yeah, it was that same pallid, anxious face he had tonight that he had back then." He dropped his head and laughed even harder as he recalled another memory from that day. "And you should have seen his face when it was born. He was so proud that you'd have thought he had fathered the damned thing himself!" he howled.

Ava laughed and it crossed her mind that she couldn't remember being happier. Regardless of dismal surroundings, less than appetizing food, sirens and babies wailing in the background, Jonathan was laughing, his gorgeous, blue eyes were shining, and it was easy to forget about the rest when the most important thing in the world to her was right again.

A knock at the door settled Jonathan's hysterics, and he tossed his napkin on the table as he rose to answer it.

"It's probably the proud papa again," he snickered.

Ava let out a quiet "Moo . . ." and he snorted, suppressing a laugh as he swung open the door, but in one fluid movement began to close it again.

"Jonathan, wait!" Ava recognized Ruth's voice and was up out of her chair.

"It's about Victor," she quickly spit out just before the door was about to be slammed in her face. Jonathan paused, the door open only an inch. He looked back at Ava, as she pushed past him and pulled the door open.

"What do *you* want?" Ava growled.

"I came here to warn you," Ruth said, ignoring Ava's presence.

"Warn us about what?" Jonathan asked.

"About Victor. He's planning something–some type of revenge. I don't know what yet, I haven't been able to find out. But it's serious, Jon. He hasn't been right in the head since he was attacked that night, and he is positive you had something to do with it. He's been acting funny for weeks. He's hardly working, he's been drinking a lot and goes off on tirades about you. And sometimes you, Ava," she said, looking at her for the first time. "He knows about the other times I came here," she said grimly. "He was paying his driver to report my every move to him."

"If you know he's going to find out, then why would you come back?" Jonathan asked.

"I'm supposed to be playing bridge with friends. I took the trolley. They'll keep my secret."

Ava looked nervously away from Ruth toward Jonathan. He had a heavily worried look about him, and all traces of happiness in his eyes and smile were now gone. That caused Ava to panic much more than news of Victor plotting revenge. He could plot and plan all he wanted, but she couldn't let Jonathan go back to that dark, distant place she had just gotten him back from.

"Thank you for taking the time to warn us," Ava said, turning to Ruth again and reached for the handle to close the door.

"I came to warn Jonathan," she said coldly, looking her in the eyes. "I know it bothers you that I still care for him, but that's the truth, Ava," she said curtly.

"Thank you, Ruth, for warning *us*," he said, placed his arm around Ava and closed the door.

"Jonathan–" Ava watched him walk to the couch and sit, preoccupied. She followed him, sat near him, and watched, waiting.

## January 15th 1930

After breakfast, Ava walked down the hall to Arianna's as Jonathan suggested and found her closing and locking her own door.

"Hey, I was just coming down to see you. Where are you headed?"

"To see the midwife Dr. Westley suggested. Will you come with me?" Arianna asked. "I'm kind of nervous meeting her for the first time."

"Sure. I heard you felt the baby move," Ava said as they headed out of the tenement.

"It's so strange," Arianna said. "It's not at all like what I expected. And I've felt it again twice this morning."

"It must be the greatest thing," Ava said, smiling at her. "Jon's been talking a lot about just letting fate decide when we have one. I'm not so sure, though."

"Oh, you should!" Arianna gushed. "That way our kids will be playmates!"

They began down the street, doing their best to ignore their surroundings.

"There's a little more to consider than that. Aren't you worried? I mean, there's so much to think about and so many things that should be in place beforehand."

"I was worried. I cried every day for a few weeks after I found out. But honestly, I'm not so worried now," she said, patting her noticeable bump. "Everything will work out. Caleb promised me."

"Well, Jon just wants to throw caution to the wind so you guys won't get too much of a head start on us. How silly," Ava said, shaking her head.

"I think Jon just wants all of our kids to grow up together in the same way they did. I think they envision little miniature versions of themselves palling around, causing trouble and sticking together the way they have."

"Well, that's assuming that we all three have boys first and fast. Who knows? Maybe we'll all have girls?"

"Here it is," Arianna said, looking the small building over.

The midwife operated out of her home, dedicating a few back rooms to her practice. Arianna knocked on the front door and a much older woman with hair piled on her head in Victorian style answered the door.

"Can I help you?" she asked, looking Arianna and Ava up and down.

"I'm looking for Mrs. Hauge."

"That's me. What can I do for you?" the old woman said and smiled.

"Well, my doctor recommended you. You see, I'm, well, I'm going to be–"

"You're with child, and you are looking for someone to care for you through it," old Mrs. Hauge interrupted.

"Yes, please."

"Come in then. I'm with a woman now, but I can speak with you shortly."

They followed her inside a modest but clean home decorated in much the same era that Mrs. Hauge appeared to have directly stepped out of. She pointed to chairs in the hallway and excused herself behind a wooden, sliding door. They could vaguely hear chattering and occasional laughter from inside the room.

A few moments later, Mrs. Hauge emerged, followed by a woman whose stomach was so large she waddled with considerable effort.

"Now, have your husband come for me the second you think it's time. I don't want you having another one before I get there," she teased.

The woman shuffled past, her enormous stomach causing her to arch her back to keep her balance as she left.

Arianna's eyes grew wide, and her head whipped to Mrs. Hauge, who was closing the door.

"*Am I going to be that big?*" Arianna asked, horrified.

The midwife laughed. "Most likely not that big unless you're having twins, but you'll be big enough. Come in and let's get to know each other, shall we?"

Arianna followed her behind the door to a parlor-like room. She sat on an old but comfortable settee, and the midwife took a fresh sheet of stationery and began asking her questions. She wrote down all of Arianna's answers and began asking her questions about her health. She pulled out a chart, looked it over, and turned to Arianna.

"Well, it appears that you'll be due in late June. But being as this is your first one, I wouldn't expect anything until well into July." She motioned for Arianna to lie back, so she could perform a physical examination.

"You're skin and bones, child!" Mrs. Hauge said, afterward. "You'd better put on some weight. Potatoes are good for that. You need to be eating lots of potatoes and as much meat as you can manage."

"I hate potatoes," she whispered aloud, rolling her eyes.

"Well, hate them or not, you'll need to be eating them for the baby. Now, I'll take you on and help you through the delivery, but you have to do exactly as I say. I've been delivering babies for thirty years, and I can count on one hand how many babies I've lost, and it was mostly due to the mother not following my instructions."

Arianna was wide-eyed hearing *babies I've lost*.

"Your instructions are to start putting on some weight. I understand circumstances are probably harsh, or you'd be at a regular doctor. But you must do whatever you can to see to a healthy baby and that includes plenty of rest and eating as much as you can with as much variety as you can. I can see to it that you have more iron supplements, and I trust you've ceased all relations with your husband?"

"Ceased rela – what?" Arianna looked stunned.

"Yes, dear. I have seen more deaf and dumb babies born than I ever cared to see because mothers did not stop having relations."

"Deaf and dumb?" Arianna squeaked.

"It truly amazes me how many women come through my door..." She leaned toward Arianna and lowered her voice. "To put it bluntly, my dear, it has been proven that intrusive and repetitive motions of that nature put a baby at great risk of being born retarded. You must bring to a halt your marital obligations if you are to have a healthy baby."

"*Retarded?*"

"Now, if your husband gives you any guff about it, bring him to me. I'll set him straight. He may tell you he will die, but I have yet to come across a husband's corpse at the foot of the bed come the time of delivery," she said with a smile and a wink.

She handed Arianna a piece of paper listing the charges for her services. Arianna paid her for the appointment and asked when she should come back.

"If all is going well, I can see you a few months from now," she said casually. Arianna left the room.

"Everything okay?" Ava was instantly concerned, seeing the expressions of shock and agony.

"Yes and no. Mostly no," Arianna whispered back.

She explained everything to Ava on the walk home.

"Are you sure she's right?" Ava asked. "I've never heard of that."

"She seemed very smart. And she's been doing this for a long time," Arianna said cautiously.

"Then forget it," Ava said. "You guys can get ahead of us. We're adopting," she said, not entirely joking.

Arianna stopped by the grocery on the way home and bought a ten-pound bag of potatoes, a pound of butter, and several cans of sardines.

Later that evening, Caleb came home and stopped abruptly inside the door. He sniffed twice and looked to see Arianna flitting about the kitchen, which smelled of perfectly baked bread, a spicy meaty smell and something sweet he couldn't put his finger on.

At the kitchen entryway, he stopped again, squinting and adjusting his eyes to make sure they weren't playing tricks on him.

"Hello," Arianna said, smiled and gave him a kiss on the cheek before turning back to the stove.

"Arianna. What are you wearing?" he asked in surprise.

"What do you mean?" She looked herself over.

"Are you wearing an apron?" he asked, incredulously.

"Yes, don't act so shocked, Caleb." She looked down and laughed.

"But it's just–I've never seen you, never *thought* I'd see you, wearing one."

"Well, naturally, I detest them," she said with a flip of her hair. "But I got to thinking, I wouldn't want to splash anything hot on myself and hurt the baby," she said.

"Oh, well, okay." He glanced over her shoulder at the full pot of potatoes on the stove. "Wow, that's a lot of potatoes," he commented. "Did you do all this by yourself?"

"Yes."

"How?" he asked, trying to understand the sudden and drastic improvement in her domestic skills.

"Well, I got to thinking about it and I want the baby to have good food. I just started paying more attention to what I was doing. Oh, I met with the midwife today."

"Oh, how was it? Is she good? Is she clean?" he asked, concerned.

"Yes on both. I'll tell you all about it over dinner. Now, go wash up," she ordered, patting him on the cheek.

"You're going to eat all those potatoes?" Caleb asked, watching her heap her plate.

"Yes. Midwife's orders. She says I'm too thin."

"You are too thin," he agreed.

"Well, I left with a list of instructions to follow if we're going to have a healthy baby."

"Good. Sounds like this woman knows what she's talking about. I want you to follow her instructions to the letter, Ahna," he said, pointing his fork at her with insistence.

"Oh, I will. I'm none too thrilled about it, but I will."

"Let's get a second opinion," he pleaded after dinner. "I've never heard of such hogwash in all my life. Retarded babies from–? If that were true, half the world would be retarded, Ahna! Think about it!"

"I'm not willing to take any chances, Caleb. What if she's right? Would you honestly risk the baby being deaf or dumb or worse?" She hadn't moved her hands from her stomach. "We have to think about the baby now, Caleb."

He sighed long and hard.

*February 1st 1930*

"Where's Arianna?" Jon asked as Caleb sat down next to Aryl, half-slamming his savings jar on the table next to the others.

"She's not coming. She doesn't want the baby to be around the noise and cigars." He turned to Ava and Claire, who were on the couch. "She wanted to know if you gals wouldn't mind having your meeting over there." He turned back to the table and snatched the cigar out of Jonathan's hand.

"What's wrong, Caleb, a little tense?" Jonathan said and smiled mockingly. Caleb glared at him.

"You know exactly what's wrong." He turned to glance at Ava and Claire who were gathering up their things and waited until they left before going on. "I swear, I'm gonna lose my mind. Everything is the baby this, the baby that. Every time I turn around I hear *think about the baby*," he said in a mocking voice. "She's learning to knit. *To knit!* I swear, I don't know who this woman *is* anymore."

"Didn't you always say that you wanted for Arianna to be more domesticated?" Aryl said and grinned. "Be careful what you wish for."

"No kidding! Let's get the cash count and checklist over with, so we can play cards. Of all the nights to not have a drink, I swear." Caleb shook his head and dumped out his jar.

They each counted the money they saved from the previous week, and Jonathan did some quick math.

"Whew. It's gonna be close," he said, rubbing his forehead. "We've got to do a little better this month."

"We had to take money out to for pay the midwife, and we aren't gonna be able to cut our grocery bill down as much as you guys," Caleb said apologetically.

"No, that's fine," Jonathan said. "Buy whatever you need for Arianna. Aryl and I can make up the difference."

"I'm also holding some back for a visit to Dr. Westley, as soon as I can convince her to go. I can't get within two feet of her anymore. You wouldn't believe what this midwife has Arianna thinking."

"We heard," Jonathan said grimly.

"You've told us three times," Aryl reminded with a chuckle.

"Just deal the damned cards," Caleb grumbled.

∞∞∞∞

"Well, isn't that the cutest thing!" Claire said, looking over the lumpy, lopsided sweater Arianna was attempting to knit.

"Shannon is a wonderful teacher," Arianna said. "I'm also learning to sew." She pulled out a small garment that looked somewhat like a sleeper made from a flour sack. It was crooked and one arm longer than the other, but the fact that Arianna had made it with her own two hands was impressive enough. "After we move and money isn't so tight, I'm going to buy some fabric. She's going to teach me how to make diapers and bedding."

"Wow. What does Caleb think of all this?" Claire asked, glancing at the perfectly baked oatmeal cookies Arianna had made for their meeting.

"Oh, he's just over the moon about this baby! He's so happy, sometimes he's just speechless for hours and stares off into space, and I just know he's dreaming about the baby."

"Well, I think it's great, Arianna." Ava suppressed a smirk and patted her leg.

"Well, the first, and really only, order in our meeting is saving money," Claire said, rolling her eyes. "Last month when we met, we made a list of ways to save, and now we need to see how that's working, and where else we can cut corners."

"Well, we started wearing clothes three or four times before washing to save hot water and laundry soap," Ava said.

"Good idea. I'll start doing that, too," Claire said.

"Well, I can't do that," Arianna said. "I need to keep things as clean as possible for the baby."

"We've gotten used to keeping the heat as low as possible, so we saw a dip in this last bill," Ava said.

"We saved several dollars this month by doing that as well," Claire said.

"I have to keep the heat a little higher, actually. I don't want to catch a cold with the baby."

"Aryl and I have started having meat only twice a week and that's helped. I also only buy my canned goods from the factory seconds."

"The midwife said I need to eat as much meat as possible for the baby, or I would do that, too. And I'm afraid the dented cans from the factory might be contaminated, and I can't get sick with the baby. The midwife said I need variety for the baby, so I had to go back to buying everything from the grocery."

"Well, why don't you tell us what you *have* done to save money this last month?" Claire asked as they stared at her.

"Well, honestly, my expenses have gone up slightly. I mean, with the midwife insisting on a better diet for the baby, and I had to buy a little yarn to start making things for the baby. I had to buy some extra scouring powder and bleach this week because I have been trying to keep things as clean as possible, you know, for the baby."

Once outside Arianna's door, Claire pulled at Ava's arm. "If I ever get like that when I'm having my baby, I want you to slap me. Repeatedly."

"Me, too. I don't know how we're going to survive until June."

"I don't know how Caleb has survived the last three weeks. I've heard a baby changes you, but this is unbelievable."

"Well, I kind of like it. She seems a little more like us now," Ava said.

"Except with us the ending to every sentence isn't *for the baby*."

They walked into Ava's apartment to the usual bellowing and laughing that went on during the mens' card games.

"Who won?" Ava asked.

"Jon. Again," Aryl said. He gathered the money they had used for the pretend bets and dumped it back into the community jar.

"If only it were real," Jonathan said. "I'd take that to the safe deposit box on Monday."

Aryl screwed on the metal lid and handed it to him. "Thirty days and counting, we're half way there."

∞∞∞

"*I* was thinking," Jonathan started as they got ready for bed, "and I decided that we shouldn't wait any longer to start a family."

"Jon, we've been over this," Ava said, exasperated.

"Yes, I know we've been over it. Several times. And you remain unconvinced."

"Due to the fact that we're not ready," she said and slipped under the covers.

"And I say we are," he said, joining her and rolling to his side. "If we keep waiting for the perfect time, Ava, it's never going to come. If we hold out until our life is more like it used to be, well, that's not going to happen either."

He moved closer to her and put an arm around her waist as she lay on her back, staring at the ceiling in the dark, unmoved by his emotional plea.

"Ava. If there is anything I have learned these last few months, it's that things can change in the blink of an eye. Six months ago, I would have never imagined that I would be living here, doing what I do for a living and happy to be scraping together pennies toward a better life. And one month ago, I couldn't have imagined that I would be lying here next to you at all, much less trying to talk you into having my baby." She didn't understand the first part of his last sentence but let him continue. "You never know when things are going to drastically change. The last few months have made my head spin. We can't live our lives waiting for the perfect time. It's never going to come. We have to go ahead and deal with the setbacks as they come."

"Jonathan." Finances weren't the only thing that made her reluctant. She took a deep breath, not comfortable speaking of Jonathan's dark time. This would be the first time she spoke directly of his depression. "It feels like I just got you back. I don't know where you went for those few months, but in both your heart and your head, you weren't here with me."

"I know and I'm so sorry. I know that was hell on you, and you have no idea how grateful I am that you stayed by my side. That time is hard for me to explain. I had to hit the bottom before I could see things clearly enough to pull myself out. But I'm not going back, if that's what you're worried about."

He found her hand under the covers, pulled it up to his mouth, kissed it, and then put it over his heart.

"I swear to you. I'm not going anywhere."

She felt his heartbeat and the warm skin of his chest and had the overwhelming urge to move closer to him. Instinctively, he moved his hand to the small of her back to hold her to him and she touched his face.

"Do you promise?"

"I promise."

"Alright, I'll think about it," she relented.

"Thank you," he whispered.

*February 15th 1930*

Following the instructions written on their homemade cards, Ava, Claire and Arianna walked into Aryl's apartment at six o'clock, sat at the table and waited patiently for dinner. A sheet was tacked over the entrance of the kitchen, and jazz played on the radio.

"Whose idea was this anyway?" Ava whispered.

"Aryl's. Since no one could buy anything for Valentine's Day yesterday, they planned to provide dinner and entertainment for the evening," Claire said.

"I can't wait to see the entertainment." Ava laughed.

A loud sizzle followed by swearing came from the crowded kitchen. Aryl poked his head out from around the sheet.

"Everything's fine, but, uh, dinner will be a little later than expected," he said and ducked back in.

Pots banged, and more sizzles, pops and swearing came from behind the sheet. The women held back laughter at the sounds of obvious struggling and shook their heads in pity.

"Maybe someone should go help them?" Claire whispered.

"No, this is good for them," Arianna insisted with a smile.

A burnt smell floated from the kitchen and there were more fervent whispers and cursing.

Finally, twenty minutes later, each of them emerged with two plates, and the girls did their best to look impressed when dinner was set in front of them; charred bits of steak, cold baked potatoes, and carrots boiled to mush.

"It looks great," Claire said.

"It does. You guys did a great job," Ava said, and leaned over to give Jonathan a quick kiss.

"I don't know if the baby likes carrots," Arianna said, picking at her food.

Caleb visibly bit his tongue as he nursed the burn on his hand.

"Have you thought of any names?" Jonathan asked as everyone started eating.

"No."

"Yes."

"You didn't tell me you'd thought of names." Caleb looked at Arianna.

"I thought we could name it after my father, if it's a boy, and my mother, if it's a girl," she said.

"Well, I have relatives, too, you know," he said, irritated.

"Actually, it's customary to name the first boy after the father and the middle name given for a relative," Aryl pointed out, trying to quell Caleb's irritation.

"Well, I decided it's going to be a girl anyway, so all that doesn't matter," Arianna said and smiled.

"How do you know?" Caleb's head whipped around.

"I just know," she said. "Maybe I'll name her after myself. After all, a little girl would surely be just like me."

Caleb's fork stopped mid-air and color drained from his face. Jonathan and Aryl struggled not to laugh and changed the subject to plans for the new building for the remainder of dinner. Arianna only interrupted three times with statements about the baby.

After dinner, Aryl changed the radio station to slower music, and Jonathan lit candles on the mantel, which illuminated Claire's mural beautifully.

"When did you finish it?" Ava asked. The bright, yellow light shone through the billowing storm clouds over the churning ocean. The quaint, white cottage set behind the lighthouse, and the sky was lit with fiery shades of red and orange on the horizon behind it.

"Just the other day," Claire said. "I'm going to hate to leave it. I think working on that has kept me sane."

"I'm sure it will make the next tenants very happy," Ava said. "And you can begin another one in the new place."

The lights were turned off suddenly. Ava gave her eyes a second to adjust. Each man migrated toward the one who held his heart and asked her to dance in his own unique way.

"Would you honor me, Mrs. Garrett?" Jonathan asked and, without waiting for an answer, took her hand and slipped an arm around her waist. She smiled and rested one hand behind his neck as he placed her other, held within his, over his heart. She looked up to tell him what a sweet evening it had been, but her words caught, paralyzed by the intensity of his eyes.

She noticed many things in that brief moment; how he carried himself with dignity, his shoulders back with confidence and, especially, the way he held her like she belonged to him. She was sure he was hers again, returned from that dark, isolated place he went to, leaving her lonely and scared. She felt it was impossible to get close enough to him.

Aryl asked silently with a desirous stare that made Claire blush as he pulled her close and began to lead.

"Would you and the baby like to dance?" Caleb asked flatly. Arianna smiled, kicked off her shoes so they would stand eye-to-eye and took his hand.

Holding her close was torture as he had been deprived of her for weeks. With a strained expression, he inhaled the scent of her hair as she rested her head on his shoulder. Against his better judgment, he let his hands follow the contours of her back, waist, and hips. He let out a ragged breath, closed his eyes, put his lips on her neck, and ignored the voice in his head that warned him he was only intensifying his agony.

One song ended and another began. Caleb wondered how long he would be able to enjoy her like this despite the fact that he would pay dearly for it later. Unconsciously he held her tighter as they danced until she pulled away. He apologized before she could scold him for squeezing her too tight. She ignored his assumption.

"I was going to tell you how nice this was. We haven't done this in a very long time." He stared at her lips as she spoke and then focused on her eyes.

"It is nice. Difficult, but nice." He hesitantly leaned in and she closed the gap between them and kissed him, soft and teasing. He was the one to pull away after only a moment.

"You're a cruel woman," he whispered. "I can't take much more of that." She grinned sadistically, arched her back, slowly devoured his neck with kisses, and ran her fingers up his neck into his hair. He swallowed hard and grit his teeth. "I really need you to stop doing that."

She ignored his pleas, toyed with his shirt buttons, and left a trail of lipstick kisses under his chin to the other side of his neck. He squeezed his eyes shut, let his head fall and clenched two fistfuls of her dress at the upper and lower back. "Arianna please, please go talk to Dr. Westley." She moved her lips to his ear.

"I did."

"You did? When? What did he say?" he was whispering loudly, but the others didn't appear to notice.

Her seductive eyes danced as she whispered, "Happy Valentine's Day."

A sharp knock on the door jolted the couples from the quiet, contented places they had found in each other's arms, and Aryl pulled away with a reluctant sigh.

"Telegram for Mr. Aryl Sullivan," a young, uniformed messenger announced.

"That's me," Aryl said. The boy handed him a paper and lingered for a tip, but Aryl had none to give. He mumbled a thank you, closed the door, and began reading the telegram.

"Who's it from?" Claire asked, turning on the overhead before standing beside him.

Caleb had ignored the interruption altogether, not caring if President Hoover himself were knocking, he refused to move one inch from Arianna.

Jonathan still held Ava close, although they had stopped dancing, and an ominous feeling came over him as Aryl looked at Claire, his brow furrowed.

"My uncle died," he whispered and looked back at the telegram to read it again.

"Oh, Aryl, I'm so sorry," Claire said.

He sat down at the table numbly, still holding the telegram. They all knew how close he had been to his uncle, growing up. Jonathan turned off the radio. Claire and his friends surrounded him as the sweet and romantic evening turned very somber. Aryl absorbed the news in silence. He held his head in his hands and sighed repeatedly.

"You need to go back for the funeral, Aryl," Jonathan said, breaking the silence.

"No." Aryl shook his head. It was obvious he was fighting tears as he cleared his throat. "That would throw our plans off. We only have two weeks left. We can't get off track now."

"It can still happen. We'll figure it out," Jonathan tried to sound assuring.

"It's too close and you know it, Jon."

Jonathan looked down, knowing Aryl was right. There was no way they could replace train fare and one week missed wages in the time before taking over the building. Arianna nudged Caleb to get his attention and Caleb followed her out the door.

A few minutes later, they returned and rejoined the others at the table.

"Aryl, you need to be with your family. I want you to take these," Arianna said, holding out a red, velvet bag. "They should be worth enough to get you to Rockport and back, maybe with some left over." Aryl took the bag and out fell two diamond earrings. "They weren't listed on the insurance paperwork when we left. We were saving them for an emergency."

"Arianna, I can't take these—" Aryl started.

"You can and you will," Caleb ordered.

"You have a baby to think about. You should use this for him," Aryl said insistently and pushed the velvet bag away.

"Believe me, Aryl, we think about the baby plenty these days," Caleb said in a serious tone. "It'll be fine. Go home and say goodbye to your uncle. For all of us," he said, reminding him that he and Jonathan had known and were fond of his uncle. He held the bag out until Aryl reluctantly took it from him.

"Thank you. Both of you." Aryl gave a weak smile through sad eyes with gratitude.

"See if you guys can get out on the train tomorrow. I'll talk to Roman on Monday," Jonathan offered.

Ava looked at the faces of her friends. Just moments ago, everyone was blissfully happy and wrapped in the arms of the ones they loved. Now there were sad faces and heavy hearts. She looked at Jonathan and remembered his words. *Things can change in the blink of an eye.* She reached for his hand and held it tightly. Aryl thanked everyone for coming and thanked Caleb and Arianna again for the earrings.

When the door shut behind them, he walked straight to the bedroom and lay down in the dark. Claire followed, nestling in next to him. He took a deep breath and exhaled hard, unable to hold himself together any longer. With a hard shake, he pulled Claire to him and cried soft, uneven sobs into her shoulder.

*February 16th 1930*

The train pulled into Boston a half-hour early. Aryl glanced around, looking for his father as he helped Claire down the step.

Walking over to the bench near the ticket office to wait, Claire gasped when Aryl unexpectedly grabbed her by the waist and pinned her against the wall. Just as Claire was about to scold him for embarrassing her with such an outward display of affection in public, a group of drunken and raucous servicemen bantered past, knocking everything and everyone out of their way.

She smiled up at him. "My hero."

Aryl decided to take advantage of the situation and stole a kiss.

"You kids and your lewd behavior," Aryl's father chided from a few feet away.

"Hey, Pops." Aryl turned to his father with a grin.

"Hello, son." He hugged him briefly and then turned his attention to Claire. "How's my favorite daughter-in-law?" he said, grinned and hugged her.

"I'm your *only* daughter-in-law, Mr. Sullivan."

"Not for long." He turned to Aryl but kept an arm around Claire's shoulder. He stopped and cleared his throat. "Your brother and his gal are at the house, so try to act surprised when they tell you."

"I will. How's Mom?"

"She's good. Been cookin' for two days straight. Lots of people have been by. Well, you know how popular your uncle was." Aryl nodded again as a lump rose in his throat. "I'm wishing now that I hadn't sold the larger house. The cottage is about to burst. Well, I better get you home soon, or your mother will skin me. She's so excited to see you, both of you. It's been a long time."

Aryl picked up the bags and followed his father, who still had an arm around Claire. He threw the bags in the backseat of the rusty Model-T Ford and climbed in, insisting Claire take the front.

"You don't mind if I hold your girl's hand on the way home, do you?" Michael Sullivan teased. Aryl winked at Claire, happy that his parents and wife adored each other the way they did.

His father filled him in on the goings on of Rockport and Pigeon Cove on the drive home: who had married and who now had children, who were involved in the latest scandal, the businesses that had gone under, folks who had lost and suffered because of the crash.

"Of course, we heard about it here when it happened. It was all the talk in the shops and down at the marina. Took a couple months to start feelin' it, though." He took a deep breath. "But I heard the news say it's turnin' around. Things should be lookin' up here soon. Heard the

President talkin' on the radio the other night, said the economy is fundamentally strong and it's startin' to rebound. It can't get much worse."

He continued on listing friends that had had to leave to find work in the city, and some that didn't want to leave were living two and three families to a home.

"Folks that fared the best owned what they have. Seems like everybody on earth had something wrapped up in that market. I'm real grateful I built that little cottage, and this old clunker is paid for."

Aryl knew all too well the direct effects of the crash. His father didn't know the extent of their hardships. Claire had censored letters somewhat, so they wouldn't worry.

Aryl took in the familiar scenery as his father talked, and he realized how much he'd missed the sound of his voice, the boisterous laugh, and the northeastern accent that sounded like home. When they got within a few miles of Rockport, Aryl's mind flashed through dozens of childhood memories and the antics of the Terrible Trio as his father had nicknamed them. Aryl waited for his father to take a breath, so he could interject.

"How are Caleb's parents?"

"Oh, all right, I suppose. Saw his father a few weeks ago at the hardware store. Come spring, your mother's going to put in a bigger garden. He's sellin' off some of his animals, wants to make room for more crops. I don't suppose he and Caleb ever got past him selling his grandfather's farm. I didn't want to bring it up."

"No. They haven't." Aryl turned toward the scenery again. "They haven't talked in several years. How about Mr. Garrett?"

"Jon, Sr.? He's doing good, I suppose. I see him every now and again. He got hit hard, you know."

"No, I didn't know."

"Yeah, he doesn't talk about it much, but that fancy car they had is gone, they've got an old clunker like this now. Rumor mill says he invested all his money with Jonathan, and when he tanked so did his father."

"I'll have to stop in and see both of them before I leave."

"How long can you stay? You didn't say in the telegram."

"Probably mid-week. I can't miss much work."

"Oh, yeah, tell me about your new job. Did Jon start a new business already?"

"Not exactly. But we are looking into some real estate." He was surprised at his embarrassment and didn't offer any more details of how he earned their meager living. He was grateful when his father changed the subject.

"How are Jon and Caleb? Haven't seen them in years. I'll bet you three are still riveted at the hip." His full laugh filled the car.

"We are. They're good. Can you keep a secret?"

"Aryl, you know I can't." The old man's eyes twinkled.

"Well, I'll tell you anyway. Arianna is expecting."

The car almost swerved off the road as he craned his neck to see if Aryl was joking. Claire let out a yelp and grabbed the dashboard.

"Whoa, Pops, keep it on the road, would ya?"

His father steadied the car. "Sorry, son, it's just, that's some news." He glanced back at him several times. "You're serious."

Aryl laughed. "Yes, I'm serious."

"Well, nothing against Caleb, you know I like the boy. And I guess I like that wife of his all right, but she just has a cat-like way about her, and it just always seemed to me that she'd be the kind to eat her young if she were to ever have any."

"You'd be surprised at her transformation, Mr. Sullivan. It's really been amazing."

"She has suddenly become very maternal," Aryl added. "And I'll admit it is strange, but it's a good thing, I think. For both of them."

"Well, Caleb's not too happy at the moment," Claire whispered under her breath. She forgot that Aryl's father had acute hearing.

His face was suddenly concerned. "He's not happy about the child? I always pictured Caleb having a whole houseful of children."

"Oh, it's not that, it's just . . ." Aryl searched for the right words. "Okay, Pops, let me ask you something." Claire turned around with wide eyes as Aryl proceeded to explain what Arianna was led to believe in rather blunt language and then, to Claire's undying mortification, asked him if it was true.

He laughed so hard the car swerved again.

"Son, if that were true, you'd be deaf, dumb, and *crippled*!" He howled with laughter.

Aryl smiled and patted Claire on the shoulder. "Told ya' so." Her face was blood red, and she refused to look at either of them.

∞∞∞∞

"Here we are."

Aryl saw the little, white cottage with several cars parked outside, and it suddenly weighed down on him again why he was here. He stepped out of the car, and the first things he noticed were the salt air and the seagulls calling in the distance. Claire waited patiently for him to open her door. One of the few rules Aryl had laid down for Claire, early on, was that she was never to touch an automobile door handle.

∞∞∞∞

Kathleen Sullivan had her back turned when Aryl walked into the kitchen. "Hey, Mom."

She spun around, already smiling. "My Aryl." She grabbed him in a tight hug. "I'm so glad you could come." She stepped back to get a better look at him. "Well, now, what have you been doing with yourself? You're as solid as a footballah!" She patted his shoulders and chest.

"Just working."

"Well, you look wonderful, son. Where's my Claire?" She looked over his shoulder and saw her, standing in the doorway.

Aryl stepped aside and Kathleen grabbed her adopted daughter in a strangling hug. "I'm so glad you could come, Claire." She finished her sentence in a whisper, "I know Aryl will need you through this." She pulled back to examine Claire more thoroughly. "You're too skinny," she said decidedly. "How are yah going to carry and nurse my grandbabies as thin as yah are?" She turned to Aryl, who was grinning at Claire's growing embarrassment. "Speaking of which, Aryl Sullivan, just where are those grandbabies? She can't do it all by herself, you know." Claire turned red again and excused herself in a fluster.

"C'mon, Mom, now you've embarrassed her," Aryl scolded, but not truly angry.

"You mean to tell me after almost five years with you, she hasn't loosened up at all?"

"She has, in her own way. I'm fighting years of ingrained training regarding proper behavior." He rolled his eyes. "It's a work in progress."

She smiled and patted his face. "You're a good boy," she said quietly, summing up all of his admirable qualities in four words.

He noticed the prominent gray at her temples, sprinkled throughout her curly, brown hair; signs of aging that he hadn't noticed when she had visited them in New York just over a year ago. Fine lines had turned to deep wrinkles, and there was a slight hunch to her back causing her to appear a few inches shorter. She had lost weight and appeared more fragile than he remembered. One day, he would have to come back here for her, but he couldn't think about that right now.

"What's wrong, son?" She read the troubled look on his face, and then shook her hands in the air and squeezed her eyes shut. "I'm sorry. For a few moments, I forgot this wasn't a reunion for joy." She looked toward the living room. "Have you seen all the family we have managed to cram into this living room?"

"I noticed them on the way in, but I wanted to see you first." He smiled.

"Well, why don't you find that ever-blushing bride of yours, and go visit with your brothah? And act surprised when he tells you his news. I know yah fathah already spilled the beans. Dinner will be ready soon."

"Don't you need some help, Mom?" Aryl looked around the kitchen at the piles of food already on the counters and in the process of being prepared.

"I like staying busy. If I do, I'll call for my Claire and see about embarrassing her some more."

"Mom—"

"I'm teasing. Now go see yah family."

"Thanks, Mom." He kissed her on the forehead.

∞∞∞

Ayl found Claire in the garden behind the cottage. "It's starting to get dark." He swung open the whitewashed, garden gate. "Are you going to come in and see the family or hide here in the garden?" he teased.

"I forgot how forward your family is." She looked slightly apologetic. Her ears and cheeks were still slightly flushed.

"Not forward really, just relaxed." He took her hand as they started to walk around the garden. "You always get used to it after a few days, remember? Soon you'll be joking right along with them. I've seen it a half-dozen times."

"I know," she said quietly. "Your parents look good." She tried to extend the small talk before going back inside.

"They're getting older." He looked at all the work that needed to be done in the yard. "Their swing is broken." He dropped Claire's hand and walked over to look at the old, framed swing. "My father built this swing when I was a little boy," he said, smiling as he recalled the story his father had told him a hundred times. "The story goes, she was very busy with two small boys, and he had to spend more and more time fishing to support us, they started growing apart. Bickering and fighting a lot. So, my father spent an entire weekend building this." He lifted the broken chain and examined cracked slats on the seat of the swing. "When it was finished, he dragged her—almost literally, out to sit with him every night after Liam and I were put to bed. After a few silent, awkward evenings, they started talking and, little by little, things got back to normal. And they've sat together every night the weather's allowed." He unhooked the chains and heaved the heavy bench closer to the tool shed in the yard. "I'll fix this before I leave." He set the bench down and held out his hand.

"Will you build me a swing?" she asked as she took his hand.

"I have plans to do better than that. I'm going to build you a lighthouse."

"How on earth are you going to do that?"

"I don't know just yet. But I will."

∞∞∞

Back inside the house, hugs and handshakes went around the crowded living room as Liam pushed his way to the center of the crowd, pulling a young woman behind him.

After a quick hug and back slap, he proudly introduced her to his brother. "Aryl, this is Sarah, my fiancé."

Aryl did a good job of looking surprised. He congratulated them both, welcomed Sarah to the family and then introduced Sarah to Claire, who instantly recognized the air of distinction about Sarah. She was from money, no doubt.

"We should all go out for an evening while you're here," Liam suggested. "Show Sarah the roaring nightlife in Rockport."

"I don't know that we can stay that long. But we'll definitely spend some time together before I leave. We should do a bonfire on the beach. Like old times."

"It's awful cold for that," Liam said. "Why not go to dinner and a show?"

"A bonfire sounds wonderful! We could bundle up," Claire said. She knew Aryl's hesitation wasn't so much about time as money.

"That might be fun, actually," Sarah agreed. "Primitive, but fun."

Once again, the light mood was brought down when Kathleen opened the door to a delivery boy, who handed a stack of programs designed and printed for her brother-in-law's service the following day. She reached for her purse, but the young boy stopped her.

"Mr. Greene said no charge. He sends his condolences."

"Well, you go back and tell him thank you and to come eat with us tomorrow evening," she said and smiled gratefully. She held out a dime for a tip.

"No ma'am. I can't take that. Not for a delivery like this." He tipped his hat and ran off quickly.

"And just when I think the youth of today is going to hell in a hand basket. What a sweet young man," she told the crowd, put the programs in the closet on the top shelf for safekeeping, and announced dinner.

## *February 17th 1930*

Aryl stood in front of the mirror, straightening his tie and dreading the day before him. Claire knocked on the door of his parents' loft bedroom and let herself in. Arianna had loaned her a black dress, and, although she looked slightly overdressed, it was better than buying something for the day.

"You look nice."

"So do you," she said, taking the tie from him and adjusting it.

"How'd you sleep?"

"All right, I guess. When did everyone finally leave?" She had fallen asleep on the couch, and Aryl had asked the remaining guests to move to the kitchen, so he could lay out a makeshift bed for her in front of the fireplace.

"Close to midnight. I'll try to find more blankets or padding of some kind before tonight," he said, reflecting on his own miserable slumber. "Too bad my folks got rid of that big house. We'd be a little more comfortable."

"It's fine, Aryl. Flat and hard is almost better than lumpy and pokey," she said, smiling as she finished his tie and straightened his jacket. "All ready. Everyone is waiting downstairs."

"I just want to get this over with."

∞∞∞

Aryl and his parents, followed by Claire, Liam and Sarah, were escorted to the front row of the chapel, as they were the only immediate family. They waited while the pews filled with friends. Aryl tried to look anywhere other than the table in front of him. It was decorated with a lace cloth, an open Bible, a framed picture of his uncle and a white urn. His eyes misted and a lump grew in his throat when he looked at the picture. He could no longer pretend he was here for another reason–a friend's wedding or maybe Easter service.

He was here to say goodbye to his uncle; a big, loveable man, an avid explorer who had a passionate affair with the sea that few people understood. He was liked by men and pursued by women, but all of his relationships ended the same way. No matter how lovely, witty or demure, no woman could compete with his lady, the sea.

More times than he liked to count, his uncle had returned home to a note that released him back to his true love, and so he never married. Never had children. Instead, he had always treated Aryl like a son, and even though his father knew him and loved him, his uncle *understood* him. They shared a love of adventure and the inability to be confined to one geographical area or occupation. Until he met Claire anyway. And even then, although his uncle was brokenhearted that their adventures would never come to be, he was gracious. He told Aryl the last time they went out to sea together that if this woman called his heart stronger and louder than the adventure, more than the freedom of the sea, more than anything else in the world then Aryl was to go with her and never look back.

Aryl had to look away again and think of something else. He went over in his mind the details of the contract he would soon sign, thought about the repairs, wondered what Jonathan was doing, and did some math in his head, anything mundane and emotionless.

The organ music pulled Aryl back to the painful present. He felt imminent tears as the minister began to speak.

"Aryl Sullivan was loved by many and will be dearly missed. Anyone who was lucky enough to know him will feel an absence in their lives and in their hearts forever. One can only be consoled by the knowledge that he is now with the Lord."

A shiver went through Claire's entire body. It was eerie and uncomfortable for her to hear the repeated reference to the deceased, as her husband and his uncle shared the exact same name, and she was anxious for it to be over. She held Aryl's hand and noticed as a few tears fell onto his pant legs. She put her arm around him, and he leaned toward her slightly; Claire being the only person besides his parents that he wasn't embarrassed to cry in front of.

After a brief opening from the pastor, Michael Sullivan stood to deliver the eulogy. He retold a heartwarming account of his brother's life, his antics, and his humor. He broke down several times as he struggled through. Aryl had been asked beforehand to say something after his father, but he found it impossible to stand when it was time.

The pastor invited anyone who wished to speak to come forward. Aryl began listening to the emotionally recounted memories, but the open sobbing of the mourners became too much for him, and he told Claire he was going to the restroom. He washed and dried his face then walked outside to pull the salt air deep into his lungs and regain control of his emotions. He walked behind the chapel and stared for a long time at the ocean.

It could have been five minutes or an hour; Aryl wasn't quite sure how much time had passed, when he noticed Claire standing beside him quietly.

"It's over," she said softly. He put an arm around her shoulder, and they walked to his parents' car and rode back in silence.

The house was overflowing with people eating, consoling each other, and reminiscing. Aryl leaned over the couch and kissed Claire on the forehead. "I'm going outside for a bit. It's getting crowded in here."

He had only planned to walk down the road, but, lost in his thoughts and following familiar paths unconsciously, he turned onto a sandy path that led down to the ocean. He stood for a bit then sat down in the sand about twenty feet from the shore, pulled his knees up to rest his elbows and picked apart a piece of kelp. Concentrating on the sound of the crashing waves and the warm sun on his back, ignoring the chill in the air, he stared at the shimmering line on the ocean that grew longer as the sun began to sink behind him.

His uncle's voice echoed above the waves.

*See that line? When you're older, we'll follow that sun line out, sailing for days and you know where we'll end up?*

*Where, Uncle Aryl?*

*A little island called Madeira. Talk about adventure, boy! I've been there! There are caves to explore, mountains to climb, exotic food and beautiful women. But you won't need to worry 'bout that part for a while.*

*Older Aryl winked and grinned.*

*It's a whole different world. You're going to love it. We'll go there as soon as you're old enough. Now get on home before your mother has my hide. We'll do some more planning tomorrow.*

"Well, some things never change." Kathleen stepped carefully down the beach, her black slippers sinking into the sand with each careful step. "I turn my back and yah gone, have to come searching for yah." Aryl rose quickly, his mother looked like she would lose her balance any moment. "Sit back down," she ordered. "And I'll sit with you for a moment." She sat beside him with a little difficulty from stiff bones. "Everyone's done eating and we're about to head out. It'll be sunset before you know it."

"We never did go to Madeira." Aryl squinted out at the ocean.

"You still can."

"It wouldn't be the same." He shook his head.

"I have to wonder, Aryl. Do you have any regrets? I mean, it is a little early to start tallying you're should-haves, but sometimes it's good to take stock before you're old and can't do anything about it. What would you have done differently, looking back?"

"I don't regret Claire, Mom." He knew what she was getting at, and it made him uncomfortable. "I know I gave up a lot when I settled down, but–" He shrugged and picked at a fresh piece of seaweed. "She's worth it."

"That's not what I mean. I can't picture yah without Claire any more than you can."

"I–" Aryl thought about it for a few moments. "would have told her family to go to hell. I know now that she would have married me without a dime to my name. I would have taken one of the boats and just run off with her," he said and smiled, repeating Claire's words and sat up a little straighter. "I would have had Uncle marry us on the open sea, and we would have just wandered from port to port, working long enough to get to the next exotic place."

"It's not too late to make that happen."

His smile dropped and he narrowed his eyes. "We're kind of wrapped up in stuff in New York."

"Things have a way of working themselves out, Aryl." She patted his hand and pointed far down the beach. "Are you going to take Claire to your special lighthouse while you're here?" she said and grinned mischievously.

"How do you know about that?" He jerked his head toward her then looked away, embarrassed.

"Yah know your fathah can't keep a secret."

"Maybe." Aryl looked down the beach. He wondered how much she knew about that night. Knowing his father, probably everything.

She looked back at the setting sun. "We better get a move on. They're probably waiting at the marina."

Aryl stood, pulled Kathleen up with both hands and they brushed sand off their clothes.

At the end of the sandy path, the old Model-T was parked on the side of the road. Aryl looked at the empty car and back to his mother.

"When did you learn how to drive?"

"Last year," she said and smiled proudly. "And I've only caused two accidents."

"Mom–"

"They hardly qualified as accidents," she said, laughing. "Little bumps and scrapes really. C'mon, hop in."

∞∞∞

Claire stood with the rest of the family, close friends, and the pastor on the dock. They boarded the small boat and Aryl and Liam pulled up the ropes. Michael Sullivan steered the boat out to sea before shutting down the engine and dropping anchor.

The family gathered at port side, faced the setting sun, and just as it dipped into the horizon, the pastor recited Psalm 23; Michael, Aryl, and Liam held the urn and slowly tipped it.

A gust of wind carried the swirling ashes away from the boat before settling gracefully on the fading white and gold shimmering line cast by the last of the setting sun.

*February 18th 1930*

"I wish you didn't have to leave tomorrow."

"I know, Mom, but I have to get back to work. And we're moving into the place that we're buying on the first. There's a lot to do." He reached for a second helping of biscuits and bacon. "I'll write you with the new address as soon as we're settled."

"Well, I don't know what you kids had planned today, but I need you to go with me this morning, Aryl. And Liam, too."

"Where to, Pops?"

His father looked down and spoke quietly. "The reading of the will. Just downtown Rockport. Won't take long."

Aryl didn't want to go, but nodded in agreement. His father had said 'I need' and therefore, he felt he couldn't refuse. "Liam should be here shortly, we'll leave then."

∞∞∞

The old car sputtered up to the family attorney's office, and all three men were hesitant to go inside. Aryl hadn't thought about the will until it was mentioned. He had had a sense of relief that the most agonizing part of this trip was over.

Inside the old office, Michael and Liam sat in front of the attorney's desk, but Aryl pulled a chair to the window, so he could tune out the attorney who droned on without emotion in his voice as he listed how his uncle's estate would be divided. Aryl busied his mind with tasks back at home again, wondering about his friends and hoping he could make it out to the lighthouse with Claire before they left. *Maybe we could pack a picnic and bring some blankets. It would be great to spend the night there—*

"Aryl, did you hear that?"

"Hear what?" He turned from the window.

Michael looked at the attorney. "Read it again, please. Just that last part."

The old man huffed his breath impatiently and read quickly. "To my nephew, Aryl, I leave my shack, four fishing boats, and all related fishing equipment to do with as he sees fit."

"Why would he leave it to me? It should go to you. You're the one still fishing." Aryl looked at his father in shock.

"He knew I was having a hard time handling what I do have. I'm getting older, last thing I need is more boats to tend."

"Nonsense, you could fix up the boats, hire men to take them out and do five times the work. Make five times the money."

"And so could you." His father looked at him knowingly.

Aryl didn't hear a word his father said all the way home but stared out the window, his brow furrowed in concentration, his mind at full speed.

"Hey, Pops, can I borrow your car?" He asked his father when they pulled up in front of the cottage.

"Sure, what for?"

"I need to go for a drive with Claire." He jumped out without further explanation and found Claire in the kitchen with his mother. He took her by the arm and led her a few feet away.

"I need to talk to you."

"What's wrong?" The look in his eyes worried her.

"Get your coat and meet me in the car." Aryl went digging in the icebox, pulling out meat and two jars. "Mom, where's that old picnic basket?"

"Right above yah head." She looked at him concerned. "What's the rush, Aryl?"

He looked shaken and preoccupied. He quickly threw random things in the basket and grabbed a few quilts on his way out the door. She smiled at the back of her son's head as she followed him to the door.

"Ah, young love," she whispered under her breath. He turned around at the last minute and kissed her on the cheek quickly.

"Pops will explain."

"I'll bet he will," she said and grinned, waving at Claire. "I don't care where yah goin', just come back with a grand baby!"

Aryl threw everything in the backseat and sped off, leaving a plume of dust behind him.

"Aryl, slow down! Would you mind telling me what this is all about?"

"When we get there." He stared straight ahead with a stone expression.

"Get where?"

"The lighthouse."

∞∞∞

"What do you *mean* someone bought it?" Jonathan sat down hard on the couch with a shocked expression.

"I went to measure the windows for Arianna again, and the owner stopped me on my way in." Caleb paced Jonathan's living room. "He was apologizing all over the place. Said an investor had come along, gave him an offer he couldn't turn down. It paid off the building with plenty left over for him to retire on."

"So, it's gone." Jonathan turned his head toward the fire.

Ava's heart began to race, her eyes fixed on Jonathan. He had been living for this, and now he might go back to that dark place.

"It's gone," Caleb repeated, his hands on his head. "This is gonna kill Aryl." He appeared on the verge of panic. "What are we gonna do, Jon? He's going to be back tomorrow night. And I have to tell Arianna something."

"Give me a minute to think." He closed his eyes and rubbed his temples, something he had always done when he was making very important decisions. It was quiet for several minutes before he stood up and looked at Caleb.

"Let's go." He reached for his coat by the door.

"What are we doing?" Caleb followed him but still looked scared.

"The only thing we can do. We're going to scour this city looking for a similar deal. Knock on doors cold if we have to. When Aryl gets home tomorrow night, we'll at least have a few leads we can work on." He turned to Ava and put his hands on her shoulders. "It's going to be fine, Ava." He bent down slightly to meet her eyes, which were starting to mist. "No, don't cry. I'm going to fix this. Something will work out. I promise you. I'm going to fix this."

"I know you will," she said and smiled through her tears, grateful to see him strong and willful.

He pulled her into a tight hug. "Don't say anything to Arianna. Not just yet."

∞∞∞

Aryl parked the car and walked quickly to the passenger side. He practically yanked Claire out of the front seat, slammed the door, pulled her along behind him over the rocks and tide pools toward the lighthouse and she struggled to keep up.

"Aryl, this isn't exactly my idea of a romantic reunion with our lighthouse," she complained to him. They got to the door and found it chained shut. He rattled them in frustration then looked toward the car.

"I think there's a crowbar in the back," he said and turned back.

She grabbed his arm. "No, Aryl. Tell me what this is about."

He looked over her shoulder, down the hill of jagged rocks at the base of the lighthouse and watched as several large waves crashed against them. Claire turned her face away from the spray.

"He left me his boats," he said softly, his eyes fixed on the sea behind her. "He left it all to me. The boats, all the equipment, everything to run a fishing business."

"What does that mean?" She stared at him, her mouth fallen open, not caring about the spray or the chill.

"It means we have some decisions to make." He took her hand, went to the car, slower this time, for the blankets and basket, and led her down to a sandy patch of beach amid the rocks. "I've rolled it over several times, and it comes down to one of two decisions." He spread out the blanket and sat down next to her. "We can sell it all and use the money for investing in real estate in New York, or we can move back here. Give it a go."

She took a few minutes to process the possibilities. He took her hand and played with her ring, twirling it around her finger and studying the engraving; a lighthouse with their initials linked in hearts at the base, identical to his own ring. "I'm torn right down the middle," he admitted.

"What about Jon and Caleb? Where would this leave them if we moved here?"

"Well, naturally, I'd want them to come, too. Get out of the city. Question is, would they?" He shook his head, discouraged. "Jon hates manual labor. Caleb wouldn't mind fishing, but I don't know that he'd want to come back here. He tried like hell to get away from this town. And with the strife with his father . . . and Arianna?" He laughed a hard laugh. "She'd go nuts here."

"Aryl."

"Hmm?" He kept his eyes on her ring.

"Look at me."

He lifted his head, and she could see the exhaustion of the last few days and the weight of the dilemma in front of him. "What do you say we think about ourselves? Just us. What's best for *us*? I know we care about our friends, but maybe this once, we can make our own decision.

Based on what *we* want." He shifted uncomfortably and looked away. "Aryl, you have been the one to keep everything and everyone together through this crisis. Jon leaned on you so hard I thought you would collapse under the weight. Caleb tried to help, but he isn't a natural leader. You are. Make a decision for us, and if they follow, great. If not?" She shrugged and gave a weak smile.

"What do *you* want to do?" he asked, hoping for a nudge in one direction or another to make the decision easier.

"I want to be wherever you are." She pushed a few wisps of hair off his forehead. He laughed and squeezed her hand.

"That doesn't help. This is big. We have to decide this together. Could you really live here? Be married to a fisherman? It's a whole different life."

"I could." She looked back at the waves crashing against the base of the lighthouse. "I'd adjust," she said quietly.

"It would be a risk, Claire. I haven't fished in years, I don't know that I'd make money right away, and I'd be gone a lot."

"Sounds like you've already thought about it then."

"I've entertained the thought." He looked around him and took a deep breath. "It's so clean here. The pace is slower and the people are familiar. When I look at people here, I don't see hard, desperate faces. It's a different kind of struggling."

"Sounds like you've made your decision."

He smiled as convincingly as he could, even though his heart was still very much divided. "I just hope the others will want to come." He saw her frustration before she looked away. "We'll come regardless, Claire," he said as he pulled her chin back to face him. "I wish you could understand how it is with us."

"I'm trying."

"Hungry?" He began pulling things out of the picnic basket.

"A little. What'd you bring?"

"I'm not sure," he said with a grin. "I threw it all together in such a hurry." He pulled out a jar of pickled beets, a half-loaf of bread, a chunk of salami and a half-pint of jam. She laughed harder with every odd thing he pulled out. He ripped off a chunk of bread and tried to dig out some jam with his pocketknife.

"I'm sorry the lighthouse is locked," she said.

"I can still break the chain, you know," he said and smiled suggestively.

"Aryl, we have a lot to do before we leave tomorrow," she said with a distant tone. He looked at her, disappointed. He could see her contemplating the drastic changes on the horizon. She got up, walked down the rocky shore, and threw bits of bread to the seagulls, who squawked excitedly. The look on her face gave Aryl the feeling that she had forgotten that he was even there.

"Maybe next time," he whispered.

∞○○∞

They were quiet on the ride back to his parents and when they pulled up alongside the house, he told her to go on inside, that he would catch up.

"I want to work on the swing. Don't say anything about our decision. We'll talk to them over dinner." He gave her a kiss on the forehead, walked to the backyard, and opened the shed to dig out tools and some scrap wood. He set to work replacing the short vertical slats on the seat and tried to rehearse how he would word the proposition to Jonathan and Caleb. Wondered, worried really, about what their reactions would be; would they decide to stay? He felt weak when he wondered if he would be able to move here without them. He couldn't picture them apart after all they had been through.

He didn't hear his father calling until the third time that Michael Sullivan bellowed his name.

"Oh, hey, Pops." Aryl looked over but didn't stop working.

"I was beginning to rethink that part about you not being born deaf," he teased as he glanced over the swing, now nearly fully repaired. "I was gonna get around to that."

"It's nothin', Pops. I needed something to do."

"It's been a hell of a week, hasn't it?"

"That's an understatement." Aryl stopped sawing and stood straight, wiping sawdust off his pants. "What time is it?" He looked up at the sinking sun, wondering how long he had been outside.

"Almost dinner. So, have you made your decision?"

"Yes." He went back to sawing the last slat and fitting it into the frame. "We'll talk to you guys over dinner."

*February 19th 1930*

Aryl hugged his parents goodbye at the train station and Kathleen cried as if she would never see them again, in spite of her mood the night before when she practically did cartwheels with the news of them moving home. The whistle blew as Aryl lifted Claire up onto the platform and then turned to wave at his parents again.

"I'll telegraph soon and let you know when we'll be back." The train jerked forward as they found their seats, and Aryl sat by the window, feeling anxious about going home.

"No matter what, right?" Claire took his hand and squeezed it.

"No matter what."

∞∞∞

"What's that smell?" Claire wrinkled her nose, looking in all directions as they stepped off the train. Aryl waited for their bags, and he couldn't help but notice the smell, too. It was the smell of an overcrowded city, a world away from the sound of crashing waves and foghorns and the heavy salt air that he was already beginning to miss.

"There's enough left to get a cab home," he said, digging in his pocket, stepping out into the street to hail one.

∞∞∞

"Caleb, stop pacing," Arianna said. Caleb continued to pace Jonathan's living room. Arianna sat with Ava on the couch, struggling with a piece of knitting. She had taken the news well, given that Jonathan had been the one to tell her and had been extremely convincing that something else would pan out long before the baby was born. She had begun to play the role of supporter to Caleb, who was worried to the point of nausea.

"I need to just get this out and over with," Aryl said and knocked. Jonathan opened the door quickly, Aryl's fist still in the air.

"Hey, we're back." He set his bags down by the door and took a seat at the table. "We need to talk."

Caleb looked from Aryl to Jonathan, confused. He sent Jonathan a look that asked whether, somehow, Aryl had found out, and Jonathan answered *no* with a narrow flash of his eyes.

"Something came up when we were in Rockport. We need to have a serious talk." The others joined him around the table.

"Something happened when you were gone, too," Jonathan started. "A pretty serious disruption in our plan."

"My news could be considered the same. Flip you for who goes first." He pulled out a quarter, and Jonathan called heads before Aryl caught it.

"Damn. The one time I didn't want to win," Jonathan grumbled. "Okay, here it is. Someone bought our building. Just outright bought it, offered the old man three times what he owes. Caleb and I have been out the last two evenings looking around, talking to people, and we haven't exactly come up with anything concrete, but a few leads might be promising. We're going to find something, don't worry about that." Jonathan waited a moment for Aryl's reaction.

"So, the building is out?" he asked.

"Yes."

"And you haven't found another deal to replace it?" Aryl's eyes narrowed, seeing the situation turned in his favor. Without the building, it might be easier to sway his friends into leaving.

"But we've been trying like hell." Caleb shook his head.

"How'd you guys like to go fishing?"

Caleb and Jonathan looked at each other, confounded.

"Look, fellas, here it is. My uncle left me his entire fishing operation in his will. Claire and I have talked about it, and we think it's a good opportunity to get out of the city and still be able to work towards being our own bosses again. We all have family that we can stay with until we get our footing." Caleb shifted uncomfortably in his chair as Aryl continued. "And with hard work, it could be profitable."

"That's some news," Jonathan said, surprised. "What all did he leave you?" Aryl listed off the inventory. "And what would we need to get this operation going?" Jonathan asked, already working on the basics of a business plan in his head.

"Nothing. Everything is in good repair. One of the boats needs more work than the others, but there's four total, so we can repair that one in our spare time. There's one for each of us. The commercial buyers that my uncle worked with know my family. We would literally step into his shoes. Hardest part, I think," he said, leaning back in his chair and searching all of the faces around the table, "is going to be refreshing my memory and teaching you two the trade."

Everyone was silent. Aryl noticed the two other wives were concentrating on their husbands' faces; studying them, waiting for a reaction, some indication of what they might be thinking. Aryl looked across the table.

"What do you think, Ava? Should we go?" Ava looked surprised that he would ask her, looked to Jonathan and back to Aryl. Jonathan nudged her leg to answer.

"Well, there's no guarantee with running your own fishing business. I mean, we'd be taking a gamble."

"We would," Aryl replied bluntly.

"That's scary," she said. "Especially after what we've been through." She was hesitant to say anything more, although she loved the idea of leaving the tenement.

"But when you've got nothing, you've got nothing to lose," Jonathan said firmly. Aryl turned to Arianna.

"What about you?"

"Well, you know what my biggest concern is." Everyone at the table collectively looked at her stomach. "I guess I wouldn't mind the idea of the baby being born in the country. I wonder where we would stay and whether we'd have our own place by the time the baby came, that sort of thing."

"Well, I want to go. I think it's the opportunity of a lifetime and I don't want to miss it. Why would we want to stay in this crummy place a day longer than we had to?" Claire asked.

Silence reigned again for several minutes. Claire nudged Aryl's leg and gave him a stern look.

"We're going. Claire and me." Caleb looked as if he'd been slapped.

"What about us? We haven't decided yet."

"Well, I want you to go; of course, I want us all to go. I want Jon to run the business, you to find buyers and work on expanding when the time comes, and I want us to each have our own boat and really make this happen. But if you decide to stay here . . . ." He looked as if he were in pain as he spoke, "I'm still leaving within the week. I know it's a lot to think about. You don't have to decide right now. Take tonight to mull it over, and we'll meet at my place tomorrow after work."

Jonathan and Caleb looked at each other, knowing now that they must decide between staying behind and hoping for opportunities or going with him and taking the risk.

Aryl and Claire left everyone sitting at the table, silent and deep in thought.

"What are you thinking, Caleb?" Arianna asked softly.

"I'm thinking that this would be the perfect opportunity, if only me and my dad weren't on the outs. I don't know where we'd stay besides with them."

"I think they'd understand." She took his hand, now leaning toward the idea of starting over in a cleaner, nicer place for the baby. He put his head in his hands.

"My mom would. But not my dad. He'll never forgive me."

"But would he turn you away? If you showed up on his doorstep tomorrow, would he literally turn you and your pregnant wife away?" Jonathan asked, knowing that as mad as he was, Caleb's father would never go that far. Caleb shrugged his shoulders. "C'mon, Caleb. You know he wouldn't. And if he started getting nasty, you know your mother would rein him in." Caleb remained unconvinced and stood to leave.

"Let's get home, Ahna."

She followed, leaving Ava and Jonathan alone at the table, the room dimming quickly as evening approached. He took her hand, and she spoke before he could.

"What do you want to do, Jonathan?"

"I want to go," he said, surprising her completely.

"Really? You've already decided?"

"Yes. I want to learn to fish or lobster or whatever it is Aryl's uncle did. I want to organize a profitable business, which I know I can do. I want to get out of Victor's building and buy us a house by the beach. Claire's right, this is a good opportunity. We should go with it." He tugged at her hand and she stood up, letting him pull her over to sit on his lap. "Who knows?" He nuzzled her neck with light kisses that sent shivers up her back. "Maybe we'll find our own lighthouse or cave or abandoned car–"

"Abandoned car?" she laughed, swatting at his wandering hands. "I hate to put on airs, Mr. Garrett, but I'm going to have to insist on at least a candlelit cave for our romantic rendezvous."

"I think I can manage that." He settled his hands around her waist and looked at her more seriously. "So, we'll go then?"

"We'll go."

∞∞∞

"Caleb, stop pacing," Arianna pleaded again. "Come sit with me."

Arianna sat by the fire with her knitting, reworking another hopelessly crooked, little sweater. Caleb paced, occasionally grumbled to himself and, after a while, Arianna got up to turn the radio on to drown him out. The evening news broadcast was mostly depressing news of the economy. Caleb's ears perked up when he heard the updated unemployment numbers and bank failures followed by contrasting reports of the stock market's rally and reports that things were good again.

"I swear," Arianna huffed, not looking up from her knitting. "They really don't have any idea what's going on, do they? It's up, down, yes, no, better, worse. I wish they'd make up their minds."

He watched her for a few moments as she stubbornly ripped out and reworked sections of the sweater. She brought her work up closer to her eyes to check for missed stitches, revealing her midsection, which seemed to get bigger with every passing day. He had insisted that she go back to the midwife while he was at work today, concerned that she was farther along than they thought.

"Ahna." He went to sit beside her, feeling like a heel. "I'm so sorry. With everything that's going on, I forgot to ask you what the midwife said. You did go today, didn't you?"

"I did and wasted money on a visit. She said everything is fine, just like I told you." She put the little sweater in a basket by the hearth.

"Did she have any explanation?"

"She did." She looked at Caleb and smiled. "She said it's probably a big, strong boy and that's why I'm so big. I just don't know, though. I really feel like it's a girl."

"I'll go with what the midwife thinks. Have you gained any weight?" He looked her over, knowing the answer.

"Well, no." She avoided his eyes. "Actually, I lost a little."

"Ahna, you need to eat more."

"I'm eating what I can."

He remembered from his youth that animals bred on the farm would get extra feed and nutrient supplements. They gained weight and produced healthy calves, foals, and kids. He sat back on the couch and crossed his arms, frustrated that he couldn't do the same for his wife. She wasn't going to have a healthy baby living on potatoes and sardines. He sighed heavily. "It's time to make some hard decisions, Ahna." She moved from the chair and sat next to him on the couch. He draped one arm around her and she leaned on him, folding both hands on her stomach. "I don't want to go," he said apologetically. Her eyes darted, anxious for him to finish his sentence. She had been certain that he would decide to go, even if only for the reason that Jonathan and Aryl were leaving. She thought surely he wouldn't want to be left here alone. "This is easy for the others. It's simply a matter of to stay here and struggle or to go there and struggle. Aryl and Claire have this whole romantic history there, and Jon is drooling at the chance to run a successful business again." Arianna wanted to say so much then, but she bit her tongue for the first time in her life. "There's a little more to consider with us." He placed his free hand on her stomach and felt a strong kick. "Hey, little guy," he said with a grin and leaned down close to her stomach. "Why don't you help your old man out here? One kick for stay and two kicks for go."

"Are you really talking to my stomach?" She looked down at him as if he'd lost his mind.

"No. I'm talking to Samuel."

"You've named him? Thanks for letting me know," she said with joking irritation.

"I figured we could decide that- Ow! Ow!" Caleb looked up and laughed. "Well, that's his two cents. Or two kicks rather. I guess he thinks we should go."

"Why wouldn't we, Caleb? Why on earth would we stay here?"

"Because we'd have to live with my parents in the beginning. My father hates me. It will be uncomfortable and awkward. I'll have to go off every day and leave you to deal with it, and I don't know how long we'd be there. I don't even know how to fish. It may be a few months before we can be in our own place." He sat back on the couch and crossed his arms again. "There's even a chance that the baby could be born at my parents' house."

"Would that be so bad? It's clean and quiet, I'd have plenty of help while you're gone, and you know it would make your mother happy to have her grandchild born in the same house you were. She's sentimental."

"Ahna, you're not realizing what this really means."

"Then enlighten me." He looked frustrated and looked away. "I'll tell you what this means, Caleb. It means you will have to face your father, and I know you don't want to do that."

"I really don't," he admitted. She couldn't see the conversation going anywhere, and she was growing tired.

"I'm going to bed. We can talk more tomorrow."

"They want a decision tomorrow."

"Then make one, Caleb." He looked over at her; how docile she looked, her facial features soft and her eyes kind. "I love you. I think you know what I want to do, but you have to be okay with it, too. I will be right here, by your side, no matter what you ultimately choose to do." She kissed his cheek, and he watched her leave the room, still amazed at how much she had changed in the last few months. He wondered if this more humane and devoted side of her recently was what her family spoke of years ago when they referred to how she *used to be*.

He sat for many hours in the dark, debating and sighing, weighing possibilities and organizing priorities until finally he made a decision he could live with. After flipping on the light and getting a pen and paper, he wrote a telegram.

'Mom and Dad. Clean out my old room. Coming home.'

## February 20th 1930

Caleb fell in with Aryl and Jonathan, who were waiting outside and talking about details of the move back to Rockport. They quieted when he walked up, watching him anxiously, waiting for his decision.

"I'm going to need to stop and send a telegram on the way home from work today." Caleb pulled out the edited paper from his pocket and looked it over.

"Does that mean you're in?" Jonathan looked hopeful. His reply was less than enthusiastic.

"I'm in."

Visible relief washed over Aryl, and Jonathan set right in on reassuring him that everything would work out with his father.

"The only question now is when should we go?" Aryl wondered aloud. The contrast of the city was so stark; the smell, grit, and commotion of the city grated on his nerves and gave him a headache. He would be happy to leave today.

"Why don't we finish the week," Jonathan suggested, "collect our pay and leave on Saturday?"

Caleb was surprised. "That fast?"

"Why not?" Aryl said. "What's holding us here?" They passed by a secondhand store and Jonathan looked in the window and added to ideas he had jotted down the night before. "We should buy a few of those steamer trunks for moving." He started walking again and handed Caleb a small list.

"What's this?" Caleb asked, reading off the note to himself.

"A list of things I need you to take care of before we leave," Jonathan said.

"Really? Who made you the boss?" Aryl teased.

"You did." Jonathan held a list out to him with a smirk.

"Well, then, boss–" Aryl took the paper and glanced over it. "It's nice to have you back."

He looked at Aryl with immeasurable gratitude in his eyes. "It's nice to be back."

They started walking again, and Caleb was completely distracted by the stress of imminent reunion with his father, and he didn't notice when Aryl handed something to Jonathan.

"I know you bought another one, but it's probably time to give this back."

Jonathan didn't say anything as he took his straight razor from Aryl's hand and slipped it in his right pocket, next to the straw cross he carried with him everywhere.

∞∞∞

"What's this?" Ava had handed Claire a piece of paper when she opened her door.

"These are things we need to do before the end of the week. Jonathan was up half the night planning and this morning asked me to give these to you and Arianna and see to it that these things get done."

Claire read over the list, nodding her head. "These are good ideas, actually. Let's go get Arianna and get started."

"Get rid of the furs!" Arianna looked horrified. Claire and Ava had had a feeling this wouldn't go well.

"It's the practical thing to do, Arianna," Claire said. No matter how domesticated Arianna had become recently, she was still, to her core, Arianna. "We'd look ridiculous wearing furs around Rockport, and it makes more sense to barter them for things we'll need more."

She huffed and fussed but went along, carrying the two fur coats she had smuggled out of the house last October down the street. The others each carried a carpetbag of fancy dresses and uncomfortable shoes that would be nonsensical to bring to their new life.

Ava pulled Arianna aside before they went into the shop with the 'Barters Welcome' sign in the window.

"Jon specifically said to tell you to be sure to trade not only for sensible clothes now, but for when you're, well, bigger. It will be easier to find the things you'll need here rather than there. Thankfully, you'll be your biggest in the summer, so you won't need to buy a second coat. Try to get some baby things as well, if they have them."

Arianna rolled her eyes and walked inside. The shop owner's eyes lit up when she saw the white, floor-length and black, thigh-length furs draped over her arm. Ava and Claire had one fur each and a half-dozen dresses that were far too elegant to be of any practical use. They saved out one nice dress for holidays and family gatherings, and traded the rest for practical clothes; cotton dresses, gingham skirts and wool sweaters. Ava suggested they each get two pair of practical and, *dreadfully hideous*, according to Arianna - shoes that would be more useful than the delicate and uncomfortable heels of their previous life.

Arianna argued with the shop owner repeatedly, demanding more store credit for the shoes that had been purchased in Paris and the dresses bought in London, and Ava intervened to help them come to an agreement. By the time they were finished, they each carried two large bags of clothes, with Ava offering to carry a third bag of baby clothes and a dozen cloth diapers for Arianna.

"Well, we can check that off our list," Ava said. "Tomorrow we'll go to the safe deposit box together."

They passed by an open door where a woman with an Irish brogue was bantering loudly. Ava stopped walking abruptly.

"Maura," she breathed. Claire could see all of the happiness and excitement drain from her face, and Ava turned to look at her helplessly. "What about Maura?"

∞∞∞∞

"*Ava*, what's wrong?" Jonathan came home to find the apartment dimly lit, Ava on the couch, her arms hugging herself and her head slumped over on the arm of the couch. He looked at the bags of clothes, which were still sitting where she set them by the door, as he walked in quickly and sat down next to her. "Are you sick?" He touched her forehead and noticed her despondent, red-rimmed eyes. "What happened?" He pulled her up and over him in one graceful motion, wrapping his arms around her. "Talk to me, Ava." She sniffled and tears welled up as she spoke.

"We have to leave Maura," her voice cracked as she cried. Jonathan looked down, holding her against his shoulder and sighed heavily.

"I hadn't thought of that," he whispered. He put his head on hers and began rocking her lightly. "I'm going to miss her, too, sweetheart," he said quietly. "She has become a very special person to us, hasn't she?" Ava nodded against his shoulder. He felt the corner of the cross pressing into his thigh and shifted so it wouldn't be damaged. He had shown it to Aryl once, who commented that it was beautiful.

*It's so much more than beautifully woven straw. It's Maura's legacy. A symbol of her love and devotion to those she cared about,* he thought. He blinked away tears as he recalled that fateful night. *It was Aryl who pulled me out of that bathtub. But it was Maura who kept me out through the telling of her family legend and selfless gift. She made me open my eyes, really see things for what they were and stop the cycle of self-pity that nearly destroyed me. And that brought my Ava back to me.*

He hugged Ava tighter and kissed her forehead. He was unsuccessful at evading tears and discreetly wiped his eyes before setting Ava up straight in front of him.

"Let's go see her." He wiped under each of her eyes and kissed her forehead. "Let's go right now. And while we're there, we'll plan her first visit to Rockport."

"Really?"

"Why not? We'll work hard and help her with the train fare. Maybe she can come this summer. How does that sound?" He smoothed her bedraggled hair and settled his hands on her shoulders.

"Oh, Jon, that would be wonderful!" She threw her arms around his neck and hugged him for a long time before she whispered to him, "You always know just what to say to make it better."

He smiled, almost blushed, but mostly felt overwhelmingly grateful; to Aryl for finding him, to Maura for breathing life back into him, to Ava for forgiving him, and to the cross for being a constant reminder of each of those things.

"Get your coat. We'll grab a sandwich on the way."

Happiness was restored with the hopes that there would be a visit soon, and Jonathan and Ava began planning it before they even got on the trolley. It was crowded with only one seat available, and Ava looked slightly shocked when Jonathan took it. He gave her a teasing look and to her great embarrassment, pulled her by the hand to sit on his lap.

"Jonathan, really!" She looked around nervously for judging faces.

"What?" He pulled her closer as the trolley wobbled down the track. "No one cares. See." She relaxed a little, and he slipped his arm under her coat around her waist so she wouldn't be jostled off his lap. "I've been thinking about you all day." The mix of breath and growl indicated just how he had been thinking about her, and she swatted at him, embarrassed.

The trolley made several stops, and it wasn't long before the seat next to Jonathan was free. Ava glanced at it and then back to Jonathan, snuggling in closer, content to stay where she was.

∞∞∞

"*I'*m so sorry, Jon, Maura's not here." Ian stepped aside to invite them in. "She went upstate with the family she works for on their winter holiday to the country. She won't be back until next week."

Ava stared at Ian in disbelief. "But we're leaving."

"Is that so? Whereabouts to?"

"Back to my hometown in Massachusetts," Jonathan said, not hiding his disappointment of missing Maura.

"Well, she should be back mid-week. Come back then, I know she'd love to see you. Would you like some tea?"

"No, no, thank you. The problem is, Ian, we're leaving Saturday."

"Oh, I see. Well, that's a problem. She'll be awful sad she didn't get to say goodbye."

"We wanted to talk to you both about coming to see us in Rockport. So, this isn't so much a goodbye as we'll see you this summer." Jonathan looked around as he spoke, remembering the crowded Christmas Eve and Tarin's exquisite voice.

"I'm sure she'd love to. I'll bring it up to her when she gets home." Ava looked on the verge of tears, and Jonathan squeezed her hand.

"Ian, I'll write down my parents' address, so she can write us. And we'll drop a letter in the mail before we get on the train. And please ask her to pass this on to Charles and Sven." Jonathan jotted down the address and stood for a moment, as if waiting for Maura to walk through the door. "Well, I guess we better get home."

"I'll tell her you came by and about visiting this summer. Maybe me and Scottie will stow away."

"We'd love to have you all."

"Have a safe trip now."

Jonathan shook his hand and turned to leave with Ava under his arm.

∞∞∞∞

"Sorry we're late." Jonathan shook off his coat. Everyone was waiting at Aryl's house when Jonathan and Ava returned. "We went to say goodbye to Maura, but she wasn't there." He joined the others at the table. "She won't be back until next week." He tried to distract himself, pulling out a list from his pocket and reading over it.

"You'll see her again," Aryl said. "I'm sure of it."

"And we can give you your baby shower, Arianna." Claire looked at Ava, who nodded in agreement, but while thinking about Maura, she was unable to get excited about a party.

"So, take our pay tomorrow, add in what we've saved and subtract train fare, and this is what we'll land in Rockport with." He passed the paper around the table.

"Not bad." Aryl leaned back. "We shouldn't have to stay with family long at all."

"Here's a list of things we need to do tomorrow after work. Ladies, here's what you need to be doing during the day and a list of things to pack. We'll be trading the radios for steamer trunks tomorrow. If you could have these things ready to pack, that would be wonderful. How did today go?"

"Good." Claire spoke up for the three of them. "Arianna is quite the haggler. She even walked away with some baby things."

"That's great. Tomorrow, we'll send a telegram during lunch to Aryl's parents. They can inform the others of our arrival time. That way we only have to pay to send one. Saturday morning, we'll finish packing and catch the two o'clock train."

"We have to say goodbye to Shannon and Patrick," Arianna said with a sigh. "And no one has mentioned my vanity. I know we can't take it with us, so I'd like to give it to her. She's helped me a great deal."

Caleb put an arm around her, encouraging her generosity. "I think that's a great idea. She would love it."

Ava wasn't sure, but she thought for a moment that Arianna was blinking away tears. She assumed that Shannon was to Arianna what Maura had become to her.

Escaping this depressing life was going to be bittersweet, after all.

*February 21ˢᵗ 1930*

The three women took a whole hour before lunch to visit with Shannon and say goodbye. They exchanged addresses and promised to stay in touch. Shannon talked of visiting, but everyone knew, due to finances, that it was very unlikely. Claire noticed the unframed painting of the angel, which hung above the fireplace and decided that she would send Shannon a beautiful wooden frame for it as soon as she could.

Ava gave Claire a certain look, and they excused themselves, claiming piles of work to do. It was only partly true. They wanted to give Arianna time for a private goodbye. They each gave Shannon a long hug, and nearly all managed to remain composed.

"I'm just goin' to miss ye so much. I know the next neighbors won't be so wonderful."

"We'll keep in touch," Ava reminded. "And maybe you can visit when Arianna has her baby?" Shannon smiled, but knew deep down that this was most likely the last time she would ever see them.

After Ava and Claire left, Arianna relaxed, letting her shoulders slump forward. Roan started to cry in his cradle and Arianna automatically went to pick him up, bouncing him gently as she walked. Aislin scrambled up onto her mother's lap. Arianna gazed at Roan as she spoke to Shannon.

"I can't thank you enough for everything you've taught me." She gave a little laugh as she shifted Roan up to her shoulder. "I know I must have been terrible in the beginning."

"Twas no trouble. I enjoyed it. And no, you weren't terrible. I was impressed with how quickly you learned. Yer a natural, you know. You're going to be a wonderful mother."

"I guess we'll see," she said wistfully. "I wish you could be there. For the first few weeks, you know."

"I do, too." She set Aislin on the couch beside her and went to the kitchen, trying not to sound too emotional. "You have your good friends, though. Don't forget that. They care about you so much, ye know."

"I know," she said quietly. "I couldn't have gotten through this without them either." It was quiet for a few moments with Aislin's giggles and Roan's cooing the only occasional noises.

"Will you stay for another cup of tea? I know ye have a lot to do."

"It can wait." She laid Roan down in his cradle again and walked to the kitchen doorway. "I have questions about the baby. When it comes, I mean." Shannon turned and saw her eyes full of tears.

"I'm really scared," she whispered.

∞∞∞

"I think Columbus might have used these," Aryl joked. It was a bustling evening as they carried three old trunks down the street after trading the radios. Once home, they set them in the center of the room, and the women packed a fraction of their belongings in the order of importance as laid out in a list by Jonathan.

Caleb and Jonathan carried the vanity down the hall to Shannon, who cried and gushed over the beautiful piece. They helped squeeze it into the small bedroom and said their goodbyes to Patrick.

After they left, Shannon opened a drawer and found a few postcards Arianna wanted her to have, a picture of her and Caleb, one of Arianna's finer dresses she had saved back and a lace chemise with a note pinned to it.

*For your week*

*February 22nd 1930*

Shannon heard scuffling in the hallway. Caleb had told her the night before that Arianna was too emotional for a second goodbye, but she couldn't help but run out to catch a glimpse of the group at the bottom of the stairs.

"Thank ye for the dress," she called out. Arianna stopped and took a moment before she turned. She managed a half-smile and raised her hand, but nothing more. "I'll come see you in Rockport, I promise," Shannon said with tears in her eyes. She watched them walk out the door and turned slowly to her own apartment as the beady-eyed one eavesdropped through her door.

They arrived at Grand Central Terminal a good while before their train's scheduled departure, unloaded the trunks, and waited while Jonathan bought six one-way tickets. Everyone was excited and talkative except Caleb, who was rehearsing his first words to his father in his head and had to be reminded to stop pacing.

Arianna noticed women as they passed in fashionable dresses, salon-styled hair, and luxurious furs. She was self-conscious, as she looked over herself, dressed plainly in a red, gingham dress with the sides let out for her growing stomach, flat shoes and a black wool coat.

Aryl pulled Jonathan aside. He recounted the events of his recent trip; shared details about the service and funeral, news about family and friends, and the town's changes in the last several years. He talked of all the things that hadn't changed; the people, the sound and smell of the ocean, the gentler pace of life than what they were used to. Jonathan became more anxious to leave as the echoing noise of the station grated on his nerves.

"Let's go get some lunch," Jonathan suggested. They waved to the others as they went to get sandwiches. Aryl bought two apples and Jonathan's mouth watered. It had been at least two months since he had eaten fresh fruit. He hoped his mother still had her garden and looked forward to the farmers market he remembered from childhood. He planned to eat a quart of strawberries and a case of apples the first chance he got. Jonathan passed out small, overpriced sandwiches and caught a glimpse of Aryl as he dropped the apples in Arianna's handbag when she wasn't looking.

The platform was growing more congested, and the group stayed huddled together as they waited for passengers to disembark the train.

"Excited?" Jonathan asked Ava quietly.

"I am. I just wish–"

"I know. Me, too. But I promise we'll bring her out. It's not goodbye. It's goodbye for now," he reminded and pulled her under his arm as people pushed and shoved past them.

The whistle blew and the conductor announced the time and destination, stepping aside as people shoved onto the train. Jonathan stopped to let two older couples board ahead of them. As someone nearly bowled Arianna over, he caught her before she went sprawling and put her in front of him. He turned around and grabbed Caleb by the front of the coat.

"I know you're wrapped up in having to deal with your dad, but that jackass nearly knocked her to the ground. Wake up and take care of your wife," he yelled and pushed him back a couple of inches with irritation. Caleb was wide-eyed and alert now. Jonathan turned to board the train and someone pulled at the back of his coat. He spun around and his face lifted in surprise. Ava pushed past him with outstretched arms.

"Maura!"

"Ye dint think I'd let ye leave town without sayin' goodbye, now, did ye?" She hugged Ava tightly with tears in her eyes.

"Ian said you were gone the whole week," Ava squeaked.

"Well, the missus' little one got sick, and she wanted him to see the doctor here in town. We just got in this marnin', and when Ian told me ye were leaving, well, I had him bring me here as fast as he could. Looks like we're just in time."

The whistle blew again, the platform crowd now thinned and the conductor announced last boarding call.

Ava didn't want to let her go. "Promise you'll come see me. Promise?"

She pulled away from Ava and held her face. "I promise, love. Ye've not seen the last o' me." Ava reluctantly stepped away, wiping her face and Maura reached for Jonathan. "You take care of yourself, Mr. Jonathan."

"Thank you, Maura." He hugged her briefly.

As the whistle blew one last time, the train lurched forward and slowly began inching along the track. Jonathan lifted Ava up into the door. He hopped up to the first step and held the railing as he turned, the train moving slightly faster now. He reached in his pocket and pulled out the cross, holding it up for Maura to see. He called out over the loud chug of the steam engine. "I've carried it every day, Maura."

Tears blurred her vision and she bit her lip. She waved briefly before turning to Ian.

∞∞∞∞

Jonathan waited until the city was well behind them before he walked back to the smoking car. He sat down, lit a cigar, and watched the scenery as it passed. Caleb joined him a few moments later, sitting silently. Jonathan leaned to hand him a cigar.

"I'm sorry to get on you like that back there, but she almost got hurt."

"No. It was called for. I wasn't paying attention. I'm glad you were." He puffed on the cigar and sat back.

"It's not just with Arianna." Jonathan looked at him gravely. "I need you to be alert and focused all round. What we're about to do." He exhaled and shook his head. "It isn't going to be easy. In fact, it's crossed my mind that we might be crazy."

"Well, I could have told you that," Caleb said with a short laugh.

"In all seriousness, Caleb, we're going to have to work night and day to make this happen. It's going to take every ounce of energy and concentration, and I can't have you distracted like this. Whatever you need to do to set things right with your old man, do it, and get it over with."

"I've been thinking a lot about that." Caleb rubbed his forehead in frustration. "I'm hoping that the baby will be somewhat of an icebreaker. Maybe soften him up a little."

"I'd have a backup plan in your pocket just in case. Look, I was talking to Aryl last night. If it gets too bad, we think you should get a place of your own sooner rather than later."

Caleb shook his head. "That wouldn't be fair. We should all get set up at the same time."

"You have different circumstances than the rest of us, Caleb. Think of—"

"If you say 'think of the baby', I swear, I'll throw you off this train. You can walk the rest of the way to Rockport."

"I was going to say think of what it will be like a few months down the road when your mother and Arianna have had nothing to do but bump around the same kitchen together."

Caleb grimaced. "I see your point."

"See your point about what?" Aryl sat in between them, holding his hand out for a cigar.

"How wonderfully Arianna and his mother will get along when they've had nothing to do but look at each other for weeks on end," Jonathan said and grinned. Aryl laughed sarcastically as he lit his cigar.

"You're some help," Caleb grumbled and dropped his head in his hands. "What am I gonna do?"

"Manage as long as you can. If it gets to be too much, say the word and we'll use savings to get you guys in your own place," Jonathan said and removed the cigar from his fingers before Caleb set his own hair on fire. Caleb grumbled again.

"Either way, I'm stuck doing something I don't want to do."

Jonathan, to a certain degree, felt sorry for Caleb. But he knew he would come through this and with Arianna distracted, he may get the chance to wear the pants in their relationship for a change.

"It doesn't matter what you want to do." He leaned forward to Caleb's head, Aryl followed instinctively, both grinning. Jonathan continued, "What you *need* to do . . ." Aryl chimed in with him, ". . . is *think of the baby*."

Caleb came up fast and shoved Jonathan hard, swearing under his breath.

∞∞∞∞

"*I*'m sorry, Caleb, your father couldn't make it." Aryl's father shoved his hands in his pockets and looked away. "He sent his truck and hired hand to help with the trunks."

Caleb looked at the shiny, black Model-T pick-up he had bought for his father a few years earlier. It looked as new as the day he had bought it, and he was glad he hadn't gotten rid of it out of spite. Or necessity. "Your mom is real excited to see you. She said to tell you she's putting the finishing touches on your room." Caleb nodded an uncomfortable acknowledgment and Michael turned to Jonathan. "Your dad here yet?"

"Looks like he's running a little late." He checked the crowds and the road. An old, decrepit vehicle pulled in and sputtered to a stop. His father and mother got out, spotted him immediately, and waved. Ava tugged on Jonathan's sleeve.

"Why isn't he driving the car you sent him?" Jonathan shrugged, although he had a good idea why.

"Jonathan, welcome home." Jonathan's mother hugged him and then Ava. "Your father and I were so happy to hear you were coming. We have a room all ready for you."

"Well, we don't expect to stay with you long. And we're sorry for the short notice." His mother waved off the inconvenience and grabbed onto Ava, leading her back to the car.

Aryl called to Jonathan and Caleb. "Monday, we'll meet at Pigeon Cove marina at dawn."

Jonathan waved as he and his father slowly walked toward the car.

"So, what's your plan, son? I know you must have a few tricks up your sleeve, or you wouldn't be here. I think it's an excellent idea, by the way, to come back home and redesign your strategy. I've been talking to some friends in Boston. They are about to jump back in. There's been a small but steady rise since Christmas, and they think it's gonna take off like a shot come spring, and they're going to ride it back up. Been dying to talk to you about how you're going to get back in."

"We'll talk later." Jonathan pointed to the old car. "What happened to the car I had delivered last year? And what is that thing anyway?" He laughed at the shoddy relic his father drove.

"Well, I appreciate the thought, but that Tudor you sent me was breaking down left and right. I spent more time waiting for parts and having it fixed than I got to enjoy it. I bought old reliable here, a 1918 Tourer. Hasn't broke down on me once."

Jonathan looked over the open cab and tattered canvas top. "This can't do too well in the winter," he assumed.

"Does just fine. We bundle up," he said curtly and climbed into the driver's seat.

Caleb and the hired hand loaded the trunks and drove carefully over the bumps and ruts of the gravel roads. They dropped off Jonathan's trunk and then Aryl's before returning to the farm. The hired hand chose to sit in the back where the trunks had been.

Caleb turned up the long, dirt road to his parents' house, and a knot grew in his stomach. The burly farmhand hoisted the trunk by himself and carried it in the back door as Caleb's mother directed him what room to put it in upstairs. When she turned, Caleb was in the doorway, Arianna holding open the screen door behind him.

"Hey, Mom." He surveyed the room but saw no sign of his father.

"Well, don't you look good!" Ethel hugged him and smiled over his shoulder at Arianna. "And you, too, but you're way too thin!" She hugged her carefully and gave her stomach a pat. "Gonna have to fatten you up. Give me a few minutes to finish dinner. In the meantime, I'll show you your room. You can get settled."

They followed her upstairs to Caleb's old bedroom.

"It's all cleaned and dusted, and we brought grandma's old bureau out of the barn and polished that up for you to use. The room is cold from airing out all day, but you can close the window, if you'd like. Of course, we'll give it a good cleaning again before the baby comes."

"Well, I doubt we'll be here that long," Caleb said, looking away from his mother. "But we appreciate you putting us up for now."

"Well, we'll see what happens. You two come down when you're all settled, and I'll have some dinner for you." She turned to leave and Caleb stopped her at the door.

"Where's Dad?" Her smile dropped and she looked apologetic.

"He's out working in the barn. Said he'd see you later tonight or tomorrow."

"I suppose nothing's changed," he said quietly, looking at the floor. She tilted her head to the side with a look of pity and put a hand on his cheek.

"It'll work itself out, don't worry. He's just a stubborn, old coot. He was happy to hear about his grandchild, though. He started refinishing your rocking horse. Remember that?" Caleb smiled, recalling his favorite toy as a child. She left the room, closing the door behind her and they took a good look around. There was a full-size bed with an ancient quilt and basic metal frame centered along the wall. On the opposite wall set the old bureau, and on a side wall was a cabinet with a blue washbasin and pitcher.

"Well, it's bigger than our old room—cleaner, too," Arianna said.

"It's pretty bad when moving in with your parents is a step up." Caleb sat down on the bed and the old, spring frame squeaked loudly. "Great."

∞∞∞

Jonathan noticed the things that weren't there; the grandfather clock Jonathan had shipped to his parents from London, several pieces of art from Paris, furniture and souvenirs from his travels over the last few years. The entire house, in fact, was sparsely decorated and seemed almost hollow.

As his father helped him carry the trunk up the stairs, he was nervous, making excuses for the missing items before even asked: given to charity or broken or out being repaired or, Jonathan's favorite, tucked away safe because of a rash of burglaries.

"Crime has gotten that bad in Rockport?" Jonathan asked sarcastically.

"Better safe than sorry, son." He avoided his son's eyes and set the trunk down carefully in the center of the room. He and Ava unpacked the trunk until his mother called them down for a late dinner.

His father passed the casserole dish and looked at Jonathan. "Did the house sell before you left, or is it still on the market? I know there are not a lot of buyers right now. Especially in the high-priced neighborhood you lived in. I hope you didn't have to mark it down too much."

"We lost the house, Dad," Jonathan spoke numbly and didn't look up.

"What do you mean you lost it? It was paid for!"

"I know."

Ava only pretended to eat, glancing nervously from father to son as Jonathan continued uncomfortably.

"When everything shook out, I owed so much money to the bank, they took everything. My cars, house, firm, furniture. Everything. It was gone in an instant. And I still owe money."

His father stared at him, dumbfounded. "Well, what have you been doing then? All this time?" Jonathan put his fork down, leaned back and crossed his arms. He had no desire to narrate the events from October to January; a period in his life that he would just prefer to forget.

"Haven't you been getting Ava's letters? She's been writing, and I know she hasn't been putting on airs about our situation."

"Yes, we've gotten them, but there was nothing saying it was this bad. It sounded like you were on your way back up. Or at least working on a plan." Jon Sr. looked at his wife, confused.

Ava's mouth dropped and she looked at Jonathan. "But I told them exactly—"

"Mom?" Jonathan watched his mother as she nervously fidgeted with her silverware.

"It was that bad, Jon," she spoke apprehensively to her husband as she explained herself. "I didn't want to alarm you. I polished up what Ava was writing and added in a few things here and there, so you wouldn't worry." Jon Sr. threw his napkin on the table.

"Well, then, since I didn't get the truth from my wife, why don't you fill me in on what's really been going on?" His father's glare demanded an answer.

"After the crash, we only had a few days to get a plan together. All we had was the money in our wallets. Less than three hundred dollars between us. We've been living in a drafty tenement, and I've been working at a shipping dock. We were saving a down payment for an apartment building, but someone bought it out from under us while Aryl was back here last week for his uncle's funeral, who left him his fishing boats in his will." The condensed version was easier to speak of than he thought. His father took a few minutes to process everything his son had revealed. His mother still hadn't looked up.

After an awkward silence, his father composed himself and spoke with authority. "Okay. All right, next week, you can go with me to Boston. I'm meeting with some friends to discuss business. They've been watching the markets, and they're almost ready to jump. We should get in on that. I have a little money saved. I'll give it to you to work that magic of yours. I know it would be hard for you, coming from being your own boss, but I'm sure one of my friends would let you in their firm with your track record and all, and you can work your way back up."

"Dad, I'm not getting back in."

"What do you mean you're not getting back in?" His father's expression mingled wary and disbelieving.

"I mean, I'm not playing the game anymore. For a lot of reasons."

"That is the most ridiculous thing I have ever heard." He looked at his wife, bewildered. "Can you believe this? The talent he has and he's just throwing it away." She glanced briefly and uncomfortably at Jonathan. His father returned his eyes to Jonathan. "Just what do you plan on doing then?" He leaned forward over his plate, his ears growing red with frustration. Ava reached for Jonathan's hand under the table, rubbing her thumb along the back, silently comforting and supporting.

"I just told you, Aryl's uncle left him his boats. We're going to do that." His father looked like he had just been told a hilarious joke.

"Do what? Fish?" Jonathan stabbed at his casserole, his face growing ruddy with humiliation.

"Yes."

Jon Sr. rubbed his face, agitated. "Well, that's great. Just great. I kept you off those boats for a reason, Jonathan. There's no money in fishing. No real money. Not like what you had. Do you honestly think–" he interrupted himself with a mocking laugh, "that you'll get rich again throwing pots all day?"

"No. But there's more to life than money, Dad. I don't need that life anymore. I don't want it." Jonathan wanted to crawl out of his skin, suddenly wanted to be anywhere but here, trying to explain what even he didn't understand.

"How can you not want that life!" his father yelled. "You had everything!"

"Jon, stop yelling," his mother ordered.

"No, Margaret, I won't stop yelling. He sounds as ridiculous as when he was younger, wanting to run off with those friends of his, playing on the beach when he needed to be here learning, working on his future."

Jonathan frowned as he thought back on all the times he asked, begged to go off with Caleb and Aryl, but his father refused to let him, insisted on molding him into a financial child prodigy.

"A lot of good it did me," Jonathan said.

His father was fuming now. "What's that supposed to mean?"

"Everything I own is in a trunk upstairs, Dad. The life I had was an illusion. It wasn't real."

Jon Sr. snorted. "Well, it looked pretty damned real all the times we came to visit."

Jonathan shook his head. "You don't understand. The way I did things, the way it was all set up, it wasn't really mine. If it was, it couldn't have been taken away so easily. I do have a plan. But this time I'm going to restructure my life better. I know that what's mine is truly mine and can't be taken away."

"Look, son, I know you're probably traumatized by what happened." He shifted his tone to sound more convincing. "A lot of folks were. But that doesn't mean you should give up and run away. Just come with me next week. Talk to these people. You won't be so afraid after you see what they are seeing."

"I'm not afraid," he said indignantly. "And your friends are wrong. I've been watching with morbid curiosity, and I can tell you that this rally is false. More smoke and mirrors. Your friends are making a huge mistake, and you will, too, if you follow them."

Margaret stood and started clearing away plates of uneaten food. Ava offered to help, begging with her eyes to get away from the tension-filled table. They disappeared into the kitchen, grateful for the busy work.

"So, what am I supposed to do?" Jon Sr. asked directly. "How am I supposed to recoup my losses? I had invested everything with you, you know."

Jonathan felt a stab of guilt so strong it brought on a wave of nausea. "I know you did," he said quietly. He had nothing to offer or suggest, and so he remained silent. His father stared at him, waiting. When it became obvious that Jonathan wasn't going to offer him a solution, he slammed his glass on the table and stormed out of the room.

Margaret and Ava reemerged from the kitchen with mugs of coffee. His mother sat across from him and took a deep breath. "I know I have some explaining to do."

"Why didn't you tell him, Mom? It would have made all this so much easier."

"I know, and I'm sorry. I had my own selfish reasons. It was wrong and I regret it now. But you have to understand, he was pinning all his hopes on you, Jonathan. Every day, even as things got worse and worse, he would talk about how you were going to fix everything, you would get back what he'd lost. After a while, I found it impossible to dash his hopes." She stared at the rose pattern on the tablecloth as she spoke, "He had to sell the car you sent him. And the clock. Most everything of value is gone, and what little is left will be gone soon. When so many businesses went under, he lost many accounts. Some of his biggest accounts have yet to pay him for last quarter's work. It's impossible to pick up any new clients, although he goes to Boston once a week and still tries. The few accounts he keeps now are for local businesses. Nothing that pays much."

"Are you in debt?"

"Not much. It's just a matter of making ends meet. You can't tell him that I told you this, but he's been working part-time at the quarry. It's terribly hard work for someone as old as your father, Jonathan. He can't secure a full-time position because the younger ones work circles around him. He's only still there because one of the supervisors is our friend and he feels bad for him. He'd die if he knew I'd told you. He's so ashamed."

"There's nothing to be ashamed of," Ava spoke up, frustrated. "He's doing whatever it takes to get by and that's commendable."

"Jon Sr. doesn't see it that way, dear. He sees it as a personal failure." She turned her head slightly toward the door Jon Sr. had stormed out of with a worrisome frown and troubled eyes that Ava recognized.

"I know how he feels." Jonathan pushed away from the table. "I'll try to talk to him tomorrow. I think that right now I'm going to get some sleep."

∞∞∞

"How are you, Ahna, did you have a good trip?" Hubert asked.

Ethel put out a large dinner and Hubert joined them late, sitting down in a business-like manner, ignoring Caleb, but acknowledging Arianna.

"We did. The scenery was beautiful."

"And the baby? Everything going well?"

"Yes. I was very sick at first, but everything is fine now. Caleb's worried I'm getting too big, though."

Hubert snapped his head up, looking at Caleb for the first time, his expression horrified. "That's ridiculous," he scoffed loudly. "You're thin as a rail." He took his hateful expression off Caleb and looked kindly at Arianna. "Me and Ethel will see to it that you gain some weight for that baby. If your husband doesn't like his women on the plump side, he's just going to have to get over it for the next few months."

"It's not that, Dad." He shifted uncomfortably, and Hubert went back to pushing his food around his plate.

Caleb stared at the top of his head when he spoke. "I know she's too thin. I'm concerned about her stomach. It seems like shortly after we found out, it just got bigger by the day. Seems like it's growing too fast."

Hubert's response was to put another biscuit on Arianna's plate and smother it with white gravy, laced with tan puddles of bacon grease.

"It just seems like that, dear," Ethel patted Caleb's hand, as he stared at his father's bent head, waiting for his comment or presence to be acknowledged. Caleb pushed his plate away and sat back, irritated with Hubert. He glanced at Arianna and reminded himself that she was the reason he was here. As long as he could put up with his father's resentment, Arianna would eat well and their baby would be healthy.

A short time later, Hubert tossed his napkin, announced he was going to bed. Ethel gave Caleb an apologetic grimace. "Give it time," she whispered after Hubert had left the room.

## February 24th 1930

"I'm sorry I stormed out last night. It was rude," Jon Sr. said quietly several minutes into an early, silent breakfast. Margaret had been glaring at him, but relaxed after his apology, which told Jonathan that it was one of those female-forced apologies.

"It's fine, Dad. I know it must have been hard to hear."

"If you're not going to change your position, I would appreciate being able to consult with you about my investments. I have to recoup my losses, Jonathan. If I don't, I'll be working until the day I die."

"I'll help in any way I can," Jonathan offered. He knew his father well, however, and was fully prepared to withstand the pressure he would surely keep on him to return to the investment world. "We'll talk about some ideas later, all right?"

## February 25th 1930

"Just look at that sunrise." Aryl was already on the boat, separating lengths of rope. Caleb was yawning despite the invigorating five-mile walk from his parents' farm, and Jonathan was still half-asleep as they stumbled on board.

"Today," Aryl said, "I'm just going to get you guys used to the boat and equipment. We'll go out together for a week or two. Then if you feel comfortable enough," he said as he pointed to other boats tied to the dock, "we'll split up, and you guys can take your own boats out." Aryl ran through a basic list of terms, pointing as he spoke. "Bow, stern, port, starboard–" He grinned as he held up a lobster pot. "money."

"What do we do?" Jonathan asked, standing on the deck, feeling completely lost.

"Well, we need to scrape and tar these pots. Looks like it's been awhile since my uncle had tended to them, some of them need fixing, and we need to untangle all these ropes. I need to study the charts to be sure of where my uncle's territory was. Don't want to go starting any trouble or losing any pots." Jonathan stared at him, clueless. "My dad talked to the other fishermen in the area. They all agreed that I, well, we could take over my uncle's territory." Jonathan looked out, the orange glow of sunrise shimmering on the vast sea, and his groggy mind tried to understand.

"Sometimes it amazes me that you grew up here and yet manage to know so little about this life." Aryl laughed, shaking his head.

"Hey, my face was in a book most of the time, remember?"

"Okay, look, we all have our own territory. It's agreed among us. If someone muscles in and tries to take over a spot without permission, it causes a lot of animosity. Lines of lost pots are very expensive to replace. But, like I said, it was agreed that we would take over his territory. And we can always go out further if it gets too crowded. Blue with a white band around the middle. Those buoys are my uncle's. We'll stick with it to avoid confusion. Come over here and I'll teach you guys basic knots and show you how to bait the traps. Then we'll head out and drop a string, just to get you guys familiar. Later, we'll do more maintenance on the equipment."

He set Jonathan to untangling ropes and Caleb touching up the paint on the buoys. He looked over the pots, found two dozen that were in good repair and set them aside. When they pulled in the lines and set out, Jonathan intently watched everything Aryl did. He was anxious to learn as fast as he could, so he could set out with his own boat. He watched as the shoreline became more distant and then turned, squinting into the rising sun.

Aryl checked his chart and compass, teaching Jonathan and Caleb as he refreshed his own memory. The sun was fully up when Aryl showed how to brick and bait the traps, tying them together in a string beginning and ending the line with a buoy. He had each of them take turns steering the boat and gave a crash course education on the engine maintenance and the sails used for backup.

Jonathan's head was swirling with new information by the time they edged up to the dock close to lunchtime. Kathleen was waiting on the dock with a basket of sandwiches and fresh coffee.

"You are a lifesaver," Aryl said with a huge smile as they bumped lightly into the pier, and Jonathan threw the rope to secure the boat.

"How'd it go out there?" she asked.

"Pretty good, they're fast learners." He turned to grin at Jonathan, who had jumped onto the pier to secure the rope. "I might keep 'em," he teased.

"It's wonderful," Jonathan said to Kathleen. "I'm going to love this. The sense of freedom out there, it hardly feels like working." She laughed.

"Just wait till it's ten below and ice rainin' sideways. It'll feel like work, all right, but yah lucky today. It's beautiful, much warmer than usual. Enjoy it, it won't last."

Aryl helped her onto the boat and she sat on a pot, visiting with her son.

"Has everyone named their boats?"

Jonathan looked up at her, and then at Aryl with a mouth full of sandwich. "Name them?"

"Well, yes, you need to name your boat. Cahn't take it out till yah do. It's bad luck."

"They're your boats, Aryl," Caleb reminded. "You should name them."

"No. Each of you needs to name the boat you're going to be taking out. It doesn't matter who technically owns the boat. It will be your boat, essentially. Think of a name."

"What did you name yours?" Jonathan asked Aryl.

"The Lisa-Lynn. After my great aunt."

Caleb and Jonathan looked at each other, instantly knowing what names they would each use.

"I got it." Caleb stared off with a goofy smile. "I'll name it the Ahna-Joy." Aryl looked at him with a cocked eye, and Jonathan suppressed a laugh and admired Caleb's ability to love his controversial wife so unconditionally.

"What about you?" Aryl asked Jonathan "Need time to think about it?"

"Oh, no. I know what it'll be," he said. He smiled at the boat he would soon be in charge of. "The Ava-Maura."

∞∞∞∞

Ava was working in the garden with Margaret, preparing for the upcoming planting season. She looked up, saw Jonathan come round the side of the house, and smiled widely. She pushed off her knees, tossed her gloves and trowel, and brushed dirt off her skirt and coat. She walked quickly to meet him and jumped up to hug him.

"Careful, I'm covered in tar."

"I don't care."

He held her off the ground for a moment.

"How was it?" she asked excitedly.

"Oh, it was great, Ava. I was worried at first, but I think this is going to work out just fine." He gave her an exaggerated kiss. "What about you? How was it here today?"

She couldn't take her eyes off his smile as they walked back toward the garden. "It was great. We got all the laundry dried and ironed, and we've been out here since after lunch. I'm helping her expand the garden and trying to plan what will go where. I'm learning a lot for when we have our own garden."

He pulled her to his side and kissed her head. "Soon, I promise."

After dinner, Jonathan found his father in the detached garage. He noticed a small crate with dusty boots and work clothes in the corner, half-covered with a blanket.

"It was great out there today. You should come out with us sometime."

"If I'd wanted to be a fisherman, Jonathan, I would have bought a boat."

"I didn't say you should work. Just come enjoy the sights and smells. I honestly didn't expect to like it this much," he spoke through a smile that irritated his father.

"You're new and being romanced by the sea. I've seen it many times. You get caught up in the salt air and crashing waves, the sense of freedom—now *that's* an illusion, Jonathan. The *freedom*," he snorted sarcastically. "But before you know it, you're tangled in those pot ropes so tight you'll never get out."

"You sound bitter."

Jon Sr. ignored him and began tinkering with the engine of the antique vehicle.

Jonathan sat on an apple crate in the corner and watched his father. "You seem to know what you're doing."

"Self-taught mainly. Mechanic friend in town gives me pointers when I'm stuck."

Jonathan watched his father with narrowed eyes, the obvious discrepancy opening up the opportunity to get his father talking honestly. "I thought it never broke down."

Jon Sr. stopped working and sighed heavily. He wiped grease off his hands, frustrated and slightly embarrassed. He was hesitant in his confession, sitting down on a crate alongside Jonathan to avoid his eyes. "When I got this, it was in pieces. The engine was shot. I've rebuilt it from the ground up."

"That's impressive."

"No, that's sad. A man, my age, after all that I have accomplished in my life." He continued reluctantly, his pride visibly distressed. "I had to sell that car you sent us. Paid some bills and had enough left to pick up this old thing, get it running."

"And the other things? The clock, art, all that was sold, too?" Jonathan tried to push his father past his pride, knowing all too well what a paralyzing vise it could be. He sighed with a reddened face and turned away.

"Yes. I'm sorry. I feel awful. They were things you wanted us to have."

After a long silence, Jonathan began his confession, "I didn't deal with the crash well, Dad. Not at all. I hated where I lived, where I worked, hated myself for a brief time. I think I even hated Ava." Jonathan scoffed at what now seemed like an atrocity coming from his mouth. His father looked up from his shame and concentrated on his son's words. "While the others were looking for a way out and seeing the tiniest bit of good in everyday things, I felt sorry for myself. And I sunk really low."

Jonathan stood and leaned against the car, facing his father.

"I don't want to see that happen to you. You wouldn't believe how easy it is, Dad." He paused, reflecting on his own inward spiral into oblivion. 'I almost lost Ava, my friends," he lowered his head and spoke quietly, "my life."

"Your life? I don't understand."

Jonathan nodded, deciding in that brief second to reveal everything. "I was so wrapped up in what I lost that I couldn't see what I still had. It was an ugly descent, really, and I ended up in a bathtub, ready to call it quits." He pulled his sleeve up with a slight jerk that got his father's attention, revealing the thin, white scar across his wrist.

His father's eyes widened and he looked up with concern. "Son, you don't mean—"

"Yes. I'm not proud of it." He lowered his sleeve and placed his hands in his pockets self-consciously. "Only Aryl knows. Ava thinks it was an accident at work. I'd appreciate it if you didn't say anything to her or Mom."

"Of course," his father said. "But I don't understand?"

"Aryl found me. Stopped me. Maura helped open my eyes."

"Maura, your maid?"

"No, Maura, my friend." One hand touched the edge of the cross. "In her own way, she helped me see that I couldn't lose what wasn't mine to begin with. But I stood to lose everything that *was* still mine by wallowing in grief for what wasn't."

Jon Sr. took a moment to contemplate his son's profound words until they wrapped themselves around his own struggles.

"I think I see what you mean." He tilted his head with a hint of disbelief. "How'd you get to be so wise anyway? Isn't that my job? Giving insight, life lessons, and all that?" He gave a self-reproaching laugh, feeling inadequate as a father.

Jonathan dismissed his father's comment with a wave of his hand. He looked outside to see the light almost fully faded, the slightest glow of crimson left in the western sky.

"I think I'm going to head to bed. I'm up even earlier tomorrow. Aryl's a real slave driver." He flashed a teasing look, his sincere smile crinkling the corners of his eyes.

∞∞∞∞

The next morning was a continuation of the crash course education in lobster fishing. Shortly after setting out, Aryl handed the chart and compass to Jonathan.

"Today, you get to find the pots."

Jonathan looked slightly shaken as he glanced over the unfamiliar chart. He tried to make sense of the markings and abbreviations. He looked up at Aryl, panicked.

"These aren't exactly the charts I'm used to looking at. I have no idea how to read these!"

Aryl pointed to places on the chart. "We're here, the pots are here." He tapped the compass. "Find them." He stood back and crossed his arms, slightly amused. He could have explained more of the topography and symbolism, but he knew Jonathan loved a challenge despite his panicked protest and decided to let him learn by trial.

Caleb busied himself with setting up pots, untangling ropes, feeling quite tempted to slip down to the berth and catch a nap. He logged ten miles a day of walking to and from the marina and, feeling a sense of obligation, helped with evening chores on the farm. It was something he resolved to do every evening to compensate for room and board. He didn't ask, but joined his father in the barn after dinner, feeding and bedding down the animals for the night while his father milked. Hubert said nothing, only glancing at him once as the two worked silently. After the animals were tended to, Caleb walked straight to their room, fell on the bed–the springs giving a piercing squeal, and was asleep within minutes. His mind was foggy and it startled him when Jonathan let out a short, maniacal laugh.

"Aha! I'll be damned! There it is!"

Caleb walked, his steps wavering against the dips and rolls of the boat, and stood next to Jonathan at the wheel, looking and sounding impressed. "How'd you do that?"

"I have no idea." Jonathan shook his head with an astonished grin.

"Okay, now, keep in mind, they've only been out one night. And it's winter. And they weren't set out that far. So, we're not going to get rich today." Aryl showed the two how to pull the pots up, by letting each of them try it out. It surprised Jonathan how much exertion was required to pull a pot, an empty pot at that, up off the bottom of the sea. He was sweating by the fourth pot. Only the fifth held four lobsters, and after opening the hatch, Aryl showed them how to hold them without getting pinched, check it for size and, finally, to make sure it wasn't an egg-bearing female. One was. It and two undersized ones were thrown back over, leaving them one lobster in the holding tank. The three stood around it, staring at their first catch.

"And that's all there is to it." Aryl grinned, proudly.

*March 2 1930*

Victor sat in his office with the door securely closed, talking in a low voice to a man who came highly recommended among the more fraudulent and corrupt executives he knew. He was someone who could get a job done, leave no tracks, and was not known for being a rat. Victor would take no chances this time on an amateur looking for a quick buck.

This job required a professional. They were working out the terms of payment when the receptionist knocked on the door, waited a moment, and then walked in with a stack of papers.

"This month's evictions." She set the papers on his desk and left quickly.

Half of them weren't true evictions, but abandonments. He was hardly concerned; they would fill by the end of the following week. As he moved them to a drawer, something caught his eye. He read the name three times before jumping up to check the cash ledger the receptionist kept in her lower drawer. He read over it multiple times and slammed his fist on the desk with an unintelligible growl that ended as a scream.

Without explanation, he left and drove himself to the building where Jonathan Garrett had lived. He took the stairs two at a time and pounded on Jonathan's door so hard that it shook the frame. He called out his name, ordering him to open the door and thumped again.

"They ain't there." Victor turned to see the beady-eyed one standing in her doorway. Although Victor was unnerving, she was unable to resist the chance to gossip. "They left last Saturday." He struggled to control his voice and sound cordial.

"Do you know where they went?"

"I heard the neighbor over there say that she would come visit them in Rockport. No idea where that is. They made a calamitous amount of noise movin' out, shuffling furniture, and dragging trunks down the stairs. And for crying poor the way they did, I was surprised they had the money to call a taxi truck. With them gone now, at least I won't have to deal with that loud-mouthed Irish–"

Victor turned and scurried down the stairs, the door to the building slammed shut behind him.

When he walked back into his office, his hired man was still waiting patiently in his office. Victor was somewhat surprised.

"I charge by the hour as well as by the job. Makes no difference to me if I sit here all day. It's your dime."

"Well, the job has changed." Victor wrote down some information and handed it, along with money for train fare and accommodations, across the desk. "I need you to go here. Find out everything you can about these people. But lay low." The man gave an annoyed look at Victor for stating the obvious.

*March 5th 1930*

Ava was bored. She walked the house slowly from room to room, looking for something to do. She was tired of reading, had no interest in knitting or sewing, and since she worked with Jonathan's mother, the housework and cooking was not enough to keep them both busy the full day. Their bedroom only took minutes to tidy, a vast difference from her life in New York where her entire day was spent scrubbing walls and floors that would never come clean. Margaret enjoyed her free time by preparing and expanding her garden. Ava walked out to the backyard, coat and purse in hand.

"I'd like to walk to Aryl's parents' house and see Claire." Margaret looked up from under her wide sunhat with a smudge of dirt on her nose.

"Well, that sounds like fun. I bet you miss your friends."

"I haven't seen them in almost two weeks."

"Do you remember the way?"

Ava looked east and then west. "I think so."

"It's only about a mile or so from here. I'll draw you a little map." She rose, dusted wet dirt off herself and went inside. She drew a detailed map with little drawings and the names of several residents along the way. "You might want to take an umbrella, looks like rain later."

Ava pulled one from the ceramic canister by the door and headed out. It felt good to be outside and alone. She had become accustomed to walking everywhere, and she was surprised how much she missed it. The scenery was so much more peaceful here. She could look all around as she walked, instead of keeping her eyes on the concrete, afraid to look up. She could nod at neighbors instead of shying away from them. She felt safe to stroll along leisurely, looking at the cute homes and cottages with their pretty trim and neat yards and dream about how she would decorate their home when they had one again.

The air was surprisingly warm and still; almost stale with a strong, earthy smell. She looked to her left and couldn't see the ocean through the trees, but saw a large wall of billowing clouds above them, smoky black with deep, violet veins. She hoped Jonathan wasn't anywhere near them and that he would be home well before those clouds got to shore.

Claire saw her as she walked up the gravel drive and met her at the door with an excited hug. "I've missed you so much!" She pulled her inside where she said hello to Aryl's mother, made a cup of coffee and slipped out the back door to sit on the swing and talk.

"How have you been? How's it going with Jonathan's parents? What do you do with yourself all day? I've been going out of my mind with boredom!"

"Whoa, one at a time. First, I've been fine. It was rough with Jon Sr. in the beginning, but he's starting to come around. Can you believe that, after all everyone has been through, he's still pressuring Jonathan to start trading again? Jonathan said never again. He has other ideas. And as far as what I do all day, I've been going crazy! Jonathan is gone so much, and I think Margaret and I have run out of things to talk about. I tried some of her hobbies, but I didn't really like them enough to keep at it. I am helping her with her garden, though. That I like, but I'll like it better when it's my own."

Claire sighed in agreement. "Aryl said maybe by May if things go well."

"Well, that's hopeful. Jon hasn't said anything either way. I don't see why we all couldn't find a place now, we have the money that they would have used for the down payment on the building, but Jon said that money is savings for the business. In case they need to repair or replace something."

"We should start having our weekly meetings again. We can visit and maybe start some projects together."

"That's a great idea. And we need to start planning Arianna's party."

Claire's eyes popped open. "I almost forgot about that! We should go see her." She scrambled to her feet as if they were going to set out right then.

"That's a long walk, Claire. Maybe someone could drive us out there this evening?"

"Nonsense. I'll drive us." She had a mischievous grin, and her eyes sparkled. Ava looked hesitant.

"Oh, come on." Claire grabbed her arm and pulled her up. "It'll be fun." She skipped ahead, dragging Ava with her and found Kathleen in the living room tending to Michael, who was home with a cold. "Would it be all right if I borrowed the car so Ava and I can go see Arianna?" She aimed her question at Michael, since she knew it would be almost impossible for him to say no to her.

"Well, I suppose. You know how to drive?" Michael asked cautiously.

"Of course," she said, smiling sweetly and convincingly.

"Well, all right." Michael struggled up, coughed for a moment, and then went for the keys in the kitchen.

"We'll only be gone a few hours. Thank you!" She gave him a peck on the cheek.

Claire sat for a moment, looking everything over.

"Just give me a minute. I've seen Aryl do this a hundred times."

"You should probably begin with starting it," Ava teased. Claire started it, put it in gear, turned to look behind her, and lurched forward five feet. Ava screamed and grabbed the dashboard.

"Oops." She giggled. They glided out of the driveway clear to the other side of the road, and she put it in drive, making a painfully slow, wide turn to get straight in the road. She paused, took a deep breath and the car lurched forward again, only to screech to a halt a second later. It sputtered violently and the engine died. Claire had to try three times to start it again, and when it did, she took off like a shot, steering wildly to stay on the road. Michael and Kathleen watched from the window.

"That girl has never driven a day in her life," he whispered under his breath.

"Well, she did bettah than I did when I got behind the wheel."

"That's not saying much, honey."

∞∞∞

They found the farm without too much trouble, sputtering and jerking up the long drive. As they neared the house, Ava couldn't help but laugh at the sight of Arianna, who was sitting on the front porch, churning butter with one hand and blowing on freshly painted nails of the other.

Claire shook her head. "Ma farmer meets Parisian party girl."

Arianna stood with a little effort and hugged her friends. "It's so wonderful for you to come see me! I feel like I'm so far away from civilization out here. And when did you learn how to drive!" She looked excited and envious at the same time.

Claire gave a sly but proud smile. "Just now."

"How on earth did you get them to let you borrow the car?"

"I lied." She shrugged her shoulders.

Arianna's face fell in shock at first, then she smiled in approval. "Well, I'm glad you did, and I'm glad you came to see me." She spun around to Ava, almost losing her balance due to her off-centered midsection. "I almost forgot! I got a letter from Maura yesterday."

"So did I, but I forgot to bring it." The latter was Ava's lie. She kept Maura's letters, three of them in only two weeks, all to herself. Even Jonathan wasn't allowed to read them. Ava would read important segments to him aloud instead. They were special, they were hers, and she wasn't going to share.

"I haven't gotten one yet," Claire said, feeling somewhat left out.

"Well, I'll go get mine, and Ava can read it aloud while I finish with the butter."

Claire and Ava looked at the wooden butter churn after the screen door slammed shut behind Arianna. "Never in my wildest dreams," Claire said, shaking her head. "I wish I still had a camera."

Arianna returned, handed the letter to Ava, and took her seat next to the churn, moving the paddle up and down and glanced to admire her short, bright red nails. Ava began reading, hearing Maura's voice in her head as she spoke. She had to speak loudly, so the sloshing and the tapping of the churn didn't drown her out.

*Dear Arianna,*

*I hope this letter finds you happy, healthy and having gained some weight. How was the train ride and how are you settling in? I think about all of you often and miss you all very much.*

Ava blinked quickly and cleared her throat before she continued.

*I am sorry I wasn't able to give your baby shower, but I'm sure Ava and Claire will do a fine job. I saw Charles on the trolley the other day. He says hello, sends his love and best wishes with the baby. As much as I miss you all, I am feeling strongly that it was good that you left the city when you did—*

"Hold on one minute, Ava," Arianna interrupted. "Mother Ethel! I'm ready!" she hollered. Ethel came quickly, with a bottle of nail polish in one hand and a large glass of milk in the other. She set the milk down on the porch rail with orders for her to drink it. Arianna moved the chair to the other side of the churn, took the plunger with her polished hand and held out the unpolished hand to Ethel. "Okay, you can go ahead now, Ava." Ava watched incredulously as Ethel finished the manicure, complete with hand massage. She shook off the surprising scene and continued reading.

*. . . good that you left the city when you did. There are scores of people without jobs and I have seen them, sometimes a block long, standing in line for free soup and bread. Petty crime is worse as well, as more folks are struggling to make ends meet. Dan's hours were reduced, but we're grateful he has the ones he does, and we've taken in an older aunt. It helps both of us, she puts a little toward the rent now, and she will have someone to care for her later in her old age. She works part-time at the library, which are my only moments of peace. She's likely to drive me to the insane asylum with her complaining of America and how she would be better off back in Ireland. I suggested that if she gets a good running start off the pier, she might land on the deck of a departing ship headed that way. And if she didn't, well, her troubles would be over either way. She didn't think that was none too funny. Write me soon. Tell me all about your life. And take care of yourself and that baby. Get plenty of rest and let folks pamper you.*

Ethel cast a look at Ava, who stifled a giggle.

*Love, Maura*

Ethel let go of the pampered hand and Arianna glanced to admire her work. "It looks wonderful, Mother Ethel, thank you so much," she said and smiled sweetly at her. Ava could see the frustration and irritation melt away from Ethel's aged face.

"You're welcome, dear." She stood and gave a loving pat to the top of Arianna's round belly.

"Would you girls like anything to drink?" she asked, turning to Ava.

"Oh, no, we're quite all right." Ava felt so bad that, on top of the never-ending, physically demanding chores that belonged to that of a farmer's wife, Ethel had Arianna to contend with as well.

"Well, let me know if you need anything. I'm going to start dinner." She glanced up at the darkening sky. "Might lose power if that turns out to be as menacing as it looks." Ava again thought of Jonathan and hoped they would return home early, well in advance of the approaching storm.

After the screen door closed lightly behind Ethel, Ava cocked an accusing eyebrow at Arianna. "Well, it looks like you're settling in quite well here," she said, with just a hint of sarcasm threaded in.

"Oh, Mother Ethel takes such good care of me. I hardly have to lift a finger. I offered to churn the butter because I felt like I should do something around here to contribute. But other than that, I really am quite bored. Caleb isn't much for company in the evenings these days."

"They work very hard," Claire acknowledged and subtly hinted. This she knew and understood but had to admit she didn't like any more than the others. Monday through Saturday, Aryl would come home after being gone twelve hours, eat an early dinner, promising to spend the evening with Claire, or on warmer nights, sit in the swing with her and look at the stars. Most evenings, however, he would fall asleep on the couch, full from dinner and warm by the fire. Claire would spread out their feather tick and blankets in front of the fireplace and gently nudge him awake. He would apologize as he crawled under the covers, pull her head over to his chest, and promptly fall back asleep. She supposed it was just as well, as their sleeping quarters were smack in the middle of the living room.

Aryl's mother had begun a habit of ringing a small bell at the top of the stairs before coming down in the night to afford at least a hint of privacy, which embarrassed her. It hadn't mattered much these last few weeks; the tiny ring only reminded Claire of what his mother *wasn't* interrupting. To say there wasn't hand-wringing frustration building in her would be a laughable lie.

"Oh, I know they do," Arianna said before taking a breath to blow on her freshly painted nails. "We'll have to plan on a vacation soon or something."

Ava and Claire exchanged a look that was both disbelieving and amused.

"Oh, sure, I was thinking about London or maybe Africa–a nice safari," Claire said in full-blown sarcasm that Arianna missed completely.

"That would be so nice," she said dreamily.

"I think the first order of business is to get a home of our own again. I don't know about you two, but I'm getting a little tired of living with Jonathan's parents." Ava crossed her legs and arms and blew out her breath.

"Are things not going so well with them?" Arianna asked, sounding genuinely concerned, although she didn't give Ava a chance to reply. "Because if they aren't, you really should get pregnant as quickly as possible. They'll turn sweet to you in no time. It's working out so well for me that I'm thinking about having five more," she said with a giggle. Claire couldn't help but laugh out loud.

Arianna turned to her, bewildered at what was so terribly funny. "What?"

Ava smiled. "You know, Arianna, eventually you will have to care for that baby, and that's no easy job. I'm not so sure you realize–"

"I realize perfectly well how much work a baby is. That's why . . . we're not going to move out right away." She whispered the last part of her sentence, and the smile on her face was devious.

"What do you mean? Don't you want a home of your own?" Claire sent a strained look to Ava. "And privacy?"

"Amen," Ava whispered under her breath.

"The way I see it, the longer we stay here, the more money we can save. And the more help I will have. Can you imagine trying to run a house all by myself when I'm tired and achy and as big as a house?" Her friends glanced at her stomach. Her rail-thin frame created the illusion of a distorted, oversized stomach. "And with Caleb gone so much, I don't want to be alone. So, we're going to stay here until after the baby is born, and I'm back on my feet."

"And how does Caleb feel about this?" Ava couldn't imagine he wanted to spend one day longer than he had to under the strained conditions.

"Well, he doesn't know just yet. I'm going to tell him this weekend."

"What if he doesn't want to stay? What if he wants his own house now?" Arianna looked at Claire, her eyes bewildered as if Claire had spoken in a foreign language she couldn't understand.

Ava glanced at the sky again, and a chill ran through her. Distracted by her visit, she hadn't noticed how much the sky had darkened and was suddenly aware that the dry, earthy smell had grown stronger. She traced the storm with her eyes toward the general direction of the sea where it was black as night.

"Aryl will get them home in time," Claire said, reading her face.

Ava smiled nervously but gratefully. "We'd better get home soon ourselves."

"Oh, don't leave!" Arianna cried. "I've missed visiting with you so much. It's just not the same now that we all live so far apart."

"We'll come back soon. I promise," Ava said.

"Why don't you gather up your husbands and come for Sunday dinner?" Ethel stepped onto the porch, wrapping a shawl around herself with a shiver; the temperature had plummeted in just the last few minutes.

"That would be lovely. Can we bring anything?" Claire asked.

"Just your appetites. We'll have a nice big Sunday dinner and visit in the parlor afterward."

"Thank you. That sounds like fun." Ava's reserved smile was for manners; inside she was terribly excited for a reason to wear a nice dress, look pretty, be sociable, and spend time with Jonathan. She blushed at the sudden idea of walking with him after dinner to find a place on the farm where they could be alone. Her reddened cheeks gave her away, and Claire smiled knowingly.

After hugging Arianna and promising many times to come back soon, Claire pulled a penny out of her pocket as they walked toward the car. "Flip you for the barn."

Ava laughed loudly and nudged Claire with her shoulder. "You're terrible!" she whispered loudly, but quickly called heads with blushing cheeks.

Arianna laughed as she watched Claire attempt to turn the car around in the narrow drive, finally resorting to making a wide circle over the grass. She stuck her arm out the window and waved as she weaved down the driveway.

Arianna raised one hand and smiled. Her eyes traveled from the car to the looming, black clouds in the distance, her smile dropped, and she inhaled deeply, hugging herself above her bulging stomach. "Hurry home, Caleb," she whispered.

∞∞∞∞

"Shouldn't he be home by now?" she asked aloud as the clock on the wall chimed five times. Ava paced the living room floor, glancing out the window every few minutes. She wrapped herself in a shawl and stood on the front porch to watch for Jonathan. She glanced down the street and up at the black sky nervously before vicious gusts of icy rain drove her back inside.

"You'll drive yourself mad staring out that window," Margaret called from the kitchen. "Come have a cup of tea with me. It'll make the time go faster."

Ava saw her mother-in-law's hopeful expression, relented, and sat beside her at the table.

"They'll be home soon," Margaret said as she gave her a steaming cup of tea. "Try not to worry."

"Have you not seen that storm?"

"Yes, but we get those frequently round here. Didn't think these spring-like days would last forever, did you? Probably wake up to snow in the morning." Ava looked nervously over her shoulder toward the door. "Ava, listen to me. As long as Jon is insistent on living this life, you will have to get used to this. Storms come up fast around here. Sometimes they beat them home and sometimes they don't. Sometimes they just work right through them. But you're going to worry yourself to an ulcer–"

"Work right through them?" Ava interrupted.

"Yes. Some do unless it gets bad enough, then they head in."

Ava fidgeted, sighed, and fixed her eyes on a door that refused to open and produce her husband.

"Jon tells me you're starting a family," Margaret said casually, pulling Ava from her staring contest with the door.

"He said that?" she asked, not at all amused.

"He did. He's extremely excited about it, actually."

"Well, I know he wants to because he's been hounding me about it for two months, but right now, there's just no way–"

"Well, of course, there's a way. Me and Mr. Garrett have been meaning to go out. We could go to Boston and see some friends, which will leave you and Jon the house for the weekend," she said and grinned as a pink hue engulfed Ava's face.

"Oh, that's not what I mean, that's not the problem." As soon as she said the words, her face burned with what they had insinuated. "What I mean is," she continued quickly, "without a home of our own, savings, furniture, that kind of thing. I mean, honestly, no one tries to have a baby when they don't even have the basic necessities for themselves. Jonathan has this romantic idea about the whole thing, I think. He's not thinking practically."

Ava flew across the room scarcely before the knocking on the front door had stopped. She tore it open to see someone who was clearly not Jonathan standing with a clipboard and a bouquet of flowers. *How silly* she scolded herself. *Jonathan wouldn't knock on his own door.*

"Delivery for a Mrs. Ava Garrett." The man wore a blue shirt with his coat open despite the freezing rain, which was coming down heavier now. The name Steve was sewn on the top left pocket, and he spoke with a heavy, New York accent.

"That's me."

"I'll need you to sign for these," he said and held out a clipboard. "Thank you, Ma'am," he said and tipped his hat, yet something about his smile sent chills up Ava's spine. She watched him as he walked away and thought it strange that he would be making deliveries on foot in such a storm.

"Who sent you those? Maybe Jonathan," Margaret suggested, answering her own question. "I know he feels badly that he can't spend as much time with you as he'd like."

Ava looked over the beautiful, long stem, red roses for a card, but found none. "I wonder?" She walked to the kitchen as Margaret filled a vase with water. She doubted that Jonathan had had time to arrange a flower delivery. In addition, it was highly unlikely that he would spend the money on a frivolity like this, knowing how badly they both wanted a home of their own. *It isn't my birthday or our anniversary, but who else could they be from?* she wondered. She pondered on this for several minutes, which distracted her until she heard Jonathan come through the door.

Ava's shoulders relaxed in relief and she sighed. He was soaked through and shivering, but to Ava's surprise, he was smiling. She went to him and helped peel off layers of soaked wool.

"Sorry I'm late. Aryl wanted to show us how to maneuver in high winds and rain. And his mother was right," he paused as a shiver ran through his body, "it does feel like work when it's freezing and raining sideways."

"Why on earth would Aryl intentionally keep you out in this?" Ava asked angrily, exchanging dripping shirts with Margaret for a large towel. She wrapped it around his bare shoulders and turned him toward the stairs before he could answer.

Inside their room, Ava opened the trunk and pulled out flannel long johns and a wool shirt while he shed his sopping pants. She threw the dry clothes on the bed, pulled the towel from Jonathan's hands, and rubbed his reddened arms and neck hard, as if she were trying to scrub off layers of grime.

"Ow!" He recoiled and stared at her. "Did you have a bad day or something?" He took the towel and finished drying himself, one eyebrow raised in question. She crossed her arms and stared at the floor.

"I was trying to warm your arms. And my day was fine, except for worrying about you. It was foolish and irresponsible for Aryl to keep you out in this."

"Ava, we have to learn how to work in this. I'd rather ride out a small storm with Aryl there to guide us than learn the hard way when I'm out there alone."

"I just don't know about this, Jon? I don't know if I am the kind of wife that can deal with this life. Watching the storms roll in, knowing you're out there, waiting for you to come home. I mean what if–" She heard the icy rain chinking against the glass outside the darkened window.

He toweled his hair quickly, stuck his arms inside the wool shirt, and took her by the shoulders. "Ava. Nothing is going to happen. I am extremely careful. Aryl is an excellent teacher. I wish you could see him out there. He's a natural. You can't worry yourself sick like this. I promise you, everything will be fine. Okay?" Raising her eyes to meet his, she relented with a slight nod. "C'mon. Let's go eat. You can tell me about your day."

Downstairs, Jonathan Sr. was preparing two plates as the storm produced the first flash of lightning and a distant, low, rumble of thunder. "Your mom and I are going to eat in our room. You two help yourselves, she made enough to feed an army. You know how she gets when it storms."

At that moment, power was lost and the entire house went black and eerily quiet. "Better eat fast, it won't stay warm long now."

"Jonathan!" Margaret called from upstairs, sounding slightly panicked.

"Coming!" he yelled back and fumbled around for the counter to set the plates down on. He felt for the cabinet he wanted and opened it to get a box of matches. He struck one and the light allowed him to find two oil lamps and set them alight.

"Jonathan!" the faltering voice called again.

He gave his son a helpless look. "You know how she gets . . . ." He set the plates and the oil lamp on the breakfast tray and said goodnight as he hurried upstairs.

Ava made their plates, and they sat down to eat with the oil lamp in the center of the table.

"Well, this is nice," Jonathan said softly. "Romantic dinner by lamplight. It should storm more often," he said with a teasing grin.

"No, it shouldn't," Ava said firmly. "What did your father mean when he said you know how she gets? She was fine earlier and trying to console *me*, actually."

"My mother doesn't do well when it storms. At night, especially."

"Well, this is the wrong place to live then. She said they happen often around here. If she hates storms so much, why didn't they ever move?"

Jonathan sat searching for the right words. Finally, he relented to tell her the truth, although it wouldn't ease her worries one bit. "Remember that I told you both my grandfathers have passed?" Ava watched his face intently, which was serious, somewhat in conflict and utterly beautiful in the amber glow. "My mother's father was a fisherman, as his father was and his father before him. Her mother didn't love the life, but she did love my grandfather and accepted everything that came with him. My mother was sixteen when her father was lost at sea. It was a beautiful, spring morning when he set out, but a nasty storm swept up out of nowhere by afternoon, and . . . he never came home," he finished grimly and checked Ava's horrified face. When she spoke, she was clearly angry.

"That is the single worst thing you could possibly tell me, after what I went through this afternoon, Jonathan!"

"Not a little storm like this, Ava, it was much worse. But the caliber of the storm doesn't matter to my mother. She still gets nervous and scared. It's all my father can do to keep her calm and distracted."

"How does he do that?" Ava asked.

"He talks to her, sings, and tells her stories. As well as other things that, as their son, I prefer not to think about." He laughed gently.

"I'm surprised at how well she took the news of you deciding to fish for a living, under the circumstances. Your father was the one who made all the fuss."

"Who says she took it well?" He took another bite. "She's come to me three times begging me to change my mind. She puts up a tough exterior, but it worries her greatly. I don't suppose she'll ever stop pestering me to quit. And my father has his own reasons for hating this."

"He wants you to make back the money he lost," she assumed, cynicism in her voice.

"Yes, he does, but it's not only that. His father was lost at sea, too. Not in the traditional way, mind you, but he died on the ocean none the less."

Ava threw her napkin on the table and crossed her arms. "I don't believe this!" She looked at him in astonishment. "You mean to tell me that you lost both your grandfathers at sea, yet you expect me to... to... just—"

"It wasn't a storm with him, Ava, not in the beginning. He slipped on some bait and hit his head. He was alone and must have floated adrift for hours, and then a storm pushed his boat to shore. My father was on the dock waiting for him to return, pacing in the rain, and worried sick. He finally saw the boat, pushed by waves toward the shore. He found his father on the deck."

"How awful!" Ava gasped. "To be the one to find him." Gruesome images of her own parents dying of the flu flashed through her mind. She quickly pushed them away, refusing to revisit them.

"That's how my parents met, you know. At his father's funeral."

"How romantic," Ava said flatly.

"It was, in a way. The tragedy they had in common created a bond, and they comforted each other through the ordeal. Comforted each other to the point where wedding plans were hastily thrown together the following spring. Before my mother started showing with me," he admitted.

"No!" Ava gasped.

"Yes. It was just as well, they were perfect for each other. She swore she would never marry a sailor or fisherman, and he swore he would never become one." He smiled. "And they lived happily ever after." He paused to butter a roll, noticed her unsettled expression, and decided to change the subject. His eyes had adjusted to the dim light, and just as he took a breath to ask about her day, he caught sight of the roses across the room. He thought perhaps his father brought them for his mother as a sweet romantic diversion from the storm.

"Where'd those come from?"

"I was hoping you'd know. They were delivered today, but there was no card." Ava's midsection grumbled, reminding her that despite the stressful afternoon and unnerving stories of storms and men lost at sea, she was indeed starving and began to eat. Jonathan continued eating, head down with a sly grin spread across his face, and said, "Maybe my mother has a secret admirer."

"No, I had to sign for them. They were for me."

"For you? Who from?" he demanded, mouth full of food. It was fine to joke of his mother having a secret admirer but not funny in the least that Ava might have one.

"I assumed you. Who else would it be?"

He pushed his chair back and she watched him dig through the flowers, looking for a card. "I take it they aren't from you."

He returned to the table a moment later, and he was not at all amused. "Who in hell would be sending my wife flowers?" he grumbled, staring at them fiercely.

"Maybe it was a mistake?" Ava offered, picking at her cold food.

"No. Someone in this town is sweet on you. And I'm going to find out who it is–set him straight. I'm gone twelve hours a day, six days a week, but that doesn't leave an open invitation for other men to move in on what's mine!"

Ava tried not to enjoy the jealous side of Jonathan too terribly much. "Jon, I'm sure you're mistaken," she said coyly as she picked at a piece of dinner roll.

"What else would it be, Ava? There are a dozen, long stem roses sitting over there. For you. Not from me. That's a problem."

She could see, even in the dim light, the redness creeping up his neck, into his cheeks and ears, a slight flare to his nostrils; things that happened only when he was truly angry. Ava had trouble suppressing a grin at his appearance. He resembled a disgruntled peacock.

"Stop worrying and finish eating, Jon. I'll throw them out tomorrow."

"I'll throw them out right now." He sprinted over, seized the roses, flung open the back door, and propelled them out. A powerful gust sucked them out into the storm. Her lips twitched in amusement of the testosterone-laden protection of his territory.

"I went to see Arianna today," she mentioned casually as he returned to his seat, proud of fulfilling his mission. He leaned back and crossed his arms as if to prove a point to someone or something invisible.

"How is she?" he asked with a tone of indifference; his mind was still struggling with the identity of the sender and more importantly, how he would find this person.

"She's fine. Fairly spoiled," she scoffed. "She has no intention of moving out anytime soon." She realized that he wasn't really paying attention to her. "Jon, please." She reached out for his hand and he reluctantly unfolded his arms.

"Maybe you don't understand, Ava." He leaned forward on the table and squeezed her hand. "You're *mine*. I don't take too kindly to someone trying to woo my wife with flowers while I'm miles away unable to do anything about it." His eyes were serious and possessive, and she wasn't entirely sure she wanted it to end. *Selfish of me*, she thought. But after experiencing the dark times with him, lonely dark times when she feared he loved another more, she would selfishly enjoy this for a few moments.

"No one is trying to woo me, Jonathan. You have nothing to worry about."

He leaned back again, still holding her hand possessively and stared at his plate. "Sunday, I'm going into town. I'll ask around and find out who sent them and when I do . . . ." He shook his head and hurled a look that finished his sentence.

"We were invited by Caleb's parents to dinner on Sunday. The whole gang will be there. It should be nice. Claire flipped me for the barn . . . and I won." She gave him a suggestive grin. He blankly stared at her, having clearly missed the meaning. She rolled her eyes, tilted her head, and smiled sheepishly at him. "Strained living conditions and close quarters might cause a couple to sneak off to the barn after dinner . . . ."

"Ahh." His face lit up and he nodded, a devious smile broke the tension in his face. "Why don't you take pity on Claire and offer her the barn on Sunday?"

"Why? I won fair and square!" she argued indignantly and rose to clear the plates.

"Well, in case you haven't noticed, there's a raging storm going on outside." He carried their glasses to the sink. "And I was going to show you the benefits of loud, pelting rain and howling wind. Makes close quarters seem . . . not that close," he spoke through a smile as his lips brushed her neck. "Leave those for the morning," he said, turning her around. The house shook with a violent wind gust, and Ava shivered from the sudden chill.

"It's not our week," she said dryly, dipping her head away and tensing slightly at his pull. "But Sunday–"

"Let's leave it to chance."

"What? Jon, how could we possibly–"

"Listen. I've thought it all through." She stared at him with the mixed frustration of their situation and longing to grant him the family that he wanted. "If we throw caution to the wind, it would take a few months, right? That's what I've heard anyway. By the time it happened, we'd be in our own place, and then we'd still have almost a year to get things ready. Plenty of time." He squeezed her shoulders with insistence, his voice convincing. She sighed and averted her eyes, still unsure. "Ava, it will be fine. I promise. I'll work night and day to make sure that you and the baby have everything you need."

"What if I don't want you to work night and day? What if I want you home with me more? You're gone all the time as it is."

"It will even out soon. We're on one hell of a learning curve right now, but it won't always be like this."

"Why do you want this so badly? It really is the worst possible time."

"And if we wait for the perfect time, it will never happen," he said with frustration. "Ava, listen to me. It's hard to explain why I want this so badly. I don't know that I *can* explain it. But I can tell you that after living through what I have, almost losing you, losing all hope, feeling so empty–" He shuddered, hating to revisit that time for even a second. He took her face in his hands and continued, his voice and eyes full of conviction. "I feel so differently now. Despite our poverty and living in one borrowed room with everything we own in a trunk, I'm happy. I feel alive. All I want to do is celebrate and make more life. A living breathing tribute to what we have, what we've been through, what we've overcome. A part of each of us creating a bond stronger than even those of our wedding vows." His eyes flickered down to her mouth, slightly agape, breaking the concentration of the stare. She inhaled suddenly, realizing she had been breathless during his heartfelt speech and as she stepped back a few inches, the world around her reappeared. She couldn't say no, not after all that, but still hesitated to agree.

The wind gusted again, slamming into the side of the house with enough force to rattle the windowpane, startling her. A distant foghorn's low moan was barely audible above the roar of the wind and sent a cold panic through her. Thoughts raced through her mind. *Were there men out there now being thrown around on violent seas, straining to see the shore, to see home in vain through the fog and rain? The lights were probably out to the whole town, so one rocky shore would seem no different than another. The solitary, incandescent glow from the lighthouse was the only guide, if it could even be seen. What if he were still out there? What if, God forbid, he hadn't come home?* She could hardly force her mind to think it, but, if one day he didn't come home, at least she would have that; a piece of him to hold forever. She suddenly and selfishly made a decision that very second. Her mouth opened to tell him what he wanted to hear.

"I'll give you some more time then," he whispered and kissed her forehead. Gentle, disappointed eyes smiled at her. He led her out of the kitchen, picking up the oil lamp on the way.

She could think of no dignified or romantic way now, as he closed the door to their room behind them, to tell him yes, she would, she wanted to more and more as every second ticked by, she wanted to.

Several minutes later, he blew out the wick, and she lay under piles of covers, trying to think of a way to resurrect the conversation. She squirmed under the covers awkwardly, voicing mild grunts.

"What are you doing?" he asked, lifting his head in the dark. Something light and soft landed on his face. Using his hands, he quickly identified it as a silken undergarment, still warm from the wearer. "What's this?" He held it up by one finger, displaying a grin she couldn't see.

"That's me . . . throwing caution to the wind and leaving it to chance."

"Are you sure?" He gave her one last chance, even though he was already reaching for her.

"I'm sure," she whispered as he pulled her under the quilts.

∞∞∞∞

Sunday morning, Ava pitched straight up in bed and woke with a gasp. The same dream had haunted her three times that week. It started out pleasantly enough, but ended with her standing atop jagged rocks, staring into the blackness of a storm, holding a black-haired baby, crying and calling for Jonathan.

She sank her face into her hands, took a few deep breaths, and then focused her eyes on brilliant rays of sunshine streaming through the window, which warmed her legs. Jonathan wasn't beside her, but she was used to that. Six days a week she woke alone, Jonathan having left for the boat hours before she stirred. But this being Sunday, she had expected him to be there. She threw on a robe quickly and headed downstairs, hoping he would be at the table with coffee, waiting for her.

There was fresh coffee on the stove but only a note on the table, which explained that his parents had gone to visit friends for the day and that he had gone to run some errands but would be back in time for dinner. Frustrated, she tossed the note on the table. *He could have woken me to go with him on the only day we have together. Now we'll have just a few hours together before the week begins again.*

She bathed and laid out three dresses to choose from for the evening. They were all somewhat plain, but she supposed an informal farmhouse dinner party wouldn't require much more. She chose a pink and white, cotton dress with a scoop neck. She pondered both the ringlet curl iron and the steam envelope for waves and decided to fashion her hair with the ringlet. She sprayed the bouncy rolls with sugar water and her hands and cheeks were sticky as a sweet roll by the time she was finished, but the curls held nicely. She prayed bees weren't out this time of year.

The idea itself came from one of Arianna's animated tales about growing up in Georgia and that sugar water was primarily used for hair setting, although not entirely practical in the summer when bees were out in full force. She had once snuck into her sister's room late on a July night and sprayed sugar water on her hair to get back at her for a mean joke she had told about Arianna winding up an old maid. She was tickled pink as the bees chased and stung her sister all the following day.

Later that afternoon, Ava was digging through the trunk, looking for a pair of stockings when Jonathan came through the bedroom door, one arm tucked behind his back. Hands on hips, she whirled around.

"Where have you been?" she snapped, although she was happy that he was home.

"I told you I was going into town to find out who sent you those flowers," he said and smiled wide.

"Well, did you? I'd hate to think that the entire morning was spent away from me in vain." His smile dropped slightly.

"No, I didn't find out. But the trip wasn't in vain." He produced a large bouquet of roses even more vibrant and beautiful than the ones previously delivered. Two dozen, not one.

"Jonathan."

"Don't you dare say I shouldn't have. First of all, it's been far too long since I've come home with flowers and second . . . ." Lowering his nose to the roses, he slowly looked up at her through his lashes. "I won't be outdone by some anonymous schmuck who thinks he's going to muscle in on my territory."

"That's hardly the case, Jon," she said, smiling and smelling the roses. "Roses in March. Must have cost a fortune. You really-"

"Ah, I said don't say that. Besides, I had an interesting thing happen today."

"What would that be?"

He removed his shirt and rummaged through the trunk for one of his nicer ones.

"Well, I was asking around at some places that sold flowers and met a guy, a reporter for the newspaper in Boston. He was doing a piece on Rockport fishermen and asked if I wanted to be featured. That's what took so long. I went to get Aryl while he gathered his equipment and he met us down by the boat. Asked us a bunch of questions about fishing and then took a picture of us next to the Ava-Maura for the newspaper."

"Your picture will be in the paper?"

"Yeah, but that's not the best part." He pulled a black sweater over his head and ran his fingers through his hair to straighten it. "I had the guy put in a quote that we'd sell for two cents less a pound than anyone else. Should have more buyers than we can handle shortly. Just in time for us to all go solo and triple our payload. I told you everything would work out," he said, grinning happily and went to the closet to choose between the two pair of slacks he owned.

∞∞∞∞

Arianna was so happy to have anything that remotely resembled a party that she was nearly bursting at her emotional seams. She fussed over her hair and dipped into her precious reserves of makeup. She grew aggravated when she was sidetracked and had to sew extra panels of fabric into the sides of her best dress to allow more room around the middle.

"You could just wear one of the dresses my mother made you," Caleb said, eying her as she worked and swore under her breath on occasion.

"A tent! That's fine for working around the house or the garden, but not for a dinner party."

"You work around the house?" His sarcastic tone was impossible to miss, but in the excitement of a get-together, she let it slide past with nothing more than a dirty look.

"I already put your clothes in the bathroom. People will be here soon. You might want to get ready," she said.

He was lying on the bed, swinging his legs off the side and the springs squeaked rhythmically. "Caleb! Stop that! Your parents might think–"

"What?" He twisted his head to look at her and asked, "That we might be having sex? No. No, we can't have them suspecting that." He stared at the ceiling, the rhythmic squeak continuing. "A young, married couple, in love for the most part, no, we can't allow them to think it's possible that we could ever or would ever." He craned to look at her again. "Say, have you managed to convince them that Junior there is a product of immaculate conception?" He focused on the ceiling again, and she stared at his head with wide eyes. "Yeah," he said with a short, hard laugh. She stood up with some effort, tossed her dress aside, and confronted him at the foot of the bed cautiously.

"What do you mean, Caleb?" Her voice was quiet despite her anger.

"Nothing." He stood up quickly. "I'm going to get dressed," he said numbly as he passed her. A long, thin arm grabbed his as he passed.

"What did you mean?" she repeated, this time her voice shaking slightly. He rolled his eyes, clearly out of patience.

"It's ridiculous for you to put on airs. But don't worry, Ahna, there's no way they're going to get the idea that we sleep together . . . . because we don't." He jerked his arm away from her grasp and left the room. She followed him down the hall, not sure herself if she were on the verge of tears or rage.

"Not that, Caleb. The other thing you said. About being 'for the most part' in love." She stood in the doorway of the bathroom so that he was unable to shut the door. "What is that supposed to mean?" she pressed. "For the most part?"

"I didn't mean it like that," he said roughly. He sighed heavily and avoided her eyes.

"Yes, you did. Is that how you really feel?" He silently lathered his face. She cleared her throat to remind him she was still there, waiting.

"Look, I don't want to get into anything before dinner. Maybe we can talk later or something." His tone was so indifferent that it stung.

She retreated but decided to stand her ground with an insistent but soft tone when she turned back. "No. I want to know what you meant. If that's really how you feel."

"You don't want to know how I really feel," he said, his voice low and hostile. His gaze was void of any feeling at all. He shaved hastily while she stared at the floor, waiting, hoping he would say something. His silence was maddening as he changed; however, sensing something was very, very wrong, she hesitated to pressure him. He passed by her, his shoulder brushing hers and stomped downstairs just in time to greet guests.

"Hey, guys, how are you all? Come in. Sit down," he called out from the steps.

Arianna swallowed hard, refusing to cry and waste perfectly good makeup. She would smile through dinner and get things straight with Caleb later. She finished her dress quickly and joined the others downstairs, surprised to see a larger than expected crowd.

She smiled from one unfamiliar face to another as Ethel introduced her daughter-in-law to several friends and neighbors. The families, some compiled of three generations, swelled the house with chatter and laughter. Arianna shook hands and glanced at her husband occasionally, who was absorbed in catching up with his parents' older friends and their children, most of whom appeared to be his age.

Another knock at the door was barely heard over the buzz. Aryl, closest to the door, opened it and stepped aside. As they filed in, Aryl cast Jonathan a look, and then his eyes touched on Caleb before closing the door.

An older couple greeted Ethel and Hubert, nodded and waved politely to Caleb, although their faces looked slightly strained. A young woman with tawny hair that fell in long curls on her shoulders and dark eyes stepped into view from behind them. She slipped her coat off her tiny frame and Ethel gave the girl a long embrace.

Aryl made his way over to Jonathan quickly. "Well, this should be interesting," he said out of the side of his mouth.

"Indeed." Jonathan could barely suppress the smirk as he sipped his drink.

Claire and Ava noticed Arianna standing alone against the wall and made their way across the parlor to her. They asked her a few questions, but it was apparent that she was completely tuning them out. Her eyes were fixed on Caleb and, more specifically, the tension in his posture when the small woman approached him. They smiled awkwardly, aware of several of the older generation's eyes on them. Arianna squinted, unsuccessfully willing herself the ability to read lips. When she set out to interrupt them, Ethel touched her arm.

"Would you be a dear and help me in the kitchen, Ahna?"

Caleb was now smiling down at his old acquaintance. "I really need to talk to–"

"Oh, it'll only take a few moments." Ethel took her arm insistently and led her to the kitchen. Claire and Ava shared a look of confusion and set out for their husbands, who appeared to be making a wager.

"All right, Jon. What's going on here?"

"Nothing, um, just talking about the game next week." Jonathan stuffed a bill back in his pocket and grinned.

"You're a horrible liar." Ava crossed her arms and glared at him.

"I'm not sure I should stir the pot, love." He stole a glance at Aryl, who shook his head in agreement.

"Is she an old flame?" Claire edged up to Aryl, hugging his arm while batting her eyes.

"Oh, no. You're not getting anything out of me."

She pouted and said, "This isn't fair. You guys know what's going on, and you're deliberately keeping us in the dark."

"Yes. Yes, we are." Jonathan smiled. The women wore indignant expressions. He rolled his eyes and slipped an arm around Ava. "Look. If we tell you what's going on, or what we think is going on, then you two are going to scurry into the kitchen and fall over each other telling

Arianna, who will cause a gigantic scene, to be sure, and may very well possibly end up going into premature labor. We're keeping the baby and Arianna's best interests in mind here. It'll come out in good time."

"Just tell us her name," Claire begged.

"Rachael. That's all you're getting." Aryl was insistent, and they didn't pressure for more. They did, however, watch the two in the corner, analyzing every smile, glance and laugh carefully and whispered in conference with each other frequently.

Ethel announced that dinner was ready and slowly everyone migrated to the dining room where the food was set out buffet style to accommodate the crowd. Chairs were set against the walls, as well as extra seats brought in from the barn. Folks filled their plates and marveled at Ethel's enormous spread of food. Jonathan was put to work with carving the ham. When Caleb held his plate out, Rachael standing close by, Jonathan leaned in close as he served a slice on his plate.

"The funny thing is, you don't even look scared," he whispered, his teasing grin fading as he met Caleb's undaunted expression.

"Why should I be?" he asked and moved along, not waiting for an answer. A boy tugged on Jonathan's sleeve while his eyes followed Caleb in disbelief.

"Oh. Here ya' go, buddy." After serving the boy, he looked back to Rachael standing next to Caleb, smiling up at him as he pointed to different dishes. Jonathan saw no sign of Arianna. No sign of Ava or Claire either, for that matter. They were standing inside the kitchen, peering into the dining room every few minutes.

"Well, I don't understand why you don't just walk right up to them and introduce yourself," Claire said.

"I shouldn't have to," Arianna grumbled and busied herself with menial tasks in the kitchen.

The women entered the dining room when the crowd had thinned. Arianna saw Caleb sitting on a sofa, his plate on his knee and Rachael sat just a few seats away, talking, and smiling comfortably.

"There's no way I can go in there now," she seethed.

"Why not? Look, the seat next to him just opened up. Walk in and sit down beside him. He'll be forced to introduce you." Ava nudged her shoulder, encouraging her. Arianna walked to the wide, arched entrance to the parlor but halted when Rachael moved to the open seat next to Caleb. She spun around, visibly boiling.

"Ava!" she ordered. "Go in there right now and tell him I need to speak to him in the kitchen." She banged her plate down, stomped away to the kitchen and plopped herself in a chair to wait.

Ava sighed resentfully, but made her way through the crowd toward Caleb. She stepped over someone's legs and felt a stab of pain as she remembered the last gathering at Maura's house. Her letters had become more infrequent now, and Ava worried she was beginning to forget her.

Finally close to Caleb, Ava leaned down and whispered in his ear. He waved dismissively at her, and she leaned to whisper again. He sighed loudly, turned to Rachael and excused himself.

Ava joined Claire in the dining room as Caleb walked quickly into the kitchen, closing the door behind him. They only heard muffled, upset voices initially, which grew louder in a heated exchange.

Aryl approached them as they huddled by the door, eavesdropping. "Honestly, ladies," he said, causing them both to jump.

"Aryl, if you don't tell me what's going on, I'll go crazy," Claire said.

He shook his head slowly and said, "If we were having trouble of some kind, would you want everyone talking about it behind our backs?"

"I'm not trying to gossip about it, Aryl. I want to help," Claire clarified.

"The best way you can help is to stay out of it for now. She'll let you know when you're needed."

A loud crash came from the kitchen. A second later, the back door slammed. Aryl poked his head into the kitchen and saw Arianna crying into her hands at the breakfast table. He looked at Claire.

"She might need you now."

He silently walked through the kitchen and out the back door to find Caleb. Arianna alternated from sobbing to furious rage repeatedly, and her incoherent words made it impossible for Claire and Ava to figure out exactly what had been said to whom or by whom. Jonathan noticed his friends had disappeared, so he entered the kitchen, pausing to study each woman. Claire and Ava were on each side of Arianna, trying to calm her.

Claire glanced at the back door. "Aryl went to find him."

∞∞∞∞

"What a mess," Caleb grumbled quietly, sitting on a hay bale, head in his hands. Aryl leaned against a beam across from him, hands in his pockets as Jonathan joined them in the barn.

"Awkward and uncomfortable, yes, but I'm not sure why this qualifies as a mess." Jonathan pulled a hay bale to sit closer to Caleb. "Is Arianna that unreasonable in her current state that she can't handle seeing an ex-girlfriend?"

"It's much more than that." He ran his hands from his chin, over his face and through his hair. "A lot more."

Aryl eyed him warily. "How much more can there be?"

Caleb looked ominously at him, then Jonathan and took a deep breath.

"It was the year before I sold my grandfather's farm . . . ."

∞∞∞∞

"Oh!" Arianna's crying stopped short with a gasp as her hands gripped her stomach. A moderately strong contraction built up quickly then slowly began to subside. She made a horrified face and whispered to Ava, "Get my mother-in-law."

Ava turned on her heels and swiftly returned with Ethel, who instructed them to help her get Arianna up to her room. The short, tight pain had passed and she walked on her own, still sniffling with jagged, little breaths from the hard cry. Ethel helped her lie down and wiped her face with a cool cloth. Ava and Claire stood back, waiting for instructions and praying she wasn't going into labor.

"Should we go get Caleb?" Claire asked.

"Oh, no. This is nothing. Practice pain, most likely from being so upset." She returned her eyes to Arianna. "You really have to try to stay calm, dear."

"How can I? If you heard the things he said to me, and then there's that *girl*. I can't stay up here while she's down there, trying to—"

"She's not trying to do anything." Ethel's voice was suddenly cold and defensive of Rachael. "It's not my place, Arianna, to say any more than this. Rachael is not trying to do whatever it is you think. She needed to see Caleb for reasons that have nothing to do with you. They have something to put to rest, so to speak. That's all." She tucked a blanket around her middle and left the cloth on her forehead. "Come get me if it happens again." She touched Ava's shoulder on her way out.

∞∞∞

"*Why* didn't you ever tell us?" Jonathan sat stunned, and Aryl hung his head, looking for the right words. Caleb shrugged.

"I didn't really want to think about it. And I didn't want it getting back to Arianna, although I guess I'll have to explain everything now. Can you see why I didn't want to come back here? So much has happened while Arianna runs around oblivious."

"Then tell her," Aryl said. "Tell her everything and while you're at it, tell her everything else that's bothering you, too."

"I don't think I have much choice."

"Go get it over with." Jonathan stood and pulled Caleb up off the hay bale. "We'll stay a while. Send up a flare if you need us," he said and grinned. They left the barn, but Caleb stopped when he saw Rachael waiting by her car. "I'm going to say goodbye. You guys go on."

∞∞∞

"*I* can't just lie here." Arianna threw back the quilt and paced the room slowly. "It's not just about this woman showing up," she explained to her silent audience by the bed. "He was angry with me before the party." She leaned her head on the window frame and sighed, "Maybe he doesn't love me any—" Her head snapped up as she squinted to focus on the dark driveway. She watched in silent shock as Rachael wrapped her arms around Caleb's neck. "That's it!" she yelled and tore across the room.

Rachael's car was just leaving the drive when Caleb turned straight into Arianna's open palm airborne toward his face. He seized her wrist an inch from his face and held it solidly in the air.

"How could you!" she screamed, trying to pull her wrist from his grasp. "You no good, two-timing bastard! And I'm pregnant!"

He turned, expressionless and pulled her by the wrist to the barn. Jonathan and Aryl watched from the shadows of the front porch.

"Well, they'll either come out with rekindled love or set on divorce," Jonathan said grimly.

"*If* they both come out," Aryl half-joked.

Caleb whirled her around and pointed to a haystack. She sat, in shock at such rude treatment.

"How dare you put your hands on me, Caleb!"

"Shut up, Ahna." He glared at her. Her mouth fell open and she struggled to get up. "Sit back down!" he bellowed. She froze on the hay, stunned. He had never, *no one* had ever, spoken to her this way. "Now, you are going to sit there with your mouth shut and listen to what I have to say." She opened her mouth in protest, but he pointed a finger at her. "So help me God, Ahna. Not until I'm done," he commanded.

She closed her mouth, clearly uncomfortable with subservience. He paced a bit while taking deep breaths, testing her ability to sit quietly. Finally, he stood in front of her, albeit out of swing's reach; a precaution for the both of them, he figured. "That was Rachael. I know what you're probably thinking, so I'm going to explain everything to you, although I'd prefer not to. This is personal and hard to talk about. But I don't have much of a choice now. Rachael and I went together toward the end of school. By the time we graduated, we were informally engaged but none the less engaged." Arianna's blood was boiling, and it took everything she had to sit still, hear about his old love, and not claw his eyes out.

"I knew that my grandfather would leave his farm to me when he died, and so we planned that we would eventually get married and take over the farm. We had our lives laid out before us. We got comfortable. Too comfortable. And she got pregnant. We only told our mothers. We figured our fathers would have killed us. They hastily began to plan a wedding, and the engagement was made formal, announcement in the paper and everything.

"A week before the wedding, we were having dinner with both families, making final plans, and she suddenly screamed." He paused and Arianna could see for the first time how hard the story was for him to recount. The pain was readable on his face, and it bothered Arianna that he didn't attempt to hide it from her. But she felt a twinge of compassion. She knew firsthand how big his heart was.

"They wouldn't let me see her at the hospital. Our fathers found out, and I thought for sure I was a dead man. At the time, that was fine with me. If she were going to die because of me, I felt I rightly should die, too." Jealousy overrode compassion and her nostrils flared. "However, she didn't die. But she did lose it. The baby. And the ability to ever . . . it left her unable to ever have children." He paused again, no longer worried about interruptions as she was speechless.

"We didn't end the engagement right away," he continued. "She got better, and we tried to just go on, but it ate away at me. She thought it bothered me that she couldn't have children any longer, knowing I wanted a big family. What was really bothering me was that I had caused this, and there was nothing I could do to fix it. I was about to approach her with the idea of adopting when she ended it with me. Just like that.

"My grandfather died, and the farm was left to me. In spite of her tainted reputation, she went on with her life and was courted by a much older man. I couldn't stand to face myself each day, so I sold the farm and left."

He paused and looked to Arianna as if to give permission to ask a question if she wanted to. For once in her life, she had nothing to say.

"I received word the next year that she got married. I wrote a letter to her, both congratulating and apologizing to her. She wrote back to thank me and forgive me. We wrote back and forth for a time. That's the reason I ended up staying in Georgia so long. I wanted to stay at the same hotel, so I wouldn't miss one of her letters." He looked at her gaping mouth, her raised eyebrows and spoke before she could come to any conclusions.

"Not love letters, Ahna." He blew out his breath impatiently. "I needed to know that she would be all right after what happened. After some letters, I knew she would be. The last letter I got included a picture of her with a beautiful baby they had adopted. She looked so happy. Come to find out, the man she married was unable to have children, too. So, they eagerly adopted. She told me tonight that the paperwork for their third child was in process and that she was so happy," he said and smiled gratefully. "She realized that there are so many children who need love. She actually said it was a blessing, what happened, because now three children, who would have otherwise grown up in an orphanage, have a loving home. And they want more.

"After her last letter, I forgave myself in Georgia and decided to move on. When I looked up from my self-loathing, I saw you and nothing else mattered."

Arianna stared at the floor now, trying to process everything.

"She wanted to see me tonight to make sure I had forgiven myself and to show me how happy she was. I told her about you and the baby. She was happy for me. She wanted to meet you. I was the one who made excuses, grateful you stayed away."

"Since you're ashamed of me," she squeaked on the verge of tears.

"No. It had nothing to do with you. I know that's hard for you to comprehend, Ahna, but the world does not revolve around you. I thought it would be very cruel to introduce my very pregnant wife to her after what had happened. I can't imagine how that might sting, no matter how happy she is with her life now." He looked at her with the slightest bit of hope. "Can you even begin to see how that might be uncomfortable for me? And her?"

"Yes," she whispered. "But earlier you—"

"Earlier had everything to do with you," he said bluntly, leaning against the support pole near her. "Between Rachael and my father, I didn't want to come back here. I did it for you. I knew you'd be better off here and so would the baby. But I've been miserable, Ahna. Even though I left here like I did, I still wanted a farm. If you remember correctly, I was searching for farmland when I met you. It was obvious that you weren't going to settle for being a farmer's wife, so we ended up in New York. And then the world went to hell, and now I'm back home. Fishing. I don't like it, Ahna. It's not what I want to be doing. I walk five miles in the cold every morning to work my ass off all day, getting pinched by lobsters and fighting seasickness and then come home to work alongside my silent, resentful father for a few hours. And when I come in, I have nothing but a pile of complaints from you."

He was growing angrier as he finally vented his frustrations. "And I hear it from my mother, too. She works herself into the ground, Ahna, and to add to that, you prance around here like a queen summoning her servants." Arianna sent him a hurtful look, but she could hardly deny it. "My mother loves you, Ahna, and she loves this baby. But there's more that you could do for yourself. You're pregnant, not crippled. And you're tiring everyone around you." She looked down shamefully and twisted the hem of her skirt into knots. "Things are going to change around here, Ahna. I was hoping I wouldn't have to talk to you about this at all because you had started coming around in the tenement when you found out you were pregnant. You were more docile, domesticated . . . and I loved it. You acted like you cared about what I was going through. But, in becoming so comfortable here, you have reverted back to full-on laziness while those around you are working themselves to death." Her head remained lowered, and he stared at it.

"Do you understand what I'm saying, Ahna?" he asked softly. A few tears slipped off her nose onto her lap, and she nodded. He looked up to the rafters of the barn and sighed. He hated to see her cry, especially when he made her do so. He resisted the urge to embrace her, kiss away her tears, and whisper things she loved to hear because he knew that no real change would happen if he showed weakness now. He did, however, squat in front of her and take her hands.

"Listen to me. These hands. They can do a lot more around here. No one expects you to plow fields or scrub floors. But you can help more. And you will." She nodded numbly with tear-filled eyes. "And see these?" He pinched a wad of fabric from his thigh. "These are pants. And I wear them. You're going to start acting like a wife. My wife. It wouldn't hurt if every now and then, you acted like you gave a shit about me."

"Oh, but I do, Caleb!" she insisted.

"Well, you have a hell of a way of showing it." He motioned for her to scoot over, and he joined her, still holding her hand. "I know why you act like you do. I know you spend most of your time behind a hard and selfish exterior scared to death and still resentful of your father for not acting like a real man and for pissing away your family's life. But I also know that you weren't always like this. I talked to your family plenty while I was trying to win you over. They told me what you used to be like." He was quiet for a moment as he chose his words carefully and spoke, "I've seen glimpses of that, and I always hoped that, if you felt safe enough, loved enough, you'd revert back to that." The next words were barely audible. "To be the kind of wife I've always wanted." His words stung and brought on more tears.

"The kind of wife *she* would have been for you," Arianna said when she could talk again. He remained silent. She felt resentful toward Rachael, who was shorter than Caleb, soft and quiet, blended in politely and blushed with any attention paid to her; humble. What bothered her most were the glances she had witnessed from her toward Caleb. No doubt there was still something there. She still adored, if not loved, him. If not for a cruel twist of fate, she would be his wife now, several children running underfoot, and lovingly greeting Caleb as he came in from a long day on his farm. Arianna seethed, boiled and hated. Rachael was the standard Caleb held for a good wife. She is what he wanted originally and what he likely thought about every time she let him down. And then, quite suddenly, she decided she would not, under any circumstance, be out done. She wouldn't allow it. Not from this pale-faced humble any more than from the most skilled and exotic whores in Paris. She looked Caleb in the eye for the first time since the fight began.

"I love you *more*," she said with conviction.

"It's not a contest, Arianna. Rachael has moved on and so have I. I don't love her anymore," he reassured.

"I'll show you." She clenched his hands, almost frantic. "I'll show you every day. I love you *more* and I will be the wife you want. I will, I promise." Her eyes were pleading and brimming with tears. "Please don't leave me," she whispered. "Don't stop loving me." He sighed and gathered her in as close as he could, her stomach intruding slightly.

"I'm not leaving you, Ahna. And stop loving you? Never. I couldn't."

∞∞∞

"*Impressive*." Victor leaned back in his chair, shaking his head in disbelief. He stared hatefully at the picture. "Posing as a journalist.

Brilliant." He pulled from his drawer a thick roll of bills and tossed it across the desk. "Did they let you on the boat?" he asked, even though he thought that would be too much good luck in one sitting.

"Let me walk all over and ask questions. Even poked around the sleeping berth."

"And you're sure of the address?"

"I was before he willingly gave it to me. I can see why you'd be inclined to clear the path. She's a looker," he said, slightly overstepping his bounds. Victor snorted. "I don't care about her. Not the way you're thinking anyway." He studied the boat carefully. "What do you know of explosives?" Now armed with the information he needed, Victor cultivated his plan with more detail.

"Enough. What do you need?"

"Knowledge. I won't be asking you to make any further trips. You've provided me with more than I hoped for. I can handle the rest. My vengeance runs long and deep. This is something I must . . . *want* to do myself. But I will pay you handsomely for the knowledge."

"A little unorthodox, but all right, let me know when, where."

"Why wait? My house. Tonight." He handed over another wad of bills. "This should cover your time and supplies."

∞∞∞∞

That evening, Victor was high on evil anticipation and he glided into the parlor, smiling for the first time in weeks. He kissed Ruth on the cheek.

"I need to talk to you," she said hesitantly, wary of his jovial appearance.

"About what?"

"Sit down," she invited politely.

"Whatever it is, just buy it or fire them or sell it." He held out his arms wide. "Makes no difference to me." He causally turned to leave her in the parlor.

"It's about Jonathan," Ruth blurted out awkwardly and he halted and slowly turned toward her. It scared her, the look in his eyes; although no longer distant and loathing, something worse now replaced it.

"What about Jonathan?" he asked. Instantly, he wondered if his new employee's services would be needed again. If Ruth would be one of those tragic loose ends he would be forced to clip and he grinned wide. *Makes no difference to me,* he reminded himself.

"I need to know where he is," she said feebly.

"Miss him, my dear?" Victor sat down slowly, watching her distrustfully.

"Of course not. I love . . . you, Victor," she said and smiled sweetly to cover her fear.

"Then why on earth would you need to know where he is?" he said and smiled sweetly to cover his rage. He was faking his suspicion–he knew she wanted to warn him, like she had before he left. She was lucky to be alive right now. The thought had crossed his mind to have her neck broken when he discovered Jonathan had, most likely as a result of her last secret visit, abandoned the apartment and ruined his first set of plans. But her best friend's husband had suffered considerable losses recently, and anyone could be bought. There had been scarcely a moment of any day, especially when Jonathan had lived near, that Victor did not know exactly where Ruth was, had been or planned to go. And Ruth had no idea the vast number of eyes that watched her daily.

She held out two letters. Slightly trembling hands betrayed her relaxed expression. He leaned back and began reading them. Short letters of swirly handwriting; the first an introduction simply requesting information, the second begged for information and explained in detail why it was needed. Victor's solid face ruptured into a smile as he read. He chuckled dryly once, and then roars of delight followed hard laughter.

Minutes later, he scooped the letters from the floor, wiped his eyes, and apologized politely. "Oh! I'm sorry, but this is simply too good to be true." He broke into hilarity again as he handed the letters back.

"I didn't think it funny in the least. It's tragic really." She felt disgust at how he always found humor in the misfortune of others. His eyes and mouth dropped into anger again, and his eyes targeted her ruthlessly.

"To me, it's hilarious. And justified. Now what to do about it, though?" he deliberated aloud as he paced. "I'll have to postpone my plans, of course, but it will be worth it to sit back and enjoy the calamity. Just for a while until it bores me." He shrugged.

"Why do you hate him so much?" The second she spoke, she regretted it as his hand shot out and grabbed hold of her throat.

"You know why," he sneered. "You want me to repeat it? You want to hear the whole story again?" he snarled just inches from her face. "You enjoy it, don't you?" Eyes bulging, she tried to deny it, to shake her head, struggling to breathe. In a crazed trance, Victor went on, "How he won the apprenticeship with his ass-kissing attitude and then had me thrown out, condemning me from proper society to rule over slums, prolific as that may have turned out to be."

The drastic change in tone to upbeat with his last sentence sent cold through Ruth's chest, convinced now that he had gone mad. His smolder continued to burn.

"Then to walk out with Ava from that dinner party, after she humiliated me in front of the last group of decent society that would receive me." He skimmed her over, repulsed. "Stuck with his *leavings*!" he growled and suddenly thrust her away from him. She gasped for breath, staggered backward and found the sofa behind her. "Now." He sat down on the sofa as though nothing had happened. "Listen very carefully, Ruth. Here is what we're going to do about this."

*March 15th 1930*

"I think I see them!" Arianna called. The girls waited with lunch baskets on the pier for the boats to come back mid-day. Arianna squinted against the bright sunlight sparkling on the ocean.

"Even if you do, it will be a while before they pull in," Claire said. "Anybody have any good gossip?"

"Gossip? Around here? Not likely. Unless it's about one of us," Ava said.

Claire chose that moment to share her news. "We started trying. For a baby, I mean."

Ava smiled at her. "So did we."

"You're kidding."

Ava shook her head. "Jon finally talked me into it."

"Aryl figures we'll be in our own place before I would have any exciting news, and then we'll have the full nine months to get things ready."

Ava narrowed her eyes and tapped her foot. "They've been collaborating. Those are the same things Jon said to me. It's a race, that's what it is. Neither of them wants his son to be the youngest." She gave a tsk-tsk, shaking her head.

Arianna yawned and stretched.

"Tired? Not too much longer now," Claire said.

"Yes, I'm tired and yes, it's a while yet. Three full months still." She poked back at a tiny foot digging into her ribs. "Yeah, I'm crowded, too!" she complained in return. "I've been getting up early to have breakfast with Caleb," she said after another long yawn.

"He gets up at what? Three am?"

"Four. I talked to his father in secret and got him to let Caleb use the truck, so he could get home quicker. His father has been grumbling about all the preparations needed for planting season, and I pointed out that if Caleb used the truck then he could help more."

"Are things any better with them? It must be awfully uncomfortable," Ava said, while spreading out a blanket on the sand.

"It's better. Hubert is still a stubborn, old fart. Caleb is the one who has changed. He goes right up to his father, bold as brass, and says what he needs to or asks something outright. At first, his father tried to pretend he couldn't hear him, so he could keep up the silent treatment. But Ethel fixed that. Bopped him on the head every time he tried it and now he answers when he's spoken to."

Ava giggled at the thought and asked, "And things with you two? Better?"

Arianna smiled mischievously. "Much better. I don't think he realizes this, but the more I dote on him, the more he dotes on me. So, when I want more attention or a foot rub or anything, all I have to do is pay more attention to him. Works every time. But don't say anything. That stays between us girls. Don't want to spoil a good thing." She squinted out again over the open water. "I'm going to rest till they get here. I'm beat." She struggled to lie down and kicked off her shoes, letting the sun warm her face and legs.

Arianna was close to dozing when a shadow cast over her face and she opened her eyes. Glancing over her, Caleb grinned.

"If you say beached whale, I'll kick you where it counts, and Junior here, will be an only child." She pulled up on one elbow, smiling through her threat. Sparing her the embarrassment of rolling ungracefully, he bent down, slipped an arm behind her, and pulled her to a sitting position. She tucked her skirt around herself modestly as he sat down beside her.

"I'm glad you came," he said and smiled while rifling through the basket. "I'm starving." Before she could raise one eyebrow and purse her lips, he slipped a hand behind her head and kissed her. "And I've missed you since the minute I left." That satisfied her well enough, and she began handing out the picnic lunch. "How's your day been?" he asked quickly before taking a large bite of sandwich made with thick wedges of homemade bread.

"We set a stew on for dinner and made bread. I finished sewing another four diapers, and I got your shirts ironed."

Caleb nodded as she ticked off her list of productivity. "You didn't leave nasty creases in the front like last time, did you?"

"Oh, no, they're perfect, darling." She kissed him on the cheek, leaving a hand on his thigh as she continued about her morning and plans for the evening.

Jonathan sat with Ava, mouth hanging open with a large bite of sandwich threatening to fall into his lap. Ava suppressed a giggle, touched under his chin and he closed his mouth to chew.

"Caleb said she was more docile, but . . . ."

Awhile later, he glanced over to see Arianna on her knees behind Caleb, kneading the muscles of his shoulders. Caleb let his head fall forward in relaxation. When he rolled it to the side for Arianna to work on his neck, he gave Jonathan a wicked look of triumph. Jonathan had to turn away or give away Caleb's expression.

Claire and Aryl were sitting ahead of them, the three couples forming a triangle of blankets on the beach. He held a sandwich in one hand and a chart in the other, showing Claire where they had been and where they would go this afternoon.

"I think we'll be out for a few days next week. I want to try this area over here." The spot on the chart he pointed to held no significance to Claire. "That might be a good time to have Arianna's shower, or you gals could go into town. Pass the time while we're gone."

"How long will you be?"

"Three, maybe four days, this first trip anyway." He continued to study the chart as she nestled in closer.

"I don't want you gone that long," she said quietly but firmly. He kissed her head without taking his eyes from the map.

"If you girls stay busy, we'll be back before you know it." He dismissed her worry and hadn't looked up to see the distress in her eyes.

"I don't like you being out there at night," she said, breaking his concentration.

"It'll be fine," he insisted. "We've got everything we need to be comfortable below." He smiled and ran his eyes down her torso and back up again. "Well, almost everything." He folded the chart and pulled her up. "C'mon. I'll show you."

They walked between the blankets. On one side, Ava sat between Jonathan's knees, leaning against him, looking out at the ocean. He locked his arms around her and rested his head on hers. On the other, Arianna was on her side, with Caleb lovingly working out the strained muscles of her lower back.

"I'm going to show Claire the boat," Aryl said. Caleb gave an exaggerated wink. Aryl rolled his eyes but the thought of an impromptu rendezvous *had* crossed his mind. Twice.

It was cozy underneath with barely enough room for two people to move around. It held a double bunk scarcely wide or long enough to hold a man, a table, and a cook stove. There was a storage area under the bottom bunk and a handmade shelf to the side of the stove, with thin wooden slats on each of the three tiers to keep objects from flying off in rough seas.

"There are only two beds," she said. "Who's staying home?"

"No one. We'll sleep in shifts."

"I just don't like the idea of you going out for that long," she said, her eyes full of concern and her mouth pulled into a pout.

"It'll be fine. I promise. We'll be back before you know it." He pulled her close in a tight hug and then nuzzled her neck. "You know, we probably have time to—"

"Aryl!" Jonathan bellowed from the pier. "Let's get a move on. Sooner we finish, sooner we can get home." Aryl dropped his head with a sigh. "Maybe next time," he whispered and kissed her quickly.

They stood on the pier, baskets in hand and watched as the boat pulled away. Ava couldn't help but think Jonathan looked perfectly natural, standing tall and proud at the wheel, heading out to sea. The thick, wool sweater accentuated his broad shoulders and arms that, despite the hard work at the shipping dock, seemed to have gained even more substance since he began work on the boat. Glancing over the rest of him, she made a mental note to buy a length of wool for another pair of pants. His current and only pair of work pants strained at the seams from added bulk in the thighs and rear as a result of vigorous work combined with better eating. One good joke from Aryl and she was afraid they'd split right up the back. She shamelessly lingered on his rear; tight, gray material where his muscles contracted on either side as his weight shifted with the slight roll of the boat. She giggled slightly as her eyes passed over the large, floppy boots, which gave the appearance of a small boy going out to play in the mud. Just before she could no longer make out the details of him, he turned and smiled, the sun glinting off his black hair, and held up his hand to throw an exaggerated kiss ashore. She pretended to catch it and waved back.

"It's amazing, isn't it?" she said aloud.

"What's amazing?" Claire asked, her eyes still fixed on the boat.

"How great things turned out. In spite of everything we've been through during those awful first few months, here we are. Our lives are completely different. We're broke and living on charity, but," she said, shrugging, "we're happy. Strange as it sounds, life seems real now."

Claire thought about it as Arianna spoke up.

"It is real now. And it's better," she said and smiled.

## March 22$^d$ 1930

The next week, they left on a Tuesday, as Aryl had planned, and returned on Saturday morning. Ava was helping his mother in the garden when she heard the swing of the gate. She scrambled to her feet, crashed into Jonathan, and covered his bearded face with kisses. He fully looked the part now; a black sea bag thrown over his shoulder, a thick, wool sweater dirty and turned up at the neck, a black knit cap pulled low, the cut of his jaw obscured by four days worth of beard.

He whispered in Ava's ear as he held her close. "You didn't happen to make that other pair of pants, did you?"

He pulled away and turned around to reveal the poorest patch job ever attempted to a split seam. She doubled over in laughter at the still-gaping hole, which revealed gray undergarments between the rough zigzags of poorly made stitches.

"You poor thing," she said between bursts of giggles. "I have them upstairs. C'mon." She led him away and he waved to his mother as he passed the garden patch, her shoulders and face slumped in obvious relief at the sight of him.

Once upstairs, Ava closed the door quietly and then whirled around, grabbing two handfuls of Jonathan's sweater.

"You can't go away like that again." She kissed him hard, oblivious of his whiskers and the salty fish smell that radiated from his clothes. He broke the kiss and, with one swift yank, pulled both his sweater and shirt over his head. While alternating kisses and bites down his neck and shoulder, she took advantage of the rip in progress by taking a firm grip of the material and pulling hard; his pants fell effortlessly to the floor. Jonathan let out a slightly shocked gasp as he looked at the pile of cloth around his ankles and lifted his eyes, slowly and deviously.

"One good tear deserves another," he said as he grabbed hold of the buttoned closures on the back of her dress.

Later, Ava lay facing the window as the very last of the day's heat shone through on their entangled legs. Jonathan had dozed off, arm securely around her waist, his fuzzy face itching her shoulder. She sighed lazily and thought of how perfectly wonderful life was. There was a light chirping outside the window and the house seemed perfectly still; as if the whole world had stopped. She closed her eyes and all that existed was the intermittent warmth from Jonathan's breath on her neck and the solid weight of his arm around her middle.

There was one other thing that existed now, but she would wait; let him wake up or maybe let him shave first. She smiled and turned slowly and carefully to face him while trying not to disturb his light sleep. His breathing was long and deep with a slight moan at the end, and, although still asleep, he instinctively drew her close until the soft skin of her stomach met his and then relaxed his arm. She thought to enjoy this particular closeness while she could, grinning again to herself. Her thoughts wandered aimlessly, for how long she wasn't sure, but she began to grow impatient for him to wake when the room took on the glow of evening dusk. She moved out from under his arm and the cool rush of air replacing her warmth was enough to stir him. He stretched, yawned, and focused his eyes on her with a smile.

"I missed you, too," he said.

"We better get up. Your parents will be wondering where we are."

"I'm sure they have a vague idea." He swung his legs over the edge of the bed. "Personally, I'd like to stay here the rest of the evening." He flopped back on the bed and lightly bit her thigh. "I'd say we still have three more days of catching up," he said. "But I'm starving. However, if I weren't . . . ." His sarcastically threatening look made her laugh.

"Jonathan, wait."

He stopped mid-movement and lay his head back down on her thigh. "What, love?"

It was now or never and hardly the way she imagined, but she had discovered that very few things ended up unfolding the way they're envisioned. These last six months had taught her the finer art of elasticity, and she went with it. She reached for his hand as she spoke.

"Do you still want to try? For a baby, I mean?"

"Yes. And I'll give it another go as soon as I get some food," he said, smiling and squeezing her hand.

"You don't have to," she blurted out. His face fell, serious and afraid.

"Have you changed your mind?" he asked quietly.

"No." She placed his hand upon her stomach. "So much for it taking a few months . . . ."

He lifted his head slowly. "You mean?"

"Yes. Apparently you're as fertile as you are charming." He stared, astonished, attempting to speak but couldn't seem to get out more than two words at a time, none of which made sense when strung together. It was an accomplishment when he managed to crawl beside her carefully as if she were suddenly made of glass and look her in the eyes.

"Are you sure?"

"Your mother took me into town yesterday and I saw the doctor. Looks like the beginning of December," she said, smiling and plucked at the whiskers on his stunned face, amused at his oblivion.

"I just didn't expect it to happen so soon," he said before quickly adding, "but I'm happy . . . very happy." He lay back with his arm on his forehead.

A knock on their bedroom door pulled him from joyous stupor, and they scrambled for bed covers, bursting into giggles and shushing each other loudly. When they were finally covered sufficiently, Jonathan called out, "Come in."

Ava ducked under the covers, mortified. Of course, his mother knew full well what they had been doing all this time, but for anyone to see them lying in bed with trampled sheets and mussed hair was too embarrassing for Ava.

"Jonathan, there's . . . someone here to see you." Her voice was odd, Ava noticed; maybe she wasn't feeling well. "I think it best if you get dressed and come downstairs."

"Hey, did you hear the good news, Grandma? Of course, you did, you took her. Isn't it great?"

"It is, Jonathan. I'm happy for you." Ava couldn't see her expression, brows furrowed, and lips tight with worry. She raised the tone of her voice the best she could, but still something strained.

He waited until she closed the door to speak. "I'll bet that's someone about the article in the paper, meaning more business, but that's a good thing." He slipped on a pair of pants, and Ava dug in the closet for a dress. "She wouldn't see it that way, though. How was she while I was gone?"

"A nervous wreck. She tried to hide it, of course." She buttoned up the front bodice of the dress and tied the waist strings around her back. "Your father didn't like it too much either." Jonathan pulled on his shoes.

"Well, more business means we can speed up plans to move out."

Ava followed Jonathan down the steps, grinning at her flat stomach and feeling grateful it would be some time yet before she looked and felt like Arianna. She tried to imagine what it would be like to be unable to see her feet. She hadn't noticed that Jonathan stopped abruptly on the last stair. She smashed into him, grabbed his sweater to keep her balance, and stared dumbly at his back.

"Oh, no," he whispered, doom touching both syllables. He turned suddenly, seemingly to run back upstairs, but froze. It wasn't fear, exactly, on his face; violent discomfort distorting his mouth, anxiety filling his eyes as if he had just witnessed some great catastrophe. For a moment, it looked as if he were drowning, unable to breathe, run, or escape.

One glance over his shoulder told Ava why. Ruth stood in the living room, prim and polite, empathizing Jonathan's shock.

Realizing no escape, Jonathan turned around but couldn't make his legs work. Ava walked around him slowly, eying Ruth cautiously. Pregnant or not, she was suddenly very ready to physically kick this woman out, hopefully retaining a handful or two of hair in the process. The intensity of rage that built up so quickly against Ruth disrupting her blissfully perfect afternoon surprised her; rage so intense that she completely overlooked the fact that if Ruth was here, Victor knew their whereabouts as well.

She stole a glance at Jonathan, thinking he would have said something by now. Jonathan's eyes were fixed–but not on Ruth. Ava followed the trail his eyes burned and landed on a woman who was standing in Ruth's shadow; a woman of pale complexion and thick, raven-black hair, which was arranged beneath a red hat adorned with beads and feathers. She wore a red, velvet dress made of such intricacy that it would have been sufficient to wear to call upon royalty. For a moment, Ava thought she might actually be royalty judging from her attire and the way she held herself.

Ava spoke first. "What are you doing here, Ruth?" she demanded. "I thought I made it clear–"

"I'm sorry for the disruption. I have nothing to say, no reason to be here except to escort an acquaintance, who has a matter to discuss with Jonathan," Ruth spoke slowly and clearly, the rehearsed words Victor had instructed her to say.

"What acquaintance? What matter?" Ava asked suspiciously. Jonathan took an unsteady step forward and held Ava tightly to his side, partially for show of loyalty and partially for support. The royal stepped out from Ruth's shadow.

"Ava . . . ." He paused to pray the next three words wouldn't destroy everything he had fought to reclaim with his wife. "This is Elyse."

If Jonathan spoke further, Ava never heard it. Wind suddenly knocked out of her, she recoiled from him as shock replaced fury in her chest; her mouth hung open, her stomach queasy.

The royal's face remained unchanged and simply watched her as she quickly went through the expected emotions. She muttered something unintelligible and anguished to Jonathan, and his face acknowledged it painfully, silently. Her eyes returned to the royal and disturbing images ran through her mind at lightning speed; flashes of sweat and skin and lust on hot, Parisian nights, the two of them entangled. She felt pitiful and repulsive in her plain, cotton dress and bare feet as she stared stupidly at Elyse. Suddenly enraged again, she turned to Jonathan and shook her head side-to-side.

"Ava, please," he implored, although he had no idea what he was begging of her. In less than as many minutes, she slipped into a third head-spinning emotion and recalled every empty, lonely feeling and every frustrating day of silent insecurity during that horrible time in the tenement when Jonathan was lost to her, and he read that fear in her eyes.

He finally confronted Elyse. "Why are you here?" He pulled Ava back to his side, rigid as she was.

"I understand my presence upsets you," Elyse spoke directly to Ava rather than Jonathan. Ava, jolted from numbness by her French accent, stared at her, unwilling to speak. "I would not be here now if it were not a matter of life and death."

"Whose life?" Jonathan asked.

"And whose death?" Ava stared pointedly at Ruth when she spoke.

"Mine," Elyse said quietly. "Please sit. There is much I must say to you." Elyse moved to the smaller sofa and sat down with regal elegance. Ruth sat next to her as if a supportive friend. Jonathan reluctantly crossed the room, pulling Ava behind him. They sat close on the sofa, and he held her hand in both of his in another show of loyalty. His parents stood inside the kitchen out of view but very much within earshot.

Elyse coughed daintily at first then produced her handkerchief as she wretched with violent spasms. Ava realized she was grimacing as she watched Elyse cough and gag uncontrollably. When she regained composure, she didn't hesitate to explain herself.

"I'm dying," she said frankly and without emotion. "Tuberculosis, aided by other illnesses common to my profession," she offered.

"Why is that any of our concern?" Ava asked coldly. Now in close proximity to her, Ava could see the yellow tinge to the whites of her eyes and a sore on the corner of her mouth, which heavy makeup could not completely conceal.

"There is no way to say this but to say it, Jonathan." Ava's blood boiled when she said his name, the way it rolled off her French tongue with lovely elegance.

"Please just say what you have to say and leave. I'd like to get back to my evening with my wife."

The royal sat up a little straighter, and her eyes locked onto his. "I did not get rid of it. He lives, he breathes, just over there," she said quietly, nodding toward the door, "waiting in the car."

Jonathan suddenly went pale and the thought crossed his mind that he might be sick. He slumped with a hard exhalation and unconsciously let go of Ava's hand.

Elyse looked down and whispered, "I should have told you, I know."

Ava needed one moment more than Jonathan to put the pieces of Elyse's words together; then blazed again so quickly through anger, shock, and fear that it was barely noticeable. She stared at the floor, numb with disbelief, waiting for Jonathan to speak.

"Why now?" Jonathan croaked. "Why come to me now? I have no money. I lost everything. I can't offer you what I could then."

"I know. I am not here for money."

"Then why come here?"

"He is my heart. I love him so." She paused, batting her eyes, fighting tears. "Aside from me, he has no one on this earth. My family has rejected him as a bastard. And me as well for the life I lead. When I die, he will be alone. To be raised in an orphanage; dirty, hungry and beaten, I cannot bear the thought of this," she said and a tear slipped down her porcelain cheek. She sniffled and her voice was more pleading now. "He has your blood, your eyes, and your name. I mean to give him to you. To finish what I cannot. To see him become a man. Try . . . to love him."

Ava, too shocked to speak, stared at Jonathan's hanging head for several minutes. Ruth slipped out unnoticed by everyone, and returned holding the small boy's hand. Ava stared at him as he passed in front of her as if he were an abomination. He walked straight to his mother and mumbled something in French. She turned him around to face Jonathan. She stroked the side of his head as she spoke and looked on the verge of tears.

"Mon chere. Il s'agit de votre papa."

The little boy, no more than five, stepped hesitantly but curiously toward Jonathan, still slumped with his head in his hands.

"Is nice to meet you," the little boy squeaked with a heavy accent of his own, holding out his hand in trained politeness. Jonathan ever so slowly raised his head and took a sharp, jagged breath when he saw his own eyes staring back at him. His black hair was straight with the slightest curl at the ends, perfectly groomed, and he smiled slowly and cautiously at Jonathan. "My name is Jean."

"Hello," Jonathan whispered and touched the child's chubby, dimpled hand.

"Excuse me," Ava said and rushed into the kitchen. Margaret was there, stunned but not nearly affected to the degree that Ava was. She held her hair while Ava vomited in the garbage bin.

"Elyse, I don't know what you expect."

"I told you. To do what I cannot; to save him from a horrendous life in an orphanage. Take him, *please?*"

Jonathan's eyes flickered back to Jean's wide eyes, and his heart lurched despite his shock. He knew of the orphanages. He had made donations frequently, although he doubted any of the money benefited the poor children who survived there. How could he condemn this child, *his* child, to that life? He looked toward the kitchen and heard Ava wretch again. How could he not? This was killing Ava. It would take months to get back to the place they were, if it was possible at all. *And what of the baby, if it holds,* he thought grimly. Such a huge upset. He prayed the shock wouldn't cause her to lose it. He felt torn over the most painful decision of his life.

"Jonathan, I do not have much time. I want to be in Paris when I–"

He nodded numbly and silently to Elyse and then to Jean, having made his decision.

"Thank you. I will leave right away," she whispered, glancing in the direction Ava had run.

She spoke with Jean quietly as Jonathan rose and walked blindly past his parents and pulled Ava from her stooping position over the garbage. He held her close, cradling her head and whispered, "I'm so sorry."

Her nausea passed and she didn't cry but held him as he fought quiet tears full of fear and regret. He held her so tightly she could scarcely breathe.

"Everything will work out, everything will be fine," he said quietly a few moments later. He wiped his eyes. "I swear, Ava. Everything will be just like it was, please believe me, please don't hate me." She tried to muster compassion over the shock. The deafening silence in the house told her the unwelcome guests had gone, and she felt relief it was over.

"I don't hate you," she said quietly. "But I do need to lie down."

Jean was standing in the front doorway, his little hand held up mid-air as he watched the car pull away with his mother in it. He turned slowly to Jonathan. His round face was pained, making a great effort to be a strong, little man like his mother requested. He held out an envelope to Jonathan. "My mother asked me to give this to you," he said, trying desperately not to cry. He turned; head slightly bowed and sat on the couch, staring into his lap.

The letter contained lists of his favorite foods, sports, radio shows, his birth date, and other tidbits of knowledge Elyse thought it necessary for his father to know. Tutored since the age of two, he was fluent in three languages. Ava stared at the boy, realizing Jonathan had made the decision to keep him without her. It was a done deal and the abomination was now theirs to care for. Her face was blank and her eyes were cold as she eyed them both. "How could you?" she whispered.

He reached for her, begging, "Ava, I just couldn't . . . you don't know what those places are like. Ava, please."

"How could you do this . . . without me?" If she weren't numb from shock and angry from betrayal, she would have been sobbing. "A living, breathing tribute. A bond stronger than those of wedding vows."

His words were thrown back at him like a knife, and they tore through his chest, ripping a gaping hole in his heart. She turned to the stairs and left him to bleed.

After a few stunned and aching moments, Jonathan retreated to the kitchen and sank into a chair. His father joined him silently. His mother stood behind him, her hands on her son's shoulders, silent. He felt like he should apologize, explain, beg forgiveness, anything. But when he opened his mouth, he asked for what he needed the most.

"Please go get Aryl."

Aryl walked through the darkened living room and into the kitchen. Jonathan sat, head resting on folded arms. Aryl spun a chair around and rested his arms on the ridge of the back.

"What happened?" his voice was serious with concern, knowing Jonathan would never call for him like this unless it was a near disaster. Jonathan's arms moved slightly, his sleeve shifted and Aryl caught sight of the faint, white scar. "What happened, Jon?" he demanded.

Jonathan lifted his head. He was still bearded and his eyes were bloodshot. "My whole world just blew up," he spoke quietly with a hint of disbelief, holding up his hands as if in surrender. "Again."

They had last seen each other at lunchtime. He had been downright jovial as they split the money three ways from their exhaustive excursion and had talked about taking Ava out on the town the next day.

"Blew up how?"

"Didn't my father tell you?"

"No. All he said was that it was a . . . 'humdinger of a situation'. So fill me in." Jonathan pulled himself up off the table and slid partially down the back of the chair, crossing his arms.

"Elyse showed up here. This afternoon."

"What in hell?" he breathed. Jonathan had no idea Aryl's eyes could get so big. Jonathan stared at the tabletop, giving his friend a moment to absorb. "Why, in God's name, would she show up here?"

Jonathan gave him an ominous, sobering expression.

"To make a delivery." He stood and Aryl followed. He turned on a low light to reveal Jean's tiny form sleeping; his cheek resting on his two hands on the arm of the sofa, dark hair falling into his eyes. Jonathan immediately noticed the dried tear streaks on his plump cheeks. Aryl's face went white, and he gawked a few seconds before he remembered how to speak.

"Holy shit. Please, Jonathan, tell me he has blue eyes." Jonathan nodded, dismissing his friend's first concern being for his own hide.

"He's mine," he said, staring at Jean with no expression.

"Now this qualifies as a mess."

They jumped slightly. Jonathan turned to see Caleb; glad his father had had the sense to fetch him as well. He stood behind them, staring, just as stunned. Jonathan turned off the light and returned to the kitchen, his shoulders slumped. Caleb set a bottle of whiskey in the middle of the table.

"Your father sent this in with me. Said to drink it up before they get back. Something about your mother not knowing he had it," he said as he poured three glasses.

"Where'd they go?" Jonathan asked.

"Didn't say." Jonathan quickly threw three shots and waited a moment with closed eyes.

"Careful there. You haven't had a drink in a while," Aryl warned as he poured a second shot for himself. "Hey, listen, sorry about my reaction. I just thought maybe you were easier to find and, since you sent for me . . . ." Jonathan shook his head. On an empty stomach, the whiskey wasted no time numbing the edges of his mind and the dead hole he felt in his chest.

"No, it's all right. Understandable. But she was already pregnant with him when you–"

"I remember now," Aryl interrupted, "but I'm sorry just the same." He sat back, rubbed his eyes, and ran his hands through his hair. Still holding a handful of loose, brown curls at the back, he leaned an elbow on the table and tried to measure up the situation.

"You remember that feeling," Jonathan started, interrupting himself with a fourth shot, "that we had that day, sitting there after it all imploded; bloodshot eyes, numb with shock, holding onto a shot glass for dear life, scared to death."

"Yeah. Not likely a feeling any of us will ever forget." Aryl slid the bottle toward Caleb, out of Jonathan's reach.

"I certainly won't. No matter how hard I tried to hold onto everything that day, it all shattered right in front of me, shattered like glass. I was helpless to do anything but watch. After everything vanished, I couldn't see the next step I was about to take. I was only amazed after the fact that I was able to take it."

"Is that how you feel now?" Aryl asked with a wary eye, wondering the current risk Jonathan posed to himself.

"Yes," he whispered, "and no."

"How no?" Caleb asked.

"Well, everything is gone again. And I watched it. Couldn't do a damn thing, but watch it shatter."

Aryl did a quick mental inventory of Jonathan's life; best friends - check, parents' support - check, boats still floating - check, a roof over his head - check, a small but precious savings tucked away - check. That left one thing. And that one thing *was* everything.

"Ava," Aryl said quietly. Jonathan leaned into a reach for the whiskey. Aryl pushed it away. "Whoa. Let's see how you feel in five minutes. I've only had three and my head is spinning."

"Bona fide lightweights. That's what we've become." Caleb laughed then turned to Jonathan more seriously. "How did she take the news?" Jonathan rolled his eyes, then his head and began recounting.

A moment later, Aryl interrupted him. "Wait. She's—"

"Told me minutes before Elyse showed up," Jonathan said, nodding slowly.

Aryl leaned back with his hands on his head. "Shit," he muttered at the ceiling and thought that this time there may be nothing he could say or do to help his friend.

Jonathan finished recounting every detail. His face was like stone, emotionless until the end, when he suddenly looked like he would break in half. "She used the same words I had said when she agreed to have a baby."

Silence reigned for a long time as all three men felt unsure of what to say and wondered whether there was anything to say that would have made a difference.

Finally Jonathan looked up at Caleb. "What would you do? With this dropped in your lap, what in the hell would you do?"

"Well, if it were me sitting over there, I wouldn't worry about it."

"Huh? How the hell could you not worry about it?" He leaned forward, pouring yet another drink.

"I wouldn't because *I'd* be dead."

Aryl cast Caleb an incredulous look. Knowing about Jonathan's past attempt, it was a damned stupid thing to say, in his opinion.

Much to his surprise, though, Jonathan started laughing, lightly at first and then harder. "You're right," he said, wiping his eyes and still laughing. "Arianna would claw your eyes out and hang them around her neck."

"No," Aryl said straight-faced. "*Those* aren't what she'd hang around her neck." Jonathan doubled over, desperately trying to smother his howls. Caleb laughed but instinctively crossed his legs.

"And no worries of it happening again, you'd be, ah, what's the word? Barren?" Jonathan slurred slightly as he finished his drink.

"No, that's women," Aryl said. "*Sterile*—or is that with bulls?" He tapped his fingers, concentrating.

"Same difference," Caleb said.

"No, that's castrated," Jonathan corrected "That's what they do to bulls. Caleb would–"

"Caleb would like to talk about something else," Caleb said, shifting in his seat, feeling the joke had run its course.

"Regardless, I take it you're still intact?" Aryl's deep-brown eyes drooped with a whiskey-induced haze.

"Yeah, not that it matters anymore." Jonathan shrugged loosely.

"What's your plan?" Aryl asked, joking aside. The air was again heavy with reality.

Jonathan let out a deep sigh. "Damned if I know, Aryl." He glanced toward the living room. "I have no idea how I am going to raise him when I'm gone all day. And I don't know anything about kids. You usually get to start sort of slow. Get to know them from birth and make mistakes before it counts. This one is–"

"Potty trained. At least there's that." Caleb interrupted with a raised glass as if to celebrate the continence of Jonathan's illegitimate child. Jonathan smiled lightly.

"I'm glad you came, Caleb." He squinted across the table at his friend. "I'd say you're fairly lit over there."

Caleb nodded slowly. "I do believe so." He was still nodding when Aryl asked Jonathan again.

"What's your plan?" He wouldn't leave until he knew Jonathan could at least see the next step he was about to take.

"I'll try to talk to Ava, although I don't think she'll listen tonight. I think I'll ask my mother to help with Jean while I'm gone. I won't ask anything of Ava regarding him. Not just yet."

"You have the same name. That's gotta be awkward." Caleb raised his eyebrows.

"Spelled differently, the French version, of course."

"I think you're right to ask your mom to help. Let Ava warm up to him on her own."

"What if she never does?" Jonathan feared out loud.

"I don't know. But I would concentrate on getting her to warm up to you first."

"That, my friend, will take nothing short of a miracle."

"Miracles happen," Aryl reminded.

Jonathan instantly thought of St. Brigid's, Maura, and all of the unexpected turns his life had taken. With words now exhausted, they swayed slightly around the table, comforted by each other's presence.

"One more for the road," Caleb said, smiling and, upon hearing a car pull into the drive, hastily split the remaining whiskey between the three glasses and tucked the empty bottle under his shirt. Just before drinking, Aryl's head jerked toward Jonathan.

"You son of a bitch!" Aryl said in accusation. Jonathan's wobbly head turned, and he raised his eyebrows in question.

"You beat us!" Aryl said with a laugh.

"Huh?" Jonathan blinked twice. "What the hell, Aryl?"

"Your son will be the oldest. You beat us, after all."

An intoxicated smile spread across Jonathan's face, and he held up his glass. "So I did."

Jonathan remained at the table for almost an hour alone; staring, sighing, hand wringing, regretting, letting a few tears fall when the fissure in his chest ached and bled.

Well after midnight, he stood somewhat unsteadily as the blood rushed from his head. He took the stairs slowly and paused at the bedroom door, looking down at a blanket and pillow Ava had thrown into the hallway. Pushing them aside with his foot, he tried the knob but found it locked. He sighed and leaned his forehead on the door.

"Ava . . . Ava, please."

He waited several moments before scooping up the bedding and turning away. He lay on the couch, not really noticing how uncomfortable it was and stared at the ceiling with his hands behind his head. A noise from the other side of the room startled him, and he remembered Jean, who was still sound asleep, leaning on the arm of the smaller sofa. Squinting in the darkness, he wobbled and carefully moved him to lie more comfortably. He reached for the afghan draped along the back of the couch and when he touched it, he immediately recognized it as his childhood blanket. He spread it over Jean and watched him sleep for a moment. Without doubt, they shared more than the same name; the shape of the eyes, shape of the eyebrows, even his lips puckered in sleep were Jonathan's. The nose and ears were Elyse's. But there was one thing that was Jean's and Jean's alone, Jonathan realized, and his heart ached. The loss. That was all his.

He astounded at how this small child, who just said goodbye to his mother forever, had remained calm as his whole life tore away from him. And then, Jonathan nearly choked on guilt. He had sat just twenty feet away with his friends, drinking, crying, and even laughing, while Jean fell asleep alone on the couch in a houseful of strangers.

*Well, I'm off to a great start,* he thought and reached out to brush a lock of hair from Jean's forehead.

*March 23rd 1930*

Jonathan stirred and touched his head. "Damn." He grimaced at the ache in his temples and squinted against the bright room. His fuzzy vision focused on Jean, who sat on the couch, staring at him.

"Er, good morning," Jonathan said awkwardly, sitting up slowly.

"Good morning, Monsieur."

Jonathan rubbed the scruff on his face and tried to smooth down the wild chunks of hair on his head sticking in every direction. It was Sunday morning, at least he thought, and he hadn't showered since the night before the extended fishing trip. He sniffed himself and recoiled violently. Jean grinned shyly.

"I don't normally look, or smell, like this," he explained. "I'm a fisherman. Lobster. And I, uh, just got back from almost a week out." Jonathan's stomach grumbled loudly. Eating, along with bathing and changing clothes, was something else he forgot to do yesterday evening, when the world had stopped. He looked at Jean again, who was slightly wide-eyed and studying him. "Are you hungry?"

*Dear God, I forgot to feed him last night, too,* he thought.

"Oui, Monsieur."

"Okay. I think I can handle that." He stood too quickly and swooned slightly. After getting his bearings, he went to the kitchen to find food to make breakfast. For his *son*. The word was as foreign to him as the pots and pans that he clumsily tilted out of the cabinet, clanging loudly on the floor. Jean peeked hesitantly around the corner.

"Come on in," Jonathan said. "Have a seat." He pointed to the table. Jean wiggled up in the chair and sat waiting with his hands tucked under his legs, watching Jonathan's every move. Jonathan glanced curiously over at him several times.

"Well, they aren't the best eggs in the world, but–" He put a plate in front of Jean, feeling awkward pressure to be a polite host. He sat across from him with his own plate.

"Merci."

"You're welcome." Jonathan watched as Jean pulled his hands out from underneath him, sit straight, and neatly placed his napkin in his lap. "Why do you do that?" Jonathan asked. "Sit on your hands, I mean."

"So I don't knock anything over," he said casually. He looked down at the plate and smiled. "This is nice," he said. Jonathan nodded with a full mouth. "There is only one fork," Jean said and held it up.

Jonathan remembered then, fine dining. "Makes it easier not to get confused, doesn't it?"

"My nanny slaps my hand when I choose the wrong one," he said with a little frown.

"Well, we don't slap hands around here. And generally we don't have more than one fork at a time. And if we do–" Jonathan shrugged and took a bite. "I don't care which one you use." He gave Jean a slight smile.

The kitchen darkened a few shades, as if a partial eclipse had stolen a few rays of sunshine. Jonathan looked up to see Ava standing in the doorway, taking in the scene.

"How sweet." Her voice was flat and her eyes were swollen. He stood up quickly and tried to get close to her, but she moved away, getting a piece of bread from the cupboard and a small glass of water.

"Can I make you something, Ava?" he asked meekly.

She turned her cold eyes back to him. "Looks like you have your hands full."

"Don't be silly, it's no trouble at all."

She stared at Jean's plate of food. "Tell me, Jonathan. When did you make *me* breakfast?" She turned to him, waiting for an answer. "Ever?" she asked and pushed past him roughly. He sat back down at the table and sighed.

"She does not like me." Observant could be added to Jean's list of above-average talents.

"It's isn't that. She's just surprised."

"You were surprised at me. But you're nice." He struggled to jelly a piece of toast with the big butter knife.

"Well, it's going to take some time, you know, to get used to each other." He kept his eyes low to his breakfast, flickering every now and then up at Jean.

"Will you tell me when I can call you by your name?" Jean asked, staring almost cross-eyed as he levered the toast, heaping with jelly towards his mouth.

"Oh, right. You don't need to call me Monsieur. You can call me Jon, I guess."

"Will you tell me when I can call you Dadee?" Jean, for a brief moment, looked his age, letting his guard down along with his manners, as he tried to reach his tongue to his nose where a drop of red jelly dotted.

"Good morning," Margaret said and smiled tentatively as she crossed the room to the coffee pot. Jonathan raised his head, grateful for the interruption.

"Morning."

She sat down with her coffee and smiled at Jean. "I'm Jonathan's mother," she said. Jean thought about this for a moment.

"What may I call you, Madame?"

Margaret grinned at Jonathan. "That little accent is so adorable," she said in a hushed voice. "Well, now." She leaned back as if deep in thought. "My name is Margaret. He calls me Mom," gesturing to Jonathan, "and being his mom, I guess that makes me your grandmother." Jean looked very serious, folding his little hands in his lap. Margaret looked over him, every inch a ghost of Jonathan over twenty years ago.

"I've never had a Grand-Mere," he said softly, looking up at Margaret, almost afraid, as if he had spoken out of turn.

"Then it's settled," she said and smiled to relieve his fear. "You'll call me Grand-Mere." She sipped her coffee and then turned to Jonathan. "I talked with your father last night. Today we can clean out the spare room. It's chock full, and it will take most of the day, but it should be ready by evening for Jean."

"That's nice of you, Mom, but I think it would be best if we started looking for a place right away. Aryl offered to dip into the business funds–"

"Don't talk with your mouth full," she scolded. He rolled his eyes, swallowed and continued.

"The money we brought from New York to help us out. And I've got some saved."

"I don't think that's the best idea, Jon." She turned to Jean who was finished eating, waiting to be excused. "Why don't you run in the living room and turn on the radio?" she said and smiled at him. He nodded and slid off the seat. "Jon. I don't have to tell you that this isn't sitting well with Ava. Do you really think it's a good idea to be gone all day, the two of them left alone? She's upset and don't forget her condition."

"You think I've forgotten for one second her condition?" He leaned back and crossed his arms, his appetite gone.

"No. But I think it's best if you stay here a while longer. Let things settle down. Let me and your father help with Jean so he's not forced on Ava."

"Look. Staying here with my wife is one thing. But now it's my pregnant wife and my illegitima–"

"Your son. Regardless of how he came to be, he's your son. And he's you to his shoes, Jonathan." She paused a moment, trying to organize her words. "Your father and I don't have a problem with where he came from. Ava does. We know very little of this woman that showed up, and we don't care to know more. What's past is past. Right now, that sweet, little boy in there has just lost everything he knows and loves. It's going to take a while for you to get to know him, and you can only be with him so much. You have to mend things with Ava, and that's going to take time and energy. So, let us help." He looked reluctantly at her and sighed.

"I'll have to insist on paying you more rent."

She waved her hand with a grunt. "I'm not worried about that." He knew she was right and agreed with a reluctant nod. He couldn't be here to take care of Jean and on the boat at the same time. And he couldn't ask Ava to look after him. She'd probably refuse anyway. "Now. I'll clean up. Go bathe. You smell," she said, smiling. "Then we'll get started on the room."

A while later, Jonathan emerged from the bathroom, smelling and feeling a great deal better. He paused and peeked through the slightly ajar bedroom door. Ava sat cross-legged on the bed, writing furiously. He walked down the hall to find his mother and Jean sitting on the floor of the spare bedroom. A cedar chest was open, and Margaret sat on her knees, digging through piles of Jonathan's things from when he was young. Jean spotted a small, tattered teddy bear and reached for it.

"What can I do?" Jonathan asked, surveying the mess of boxes and crates.

Jean looked up, slightly shocked at Jonathan's clean-shaven face and combed hair, and smiled.

∞∞∞∞

"Ruth?" Elyse watched the countryside, wobbling in her seat next to Ruth as the train steamed toward New York and away from her child. "Do you think he'll be happy here?"

"I do. Jonathan will be good to him. I'm sure of it. He's got a big heart." Elyse looked at her with compassion.

"You care for him." It was more a statement than a question.

"I do." Ruth looked down. "I always will."

"But your husband is a good man to arrange for our travel, to help and be so hospitable. I still feel I must repay him for what he has done. He has been very kind."

"Victor has his own reasons for helping, and they have nothing to do with kindness. Jonathan is good, kind, and strong. Victor is . . . nothing like Jonathan."

"Tell me." Ruth thought twice before confiding. She cautiously wondered whether Elyse was yet another spy to watch and report. But what would Elyse have to gain? She was dying and had her own money.

"You know, I'm probably signing my own death certificate, but . . . ." She proceeded to tell Elyse about the two men's entangled past. It left Elyse slightly wide-eyed with shock and worry. "You know, sometimes I think that's the only reason I've stayed so long. I feel like I might be able to keep an eye out for Jonathan this way. Maybe warn him. Victor gets more secretive as time goes on, though. And I think he knows. I think he knows I still care for Jonathan and that I would betray him in a heartbeat to protect Jon."

Elyse laid a hand on Ruth's, surprised and grateful that she didn't shrink away, the way most polite society did. "I still care for him greatly myself. If there is anything I can do, please tell me," she offered. Her eyes held sympathy and the two women sat quietly for a moment, holding hands and reflecting on their common love. Ruth looked at her and felt obliged. Even in her own moment of grief, she was kind enough to reach out and listen.

Several moments later, an idea came to her. "There is one thing," Ruth began, breaking the silence.

∞∞∞∞

Shortly after a formal dinner, Victor excused himself and Ruth, leaving Elyse to finish her dessert in silence. Victor led Ruth to the parlor and closed the door behind him. He interrogated her and demanded to know the exact words exchanged and made her repeat, twice, Ava and Jonathan's reactions in detail. He grinned to himself, enjoying the fact that Ava was upset to the point of physical illness.

*Go to hell, you filthy, evil bastard. You're not a fraction of the man he is. Go straight to hell*, Ruth thought as she stared at the floor to hide her hatred.

"If that's all you need, I'd like to go to sleep. It's been a long day," she said softly and he waved her away. Elyse was also in the process of leaving the dining room to retire for the evening, and Ruth watched her climb to the top of the stairs. Elyse stopped, looked down, and gave a scant nod.

Elyse later slipped downstairs quietly and found Victor in the parlor alone. Several glasses of brandy and malicious satisfaction twisted his mouth into a smile as he stared at the dying fire. "Monsieur. I wanted to thank you once again for your help, your hospitality, and your kindness."

"It was no . . ." She glided across the room toward him, her sheer gown flowing behind her, leaving nothing to the imagination. ". . . trouble." She sat in the chair next to him, leaning over to let her gown expose full cleavage.

"I just wish I had a gift to express my gratitude. Some way I could," her eyes flickered up with insinuation, "repay you."

He grinned and reached out, tracing a finger along her collar bone and down along her cleavage to draw the seam of the gown further apart.

"I'm sure we can think of something."

∞∞∞∞

Elyse boarded the ship bound for her homeland at noon the next day. She was at peace with her son safely delivered to his father; the last of her affairs now in order. And by fulfilling Ruth's request, her parting gifts to Victor–syphilis, tuberculosis, and a wasting liver disease.

*March 31ˢᵗ 1930*

Claire walked leisurely down the beach, picking up shells, unique rocks, and small pieces of driftwood to paint. She glanced at the sun, which hung low in the sky and wandered away from the blanket and picnic basket she had laid out. It had been Aryl's idea, she remembered with a smile, to start having Friday dinner picnics on the beach whenever the weather allowed, which provided a few precious hours to be truly alone and talk freely about anything. They talked about the frustrations of communal living, about the other couples' current strife, but mainly they talked about their future.

He kept a list of all their hopes and plans in his pocket. Some were nothing more than outlines of far off things that were too early to detail. Others were detailed to the point of color choices for their new home one day and names for their future children. They went over the lists every Friday as they ate, adjusted plans where needed and added new details that came to mind.

He was late, and she stood, holding her hand over her eyes for a long time, watching the ocean for a sign of his boat. She suddenly startled as a bit of sand grazed her leg. She looked down to see a little girl, maybe six, playing in the sand a few feet away. Pixie cut, strawberry-blond hair surrounded her face as she dug deep into the sand.

"Sorry," she said softly with a grin and quickly went back to her sand play.

"That's all right." Claire hugged herself with crossed arms, smiling. "You're not out here all alone, are you?" she asked while looking around for the girl's family.

"No, my momma's over there." She pointed to her without looking up from her sand pile. "I have to go soon," she said with pleasant finality. Claire looked in that direction, and, even though she could only see a foggy silhouette down the shoreline, she waved.

She bent at the knees and dug lines in the sand with a stick.

"I'm Claire. What's your name?"

"Beatrice Joy," she said with oomph, beaming, terribly proud of her name. She patted her sand castle, frowning occasionally, unconscious of her tongue poking out the side of her mouth in concentration. Although Claire hadn't heard anything over the ocean waves, she noticed the mother now within calling distance.

"Beadie, what did I tell you about running off?" she said with a frustrated smile, shifting a baby boy in her arms. "I hope she wasn't any trouble," the mother said to Claire.

"No, none at all. We were just talking." Claire stood and raised her hand again against the glare. The woman stood a foot taller than Claire, and the sinking sun behind her illuminated her red hair in a radiant silver and gold circle of light. One large hand cupped the bottom of the baby boy who laid his head on her shoulder, and she held her other hand out. "Come now, Bea. It's time to go home." Without hesitation, the little girl rose, leaving the sand tools she had scavenged from nature behind and ran several steps to take her mother's hand. Claire watched until they were almost out of sight, and the little girl turned at the last, looked over her shoulder and waved with a contented smile as they vanished into the brilliant core of the sunset. Claire raised her hand, holding it still in the air until they vanished.

*April 5th 1930*

Jonathan stood outside the bedroom doorway, debating and then leaned in, only exposing his left side. The last two times he had attempted to talk to her, he needed to dodge whatever happened to be within Ava's reach. This way, he figured he could duck out easier, if he needed to again. He poked his head in, resting it on the inner frame, and his voice cracked with hushed imploring.

"*Ava*, it's been *two* weeks." She glanced at the calendar and back at Jonathan with a blank expression. *Well, that's an improvement from burning hatred,* he thought hopefully.

She sat on the bed, legs folded under her skirt, back against the wall, and suddenly gathered her letters to hold them to her chest protectively, scowling at him.

With her hands occupied now, he took a few tentative steps into the bedroom.

"Looks like Maura wrote you." She looked down at the letters she cradled, nodded slightly, and fixed her vacant stare past him. "My mother said you got several letters at once. I wonder if some got delayed along the way." Her shrug was barely noticeable as she looked down at them again. "Listen, I have to go into town today. I was wondering if you'd go with me. Might feel good to get out of the house."

"I have been. I've spent almost every day with Claire," she said under her breath. Each day, she hastily did her share of chores and then spent the rest of the time alone in the locked room or visiting Claire. Jonathan had effectively been kicked out.

"I know," he said, nodding. "I meant out of the house *with me*." He leaned with crossed arms waiting for her rejection. He could see her thinking and dared to feel hopeful.

"I have to pick up a present for Arianna."

He nodded quickly. "We can do that."

"And I have to get a few things for her shower." He'd have let her shop their entire savings away as long as it meant spending time with her, closing the gap between them. He missed her; it picked at his heart's wound to be in the same room and have her barely acknowledge him. He inhaled her familiar scent just out of reach, tortuously forbidden to reach out.

"Whatever you need," he spoke dully, disguising his elation. He chose a lightweight, forest-green sweater to go over a white shirt. Tan or black dress pants were his only choices, so he chose black and headed for the bathroom.

More promptly than usual, he appeared in the living room shaved, styled and with a bit too much cologne applied. He tucked his wallet into his back pocket and caught the keys his father tossed to him. As Ava walked out ahead of him, he grinned hopefully at his parents.

"Don't wait up."

Less than a mile down the road, Ava began wrestling with the window lever, struggling to breathe.

"Oh, it's been jamming lately." He pulled over and leaned across to tug at the rusted handle. She leaned back on the seat and he came up slowly, smiling sweetly. "There you go."

She coughed a 'thank you', overwhelmed by the reek of liquid persuasion.

"Did you spill it or something?" she asked, slightly irritated, leaning closer to the open window.

"Yeah, on my pant leg," he lied gracefully. "I would have changed but, you know, I figured you wanted to get going."

As minutes of silence passed, Jonathan scrambled to find something to say. "Are those your letters from Maura, or are they some you need to mail?" he asked, referencing the stack of letters she held.

"Both. Maura's and invitations to the baby shower. Arianna wanted to send some to New York, even though she knows none of them will be able to come." She stared at the countryside. "I already wrote to Maura this week."

Jonathan thought he detected the slightest bit of warning in her voice. There was a flash of cold fear in his gut, and he reaffirmed his effort to change her mind. He wished Maura was here. She could talk Ava out of leaving, if that's what she was planning. Maura would walk in disconcerted, swearing, demanding answers and a drink. Then she would sit them both down and tell Ava how unreasonable she was being. He could almost hear her as he drove.

*"Now what's goin' on this time? The two of ye sittin' on opposite sides of the couch again, I thought ye were well past that by now. What'd ye do, Mr. Jonathan?"*

He'd plead his case, profess his love, and then Maura would turn on Ava and set her straight. After more cursing and loving threats, she'd leave and all would be well.

He opened his mouth and closed it, fighting the rising lump in his throat. He swallowed hard and tried again. "How is Maura?"

She recognized something in his voice that made her heart ache even more for Maura, and for a few moments, she ignored her anger at him.

"Not all that well, I'm afraid. Ian lost his job. She's still working, but she says things are getting bad in the city. Tarin has been working at the cannery, but that's not going well either. The supervisor likes to get friendly with the girls, and the first time Tarin came home in tears, well, Maura took care of him well enough."

He heard Maura's concerned voice in his head as the story came to life in his mind.

*"Why, Tarin! What's the matter, love?"* Tarin collapsed onto the couch, sobbing. Maura went to her immediately, stroking her hair and trying to comfort her. *"Now, tell me, love, what's got ye so upset?"*

*Tarin proceeded to tell Maura of her new supervisor and his wandering hands. "Mr. Craig does it to all the girls, auntie. Grabbin' and pinchin', slappin' their bottoms when they walk by. He hadn't paid much attention to me, but today he . . . ."*

*Maura's face was set hard and almost as red as her rich, auburn hair. Her green eyes flashed, narrowed and she urged Tarin to continue.*

*"Well, he's done worse to other girls, that's for sure. But today he grabbed at my bodice, slapped me rear, and laughed the whole time, like it was entertainin'. He's a gross, fat man. An' he smells."* She wrinkled her nose; most of her tears now subsided.

*"Well, Tarin, ye can go to work tomorra' without worry of this ever happenin' again."* She kissed her on the head and crossed the room, lifting the black, metal tongs from its peg on the hearth. *"Auntie will see to that,"* she professed as she walked out the door coatless, headed down to the cannery.

"Did he live?" Jonathan asked, laughing. "Or are your letters now addressed to the women's penitentiary?"

"Oh, he lived. Maura can be quite convincing when she wants to be. And she convinced Mr. Craig not to even so much as look in Tarin's direction again," she said and smiled, squinting her eyes against the sunlight. She felt the slightest twinge of jealousy toward Tarin, wishing Maura were here to put Jonathan in his place. She smirked at the visual of her standing before him with a set of fire tongs in her hands. She continued with the story.

*Maura walked into Mr. Craig's office without knocking. Before he could register the fiery whirlwind that blurred through the door, Maura had the fire tongs buried neatly in his crotch, the tongs above and below, grasping his bits and parts with constriction that demanded attention.*

*"What are you doing, you mad woman!?"*

*"Ye'll lower your voice, Mr. Craig,"* she said. *Her voice was low, insistent and unwilling to negotiate.* *"And ye'll hear me out, or I swear on everything that's good and true, I'll rip off yer parts, and ye'll have to choke your own throat to get yerself off because that's where I'll have stuffed yer wee piece."* She applied pressure to the tongs to emphasize her point.

*He squealed an unnaturally high octave and held his hands up in surrender.*

*"Now. Ye know of a girl named Tarin? Sweet Irish lass just started workin' here a few weeks ago?"*

*He nodded quickly, wide-eyed with the sudden realization of the meaning behind the visit.*

*"She's the one ye had your nasty paws on this afternoon. Well, Mr. Craig, I'm here to tell ye that if ye so much as look in the direction my niece happens to be . . . our next visit won't be quite so pleasant."* She added pressure as she finished her sentence.

*He gasped and groaned, clutching the arms of his chair. "Please," he whispered.*
*"Do we have an understandin' then?" she asked suddenly smiling sweetly at him.*
*He was convinced this woman was stark raving mad. "Yes," he whispered.*

Jonathan laughed until he could hardly see the road, and despite herself, Ava laughed, too.

"God help anybody," he said, wiping his eyes, "who crosses that woman."

Ava gave him a quick glance and wished Maura were here now, handling him much in the same manner. They fell into silence for many miles, Maura heavy on their minds. Suddenly, he arched his back, leaning on the steering wheel with a wince and a groan.

Ava glanced at him. "What happened?" she asked indifferently.

"Oh, it's nothing. My back hurts. The couch is rather uncomfortable." He eyed her sideways, hoping it would lead to a compromise of letting him back into the room. "So, how have you been feeling?" He noticed she was re-reading one of Maura's letters. She folded it quickly and stuffed it back in her handbag.

"Oh, yes. I'm pregnant," she snapped sarcastically. "How nice of you to remember."

"I didn't forget, Ava. You haven't been talking to me, remember?"

"I've been pretty sick to my stomach." She watched the passing landscape with little interest.

"Morning sickness, huh?"

"Among other things," she said, her voice cold again.

They were silent the rest of the drive to Boston.

Jonathan went into a hardware store, searching for a few things his father had requested. He made idle small talk with Ava as best he could while she followed him around numbly. She simply stared at him or through him; Jonathan wasn't quite sure which.

Next, they went to a department store, and Ava wandered off to pick out a gift for Arianna. Jonathan used the time alone to look for a present for her birthday, which was only a week away. He found a bottle of perfume that he loved and was fairly sure she would like, and with pink-faced embarrassment, wandered into the department for women. He bought three pair of silk stockings and had all of it wrapped in a beautiful box. He found Ava in the baby department, holding tiny outfits in front of her with a grin.

"That's adorable. We should buy it," Jonathan said, sidling up to her.

"This is a girl's outfit. We don't even know what ours will be. And since when did we have so much money to spend?" She stepped away to a display of blankets and swaddling cloths.

"Well." Jonathan followed her. "Since we're staying with my parents a while longer, we can use a little of the savings. That four-day trip was very profitable, and we've been saving so hard for so long. We deserve it." He touched her shoulder. She glared at his hand and then up at him. He removed it. "Sorry."

"I found this for Arianna," she said, putting a lovely red, silk sleeping gown in Jonathan's hands. "I need to find something for the baby, and I'll be finished."

"Their baby or ours?" he asked quietly.

She looked at the piles of gowns and outfits. He was almost sure he saw a flicker of emotion and one or two of the bricks crumble from the wall she had built around herself.

"Theirs," she whispered.

He prolonged their time in the city by suggesting they get something to eat before heading home. They sat across from each other in a booth by the window of a small restaurant.

"Hungry?" he asked cheerfully, even more determined to break through the rest of the fortified barrier that was keeping her from him. He now knew it was penetrable.

"A little." She hunched over the table peering at the menu. He ordered a Reuben and soup, but she only wanted soup.

"I know it's early, but have you thought about any names yet?" he asked. She shook her head and focused her eyes across the room. "What are you hoping for? A boy or a girl?" he asked. Her eyes rolled back to him with a slow, irritated blink.

"What are you hoping for, Jonathan?" There was no right answer and he knew it. If he said a boy, she would call him a liar because he'd already gotten his boy; claiming he only wanted to make her feel better that she could produce a child equal to what Elyse had produced. If he said a girl, she'd call him a liar as well; claiming he only said it to avoid a riff with wanting a boy and to avoid being forced to choose who produced the better boy.

This was his fear anyway. Since she had been so emotional and irrational lately, it wouldn't surprise him if his fear turned out to be well founded. He went with both honesty and diversion.

"I want a healthy baby and a quick delivery with as little discomfort as possible for you." She nodded at his acceptable, albeit safe, answer. They were served lunch and it was left to Jonathan to break the silence once again.

"Tell me more about Maura," he said quietly, cooling a spoonful of soup. "You said things were getting bad."

"They are." As soon as the subject of Maura came up, her voice softened and she spoke easily. "She said that there are a lot of people out of work. She sees bread lines every day now, sometimes over a block long. Families are moving in together to save money. There's also a bunch of people living in Central Park. She said it's like a city of tents and shanties. The city doesn't like it, but there's nowhere else for them to go. They shoo some of them away, but they show up again in a few days." She crushed crackers into her vegetable soup with a furrowed brow, worried for Maura.

"How are she and Ian doing? I mean, is it that bad for them?"

"Not yet. Maura is still working for the family she went to after us, but they've shortened her workdays. Her aunt lost her job at the library, so she's home every day to tell Ian how poor a job he's doing of raising Scottie. To make ends meet for now, they are dipping into the money saved to bring Maura's mother over. She's heartbroken over that."

"I wish there was something we could do." He stared at the table, his soup growing cold, trying to brainstorm a solution to help. Several moments later he sighed, resigned to helplessness.

"How about Shannon and Patrick? Have you heard from them?"

"Yes. It's getting rough for them, too. Patrick still has his job, but every day he wonders if it will be his last. I guess they're laying off men every week. And Shannon is worried she's pregnant again."

He looked up with raised eyebrows. "Lord, that's the last thing they need."

"I guess Patrick has a new hobby of yelling at the radio, especially when the President says things are okay now and continue to get better every day. He yells that maybe His Highness should take a stroll down to Central Park or any number of alleys in the lower east side to see the people huddled in them or to the factories and docks to see how many men continue to walk away without a job every Friday."

Jonathan laughed at her attempt to impersonate Patrick's thick, Irish brogue. "I miss them," he said. "I wish there was something we could do." It was all they could do to save a bit toward their own future home and contribute to living expenses; but now with another mouth to feed and yet another to come the end of the year, she wondered if they would ever be able to move out.

"I was thinking about planning a picnic next weekend," he said, abruptly changing the subject.

"Why?" Her eyes glazed again as her smile faded.

"Well, for one, I like spending time with you, for two, the weather's been beautiful, for three, Jean asked if we could have one. The three of us."

"I'd rather not," she said curtly and went back to her cold soup.

"Ava, he's just a child. He has no idea—"

"He's yours and *her* child. And I don't want anything to do with him. I thought I made that clear."

"I'm not asking you to love him, just—"

Her eyes flashed full of anger as she leaned toward him.

"You made this decision without even consulting me. You chose her wishes over mine. And I will never forgive you." She gathered her hat and gloves to leave.

"Ava, wait!" He grabbed her wrist and she jerked it away. "You're right. I should have talked to you first. I'm sorry, all right, a thousand times, I'm sorry." His voice was hushed. "I was in shock—completely stunned, I couldn't breathe ... I ... ." He leaned his elbow on the table, held his forehead in his hand, and looked at her pitifully. "I miss you," he whispered.

She looked away quickly, but not quick enough; he saw one more brick fall. He ordered tea for both of them, and they sat quietly for a long time. "I need to know," he said, sitting up straighter and running his hand through his hair. "Are you leaving me?" Her head jerked and for a brief second, she looked insulted.

"Do you want me to leave?" she asked spitefully.

"No. Of course not. I just thought, under the circumstances of you writing Maura so much, you might be thinking about it."

More silence. He sighed and let his hand fall onto the table with a thud. "Jesus, Ava, just tell me yes or no. I need to know."

"I haven't decided yet," she said quietly. "I just don't know if I can do it, Jon. If I can look at him every day. You have no idea how I feel or what goes through my mind. And I don't know if I can look at you every day. I don't even know if I want this baby." His eyes widened and dread balled up in his stomach.

"What do you mean?" he asked cautiously.

"I don't know," she whispered with tears in her eyes. She reached for her hat and gloves again, and this time he didn't try to stop her. He walked a few paces behind her to the car.

∞∞∞

After a silent ride home, she went directly to their room, closing the door behind her. Jonathan sat on the couch, and Jean scrambled up to sit beside him, showing him several drawings he had done that day.

"Wow." He looked at Jean and back to the drawings. "You did these?" Jean grinned shyly and nodded. "They're very good." He studied the drawings, stunned, and glanced at his mother.

"Jean drew those for you," she said, confirming Jonathan's questioning look. He shook his head and rubbed his chin, amazed. "You're a good, little artist. I bet you'd enjoy meeting Claire. She's an artist, too. She paints."

"I love to paint!" he said and smiled widely. "When can I meet her?"

"Well, you know that picnic? Maybe we could invite Claire and her husband and our other friends, too?" *That way Ava would have to go,* he thought.

"Oui, can we please?"

"We can," Jonathan said with a tired smile.

Jean scooted off the couch, announcing, "I have to go to bed now." He headed toward the stairs, pausing to hug his grandmother on his way. "Good night, Grand'Mere."

Jonathan had just placed his bedding on the couch when he heard footsteps on the stairs. Ava went to the kitchen for a drink of water and then stopped at the landing of the stairs, gripping the rail tightly.

"You don't have to sleep on the couch anymore," she said. Her voice was strained, as though the words were forced at gunpoint. "I know you work hard, and I won't be responsible for causing someone pain." She glared at him pointedly. "But mind the line."

When he walked into the room, he saw she had taken a pen and physically drawn a line down the center of the white sheet.

*April 7th 1930*

"So, did you make any headway Saturday?" Aryl's pace was slowing, tiring from the repetitive hand-over-hand motion of pulling up the heavy pots.

"Yes and no." Jonathan took a large bite of apple and then tucked it in his pocket as the first pot emerged from the water. He leaned to haul it up and over as Aryl began pulling up the next pot. "I'm off the couch. But she still barely talks to me."

"What about the kid? How is she around him?" Aryl paused to wipe sweat off his forehead with his sleeve. "Damn, it's getting warm," he muttered and went back to his tug of war with the sea.

"She ignores him. I guess it could be worse. She's not outright mean to him. She spends a lot of time with Claire and Arianna and when I'm home, she spends a lot of time in the room or the garden."

"You're getting the next string," Aryl grunted as he pulled up yet another pot swollen with a red mass of black beady eyes, claws that snapped with a tight sinister pop and antennae that wildly poked out of the pot in all directions. Jonathan opened the pot and grimaced as he carefully transferred them to the water hold, occasionally throwing one back overboard.

"I still say these are the ugliest things," he muttered.

"Well, feel free to trade me places. My arms are killing me."

"I will, next string," Jonathan said and grinned. "Anyway, I hope the picnic this weekend will go all right. She didn't like the idea of just the three of us having one."

"Do me a favor," Aryl said as he pulled another pot over the edge. "Go over there and kick Caleb. Nap time is over." He glanced over his shoulder at Caleb, who slept curled on his side with a coat over his head. Jonathan nudged him on the shoulder.

"Hey, wake up. Wouldn't want you to miss all the fun."

Caleb pushed the coat off his head and squinted in the sunlight.

"How long was I out?" he asked groggily while rubbing his face.

"Couple hours." Jonathan went back to sorting lobsters. Caleb wobbled to his feet.

"Sorry 'bout that," he grumbled.

"Arianna still keeping you awake?" Aryl asked. Caleb nodded mid-yawn.

"She can't get comfortable. Her back hurts, her feet are swollen, and she has to use the bathroom every hour. And she's having more and more of those practice pains. I guess they don't hurt that bad, but they wake her up, which wakes me up. I'll be glad when this is over," he said, rubbing his eyes again.

"Aw, you can't stop now. I've always pictured you with at least a dozen kids running around that farm," Aryl said. Caleb glowered at him as he started unloading a pot.

"Just *you* wait," he warned.

"I can't wait to have kids." Aryl smiled.

"You say that now, but I think you'll be singing a different tune when Claire is," he paused, and even though they were in the middle of the ocean, he lowered his voice to a whisper, "as big as a house and crabby and crying and throwing things." Caleb shuddered. "But that's not what bothers me the most," he continued, setting aside the empty pot and dragging another away from the wall. "There isn't a damn thing I can do to make it better." He shook his head in frustration. Aryl pulled the last pot up and sat down hard, completely spent.

"It's almost over, Caleb. Couple more months." Caleb nodded, yawned again, and finished working. "Let's go in after this," Aryl said. Jonathan stopped working and stared at him for a moment.

"Are you, actually, calling an early day? Have you gone mad?" he teased.

"No. Just really tired. I think I might be catching a cold or something," he said, rubbing his sinuses with a grimace.

∞∞∞

*A*va came up out of bed with a strangled scream, sweat covering her face and chest. She gasped, cold and numb with fear, trying to catch her breath.

"Hey, hey, what's wrong?" Jonathan sat up and leaned to try to see her face. She dropped her head into her hands and tried several slow, deep breaths.

"Just a bad dream," she whispered. The same dream that haunted her for several months had revisited her. This time, Jean followed her along the black, jagged rocks where she cried and called for Jonathan. No matter how many times she turned to yell for him to go away, to leave her alone with her own baby screaming in her arms, he clung to her skirt and called her Mother.

"Talk to me," he said softly and slipped the fallen arm of her sleeping gown back up onto her shoulder. She shook her head, dropped her hands to her legs, and kept her head down. "It might help." He put her hand into his and was pleasantly surprised when she didn't pull it away.

"I keep having the same dream, at least once a week. This time . . . it was worse." Her voice was hoarse from sleep and fright. He turned toward her and massaged her hand.

"What do you keep dreaming about? Tell me," he whispered. She sighed, long, slow, and rolled her head over to him.

"I can't." The house was perfectly still; the only sound the faint ticking of the bedside clock. The glow of the moonlit room was enough light just to make out shapes and outlines.

He pushed the hair from her face. "I meant what I said last Saturday." She searched his face, wondering which phrase he was talking about. "I really miss you," he whispered. She could barely make out his eyes; they were so sincere that she felt her heart's ice begin to melt, and he could sense it. "It kills me to be this close to you. I'd do anything to make things right again. I just want things to be like they were . . . when we were happy." He leaned to kiss her and she didn't pull away. She let him do what he would, leading the kiss tentatively, as she grappled between anger and loneliness. After a moment, loneliness won and she grabbed two handfuls of his hair, urging him on.

"Michael. Michael! What's that?" Margaret sat up in bed, unnerved. "I think someone is trying to break in," she whispered. He listened intently for a moment and then suddenly let out a quiet, hard laugh. "What is it? Why are you laughing?" she whispered with a hint of irritation.

"No one is trying to break in, Margaret. I think Jon and Ava worked things out." Three seconds to process and Margaret giggled, slightly embarrassed. "Well, that's good," she said with a smile, reclining again.

"Hey, hold on now," he said and smiled down at her. "Just what are you doing?"

"Going back to sleep since we're not being robbed." She leaned up, pecked him on the lips, and then settled under the quilts.

"I have a better idea," he said, grinning in the dark, hovering over her. "Let's give 'em a run for their money." She giggled wickedly and pinched him playfully on the thigh.

∞∞∞∞

The next afternoon, Jonathan returned home early. He had worked at a breakneck pace to get home as fast as possible to Ava. He practically skipped home, swinging his lunch pail as he walked, whistled, and greeted some birds nesting in a tree with a cordial hello. He stopped only briefly to pick some wild daisies that grew alongside the patchy, gravel road.

Once inside, he waved to his parents, who were on the couch listening to the radio with a glow of their own. He stooped toward the floor to pat Jean's head as he was creating a new drawing. He took the stairs two at a time and pushed the door open, smiling.

Ava glanced up and immediately went back to her letter writing, sitting on the side of the bed. In one graceful movement, he rounded the bed and pulled her up by one arm, spun her around and dipped her back, kissing her. He pulled away briefly with a lopsided grin. "Honey, I'm home." He leaned in again, and his lips landed on her cheek.

"Jon, what are you doing?" she asked with annoyance.

"Well." He lifted her up. "I was trying to come home and sweep you off your feet, but you don't look very . . . swept." He raised one eyebrow curiously. She backed away from him, gave a little shove in the process with an annoyed look and bent to gather her scattered papers.

"Everything go okay here today?" He pulled off his wool cap and scratched his head.

"No better, no worse," she said quietly.

"Well, then, what's wrong?" he asked. She ignored him and continued gathering her things. "Ava, I thought–" She spun around, stopping him mid-sentence.

"Look, Jon." She crossed her arms and exhaled roughly. "Last night, well, it doesn't change how I feel."

"But," he began, staring at her in disbelief, "I thought things were okay with us now. I mean, with how you were last night."

"That was purely . . . need," she said firmly. His head fell slightly as he gaped at her. He looked down over himself and back at her.

"You . . . *used* me?" he cried.

"No more than you used me," she said coldly and turned away.

"Hold on. I didn't use you. I was the one saying I love you, remember? I said that I missed you, and I was so happy to be close to you again."

She looked back before leaving the room. "I'm sorry you misinterpreted it."

*April 10th 1930*

Ava sat staring at the silver and white box on the bed. The tag read Happy Birthday in beautiful script. She had forgotten her own birthday and struggled with whether or not to open it. She wondered briefly if it would sting him to find it unopened on the bedside. She didn't wonder what was inside, only whether or not to take the opportunity to emotionally slap him one more time. She sighed heavily and decided to wait, gathered her clothes and set out for the shower. She found the door locked and waited patiently outside, leaning against the wall. A few moments later, Jean opened the door, and she met his smile with a cold, unyielding expression.

"Good morning, Madame." Ava walked into the bathroom, closing the door just as Jean squeaked out, "Happy Birthday."

An hour later, she sat down to breakfast alone and picked at her oatmeal. Margaret had taken Jean out to the garden with her after their breakfast. On the counter, she saw unfrosted layers of what was going to be her birthday cake. *Everyone will expect me to smile while they sing and be happy as I blow out candles.* She was tempted to grab the platter and run out to dump the layers in the thick shrubs that lined the front yard. She decided she would go to Claire's instead and hide out until bedtime, if necessary. *They can just eat cake without me. And choke on it.*

∞∞∞∞

"Jon, I'm not the smartest guy in the world, but I really don't think that's such a good idea," Aryl said, leaning against the side of the boat and shaking his head slowly.

"Well, I think it will work," Jonathan insisted. "If she thinks some other gal in town has taken an interest in me, it'll get her attention. Lately, all I've done is mope around and beg her to talk to me. I plead with her to stay with me and I swear, I think she likes it."

"Of course, she does, dummy. You're paying retribution," Caleb snickered.

"I shouldn't have to. This isn't my fault. The entire relationship happened before Ava, even Jean happened before Ava, and I had no idea the kid even existed! I know it's a shock and not the ideal situation, but she is hell bent on making me hurt every single day and I'm sick of it. I think she needs to be under the impression that there's a little competition. Make her realize what she's taking for granted." He crossed his arms, delighted with his master plan to win back Ava's affections. Aryl shook his head with a grim look.

"No. I wouldn't go through with it. You've got a woman scorned, a *pregnant* woman scorned." He shook his head. "I think you'd be walking into very dangerous territory, my friend, and me and Caleb can't run this show without you."

"We'll see how her birthday present softens her up. I'll keep it in my back pocket for now."

∞∞∞

Ava found Claire sitting on the swing in the backyard, blankly staring. Her voice pulled Claire from her faraway gaze. "What are you dreaming about?" Claire blinked a few times to adjust her eyes.

"Oh, nothing, really."

"No, c'mon, what's wrong?"

Claire brought her shoulders up to her ears and held them there for a second. "It's just that . . . ." She dropped them and smiled. "It's just that now that we've decided to have a baby, I'm not sure if it's the best time, you know? Things still seem so unstable. I feel like everything could fall apart in the blink of an eye. And what then?"

"Well, I'm sure you've got some time to think about it. It only happened on the first try with me because it was the cruelest possible twist of fate."

"Ava, what's happened to you?" Claire asked brusquely.

"You know full well what's happened to me."

"Yes, I know, but . . . you're not doing yourself any favors by alienating yourself from Jonathan. You're only making it harder on yourself."

"Oh, am I? If Aryl had his bastard child dumped in your lap, I suppose you would handle this with so much more grace and tact than I have. You'd just accept him with open arms? Tuck him in at night and bake him cookies?"

"I'm not saying that, Ava," Claire said, frustrated. "I just think that there's nothing you can do to change the situation. So, you might as well try and make the best of it. Aryl tells me a lot of what Jon tells him while they are out. He loves you, Ava, and this whole situation is killing him. He wants to make it better, he just doesn't know how."

"He can put it back on a boat to Paris, *that's* what he can do," she said coldly.

"He's just a *child*, Ava. This isn't any more his fault than yours."

Ava refused to answer her, staring forward with a set face as they swung slowly. "You don't understand," she spoke softly. "No one understands except–" Her eyes blurred with tears. "Except Maura."

Claire turned to face her. "And what would Maura tell you to do?" Her tone was icy. Ava pushed off the swing and quickly walked away. "Ava, don't leave," Claire called after her.

∞∞∞

Jonathan found Ava in the room, lying on her side, staring out the window. He spotted the present unopened in the garbage bin as he turned to walk back out of the room.

"She won't come down," his mother told him when he sat down to dinner. "Said to have cake without her." Jonathan began eating while Jean filled him in on his day.

### *April 13ᵗʰ 1930*

Sunday afternoon was beautiful and despite a light, salty breeze, the perfect temperature for a picnic. Ava spread a blanket under the shade of a nearby tree and opened her book. The others gathered around the picnic table as Jonathan introduced Jean to each of them. Arianna immediately began having a conversation with Jean in French, and he seemed overjoyed to find someone to converse with in his native tongue. Everyone, despite Ava's occasional glares from afar, thought he was the most adorable thing. They gushed over his manners and remarked in very hushed voices of how much he looked like Jonathan, who was beginning to take on the beam of a proud father. Claire began to talk to him about drawing, and he pulled out some of his pictures from his knapsack to show her. Like Jonathan, she looked at the drawings and back to Jean repeatedly, astonished. "These are amazing, Jean," she said.

Arianna made sure Jean understood. "Magnifique! Superbe!"

"Merci," he replied to Claire.

"That means thank you," Arianna said.

"We know," Claire reminded her, laughing.

Jonathan called Ava over when everyone began to eat. Whether ignoring him or not hearing him, she didn't respond, so he walked over to where she lay in the shade.

"We're all eating now."

"That's nice," she said, eyes on her book.

"Aren't you going to join us?" he asked with a hint of frustration.

"Maybe in a little while." She glanced at the group encircling Jean. Jonathan turned to leave, muttering a frustrated, "I give up." as he went.

After lunch, Aryl pulled out a baseball and a couple of gloves from his bag. "C'mon, Caleb," he said as he tossed him one of the gloves.

"Nah, I'm gonna stay here with Ahna." He tossed the glove to Jonathan and went back to rubbing Arianna's back. "You'll have to make do with him."

"Funny." Jonathan got up and walked past Ava, far enough away to catch one of Aryl's powerful throws.

After some impressive throws, Jonathan saw his opportunity.

She stood about fifty feet past his friends, playing with a small dog. He took a deep breath, pulled his arm back, twisting to the side and threw the ball with every ounce of strength he could muster. It catapulted through the air, arching so high and traveling so fast that Aryl didn't even bother to run for it but simply watched as it flew overhead and well past the group. The collective oohs and ahhs from the group caught Ava's attention, and she looked up.

"Sorry!" he yelled. "I'll get it." He started running toward the ball and as if rehearsed to perfection, a young brunette was already heading to pick it up for him.

Once well past Aryl, he slowed to a walk and checked to see that Ava was still watching him. The woman now walked toward him with the ball, and Jonathan flashed his most charming smile.

"You lost your ball," she said, smiling.

"Well, thank you. You want to play?" he asked, using his eyes on her, dazzling and deep blue.

She blushed before replying, "Oh, no, thank you." Ava sat up a little straighter and craned her neck.

"What's your name?" he asked. He was being cruel now, using his charm to his advantage. This poor unsuspecting girl had no clue that his only intent was to get his wife's attention.

"Debbie," she said with a smile and twisted one leg on her toe nervously. "What's yours?"

"Jonathan," he said, taking a step closer, drowning her with his eyes.

He continued to talk while the stunned group looked on. Ava threw daggers with her eyes while Aryl walked over and stood by his side, looking none too happy.

"What the hell are you doing?" he asked out of the side of his mouth.

"I told you earlier," he said quietly and turned back to the girl, speaking seductive sentences in French, using his eyes for emphasis. "Il était très agréable de vous rencontrer. J'espère que mon idée n'était pas une faute et ma femme me bat plutôt."

The girl giggled and blushed, too smitten to make any further intelligible conversation. She looked completely spellbound as Jonathan flashed one last smile over his shoulder when he walked away. Ava sat up against the tree with crossed arms and watched from afar. Red crept up her face as her blood boiled. Aryl smacked him on the shoulder.

"Jon, I thought I told you that wasn't a good idea. What the hell were you saying to her anyway?"

"I said 'it was nice to meet you and that I hope my idea was not a mistake and my wife beats me for it.'"

Aryl couldn't help but laugh. "Oh, she will."

Jonathan nibbled on leftovers at the picnic table for a good ten minutes before he joined Ava.

"Looks like you made a friend," she said curtly.

"Oh, her? Just someone new in town. Nice girl," he said with a far off voice as he glanced in Debbie's direction. Ava glared at the side of his head.

"Did you need to talk to her for so long? I mean, how long does it take for you to take a ball from someone and say thanks?" He turned to her, his eyes attempting to work their sapphire magic on her as well.

"I was just being nice, Ava." She was the first to break the stare. He leaned toward her slightly. "Are you jealous?" he whispered.

"No!" she insisted, gathered her book, and walked over to sit with Arianna.

Aryl and Caleb were trying to teach Jean how to throw, and the girls had the blanket to themselves. Claire reported rapid-fire as Ava sat down, "Okay, Aryl just told me that Jon only did that to make you jealous, so you'd pay attention to him. He wanted me to tell you because he's afraid you're going to kill Jon, and he doesn't want to have to do his share of the work on the boat."

"I'm not going to kill him," she assured. Her cheeks and the tips of her ears were red, her lips pursed.

"What are you going to do?" Arianna asked. "See, Caleb and I may have come to an understanding about certain things, but if he were to flirt with another woman in front of me . . . ." Her eyebrows arched and she let out a long, slow whistle that sounded much like an incoming mortar. Ava shrugged as if she didn't care, but her insides were churning with jealousy. Jonathan was holding a charming smile for her when her eyes flickered back to him. She looked away quickly, angry for letting herself want him again.

It was sunset when everyone headed to the cars. "See you Saturday!" Arianna yelled, waving. Caleb turned in Jonathan's direction, moving his hand to his mouth as if he were throwing back a drink. "See you Saturday."

"We decided to get together at our place while you gals are doing the baby shower," he explained briefly, and held the door open for Ava. Jean climbed in the backseat and as Jonathan pulled out onto the road, he yawned. Jonathan smiled at him over his shoulder.

"Tired? I think Caleb and Aryl wore you out, didn't they?"

"They are very nice," Jean said. "I think they like me."

"Well, why wouldn't they?" Jonathan asked. Jean glanced at the back of Ava's head. "Yes, they like you. Arianna would like you to spend the weekend with them sometime. Would you like that?" he asked, grinning.

"Oui, please!" Jonathan smiled, and caught Ava watching him. For the first time in weeks, her face was soft and curious.

∞∞∞∞

"*I* was jealous." Ava sat down on the bed, staring out the darkened window as Jonathan readied for bed. Clouds had quickly moved in after the picnic. There was no moon to be seen tonight. He stopped tying the strings of his sleeping pants and looked at her.

"Were you?"

"What would Maura do?" she whispered. "That's what I've been asking myself for weeks. If she were me, what would she do? How would she handle this situation? And you." Jonathan sat beside her, close enough to show he cared but far enough to give her space.

"I'd like to think she would try to make the best of it."

"She would. I just don't know that I . . . I can't promise you . . . I feel like everything . . . ." She gave up trying to complete the sentence and hung her head to hide her tears. He put an arm around her, and she slumped over against his chest. Silent tears and a rigid form gave way as the brick wall further crumbled and fell away. With sagging shoulders, she softened and he gathered her in closer as she disintegrated, sobs filled with anger, betrayal and loneliness. He held one arm around her waist, supporting her weight and the other behind her head as she cried into his neck. Arms limp at her side, tears streamed down her cheeks and onto his chest. With a set jaw, he endured the sting of each one as it trailed over his heart and he let her cry for a long time.

"I'm sorry," he whispered. "What can I do?" he begged, helpless. He would do anything for her, short of sending Jean to an orphanage, and he feared that's what Ava wanted him to do.

Silent moments passed. There was nothing he could do, but there was certainly much he could say.

"I don't see her when I look at him," he said honestly. She tensed slightly. "I know that's what you think. But I don't. I see a lot of me, and what isn't me, I pretend is the best of you," he said softly, with a squeeze around her waist. "I only think of Elyse when you cry or yell at me or act like you hate me. It reminds me of how much I hurt you, long before I even knew you." Ava was quiet and he cautiously continued. "It also reminds me of how she acted when I told her I wouldn't marry her, and she threatened to abort Jean. I had to accept the fact that she would. There was nothing I could do back then. But I'd like to think there's something I can do now, if you'll let me." She wiped her face but wouldn't look at him.

"Would you do anything?" she whispered. His stomach twisted in knots.

"I won't send him away, Ava." He tried to infuse as much love as possible into his words. "He has *no one*. And, even though it's a disruption in our life, he's mine. I can't just turn my back on my responsibility." A silent, emotional standoff lasted for several moments.

"You asked Elyse what she expected of you. Now I'm asking you what you expect of me."

He didn't hesitate. "Don't leave me. Don't stop loving me. I can't do this without you." He put a hand on her lower back. "I love you more than anything." He took a deep breath and resigned himself to explain everything if he needed to but prayed he wouldn't. "You were the only thing to pull me back, Ava. Nothing else on earth had the power on my heart and soul enough to pull me back from the edge of my grave." Her foggy, emotionally charged mind tried to rationalize his words about that dark time. It was Maura that had changed him. Her green eyes saw things, things that lurked deep in the core of a person. Her wise words infused with hard love worked miracles on the soul. She let her mind wander to Maura's last letter, her advice and most of all, the sentence she had written on the bottom of each and every letter since Jean's arrival.

"*It's not the end of the world*," she whispered. "That's what Maura says."

"It's not." A cold shiver went through Jonathan as he remembered the night Maura said those words to him and he realized Maura, too, was worried about the extent of Ava's depression. "Is this what it was like?" he asked, trying to smooth down her rumpled hair. "When you watched me sink into oblivion?"

She thought she was incapable of producing more tears but more escaped.

"Well, I'm sorry for that, too," he said softly. "I don't expect anything, Ava. All I ask you to do is leave yourself open to the possibility of being happy again. *Us* being happy again. Don't close yourself off. I really think it's possible." He lifted her chin. "I will die trying to make it happen. I won't give up, I promise you."

"I just don't know that it's possible . . . for things to ever be like they were," she said bleakly.

"They won't be the same, Ava. So much has changed since October. It makes my head spin to think of how many times we were blindsided and forced to adapt. No, things won't ever be the same. But," he took her face in his hands, "that doesn't mean that they can't be good."

*April 26th 1930*

"Oh, it's adorable!" Arianna cried as she pulled the red, silk sleeping gown out of the box.

Ava smiled and said, "I thought you'd like it."

She held it up to herself. "I just wonder if I'll ever be able to fit into it!" she laughed as her large stomach distorted the sleek gown.

"You're still thin as a rail, Arianna. It'll fit wonderfully after the baby is born." She handed her another box. "We got this for the baby." Arianna drew from the box a sleeping gown for the baby; white cotton with embroidered yellow bunnies and teal-colored teddy bears sewn along the hem with thin yellow ribbon ties at the neck.

"Thank you. It's beautiful." She reached up to hug Ava as Ethel walked in with a tray of small cakes and slices of pie.

The parlor was modestly decorated; a table held a small pile of presents and cards from a few friends abroad. Ethel set the tray down on the coffee table and handed Arianna a large box that was impossible to balance on what little lap she had left. Claire helped her to set it on the floor and then opened it for her, handing her the contents.

"This is from me. Hubert has something of his own he'd like to give you," her mother-in-law said and lit up with a wide smile.

"Oh! Thank you so much!" she cried as Claire handed her pile after pile of cloth diapers Ethel had made, knowing from experience that Arianna hadn't made nearly enough. Beneath those were a dozen infant gowns, a few knitted sweaters, and a crocheted yellow and white blanket made by Ethel as well.

"There's more?" Arianna exclaimed as Claire handed her yet another pile.

Ethel told her, "These pieces aren't new, but I thought I'd throw them in, just in case."

"Just in case?" Arianna questioned and then understood. There were several folded pieces of Caleb's baby clothes: tiny overalls, blue sleepers, miniature flannel farmer plaids, and one very well loved baby blanket. Ethel had preserved these pieces beautifully, and Arianna giggled as she tried to picture Caleb as a tiny seven-pound squirming mass of chub and spittle.

Just then, Hubert struggled through the door, awkwardly carrying a rocking horse. "This was Caleb's as well. I cleaned it up a bit," he said modestly. "I hope you like it." Arianna looked up at Hubert, touched.

"It's beautiful," she whispered, admiring the dark mahogany of the horse's head and curved rails, the carefully retouched colorful saddle and newly set mane made of black yarn. She struggled to her feet despite his protests and hugged him tightly. Her stomach pressed against his, and the new one kicked hard against him. Hubert pulled back, laughing. "Now don't you start!" he scolded her stomach with a smile.

Claire led Arianna out to the porch to show her their gifts.

"Aryl made it," she said proudly. Arianna smiled at the miniature version of his parents' backyard swing, sanded soft and painted white. A small cradle hung from the hooks and beside it was a seat leaning back at a sharp angle that would replace the cradle once the baby was old enough to sit up.

"Oh, Claire, it's wonderful! It's so . . . wonderful!" She touched the swing, amazed at the craftsmanship.

"Those are from me," she said, pointing to a small stack of paintings. She bent to pick them up and show them to Arianna; stunning, colorful animations of animals. There were four seasonals; winter snow bunnies, springtime blue robins, chubby pink pigs, a gelding standing under a tree vivid with foliage. Arianna was speechless and emotional. She hugged her friend tightly and retreated inside to the rocking chair, spasms in her back growing stronger.

Ava pulled out a pencil drawing from her bag, unframed and slightly creased. "He . . . Jean asked me to give this to you. He said he would give a gift to the baby after it is born. He wants to know what it is first."

Arianna beheld the picture so amazing in detail of herself standing at the base of the Eiffel tower, the cityscape sketched to perfection in the background.

"I'll thank him the next time I see him. And I'll find a frame for this," she said softly. "He is so sweet."

Several of Ethel's friends had stopped by, each delivering a handmade gift, and having a piece of cake, spilling advice to Arianna to the point of making her head spin. She felt thoroughly panicked by the time everyone left. She wondered how in the world she would remember everything and feared for her child's life due to her own ignorance.

∞∞∞∞

"Congratulations, Caleb, here's a little something for you," Michael said and handed him a bottle of brandy wine with a big smile.

"Where did you get this?" he asked.

"I know a guy. Sit, have a drink and let us enlighten you of the horrors–I mean, ah, *joys* of fatherhood." He chuckled and called for Aryl and Jonathan, who stood outside enjoying one of Jonathan's preciously rationed cigars.

"So, how are things with Ava?" Aryl asked.

"A little better," Jonathan said. "A far cry from where we need to be, but I can see she's trying."

"Trying not to hate you or trying to make it better?" Aryl asked with a laugh. "There *is* a difference."

"I know. She's trying to be open, trying not to shut me out, trying not to see Elyse every time she looks at Jean. And I guess, to a certain extent, trying not to hate me," he said. "We're just going to take it very slow."

"That's all you can do."

"What about you–" he asked in return. "I never hear about you and Claire. What are you? The perfect couple or something?" he scoffed jokingly.

"Far from it," Aryl said, smiling. "It's hard, she really . . . ." He tried to find the right words. "She depends on me to keep her spirits up. It was worse in the tenement, of course, which is what fueled me to find something, anything to give everyone some hope, especially her. Even now, she still has a hard time. I get tired trying to keep her up, but I'd never tell her that." He cast his eyes downward.

"We all depended on you, Aryl. I wouldn't be here, in more ways than one, if it weren't for you. We all wouldn't be here in Rockport with at least a fighting chance at a new life. Hell, I sent for you first thing when Elyse showed up. I talked your ear off every day with all my problems, and Caleb, too. That had to be tiring." He felt a small sting of guilt for his consummation with his own trials. "So, how are you then? You and Claire. What's going on with you guys?" he asked.

Aryl shrugged. "Well, we decided to try for a baby. She swings back and forth, worries that it's not the right time, like something is going to fly out of nowhere and make us regret it."

Jonathan thought for a moment and said, "I think once you've lived through what we have, you don't ever stop looking over your shoulder. You always feel like something is about to swoop in and destroy you."

"Very true." He nodded slowly. "I still feel like that a lot of the time. I know she does, too." Aryl smiled. "I'm taking her to our lighthouse next month for our anniversary. It's a surprise. My dad is helping me set everything up." As if on cue, Aryl's father's laughter boomed from the house, something at Caleb's expense, to be sure.

Aryl grinned toward the house. "I tried to think of what I could do to top last year's anniversary, but, under the circumstances, of course, I can't." He shrugged helplessly as he looked far off, past the yard.

"Paris, wasn't it?" Jonathan tried to remember where they disappeared to for two weeks last year.

"No, London."

"Ah. That's right. I've got until August to figure out something. Hopefully things will be better by then. I just keep trying to remember what you told me that first night when Jean arrived."

"I'm surprised you remember anything I told you," Aryl teased.

"No," Jonathan said seriously. "I remember. *Miracles happen* . . . that's what you said."

Aryl smiled, brown eyes crinkling at the edges, and said, "They do. I really believe they do."

*May 7th 1930*

Ava stood at the edge of the pier, waving frantically as the boats came into view. Jonathan squinted, watched her for a moment, and realized something wasn't right. He waved to the others to hurry along. Edging up to the pier, he threw the rope over.

"What's wrong?" he asked, dropping off the side of the boat to the pier and tying down the boat.

"It's Arianna," she said breathlessly. "She's in labor." Jonathan stared at her stupidly for a moment, and then turned to yell for Caleb as he edged up to the pier. He ran to his boat, jumping the three feet over open water to the deck.

"Go. Arianna's in labor."

Caleb stood frozen. Jonathan gave him a shove, and he jumped to the pier, lost his balance, and nearly rolled off the other side into the water. Ava ran up to him and grabbed his sleeve, pulling him up.

"It started this morning, right after you left." She guided him toward the car where Aryl's mother waited in the driver's seat.

"Your mom tried to stop it, had her go back to bed, but–"

"It's too early," he realized suddenly, turning to her with wild eyes. "Ava, it's too early!"

"I know. Your mother has sent for the doctor. For now, she and a midwife are taking care of her. But she wants *you*." She shoved him in the car, slammed the door and jumped into the front seat as Aryl's mother sped off, leaving a plume of dust and sand in their wake. Aryl and Jonathan locked serious and fearful eyes and hurried to wrap up the boats' work, so they could try to be of some help.

∞∞∞∞

"*Arianna!*" Caleb took the stairs two at a time and nearly knocked the midwife over, who was heading downstairs for more towels.

"Easy there!"

"How is she?" he asked, a lost, frightened look as sweat beaded up on his forehead.

"She's all right. She'll be glad you're here. Why don't you go in, see her for a moment, then settle yourself downstairs with the other men. It won't be much longer now."

"It won't?" he asked in shock.

"No, her water broke just after dawn. The pains are only a few minutes apart now," she said, patting him on the arm. "Now everything is going to be fine, don't you worry." He ran his hands through his hair and shifted his weight nervously.

"It's too soon," he whispered. His eyes darted around nervously.

"It's early, true. But I've delivered earlier that's survived. It'll need a bit of extra care and nourishment, but we need to hope for the best. Now go see your wife. She's very tired. It's been a long day for her. And no talk of the baby coming too soon. She's scared enough as it is about that. No need to upset her more." After giving the firm orders, she turned away, leaving Caleb to stare at the closed door.

He knocked softly and heard Kathleen's voice call to come in. He entered hesitantly and took in the whole room. From afar, Arianna looked no different than when he left in the early morning.

"Caleb," she whispered as he walked quickly over and sat on the edge of the bed. Closer now, he saw her ghostly pale face with cheeks red from exertion, dark and sunken eyes, and hair matted to her head with sweat.

"Ahna, honey, how are you?" He ruled his voice steady despite his panic, held her hand, and wiped the wet strands of hair out of her eyes.

"It *hurts* . . . ." she cried. Her eyes lost focus and her face grimaced, involuntarily drawn up to a half-sitting position from the pain and growled through her teeth. Caleb went white.

"What do I do?! *What do I do?!*"

"Just help hold her up," Claire said. She handed him a wet cloth with a shaking hand. "Wipe her face and arms with this when it's over."

It ended suddenly, and she fell back on the bed, gasping. The midwife returned with an armload of supplies and began laying everything out where it needed to be for the doctor when he arrived. Caleb sat with her through five more pains. The last one in particular was violent and seemed to be a signal to the midwife.

"I think it's time you head downstairs," she said, gently laying a hand on his shoulder.

"No." He kept his eyes on Arianna, who lay spent, eyes closed, relishing the brief moments between pains. "I'm not leaving."

"Caleb," she said his name as if she knew him personally. "I need to check your wife's . . . progress. That's a rather intimate procedure, and I think it best if–"

Irritated, he turned to her. "I've seen it before," he said sharply. "Do what you need to do. I'm not leaving." He turned back just as Arianna's shoulders came off the bed, no longer growling, but screaming through to the end of the contraction.

The midwife moved to the bottom of the bed as Claire and Kathleen held the sheet up for privacy.

"Kathleen."

The midwife's voice was too calm. Kathleen focused on the midwife's horror-struck face and then followed her gaze. It landed between Arianna's legs; more specifically, to the tiny arm that protruded out.

"Go get that doctor. *Now!*" she whispered with urgency. Kathleen rushed out of the room. The midwife did what she could to get the little arm back inside, so she could turn the baby, but every attempt resulted in Arianna screaming bloody murder, gasping and wrenching out long streams of profanity.

"Caleb." She moved beside him, pulled him up by the arm, and looked at him squarely. "I need you to go downstairs and–"

"I told you I'm not leaving!" he yelled at her. She grabbed his shirtsleeve and pulled him to the door, whispering through gritted teeth.

"Caleb. The baby is turned the wrong way. I need to move it, and I need you not to be here when I do it. It will be difficult. I need you to boil as much water as you can. If you want a healthy baby, then for the love of God, go boil some water!"

The midwife held her hand gently after Caleb left. "Arianna. The baby is turned the wrong way, dear. I'm going to need to move him. It's going to hurt," she said. Arianna met her eyes and nodded weakly. The midwife knew from experience that this process would be so arduous that Arianna may not have the energy to push when the time came. She called Claire over, who was now pale and shaking with fear.

"Go downstairs and get another woman. We're going to need help." Claire nodded, ran down the stairs, and bounded into the kitchen, looking for Ethel.

Aryl spotted her and quickly made his way across the room. "Claire. What's wrong?"

"We need help . . . It's, uh . . . ." She looked at Caleb across the room, who was yelling at a pot of water to boil faster. Jonathan was by his side, trying to calm him. She looked back at Aryl as a drop of sweat rolled down her temple. The panic in her eyes told him something was very wrong.

"Tell me," he whispered and pulled her into a tight hug. She spoke quietly in his ear. "The baby is turned around. One arm is . . . sticking out. Arianna is exhausted and we need someone to help us turn it." She pulled away to peer for Ethel or Kathleen.

"Is she going to be all right?" he asked in a hushed voice.

Uncertain eyes met his. "I don't know."

"I'll help."

"Aryl, no, it needs to be—"

"A woman? Well, there's no other woman here. Ethel and Kathleen went to find the doctor, and Margaret and Ava went with Jean to get food from her house."

He put an arm around her, turning her toward the stairs. "I'm *not* going to let Arianna or her baby die for the sake of modesty. Let's go." He took her shaking hand and pulled her up the stairs.

The midwife positioned Aryl and Claire on each side of Arianna. She felt for the baby then laid their hands where she wanted them and instructed them what direction to apply pressure when she gave the word. They stood waiting, hands at odd angles on Arianna's massive stomach, locked eyes briefly, more frightened than they had ever been in their lives. Arianna lifted a limp hand and laid it on Aryl's. "Thank you," she whispered. She looked as if life was draining from her by the second, and the horror of it must have shown on his face.

"She's very tired, but she's a fighter," Claire reassured and smiled down at Arianna, who attempted to return the smile as another pain consumed her suddenly.

"Keep the position of your hands. We'll turn after this pain," the midwife ordered and they stood stock-still and helpless as Arianna screamed through another twisting pain. Aryl instantly regretted taking his eyes off Claire as he caught sight of the tiny protruding arm, now turning blue from the constriction of the contraction. His face went white and his stomach did a little flip.

"Now!" The midwife gently worked the little arm back inside as Aryl and Claire applied pressure, and then to Aryl's shock, her own hand disappeared to the wrist. He looked a little green and felt slightly queasy as he helped push the unyielding mass from above.

"Stop!" she called just as another contraction racked Arianna, who passed out immediately after it, and they set to work again. There was a sudden shifting under their hands with the third try, and they gawked with wide eyes.

"Did that work?" Aryl breathed. Before the midwife could answer, there was a rush of liquid, splashing the bed and up onto the midwife's birthing gown.

"I thought her water broke this morning?" Claire asked.

"It did. This must have been behind the baby. When we moved him, it was free to flow. By the size of her, she's made too much fluid. I've never seen so much . . . ."

Aryl took a step back. "Do you need me anymore?" He wiped his forehead and looked at Arianna's unconscious face pitifully.

"No, thank you, Aryl, very much. Why don't you go down and make sure Caleb's doing all right?" He opened the door to see Margaret, Kathleen and Ava rushing up the stairs with Ethel leading the group. Aryl stepped aside as they streamed in.

"You missed all the fun," he said shakily.

Ethel ran straight to the midwife. "The doctor is on an emergency. He can't come." She glanced at her unconscious daughter-in-law and back to the midwife.

"We've handled it," she said proudly. "Shouldn't be long now."

Soon, Ava came downstairs smiling. "It's showing. Should only be a few more minutes." She took a pot of boiling water back up with her, so Caleb wouldn't think that his water-boiling efforts were in vain.

"*What's* showing?" Caleb asked.

Jon laughed and put a hand on his shoulder. "C'mon, Caleb. You know how this works."

Caleb paced the kitchen, now mumbling to himself.

"It's been too quiet," he muttered anxiously. "What if something went wrong?"

"I'm sure it's fine, Caleb," Aryl reassured. "They'll call you as soon as it's born." Everyone looked at the ceiling as there was a loud commotion and a blood curdling scream from Arianna.

"I need to be in there." Caleb made for the stairs.

"Now, son, I think it best if you just let the women do what they know how to do. You'll just be in the way. They'll call you when he's here."

It was the first full sentence Hubert had spoken to Caleb since their arrival. Caleb turned and asked sarcastically, "Oh, are you speaking to me?"

"Yes. And I'm telling you to let the women be. They know how to handle this."

"That's my wife and child up there."

Arianna let out another guttural scream. Caleb looked up at the ceiling. "How many damn times growing up did you wake me up in the middle of the night to help with a calving? If it was important for me to be there for the birth of a cow or a horse, don't you think maybe it's important for me to be there for the birth of my own son?" He didn't wait for a reply, but ran up the stairs.

"Darn kids and their newfangled ideas, being in the room during a woman's labor. Humph." Hubert crossed his arms indignantly.

Caleb let himself in the room and ignored the midwife's minor protests. He stood beside the bed. Arianna looked too weak to continue.

"Caleb, with the next pain, sit her up as high as you can." A second later, he lifted her and they all yelled for Arianna to push as hard as she could while the midwife counted. The midwife blew some hair out of her own face and wiped her forehead with a bloody sleeve.

"This should be it," she panted.

And it was.

With one more gut wrenching push, Samuel Robert slipped out of his mother and onto the bed. Arianna lay back gasping, and Caleb stared at the little blue and white baby as the midwife cleared his mouth and smacked his bottom, causing him to let out a piercing cry. Caleb laughed with relief, and the midwife held him up for Arianna to see.

"He's perfect," Caleb said, smiled wide and kissed Arianna on the forehead. "Just perfect."

"His arm is a bit bruised," the midwife pointed out. "But not broken. It will heal." She handed him to Caleb, who knelt by the side of the bed and laid the baby between himself and Arianna.

"You should try to get him to nurse. He's probably hungry." The midwife smiled down on the three, pleased with her efforts that most likely saved both mother and child. Caleb helped Arianna reposition herself, and she cuddled Samuel close. He latched on without any help or prodding and began to nurse ferociously.

"Goodness. That was easy," Arianna said, her voice weak but happy. Caleb helped pull her bedraggled hair back and washed her face and neck with a cool cloth. She leaned her head back to enjoy the relaxing moment. The room was quiet except for the small grunts and slurps of the newborn nursing.

Suddenly Arianna's head pulled forward and she grunted.

"That's the afterbirth. It's not near as bad as labor pains," the midwife reassured a newly frightened Caleb as Arianna eased down off the contraction. Without warning, another pain overtook her causing her arms to go limp. Caleb scooped Samuel up. The midwife lifted the sheet, and her eyes bulged. "*Oh my God,*" she whispered.

"What! What's wrong?" Caleb yelled out in confusion as Arianna yelled out in pain and Samuel yelled out in hunger.

"There's another baby!"

"What?!" the room cried out in unison.

"I don't know why I didn't see. Claire, hurry, get me more towels!" The whole room burst into a flurry of activity, as one contraction surged into another, hardly allowing Arianna time to catch her breath. Aryl and Jonathan stood in the hallway, listening, hands in pockets and heads lowered in concern.

"How can there be another baby!" Caleb cried over Samuel's intense, choppy wails.

"She's having twins!" the midwife snapped impatiently, motioning Kathleen and Margaret on each side to hold Arianna's legs. Caleb looked helplessly between the howling baby in his arms and Arianna.

Ava took the baby. "Help Arianna," she said, worried he was so frightened he very well might drop Samuel.

"Is there anything we can do?" Aryl asked into the small opening of the door. Ava walked into the hall and handed Aryl the baby.

"Hold him," she ordered and hurried back into the room. Arianna's grunts and cries were near constant, but she couldn't rise with each contraction any longer. The midwife yelled for towels and twine. Caleb dropped to his knees, kissed Arianna's hand, and felt completely useless.

"Caleb! Get up! You have to help push the baby out," the midwife shouted.

"What!" he cried with owlish eyes.

"She doesn't have the strength to do this." He slipped an arm behind her to push her upright, but the midwife stopped him. "It doesn't matter if she sits up if she has no more strength to push!" she yelled. "Here, when I say push, push here." She positioned his hands at the top of her stomach, and Caleb braced himself, waited for the cue. Arianna lay with her head rolled to the side, only the peak of the pains stirring her to light consciousness now.

"Push!" Caleb gave a little downward pressure and the midwife yelled for more. "A little more, Caleb, you're doing fine, keep it up." Sweat rolled down his temples, and although he was hyperventilating, he felt like he was suffocating.

"Here it is!" the midwife yelled with relief. Caleb saw a tiny scalp covered in white balm tinged with blood begin to crown before receding again. A moment later, almost effortlessly this time, the babe glided into the waiting and warm hands of the midwife.

"It's a girl," Caleb whispered. "Ahna, it's a girl."

Arianna was unconscious and breathing long and deep. The midwife worked quickly, clearing the airway, rubbing the little body to aide circulation, and tying the cord. The room fell silent as everyone waited for the cry. The babe was lifeless and silent; blue, flaccid limbs splayed open. The midwife's face was set in stone, determined not to lose this child. She rubbed the baby furiously, cleared the little airway twice, but the little girl still appeared lifeless. Grasping the infant by the ankles, she held it high in front of her.

The second smack on its bottom was much harder than the first, and the baby sucked in a ragged breath and let out a piercing scream. The whole room exhaled in relief, and Caleb sunk to his knees by the bed with his head in his hands. The midwife swaddled the baby, who was smaller than her twin, and handed her with shaking hands to Caleb. She had a tuft of raven, black hair and her mother's pointy nose. He smiled with incredulous wonder at the little surprise and then panicked.

"Waitaminute!" he called out, frightened, his eyes searching the room. "Where's the other one?"

Ava laughed and said, "Aryl has him. I'll go get him." She poked her head out to see Aryl in the hall with Samuel sleeping on his shoulder as he patted his little back and paced with a light bounce.

"Aryl, you can bring him in now," she said softly. He made his way to the door with the slow bounce-walk. Jonathan pushed off the wall opposite the door and hugged Ava.

"*That* was intense," he whispered.

"Yeah. And it was worse in there," she teased. "But they're both here and healthy. It's a good day," she said and smiled, glancing back at the door.

"Are you scared?" he asked, with a nod to her stomach.

"Terrified," she spoke wide-eyed with a smile.

"Will you let me be with you? When it's time?" he asked timidly.

"I expect you to be with me," she said quietly and seriously, meeting his eyes.

∞∞∞∞

*A*rianna had stirred into awareness and looked on wearily as Aryl laid Samuel next to his sister on the bed between Arianna and Caleb. "I thought it was a dream," she said with a hoarse whisper. "Are there two of them?"

"There really are," Caleb said, running a finger lightly over each of the tiny foreheads. "We didn't think of a girl's name. I guess we better get on that," he said with a smile. They stared in awe at the two small bundles snuggled in next to each other and perfectly content; tiny, pink, rosebud mouths appeared totally relaxed, but their little transparent eyebrows still held a lingering grimace from their arduous journey into the world. Friends and family gathered quietly at the foot of the bed enchanted by the peaceful new family.

Little Girl began squirming, her arms escaping the swaddling and let out a sudden wail of discontent. Samuel frowned and pouted in annoyance and then joined her in howling as her little fist flew over and popped him in the mouth.

"Hey, now, it's a little early to start fighting," Caleb said with a laugh. He tucked her arms back in the swaddling and placed his hand over the bundle, slowly rocking her back and forth until she settled before he leaned over his babies and kissed Arianna. "You did good," he said, touching his forehead to hers. "You were amazing. I had no idea you were that strong."

"Neither did I. But I couldn't have done it without you," she whispered.

Several hours later, when all of the friends and family had left, Caleb went downstairs, holding Samuel tight against his chest. His father sat at the kitchen table. An oil lamp burning in the center gave an amber glow of comfort to the kitchen. Caleb stopped at the bottom of the stairs for a moment and stared at his father's back. He sat hunched over his coffee with his head bowed. Every third breath ended with a deep exhale and he sounded very tired.

"Mom go to bed?" Caleb rounded the table, facing him from the side.

"Mmm." Hubert kept staring inside his mug.

"Does 'Mmm' mean yes or no?" he demanded.

"Yes."

"This is really getting monotonous, Dad."

"Mmm."

Caleb's eyes flared as he blew out his breath in frustration. Hubert rose to leave the room without meeting Caleb's glare. Caleb stepped in front of him while moving Samuel to cradle his small head in the crook of his arm.

"If that's the way you want it, fine, Dad," he said, taking a step closer to him, his voice low but imperative. "You can hate me until the day you die. But you're *not* going to hate him." He pushed the baby into Hubert's arms and Hubert sat down again. He held him awkwardly for a moment, looking back at Caleb with an astonished expression. Caleb took a step away, keeping his eyes on Samuel. Hubert slowly looked down as Samuel pursed his lips and scrunched his face, threatening to cry but quickly changed his mind and drifted off again.

"No, hold him like this." Caleb stepped forward to rearrange the baby in his arms. As he stepped away again, he grumbled, "I know you remember how." He collapsed into a chair from exhaustion.

"What did you name him?" his father asked quietly, worming a finger into the baby's fist.

"Samuel Robert. After both of our grandfathers."

Hubert nodded tightly and cleared his throat, unexpectedly moved with emotion. "He looks like you," he said a moment later, his voice cracking.

"Darker hair, though." He touched the wisps of dark brown hair that lightened to a deep auburn color at the temples.

"I'll be right back." Caleb left abruptly, returning a few moments later with another small bundle. "Got two for the price of one," he joked and held the other baby out. Hubert looked lost for a moment and then shifted Samuel further into the crook of his arm, allowing Caleb to rest the second baby in the crook of the other.

"Oh, now, she's her mother to her toes," he said and grinned. "What did you name her?" Caleb laughed a short laugh.

"Well, we never talked about girls' names. For now, we're calling her Little Girl. We'll come up with something. We're accepting ideas if you've got any."

"I'll think on it," he said softly. They sat in silence for a long time, listening to the even breathing, soft grunts and squeaks from the babies. "I don't hate you, Caleb," he said suddenly, with his eyes on Samuel. "I've been mad as hell for a long time . . . but I don't hate you."

Caleb nodded and took his words head on. "What can I do?"

His father shook his head slowly. "Nothing. I'll just have to get past it."

"How?"

Hubert took a deep breath and blew it out slowly. "I suppose, if you hadn't sold Dad's farm and run off, you wouldn't have met the wild one." He paused to glance up at the ceiling with a smirk. "Somehow managed to tame her and then go on to have these two precious little things." He gently bounced his elbows to keep both babies pacified.

"I guess that's one way to look at it," Caleb said, though fatigue marking his words, he was grateful for the breakthrough with his father.

"I guess I'm a grandpa," he whispered, looking back and forth to each baby.

"I guess you are."

He looked up from the babies with peaceful eyes. "You did good."

*May 13th 1930*

"*How*'s that easel working out?"

"Wonderfully. Thank you so much for making it, Aryl," Claire said, smiling as she painted. He walked up behind her and put his hands on her shoulders.

"Another lighthouse. This one seems happier."

"It is."

"But not perfectly happy." He pointed to a dark spot far off over the ocean. "Is that a storm lurking?"

"There's always a storm lurking," she said quietly. He watched her work for a moment, as she tipped the rolling waves with white paint.

"Let's go for a walk." He hadn't presented it in the form of a question and walked to the closet for her sweater before she could answer.

"But we're due at Arianna's in an hour." She hadn't taken her eyes off the painting. "I want to see those babies again."

"We'll be back in plenty of time," he assured. Outside, she shivered and was glad he had brought her sweater. "Cold snap. Hope it breaks before Monday," he said, glancing up and around as if the sky would tell him whether Monday would hold favorable working conditions.

"Where are we going?"

"Not too far," he said and smiled. "There's something I want to show you. I've been waiting to see if it was going to work out. And it did. I think you'll like it." She gave him a confused look, and he put an arm around her shoulder. "You'll see." They had walked a short way to the west then a short way to the north when Aryl stopped and faced her. "We're moving out of my parents' house," he announced.

She looked at him curiously, as if he were fibbing.

"Soon as we can get packed, actually," he continued with an excited smile.

"Aryl, how? Where? Wh—"

He turned her by the shoulders, and she faced a small, white house with black shutters. The yard was neglected and the short, wooden fence needed repair.

"Aryl . . . how?" She stared at the little house and thought surely it was too good to be true that they could have a home of their own again so soon.

"The owner of a small shop in town, well, he went out of business. He's moving his family in with his parents and wants to avoid losing this house. When times are better, he's hoping to move back in. But that's down the road. There's plenty of time for us to save and plan. So, what do you think?" he asked and grinned at her speechless expression. She threw her arms around him, laughing.

"I think I'm going to love not sleeping on a feather tick in the middle of your parents' living room!"

"That's the best part," he said, hugging her back. "The owner is leaving all the furniture. He can't store it at his parents' house, so we get to use it all." She pulled back, resting her hands on his shoulders and looked at him, stunned and pleased.

"I would have been happy to drag that old feather tick over here and sleep in our own living room in front of our own fireplace," she said with a sincere smile.

"I know you would," he said and smiled with a sympathetic look. "God knows you shouldn't have to, though." He pushed a lock of hair behind her ear. "Sometimes it amazes me that you're still here," he said quietly. She looked at him with confusion. "When I met you, I had nothing and I worked my ass off to build us a life, and then . . . there it went and I was back to nothing. Yet, here you are. Still."

"Of course, I am, Aryl." She didn't know whether to be flattered or offended.

"I'm just really thankful for that is all," he said softly.

"Aryl." She slid her hands from his shoulders up his neck, fingers tangling in the hair at the back of his head. "Don't you understand? I can't be anywhere you're not," she whispered, temporarily losing herself in the depth of his dark-brown eyes. "No matter what we have or don't have, it isn't possible to live without you."

He smiled and pulled her tight against him. "I love you," he whispered just before he kissed her. He broke the kiss and touched his forehead to hers. "Even if we had to spend the rest of our lives on a feather tick in my parents' living room?" he asked and grinned playfully.

"Yes. Even then." She glanced at the house. "But this is great, too. Much more–" She flashed insinuating eyes, "*convenient* to have our own place."

"I agree. I think I'll spend the whole first day walking around entirely naked," he announced with a sly grin. She laughed and released his head. "C'mon." He took her hand and pulled out two keys. "I'll show you the inside."

∞∞∞

"*How* fah away is that rental?" Kathleen asked and grinned mockingly as Aryl and Claire came up the walk.

"Oh. Well, you know, we had to do a thorough walk through, make lists, measure windows, that kind of thing," Aryl said nonchalantly as they walked past her. Claire refused to look directly at her mother-in-law's insinuating grin.

"Well, that's good. Aryl, yah fly's open and yah shirt's stickin' out in the back," she snickered. Claire blushed crimson and scurried past them into the house.

"Kathleen, leave those poor kids alone. I swear, you do love tormenting them." Michael shook his head hopelessly. "Make 'em self-conscious about it and you'll never get those grandbabies." He shook a finger in warning.

"Oh, I'm only teasing." Her mouth twisted into the same mischievous grin that Aryl's did when he was teasing Jonathan and Caleb.

∞∞∞

Ethel and Hubert's house was brimming by the time Jonathan, Ava, Jean and his parents arrived. Arianna sat in the corner of the living room in a rocking chair, a blanket thrown over her shoulder as she nursed one of the babies.

"This is all I do," she said, not entirely joking. "I'm a walking dairy." She peeked under the blanket, arranged herself, and then handed Samuel to Caleb, who then deftly handed her Little Girl. Everyone crowded around Arianna, and Little Girl screamed in protest, preferring food over attention.

Caleb closed one eye and stuck a finger in his ear. "She's the loud one," he said and grinned. Arianna threw the blanket over her other shoulder and the wailing stopped quickly.

Aryl smiled at Samuel, who was perched high on Caleb's shoulder. "Hey, little guy, remember me?" Caleb turned around.

"Oh, that's right. You two have met." He rubbed his sore arm and handed Samuel off to Aryl. "She feeds and I hold. And neither one of us sleep."

"The whole house doesn't sleep," Hubert interjected, sitting by the fireplace, grinning. Everyone laughed in sympathy. He stood up with the grunts of old age and stiff bones. "I'll get you a hot pad for your arm while you've got your friends here to do the rocking for a while," he said and smiled, patting Caleb on the back as he passed.

Jonathan watched him leave and then looked with question at Caleb. Caleb shrugged and blinked with a grin, telling Jonathan it had all worked out. Jean tugged at Jonathan's shirt. Jonathan bent over while Jean whispered something in his ear.

"Oh, okay, well, let's introduce you then." He took Jean by the shoulders and walked him over to Aryl, who sat down on the couch to let Jean get a better look at Samuel.

"He's so little. I've never seen a bebe this close before," he whispered.

"Well, here." Caleb picked Jean up from behind and sat him next to Aryl. "Why don't you hold him?"

Jean looked up with wide eyes. "I won't hurt him?" he asked panicky.

"You won't hurt him." Jonathan rumpled his hair as Caleb took Samuel from Aryl and helped position him in Jean's arms.

"No," he whispered. "I would *never* hurt him." He looked over the little baby in awe. Samuel reached up and grabbed Jean's finger, gripping it tightly. Jean's face lit up as he looked from Caleb to Jonathan. "He likes me!"

"Of course, he likes you," Jonathan said. In getting to know Jean, he had recognized the pattern that Jean's first and foremost concern was whether people liked him, and he grew very insecure when they didn't. He still fretted over Ava's chilly disposition. Jean's brow furrowed in concentration.

"What is he? To me, I mean." He looked up at Jonathan with big eyes.

"Well . . . ." Jonathan narrowed his matching eyes.

"You're his cousin," Caleb said, squatting down in front of him.

"I'm his cousin? What do I do as a cousin?" he asked with concern.

"Well, when he gets older, you can play with him, be his buddy, and teach him things, and look out for him," Caleb said, "like your dad did for me when we were kids." Jean looked down at Samuel with all the seriousness he could muster.

"Oh, I will," he vowed.

## May 17th 1930

"Dinner's ready." Ava stepped into the living room, wiping her hands on her apron. Jonathan was sitting on the couch, hunched to the side, Jean whispering in his ear.

"I'm not sure," Jonathan said, returning upright. "But I'll find out and let you know, okay?" Jean nodded, slid off the couch, and walked past Ava into the kitchen.

"What was that all about?" she asked with the usual tight-mouthed, reserved expression she used with topics that revolved around Jean. Jonathan motioned for her to come closer.

"He wants to know what to call you. He realized today he's never called you anything. He's only spoken to you when you happened to be looking his way or within earshot."

"Well, I have a name. He can use that," she said while untying her apron and wadding it up into a ball.

"I suggested that. But . . . ."

"But what?"

"He said that being here with us almost feels like a real family. In Paris, he only had his mother, and now there are two parents. He feels like it's too *formal* to call you Ava. He wants me to find something else."

"Well, he's not calling me Mother, if that's what you're getting at." She crossed her arms.

"No, he doesn't want to call you Mother," he said. "Just think about it, okay? What you'd like him to call you. He's going to need to address you at some point."

"I'll think about it," she said quietly as he walked around her and into the kitchen.

The three of them sat down to dinner. Jonathan's parents had gone out for the evening and the mood was tense. It was left to Jonathan to make conversation.

"Did Claire tell you that she and Aryl are moving out?" he asked.

"She did." Ava's eyes remained on her plate. "We're supposed to help them move in on Saturday."

"Well, that shouldn't take long," he joked. "You want to do something after that?"

"A picnic?" Jean suggested with Jonathan's grin. "You can teach me how to throw the ball *very far* like you did the last time."

Ava threw Jonathan an annoyed look, recalling that throw and the subsequent flirting in an effort to get her attention. He read her face and grinned back at her.

"Well, it worked," he said with a wink. "Do you want to have a picnic? Or maybe do something else?" he asked, inviting her into the conversation.

"It doesn't matter to me," she said indifferently. Jonathan watched as Ava avoided looking at Jean completely while the child stole little peeks in her direction every few minutes. Toward the end of dinner, which had remained for the most part silent, there was a sharp knock on the door.

"Who in the world could that be?" Jonathan asked as he rose. Jean stole a timid glance at her, and after he looked away, she stole one of him.

*The eyes. They're exactly the same. If only I could look at his eyes and nothing else,* she thought.

There was a loud thud in the living room, and Ava jumped up to see what it was. Two deliverymen walked out the door, having deposited a large trunk in the living room. A delivery boy from the telegraph office waited while Jonathan dug in his pocket for a tip.

A moment later, he opened the telegram and as he read, his face wilted into something between sorrow and gloom.

"Who's it from?" Ava asked, glancing over his shoulder. She read it, took a step back, and looked at the floor, waiting for Jonathan to say something. She turned for the kitchen as he spoke.

"I need to talk to Jean alone . . . . Jean, come sit, please," he said, dreading the task before him. "I have something to tell you. It's not . . . good news." Jean stared at him, not yet connecting the telegram with the trunk delivered from Paris. "Jean, your mother, she's gone. She passed away last week." Jean stared at him for a moment as if he hadn't heard him at all. He looked down at his empty hands lying palms up on his lap. When he raised his head again, his eyes were full of tears. His father scooped him up and held him close before they fell.

Ava peeked around the corner and saw Jean sitting on Jonathan's lap with his arms tight around his neck, sobbing as quietly as he could. Jonathan rubbed and patted his back alternately, and bent his head, speaking to him in a voice too low for Ava to hear. She retreated into the kitchen and leaned against the wall. Her eyes filled with tears, not for Jean's heartache, but because she was glad. And she was sure she would burn in hell for being relieved that another human life had ended. But she was. She hated herself for hating Elyse and for rejecting Jean. In her rational mind, she knew he was only a blameless child caught up in this mess. But the emotional side refused to communicate with the rational.

Every time she had opened her mouth to speak sweetly or be kind, the intention shut itself down and what came out were monotone and cold words.

"Did it hurt?" Jean cried between sobs.

Ava gasped, and then her breath came quick. *That's what I asked my aunt when they died,* she remembered. She closed her eyes tight against a flood of memories conveniently locked away for many years: being called up to say goodbye to both of her dying parents only one day in between, seeing them pasty white, still glistening with sweat from a fever that cooked them from the inside out, their eyes red-rimmed and sunken, mouths that wouldn't stay closed. All this had scared her, and she felt guilty for it. And then later, she asked her aunt if it hurt when someone died. They looked like it had hurt.

She fled the kitchen quickly, running through the living room and upstairs to the sanctuary of their bedroom and sobbed. She tried to shove the images, ones she never should have been allowed to see as a child, back down into the recesses of her mind and, in the process, had her first warm thought toward Jean. She was grateful he hadn't been there to watch his mother die. And although the thought blindsided her to the point of her tears ceasing abruptly, she was appreciative that Elyse had had the decency to send him away beforehand, instead of selfishly keeping him as a comfort right up until the last.

*June 13th 1930*

"*Do* you have everything?" Jonathan adjusted the straps on Jean's knapsack, bursting with everything he could possibly need for the weekend.

"I think so." He turned around and reached up to Jonathan, who picked him up and gave him a bear hug with growls that made Jean squeal with giggles. He gave his son a solid kiss on the cheek before setting him down.

"Be good. Mind your Aunt Ahna." He tousled his hair one last time. Jean waved to Ava and then ran to Arianna, who was waiting inside the Runabout. He hopped in the front seat, reached to hug her and began talking animatedly in French.

"Seems like he's doing better," Caleb said.

"He is, I think. It's been a month." Jonathan shrugged, wondering what the usual amount of time is for childhood grieving. The first few days, he cried off and on from morning till night and, for the most part, stopped eating. After a week, he began to come around; at least the hollow look in his eyes had faded and he would nibble at his food. The end of the second week was when Jonathan saw the most improvement. And it was in no small part, in his opinion, to the talk that Ava had had with him. Jonathan had come home early and found them on the couch. One cushion apart but clearly having a private conversation. He never asked either of them what they had talked about and neither one volunteered. But there was a peace between them now that didn't exist before. The last week had been hit or miss. Some days, Jonathan came home to him sobbing in his bed, clutching the framed picture of his mother and other days, he would find him drawing at the table, somewhat contented and it was Ava who was crying.

When Caleb offered to take Jean for the weekend, Jonathan jumped at the idea. "I really think this change of scenery is what he needs. Get his mind off things till the sting starts to wear off," Jonathan said.

"Well, we'll take good care of him," Caleb promised as he turned to leave.

"See you Sunday night." Ava and Jonathan watched from the porch as they drove away, Jean's little hand waved wildly out the window. Jonathan pulled Ava close to his side as a sly grin spread across his face. "We have the *whole* weekend to do whatever we want."

"I know. I hardly know what to do first. Oh! Let's go to the movie house in Boston!"

His suggestive smile faded to a pleasant one. "Or we could do that."

∞∞∞

"Where are the bebes?" Jean walked into the kitchen and dropped his knapsack by the back door. He gave Ethel and Hubert a passing hug and darted into the living room to look for them.

"They're upstairs sleeping," Ethel said with a smile.

"Alone?" he cried with wide eyes. "What if they need something?"

"It's all right, Jean. If they need something, they'll cry and we'll hear them."

"Can I go sit with them?" he asked with pleading eyes.

"Well." Caleb looked at Arianna.

"Don't you want to play outside?" she asked. "With the piglets maybe? Or Caleb can take you for a ride on the horse?"

"Not now. I'd rather sit with the bebes."

"Well, all right. Just don't wake them up, okay?" Jean nodded so fast it looked like his little head might pop off, and he took off wildly up the stairs, slowing to light steps at the top.

Arianna peeked in on him sometime later to call him for dinner, and he was lying on the floor in the middle of the room, coloring. Every ten strokes or so, he would pop his head up like a gopher and take a look at the babies, who lay sleeping together inside a floor pen, and then go back to coloring.

"Le temps pour manger, petit homme." He looked up and grinned.

"Bon. J'ai faim," he whispered. He dropped back into English as Arianna closed the door softly behind them. "I didn't wake them."

∞∞∞

"I didn't know I got letters." Ava picked up two letters from the kitchen table.

"Mail must have run late today." Jonathan rummaged through the icebox for leftovers to reheat. "You mind eating before we go?"

"That's fine," she said distantly as she began reading a letter from Shannon. "Oh, no," Ava breathed.

"What's wrong?" Jonathan set a pot of vegetable stew on the stove and lit the pilot light.

"Patrick was laid off, says that jobs are harder and harder to come by, says what Maura said, that it's good we got out of the city." Jonathan sighed heavily.

"I'm sure he'll find something. He's very versatile."

"I hope so," she said as she opened the other letter, from Maura.

"What?" she yelled out. "Ian lost his job, too." She leaned forward, chewing on her thumb as she kept reading—more about the bread lines, small food riots and the break in. She looked up in disbelief. "They got robbed." She stared at Jonathan, her mouth hanging open.

"Oh, no." Jonathan leaned against the stove with crossed arms. "What did they lose?"

"Food. That's all they took. Wiped out their icebox and cupboards. Didn't even look for valuables, not that they had any." She continued reading, shaking her head slightly.

"Does Maura still have her job?"

"I think so, she hasn't said otherwise," she said and smiled wistfully at the last line of the letter, *Oh well, it isn't the end of the world.* "How can she keep such a good attitude with all this?" Ava wondered out loud.

"It's admirable."

She crossed the kitchen and hugged Jonathan tight around the waist, resting her head just under his chin.

"She said to tell you hello. Do you think?" She paused, not sure if she wanted to hear the answer. "Do you think sometime, we could go visit her?"

"Maybe." He kissed the top of her head. "I miss her, too." They both turned to the entrance of the kitchen, hearing the front door close with a thud. His father walked through first, slowly, with a tightly drawn face. Margaret followed, sitting down unhurriedly in a chair.

"Did you have fun?" Jonathan asked with a wary eye.

"We didn't go out to have fun," Jonathan Sr. said grimly. "We just needed to talk privately."

"Everything okay?" He shifted Ava to his side, his arm around her shoulder.

"Not really, son." He sighed heavily and sank his head into his hands. Jonathan felt what had come to be a familiar knot of dread in the pit of his stomach. Life had been tumultuous, so unpredictable, that the sensation hardly had a chance to fade before providence dealt another crisis. If he could do with his body what he had become accustomed to doing with his mind, he would be the greatest running back of all time; dodging formidable players with minds set to knock him to the ground and keep him there, making split-second decisions on which play has the most chance of success.

His father sighed and said, "That part-time job I had at the quarry. The one I pretended I didn't have? Well, I was let go." Ava looked at Jonathan, waiting for his reaction.

"Okay." He nodded slowly and decided, "So it'll be a little tight around here. We'll pitch in more."

"It's not only that." Jonathan Sr. looked at Margaret with apology and angst but directed his words to Jonathan. "You were right," he said softly.

"I was right about what?" Jonathan asked cautiously.

"Getting back in. I didn't say anything. I had big plans when the payday came." He rubbed his face hard with his hands. "I should have listened to you," he said softly.

"What in hell are you talking about, Dad?"

"I went all in. The end of March. Every last cent of my savings. Gave it to a friend of mine in Boston, the one I wanted you to start working for, Jack. He said it was at bottom, nowhere to go but up. Get in while it's good." He shook his head remorsefully. Jonathan closed his eyes and dropped his head. "It's all gone. What little we had saved is gone," Jonathan Sr. said apologetically. "I'm sorry. I should have listened to you."

"You're damned straight you should have. Did I not tell you that it was unstable, Dad? Didn't I tell you that it wasn't finished shaking out?" Jonathan Sr. nodded, eyes cast down like a child being scolded. "When it all started sinking again," Jonathan began, shaking his head in disbelief, "didn't you think to get out then? Right at the beginning when you still had something left. Did you have to ride it straight to the bottom?" he demanded. Unconsciously, his grip on Ava's shoulders had tightened like a vise and she squirmed under the pressure.

Jonathan Sr. nodded. "I wanted to, but Jack kept saying—"

"Kept saying what? Ride it out? It'll rally, it'll all be okay?" Jonathan shook his head at the ignorance. "Dad. They've been saying that since October of last year. People are still losing their jobs left and right. Families are doubling and tripling up to survive, more and more businesses and factories are closing. There are soup lines and bread lines in New York, in every major city for that matter, which are blocks long.

Our friend was just robbed and you know what they took? Food. Didn't bother with anything else. I don't care what the weekly address says, it's bad and it's only getting worse . . . ." he trailed off, with a hanging jaw, not sure how to further emphasize the magnitude of what was going on in the world around his father.

"I'm sorry," Jonathan Sr. said into his hands. Jonathan sighed deeply and glanced at Ava, signaling her to follow him.

"I'll be right back," he said as they walked out the backdoor. He led her to the old car in the carport and opened the door for her to get in, then walked around and climbed into the driver's seat.

"Of all the stupid things," he said and then turned to Ava. "I made a huge decision without you recently, and I'm not about to do that again. I need to talk to you about this."

"Okay." She waited curiously for what he might have thought of in the last three minutes.

"His savings is gone. His part-time work is gone. He still has a couple of accounts he does on the side, but that's not enough to live on, and I doubt those businesses will survive much longer anyway." He rubbed his forehead with a grimace. "I don't think we have a choice but to stay," he said with resignation. "Take over the bills. Keep the boat afloat so to speak. I'll have to work more, but there's no way they can survive now. It'll only be a matter of a few weeks, and they'll lose the house and be starving. And honestly, with Jean and our baby, it'll be damned hard for us to make it alone as well. We're not getting as much for the lobster; it's getting vicious. Everyone's undercutting prices so they'll at least walk away with something."

"I would want to anyway, Jonathan, even if we could make it on our own. They helped us when we were at bottom." She reached over and took his hand. "I remember when you had a very similar look on your face, lost and scared, wondering what we were going to do. There's no way we can abandon them now." He nodded slowly, staring through the cracked windshield. Ava watched him as his eyes narrowed in concentration. She felt it an absurd question but asked it anyway. "What are you thinking about?" He picked at the thick cracked leather of the dashboard.

"Patrick."

"Why Patrick?" Her brows came together in confusion.

"Because he's resourceful and purposefully versatile. I was just thinking that with his approach, it'll see them through." His voice was soft and distant as he retreated into his mind, racing through ideas and possibilities, giving them undivided attention.

"I'm glad for him, but I don't understand what that has to do with your father?" She watched his eyes as they flitted back and forth, deep in contemplation. She knew from experience that if she asked him anything now, he either wouldn't hear her or would answer unintelligibly. She waited several moments for him to come back, entertaining herself with the daydream of a trip to visit Maura. In her mind, they were walking along Broadway with linked arms, talking and laughing.

Jonathan snapped his head back slightly. She looked over with a smile.

"What'd you figure out?"

"It just might work, won't make a lot of money, but it'll keep him busy, make him feel productive."

"What will, Jon?"

"Let's go back inside." He grabbed her hand and pulled her out the driver's side door. "I'll explain, don't worry."

∞∞∞

"Huh?" Caleb jerked his head up, looking left and right, startled.

"She's ready to go down," Arianna whispered. He stood, stretched, then shuffled to the rocking chair, yawning and took Little Girl.

"We really need to give her a name," he whispered as he cradled his daughter in his arms. Arianna nodded but was too tired to think. "What kind of parents let their baby go over a month without a name?" he asked with guilt as he walked toward the stairs.

"The kind who didn't expect her in the first place and are now too tired to put serious thought into it. Long as she has one by the time she starts school," she said and grinned as she stood, arching her tired back. Jean walked over to her, tugging at her skirt.

"I had a friend in Paris. She liked me and she had a pretty name," he offered.

"Oh, really, what was it?" Arianna asked, pushing his hair back off his forehead, smoothing it into a neat side-part.

"Savrene." It rolled off his accented tongue with an elegant flair. Caleb stopped at the doorway of the living room and turned around.

"Say that again?"

"Savrene."

"No, in English."

"That is in English, silly. Suh-vreen." She enunciated without the French intonation, smiling at Jean. "And I like it." Caleb looked down at Little Girl.

"I like it, too." He turned to Arianna, eyebrows raised.

"Then it's settled. Little Girl finally has a name. Savrene," she said pleasantly. Jean stood very close, smiling. "Thank you for helping us name our baby," she said, hugging him to her side.

"You're welcome," he whispered, proud but slightly embarrassed. Caleb disappeared upstairs and Jean stood quiet for a moment. "If I ask you something, Aunt Ahna, will you tell me the truth?" She put an arm around his shoulders.

"Of course, what is it?"

"Well, I have two questions." His little face was mixed with seriousness and fear. Arianna walked, holding his hand, to the couch and sat him down beside her.

"Now, what are your questions?" She wrapped her arm around him and he sunk into her side, leaning his head on her soft, warm bosom and feeling maternal comfort for the first time in months.

"Is my Dadee going to die?" he blurted out without emotion, as if he were asking what was for dinner. "And if he does, can I come live with you?" He looked up at her with wide eyes, misty with the beginning of tears. Arianna gasped with surprise.

"Sweetheart, what on earth makes you think your Dadee is going to die? No, no, he isn't. Don't you worry about that." She rubbed his shoulder and he continued to stare at her, waiting for her answers. "Jean." She turned to face him more fully and held his face between her hands. "Your Dadee is not going to die. But if he did, yes, you could come live with me." His face relaxed, and he settled into her side again. "Why would you worry about such things?" she asked, instantly feeling foolish. *Of course, he would worry about Jonathan dying. His mother just died and Jonathan is all he has. Perfectly natural,* she thought.

"My mother told me," he started, swallowing hard before going on, "that my Dadee had to leave Paris before I was born. She said it was the only way his heart would be happy. There was a man on the boat when we were traveling here, who died. I heard someone say he had a bad heart. What if Dadee's heart isn't happy anymore and goes bad?" Arianna was momentarily at a loss for words.

"Jean, I don't think your mother meant he had a bad heart as if he were sick. I think she meant . . . ." *Dammit, Jon, what the hell am I supposed to say,* she growled in her mind. Caleb crossed the threshold into the living room and sank into the comfortable chair by the fire.

"Hurry. They're both asleep, we might be able to get a ten minute nap," he said, leaning his head back with closed eyes. Arianna looked back at Jean.

"I think this is something you should talk to your Dadee about," she said in a whisper. "But I can tell you that he is not sick, he does not have a bad heart, and there is no reason to worry that he is going to leave you, all right?" She stroked his hair as he nodded weakly.

"But if–" He looked up again with big, pleading eyes.

"If so, yes, you can live with me, all right?" she said softly and he snuggled back into her side, content with her answer.

"Can I ride the pony tomorrow?" he asked sometime later as his eyes started to close.

"Oui, vous pouvez monter le poney demain," she said, kissing the top of his head.

∞∞∞

"*Okay.*" Jonathan walked into the kitchen and sat across from his father with his proposal. Ava stood behind him, glancing from Margaret's worried eyes to Jonathan Sr.'s bleak expression. "Here's what we're going to do," Jonathan started, leaning forward to rest his elbows on his knees. "We're going to stay on here. Take over the bills–"

Jonathan Sr. threw his head back and opened his mouth to protest, but was quickly muted by his son. "You'll be homeless and starving in a month, Dad, and you know it. If we were to move out, we'd have to pay all the same bills. Why not pay them here? Just until things get better." His father shook his head, feeling slightly disgraced and blew out a hard breath. "And here's what you're going to do," he continued, not letting his father get in a single word of opposition. "You're to use what you've got. When you got rid of the new car I sent you and bought that old, rusted piece of junk–"

"Hey! That old piece of junk runs just fine now," his father yelled indignantly. Jonathan smiled widely.

"*Exactly*. Did you know how to rebuild an engine before you bought it?"

"No. I learned out of necessity." He folded his arms, wondering what Jonathan was getting at.

"Well, now you're going to take what you learned out of necessity and use it for profit. Marginal, at best, but profit nonetheless." He leaned back in his chair, mirroring his father's posture, staring victoriously into uncertain eyes. "I'll talk to the guys Monday, but I don't think it will be a problem. I'll replace the money over time, if it doesn't work."

"If what doesn't work? Talk to them about what?" The forlorn form had given way to a straightened posture and a curious eye.

"I'm going to borrow some money from the business savings. You," he pronounced and pointed a finger at Jonathan Sr., "are going to take it and find another jalopy like the one out there. The worse condition and the cheaper the better. Then you're going to spend your days fixing it up. Save back some of what I give you for parts. When it's done, we'll put the word out and you can sell it. There are a whole lot of people right now looking for cheap transportation. It's a pattern I don't see changing anytime soon. And then," He reached across his chest and put his hand on Ava's resting on his shoulder, and squeezed it lightly. He could almost feel her smiling behind him as he continued. "you're going to take that money and do it again. With each sale, you can pay down the loan. It won't make you rich, but it'll keep you busy, and it'll bring a bit of money in." He and his father sat, eyes locked. Jonathan's expression was satisfied and slightly triumphant; his fathers' was unreadable.

"Jon." His mother turned to him with grateful eyes. "That's a wonderful idea." She reached for his hand, and he let go of Ava's to accept it.

"I thought so." He tilted his head, grinning arrogantly.

"It is," his father said quietly. "Good thinking, son. Thank you. I should have been thinking along those lines."

"I'm sure you would have thought of it as soon as the shock wore off," he said graciously. Jonathan Sr. rubbed his face hard, skin loose with finely aged wrinkles moved by his fingers on the once handsome face, and he tiredly spoke through his hands.

"Maybe. Maybe not. I might have ended up in a bathtub, too, if–" He froze the moment he said it. Caught up in relief, reveling in a sliver of hope when only a moment ago he had been consumed by despair, he had let the words slip out. He dropped his hands in his lap with a thud. "I'm sorry," he pled to Jonathan's stunned expression. "I didn't mean–"

"Forget it," he ordered with hard eyes and a clenched jaw. His father nodded and lowered his eyes. Margaret and Ava exchanged puzzled expressions.

∞∞∞∞

"*Do* we have to leave tomorrow?" Claire asked lazily as she stretched.

Aryl lifted his head from her stomach. "Well." He craned his neck to see their small crate of food across the room. "If we ration, we might be able to make it a week," he said and grinned happily.

"I'll starve," she said, smiling and tangling her fingers in his hair. "Let's stay."

"I wish we could." He looked up at her, folding his hands on her stomach and resting his chin on his knuckles.

"Are you sure this is all right?" He gave an admiring gaze at the bare breasts between their smiles. "I mean, I'm perfectly content to do this for days on end. But I do wish I could have done more for you."

"It's wonderful. Just as it is." She looked around the room. "Just being here again. Planning it all, it was the perfect anniversary gift." He smiled gratefully and turned his head to the side, sliding one arm down to hug her hip. They lay quiet, his head rose and fell with her breathing, listening as the wind picked up and rain began tapping the windows of the lantern room.

"You know," she said, running her fingers aimlessly around his scalp. "We won't be able to do this after the baby is born."

"I know," he whispered and raised his head look at her. His eyes were dancing, but to Claire's surprise, there was no shock. Not the expression that normally strikes the faces of men just told they were going to be fathers.

"How did you know?" she asked, slightly deflated.

"My mother," he said apologetically.

"But I hadn't told her! I hadn't told anyone. I wanted you to be the first to know!" She was thoroughly disappointed and angry that his mother, who took far too much interest in the intimate side of their marriage to begin with, had stolen her moment. She pushed his head off her stomach and sat up, pouting.

"She didn't know, she only suspected." He turned around to sit in front of her. "She's been watching the laundry."

"Oh, my Lord!" Claire stared at him open-mouthed.

He grinned apologetically. "She really wants grandchildren. She talked to me yesterday about her suspicion and I told her to keep quiet, so you could tell me." He lifted her chin. "And I was really hoping she was right," he said and smiled, his brown eyes were genuinely thrilled.

"I wanted it to be a *surprise*," she whined with tears in her eyes, pulling her chin away and dropping her head.

"Well, it was . . . sort of." He sat for moment, thinking. "Here. Lay back down."

"What?"

"Lay back down," he said. "We'll re-do this."

"We can't redo it," she said sadly.

He nudged her shoulders back down on the feather tick. "Yes, we can." He repositioned his head on her stomach, lifting it and laying it back down several times to get it just right. "There. No, wait." He moved his arm to hug her hip. "There." He looked back up at her briefly. "You had your hands on my head," he reminded and rested his head back down. She plopped her hands on his head lethargically.

"Okay," he said, satisfied. She lay staring at the ceiling, growing angrier at his mother with every minute. She would do something about this—teach her a lesson. She rolled several possibilities around in her head. She was lost in her ideas of retribution when Aryl cleared his throat as a cue. He lifted his head again. "Here's where you tell me," he whispered and quickly dropped his head. She smiled down at him for his effort.

"Aryl, we're having a baby," she said monotone and sarcastic.

He threw his head up with eyes nearly popping out of their sockets. "What?" he asked and stared at her with a ridiculous expression that made her laugh. "I . . . just . . . never saw this coming! I mean, how? Okay, well, I know how, but when? When will it be here? What will we name it?" He rolled onto his back and put his hands on his head. "There's so much to do. We have to get to work. No, you rest, I'll work." He flipped to his side and felt her head, patting all over her face and neck. "How are you feeling? Are you sick? Hungry? You're not in pain, are you?"

She was giggling hysterically now, and just as he launched into another outburst, she put her hand over his mouth.

"Aryl, *stop*." He froze, watching her flat expression as it melted into a smile. "Thank you. That was very entertaining. And sweet."

"I'm sorry it didn't happen the way you wanted it to," he said. She looked around the room, recounting at lightning speed the whirlwind her life had been since the first time they were here.

"It's all right," she whispered. "But your mother!" She laughed a low, evil laugh. "I'm going to find a way to get her back for this."

∞∞∞∞

"The wind is really picking up," Jonathan said casually, glancing at the window over the sink. Jonathan Sr. had excused himself to bed and Margaret followed, leaving Ava and Jonathan at the table.

"It is. Think we'll lose the lights?" She picked at the tablecloth and felt the sudden apprehension in the air. Jonathan shrugged and stared into the doorway of the dark living room.

"I'm sorry we couldn't make it to the movie house."

"I guess we shouldn't spend any money anyway, under the new circumstances." She sighed in resignation.

He leaned his head back, speaking into the air. "I'm sorry. Just when things were starting to look up."

"What did he mean, Jonathan?" He tensed, crossed his arms, and took a deep breath.

"He's just upset, in shock, talking nonsense." He wouldn't look at her but felt her eyes boring into him. He prayed silently she would let it pass. A month ago, he was prepared to tell her everything, if he had to–if it meant her emerging from behind her brick wall. But now, for reasons he didn't understand, he wanted to bury it back down, forget about it. He didn't want to explain himself, especially during what should have been a relaxing and romantic weekend.

"If he was talking nonsense, why did he apologize to you? The look on his face, he knew he messed up, and his apology was directed at you. Ending up in a bathtub?" She looked at him confused. "Why would he be sorry to you for saying that?" His eyes focused on the rose print of the tablecloth.

"I'm not sure I want to go into it tonight," he said, almost pleading, but acknowledging to himself that he would, at some point, have to go into it.

"So, there *is* something else you haven't told me." She crossed her arms, staring into her lap. "How many times has this happened," she said sarcastically. "Honestly, I should be used to it by now."

"There's just this. And one other thing. But neither one is what you think."

"Two things. Wonderful. Then why don't you enlighten me, so I don't assume the worst."

He pulled a quarter out of his pocket and flipped it in the air.

"What are you doing?" She looked at him, irritated. It was getting late, her plans for the evening were ruined, and now he wanted to play games.

"Heads or tails. I'm letting fate decide what to talk to you about first," he said. "We might as well get it all out, I suppose, so tomorrow we can try to have a nice day." He raised his hand to peek. "Shit. All right, let's do that one first." He sighed in resignation and rose. "I'll be right back."

He left the room, took the stairs with sluggish steps, and rustled around upstairs. A moment later, he returned with an envelope.

"I was saving this for the right time. I'm not sure when that was ever going to be. I guess now's as good a time as any." He turned it over and she strained to see the feminine script on the front of it. He pulled out a smaller envelope from inside and placed it in front of her. "I found this in the trunk of Jean's things when we got the telegram. There was a letter addressed to me, asking me to give this to you when you were ready. I'm not sure what she meant by ready, but here it is."

She looked up from the letter at Jonathan as if she had been stabbed. "It's from . . . *her*?"

"I guess there are things she needed to say to you."

Ava didn't break her expression of disbelief. "Oh, I'll bet there are. Only now, she's dead and I can't have my say in return." She shoved the letter across the table. "I won't have a one-sided conversation."

"Ava, please."

"No!" she screamed suddenly. "No more *Ava, please*!" she spit the words mockingly. "Every time I turn around you're saying *Ava, please*. And I'm done." She shoved her chair back and stood up, glaring down at him. "No. This time, it's *Jonathan, please*. Jonathan, please understand that I am sick and tired of your past haunting me. I had nothing to do with it, and it's not fair that it's wormed its way into our marriage and ruined my life."

"I hardly think it's ruined your life."

"It's *my* turn to talk, Jonathan!" He recoiled slightly as she screeched at him. "Your past, everything from who you slept with to how you ran your business has affected me, and all you can say is *'Ava please'*. I'm forced to cope with the fallout of every decision you have ever made, things I never had a choice about and *then*!" She laughed, short and maniacally. "I have your bastard son to suddenly contend with." Anger flashed deep in his eyes. "Someone that will always remind me, and you, for that matter, of *her*. I have to be reminded every day of the other woman you loved. And now you want me to read a letter from her. I will not, Jonathan. You can go straight to hell." He opened his mouth to counter but she had only paused to take a breath. He folded his arms and tilted his head to the side, waiting for her to finish. "I lost everything with you, I lived in that horrible tenement with you, waiting for Victor to torture us, scared of what he'd do next, I stood by you while you crumpled into someone who didn't care about anything anymore, I took care of you when you were attacked, I half-starved with you and every day I told myself that you were going to snap out of it. You were going to fix everything and be the hero that you love to be. It didn't once cross my mind to abandon you!" Fury was boiling through her, months of repressed anger and frustration welling to the top, causing words to spill over without concern for their consequences. She walked over to the sink. He raised his head, yelling at her back.

"Yes, it did! You said you were going to Maura's after Christmas. But she wouldn't take you in, so you stayed. Don't act like you did me a favor by staying, you had nowhere else to go!" He looked away and bit his lip with instant regret. Without thinking, she spun around, picked up a plate from the drain board, and hurled it across the kitchen. It shattered against the wall with a thunderous crash, shards of ceramic flying in all directions. He ducked, covering his head. Her breath was ragged with adrenaline, fuming with rage, trying to arrange the most hurtful words possible.

"I could have gone back to him," she snarled. "To Victor. He would have taken me in, even if only to finally beat you at something," she spoke slowly, intentionally, seething. He was utterly shocked and instantly enraged. His hand curled around the sugar bowl and hurled it across the room, leaving a gash in the plaster by the kitchen window.

"How dare you!" he roared. "You would be a whore for him, wouldn't you? Yet you condemn Elyse for caring about me!" He stood, absentmindedly groping for something else to throw. Both fully consumed by deep hurt and irrational rage, there was only one mission now and that was to hurt the other as mortally as possible.

Jonathan Sr. poked his head in the doorway with frightened concern. "Jon. Everything okay?" he asked timidly.

"No!" he yelled at him. "Everything is definitely not okay." He went back to staring at Ava with revulsion. "Go away and leave us alone." They stared intently at each other with narrow, hate-filled eyes that dared the other to speak, or look away.

"Take it back," Jonathan ordered with a low voice, thick with warning. "Take your words back before everything we have is destroyed."

"I'll take it back, if you send him back," she challenged unreasonably.

"I'm not sending him back. He's my son and I love him!" The words surprised both of them. In his own heart and mind, he had admitted to growing fond of Jean, forging a bond, and even beginning to feel fiercely protective of him. But he hadn't admitted, until this moment, that he loved him. He sat down hard in the chair and lowered his head. "I love him," he repeated. "And he's staying with me." His slightly shocked but resigned expression told her this was no longer negotiable.

"And what if I said it's me or him, Jonathan? Who would you choose?"

"You wouldn't make me choose. You're angry, you're pregnant, and your emotions are running high." He looked down, his fury somewhat diffused from those realizations.

"You'd choose him," she whispered. He shook his head slowly.

"It would be an impossible choice, Ava." He rested his arms on his knees and hung his head down, closing his eyes, suddenly very tired.

"Tell me, Jonathan," she started, "after Elyse, Ruth, Jean, and even Aryl and Caleb, is there anyone else you love more than me? Just so I can place myself in the proper pecking order." He sighed heavily, feeling frustration welling up again.

"Elyse is dead and I never loved her like you think I did. Ruth, I didn't really care about in the first place. Jean is my son and I'll protect him like I protect you, or from you, if necessary. And leave my friends out of this. Especially Aryl."

"Even *him* before me?" She looked around in disbelief. "I had no idea I ranked so low." He sprung from the chair, a split second later an inch from her face, gripping her shoulders.

"There is nothing I love more than you. *Nothing!*" he said through his teeth. "But you don't believe me, do you? You want me to prove it? I guess there's only one way to do that." He took a step back, yanked up his sleeve, and thrust his wrist in her face. "Christmas Eve. While you all were walking to Maura's, warm with hot buttered rum, I was sitting in the bathtub with a razor to my wrist. That's what my Dad meant, Ava. I had completely given up. I wanted to die so badly and was within a few seconds of accomplishing that when Aryl found me."

Her mouth fell open, all the rage drained away as she stared at the thin, white scar in shock while he spoke. "At first, nothing he said made a difference. In fact, while he was rattling on, I had decided to move the razor to my throat and pull very quickly because that way there would be no time for him to save me." He winced at the memory before going on. "But then he talked about you. See, I thought you'd be better off without me. Thought I was doing you a favor. He didn't mention you to convince me that you *needed* me or even that you *loved* me, after all I had put you through. He worked an angle he knew would get my attention. He told me that if I did it, he would take you to Victor. That he would hand you over to him the first chance he got. His act was very convincing. That's the only thing that stopped me." He stared at her eyes, which were fixed on the scar, brimming with tears. "He pulled me out of that bathtub, and I did what he asked of me. I put one foot in front of the other and kept going. That's what I did until I gradually returned to myself. But you." He lowered his arm, sliding the sleeve over it. "You were the only thing to pull me back." She reached down and circled the wrist with her fingers as she contemplated his words. "The thought of him taking you to Victor ... And then you threaten me with the same thing." He yanked his wrist from her grip and glared at her.

"I'm sorry," she whispered, refusing to look him in the eyes.

"You *should* be." He walked back to the table and sat down hard, leaning his elbows on the table, holding his head in his hands.

The wind had begun to blow in small gusts and the tip of a tree branch scraped against the windowpane. The noise sent shivers up Ava's spine as she stood against the sink, wiping tears. He took deep, ragged breaths and touched his own eyes discreetly.

"I'm sorry," he said with a sigh, "for everything." She stared at his bent head, unsure of what to say. Too much had happened for her to just tell him *it's okay* and be done with it. She wanted to comfort him; he looked remorseful enough, but she willed herself against the sink, determined to hash this out so she'd never have to hear another *Ava, please*. He sniffled and wiped his face with both hands. "I'm sorry," he repeated. "All I ever tried to do is protect you. From everything. Seems like everything I tried to protect you from found a way around me and hurt you anyway."

"If you had just told me everything from the start, Jonathan."

"I know. You're right. I should have talked to you when I saw everything start to fall apart. I should have told you who we had to rent from."

"That would have been better than the way I found out." She nodded in agreement. He sighed, recalling their first major fight and then quickly shook his head.

"No. I never should have agreed to it. Even if it meant leaving our friends and moving you here, *that's* what I should have done. Found something else or brought you to Rockport. I should have thought more of you when we were there," he continued. "I got lost in my own self-pity, and I'm sorry."

"It was a bad time for us all, Jonathan," she said quietly.

"No, I was selfish. I should have told you about Elyse, too. I just didn't want you to think badly of me. It was an odd arrangement, I admit. But most importantly, I didn't want you to know because I never wanted you to feel like you had to compete or weren't good enough."

"It would be hard for any woman to not feel less than average standing next to her," Ava said with a hint of venom.

"Only for the reason that you don't see what I see," he said, looking up at her with tired eyes. "There is no competition. And I should have told you about Ruth." He leaned back, folded his arms, and stared at the tablecloth. "I can't begin to tell you how unimportant she was, Ava. I explained why I didn't mention her when we first met, but I should have told you later." All she could do was nod, suddenly exhausted and unable to hold onto her burning anger with her husband pouring his heart out. "I didn't know about Jean, so there is no way I could have warned you about that," he said with a helpless shrug. Some of the anger she thought she was too tired to feel returned with a vengeance, and her ears burned red. She opened her mouth with a string of hurtful words at the ready. "But I should have talked to you before deciding to keep him," he said, before she could hurl them across the room.

"Yes, you should have," she said firmly.

"And about my grandfathers." He sighed long and hard. "There's so much I *should have* done, and I'm sorry." He stood and walked over to her, wrapped his arms around her slowly and buried his face in her hair. Her folded arms stayed wedged between them, her body slightly rigid as he slowly rocked her.

"Please forgive me," he whispered. Ava blinked away tears, unfolded her arms, and placed her hands lightly on his waist. A strike of lightning lit the room with an intense flash and a deafening thunderclap overhead shook the house. Jonathan instinctively pulled her closer and then laughed.

"What's so funny?" Her voice was muffled against his shoulder.

"I just keep doing it. Trying to protect you, I mean. I'd throw myself in front of a bolt of lightning for you, you know." She meant her laugh to be endearing, but it came out as a scoff.

"If you didn't push me in front of it first," he added with a twitch of his lips. He moved, his eyes closed and bent his head to rest his forehead on hers. "I love you so much, Ava."

"There are things you can protect me from, Jon. And I want you to when it's needed. I love that about you. You've always been there, standing in front of me, strong and confident." Her hands moved over his shoulders, taking a moment to enjoy the depth and width of them. She covered every inch of them and then she rested her hands, fingers spread wide, over his chest. "But you can't protect me from everything."

"But I want to. I need to," he admitted with a whisper. He hugged and rocked her again, holding her so tight she could scarcely breathe. Suddenly, his eyes flew open.

"I thought of something I should tell you," he said hesitantly and felt her stiffen under his arms. "But it's not what you think. It's nothing really, I just don't want you to hear about it later and be angry or think something else of it." She wiggled out of his hold and stood back, staring at him, braced and ready. He held the hands she kept rigid at her side. "Before you, on one of the trips to Paris, well, you know by now what an outrageous mess Arianna was. One night we were all playing cards with a handful of clients. We were intoxicated, but Arianna was way ahead of us as usual. I excused myself to the restroom and when I came back to the table, she, well, she was topless. Dancing. I saw, well, the whole room saw her–" he glanced down at his chest. "I didn't mean to," he said in his own defense.

Ava stared at him expressionless and then her face cracked into a smile, and then a laugh. A small wave of relief washed over his weary face.

"I can hardly blame you for that, Jonathan," she said. "I'm sure half of Paris has seen Arianna's breasts." He laughed lightly, nodding in agreement, and gave her a sheepish grin.

"Yours are nicer," he whispered. Her lips twitched in appreciation, her eyes flickered up to his, then away. They were surrounded by awkward silence again, and she shifted her weight uncomfortably with a sigh.

"Let's go to bed," he suggested with a slight tug of her arm.

She shook her head. "You go ahead. I'll be up later." His eyes dropped in disappointment, but he turned from her slowly and left the room.

Ava sat at the table and turned the letter repeatedly in her hands as she made her final decision. Much emotion welled up in her again, and tears spilled over. With a ragged breath, she wiped her wet cheeks, ripped the seal, and began reading.

She pushed the bedroom door open sometime later to find Jonathan sitting in the dark on the side of the bed, his hands and head positioned as if in prayer. She held the letter limply at her side.

"She loved you," Ava whispered. "She loved you enough to make peace with me, so I wouldn't keep putting you through this. She didn't want either of us to be tormented by the past." He remained motionless, except for a deep, grateful exhale. "She said a lot, actually." Ava glanced down at the letter that hung by her side. "Explained a lot. There's not a lot of it I want to talk about. I just wanted to tell you, it's over. I'll never bring her up in anger again." He reached one hand back to her without looking up. She crossed the room slowly, dropping the letter on the foot of the bed and took his hand. He didn't change his posture as he guided her to settle beside him, and they sat in hushed darkness for many moments, neither one knowing where to start. "I'm sorry," Ava said remorsefully, "for bringing him up, suggesting that I would go back to him. I was really angry."

"I know. But still, I never want his name spoken again. By either of us."

"You really were going to do it," she said, turning his hand over and running a finger over the slightly raised scar.

"I was." He nodded, in shame. "I'm not proud of it, and I never wanted you to find out." He self-consciously turned his hand over. "And honestly, I thought you'd have more of a reaction."

"I guess I didn't because it had crossed my mind recently, too." Her words were laced with shame. His eyes squinted to see her face in what little moonlight shone through the window. "When Jean showed up, and I saw her, after just telling you I was pregnant. Of course, I couldn't do it. But it crossed my mind, and I wished for a long time that I wasn't pregnant, so I could. I just felt like that was the final straw, you know? I couldn't deal with everything that had happened and right when you started acting like yourself again, here was Jean and I was sure that I would be pushed to the side for him." She stared at the floor during her confession.

"You know that's not true, don't you? I've tried so hard to show you that it wasn't going to be that way."

"You have. And I don't feel like that anymore."

Jonathan watched her for a moment before he leaned over to the bedside table, pulling open the bottom drawer. He dug around blindly. "Aryl found me and thought quickly to save me. But Maura helped, too. Remember on the walk to the church she wanted to talk to me alone? She knew. I don't know how she knew, but she talked to me all the way to the church. Got me thinking and gave me this. I carried it in my pocket for months, like a kid with a security blanket. It came to mean a lot more to me than the story behind it or even the things Maura tried to get across to me. I've stopped carrying it with me everywhere only recently. Like her, I have the story and the meaning in my heart." He handed her the cross.

"It's beautiful." She turned it over in the dim light, not really seeing the detail of design or the antique strand that ran throughout. "That was nice of her to give it to you."

"Well, now I'm giving it to you," he said, closing her fingers around the heart of it. "Maura told me it should always be with someone who needs it. It's yours now."

"Thank you, but . . . ." She looked up at him, astounded. "How can you give me something after all the horrible things I said? I yelled at you, threw things."

He took her head between his hands, squeezing it slightly for emphasis.

"Don't ever question the fact that I love you more than anything."

She met his concentrated stare.

"Don't ever keep anything from me again. I don't care how small it might seem at the time, or how difficult it may be to tell me. Don't you ever keep another secret from me." He placed her hand over his heart and held it there. She could feel it beating strong beneath the thin material, slightly damp from the balminess of the incoming storm.

"I swear. On my life, Ava. No more surprises."

With nothing left to explain, he lay down, tucked an arm behind his head, pulled her close to him.

The wind blew the sheer, white curtains away from the frame into large swells that suspended momentarily, then rippled to the side with a graceful shimmer and quickly gusted out again. The hypnotic motions in the silvery moonlight lulled both of them to sleep quickly.

*June 15th 1930*

"*L*et's stop by on the way home and tell them."

"You sure?" Aryl cocked an eyebrow at her from behind the wheel of his parents' car.

"Yes," she said and smiled sweetly.

"You're going to be nice, aren't you?" Aryl looked from the dirt road to Claire and back several times, warily.

"Yes, I'm going to be nice. All smiles," she promised with a big toothy grin. They bumped along the rutted road in silence for a while before Aryl began apologizing again.

"I'm sorry we couldn't stay another day. I have to get ready for tomorrow and–"

"I told you, it's fine, Aryl. I had a wonderful time. Very relaxing." She gazed out the window at a patch of dark clouds that lurked out over the ocean. "Wonder when that'll blow in?"

"Probably later this evening," he surmised as he sized up the shadowy billows.

They pulled into the driveway and Aryl honked twice. His mother was at the door in seconds, waving and smiling. Claire walked along the cobble path to the door ahead of Aryl and he peeked around her, glaring at his mother, putting his finger to his lips.

"I know you're right around the cornah, but I miss yah so much!" She hugged her son tightly and then Claire. "So," she said with dancing eyes and a smirk that gave away her knowledge. "How was it?"

"Oh, it was lovely," Claire said and smiled as she sat down in the living room, folding her hands in her lap, staring at her mother-in-law with a sweet, innocent expression.

Kathleen fidgeted with the fold of her apron. "Just lovely?" she asked, her voice slightly high in pitch. "A plain old lovely weekend?"

"Just lovely." Claire stared at her, waiting and enjoying watching her squirm.

"Huh." She turned to Aryl, her forehead scrunched up in question. "Nothing exciting happened then?" She looked slightly deflated.

"Oh, I didn't say that," Claire said, pulling her attention back.

Kathleen lit up and wiggled slightly in her seat, as if wanting to be settled just right to receive the news of her first grandchild. She smiled, waiting eagerly. Claire spoke with a perfectly straight face.

"We had sex a lot. And I mean, *a lot*." Aryl snorted, coughed, and left the living room. Kathleen's face had frozen in place as Claire continued. "Practically all we did. Thank you for sending the biscuits and jam, by the way. They were delicious."

"You're w-welcome." Kathleen stared, dumbfounded.

"When I first walked up the stairs, I was completely amazed. Aryl had it set up so beautifully. Everything was almost exactly the way it was the first time we were there. Only this time I didn't have to pick splinters from my rear the next day, since he thought to bring the feather tick. Aryl is so," she looked toward the kitchen with a sigh, "well-endowed. I hope for *your* sake that runs in the family," she said and grinned playfully at her mother-in-law. "And it was good that it stormed almost the entire time we were there. That thunder was loud, wasn't it? Not as loud as us, mind you. Good thing there were no close neighbors—"

"Claire, I'm not sure this is—"

"It really was pointless to go on and on like we did," Claire interrupted, "from a procreative point of view, since I'm already pregnant. *But you knew that, didn't you?*" She tilted her head and smiled sweetly at her clever mother-in-law. Kathleen still hadn't moved her statuesque posture, eyes still wide with shock at the unique confrontation.

Claire stood up, gathered her purse, and called out to the kitchen. "Aryl, darling, we'd better get going." She rolled her head back to Kathleen with her eyes bugged out. "I *really* need a bath." Michael's laughter came in spurts of coughing fits from the kitchen, and Aryl walked to the door quickly, his own face quivering as he tried desperately to contain his hysterical outburst. Outside, he bent over laughing for a moment and then grabbed her arm to pull himself up.

"What in the world got into you?" he asked.

"Well, I decided that since she stole my moment, I was going to steal hers." She nodded triumphantly. "Think it worked?"

Aryl laughed again. "Oh, I think it worked, served her right, too." He closed the passenger door behind her, laughing still.

∞∞∞

"Maybe she doesn't like her name?" Caleb paced the living room with Savrene wailing on his shoulder. "Ever since we gave it to her, she's done nothing but cry."

"Don't be silly." Arianna peeked at the baby over his shoulder. "Try holding her the other way."

"I've held her every way there is to hold a baby. Nothing helps." He began pacing again, patting her back with a bouncing shuffle. Jean sat on the couch with a worried look and his fingers in his ears.

"It's colic." Hubert leaned on the doorjamb with a look of sympathy on his slightly reddened face. "You had it something awful when you were about this age. Seems to be when it starts. I think you cried for two months straight, didn't get a wink of sleep." He shook his head reminiscing.

"Well, I'm sorry I was such a difficult child, but how do you fix it? There has to be something we can do." He looked down anxiously at Savrene, whose little red face was quivering with one piercing cry after another.

"Well, if I remember correctly, the only thing that quieted you down was a ride in the wagon. Damn near drove two of my best horses to an early grave from exhaustion."

"Again, sorry I was so much trouble," he said sarcastically. "Maybe I could try that."

"Can't. Got rid of the wagon last year. Maybe you could take her for a horse ride, though." Hubert wiped sweat off his brow with his sleeve. "Sure is getting hot," he said. Caleb glanced at Arianna in concern, then watched his father closely.

"You feeling okay, Dad? You don't look so good."

"Just getting a cold." He lumbered back to the kitchen. "Maybe I'll turn in early tonight," he called.

"Mom's not back yet?" It would be dusk soon, and he didn't like the idea of his mother being out alone at night.

"You know how she gets when she and the other hens get together." He flapped his fingers to his thumb several times. "The gossip alone could go on for hours before they ever get to playing cards. I'm just glad they have their meetings over at June's house." Caleb stood at the back door, staring through the screen.

"Maybe a walk outside would calm her down. We've got that old pram."

"I'm willing to try anything. You want to take her or do you want me to do it?" Arianna asked.

"Why don't both of you get some fresh air. I'll stay here with Jean and Samuel," Hubert offered, leaning over the table to light the oil lamp. The amber light from the small flame brought out the shadows and sallow color in his face. "C'mon, Jean, I'll show you where Ethel hides the cookies," he said.

∞∞∞∞

Less than twenty paces from the house, distracted and calmed by the bounce of the pram as it wobbled along the dirt drive, Savrene quieted and nodded off.

"Great. We'll just do this all night," Caleb said sarcastically with a sigh. Arianna hooked her arm around his and leaned her head on his shoulder as they slowly made their way down to the main road. When they got back, Caleb slowly and carefully lifted her from the bed of the pram and she wailed instantly. His head fell in frustration and he laid her back down, tucked her in, and then turned to make the trek once more.

∞∞∞∞

Hubert reached to the top of the pantry and pulled out a large jar. He held it out to Jean. He smiled with effort, his face glistened with the sheen of a cold sweat, and his breath was hard and short.

"Here you go. I think I better sit down," he panted while groping for the chair in front of him. "Think you can manage the milk from the icebox?" Jean nodded and skipped to the icebox, having to move several items around to get to the round milk pitcher.

"Jean."

Jean turned toward Hubert's pained whisper. His mouth was open in a silent scream, his hands clutching his chest and then, to Jean's horror, watched him fall onto the table, tipping it over. The lamp skidded across the room, spraying oil in a circular pattern as it spun on its angled side. The fire quickly jumped from the wick and chased the oil in all directions. Jean stood frozen in fear, watching the fire grow. He heard Samuel's crying from upstairs and looked around anxiously.

Fire, a foot tall in some places, stood between him and the stairwell. He watched frantically as the fire jumped to the curtains of the back door and the kitchen quickly filled with smoke. He dumped the pitcher of milk over his head and ran full on at the fire, jumping over it in spots and raced up the stairs.

Samuel was screaming hard, choppy wails as Jean stood on tiptoes to reach him in the crib. He couldn't quite reach him; he dropped to his knees to reach a thin arm through the bars and pulled him close to the edge. Back up on toes, he grabbed two fistfuls of Samuel's sleeper and pulled with all his might to raise him over the edge of the crib wall.

∞∞∞

"Make sure she's tucked in," Arianna said. Dark clouds from the approaching storm caused dusk to fall quickly, and Caleb noticed the threatening clouds in the distance on their third trip down the drive.

"Looks like it's going to be a hell of a storm tonight," he mentioned, too tired to sound more than casual. Arianna nodded, head down, watching the pebbles fly in all directions as she drug her feet.

"Do you smell that?" He sniffed the air several times to the left and right.

"Maybe the lightning caught something." Arianna shrugged. A sizzling pop from behind them caused Caleb to turn around slowly and his eyes grew wide. Flames reached high out of the kitchen window and teased at the door below billows of black smoke. The screen door hung to the side, the bottom-half glowing red.

"Samuel!" Arianna screamed and scooped up Savrene as they both began running toward the house.

It was a long road to begin with, but in this moment, it seemed to go on forever. Caleb lowered his head, willing his legs to run faster and Arianna screamed for Jean and Samuel in turn.

Caleb stopped at the edge of the porch and pumped the well handle furiously, drenching himself as best he could, instantly grateful his mother had insisted on a well pump near the kitchen. He ducked his head under the stream one last time as something caught his eye. He pulled his head up, shook it wildly, and wiped his eyes. He made out a little figure engulfed in the smoke and a second later, Jean emerged, coughing and holding Samuel tight to his stomach, his little fists locked under the infant's arms. The baby began to slide from Jean's hold, and Caleb took a huge step to catch the baby before he fell to the porch. He tossed him onto his shoulder and then scooped Jean up, hugging him tightly with one arm.

"Thank you, Jean. Thank you," he whispered repeatedly as he raced to Arianna. She laid Savrene on the ground and grabbed Samuel in one fell swoop, dropped to her knees and pulled Jean to her, holding them both tightly as she cried in relief.

"Jean, where's my dad?" Caleb asked frantically.

". . . kitchen . . . ," he replied through a cough.

Caleb took off again toward the house, covered his mouth and nose with his shirt, and lowered his head as he entered the burning kitchen. Arianna scarcely breathed as several minutes passed and Caleb hadn't returned.

"Jean. Stay here with the babies. Don't move, all right? Ne bougez pas!"

He nodded wide-eyed, moved himself between the babies, and held each of their hands. Arianna raced to the porch and could feel the wall of heat radiating from the house. She looked around frantically for the bucket at the other end of the porch. She grabbed it, returned to the pump, filled it with water, and threw it in the doorway that was now thick with flames.

Someone from behind her yelled, "Form a line!" She turned to see more than a dozen neighbors, all with buckets in hand, forming two lines from the well pump to the door.

"Caleb!" she screamed desperately over the roar of the flames. Arianna stumbled backwards from the burning doorway.

"There he is!" someone yelled, pushed past Arianna and stepped into the smoke to help Caleb pull his father's body out of the house.

A safe distance from the house, his limp body dropped to the ground with a deafening clap of thunder overhead. Caleb leaned over him to listen for breath, ripped open his shirt and put his ear to his chest but heard nothing. Arianna stood over him with her hands over her mouth, crying.

"He's gone," Caleb whispered, looking up at Arianna with tears in his eyes. "He's gone." He remained on his knees by his father's body, staring blankly at him while a number of neighbors raced to save what they could of the house. A flash of lightning followed by another thunderclap preceded a sudden downpour by only seconds. Arianna ran to the children to move them to the dry barn. One of Hubert's friends stood behind Caleb and gave him a sympathetic pat on the shoulder. He reached around and handed him a wadded up sheet that he had pulled from the clothesline. And even though it was already wet from the sudden rain, Caleb draped the sheet over his father and slowly rose. His eyes found Arianna standing in the threshold of the barn, safe; he turned his attention to helping the effort to save the house. He grabbed a bucket and began racing in and out of the house with the others.

Jonathan tore onto the property, skidding to a stop with a muddy fishtail in the pouring rain, and Aryl screeched to a halt behind him; the oldest of the neighbors who had been dispatched to fetch them was left several miles back. Aryl ran toward the house, the fire now reduced to a smoldering mess, and picked up a stray bucket along the way. Jonathan looked across the yard where Caleb held his mother's shoulders as she cried over her husband's body.

"Dadee!"

Jean ran from the barn and scrambled up into Jonathan's arms. He hugged him tight and then pulled him back to look at him.

"Are you all right?" he asked, caressing his hair and sooty face. He nodded with eyes full of tears as Jonathan carried him back to the barn.

"I was scared," he whispered in his father's ear.

∞∞∞

"Jonathan," Arianna said, as she sat against a bale of hay, feeding Savrene. Samuel lay on his side next to her leg. She looked like she was ready to drop, if she weren't already sitting, from the combination of exhaustion and the letdown of adrenaline. "Thank you for coming." Jonathan looked at each of the babies and thought her gratitude absurd.

"I'm glad you all got out all right," he said, running his fingers through his hair and looking back to the black hole in the side of the house.

"Jonathan, Caleb and I were out walking Savrene when it happened. Jean was in the house. He said Hubert fell on the table and the lamp started the fire. He ran upstairs and saved Samuel. I don't know how he got him out of that crib, but–" She looked at Jean with more love than any mother could possess. "He saved my baby." Tears filled her eyes, and she simply lowered her head and sobbed.

Jonathan set Jean to standing and lowered himself to his level. He wiped the soot from his cheeks and forehead with his sleeve and pushed his hair out of his eyes. He held his little head between his hands, looking him in the eyes.

"You did a very good thing tonight, Jean. A very good thing. I'm so proud of you."

Jean's bottom lip quivered and he fell into Jonathan's hug.

The rain drove down, and Aryl had to speak loudly to be heard.

"You'll need to get the coroner," he told one of Hubert's older friends. "We should get him out of the rain." He took off his jacket and put it around Ethel's shoulders, though it didn't help much. It was soaked through within minutes. He walked around to stand behind Caleb, touching his shoulder briefly.

"Help me get her out of the rain," Caleb asked when he looked up.

Aryl bent down. "Ethel. Let us help you get into the barn where it's dry. You're going to catch cold." She shook her head violently.

"No! I won't leave him!" She grabbed two fistfuls of his flannel, refusing to let go.

"You need to get out of the rain. It's getting worse," Aryl said gently as he looked up and squinted his eyes against the storm. It had been the house's saving grace. Without it, Aryl knew that a dozen men with buckets would not have been enough to keep the fire contained, much less put it out.

"No!" she screamed, still staring at Hubert's bloodless face.

"Mom–"

"Leave her." Aryl took his arm and lowered his voice. "This is the last few moments she has with him. Let her have them."

Caleb crumpled roughly beside his mother in a puddle of muddy rain that had collected around the body and dropped his head into his hands.

"I need to go look at the damage to the house and check on Caleb." Jonathan told the women huddled in the barn. "Jean, you stay here, you'll get soaked if you go out there." Jean shook his head and grabbed onto him.

"I'll be right back, I promise."

"Jean."

Jonathan turned slowly toward the sound of Ava's voice and saw her outstretched hand.

"We need someone to stay here and protect us. Will you?" He looked over the women and babies and nodded to Jonathan that he would stay. He walked over and sat as close to Arianna as possible, stroking the forehead of the baby she was nursing.

∞∞∞

"*L*ooks like the kitchen is completely destroyed. There's smoke and water damage a few feet into the living room, and the first five stairs are gone along with the banister," Aryl assessed. Jonathan and Aryl walked slowly through the darkened house, each holding a kerosene lamp to light the way. Jonathan turned to look at the charred hole where the door once stood.

"Well, they can't stay here. Not until all this is repaired."

"Caleb, Arianna and the babies can stay with us. We have the extra bedroom," Aryl offered.

"What about Ethel?"

"I think it would be best if she stayed with one of her close friends. She'd be more comfortable."

"You're probably right."

They walked out onto the smoke-blackened porch and saw that all of the volunteers had migrated to the barn. Caleb was helping Ethel walk, who looked on the verge of collapse. A fresh wave of hysteria and tears erupted as the coroner arrived to take Hubert's body.

Jonathan explained the extent of the damage and the sleeping arrangements for the night. Ethel's best friend, June, stood by her side with an arm around her.

"Ethel can stay with me as long as she needs to."

"All right. Caleb and I can go back inside and try to get whatever you might need for the next few days. The things upstairs should be fine, except for the smell of smoke." June rattled off a few things Ethel needed; Bible, toothbrush, robe, hairbrush. Jonathan made a mental list while telling Caleb to grab everything he could carry for the babies.

∞∞∞

Close to midnight, Arianna got the babies settled in the corner of the extra bedroom of Aryl's home. Jean's head wobbled heavily, but he fought to stay awake, clinging to Jonathan. He carried him inside Aryl's house, and Jean nodded off briefly on his shoulder while Jonathan said the usual words of consolation to Caleb. Caleb thanked Aryl for housing them and excused himself to bed, exhausted and emotionally drained.

Jonathan stood with Aryl after their friend had disappeared upstairs into the bedroom. He shifted Jean on his shoulder as he spoke.

"Rebuilding is going to begin as soon as the storm is over," Jonathan said quietly. "I know I don't need to ask, but I thought we could take some out of the business savings for supplies."

"Of course," Aryl agreed. "We're going to have to take some time off work. Maybe a week if some neighbors pitch in to help. What about Hubert's funeral? Who's going to be organizing that?" Jonathan went over his mental checklist, organizing the things he needed to address right away and things that could wait.

"I heard Caleb say his mother would with the help of their friends. I'm not so sure that's something he can handle right now." Aryl slumped down on the sofa, looking up as Jonathan continued. "I think it's best to keep Caleb busy. I'll come back in the morning. We can go back to the house and start making a list of things we'll need for rebuilding." Aryl nodded with a yawn, closing and opening his eyes in an exaggerated blink.

"I'm beat."

"We all need some sleep," Jonathan said as he made his way to the door. "I'll see you tomorrow then."

He walked out to the car where Ava was waiting and set Jean in the center of the narrow bench seat. He woke briefly, looking around in confusion and then slumped over onto Ava's arm. She moved hesitantly as she lifted his head to free her arm and put it around his shoulders. He melted into her side, and she held him loosely with both arms to keep him from falling forward in his deep sleep. Jonathan watched from the corner of his eye, silently relieved and deeply hopeful.

*June 16th 1930*

Ava was jarred from her sleep in the early hours of morning as howling winds shook the frame of the house. Poking her head out of the covers, she saw a light coming from the hall and that she was alone in bed. She pulled herself up groggily and slipped into her robe.

From the doorway, she could see a dim light coming from Jean's room. The door creaked briefly as she pushed it open and peeked inside. Jean lay on his stomach on the edge of the mattress with his arm hanging over the side, his hand connected to Jonathan's, who sat with folded arms on his knees, his back against the wall. He looked up and shrugged.

"Nightmares," he whispered.

"He's asleep now," she whispered back, walking toward him with a watchful eye on Jean.

"Every time I leave, he wakes up. After the third time, I just decided to stay." He leaned his head back on the wall and closed his eyes.

"What a terrible day," she whispered, sitting down next to him. Jonathan nodded in saddened agreement.

"Do you think Caleb will be okay?" She laid her head on his shoulder and held onto his arm.

"Eventually," Jonathan whispered back. "There's something he hasn't thought of yet, and I'm not sure whether to bring it up or let him come to it on his own."

"What?" Ava looked up at him.

"With his father gone, someone is going to need to run the farm. Caleb has been wanting off the boats. This may be his chance. Problem for us is that we need a third man. I'm not sure what we'd do if he decided to leave the operation." He stared ahead in the dim light, searching for solutions.

"Maybe he won't," Ava said and shrugged lightly.

"No. I think he will–" Ava put a finger to her lips as Jonathan's voice grew above a whisper.

"Think about it," he continued in a lower voice. "There's a lot that little farm produces that they can't do without. Milk, eggs, butter, and meat, not to mention the acres of wheat they use every year. Caleb has two children now. If anything, he needs to increase productivity." Ava laid her head back on his shoulder, too tired to think. Just as she dozed off, her head slid off Jonathan's shoulder and an image of Shannon holding one of her babies in the homemade sling flashed into her mind. Her head whipped around to face Jonathan.

"Patrick!" she cried. Jean stirred and shifted under his quilts. "Sorry," she whispered. "Patrick, Jonathan! He can take Caleb's place. He lost his job and they are on the verge of total ruin. They could make a new life here!" She could barely keep her excitement contained to a whisper. Jonathan grinned at her.

"That's a damned good idea," he said, nodding. "Good thinking, beautiful." She grinned back, albeit selfishly, at the thought of Shannon living close again.

"I'll talk to Aryl. Caleb, too, for that matter, so he knows there's no pressure. I can telegram Patrick and maybe you could follow up with a letter, explaining the details? We might could even help a little with getting them out here, depending on how much it costs to rebuild part of the hou–" He interrupted himself with a hearty yawn.

"Go back to bed," Ava whispered, but Jonathan shook his head and looked at Jean helplessly.

"I'll just be back here in ten minutes."

"Go. I'll stay."

"Are you sure?"

"I am. Go. You need your rest. You've got a house to help rebuild." She slipped her hand in between Jonathan and Jean's and took his place against the wall. He bent down and looked at their hands briefly before giving her a long but modest kiss.

"Thank you," he whispered. Ava gave him a little smile and leaned her head on the mattress, Jean's hand curled inside hers.

∞∞∞

Everyone met outside the farmhouse just before noon as neighbors came from miles away to help in what small way they might. Caleb set to work taking care of the animals that had been neglected the previous afternoon. Deep-set brow lines and bloated eyes hid the joyous milestone of the babies sleeping through the night for the first time. They had woken twice, fussed briefly and, just as Caleb pulled his eyes open, settled quickly.

Aryl walked through the house with a notebook along with one of the older neighbors, skilled in carpentry. He pulled away large chunks of blackened plaster in the kitchen to reveal little damage to the framework. "That's going to make our job a lot easier," the old man said and smiled. "I'd say a week, give or take a day. Should have this place livable again." He looked around as he spoke, grimacing at the grunge covered icebox and stove. "I'll ask around, see about getting some appliances."

"That's great. Thank you for all your help." Aryl followed him around as he finished inspecting the damage, taking notes and making lists.

∞∞∞

Jonathan joined Caleb in the barn and quietly took a seat next to him as he milked their cow, Hannah.

"She's hurting," Caleb said as he worked. "Missed two milkings." Jonathan watched his hands' rhythmic motions as Hannah made low grunts of relief.

"I wanted to talk to you about something. I was going to wait, but the sooner we get a plan together, the better. I already spoke with Aryl." Caleb remained focused on Hannah's udders with a scowl. "Look, I know you've wanted off the boats for a while now. I think there's a way we can make that happen." Caleb stopped milking and looked up at him.

"How?"

"We could send for Patrick. We can help him and Shannon get here, and he could take your place. You'd be free to work here full-time." Caleb rubbed his forehead, deep in thought and shook his head in disappointment.

"I just can't see how . . . I need to do both, Jon, and I don't know how I'm going to do that."

"What do you mean, do both?"

"I need to keep things going here, even just producing for our own use, but I need to make money, too." His shoulders drooped and he looked up, discouraged. "I don't know how I'm going to do both."

"Why don't we do this?" Aryl walked in and leaned on Hannah's left haunch. "You take some time off, get things in order around here. We'll ask Patrick. He's a quick study, so it won't take him any time at all to outwork the both of us combined. We'll save every cent and get that fourth boat up and running. You can use that." He nodded out toward the acre of blueberries visible from the barn window. "And spend time here. You might need to hire a hand to help–" Caleb opened his mouth to protest. Aryl raised his eyebrows and continued. "There are a lot of folks that need work right now and will take what pay they can get. Maybe next year Arianna can expand the garden and for now, you can pay a hand partially in produce come fall." He shrugged his shoulders with his suggestion and waited. Caleb sat pondering the suggestion.

"I don't see how I can pay for the boat repairs; we've parted the hell out of that thing-"

"Let us worry about that," Jonathan said. There was a long pause before he looked up with gratitude.

"I don't know what I'd do without you guys," he said quietly. "Thanks."

"Don't mention it." Jonathan turned to leave, immediately kicking the plan into action. "I'm going to run into town to send Patrick a telegram, and Ava can get started on a letter."

"Think he'll go for it?" Caleb called after him.

"I do. It's getting bad in the city. They've got nothing to lose," he said as he rounded the corner with long strides.

Aryl looked around the barn. "What else needs to be done in here?"

"Pigs. They need to be fed and their bedding changed." Aryl walked over and smiled at the massive sow surrounded by noisy, wiggling, pink piglets. He filled their trough with feed from a large drum outside the pen and cleared the hay while they were distracted.

A small shadow caused Caleb to look up, and he halfheartedly smiled at Jean. "Hey, fella. What are you doing?"

"My Dadee left. Can I stay with you? Can I help?" The large cow swung her head around to look at Jean and let out a long "Moo" that made Jean giggle.

"Sure. We'll find something for you to do," Caleb said with a smile.

"What about the chickens?" Aryl asked from across the barn. "Want to feed the chickens?" Jean nodded excitedly, and Aryl grabbed a bucket as Caleb directed him to the chicken feed.

Outside, he showed Jean how to scatter the feed, and Jean squealed as all the chickens surrounded him, clucking wildly, and pecking the food from the ground. Ava stood by the front of the house where the women had gathered to assign the needed cleaning work and designate who was to provide food on which days. Jean's giggles grabbed Ava's attention as the chickens chased him, then he turned to chase the chickens, feed spilling out of the bucket as he ran. She smiled, remembering that it was her daily chore with her aunt to feed their small flock of chickens. It was her favorite responsibility as a child.

One of the older women handed her a note with her jobs and days to provide lunch listed, and she walked over to the chicken coop, tucking the list into her pocket.

"Did you know they have names?" she called. Jean turned, startled at her voice and smiled shyly.

"No. What are they?" he asked.

"Well, that one is called 'fried'. And that one is 'roast'." She pointed as she spoke with a grin. "That's 'casserole' over there and 'cordon bleu' is in the corner." He giggled and walked over to her.

"Want to help me?" he asked, holding up the bucket.

"Sure." She went into the pen and took a handful of grain. "Spread it like this." She spread the grain in a sweeping motion in front of her. "That way they can all get some, and they won't fight over a small pile." He nodded and spread it into hardly more than a scattered pile.

"Keep practicing," she encouraged and showed him again. Aryl stood at the entrance of the barn watching them with a half-smile.

"Hey," he called to Caleb. "Come look at this." Caleb stood with Aryl for several minutes as they watched Ava and Jean's first authentic interaction.

*June 18th 1930*

*W*ork on the house stopped for the day of the funeral. Jonathan Sr. and Margaret offered their house to receive mourners afterward. The work of preparing food for the guests had kept them busy late into the night. The hushed atmosphere of soft music, sniffles and tears, and long, silent hugs lingered heavily in the house. Ethel sat in the corner, dressed in black with sagging eyelids, the corners of her mouth turned down, and although it took concentration she would not remember rallying, she acknowledged loved ones and friends as they took turns to sit near her, and offer their condolences. She gave a weak smile and a polite thank you to most, cried with some and laughed modestly with Hubert's men friends, who told stories of Hubert's antics and sense of humor; their way of consoling indirectly. Praise and gratitude was extended to Jean whenever the story was shared of his heroic act in saving Samuel. He beamed with pride and watched Samuel with brotherly love. The sudden appearance of Jean and his questionable origin was not spoken of by the majority, but the few who dared to whisper impolitely had recoiled from the sting of Arianna's harsh tongue.

Caleb avoided the crowd and direct sympathy by remaining outside. Jonathan and Aryl wandered in and out of the house alternately, never leaving him alone for more than few minutes. They brought him a plate of food and sat together on the wooden bench at the back of the house.

"Remember when we sat back here as kids?" Caleb gave a short laugh.

"We got caught doing something and were in trouble. I don't remember what we did, do you, guys?" Aryl asked, grinning.

"God only knows. There were so many times."

"All I remember is us sitting here while we waited for Jon's dad to go get our folks," he said.

"I remember," Jonathan said, smiling. "Sitting here, I mean. And I remember getting whooped, but I don't remember what for. Must not have been that bad." He shrugged, picking at his food. They sat quietly, each remembering numerous times they awaited punishment together on the bench for childhood antics that seemed like a really good idea at the time.

"I'm glad I made peace with him before . . . ." Caleb said quietly.

∞∞∞∞

"*D*adee!" Before Jonathan stirred, Ava woke, slipped out of bed, and tiptoed into Jean's room.

"Where's Dadee?" he asked, his cheeks stained from tears.

"He's sleeping. He's very tired. Is it all right if I sit with you?" she asked.

He nodded, scooting over for her. She sat with her back against the headboard and pulled the covers back up over him.

"Nightmares again?" she asked. He nodded and sniffled.

"I had many nightmares when I was a child after my parents died. What do you dream about? Sometimes it helps to talk about it," she said.

"The fire." His voice was shaky. "I dream I can't get Samuel out of the crib... and the fire burns us."

"You wouldn't have left him there, would you?" She spoke the obvious with admiration. "If you couldn't have gotten him out of the crib, you would have stayed with him." She pushed his bangs from his forehead, so she could better see Jonathan's eyes in the dim light.

"Yes," he said without hesitation.

"That's very admirable, Jean," she said with a sigh. "There are many adults who couldn't be that brave."

"I don't feel brave when I dream," he said shamefully.

"Do you know what you need?" she asked. "A good luck charm. Something to keep the bad dreams away."

"Is there such a thing?" he asked, raising his head off the pillow.

"I'll be right back." She disappeared into the dark hallway. A moment later, she reappeared with something in her hands and repositioned herself beside him.

"This is very special. I want you to take good care of it, all right?" He nodded with sincere, promising eyes as she showed him Maura's cross.

"Someone special gave this to Jonathan when he was having... nightmares, and, just recently, he gave it to me when I was very sad. He said it should always be with someone who needs it. And I think," she lifted the corner of his pillow as she spoke, "that if you keep it here, it will keep the nightmares away."

"Do you believe this?"

"I do. It worked for me. Will you give it a try?" she asked with a smile, and nudged his head back down.

"Will you stay here until I fall asleep?" he asked, yawning.

"I will." She put her hand lightly on his back as he closed his eyes.

"Thank you," he whispered.

The child spoke the words, but she heard Jonathan's voice.

*June 19ᵗʰ 1930*

The formalities of mourning now behind them, people arrived at the farmhouse and began the healing process with the sweat of labor. Jonathan helped Caleb pitch hay into a pile for Hannah, then they surveyed the bustling work site from the barn door. Older women stood around a large, metal tub over a fire. Each of them held a washboard and scrubbed the pungent smoke out of any fabric washable from the house. Jared and Sam, two of Hubert's closest friends, carried long two-by-fours on their shoulders into the house, which produced the typical sounds of construction: hammering, clanking, occasional clatter of burnt rubbish thrown out onto the porch, whooping laughter and a string of curses that set one of the washing women off into a long-winded reprimand which included her husband's full name.

The younger generation worked in the garden, trying to save what they could from the storm's damage, and the youngest walked around with buckets, picking up garbage and burnt items tossed from the house.

"I don't know how I can ever repay them," Caleb said, clearly moved.

"Maybe we could have a party when it's finished. A big picnic," Jonathan suggested. "We could shoot old Hannah there and have steak," he said and grinned.

Caleb let out a laugh. "No, we need her for milk . . . but we could have *pork*." They both looked back slowly at the sow in the pen.

"I was going to wait until fall, but . . . ." He watched the many people who took time out of their busy, struggling lives to help. "I think that's a good idea."

On their way back to the house, an old truck came rattling up the bumpy drive. A metal clanking sound came from the bed, but the old cast-iron wood stove wasn't visible until the truck backed up to the porch. Abe Prescott threw the driver's side door closed with a tinny slam and waved at Caleb. "Got something for yah," he yelled and motioned for him to come closer. "Had this laying around, needs cleaning up, but it'll work fine until you can replace it," he said, smiling wide and toothless, motioning for help to lift it out of the truck. It took eight men to lower it to the ground and the women descended upon it with rags and scrub brushes, admiring the old relic.

*June 21ˢᵗ 1930*

The bulk of the major renovation reached completion by early Saturday afternoon, and a group of women armed with buckets went to work cleaning every inch of the smoke-damaged interior. Ethel walked around in amazement. This was her first return to the house since the fire. She looked tired, but with the early stage of shock past, Caleb could see she was moving into the long process of grief adjustment as he walked with her quietly.

"It's amazing," she said, moving from the kitchen to the living room. "It was so wonderful of everyone to help."

"There's work until Monday, and then we should be able to move back in. I thought we would have a cookout on Tuesday afternoon to thank everyone."

"I think that's a great idea," said two women in unison from the hearth where they were scrubbing.

"I know it'll be hard, Mom. We can move some stuff around." She looked over the living room slowly and then set her gaze to the window facing the blueberry trees.

"He's still here. I can feel it."

"Let me know if there's anything you want me to, you know, take out to the barn." She followed his eyes to his father's chair where he had sat every night.

"No. Leave it there," she said with a wistful smile. "Please, leave it there. So I can sit with him."

∞∞∞

"I can't believe how great you look. It hasn't even been two months, Ahna!" Claire said. "I hope I bounce back that quickly." She turned to Ava, who was holding Samuel while Arianna fed Savrene. "How are you feeling?"

"Fine now. I felt sick a lot during the beginning, but everything has been so hectic, I hardly noticed. I'm going to have to start letting out my clothes soon, though." She looked down at her dress, which strained slightly over the small bulge of her lower stomach.

"Just think! Next summer, we're going to have four children between us." Arianna laughed in amazement. "How did that happen?"

"Five," Ava said quietly, picking at the grass with her free hand.

"Yes. Jean." Arianna glanced at Claire, then Ava. "I just didn't know how you'd feel if, well, if I included him."

"Well, he's here. He's a child. He's Jon's, so . . . ." She raised one shoulder in concession. "That makes him mine, too, I suppose." Ava gave a strained smile.

"What changed?" Claire asked bluntly.

Ava looked out into the yard at the shiny, new door on the old house bustling with volunteers, then to Aryl and Jonathan laughing together near the barn as Jean clung to his father's leg. She didn't tell them about Elyse's letter, Maura's love and support from afar, Jonathan's confession, or giving Jean the cross.

She answered with tranquility, "Everything."

*June 22ᵈ 1930*

"You're taking a trip, Mr. Drayton?" Grayson stood at the bedside ready, if asked, to help Victor pack his suitcase. His employer packing his own luggage was unusual.

"Yes. I'll be gone until mid-week or so. Make sure Mrs. Drayton doesn't stray far while I'm gone, would you?" He gave at tight, irritated smile.

"Of course, sir. What time shall I have the car ready to leave?"

"Have it ready in an hour. But I won't be taking the train. I'll be driving myself."

Grayson smiled nervously. "Going on an adventure, sir?"

"Yes, Grayson, something like that." His black eyes flashed. "Where's my coat?" he asked.

"It was laundered last week. I'll call the maid to retrieve it, although it *is* rather warm for a coat, sir."

"Just go get it." Victor waved him away, annoyed, and resumed his packing.

Grayson returned with the long, dark coat over his arm and looked even more unnerved. "There's someone here to see you, sir." Victor snatched the coat and tossed it into the leather bag. He glanced at his watch and cursed under his breath.

"He's early," he growled. "Grayson, get the car. I'll be leaving sooner than expected." He zipped the bag and headed downstairs.

Outside, Victor was handed a set of instructions. Two good-sized boxes were tucked in the back seat. "Be sure to follow these instructions *in the order* I've written them."

"You've told me and showed me a dozen times. I can handle this," he said, stuffing the paper in his pocket.

"I still don't understand why you won't send me? This is, after all, my area of expertise."

"For the reason that this is personal, that's why. I want the satisfaction of a job well-done *by me*." His smile was unsettling. His malevolent educator raised his hands in submission.

"Besides," Victor said, taking a step closer and lowering his voice, "if I sent you to do this, you wouldn't be here to take care of my other problem." He glanced toward the house. "Remember," Victor held up a finger in warning, "what I said. Quiet and neat. No loose ends."

"A man doesn't get to charge what I do by being messy or leaving loose ends," he said with confident arrogance. Victor hurled him a final smug look before pulling out onto Fifth Avenue.

*June 24ᵗʰ 1930*

"We really appreciate you putting us up, Aryl," Caleb said sincerely as they carried armloads of things upstairs in the rebuilt home.

"It's no trouble." He pushed the bedroom door open and let his armload spill onto the bed. "I'm just sorry for the circumstances."

"Me, too." Caleb set a stack of diapers and blankets inside the crib, and then stopped to stare at a stuffed bear that was propped in the corner. "You know what's strange? The babies have slept through the night ever since it happened. And Savrene's colic has all but disappeared." Aryl raised his eyebrows.

"Really? That's great."

"It's strange."

"Don't question it. Just be grateful for it," Aryl said as they returned downstairs.

Ethel had begun teaching Arianna the art of cooking on a wood-fired antique. Jonathan bounded onto the back porch and into the kitchen.

"Caleb," he said breathlessly. "I just got a telegram from Patrick. He said yes. It must have gotten delayed somehow, but they are going to be here on the noon train tomorrow."

"That fast?" Aryl pulled a chair out and sat down. "We haven't even talked about where to put them up."

"Well, we have plenty of room here," Caleb said, "until we figure something else out."

"Once Patrick is taught, you're free." He understood the misery of doing a job every day that you hated; or, at the very least, *didn't love*. Jonathan had come to love fishing. And Caleb loved this small farm.

He leaned back and smiled. "I really appreciate that. But I'll still go out with you guys a couple days a week."

Earlier that morning, Aryl had started the roasting fire in the pit and Jonathan and Caleb had heaved the massive swine from the tree where it drained to the fire pit.

"You boys better check on that pig if there's going to be a dinner. Folks'll be showing up here this afternoon," Ethel warned while preparing to make a vat of potato salad. She had gone into work mode, Caleb noticed, and kept her hands and mind busy every waking moment of the day.

Ava was all smiles, looking forward to seeing Shannon again and helping them resettle in the town. Jean stayed close to her side.

Just before dinner was called, Caleb stood up and got everyone's attention. Many families were scattered about the yard; some at small tables and others on blankets circling out from the main food table. They all quieted down to a hush.

"I just wanted to thank everyone for everything you've done. It's amazing," he said, admiring the house. "And it's hard to believe it only took a week. Thanks to everyone for all your hard work. This dinner isn't nearly enough to repay all of you. Or express our gratitude–"

"It's plenty enough, we're starving already!" toothless Abe yelled out. Caleb laughed. "All right, everyone. Let's eat!"

He carved piles of pork for a large platter and thanked each person as they helped themselves to the meat. Caleb glanced over at Arianna sitting on a blanket. The dozing babies lay close together, and Savrene tightly held a fistful of Samuel's sleeper. When everyone had filled their plates, Caleb walked toward his family with two plates of food. Friends, old and young, adorned the multitude of blankets and quilts that dotted the yard; a simple meal and fellowship the reward for a week's worth of hard work and charity. Jean sat in between Ava and Jonathan under a small tree. Aryl and Claire sat close together in the sun by the porch. Claire was listening intently as Aryl talked nearly nonstop, pausing occasionally to eat. It was quieter now as everyone feasted, and Caleb was grateful for a peaceful moment. He lowered a plate of food to Arianna as she smiled, squinting up against the sun.

"Thank you."

"You're welcome. Are you excited about Patrick and Shannon?" Arianna moved so Caleb could snuggle in between her and the babies.

Nodding, she said, "I'm so excited." She covered her mouthful of food with her hand. "I've missed her so much."

"I think she's going to be quite impressed with you. How much you've changed." He shook his head slightly as if he himself still couldn't believe her transformation.

"Are you okay?" she asked after several moments.

"Everyone has helped so much that it astounds me. I guess we spent so much time in the city that I forgot how decent and charitable people can be." He looked over the gathering and smiled. "It really helps with what happened. I don't know whether it should or not." He looked at Arianna as if waiting for her to agree or disagree. "I feel like I should be grieving harder, mourning deeper. I almost feel guilty for being so, well, *happy*."

"Don't feel guilty. Your father wouldn't want you to wallow in grief and stop living life. I think you're doing and feeling exactly what you should be right now." She slipped her hand into his. His eyes panned over the small farm that was now his. It was made official with the reading of the will at the dining room table the day before. The two conditions of the inheritance were simple and Caleb had no problem with agreeing to them; his mother was to stay on with him for the rest of her days, and he was to never, ever, sell the farm to any non-blood relative.

Just before dusk, Aryl made the suggestion while leaning against the porch rail.

"Jon, why don't you go and pick them up? Me and Caleb can handle it tomorrow." All of the neighbors had gone home, full and tired; Caleb had put away the last of the extra tables and chairs in the barn while

Arianna settled the babies upstairs. Ava and Jonathan sat on the porch swing and watched Jean run around the yard with a mason jar trying to catch crickets.

"Sure," Jonathan agreed. "I hate to miss another day, though. We're already so far behind."

"Well, one of us would miss a day regardless, and the next day Patrick will be with us, so we'll make up for any lost time." Aryl lifted up his arm as Claire ducked under it and wrapped both arms around his waist.

"True. Okay, I'll go get them and bring them here. Let's all meet up in the evening. There's got to be enough leftovers for another dinner."

"Several dinners," Claire said. She had just finished helping Ethel put away the food for the night.

Ava's head jerked as Jean's bloodcurdling scream crossed the yard. She jumped from the swing and ran down the stairs, but was unable to see what was wrong in the dim light of the remaining sunset.

Jonathan was behind her, but she already had Jean scooped up in her arms by the time he caught up with her.

"Bee sting," she informed with a pout. She carried him into the house as he shook his hand and cried on her shoulder. Claire followed her and helped as Ava pulled the still pulsing stinger out, packed the throbbing finger with a baking soda paste and wrapped it up in a piece of cloth. His tears had slowed to a whimper by the time she carried him back out to the porch where Jonathan and Aryl abruptly ended a private conversation.

"All better," she said, putting him down in front of Jonathan.

Claire resumed her place nestled against Aryl and yawned.

"Come on, let's get you home," he said quietly. "You've got to be exhausted."

"In a few minutes," she sighed.

Arianna's figure cast a shadow on the porch as she closed the screen door behind her softly. She smiled and waved as Caleb emerged from the dark yard into the light. "They're finally asleep," her whisper heard just over the crickets and light winds rustling through the trees. Caleb stood next to her and she kicked off her shoes to stand equal height to him.

"We should all get together more often. We don't do that enough anymore," he said, taking Arianna's hand and looking at his friends.

"We should," Aryl agreed. Jean climbed up onto Jonathan's lap and whispered in his ear. Jonathan smiled and gave a little laugh.

"Yes, Jean, they'll like you." He rubbed his head. "Don't worry about that." Jonathan whispered in Jean's ear and his cheeks swelled with a large smile. "Go ahead," Jonathan whispered. "Ask her."

Jean looked hesitant as he stared at Ava for a moment. Finally, his voice barely audible, he asked his question.

"Do you like me . . . now?" Her eyes remained fixed on his; she realized, then, all the pain she had caused him with her rejection. The last slivers of ice in her heart melted, she held out her arms to him and he eagerly climbed into her lap.

"Yes, I like you, Jean," she said, hugging him tightly, the porch swing swaying lightly. The others looked on with appreciation for how difficult the last few months had been for them and in awe at how far Ava had come. In respect for the private moment, Aryl motioned with his eyes to Claire that they should leave.

As they walked down the squeaky steps, Jonathan called to him, just before they stepped beyond the soft glow of the front light.

"Aryl, you were right." He looked back to see Jonathan with Ava close at his side, holding Jean with her head resting down on his as they gently swayed. He narrowed his eyes in concentration and then followed Jonathan's quick glance at Ava. He smiled then, eyes full of conviction.

"Oh, yeah. *Miracles happen*," he said. He walked with Claire into the darkness of the yard, holding up one hand as he left.

*June 25th 1930*

Dawn came too soon for Caleb and Aryl, who boarded their boats with yawns and stretches. Caleb cursed under his breath as his boat's engine chugged and sputtered but refused to start.

"Hey, don't go yet," he yelled to Aryl. "I can't get her started. I might have to go with you." Aryl nodded as his boat engine idled roughly, but just as Caleb climbed on board, it cut out with a popping sound followed by a puff of black smoke.

"Great." Caleb held up the frayed ends of melted wires. "You're not going anywhere either." Aryl dropped his head, tired shoulders slumped, in worry of how they would be able to afford the unexpected repairs.

"C'mon, let's take the Ava-Maura. Jon won't mind," Caleb decided. "We need to make some money today." Aryl shrugged, yawned, and nearly tripped over a pot.

The sun had risen by the time they were underway, the Ava-Maura chugging reliably out into the open ocean.

The eastern sky was brilliant with a red sunrise.

∞∞∞∞

Ava and Arianna waited with excitement at the farmhouse as Jonathan took the Runabout to the train station. Ava took Caleb's place in changing, walking, and rocking one baby while Arianna nursed the other.

"Claire didn't want to come?" Arianna asked, disappointed.

"We stopped by to pick her up, but she wasn't feeling well. She'll be by this afternoon with Aryl after the sickness passes." Ava propped Samuel on her shoulder, patting his back.

"I never thought I'd be glad to see anything from that time in our lives." Arianna rocked slowly with Savrene, who was covered by the shoulder blanket. "But I'll be so glad to see Shannon."

"Me, too," Ava said, distracted by Maura's letter. She was excited to see Shannon, though, truth be told, if she had her choice of brash and loving Irish friends, it was Maura she would rather see and live close to.

She also knew that this was the end of the trio; the three women had been together through this entire ordeal, complementing each other's contrasting personalities in good times and bad. It never occurred to Ava that this would ever change. She had been sure, more in the throes of poverty than ever in the spoils of luxury, that it would always be just the three of them. But now there would be four. She wondered where Shannon would fit in and worried about who might be pushed out.

∞∞∞

"*P*atrick!" Jonathan stood on a bench, searching the crowded platform. He spotted Aislin sitting on Patrick's shoulders and waved. "Patrick!"

He looked around, focused on Jonathan, and lit up with a relieved smile. Jonathan hopped off the bench and waited for them to cut through the throng of travelers.

"Jon! Good to see you again!" A hearty handshake and back slaps were as close to an embrace as the two felt comfortable giving in public.

"You look good, Jon," Shannon said, grinning and reached to hug him. Patrick looked him over and then centered on his face. "Somethin's different." He pondered while Jonathan shrugged. "But fer the good, Jon, fer the good. Ye look better."

"Come on, I'll help you get your luggage," he said, taking the attention off himself. "I brought Caleb's father's . . . well, I guess it's Caleb's truck now. The telegram said you had three?"

"Two. Pared down last minute. We couldn't pay the extra fare for the third." They located the well-traveled trunks, and the men each took an end to heave them onto the bed of the truck.

"We really can't thank you enough for coming, Patrick," Jonathan said as he pulled onto the main road. "I know from experience that it's not easy for a man, a family, to just pack up bare necessities and leave a way of life behind."

"Nay, it's me who should be thanking you. I've never been so glad to leave a place before." He looked to Shannon, wedged between them, Roan sleeping on her shoulder. "I don't know what ye might have heard, but it was getting bad where we were. All over really. I guess it wasn't hard ta' pare down when there wasn't much to pare."

"Aside from selling a few things to get by, we were robbed three times. Almost everyone in the building's been robbed. If you're lucky, they wait until you're gone. But the one time, though, Shannon here hid in the bathroom with the babes while they had their pick of the place."

"Really, Patrick?"

"Aye. Tis a sad thing to be glad yer out o' work, so ye can protect yer wife and young." He shook his head in disgust.

"Well, you'll have a better life here. You won't be rich, but you can leave your family without worry."

"How is Arianna? And the others? I haven't heard from them in a bit now," Shannon interrupted.

"They're good. My Ava and Claire are expecting, but I'm sure you knew that from their letters. The twins are doing well. They keep Arianna very busy. That's probably why she hasn't written in a while."

"And Jean? How is he?" Shannon asked casually.

Jonathan looked uneasy for a moment. "Ava wrote you about him then?" he asked, wondering exactly what knowledge of him they had.

"Aye, she did, just a few weeks ago. Said he was settlin' in and lookin' forward to bein' a big brother."

"He is," he said slowly. He hadn't thought of how he would explain Jean to them.

"Tell me what I'll be doin', Jon. How big is this operation you've got up here, and where on earth are we sleepin' tonight?" Patrick relieved Jonathan with his curiosities.

"Catching lobster. That's what you'll be doing. And the operation is only three boats right now, but we're going to fix up the fourth, so Caleb can fish part-time. And you'll be staying with Caleb and Arianna until we get you set up in a permanent home. It's a large house, so you should be comfortable enough."

"Well, Jon, I can't tell you enough how grateful we are for the opportunity."

Jonathan laughed. "And I told you, Patrick, *we're* the grateful ones, especially Caleb. We're all having a picnic tonight to welcome you."

Aislin whined and wiggled in Patrick's lap. An entire day of sitting still had reduced her to a squirming mass that wanted to run, jump, and scream about. Jonathan looked out at the dark billows forming in the eastern sky.

"But we might have to change plans, if that comes at us too quickly."

"Looks threatenin' enough. Get lots o' storms like that around here?"

"Some don't turn out to be much. You can still work through them. But others come hard and fast with very little warning. There have been a couple of times when we've raced back to shore just before a powerful one hit." Shannon's mouth dropped open with a horrified expression. "But we know better now. We're very careful, and there hasn't been a close one like that in a long time. In fact, Aryl and Caleb, will probably be back in plenty of time before dinner."

∞∞∞∞

Caleb had picked up his pace and urged Aryl to do the same. Greenish, gray clouds and humid gusts of salty air had replaced the warmth of the early summer sun. Caleb scrutinized the storm in the distance with concern.

"We need to beat that. It's moving fast. Let's pull one more string and then head back. The rest can wait till tomorrow."

Rain began to fall, and the wind picked up considerably. Aryl sorted while Caleb pulled and they worked frantically. After the last pot in the string, Caleb nodded for Aryl to start the engines and head home. The rain fell in large, hard droplets now propelled by vicious winds that stung their faces and made it hard to see. Aryl frowned after the third attempt to start the engine failed. Just when Aryl thought they might have to hoist the sails that had never been used, the engine sputtered to life, and Aryl let out a deep, relieved breath. He wiped his soggy hair from his face and tilted his head to give Caleb an odd look. Caleb had heard it, too. He strained his ears against the roar of wind. They briefly heard a distant, muted ringing. Aryl stepped toward the entrance of the berth.

Slammed against the wheel, he had felt it before he heard it; the detonation merged with the screech of ripped metal and crunches of splintered planks, which drowned out Caleb's guttural scream. Aryl slid to the deck as profuse blood stains instantaneously materialized through the back of his shirt. Caleb was to him before his body had settled. He rolled him over and shouted breathlessly up to the dark heavens.

Aryl was still breathing.

He gripped two fistfuls of Aryl's shirt and shook him hard. Aryl's eyes rolled, found Caleb's face and he nodded weakly. Caleb struggled unsteadily to help him to his feet. Aryl's mouth moved and his eyes implored his friend frantically, but Caleb could only watch; his own ears ringing. He was helpless to understand or answer him. He dragged Aryl along while he began to pull wildly at the sails in an ingrained drive to save his own life, praying that the wind would push them back to shore before the boat sank. Aryl soberly stared at the sharp slant of the deck and the water lapping at his shoes.

Caleb screamed again, not from the stinging rain that welted his face and arms, but from the sight of the sails now pulled several feet into the air. They had been cut. Long, clean, and deliberate slices that continued to tear into sloppy shreds as Caleb grabbed hold to yank them violently. He skimmed the ocean through the storm-shadowed distance and saw a few boats heading in to beat the storm; it was unlikely they had witnessed the explosion and smoke through the swirling winds and heavy rain.

Paralyzed in every aspect, Aryl's crazed eyes powerlessly met the towering rogue wave that barreled toward the crippled boat off the port side. Ears bleeding, he could hear neither the roar of the ocean nor the splintering of the boat from the second explosion.

He had only one thought–*Claire*.

The massive wave entrenched it all and washed both men into the Atlantic.

∞∞∞

"*I*'m so glad to see you again!" Arianna said as the two women hugged and traded babies to cuddle.

"Ye have no idea how wonderful it is to be here," Shannon said, smiling. "It's so clean, so fresh . . . like *home*." Through the kitchen window, she watched Aislin running in the yard with Jean, the darkened sky just beginning to spill. "I'm just so happy ye thought of us when ye needed help. It'll help the both of us, to be sure."

"Come on, I'll show you your room. You'll all have to share, but Caleb was talking about refurbishing the old cabin at the edge of the property and letting you use that."

"A cabin?" Shannon asked, delighted.

"Yes, but it's old and uninhabitable right now. But with some hard work, we could make it nice."

Claire sat close to Ava, already feeling somewhat pushed to the side as Arianna and Shannon reunited.

Upstairs, Shannon was appreciative of the clean and quaint room provided, although it was small for four people. Arianna had rearranged it so that the children would be on one side and the parents on the other.

Jonathan showed Patrick around outside and kept an eye on Jean and Aislin. Patrick was cheerful as he admired the large garden and barn. Jonathan Sr. and Margaret were the last ones to arrive for dinner and Aryl's mother accused them of parking on a deserted road along the way. Jonathan Sr. grinned and contemplated going along with the tease until Margaret poked him in the side.

"I had to clean up the grease and muck. I have that old truck almost running," he said proudly, smiling at Jonathan. "And I've had two inquiries on it, too. Might have it sold before it's finished." Michael, who looked somewhat interested, moved to talk to him about his project.

Jonathan sat down beside Ava and glanced at his watch. "I wonder where those guys are?" He jumped, smiling. "What are you doing?" he whispered out of the corner of his mouth. She grinned devilishly, as she slid her hand up Jonathan's thigh.

An hour later, Ethel called everyone to dinner. "We're not going to wait for the slowpokes. It's hot and ready, so help yourself."

Everyone filed into the kitchen, served themselves, and then crowded around the table. Arianna and Shannon huddled together talking and giggling, making plans for the following week. Ava sat beside Jonathan but watched Claire, who stood at the kitchen window staring out into the driving rain.

A few moments later, she saw a vehicle pull into the drive and faced the room with a relieved smile. "They're here," she said and began making a plate of food for Aryl. Arianna, wanting to show off her new skills of domestic devotion, jumped up to join her.

"Sheriff Vincent." Jonathan opened the door, but his smile had disappeared. "What can we do for you?" The sheriff removed his hat, shook it outside the door, and stepped gingerly inside the kitchen that had suddenly fallen quiet. His eyes were grave and only made contact with Jonathan's.

"Ah . . . I'm afraid there's been an accident," he said regretfully with a heavy northeastern accent.

"What kind of accident?" Jonathan asked. Claire stood stock-still at the stove, staring at the wall behind, plate suspended in mid-air. Arianna turned to face them and put a hand on Claire's shoulder to steady herself as all the blood drained from her face.

"The details are sketchy, but there was an explosion. And the storm–" He turned to glance out the door. "No, that didn't help, but, ah, well," The Sheriff always hated this part of his job. There was no piece of good that could be pulled from informing people of a loss, a tragedy. The air was thick with anticipation and dread as he cleared his throat and finally said, "The Ava-Maura went down earlier today–"

The plate fell, shards of glass and food lay at Claire's feet. The hand that dropped the plate now gripped Arianna's arm, fingers digging into her flesh; Claire hadn't turned from the wall.

"Wait, the Ava-Maura–but that's *my* boat!" Jonathan cried.

"Like I said, Mr. Garrett. The details are sketchy at present. All we know is that there was an explosion. The Ava-Maura was lost, but luckily there was another boat in the area when it happened. There was one survivor."

"*One*," he whispered.

"I am very sorry."

Jonathan stared in disbelief as the Sheriff nodded grimly.

"Which one?" Jonathan asked, blinking, as a lump rose in his throat.

"I don't know. He's being treated at the hospital in Gloucester with minor injuries. Deputy will give him a ride home after he's released an–"

"*Which one!*" Jonathan roared. Everyone in the room startled, including the sheriff despite his training.

"I told you, sir, I don't know. I got the message third hand. *Everything I have told you is everything that I know*. Deputy will bring him by, probably a few hours from now." The sheriff bowed his head in condolence as he left the silent room and closed the door behind him. Jonathan roused from his daze and followed him out the door.

"Wait!"

Sheriff Vincent turned, shielding his face from the driving rain.

"The *other* one, we should be *looking* for him," Jonathan said desperately.

"It's too rough out there, Mr. Garrett. We'll assemble a search party when the storm passes."

Jonathan jumped off the porch and grabbed him from behind. He spun him around and slammed him against his vehicle.

"No! We need to be out there looking, we can't just, just *leave* him!" he yelled over the storm's wind.

"Mr. Garrett. I understand your grief, but you need to *calm down*, and more importantly, take your hands *off me* before I'm forced to take you in."

Jonathan let go of the uniform with a slight shove and glowered at him.

"I can't just leave him out there," he said piteously.

"I wish there was something I could do. I know every man in the area will volunteer to join in a search once it's safe enough to go out. I'm afraid that's all that can be done."

Jonathan stared at the ground helplessly, oblivious of the complete saturation of the storm.

Inside, everyone sat in stunned silence. Arianna and Claire held hands by the stove, supporting each other. They locked eyes for what seemed like an eternity.

One of them was looking at a widow; each selfishly, guiltily, prayed it wasn't herself.

Jonathan returned, soaked through and avoiding eyes. "Could someone make a pot of coffee? It's going to be a long night." He sat down hard and wiped his face dry with some napkins. Ava stood behind him, bracing his shoulders tightly, and they all began the long wait. Jean and Aislin sensed the tension and played quietly in the living room, breathing nothing above a whisper for the next few hours.

By ten o'clock, the rain had nearly stopped, and the wind had died down to a heavy breeze. The engine rolling up the driveway was easy to hear above the silence of fearful expectation. Jonathan's head suddenly jerked up. Everyone looked at Arianna, whose breathing had suddenly become loud and erratic, tears streaming down her face.

"I can't," she whispered. "I can't go . . . I don't want to . . . What if?" Patrick and Shannon each supported an arm and guided her as she moved toward the porch to learn her husband's fate. The older women rocked the babies, sharing looks of fear, doubt, and apprehension.

"Claire?" Jonathan held out his hand. Her head bobbed slightly as her eyes traveled from the door to Jonathan and back to the door again. She took an unsteady step. He moved quickly to her side and then walked with her slowly, a strong and supportive arm around her. Ava held her other side and her hand.

They stood together on the porch, and the car seemed to take an eternity to crawl the drive. The deputy parked at an angle, and although they strained, they couldn't make out who was in the passenger side; the light not sufficient to identify a face. The deputy stepped out and walked around the car.

Jonathan tried to steel himself. In a moment, everything would change. One of his childhood friends, a brother, was gone, lost to the sea. The anticipation of this was agony; and in the last moment, he suddenly didn't wish to know. *It's better to wonder than to grieve,* he thought and he held onto Claire as much for himself as for her. Patrick watched Arianna closely. The deputy opened the passenger door and leaned inside for a moment.

No one breathed.

The deputy placed Aryl's sea bag on top of the vehicle and Arianna let out a ragged, strangled cry.

Then Caleb's head slowly rose above the car and turned toward the house.

Claire screamed and collapsed to her knees. Jonathan buckled beside her, his hard face shattered. He held Claire's shoulders tightly. She was momentarily silenced by shock, eyes wide in disbelief, her arms bound to herself tightly. When she found her voice, a gut wrenching and primal scream shook her whole body. She grabbed Jonathan and tore at his shirt as another scream doubled her over. He went over with her, his own muffled sobs joining hers.

Arianna looked down at her, briefly felt agonizing guilt for her own relief, and then rushed down the stairs to Caleb. She crashed into him, nearly knocking him over, his bandaged arm cradled in a sling wedged between them. Her hold around his neck nearly choked him, and she sobbed unevenly. Caleb could barely make out through his tear-filled eyes Claire's crumpled body on the porch, as she shook her head violently in defiance of reality, still grabbing at Jonathan, crying "No! No! No!" woefully.

Caleb withdrew his gaze, lowering his head to Arianna's neck as Claire began to beg Jonathan. She pleaded for him to tell her it wasn't true, and when he couldn't, she scrambled suddenly to her feet, trying to push Jonathan off the porch.

"Go get him, Jonathan! Please! There's still time! He's out there! You can go get him! You can save him! Please!" Jonathan shook his head in regret. She screamed at him so strongly her voice cracked.

"He saved you! You have to save him!"

Jonathan felt his heart rip out of his chest and he lowered his head, shaking it. "I can't, Claire. I'm so sorry. There's no chance . . . ."

Her outraged face blurred, and he choked back another sob. "If I could, Claire, I would have already been out there."

She started beating him on the chest and shoulders with fists, screaming. He grabbed her wrists, and she writhed against him with grunts and cries then went limp with a long wail and disintegrated into a brokenhearted mound on the porch, weakly attempting to beat the wooden planks. He knelt again and hovered over her, letting her cry and curse him. Ethel had moved past Claire quietly and hurried to hug her son.

Michael and Kathleen had retreated into the living room at the first sight of Caleb. They sat together; crying, grieving for their son.

∞∞∞∞

In the early hours of the morning, the doctor came down the stairs, rubbing his bloodshot eyes. "She's sleeping. She should be out for several hours." He placed a wrinkled hand on Jonathan's shoulder. "It's anyone's guess whether she'll lose the baby. But it's best to keep her as calm as possible." He set an amber bottle on the table in front of Jonathan. After taking a hard look at him, he moved it in front of Ethel. "Give her two teaspoons of this every few hours when she wakes up. There's enough for several days; try to keep her sedated through the funeral."

"All right," Ethel agreed and nodded her head toward Jonathan, who sat with beard stubble and vacant, swollen eyes.

"Why don't you let me give you something for rest, too, Jon?" he offered. Jonathan jerked a little; he shook his head and downed the last of his coffee.

"No. It'll be light soon. We'll be heading out . . . to look." The doctor relented with a sigh and ambled toward the door.

"I'll be back in a day or two. Send for me if you need me." He bestowed a look of sympathy to all in the room and left quietly.

∞∞∞∞

"*No!*" Arianna demanded, pulling at his shirt. "You can't go! I won't let you!" Just before dawn, Caleb had spent several minutes trying to calm Arianna, who refused to let him go.

"Ahna, I *have* to. I have to try to help." He cleared his throat and squeezed his eyes against fresh tears. "He's out there," he whispered. "And we have to find him." A loud and pitiful cry came from upstairs and he looked painfully toward the stairs. "If it had been me–" he began and Arianna shook her head violently.

"Don't say that, don't ever say that."

"But if it had been, Ahna, wouldn't you want them to bring me home?" Tears slipped down their cheeks at the same time.

"Thank God it wasn't you," she said and hugged him tightly.

*June 26th 1930*

Morning's first light found three dozen men volunteering their time and boats to search for one of their own. There was little hope of a recovery, but no one would say that out loud. And so they did what they would want done if it had been one of them; at least *look*.

Jonathan laid out a chart on the hood of Caleb's truck and assigned each man a different area to search. Caleb pointed out his best guess of the area where the explosion took place. Jonathan ordered two boats to that location and another two vessels were to scout the shoreline twenty miles in each direction. Everyone else was assigned an area extending from the shore to the accident site. Then Caleb and Jonathan boarded the harbormaster's vessel.

Caleb sat against the side of the boat, his head in his hands. He swayed slightly as the boat rocked and kept his head low as he choked randomly and cleared his throat hard several times. Jonathan sat beside him and looked briefly at the sky, prepared now to know.

"What happened?" he asked numbly. Caleb shook his head, still cradled in his hands.

"It happened so fast," he started, having to clear his throat again.

"Start at the beginning. How did you end up in my boat?" Jonathan's bloodshot eyes focused on the side of Caleb's bent head, and he tugged at his sleeve. "Talk to me." Caleb took a deep breath and recounted the day. Jonathan stopped him several times, having him repeat accounts of the explosion and then the shredded sails.

"Shredded? But they were fine—"

"I can't figure it out. I think there was a second explosion . . ." he trailed off and stared blankly ahead as he spoke. "There was a wave so big. I've never seen one so big . . . next thing I know, I'm underwater not knowing which way was up. When I finally found the surface, I saw the bow of the Ava-Maura just before it went under. It was so hard to stay afloat with the waves and the wind, it was hard to see . . . but I saw Aryl. I know he came back up at least . . . for a moment. He was maybe ten yards from me. He was pointing at a smaller fishing boat headed our way. I bobbed as high as I could so they would see us and screamed as loud as I could. There were pieces of the boat floating all around. I hung onto one until they got close. When I looked back . . . he was gone. He had lost a good amount of blood, Jon." Caleb was nodding firmly. "He probably didn't have the strength—"

"Lost blood?"

"The first explosion threw him across the deck," Caleb said, painfully remembering. "The back of his shirt was bloody."

"That changes things," Jonathan said grimly.

"I know." He took a ragged breath and gave into the grief. "We're not going to find him, are we, Jon?" His voice was frayed.

"No. I don't think so." He put an arm around Caleb's shoulder; they gave up hiding tears from each other as the harbormaster guided his boat over every square inch of the assigned search area.

∞∞∞

"Anything?" Ava rose quickly from Hubert's chair with anxious eyes, shifting Samuel on her shoulder. Jonathan dropped his eyes and shook his head. Caleb's newly inherited farmhouse had become the gathering spot for family and friends, except for Aryl's parents, who chose to be alone to mourn privately.

"How's Claire?" he asked as he glanced at the stairs.

"Not good. The medicine makes her sleep. But she wakes up screaming every few hours. She won't eat." She wiped her eyes with the back of her hand and sniffled as she laid Samuel in his floor pen and then hugged Jonathan tightly around the neck. "How are you?" she asked. Her tears had been for Aryl, even more for Claire. But some had been shed in relief that Jonathan hadn't been on the boat; that he had gone to pick up Patrick, that her recurring dream had not been a premonition.

"They're going back out tomorrow, even though everyone knows . . . I'm not going with them, though. I'm going to the Sullivan's to help arrange the funeral. Claire isn't up to it." She pulled back with a dire expression.

"You're giving up?"

His eyes were dull, lifeless, and his voice broke when he spoke. "He's gone, Ava," he whispered as a single tear spilled. She pulled him close again and held him while he racked with strangled sobs of grief and exhaustion.

Jean walked in quietly, wrapped his arms around Jonathan's leg and rested his head against his hip. Ava placed one hand on his head and stroked his hair while he looked up at her, somewhat fearful of Jonathan's breakdown. The few other inhabitants of the house tactfully avoided the room.

*June 27th 1930*

At the end of the day when all of the boats had returned, the search was officially called off. Ava was sitting in the living room holding Jean on her lap when Jonathan returned from the Sullivan's. His face wore the hollow, red, and swollen eyes of mourning. Ava and Jean hugged him in turn, and then Ava took Jean upstairs to put him to bed.

Downstairs, she found Jonathan in the kitchen sitting sloppily, as if he were a rag-doll thrown into a chair.

"Sunday," he said wearily. "We're going to have a service on Sunday. That's what Michael and Kathleen want." She slid into the seat next to him and took his hand. "We're going to have a box. Just a small one, so people can put," he paused, looking upward, blowing out his breath and blinking fast, "put in things that are special." He shifted in his seat. "Michael sent me into town with a list of family and friends to send telegrams to. I'm not sure how I'm going to get through that service, Ava." He stared ahead with a clenched jaw. "Everything we've been through, everything we've lost . . . ." He clutched a handful of his shirt, right over his heart. "It was *nothing* compared to this," he whispered.

They heard a small noise and turned to the doorway.

"Dadee?" Jonathan straightened in his chair and sniffled, wiping his face.

"Yes, Jean. What is it?" Jean walked to Jonathan's side and curled his little arm around his back. He seemed to struggle for words, and then his face relaxed.

"Here. I don't have nightmares anymore," Jean said as he placed Maura's cross on the table in front of Jonathan. He scurried back up the stairs.

Jonathan stared at it for a long time. He was out of tears, but his eyes burned as he held it for a moment and then slipped it into his pocket.

After a long silence, there was a soft knock at the door. Ava opened it to a disheveled and intoxicated Caleb.

"Is Jon here?" he asked woozily.

"He is. Come in, Caleb."

He walked into the kitchen and dropped into a chair without acknowledging Jonathan, and the knapsack he put on the table made clinking sounds as it settled. Ava leaned over Jonathan, kissing the top of his head.

"I'll be upstairs if you need me."

He looked up with grateful eyes.

"I love you."

She touched his face, smiled compassionately, and left the two to whatever distraction Caleb had smuggled in.

"Compliments of the local law," he said as he pulled out two bottles of whiskey from the bag.

"The sheriff?" Jonathan asked incredulously.

"He gave them to me, to us . . . in not so many words," he explained as he pushed one bottle toward Jonathan.

"How many words did he use?" Jonathan asked suspiciously.

"He confiscated these yesterday from a runner. He stopped by this afternoon to give his condolences." He paused to tilt the bottle up for several seconds and whistled at the burn. "Said he had some business to take care of on the other end of town, asked me if I'd do him a favor and dispose of it properly, since he didn't have time." One corner of his mouth twisted but his eyes remained heavy. "I assured him that I would." He held up the bottle and swigged heartily again.

They sat quietly, avoiding each other's eyes, listening to the crickets' songs through the open window.

"It's hot," Caleb said, glancing at the back door. "I'm going outside." Jonathan knew Cable was most likely on the verge of tears again and preferred them hidden by the dark. He grabbed his bottle and knapsack and pushed open the screen door. Jonathan followed.

They sat on the bench against the house with two feet of space between them; the spot where Aryl belonged.

The missing element was overwhelming and neither could bear to look at the gap.

*June 29ᵗʰ 1930*

Claire sat by the window, staring through it with blank eyes as Ava changed her bed sheets. The doctor suggested they talk to her about random things, and so she did; the roses blooming outside and the weather, how lovely the quilt was, what the quilter might have been thinking when she created the design. Claire didn't answer or give any indication that she had even heard her. After making the bed, she sat in front of her friend with a tray of food.

"You need to eat something, Claire," she pleaded and held a spoon to her lips. Claire remained motionless. "It's been three days, Claire. Please eat something." She touched the spoon to her closed lips and sighed in frustration at her catatonic state. Ava wiped Claire's mouth. "Stand up, honey. We need to get you dressed." She pulled on both arms, and Claire stood limply, swaying, staring past her. Ava pulled the gown over her head and replaced it with a black dress, high in the neck with dozens of small satin buttons lining the bodice. She straightened it around her waist, and reached around to tie the high waist back. She shook out the skirt around her calves and lastly, she bent and pulled off her house slippers and replaced them with low heels. She guided her back down in the chair and Claire's arms hung limply at her side. Ava moved behind her and brushed her dirty hair, smoothing tangles. She placed a newly purchased cloche hat low around her ears, so only the curls of the ends of her golden blonde hair showed. Ava was grateful that the hat covered most of her matted hair. She walked around and stooped to eye-level with Claire.

"Honey, I'm going downstairs for a minute. I'll come get you when it's time, all right?" She touched Claire's wet cheek as a few more tears overflowed from blank eyes.

∞∞∞

Downstairs, the house was beginning to buzz loudly as more and more people arrived, wanting to be included in the funeral procession. Dozens of people crowded the living room and kitchen. Piles of prepared food accumulated quickly on the counters.

"She's dressed," Ava told Arianna and Ethel as she sat down to a strong cup of coffee. She glanced into the living room and saw Caleb near the window with hands shoved in his pockets, eyes cast down.

Jonathan stood by the fireplace, leaning on the mantel, only half-listening to those around him. He looked extremely handsome in his black suit, and Ava wished it was for any other reason that he was dressed formally. She felt a pang of guilt for even noticing his beauty at a time like this.

Just in the short time she had been focusing on Jonathan, there had been three knocks on the door. Each time Ethel scurried across the room to answer it, let people in or receive a gift of sympathy for Claire or Aryl's parents. Grateful as she was, she was becoming more flustered. A fourth knock sent her hands up in the air and the dishtowel flying across the room.

Ava rose and took two quick steps. "I'll get it, Ethel," she said and smiled back at her as she swung the door open.

Her eyes flew open wide and she gasped, slapping both hands to her mouth, making a whimpering sound from behind them.

"Where is she, love?"

Ava stepped forward with tears stinging her tired eyes and fell into Maura's arms. She sobbed loudly and clung to Maura as she patted her back.

"There, there, Miss Ava."

"You're here." She pulled back and put her hands on Maura's cheeks. "You're really here," she said with a quivering lip.

"I received Mr. Jonathan's telegram and was on the train first thing this marnin'."

Over Ava's shoulder, her eyes found Jonathan, standing in the archway to the living room. He returned her gaze with a tired, relieved expression, very close to breaking down. She walked to him and stood on tiptoe to hug him.

"I'm so glad you came," he choked, unable to hold back his emotion. "Thank you." He worried briefly about how she would absorb the cost of the trip with Ian out of work and tried to remember the exact balance of the account that held the business funds. It didn't matter. He was so relieved and soothed by her presence that he would mortgage his soul, if need be, to pay for the visit.

"You look so tired, Mr. Jonathan." She touched the side of his face.

"I am tired, Maura." He wanted to say more, but he remembered that Claire's loss was the greatest amongst them. He motioned to the stairs. "She's upstairs."

"We need to leave soon, Jon. Do you think we can get her downstairs?" Michael Sullivan asked as he passed, placing a hand on Jon's shoulder.

"We will," Jonathan said, looking at Maura.

Ava held onto Maura's hand and led her to where Claire sat, void of emotion.

"She hasn't eaten in three days, she doesn't talk, and she just stares." Ava stepped aside and let Maura do what she did best; touch people's hearts. She knelt down in front of Claire and smiled pitifully, pushing stay strands of hair out of her face, tucking them under her hat.

"Claire, love." She took her cold hands and put them together between hers, squeezing them. "It's time to go." Claire's eyes flickered but lacked focus. "This will be one of the hardest things ye have ever done. Goodbyes are never easy . . . but it's something ye must do." Claire's eyes welled with tears as she stared past Maura's shoulder. "Claire." Maura commanded her attention with loving authority. "Ye have to get this day behind you. Ye won't be able to truly grieve and begin to heal until you've properly said goodbye. Today begins that long journey, love," Maura said with a sigh. "And ye must get to the point of healing. Aryl's babe, he depends on ye. He needs you. And you need him. Aryl left a part of himself with you. You have to do this." She put a hand on her still-flat stomach. "Fer him."

Claire rose from the chair slowly and held onto Maura as they made their way to the door. Ava followed, tears streaming down her face.

∞∞∞∞

The long line of cars stopped along the sandy road, and Caleb looked hesitantly down at the beach. It was Michael's idea for a beachfront service, his brother's memorial still too raw for him to withstand sitting in the same chapel to say goodbye to his son.

A small alter faced the crowd; below it rested an oak box in the sand, its lid leaning off the side. Many families had offered the use of their chairs and the mismatched seats were lined up in neat rows.

Aryl's mother walked slowly, already having begun to sob, supported by her husband, his face set in strangled stone. Jonathan signaled to Caleb as he stepped out of the Runabout. He walked quickly and took his place on one side of Claire, Jonathan on the other, both partially holding her up as she weakly made her way through the sand. Maura followed with Ava and Arianna close behind. Kathleen and Michael sat in the center of the front row, next to Aryl's brother, Liam, who appeared shell-shocked, eyes avoiding the empty box a few feet in front of him. The pastor leaned down with a sympathetic hand on each of their shoulders and spoke quietly with them in turn.

"Kathleen would like a quick service if you don't mind," Michael told him. The pastor nodded understandingly and took his place at the pulpit. The seats filled completely, and there were a few dozen people standing behind the rows, handkerchiefs in hand. They guided Claire to her seat on the left side of the front row, and Jonathan and Caleb sat on each side of her, holding her hands. Ava and Arianna sat on the other sides of their husbands. Maura took a seat in the second row.

"No. You sit with us." Jonathan pointed to the one seat left in the front row.

The pastor raised his hand, silencing the low hum of weeping. For a moment, only crashing waves and calling gulls filled the air as the crowd of over a hundred both sat and stood in reverence.

"Aryl Sullivan was loved by many and will be dearly missed. Anyone who was lucky enough to know him will feel an absence in their lives and in their hearts forever; one that can only be consoled by the knowledge that he is now with the Lord."

Claire let out a strangled sob as she recalled those exact words spoken just months ago at Aryl's uncle's memorial. Jonathan put his arm around her shoulder. His other hand gripped Ava's unbearably hard. Jonathan tuned out much of the service. He went somewhere deep inside his mind, only intermittently brought up to light consciousness by the occasional cough or muffled sob. He held Claire by the shoulder to keep her from falling forward. The pastor explained the request of the family for a brief service and that they would forgo public speaking.

"Under the circumstances of Aryl's untimely departure, we will be laying to rest a box of letters, sentimental items, and private thoughts. Anyone who has such an item is welcome to come forward and place it inside." Several people stood and made their way to the front, forming a line. Odd things were gently laid inside that only meant something to the mourner; notes, cards, a set of jacks, a deck of cards, an empty flask, a few bottle caps, some fishing hooks, flowers, a Bible.

"Are you sure, Claire?" Jonathan whispered. Claire, crying, was working her wedding ring off her finger. She reached for his arm to stand. He walked slowly with her to the box, and she knelt down to touch the edges of it tenderly. She wrapped the ring in her handkerchief and tucked it into the corner. While trying to control her sobs, she stumbled and Caleb rushed to help her back to her seat.

Something unintelligible rose from Jonathan's throat as stared down into the box. A thousand memories of Aryl flashed through his mind from early childhood to the present. In mere seconds, his mind touched on a thousand conversations they'd shared. He remembered Aryl's face happy and grinning as a boy on the beach, solemn and sincere the day he married Claire, hollow and stunned the day they lost everything. Remembered him dressed as a woman on Halloween, making their first day in the tenement one they would always look back on with laughter, remembered the hurtful expression of betrayal as he sat beside the bathtub where Jonathan had tried to take his own life. And finally, the very last time he had laid eyes on him. He had turned around, his face barely visible in the darkness, but Jonathan could see his smile.

He reached into his pocket and pulled out the worn cross. Looking briefly over his shoulder, he saw Maura with tears in her eyes. She gave a small nod. He bent down and placed the cross in the box.

"Goodbye, Aryl."

"How's he doing?" Elizabeth asked from the darkened doorway. Cecile wiped his forehead with a cool cloth, and her aged finger pushed the hair away from the temples.

"Fever broke this morning. Looks like he's going to make it." She wiped her own face in relief, having sat thru a two day vigil in an attempt to save the young man's life.

"Does he know yet?" Elizabeth stepped out of the shadows to the bed stand and turned up the wick in the oil lamp. It illuminated the young man's face and her striking features.

"No. I asked the last time he woke, but he still–"

"He looks better," she interrupted, smiling at her mother, her brown eyes crinkled at the edges.

"He does. I think he's going to be just fine. Tomorrow I can go into town and talk to the sheriff and the newspaper–"

"No, you won't," Elizabeth said calmly. She sat at the side of the bed, placed a hand softly on his knee, and watched his face adoringly. "He's mine. I'm keeping him."

"He belongs somewhere, Elizabeth. He must have a family, people that miss him. Your father told you we would only see him recovered and then–"

"I want to be here when he wakes up again," she said with resolve, ignoring her mother. Cecile eyed Elizabeth warily and stood to stretch her achy bones.

"Ah, now, that's better," she groaned with two snaps from her spine. Elizabeth's narrowed eyes suspiciously watched her mother leave the room. She turned back to the young man in her bed. She pulled his hand out from under the covers and held it, stroking the back of it with her fingers. The gold band on his ring finger caught her eye and she played with it, spinning it around his finger, deep in thought. She decided quietly as she worked the ring off.

"I'm sorry. *I* need you more."

She held the ring up to examine it in the dim light. She placed his hand on his stomach, noticing that the white stripe of flesh gleamed in contrast to his tanned and work-weathered finger.

The band was wide and gold, thick and of good quality. She slipped it onto her own finger and caught sight of an engraving. Walking over to the lamplight, she tilted her hand until she could see it clearly. The extra width of the band accommodated the engraving.

The outline was that of a lighthouse with two hearts engraved on each side of it; an *A* set in the center of one heart and a *C* set in the center of the other.

He began to stir and Elizabeth rushed back to the bedside. She gasped slightly as his eyes fluttered open and tried to focus. He took a breath to speak but began a violent coughing fit; a fit so strenuous that it lifted the top-half of his body a few inches off the bed and made his eyes bulge and water. Cecile rushed through the door and saw to him in a flash, patting his back, trying to help bring up the sickness.

"There, there, you're better now," she soothed when the racking stopped and he fell back on the pillow, gasping. He looked down to the foot of the bed and saw Elizabeth, her shoulder-length brown hair swept up into a messy bun.

"We were mighty worried about you. You've been asleep for days. Double pneumonia. Looks as if you're over the worst of it. Can you tell us now–what's your name?" Cecile sat on the side of his bed, distracting him from the vision at the foot of his bed. She pushed the brown curls off his forehead and felt again for fever. She cast a nervous glance toward Elizabeth, who glared at the side of her mother's head.

Cracked lips parted to whisper with a voice he didn't recognize.

"I don't know."

# Coming Soon

## Elizabeth's Heart

by
M.L Gardner
www.mlgardnernovels.com

Made in the USA
Lexington, KY
02 June 2011